The Eleventh Hour

More by Brooke Shaffer

The Timekeeper Chronicles

The Chivalrous Welshman
Time to Kill
Tick Tock
Windup
Stopwatch
Free Time
Leap Second
Imminence
Synchronization
Turning Point
The Eleventh Hour

The Fifth Horseman
Famine (Winter 2025)

The Hands of Time
In the Hands of the Enemy
The Hands Pulling the Strings
The Hand Holding the Knife

The Lone Wolf
Wolf Pack
Alpha Wolf
Lone Wolf

The Akari Bearer
Bearer of Bad News (Summer 2025)

Singles
Of Saints and Sinners
Chasing the White Bear

The Eleventh Hour
Book Ten of The Chivalrous Welshman
The Timekeeper Chronicles

Brooke Shaffer

Black Bear Publishing

ISBN:
 Hardcover: 978-1-953113-40-5
 Softcover: 978-1-953113-41-2
 eBook: 978-1-953113-42-9

For You

After Ryan left, Walter decided to limit the number of children in his household to exactly one. He'd never actually intended on having children, not after his disaster of a life, but Tommen was a special case. Tommen was a good kid at heart, bright, brimming with curiosity. Walter could see that he'd been damaged by Ryan's stay, and that only made him feel guilty. So, he decided on no more children. It would be just the two of them, sharing the bond of blood and Time. Besides, he was too old to get mixed up in this more than he had to. He'd never realized how old he'd gotten or how much energy he'd lost since he discovered he could hardly keep up with his son.

A few times, he considered dating, maybe finding a wife, a mother for his child, but such things never came to pass. He was already working more than he preferred and was away from his son more than he wanted to be; there was no way he could give a woman the attention she deserved. The furthest he ever got with a woman was a couple of coffee dates. Then the guilt would come back to gnaw at him, that she would grow old and he would not.

When Tommen started noticing girls, he sometimes asked Walter about it, why he didn't date or pursue women in any fashion. At first, Walter just said he worked a lot and he wanted to focus on what he had rather than pursue something he didn't have and didn't precisely need. Only later, once Tommen got more into Timekeeping and studying for his Apprentice review did he really put it together.

"So you do it for her sake," Tommen stated. He was perhaps thirteen or fourteen at the time and Walter had just picked him up from the bakery.

"Yes," Walter confirmed sadly.

"What about finding another Timekeeper, or any Time Agent?"

"Honestly, Tommen, I just haven't had the interest, not really, not for a long time."

"Why?"

Because of my failed marriage, my dead wife and daughter, the fact that we have a deeper family bond than you could possibly know right now? "I've had you. And I'm glad to say that. I've been happy to raise you."

"But what about after that? After I'm up and gone, are you just going to sit at home alone in your recliner like a cranky old miser who chases kids off his lawn?"

"I don't know what I'll do. Maybe I will find a female Time Agent to share my life with. But seeing how we have a longer lifespan than most, I'm in no rush. And I'll worry about it after you've gone. One life at a time."

"How do you know which life is your last, though?"

"You don't. You know that every morning when I leave for work, it could be my last day. Bending Time does not make us indestructible."

"Then why not do the things you want to do? Take a vacation, find love, things like that?"

Walter sighed. "Kid, you're too philosophical for your own good sometimes."

"I lie awake in a pool of existential crises at night."

"Apparently. Are there any other crises you want to work out?"

"No."

He was lying, Walter could tell, but the kid was becoming independent. He wanted to work some things out on his own. That could be good or bad, but it was just part of growing up.

Sometimes Walter wondered if things would have been different if his son had had a mother.

A wave of cooler weather had moved through the area, bringing much-needed rain and helping to dissipate the oppressive heat that had lain over the city most of the summer. It was only mid-August, but everyone knew fall was on its way.

In other words, it was a good day to help someone move, even when social circumstances were less than ideal. Tommen could feel his future father-in-law watching his every move from the large windows in the living room. He told himself that his skin was red from the hard work and not from embarrassment and the lingering fear that the old Jewish man would still take a knife to his cock, and not for religious circumcision.

Upstairs in what was now her former bedroom, Becky was chasing Mr. Snuffles around and trying to reach him under the bed so she could put him in his crate. The long-haired gray cat was not having any of it. Becky, still struggling with the events of the last few days—and, if she was to be believed, the last month—was too frustrated to give much more than two minutes' worth of effort at a time, and Tommen found her sitting cross-legged on the carpet, head in hand, looking ready to cry.

"Is he still not coming?" Tommen asked.

"I've tried to get him, but he's just not having it," Becky told him, closing her eyes, the stress very much in evidence on her face.

"All right, I'll get him. Back up."

She did so. Tommen closed the bedroom and closet doors and pulled the bed away from the wall. The cat streaked out of his hiding spot but could find nowhere to go. When he hit a corner, he turned around, fluffed up his fur, and hissed. Normally Mr. Snuffles was very agreeable and even affectionate, at least toward Becky, but once the crate came out, so did the lion, apparently. Nevertheless, the little furball had nowhere to go. Tommen endured a flurry of claws and teeth to put the bad-tempered feline in his crate where he went from ferocious lion to the poster kitten for all those humane society commercials, meowing pitifully and rolling around on the blanket inside as if he were dying. The cat was the last piece of the puzzle before the move.

Three days ago, on Wednesday, Tommen and Becky had sneaked away from his birthday party at her house, returning to his house which was empty since his dad had gone to work, and had a little birthday sex. Okay, a lot of birthday sex. It had been damn good as far as he was concerned, right up until she had passed out and needed to go to the hospital. Then, not only were their exploits revealed to her strictly religious parents, but she confessed that she was pregnant with his child, about ten weeks along.

It had been decided that she would move in with him. Becky had a lot of brothers and sisters and more extended family with a lot of kids, and everyone had agreed that it was best for her to have a quieter environment, such as living with Tommen and his dad who were the only ones in their home. Of course, they lived only a quarter mile apart, if that, and Becky's mom agreed to keep all of her sewing stuff so she could reopen her tailoring business, or at least make her own baby clothes.

Furthermore, as of yesterday afternoon, Tommen and Becky were officially engaged. Dr. Polski had all but called up a rabbi on the spot, but Mrs. Polski calmed him down and got him to agree to a wedding next summer, after the baby was born, after Becky had lost some of the weight, and after Tommen was graduated from high school. He would literally walk down the aisle for graduation, and then walk down the aisle to get married.

Yeah, that was a little embarrassing. With her due date in March, Tommen had looked at his school calendar and determined that in the week between his final semester of high school and his first semester of college, he would become a new dad. Fuck, but that was still enough to make him light-headed.

They went downstairs and out to the van. Mrs. Polski had said they could use it to take all of Becky's stuff at once so long as he didn't damage it and remembered to put all the rows of seats back up when he was done. She had grandkids and great-grandkids to shuttle to Mass in the morning. He got in the driver's seat and Becky in the passenger. Normally she couldn't ride shotgun because of her short stature — she was only three-foot-nine — but for the quick jaunt up the road, she would make an exception. Mr. Snuffles, in his crate on her lap, *mrrow*ed and begged to be let out.

There had been some debate over whether to bring the cat. For one, Tommen's dad was allergic to cats, and he wasn't very fond of them anyway. Second, his dad had declared that he wasn't cleaning the litterbox, and Becky most certainly couldn't clean the litterbox, which just left Tommen. In the summer it was fine, because the cat was a good indoor-outdoor cat and could do his business outside, but during the winter, he holed up indoors, usually under the blankets, and then it would be box cleaning time. Tommen had decided that cleaning the litterbox wouldn't be such a big deal, and Mr. Snuffles offered comfort to his girlfriend. Fiancée. Damn, that word still sounded foreign to him. He was engaged. He had a fiancée. He was going to be a dad.

Tell that to him two years ago and he would have just laughed.

Life was changing, and it was changing big time.

He hadn't told his shrink yet. Actually, he'd called off his normal Thursday night, pleaded sick. If Nathan suspected anything, he hadn't said so over the phone. Just a see-you-next-week.

Tommen was a little afraid of that conversation, honestly, not because he feared Nathan and thought the man would do something to him, but because he hated seeing all the disappointment. He would never forget the look of disappointment on his dad's face; he didn't know if he could handle it coming from Nathan, too.

All this time, everyone had called him the Chivalrous Welshman. Since getting his act together the last couple years, he'd prided himself on living up to that title, even if he knew he really hadn't been by sleeping with Becky. But that had also produced a small seed of resentment. He was called chivalrous, and that projected a certain image. He was expected to live up to that image, a facade. In a way, he himself felt ignored, as if he didn't have dreams and desires of his own, but the image was all that mattered.

Maybe that was another reason he was scared to talk to Nathan. Since being afflicted with the accelerated aging on account of Time, the Akari was all he'd had left, and Nathan had been his mentor. Nathan had been a good mentor, a great teacher. But with the Wheel of Time hostile to the point of being inaccessible, the Akarin scattered, and the Order out for blood, it all felt like a facade, a strange game that only select members played, a cult in its own right.

This was what was happening, here, now. His girlfriend—ahem, fiancée—was pregnant with his child. He was going to be a husband and father; he didn't have time to worry about fairy tales, even though he knew the fairy tales were true. And so were the nightmares.

More than once he'd glanced over his shoulder, wondering if he were being watched and by whom. Rifun was still in jail after his conviction, and Tommen wasn't convinced that his men, the Miaramila, or their new leader, Godwin Lore, would look out for him in the same way. If being manipulated into war could be called looking out.

But they were still the better option to have watching him. He had no desire to run into Julianna or any of her minions. Her courthouse moles had been deposed, but that was the last report he'd heard. Were the Miaramila able to keep up the charade? Did Julianna suspect his involvement? What would she do about it? It was a prospect Tommen did not want to consider, and he hoped her goals were lofty enough that he didn't even register on the radar, threat or otherwise. At this point, he just wanted a normal life.

With everything he'd gone through in the last two years, he had great suspicions that he wouldn't be so lucky. He never was. Always, there was something that demanded his attention. Well, this time around, he was determined to keep his attention fixed on the present, the here and now, and not worry about anything that didn't directly affect him and his family.

Family. His family. He felt light-headed again.

He backed in his driveway where his dad and Miach were waiting to help unload the boxes. It was going to have to be a quick job. Miach had some business to catch up on, and Tommen and his dad had a funeral to attend. They'd asked Becky if she wanted to attend, but she declined, saying she would be content to stay and unpack her boxes, rearrange things in Tommen's room and make herself at home. While Tommen understood that he was going to have to learn to share, he wasn't sure how he felt about her rearranging things. The last few days of stress aside, Becky could be a forceful personality, a regular typhoon of spit and vinegar.

With Becky around, the men's use of Time was limited but strategic, and somehow they managed to get all the boxes in the house in about twenty percent less time than they might have normally. If Becky noticed anything amiss, she didn't say so, and she began rummaging through the boxes, looking for this and that. Most of the boxes were in the bedroom—not just his bedroom anymore, but their bedroom—but a few sat in the living room, things to make the house a little more homey. Tommen thought the house was just fine, but his dad cautioned him against saying so and told him to never underestimate a woman's touch on a place.

Tommen and his dad had lived together with no women in the house for the last ten years. The best that Tommen could picture were old memories of his ma spinning wool which she later dyed and then wove into rugs to cover the cold floor of the tiny mountain cabin. What he wouldn't give to have her here, to tell him what was going on, what to do, what to expect, tell him everything was going to be okay. His dad had given him a little advice, but there were times when he just wanted his ma. And his pa, too. And his brother Teo.

"Are you sure you don't want to come with us?" he asked, walking in the bedroom where Becky was busy sorting her clothes. Tommen had gone through his dresser and closet a couple days ago and cleaned out a lot of old stuff, setting them aside to be recycled and making room for Becky. She said she had done the same thing, but she'd always had more than him because her family was rich, so his idea of cutting back and her idea of cutting back were probably very different. Her expression readily conveyed this thought.

"I'm sure," she told him. "It's one of your dad's friends, and he was there at the warehouse. I would just get in the way. Besides, I have to have some of these boxes out of the way tonight or else we won't be able to sleep here."

It was an excuse and they both knew it. She thought she would be a distraction at the funeral. In the same breath, she had chastised herself for being so selfish about this opinion, but she just felt very conspicuous now. Everyone knew Walter was going to be a grandpa. Everyone knew Tommen and Becky had been dating for over a year. It didn't take a genius to put two and two together. She was embarrassed. Tommen told her not to be, that everything would be just fine and no one would dare say anything about it. Still she declined and told him to go pay his respects.

So for as much as he wanted to stay and help her unpack—that is, keep her from completely destroying and-or remodeling his room—he had to get ready for the funeral, which meant showering to clean the sweat from moving boxes, finding something decent to wear, then returning Mrs. Polski's van, all nice and clean and with all the seats in their upright and locked positions. Then he walked home where his dad was just buttoning up his uniform and Miach was getting ready to leave, having rented a car for just a couple days so he could get around, and so he didn't have to try to bike with a suitcase. The bike he was leaving in their garage for anyone to use.

"Leaving so soon?" Tommen asked, trying to pretend that it was no big deal that his crazy uncle was leaving.

Miach shrugged. "For a little while, anyway. Got stuff at home to take care of."

"Infiltrating Irish courts now, are you?"

"Ah, nothing like that I don't think, but I'll let you guys know."

"Word from the Akarin or the Order?"

"I don't know yet. Like I said, I'll let you know if it's anything major. But you, man, you need to focus on your family."

Tommen let out a breath. "Yeah."

"You're taking some big steps into adulthood." Miach held out his hand and Tommen took it. "And I congratulate you for it."

"Thanks, Micah."

"I want to see pictures."

"Well, naturally."

Walter came to say his goodbyes, wishing Miach well in his endeavors, especially his first and foremost task of finding his own apartment—ahem, flat—so he didn't have to be cooped up with his cousin and his family. Miach wished Walter well in his upcoming retirement and expressed his condolences for the funeral. Then the Irishman got in his rental car and drove away.

Tommen thought he had seemed a little jumpy, but he knew why. It was almost a year to the day since Micaiah was murdered, or supposedly so. One of Tommen's Books had revealed his apparent survival, this confirmed by Nathan not long ago. But Miach didn't know that, and Tommen had been instructed not to tell him. Leave it between the brothers, he'd been told. But was that a smart idea?

"All right, kiddo, you ready?" Walter asked, jerking him from his thoughts.

"Yeah, I guess so," Tommen sighed. He hated funerals, especially under such wretched circumstances.

"Is Becky coming?"

"No, she wants to stay and unpack and stuff."

"And you're going to let her?" His dad's tone was joking, referring to Becky possibly completely redecorating his bedroom.

Their bedroom.

"I don't have a choice."

"Good answer. All right, let's go. Greg wanted everyone there early so we can meet people at the door."

"Is it being treated like a line of duty death?"

"No, but we should still be there early. It's a respect thing."

Tommen could understand that, and he ducked into his dad's car, a little stiff in the suit. He'd hoped that the verdict was the last time he had to wear the suit, but apparently not. But he wasn't going to complain about it. Complain for court duty, fine. Everyone complained about that. He wasn't going to complain about a funeral.

They drove into the city where the morning rush had come and gone and the lull was giving way to the beginning of the lunch rush. It wasn't hard to figure out where the funeral was being held, judging by the number of city and state police cruisers lurking about. It even appeared as though the county sheriff had showed up, too; his was the only county car Tommen spotted.

With all the cruisers around, people were more apt to obey the reserved parking signs, and Walter had little trouble finding a parking spot. They got out of the car and spent a short amount of time straightening jackets, adjusting ties and sleeves and everything else. Tommen just had his suit, but his dad wore his dress uniform. He looked rather dashing, actually, Tommen thought, but he didn't say this out loud.

Walking into the funeral home was like walking into one of those black-tie fundraisers the city precinct held every year to shmooze the upper crust into donating large amounts of cash in the name of supporting the local fuzz and not raising taxes on everyone. Those who weren't in crisp black uniforms were in fine suits, or long skirts and blouses as evidenced by Connie's attire.

Greg Steggmann was not difficult to spot. The warehouse survivors had formed their own little social club, and he was the biggest of them all. Tommen thought he remembered his dad saying that the man wore a size 15 shoe. He was big and tall and looked a bit like Frankenstein, just without the bolts. With his eyeline above the general crowd, he picked out Walter and Tommen easily and motioned them over to politely inform them that they could go in and see the memorial for a few minutes beforehand if they wanted.

They went into the parlor where a large, gleaming casket sat, the lid closed. Dan had put a .45 to his head, so there would be no viewing. Instead, an enlarged portrait of him had been set up on an easel. He looked a little younger than Tommen remembered him being, but it was the lack of scar on his neck that told Tommen the photo had been taken before the warehouse.

He glanced at his dad who pulled on his dress gloves and put his hands on the casket. He stared at the floral arrangement resting on top, not saying a word. Tommen thought he watched his dad age ten years in the ten seconds he stood there staring, and he knew there was no choice now but for him to retire. He'd been through too much and his heart, his very soul couldn't take much more. He needed to slow down, maybe even settle down.

Walter walked away, still without speaking, and Tommen somberly followed. Outside, conversation was remarkably light. Most of the grieving and anger had been done after the dinner a few nights ago, and now fond memories came to the surface. Tommen probably heard the same glitter bomb story forty times before Greg called for them to stand at the doors and meet the incoming public.

Dan was not married and had no kids. According to those around, he'd been dating a girl before the warehouse, but after the incident and his depression and emotional rollercoaster, she'd left him, which certainly hadn't helped things. His family attendance included both his parents and stepparents, his brother, and one sister who looked like she'd just gotten off the plane from San Francisco.

In another room off to the side of the lobby was the memorial room, decorated wall to wall with posters, collages, and framed photos of the man who lay with only half a head in the casket in the parlor. On one table was a collection of artwork; apparently Dan had been big into watercolors and he loved birds. Dozens of canvases depicted songbirds in trees, robins in a birdbath, blue jays and cardinals fighting at a bird feeder. There was also some of his bird photography on display. A sign on the table said all artwork was for sale and proceeds would go to the Fallen Police Officers Foundation. A few people were already walking around with the smaller canvases and photos.

Tommen was looking over all the posters when a hand touched his shoulder. He looked to see his dad making a silent gesture to follow. They headed into the parlor where half of the seating was filled with officers. Most of them were in uniform, the warehouse survivors being the only notable exception. Tommen was shown to a seat just behind the officers while his dad went closer to the front. There was enough brass in the room to make a statue of the deceased.

The service was short and sweet, the sermon making way for speeches from Steggmann, Pat, and even Walter. Tommen hadn't known his dad had been working on a small speech, but then, he'd been too wrapped up in his own issues.

His dad talked about how Dan had always been the free spirit of the precinct, only loosely bound by propriety when it came to office politics and conduct. Again, his penchant for pranks involving glitter and confetti came up, Walter being the unlucky discoverer of one of his infamous glitter bombs. Dan was a good soul who enjoyed the outdoors, especially his birds. He also had a rock solid commitment to ensuring that everyone went home. When an officer was in trouble, he would step in. When Tommen was taken, he'd been ready and willing to give his life to see father and son reunited.

"That's how I choose to remember him," Walter finished. He folded his paper and sat down.

Few speakers mentioned Dan's activities after the warehouse, as it was all one big downward spiral. Dropped out of seminary school because of problems with his own faith, a good businessman for the company he worked for but largely unhappy and on several different medications, not including the self-prescribed ones. It was a death two years in the making, Tommen thought grayly.

Dan's brother Tim was the head pallbearer, and with him was Steggmann, Pat, Walter, Connie, Standish, all the warehouse survivors. Sean Tanner followed close behind in his wheelchair, his service dog padding along beside him.

Down the steps to the hearse, and then it was time to put out the purple flags for the cars in the procession. It was not a full line of duty procession with every police cruiser, fire truck, and ambulance in the city in line, but there were a couple cruisers at the front and rear, dutifully clearing the way.

The only ones at the graveside were the family and the warehouse survivors. There was another short sermon as the preacher read a few verses. The floor was opened up again to any who maybe wanted to share more intimate stories with the inside crowd, but none did. For a long moment, the only sound that could be heard was the weeping from Dan's mother, her husband rubbing one shoulder, her ex-husband, Dan's father, rubbing the other.

The preacher dismissed them, but it was another minute or two before anyone moved. The policemen were the first to clear out, leaving the family to their own affairs. Tommen returned to the car, taking the purple flag and giving it to the hearse driver, then waiting for his dad who stopped to talk to the others for a few minutes. Tommen got out his phone and poked around on a game for a bit until his dad was ready.

He'd kind of hoped that it would be a quick chitchat, but it wasn't. In fact, the only reason the cops cut their conversation short was because the family was getting ready to leave and they didn't want to be seen as a bunch of gossiping hens, which they were anyway.

"Ready to retire?" Tommen asked as his dad got in the car.

"More than you know, kid."

The ride home was silent. Mostly it was Walter lost in his own thoughts and Tommen not wanting to interrupt him. When they arrived home, the lights were on in the kitchen. Walking in, it was like entering a fine restaurant. Several pans were on the stove and another was in the little toaster oven. Becky moved back and forth doing this and that.

"Oh, you're home already? I thought it would be a longer service."

"What's all this?" Tommen wondered. His dad kicked off his shoes and went down to his room to take off his uniform.

"Dinner. You do eat dinner here, don't you?"

"Yeah, but...I don't know."

"What?"

"Nothing."

"What?"

"Nothing. Just...have to get used to things changing."

"You haven't had a woman in the house for a while, so, yeah, things are going to be a little different."

One thing that didn't change was how small the kitchen was. It was just enough for one person, enough for two assuming one person didn't mind standing. Three people had to move out to the living room. Walter reclaimed his recliner and Tommen and Becky took opposite ends of the couch, their plates resting on the armrests. Dinner was baked barbecue chicken wings with mashed potatoes, gravy, corn, and peas.

"You get all your stuff unpacked?" Tommen asked, feeling conspicuous having the conversation in front of his dad.

"I got my clothes put away and a few things unpacked, but there are still a few boxes left," she told him. "I got bored and decided to make dinner."

"Is dinner going to be a regular occurrence?" Walter wondered, taking a bite of chicken.

"Probably, as long as I can. We'll see how things go with classes and...being pregnant and everything else."

"What classes do you have?"

"Advanced English, Calculus, Biology 201, Bio Lab, and Intro to Genetics."

"Isn't this your first semester?"

"Yes, but I took enough AP classes in high school to get me through a lot of the lower classes."

"That's good. This chicken is good, too."

Becky beamed at the compliment and self-consciously took a bite of potatoes. She kept all of her food generally separate. Tommen had mixed his corn and peas in with his potatoes. Made it easier to eat the corn and peas. That was his story and he was sticking to it. He even went back for a second helping. He was getting better about his eating and recovering from the accelerated aging, but Becky was a good cook. He glanced at his dad and knew they were thinking the same thing. They were going to need bigger pants.

Once all the dishes were done and leftovers portioned out, Becky called Mr. Snuffles in for the night and Tommen followed her back to his — their bedroom. He stopped in the doorway.

Well, she'd certainly made herself at home. It wasn't all girlied up, thankfully, because Becky wasn't much of a girly-girl, but her presence was definitely known. Where once his bookshelves had housed some books and a few trinkets with respectable space between them, now everything was pressed tight together, her own book collection squeezed in beside his own with very little open space left. Her trinkets sat beside his trinkets. If there was any order or system to it, it was lost on him. On the walls, she'd brought over a few of her favorite book, movie, or band posters and covered up what little wall space was left.

In the dresser, it appeared as though all the clothes had been removed and put back in, because Tommen knew his folding job wasn't that neat. All folds were crisp, everything stacked one on top of the other, his clothes definitively on one side, her clothes definitively on the other. Her clothes looked like children's clothing, but that wasn't the point. The closet was a similar story, everything rearranged neatly, his clothes on one side, hers on the other. A few unopened boxes sat in the bottom beside the shoes. The top shelf looked like it hadn't been touched.

"I'd say you were busy today," he observed.

"Just a little. I didn't want to intrude too much but I did have to reorganize a few things to get my stuff to fit," she told him.

"No, that's fine, just...wow."

Even the bed had been made, crisp and clean. The desk had been organized, her college textbooks stacked neatly in one corner. All in all, it looked very neat, very homey, less like a teenage boy's room and more like, well, a bedroom for a couple college kids. Fucking hell, life was moving fast suddenly. He sat on the bed and Becky crawled up beside him, resting her chin on his shoulder.

"Maybe when I'm bored in class I can come up with a few ideas on the where and how to put a crib and everything else."

Right. That. It had been his room. Now it was their room. In about six or seven months, there would be a third one in the picture. Well, the good news was, his dad was retiring and would be moving. Once he did, and if they did buy the house from him, they could move into his room and the baby could have its own nursery. Because the three of them were not going to fit in this room very well for very long.

"I don't think you'll get bored in class," he told her, turning his head to kiss her. "You're too smart and too eager for that. And besides, I'd like a little say in it, too."

"I know, and I'm sure you'll have plenty of time to be bored sitting in your classes, too."

"Maybe we can compare notes."

"At least no one can accuse us of cheating."

"No, never." He kissed her again.

She sighed and weaseled her way under his arm. "It's going to be different, sleeping here. Sleeping next to you."

"I think there might be a lot of tossing and turning at first and waking up wondering who's here with me."

Tommen did not voice his real fears, that he could get violent. Nightmares still plagued his sleep, and if the Shadows got involved, guaranteed they would try to go after Becky and the baby. If they could use him to get to them, so much the better. Tommen steeled his resolve and told himself that he would not do it, he would not hurt them, consciously or unconsciously.

"Are you going to Mass in the morning?" he asked suddenly. Normally she went with her mom. While not impossible for her to walk down and hop in with them, he would be expected to drive her since she was living with him now and she could not drive herself.

She sighed and finally said, "No. Not this week. I don't know if I could quite handle it. And they would try to marry us on the spot, I just know it." She rolled her eyes. "But thank you for asking."

He lay back on his bed, noticing that there were now two pillows here instead of just one. She lay back beside him. He turned and put a hand on her stomach. "So, you knew for a month before telling me."

She blushed hard and said quietly, "Yeah."

"Did you think I would be mad?"

"I don't know. Maybe. I mean, we both had plans for our lives..."

He shrugged and slipped his hand under her shirt, still on her stomach. "Plans change. Doesn't always mean it's a bad thing."

"I know. And every reason I come up with for not having kids just sounds so...selfish. Like, it's not about me anymore."

"Well, you've done a good job taking my room and turning it into our room. I've never really liked the idea of giving up my bachelor pad, but now that it's done—it's going to take time to get used to, but I like it. Feels like a home."

"A tiny home."

"Our home."

Tommen would admit that he had his fears and misgivings about Becky moving in, but he was smart enough not to voice them aloud. Ultimately, they were only nebulous fears of the unknown, not anything they had control over, nothing anyone could really do about or prepare for except to experience it. That thought alone was terrifying enough.

They stayed up for a bit, Becky succumbing to fatigue first, Tommen following suit if only because he wasn't sure how this sleeping together thing was going to work and he didn't want any surprises the first night.

His first sensation was that he was falling off the bed just because he was used to sleeping in the middle, not on one side. His next sensation was that someone had stacked a bunch of pillows beside him, but it was only Becky's small form. His first fright came when Mr. Snuffles jumped up on the bed and started meowing, looking for Becky. Becky sighed, rolled onto her back, and started petting the cat.

"Can't sleep, huh?" Tommen said.

"Nope." She sighed and rubbed her face. "I am so tired, but I keep bumping into you and can't sleep."

"Same here."

They lay there in silence. He was the first to roll onto one side and pull her close to his body. A second later, she wriggled away.

"Too warm," she breathed.

No denying that. It was already warm; having another warm body in bed wasn't helping. Having a warm, furry cat wasn't helping either, and Mr. Snuffles went down to the end of the bed to curl up on a blanket.

Tommen rolled over onto his other side and closed his eyes. He could only assume that he fell asleep because of exhaustion and not other normal, natural processes because it was like diving off a cliff. The blackness covered him as though he were diving through ink. It coated him, stained him, and still he fell with little or no resistance. His dive quickly turned into a panicked free fall. He heard hissing, laughing. At the last second, there was a flash of white. He no sooner registered that than he hit concrete. He felt his body break, and it wasn't just his bones, but it was like in a cartoon where arms and legs are broken off in ways that were anatomically impossible to be random. He lost all feeling, yet his head was still functioning. All around him was a swirling, inky darkness, but high overhead, he could see light.

"Tommen..." someone said, the voice echoing.

He swallowed and tried to look around, but his head would not respond, only his eyes and face.

"Tommen..."

He made a sound.

"Tommen!"

He jolted awake with a wild fist flying through the air. A huge hand caught his wrist and jerked his arm down, pinning it to the side of the bed and dragging him down with it, twisting his body so his arms were trapped. He found himself looking in his dad's face. For a second, he just stared at his dad, mouth slightly ajar. Then it registered. "Oh, shit."

His dad let him go and he twisted around, looking for Becky. She was out of bed, standing in front of one of the bookcases.

"Oh, shit, what happened? Did I hurt you?" He got himself sorted out and got out of bed. He went to Becky and put his hands on her shoulders. "I didn't hurt you, did I?"

She was trembling but managed to shake her head no. "No, you scared me more than anything. You weren't really yelling, but you were just wrenching and twisting and everything else. I tried to wake you up, called your name. Your dad came in and told me to stand back. Guess it's a good thing I did."

"You okay now, kiddo?" his dad asked, standing.

Tommen let out a breath and rubbed his eyes. "I don't know, I guess so."

His dad looked uncertain. "If you want, you can sleep in my bed or come out to the couch."

Tommen shook his head. "No. I'm not going to give up that easily."

For a long moment, there was silence. Finally his dad nodded toward his night stand. "Either take one, or the next time I have to come in here, I'm moving you myself."

Then he was gone.

Mentally kicking himself, Tommen rummaged in his night stand drawer. Instead of bringing out the bottle of sleeping pills, however, he took a lighter and lit the candle Chandler had given him. The candles were usually infused with herbs to help him sleep. Hopefully it would be enough. Then he collapsed back onto his bed. Becky gingerly joined him.

"I'm sorry," he said, bringing her close again for just a second before releasing her. "I don't want to hurt you."

"I know," she told him.

"If you want me to go, just tell me."

"No, not so soon. I want a chance for this to work itself out."

"Okay." He kissed her cheek, then carefully rolled over. His whole body had begun to ache from his thrashing, and he focused on that in order to get back to sleep, hopefully a normal sleep.

The thing that woke him up next was not a nightmare, but actually a tactile change, and he jerked awake to find himself in an unfamiliar room. As his eyes adjusted to the dim light, he recognized his dad's room, the man standing at the end of the bed.

"What—?"

"I decided to just skip the argument and go straight to the segregation," his dad said. "You didn't take a pill like I told you to."

Tommen sighed. "I don't like the pills; I don't want to be medicated."

"Not about you anymore, there, kid. What happens if you start throwing punches? You hit Becky just right, she could lose the baby. You hit Becky at all, her dad comes after you, to say nothing of me."

He rubbed his face. His dad was right, but he really didn't want to be dependent on drugs just to sleep. At the same time, he didn't want to be responsible for the death of his own child, especially when it wasn't something he could control. "Okay."

"Sleep here for the night; I'll take the couch in the morning. Becky's already gone back to sleep. Tomorrow night, you start taking your pills."

Tommen reluctantly agreed, and his dad left the room, closing the door behind him. Shame and embarrassment flooded through him. Some husband and father he was turning out to be.

He closed his eyes and quickly opened them to find himself in a cave, one he knew well. It was full of handmade pottery, candles, woven rugs, all of it made and overseen by one man who now sat by the fire in the center, poking the coals with a stick as he added smaller logs to coax out the flames.

"Congratulations, Dad," Chandler said emphatically and with a smile.

"Thanks," Tommen mumbled. He went and took his familiar place by the fire, to Chandler's left. "Did you know?"

The Native man dipped his head, not looking at him. "I did know."

"Why not tell me? Why let it get to that point?"

"Because it was the least bad outcome. Sometimes, that's all we can hope for."

Tommen had learned long ago that it was pointless to argue and try to get the man to speak clearly when he didn't want to. Instead he changed the subject. "Did you watch the trial, or...I don't know, investigate it? Did I do okay?"

"You did exactly what you did."

Tommen gave him a look as he considered things. "We could have gotten him off. The only real charges he was convicted of were against me and my dad. I forgave him. Maybe my dad could have been persuaded to do the same. Then he would have basically walked free, the petty charges notwithstanding."

"Forgiveness and justice," Chandler said seriously. "Is an affair between me and you anyone else's business?"

Tommen frowned. "He's going to die, isn't he? Between his blindness and seizures, he isn't going to last long, especially when Julianna comes for him because of this double-agent business. She tried once, I think, during the trial. She'll try again."

"Your paths have diverged." Chandler used a stick to roll a log just so. "What's done is done, and what will be, will be."

A flicker of movement caught Tommen's attention, and he looked to see the White Hawk bird-walking toward them. A couple weeks ago, the bird of prey had gone into the shadowy forest on some secret mission of the Author and been attacked by multiple Shadows. He appeared to have healed, so what was keeping him here was anyone's guess.

"Still keeping each other company, huh?" Tommen said.

"I am a creature of the air and I am kept in this cage," the hawk said irritably.

"I've never stopped you from going outside," Chandler told him.

"But what am I supposed to do? Hop around on the ground like the turkey? Even the turkey can fly."

"Your wings will heal in time."

The hawk made a sound and flitted up to perch on Chandler's shoulder. The man grimaced at the bird's talons but did not shoo him away. Rather he offered up a piece of meat which the hawk snatched and devoured greedily.

Tommen slowly let out a breath. "Chandler, I don't know what to do."

"What seems to be the dilemma?"

"I'm...excited to have a family. I really want to be a dad, a good dad. But...I just...I can't just leave all of this and pretend like none of it ever happened, or couldn't happen again. I'm not ignorant. I want to keep Becky and our baby safe."

"As well you should."

"That includes sleeping together and not beating her up in the middle of the night and possibly hurting our baby. I lit your candle, but I don't know, I guess I still had nightmares or something because my dad moved me to his bed. And what was up with the calling card?"

"The candle and card was a birthday gift, Tommen," Chandler told him. "The wolf print was me, and the rabbit print was the rabbit.

Happy birthday. Nothing magical about it, though I fear the teaching may have been lost on you."

"Apparently."

"I've already told you the seven sacred colors."

"White, yellow, red, black, blue, green, and brown."

"Yes. They also correspond with the seven sacred directions."

"You mean there's a map that goes with this?"

Chandler grinned. "Of sorts. A map of life. White for the north, yellow to the east, red to the south, and black for the west. We also have blue for up, green for down, and brown for exactly where you are. The blue was at the top of the candle, green at the bottom. We all come from the sky, from the Creator, descended to the earth. In the same way, as the Creator gives us life, our lives slowly burn down to death."

"What does that have to do with keeping Becky and our child safe?"

"If you move the center point, if you were to move from here to the outside, do the cardinal directions change?"

"No."

"North is still north. And the wick of the candle, the direct line from the Creator to you, still flows through you. You may ask for help at any time. The wick and the wax cannot be easily separated except by brute force that results only in destruction."

"You could have just told me to pray about it."

"I prefer the object lesson."

Tommen shifted his position. "Does prayer actually work, though? If I ask the Author for help, does God get offended? Is there a God? Is the Author a proxy, like Catholic priests? If we're all just in a book, where everything has to be written out by the Author anyway, is there a point to praying when she already knows what's going to happen, what we're going to say?"

Chandler chuckled. "Such musings can be good for the soul and help to keep one's ego in check, but for your purposes, you are thinking too high on the blue end. Return to the brown, exactly where you are."

"To be fair, my body is in my dad's bed, and my mind is here. I am in two places at once, so tell me how that works out."

"Means you're too smart for your own good. Focus on your family, Tommen."

"What about the Akari and everything else? If it only gives longer life..."

"Tommen, even small acts of kindness can be righteous. It's not all about going to Mass and taking communion and participating in rituals. A stranger who pays for a woman's groceries, a family who befriends a homeless man, a father who plays with his children, these can be acts of righteousness.

"The Akari is a great and powerful thing, but many lose sight of it beyond a tool for power. It is a living thing of and sent by the Author. Stay with your family, and if you need to defend them, simply ask for help and it will come. Maybe it won't be as dramatic as pillars of fire or calming storms, but it will always be exactly what you need."

Tommen considered this for a long moment before finally nodding. "So you're saying I should stop training with Nathan."

Chandler leaned back a bit. "I am not going to tell you yes or no, only that you must focus on the here and now, where you are. You must figure out what that means in your situation. Your life is changing and you will have to rearrange your priorities a little."

"Okay. I think I get it." He stood. "Feel better, Hawk. Don't hurt each other too much while you're cooped up together."

The hawk made a few chittering noises and his feathers were noticeably and literally ruffled, but before he could say anything, Tommen turned and found himself nearly falling off the bed. The sudden change in perceived direction confused him for a second, but he managed to save himself and scramble back onto the blankets.

He looked at the clock. Seven-thirty. For him it was sleeping in, but still pretty early for the rest of them. He sat up, stretched, rubbed his eyes, and looked around. After a minute or two of consideration, he pushed back the blankets and crept out of his dad's room back to his room. Becky was still asleep. Trying to be as quiet and unobtrusive as possible, he lay down next to her and put his arm around her.

"Are you okay?" she mumbled sleepily.

"Yeah, I am," he whispered. "I'm awake, though, so it's all good. You go back to sleep."

He wasn't sure that she'd even been awake enough in the first place to comprehend her own question, much less his reply. Nevertheless, her breathing deepened again and she lay still against his body. He breathed in the lingering scent of her shampoo, much finer fare than the cheap stuff he and his dad used. He liked it.

Tommen didn't know how long they lay like that, but he figured he must have dozed a little bit. The next thing he knew, Becky was moving, rolling over to face him. She kissed him. He kissed her back. Then she was unzipping his pants and he took off her shirt.

Some things changed.

Some things stayed the same.

Chapter Two
The Package

Sunday was spent helping Becky unpack the rest of her things. Tommen thought the room seemed a bit more cluttered and smaller than it had before, but that was to be expected, he supposed. Sunday night, he ended up taking one of his sleeping pills. Two would completely conk him out, but one would put him sufficiently under that he did not endanger Becky. It made it harder to get up, though, as his alarm went off and he slogged out of bed, head stuffed with cotton, eyes barely open. In bed, Becky softly murmured something and rolled over.

Mr. Snuffles, however, was at first rather miffed that he had been woken up. Then he decided it was an excellent opportunity to beg for food. Tommen got up and around, bathroom routine, getting dressed, putting in his hearing aids and everything else, all the while listening to meows, *mrows*, *prrths*, *rrowrows*, and other assorted cat sounds. The cat's food and water was in the kitchen, and Tommen was obligated to see that the cat was fed before he even thought about making food for himself.

He was just about to head out the door when he stopped and remembered himself. He returned to the bedroom where Becky was still sleeping. When he touched and kissed her, she sighed and opened sleepy eyes.

"Where are you going?" she mumbled.

"Work," he told her.

"Oh. Yeah, I guess you do have to do that, don't you?"

"Just a little. I'll see you tonight, okay? Have fun at your first day of school."

She waved him off and stretched out for a moment, then relaxed. He kissed her again, then headed off to work.

Tuesday, Tommen had stayed home from his construction job on account of his dad telling him about Dan's suicide. Wednesday had been his birthday which he'd already arranged to have off. Between Monday and Thursday, a lot had changed.

Thursday his coworkers said he looked like a ghost, and that was saying something. When he told them about Becky's pregnancy, he was surprised they didn't break his spine for all the back slaps they gave him—after he assured them that it was cool, he was excited for it, and they were sticking together. Otherwise they might have just broken his spine and been done with it. That day had been filled with congratulations and jabs and they'd all called him "Dad" all day long.

Friday had been some of the more serious questions, things like, "Are you even out of high school yet?" and "Where are you going to live?" Most of the questions were simple to answer, but that didn't mean it wasn't embarrassing to some degree. It was one thing when it was a dude and his girlfriend living in their own apartment, maybe in college, maybe working, but they were on their own. It was another thing when he was still in high school and they were living with his dad.

Tommen recalled a conversation he and Becky had had some months ago, complaining about how it wasn't fair for people to judge them. What if someone just fell on hard economic times that were out of their control? How was it any different? Well, now he was understanding how it was different. At the same time, he just had to keep on with Chandler's advice, focus on his family, the here and now. It wasn't going to be easy, but he would try his damnedest.

They had finally moved on from the old Victorian home and were just starting on a new house being built northeast of the city. It was a huge undertaking, something like seven thousand square feet, half-buried in the mountain it sat on. Vaulted ceilings, enormous windows. It was going to be the castle of the modern world. Chris, the foreman and owner of the company, had been speaking to the homeowners at length. The homeowners, an ultra-wealthy couple from New Jersey, had made it abundantly clear that no expense was to be spared and they expected to move in next April.

It was August now, which meant they only had so much good weather left to get the basement walls poured, and then it was going to be half a nightmare getting the walls and roof up. The framing was always the worst part, but once the skeleton was up and they got it covered in plywood and siding, got the roof on, the interior could be worked on in any weather.

It was going to be an interesting project.

As with most construction that started from scratch, there were a lot of trees in the way, and the landscape was typically less than favorable. Trees had to be cut, stumps pulled, and huge mounds of earth moved around. Tommen had only just been made a full part of the team, and he was excited to learn all the steps, all the tools, from start to finish. Project number one, safely cutting down trees so they didn't get caught up in neighboring trees or crush anything of importance, especially your coworkers. Tommen had run chainsaws before, but the trees were typically smaller, the cuts easy, the direction obvious, and no one else was around. This was a whole new experience for him.

And that was basically his day. There was more standing around than he originally anticipated, but with the amount of land that had to be cleared, processors were the preferred choice for clearing trees, as the terrain allowed.

The clearing had started on Friday afternoon, and with the efficiency of the processors and clean-up of the chainsaws, the marked off area was done by Monday afternoon. Lunch was later than normal, but they all kind of just wanted to get it done. Then they could take a break, eat lunch, the processing guys could pack up and go home, and they could move on to step two: stump removal.

An excavator was brought in for that, digging or ripping up stumps with mostly minimal effort and moving them into a huge pile right where the front lawn was projected to be.

"That's going to make a nice bonfire," Matt commented to Tommen.

"Do we actually get to light it?" he asked.

"Heck yeah! Frank will get them all set up here today, then he'll move them a little out of the way so we can keep working this week—it's usually better if we get this done on like a Friday, but whatever—and then Friday or Saturday, depending on the weather, after we're off, we douse it in gasoline and light it."

Tommen nodded. "Nice."

"Good for morale," Matt agreed. "Lot better than just shipping it off to get turned into mulch or fertilizer, know what I'm saying?"

He did. Fire was fun. Well, sometimes.

With the excavator doing most of the work with the stumps, the general labor was permitted to leave early while the foreman and some of the more senior members of the crew took a step back to observe the landscape and make the plans for the next few days. Tommen did not argue, simply got in his car and headed out.

He liked the Victorian house better; it was on his side of the river and he didn't have to drive through Charleston to get there or home. He was in a decent mood, but he still did his best to detour around the city.

There was no question that construction paid well, and Chris had mentioned giving him a raise because he was now eighteen and could do all the stuff, or he should be able to. Tommen was happy and grateful, but now, with an upcoming wife and kid to support, suddenly he wasn't so sure it would be enough. They both had scholarships, but he didn't want to leave before he got some kind of degree, or her for that matter, and college was expensive. Forgoing the dorms was great, but those costs would be right up on them again if they bought the house from his dad. Maybe they'd work something out, but they'd still have utilities and taxes and everything else.

Real life was hard.

And those were just the financial factors.

He let out a breath. Before his brain had time to form another thought, a voice from his passenger seat nearly caused him to swerve off the road.

"Oh shit!" Tommen cried, righting the car, enduring a myriad of horns and likely very angry curses. He glanced at the figure in the seat but still did not quite see who it was as he fought his way over to the appropriate exit and got on the ramp without further incident.

"What the fuck?!" he demanded, finally looking to see who had intruded. It was Godwin, looking rather smug about the whole thing. Tommen repeated, now more angry than surprised, "What the fuck? What the actual fuck, man? I could have killed us."

Godwin laughed, and it was no less patronizing than his expression. "You get your girlfriend knocked up and suddenly you realize that manipulating the physics of the universe isn't all it's cracked up to be. And you forget every bit of it."

Tommen growled under his breath. "You still surprised me."

The mercenary chuckled again. "Better me than Julianna, wouldn't you say?"

Still trying to stay focused on driving, Tommen could only give the man a side glance. "What's she up to now? Any news from Hlohi?"

"The Krydik are less than forthcoming about their situation. I choose to see it as, if they do ask for help, they are in dire straits indeed."

"No news is good news."

"Something of the sort."

Tommen made a turn, leaving the last of the city's tentacles behind and entering the more suburban areas. "And the Miaramila have their base of operations?"

He could see Godwin dip his head. "We do. Our current goal is to become entrenched and strengthen ourselves and our positions as much as possible before the Order notices where we are. We're still using *Runner's Refuge* as a mobile ops base."

"And what about Rifun? When are you breaking him out?" When there was no swift answer, he went on, "Trial's over. You got

Julianna's moles. I'm assuming you have some kind of plan seeing how you switched places or something. Or are you waiting until the sentencing and whatever, just to buy yourselves that much more time?"

"That is one thing we have considered," Godwin answered evasively.

Tommen pulled over and put up a Band. "I know I made some comment about it, but is Rifun really going to allow himself to go to prison? And you're going to let him? Between his blindness and seizures, without his Akari abilities, prison gangs will eat him alive."

Godwin's tone turned serious, commanding, but mechanical. "The Miaramila are under orders to keep watch over certain chosen ones of the Author. You are one of them."

"The last Book I got was *Synchronization*. I know *The Hands of Time* is Rifun, Cassius, and Julianna. Obviously we know how that's working out. I know *Chasing the White Bear* is Kayla and *The Lone Wolf* is the Krydik, and they're happy to be left alone. I know *The Akari-Bearer* is Miach and Micaiah, and I know Micaiah is alive somewhere. Are you watching over them?"

"In a certain sense."

"What does that mean? This is serious, Godwin, we can't just play twenty questions like a bunch of kids. Lives are at stake."

"And how is knowing who's who going to influence your choices? If I said yes, we're watching this person, or no, we're not watching that person, what are you going to do?"

Tommen gave him a look. "Then why tell me at all?"

"Because Faharoa asked me to. Sometimes people need to see their guardian angels."

"You're too ugly for that."

Godwin barked a laugh.

"And you didn't answer my question," Tommen pressed.

"Miach is going to be recruited into running a few errands for us. He will be our eyes and ears on Earth."

"Going to be? He hasn't agreed to it then. What about me?"

Godwin let out an even breath. "You have your own worries. Rifun believes you should focus on them. I agree, if for differing reasons."

Tommen shifted position. "In Rifun's Book, you mentioned that you'd been married and had kids before, multiple times. How did you do it?"

The mercenary raised a brow. "I think you're well-versed in the birds and the bees." At a look, he sighed. "Funny thing about war. It ages a man. I never had trouble meeting women, and in older days, it was easier to get married, or so it felt."

"And when your kids grew up and you got too old, you just...went off to war again, faked your death."

Godwin nodded. "Basically. There is never a shortage of wars to be lost in."

"Were none of your families worth aging for?"

"At what point? I raised my children, watched a few get married and have children of their own. It's all nature expects of us. More than it expects of us, really. I just had the opportunity to go out and do it all again as I chose."

"What about your wives?"

"Remarried, taken care of by men who would age with them."

Tommen frowned, unsure how to respond. Finally, he changed the subject. "You're right, I do have my own worries now. But if I'm going to focus on them, I can't watch everything else. Please tell me if you get any intel regarding me or Becky or my dad or anyone or anything close to us. Whatever mission you've got Miach on, or going to try and rope him into, can I make that one request?"

Godwin nodded, and his expression was sincere. "Most people call mercenaries heartless moneygrubbers. I'll never say I wasn't greedy, but I will never kill a babe. And I'll be damned if Julianna goes after your child. Any woman who murders children is no woman, and I've no qualms about killing the cunt who tries."

Tommen sighed. "My inner chivalry says to be gracious toward women —"

Now Godwin's tone changed, like flipping a switch. "You fucked your girlfriend and got her knocked up; don't even fucking pretend like you're some poster child of chivalry. As for Julianna, she's a cunt and a witch. Nothing more."

Tommen couldn't help but laugh.

"All right, enough feel-good chitchat. I have other things to do, like talk to your hard-headed Irish friend."

"What makes you think he's going to help you?"

Godwin gave him a look. "Because his brother already is."

Tommen shifted again. "I knew Micaiah was alive, but Nathan said he's in bad shape."

"He is, yes. But—"

"How is he?"

The mercenary hesitated. Then, "With a lot of careful use of the Akari, he may recover to be almost the man he once was, but it's going to be a long road." Tommen opened his mouth but Godwin shook his head and said, "That's all I'm going to say about it. We never know when the next Book will emerge and yours especially have a propensity for tattling."

Tommen opened his mouth again, shrugged, and said, "Fair enough. But—"

He did not get a chance to say more as Godwin opened a portal and disappeared, leaving him alone on the side of the road in his car. After a moment, Tommen dropped his Band and pulled back onto the road.

He arrived home to find his dad already gone, but Becky was home, sitting at the desk in their bedroom already poring over a textbook. She looked up as he walked in.

"You're home early," she observed, kissing him. "Everything okay?"

Tommen rubbed his face. "Yeah, just...a lot going on. I kind of want to take things one at a time, but everything just feels like it's piling up at once." Rather than go into any details, he changed topic and asked, "So, how was the first day of school?"

"I haven't had this much fun since first grade," she told him, suddenly getting excited. "It seriously makes me excited for school again. Like, I want to go, I want to learn, I want to get my degree and do something with myself."

"That's always good." He sat on the edge of the bed. "You make friends with your teacher and your classmates?"

"Not yet. They're still getting over the weirdness factor, you know? Same as everyone, just like you had to get over my weirdness the first time I walked into AP Physics."

"Okay, fair enough. What class did you have today?"

"Advanced English. Tuesday and Thursday is Bio 201 in the morning with Bio Lab in the afternoon. I think I might just stay on campus to look around, get a feel for things, study a little. Wednesday is Calculus and Friday is Intro to Genetics. It's an appropriate way to end the week, I think."

"Sounds like a full load. And a lot of traveling."

"Yeah...but my mom is taking me, so it's all good. I figure that in a week or so, once I get my full workload and figure it out, I'll go back to sewing. Make some money and stuff. Start stashing away diaper packages and whatnot."

Tommen nodded. "That would be a good idea." He lay back on the bed. "I still have no clue what I'm doing."

"Welcome to the club."

"Yeah, but you have your mom and sisters and everyone else to fall back on. I...I'm too afraid to ask my dad."

Becky folded her arms. "Aren't you adopted?"

"My dad was married once and had a daughter. Before I was born."

"What happened?"

"Um...she divorced him and her second husband murdered her and the baby."

Becky put a hand to her mouth. "Oh no."

"That's kind of what motivated my dad to become a cop."

"Oh, that's terrible."

Tommen shrugged. "It is what it is."

"So all of this with me and you has to be kind of hard on him, huh?"

"It's bringing back some buried memories, yes."

"Oh, I had no idea." She stared at him for a second before her expression changed, as if something had just dawned on her. "But I did just remember. Your dad brought this back this morning." She rummaged under the desk and brought out a box made of heavy cardboard. "It's for you. I haven't opened it."

"That's unusual," he joked, taking the box from her and setting it on the bed.

"Well...it seemed kind of private and personal. I figured I would just let you do the honors."

Looking at the top of the box told Tommen everything he needed to know about what was inside. "Case number: 4-078-4f9-16, Forbes, Tommen, August 12, 1997" was written in black marker along with some other information about the county courthouse, child protective services, foster care services, and the State of West Virginia. This was his adoption box, all the court papers and case files, all the reports from his time in foster care, the adoption records, the police reports, all of it.

Some kids in school who had similar boxes were too eager to rip into them, to get all the information they could to track down their birth families and instantly reconnect, make up for all the years lost to one bad decision or one regret. Others wanted nothing to do with anything and probably burned the box as soon as looked at it. Some kids were old enough to remember the beating, the neglect, the sexual abuse, the drugs and alcohol, all the things that rightly got them removed.

Tommen was old enough and smart enough to know there would be very little of interest inside. Records were great, but there would be no letters from family hoping to reunite. There would be nothing at all about his birth family, except maybe to state that when he was first admitted to the hospital, they all thought he was nuts because he proclaimed himself to be *the* Tommen Forbes, for whom Forbes Cave was named. Shit, ten years later and he still couldn't shake that label that he was crazy. Sometimes he wondered if he really was crazy and should check himself into a mental hospital.

The box wasn't as light as he thought it would be, and when he finally took the lid off, he was surprised at how much there was. No one had been thoughtful enough to put it all in chronological order, but considering legal paperwork came in stacks of a hundred, it wasn't super difficult to sort out.

His only real surprise came when he discovered the police report and the newspaper articles, the first one describing the death of the Forbes family from carbon monoxide, one child still missing; the second talking about how the missing Forbes child had been found, hit by a car after running down the hill from Forbes Cave. These things were a surprise because they were completely fake. Not only that, but it was a story they'd only come up with in the last year or two. Adoption boxes were more heavily guarded than politicians' tax returns, so his dad would have had to sneak these in retroactively, probably Banding to do it.

He found the "Unknown Child" records from the hospital when he'd first been admitted, detailing his injuries and apparent insanity, how they'd made contact with the police to report him. Walter Forbes was the responding officer, his initial "Found Child" report also included.

Tommen also found the name of the first foster family he'd been placed with. They'd already had eight children ranging in age from under a year to thirteen. Tommen only vaguely remembered them, but he remembered feeling awfully overwhelmed by all the activity. It was why he'd been placed with his dad in a much quieter, more personal environment.

Then there was the adoption case itself. There were a lot of hoops to jump through, Tommen saw, especially in a case like this. The state didn't want to just give away a kid without looking for more family. But in this case, they'd been...successful?

Tommen pulled out a massive multi-page report from some lab in the area, detailing these and those characteristics and alleles and chromosomes and —

"Translate," he said, perhaps more sharply than intended, handing the report to Becky.

She skimmed through it, speed reading and occasionally looking back at this or that. Finally she said, "Well, in a nutshell, it's genetic proof that you and your dad are related, the strongest and most likely relationship being uncle-nephew."

"Son of a bitch," Tommen sighed, taking the paper and looking through it again, most of it going over his head. "They always knew."

"You mean you didn't know?"

"Not until a couple years ago, after the warehouse. I mean, it would make a ton of sense. A single dad isn't going to win out over a full family unless he can make a stronger blood relative case. Just...I don't know why it surprises me. Maybe just seeing the actual evidence here in front of me."

Unable to stop himself, Tommen took out his phone and called his dad.

"Hello?" his dad answered.

"They always knew, didn't they?" Tommen asked.

"Who knew what?"

"The courts. They always knew we were related. That was why they let the placement and adoption go through."

His dad was silent for a long moment, then, "Yes. I knew I was going to lose to the Robertsons, so I did play the family card, asked for the genetic test to be done to prove it—immigration records are sometimes incomplete when it comes to family ties, and I wasn't in the best standing, anyway—and when it came back solid...yeah, that's how I won."

"So you were always going to tell me."

"Of course I was. I may not have wanted to, especially after hiding it, but it was going to come out eventually. I'd hoped it wouldn't be how it did, but there it is."

"Yeah. Okay."

"Find anything else interesting in the box?"

"Just the police reports and newspaper articles and stuff."

"Well, we can talk about it later if you want."

"Okay. Stay safe tonight, Dad."

"I always try."

The call ended and Tommen stared at the genetic test papers a minute longer.

"Why didn't your dad tell you before?" Becky asked.

"He said he didn't want to confuse me," Tommen told her, which was the truth. "Early on, because he and my pa weren't exactly friends, he didn't know what my pa told me about him. And I'd never seen him before; he sort of looks like my pa but I don't remember him...very well..." He frowned and looked away.

"Is this him?"

He looked at Becky, then at the paper in her hand. It was a photograph, an old one, so old that people still weren't smiling in them. There were maybe forty people in the picture, but it was the two in the middle that he focused on. He was dressed in a nice, clean shirt, pants that fit, a small flower sticking out of the pocket of the shirt. She wore a dress that may have been white or cream, her flower bouquet decorated also with feathers that were most likely brightly-colored, because she loved color. He had angular features and a thick mop of brown hair. She had softer curves but bright chocolate-colored eyes. Tommen wasn't sure how much he was getting from the picture and how much he was remembering. He could only conclude that the extra people one either side of them were their families, his grandparents and uncles and aunts and cousins. But Walter would not be included as he'd been in jail.

He turned the picture over. "Teo Owain Fforidd a Maisy Gwynedd Williams, June 3, 1836, Llyranffod, Cymru." He could see where it had been written once, then faded, and then gone over again lightly with pen.

"How do you say all that?" Becky wondered.

He told her, the words rolling off his tongue like half-forgotten memories coming to life. She nodded. "I think you look more like your dad."

"My pa, yeah. Except for the eyes, my dad tells me. I don't know how that would explain my color-blindness, though. I know, I know, carries through the mother. But still..."

"The old-timey wedding theme was cool, though."

Theme. Yeah. That's all it was. "Yeah."

Tommen hadn't expected this box to affect him as much as it was, but it did. Maybe because it wasn't just about police reports and hospital records, but this was all he had left of his birth family. At school, he knew of some kids who came of age and swore they would never talk to their birth family ever again after that first meeting. He wanted to shake them by their shoulders and make them understand that he would give anything to have his family back. He would give anything to hug his ma, wrestle his brother, talk to his pa, even just meet his sisters. He was not an orphan. He was not an only child. But some days he felt as though he were trapped in a glass box and could only watch the same things over and over, the same fragmented memories of a child who no longer existed.

He found a small coal of resentment burning in his gut, that his dad wasn't here to go through it with him, talk to him, explain things. He'd dropped it off with Becky and then run off to work.

Even as he thought it, Tommen knew the resentment and anger was unfair. They both missed their family. Tommen had it taken away, Walter pushed it away. And now they were dealing with the consequences. In a way, they had to process everything separately before they could get together and talk, otherwise they would just be staring at each other, confused, wondering, but having little to say. But at least they could deal with it as family.

"You okay?" Becky wondered, lightly touching his shoulder.

"Um...yeah. Yeah, I'm okay," he said, knowing his lie was hardly convincing.

He looked through the box again, this time finding a few envelopes, all addressed to him in his dad's handwriting. They were letters, four of them. Tommen glanced at Becky. "Can you please not read over my shoulder?"

She sat back and nodded, then got off the bed. "Yeah. No, I'm sorry. I'll, um, I'll take my books out to the living room or something."

He did not stop her, and he did not turn his attention back to the letters until she was gone, quietly closing the door behind her. Even then, it was a long moment before he unfolded the papers. With only four letters, it wasn't difficult to sort them into chronological order. The first was dated April of 2006.

Dear Tommen,

At this time, you're eight years old, and the adoption papers just went through. As far as you know, I'm just a stranger you have to live with, who you call Tad because you don't know any better. You cry at night, asking for your ma or pa or your brother. I have nothing to give you but me, and if that's terrifying for me, I can only imagine what it feels like for you.

If you're reading this letter, it's because it's in your adoption box, which you get when you turn eighteen, which means you've probably already discovered our relation. And if not, I'll confess it now that I am your biological uncle. Your pa was my younger brother. I'm sorry I never told you. Your pa and I didn't exactly see eye-to-eye, and I wasn't in good standing with the family. I reasoned that the best break was a clean one, without dragging you into old family fights. Maybe that was a good choice, maybe a bad one. Only time will tell, I suppose. Maybe you'll work it out for yourself, or maybe I'll tell you, and those fears will be immaterial by the time you get this letter.

I have to admit, I don't know what I'm doing, as a dad. My own marriage ended in disaster. That was primarily my own fault. And now I have a son? I must be insane. Regardless, you are family, and I'm not letting you go.

By that same token, however, I also know that the only stories you will ever hear about your family will come from me. I have only one picture of your ma and pa, taken at their wedding, which I was not present for, again to my own shame. Their first child was your brother Teo, born in Wales. When they came to America, they had Eileigh and Irene, your sisters. Then you came along. I'm told there were others, but miscarriage and exposure are not uncommon in the mountains. When it all ended, your mother was expecting another. I hear it would have been another sister. Our family seems to be very good at having only two sons and a multitude of daughters.

If I continue writing, I expect I will start to ramble, so I'll end this letter here, including the photo of your ma and pa. Take good care of it. If you don't want it, I'll take it back. There will probably be more letters in the future, but I've never been very good with words.

Love, Tad

The second was dated a couple years later.

Dear Tommen,

As I write this, I feel a blanket of stress lifting even as another blanket of guilt lays down over me. Ryan has just left our house. With any luck, you've forgotten him, but with the amount of damage he did, I highly doubt it. If I had known that all this would have happened, I never would have agreed to take him in, or maybe I would have done things differently. Even now, I question my own motivations.

There were ten years between you and Teo, but the memories you do have seem to be fond ones. Perhaps I was trying to give you a brother, someone you could grow close to who wasn't me, who could show you things as only a brother can (at least, I've heard of such things. My own experiences are less than worthy of repetition). Maybe I was hoping to rehabilitate him, prove to myself that such people could be rehabilitated and so make myself feel better. Whatever the case, I apologize.

He hurt you. He hurt me. And I worry that from it, you may blame me, that maybe I should have known he was a bad seed from the start. Maybe that was my pride getting in the way, my own ego and my work as a police officer telling me that I could rehabilitate him. I fear you may mistrust me, that it may have been punishment for something you did. Nothing could be further from the truth. You are a sweet, loving boy. Unfortunately, the road to Hell is paved with good intentions, and it seems to be a habit of mine to ignore the road signs that line the road as well. But most of all, I fear that it may have damaged your memories of your true brother, Teo, that you may overlap memories unintentionally, blame him for things Ryan did, or think he was a bad brother when I know he was anything but.

I fear that Ryan may have also damaged your sense of trust in relationships as a whole, how you interact with others and make friends. You're a good kid, but because of your unusual upbringing and difficulty with English, you have a hard time making friends. And all of this isn't even considering Tyler and the bullies at school, or my line of work which often interacts with people at their worst. For as much as I try to put on a good face, you're smart. You know what I deal with. I fear all of this will only make you mistrustful, cynical, and bitter. Please don't be that way. The world is full of good people who do good things.

Part of me hopes that maybe you would consider me one of them.

Love, Dad

Tommen set the second letter aside and took a breath. Perhaps the hardest part about all of this was that they were written in Welsh. They'd never really spoken Welsh in the home until a couple years ago. He'd always felt alone in that. He couldn't even muster up any anger at his dad for not doing so. Now to see his dad's handwriting and his dad's words, communicating honestly, somehow it was the Welsh that made it seem true, that made it feel like family.

He picked up the third letter, this one dated just after he turned thirteen.

Dear Tommen,

You're a teenager now, and suddenly I'm feeling my age. Mostly because you don't seem to feel yours. I always thought the concept of 13 going on 30 was for girls who wanted to wear makeup and jewelry. Apparently it applies to boys, too. To hear you say it, I would think you planned on driving, going to college, and getting married all in the next month. If I ever had any misgivings about you adapting to modern society...sometimes I wonder if I didn't imagine it all, your struggles as a kid.

Of course, I know that part of it has to do with your friends, Eric and Varad. They're the more modern kids. Even Eric, whose family has no electricity or running water. I know they've been helping you navigate the big city and technology and helping you cope, especially when Tyler makes you his target yet again. I also know that coping has gone beyond mere friendship and into something like self-medicating.

Yes, Tommen, I know. And you might expect me to come crashing into your bedroom for a confrontation, but I won't. First of all, I have bad guys who need more watching than you do, and I don't want to come home to a petty fight. Second, some things can only be learned through experience, and the more I try to forbid something, the more you're going to want to do it. Sometimes, it's best to just let things run its course. So, yes, I know it's not just a stomach bug or a migraine or a midnight snack. I know what you're doing, and I do keep an eye on it. If I have to confront you, I will, but I know you, and I know you'll come back around. You're the Chivalrous Welshman, after all, and you know right and wrong. A season for everything.

I also know that it'll run out eventually because you try so hard to hide it, both working and training. Honestly, it's almost funny to watch, sorry to say. Maybe it's the cop in me. You're a good kid, Tommen. Maybe you don't always make the best decisions, but I still love you, and I have faith that you'll come back around eventually.

I'm sorry my letters aren't longer or more frequent, but I've never been good with words. But you probably knew that.

Love, Dad

The fourth letter was dated less than two years ago, right after his dad got out of the hospital. Tommen paused for a moment and considered that. When the truth came out, Tommen thought they had been pretty open and honest with each other at that point. Cautiously, he unfolded the paper.

Dear Tommen,

You're probably wondering why I bothered to write this letter. It's less than two years until you turn eighteen, and a lot of truth has come out recently, but I feel the need. Maybe because I almost didn't get to tell you, and that would have left you sitting with only a box of legal documents, three letters, and one photograph to explain things, plus whatever commentary Micah and Micaiah could give.

I'm not going to rehash the warehouse. You were there. I'm not going to rehash our talk in the hospital. You were there, too. So then, what's left to say? Maybe only that I'm sorry. Sorry that I wasn't a better dad, that I wasn't upfront with you, maybe even that you didn't have a mom, too. I don't know. Maybe I'm just being sentimental, but I also almost didn't get a chance to write this letter or do any number of things that I probably should do.

On the other hand, there is every chance that I won't be around when you get your box, and not because something happened to me, but because I'm a coward. Probably I just left this on your bed and went out to do something, "volunteered" to cover an extra shift at work so I wouldn't have to be there. I hope you can forgive me for that. Old habits die hard, and in my life, those old habits have become like diamonds. Once a coward, always a coward, I suppose.

But again I ramble. Before I go off on another self-pitying tangent, let me just say a few things. First, I love you. You are my world. Second, I'm proud of you. You're a better man than I could ever be. You are the spitting image of your pa and are just like him in almost every way. And in ways that you aren't like him, you're like your ma. I think your pa would agree that she's the better one to imitate, but they were both fine people. You were lucky to have them for parents, and they were lucky to have you for a son. And so am I.

I could spend all day writing out apologies, but it wouldn't be productive for either of us, so I'll just leave this where it sits. I imagine we'll be speaking soon anyway.

Love, Dad

P.S., Look in the mail.

Tommen stared at the letter a second or two longer before folding it up and placing it with the other letters. Four of them. Or more? He rubbed his eyes and ambled out of the bedroom. Becky was on the couch and she looked up.

"Hey. Are you okay?"

He looked at her, momentarily forgetting why he'd come out. Then, "Did the mail come yet?"

"Um...I think so. I don't know, I didn't check. Didn't even think about it."

Tommen made his way outside, momentarily stunned by the sudden wave of heat and humidity. He'd completely forgotten about little things like the weather. Still, he calmly walked out to the mailbox and checked. Electric bill, credit card offers, bank statement, sale paper from Best Buy, and a handwritten letter addressed to him.

He returned to the house, dropped off the pertinent stuff on the counter, discarded the junk mail, and returned to his room with the letter. He could feel Becky watching him the whole way, but she said nothing and made no move to intercept. He hoped she could feel his gratefulness as he closed the bedroom door.

He ripped open the envelope and took out the letter. It was dated just a few days ago.

Dear Tommen,

In the event that something happened to me or that you hated me or something else transpired where we couldn't talk, I had always planned to send you another letter after you turned eighteen, sending it in the mail so it arrived on the day you got your box. This was intentional.

It's not the letter I thought I would write. Honestly, I'm writing this on the side of the road at about three-fifteen in the morning. An idle mind is a dangerous thing, and this could be a long letter. I don't do second drafts, if you get what I'm saying.

Sometimes you scare me to death, kid, and it's a wonder I haven't dropped dead already. Used to be just about you looking both ways before crossing the street, then it turned into the bullying, then your slightly wanton ways of drug and alcohol use, then driving (oh, God, driving). Then it was just the thought of you turning eighteen. And that's not even considering all the stuff in between.

Every parent has hopes for their kids, and I had hoped that this letter would be about you going off to college, getting an education, continuing your training, maybe finding a girl. I had hoped that this letter would be about your questions about faith and religion and all the things you grew up with, how life changed, and all the confusion that happened when you were eight years old.

Turns out, this letter is about all those things, but in a different way. I'm not mad about you and Becky. Actually, I am very happy for you two. Honestly, I think you're going to be a great dad. Better than I was, anyway. You're going to take after your pa, and that's not a bad thing. You are dedicated, honest, loyal, hard-working, compassionate, kind, loving, strong, and also merciful. I think you've found something at eighteen years old that some people never find in a lifetime of searching and secular or vaguely philosophical wisdom. Never, ever let go of that. Don't make the same mistakes I did.

A lot of things in your life have been out of your control. Your family, your training, the warehouse and all ensuing events. In a way, that second life was forced on you. Maybe rightly so, maybe not. I did it only to try and keep you safe, and one fight with Tyler Freeman was all it took. But now things are up to you. You're an adult. You're a man, a father-to-be. It's time to make your own choices now. For real. I don't know where those choices will take you, and it's hard to let go.

I know you've had a lot of questions about God, whether He's real, whether He's really all that loving, whether He's really all that powerful. And you've had to endure more than most, with some very unique questions and perspectives. I'm not a preacher. I'm more theologically challenged than I probably should be, and I don't have all the answers. I guess all I ask is that you don't give up. Everyone needs someone to look to because there will come a time when all your strength and all your will is not enough, and mine isn't either, assuming I'm there. A lot of good men look to God. Maybe it's a start. And as a dad, you're going to need all the help you can get. As a husband, you're going to need even more.

I guess I always thought that if I didn't want something enough, if I said I did not want it over and over again, maybe it wouldn't happen. Maybe your eighteenth birthday would just slip by the same as every other birthday and everything would go back to normal by the next day. It's a foolish thing to think in the first place, and by now, there is no going back. For either of us. You've done it. You're grown up. You are a man with your own life. But just know that no matter what, as long as I can, I'll still be there for you. When Becky is pregnant and cranky for no good reason. When your child is being obnoxious and not letting you sleep (at any age). Or when you just want someone to talk to, have someone to listen. I'll still be here.

I love you, kiddo. And I'm proud of you.

Love, Dad
(Grandpa)

Tommen folded up the letter and wiped his face, silently scolding himself even as he sniffed hard and let out an even breath. He hadn't realized it until now as the heaviness lifted that he'd been absolutely terrified. Afraid his dad secretly hated him, was going to somehow disown him, give him a stern lecture from his own pulpit, tell him he was on his own with Becky and their baby. Somehow, forgiveness and acceptance hadn't been on the table in his mind, not really; they'd appeared more as a smoke screen.

Except it wasn't. His dad could have written a million things under the cover of physical and temporal distance as well as a certain degree of obvious anonymity. But he hadn't. He'd been honest, and acceptance was part of that. Everything was going to be okay.

He called up his dad again.

"Hello?"

"I love you, too, Dad," Tommen said softly, willing his voice not to break and failing.

"Dammit, kid, you can't go get me crying now," his dad told him, his voice wavering instantly. "I have to be an asshole cop, remember? Asshole cops don't cry."

"You're not an asshole cop. So you're allowed to cry."

"I take it you read the letters?"

"Yeah. And the one that came today. You have impeccable timing with the mail."

"It's not that hard, especially when you send it to yourself, basically. What is the post office going to do, return to sender?"

Tommen barked a laugh. "Yeah, no kidding."

His dad took a breath. "Listen, Tommen, why don't we talk about this later, when I get home? You'll be getting up for work about then."

"Yeah. Yeah, okay, sounds good. I love you, Dad. You take care of yourself out there."

"I love you, too, son."

Tommen hung up and wiped his eyes again. He took several deliberate breaths and looked at the box and the letters beside it. Carefully, he gathered up the letters and put them in his closet in a small safe with his birth certificate, social security card, and everything else. Then he took the old picture of his parents and set that on his bookshelf, telling himself he needed to find a good frame for it. He'd probably have to do some research into how to preserve old photographs so it didn't discolor or disintegrate.

He bored himself for a few minutes, burying the memories

and emotion by looking through all the boring legal paperwork, all the judges and lawyers who had been present for all the proceedings, the doctors and nurses, the hospital psychiatrist, this report, that report, all of it very dull, until his composure was restored. Only then did he put everything back, put the lid on the box, put the box in the bottom of his closet for the time being, then making a quick stop in the bathroom before heading out to the living room, plopping down on the end of the couch opposite Becky.

"Hey," she greeted softly. "You okay?"

He rubbed his face and rested his head in one hand. "Yeah. Yeah, I'm fine."

"More in the box than you thought?"

He nodded. "A lot more."

"Anything you want to talk about? I can be a sounding board."

"No, that's okay." He rubbed his eyes and sighed. "Thank you."

After a minute, he reached for the remote and found some mildly interesting show to attract his attention. It took a few minutes and a bloc of commercials before he really paid attention, however. Just as the show was coming back on, Becky lightly touched his shoulder. He looked and she handed him a plate of leftovers from the night before—tacos with Spanish rice—and a second saucer with four cookies.

"You looked like you needed it," she told him. "Mostly the cookies."

"Starving to death, am I?" he wondered.

"One could make that argument."

"Not with you cooking for us now."

"I'm beginning to think you two have gone without a woman in the house for far too long."

Well, she wasn't knitting doilies for everything, so that was something. And it was kind of nice to have dinner. And while Tommen and his dad had always been good about keeping house, Becky just seemed to have a more discerning eye for cleanliness.

Maybe it was the euphoria of not having to do it and they weren't going to argue with free help. The only thing she couldn't do was use the heavy chemical cleaners, which was fine. It didn't bother Tommen a whole lot to clean the bathroom. Nothing out of the ordinary for him.

Actually, if anyone was being spoiled, it was his dad. In the four days since Becky moved in, he hadn't done any cooking or cleaning. His chores were strictly garage and outside work, which was fine with him, if still a little awkward.

Tommen finished off the food even while he absently watched the show on TV, getting through three half-hour episodes before finally scraping up enough motivation to get off the couch and go wash his dishes. He did so silently, maybe even two or three times, before drying them and putting them away.

His mind was distracted, but he wasn't preoccupied with anything in particular that he could think of. He couldn't pin down any one thing that captured his attention. Everything was just happening at once. So many changes coming at him. Well, there was one thing that wasn't changing right away, and that was going back to school. Still, he was returning with a new perspective on things. Fucking hell.

He was almost grateful when it came time for bed, though he was a little confused when Becky joined him.

"You don't have to go to bed the same time as me," he told her, kissing the top of her head before lying on top of the blankets. "You can stay up and watch TV or whatever."

"What are you talking about? I've been forcing myself to stay up with you. I've been forcing myself to do a lot of things lately in the name of keeping up appearances. Now that everyone knows I'm pregnant, I don't have to. Frankly, I'm exhausted."

She crawled into bed beside him and snuggled close for just a few seconds before deciding it was too warm for that. Summer seemed to be lingering a bit, and the house was still quite toasty. Still, he pulled her close and put a hand on her stomach. "So when is that baby bump supposed to appear?"

"It could be sooner than normal, me being as small as I am," she told him, her tone slightly teasing. "But don't worry; it'll come. Weren't you the one freaking out earlier over everything changing and happening so fast?"

"Believe me, I still am. But I'm still excited all the same."

"That's good. So am I."

She fell asleep before he did, and Tommen lay awake for what felt like a long time, long after his sleeping pill should have kicked in. Should he take another? Was his mind really racing that fast? He still couldn't say what specifically was bothering him. Maybe just a nebulous fear of the unknown. Maybe a nebulous fear that he would never know, not really, and that applied both to being a dad and knowing his birth family.

He would never know what life would have been like if he'd never wandered into Forbes Cave that day. He would never know what life would have been like to have his ma and pa and siblings around him, maybe even Uncle Owain later in life. When he'd been trapped in the in-between dimension and could sort of pseudo-time travel, he'd seen what their lives had been like without him, but it wasn't quite the same.

He still remembered watching the deaths of his parents and his brother, and he felt a surge of homesickness worm its way into his chest. What he wouldn't give to have them by his side now, to chastise him for dishonoring his girlfriend, to give him advice. But he didn't, and he would never really know. Even his dad admitted that he couldn't give him everything because he'd been too selfish at the time to care. Walter wasn't even in his brother's wedding picture because he'd been in jail. That probably did a number on him, had been eating away at him for decades.

Tommen took an even breath and closed his eyes. Maybe the sleeping pill was just now kicking in. Either it was delayed, or his mind was racing faster than he thought and it only felt like longer. Everything was changing at once, and yet it seemed to be a game of hurry up and wait. Hurry up and wait. He had a kid on the way. Hurry up and wait. He was finishing school. Hurry up and wait.

He felt the pill start to really kick in, and it was a bit like undergoing anesthesia, like when he'd gotten his wisdom teeth out. His mind was still there for the moment, but there was also the disconnect between mind and body. Could he move his arm? Meh, if he wanted to, he supposed. He vaguely felt Becky roll away from his grasp, but didn't have the willpower to do anything about it. A small part of him didn't like this feeling, that something outside his control was dragging him down like this and it wasn't going to be easy to wake up. He could fight it, if he wanted to, but his will was slowly dissolving. Even his paranoia tapered off to a grudging mumble. He knew almost the exact moment that he fell asleep as murky blackness enveloped his consciousness and he dropped off.

Chapter Three
Generations

Walter didn't like surprises. He didn't like change. There had been a lot of both going around the last week or so. He figured he slept soundly, but he still woke feeling exhausted, or more than usual, anyway.

Several days had passed since Tommen had gotten his adoption box. Several days had passed since he read the letters, gotten the photograph, and they'd had a rather lengthy, brutally honest talk, emotions raw on both sides. Walter had never realized how much Tommen missed his family; even Tommen had seemed surprised since he himself admitted his memories of them were few. Concrete memories, anyway. Then he'd explained more of his escapades in the in-between dimension. Walter had also pointed to Tommen's stories, half-remembered memories manifesting themselves as fiction. That had ripped open a few old wounds, too.

As for Walter, he was forced to guiltily admit—again—that he didn't know a whole hell of a lot about his brother or his family at large. He could name all the people in the photograph, help build the family tree, but intimate knowledge was limited. He could see Tommen's disappointment, which only compounded the guilt and shame.

Now he was heading to work again, his mind still muddled with everything that had happened the last few days. It was almost too much to process. Thank God for impending retirement, even if it was still ten or eleven months away. He still wasn't sure how he was going to pull it off with paperwork in the Wheel, and then he considered that maybe he would just skip that this time. He would forgo the effort of building a new life, at least for now, and simply move on like a normal person. Maybe he would head back to Texas; that hadn't been bad, in all reality. Of course, he'd felt like a younger man back then, with drive and a purpose. Now he'd found his missing kid and that kid was making him a grandpa.

As Tommen would say, fucking hell.

The couple had already made it clear that they were going to find out the sex but wouldn't announce it until at least Thanksgiving, maybe Christmas. By then, they would have a name picked out and they didn't want your opinion thank you very much. When asked which they would prefer, neither would give a straight answer.

Walter figured that if he had to do it all over again, meaning, if and when he got called on to babysit, he would probably prefer a boy. He had experience with boys, good experience he thought. He was one, for starters. He'd raised one. Girls...Becky was the first female in his house in forever, and all of his experience with women had been terrible, with exception of his mother, but that was a whole different dynamic.

He wasn't even sure what it was like to be a grandpa, not just because he'd never been one before, but because he'd never had much of a relationship with his grandparents. He may have met them twice in his life before things started going downhill. All of his grandparenting knowledge came from watching others, most notably Pat, who had half a dozen grandkids. Maybe he'd call him up at some point and see if he had any advice.

At least these musings were a more neutral occupation of his brain, versus the raging storm of most anything else he could consider, and he pulled into the station parking lot no worse for wear.

"Evening, Walt," Kate greeted. She was the night Sergeant, thirties, blond, maybe five-six, one-sixty, and one hell of an attitude if the going got tough.

"Evening, Kate," Walter said, punching in and filling his thermos.

"You look like hell, Walt. Adoption box not go well?"

The first night after his and Tommen's chat had been his night off. Last night had been her night off. It wasn't exactly something he was keen on discussing, but the question was there. Apparently his somewhat neutral mood hadn't made it to his face. He answered, "Depends on how you define well. He has no family to contact because they're all dead, and I'm worse than useless because I don't know jack shit about them because I was the outcast and didn't have much contact with them in the first place."

"Feeling a little guilty, huh?"

"More than a little."

"I'm sorry."

He shook his head and took a drink of coffee. "Nothing anyone can do about it now."

"How's he getting along with pregnant girlfriend? She driving him crazy yet?"

"So far so good, I guess. I haven't heard anything otherwise. I think the box is kind of at the forefront of his mind right now, though. That's going to segue into his own fears about being a dad because he doesn't have a family." Walter rubbed his face.

"Don't beat yourself up, Walt. You can't change the past. You can only deal with what's in front of you. Same with Tommen. Okay?"

"I know, believe me."

"Don't make me make it an order. We got a whole stack of complaints to investigate."

"Lovely."

"And besides," she told him, punching him in the shoulder, "he does have family. He has you. I'm sure he'll be coming to you with all sorts of questions and requests for advice."

"I have no idea what I'm going to tell him."

"You'll think of something." She shuffled through a stack of papers. "Eeny-meeny-minie-mo, here is one, take it to go." She handed one to him. "All yours. I don't know what it is."

Walter took the paper and looked at it. "Break-in at a residence. On it."

He went out, grabbed a set of keys, and made for the garage to grab a cruiser and go. The call had come in about ten minutes ago, and it took another fifteen to get to the house.

It was a bona fide break-in. Homeowner had come home from work to find the front door busted off its hinges, bedroom rifled through. Wife was away for the week so she had her purse and a little jewelry, but all the really expensive stuff had been taken. It was so textbook, a rookie could have taken the call.

Naturally, there was a little adventurous paranoia that it was so textbook perfect as to be too textbook perfect, and maybe the homeowner had staged it in order to defraud the insurance company; it wasn't impossible, and it had happened before, at least in the city. At the same time, not everything was an episode of *Law & Order*, or whatever it was. Actually, the whole thing resolved itself pretty quickly.

The neighbor across the street claimed to have heard the door being broken off and a man entering the building. One next door neighbor said he saw a tall man leaving out the back door. The other next door neighbor said that as he was driving down the road, he saw a third neighbor from the next block down running away down the sidewalk—not running, as in, jogging or anything recreational, but running like a bat out of hell, a small sling bag in his hand.

When Walter walked down the sidewalk, in the path of this mystery neighbor-slash-thief, he came across a diamond earring in the grass, just off the lip of the sidewalk. He returned to his cruiser and casually puttered up the road to this neighbor's house. That was where it got fun.

At first, the neighbor tried to claim he was breathing heavily because he'd been working out. Yes, he was fat, but you had to start somewhere, right? Better than being on the couch daydreaming about being fit, right? When Walter asked where he'd been running and if perhaps he'd seen anything relating to the robbery, the man almost looked ready to fess up, then he decided he wanted to take his chances and try to make it out the back door to the woods beyond.

His problem came from a problem he admitted to not two minutes before. He was fat and unhealthy. If rumors were true, he'd just run a quarter- to a half-mile, something he was clearly not accustomed to, and there was no way he was going anywhere faster, except to jail. At the same time, a fat guy was not as easy to tackle as a thin guy, and it was a fight to get him to the ground, even with Walter throwing his own weight around a bit.

"Maybe you should have taken up running a little sooner," Walter told him, hauling the big man to his feet after reciting the man's rights. "That was at least one charge of evading and eluding. You want to confess to the robbery, too, or do I need to get a warrant?"

The man was not defiant, instead looking almost defeated. "Computer desk, left bottom drawer; there's a false bottom."

Walter retrieved the bag filled with jewelry and a little cash, as well as a few crude lock-picking tools.

Only the first complaint of the night, but at least it was a pretty straightforward, if not an easy case. Walter wrapped things up, dropped off the new criminal to the bookies, and topped off his thermos before heading back out.

There never seemed to be a so-so night, as far as criminal activity went. It was either wide-open action with all the worst baddies out doing the craziest, weirdest stuff all at once, or else it was endless hours of sitting on the side of the road waiting for the clock to tick quitting time.

Tonight was the former. It started with the jewel thief and went downhill from there. Most of it was drug-related. West Virginia had a terrible problem with prescription drugs, and it was estimated that if all the pills were distributed equally, each resident would get between five and eleven thousand pills a year, depending on which statistic you believed. Seeing how every resident did not have between five and eleven thousand pills, that meant that someone was sitting on upwards of a million pills and selling them for a fortune. And it wasn't always the heroin junkies who started smoking at twelve, dropped out of school at age fourteen, got tattoos at sixteen, and knew the criminal justice system inside and out, graduated with a PhD from the School of Hard Knocks.

Sometimes, the victims were those like Walter, who had been injured and become addicted to pain pills. When the doctor stopped prescribing, they needed to get it from somewhere. Not always a dark street corner, but from an opportunistic, low-level teenage entrepreneur who was but the front man for a larger criminal empire, even if that teenager didn't realize it yet. They were the victim's neighbor, the victim's friend, who knew what happened, who wanted to help, who didn't believe that The Man was doing enough. So they offered these off the market pills for just a little cheaper than co-pay. Want more? He knows a guy.

Walter knew plenty of guys. He also knew where the evidence was kept, and he had the power to bypass the security, both legally and illegally. He'd done it, too. He might be—no, he would definitely be in worse shape if not for his encounter with the blue Borelian.

The kingpins, he had no sympathy for. They were entrepreneurial scumbags who knew exactly what they were doing, knew they were harming people but didn't care as long as they made a buck.

The victims, those who had been hurt and so ended up in this downward spiral, those he had sympathy for. And more than once he called an ambulance before he broke out the handcuffs, telling the person to go to rehab before going to jail. Ask for this doctor, that program, and this was the best withdrawal drug he knew of to help. Most often, the victim was too ashamed to say much, and it was the girlfriend or boyfriend or spouse or children who ended up thanking him.

It wasn't right. The kingpins needed to go away. But the victims needed help. They had enough problems with the drugs. Jail wasn't going to help. In a way, that was one of the advantages of being a police officer. As much as his job was to enforce the law, he also had a little wiggle room to exploit some loopholes.

And on top of all of that, there weren't enough jail cells to house every person who was statistically likely to be an addict or even a low-level dealer. There weren't enough hospital beds or rehab centers, either, but at least those were more comfortable and theoretically less prone to spontaneous violence.

Walter rubbed his face as he turned over his latest report to begin filling out the back side. It wasn't even ten o'clock. He let out a breath. Less than a year until retirement.

He nearly came out of his skin when there was a knock on his window and he cracked it open, just enough to speak.

"Can I help you?"

The man on the outside could have been anywhere between thirty years old—on drugs for over a decade—and sixty years old—at least drinking and smoking for over a quarter, if not doing drugs, as well—with short hair, a graying beard and mustache, and a rather blank stare, not fully glassy, but not fully lucid either.

"I don't know," the man said blankly. "I think I need help."

"What do you need help with?" Walter asked.

"I'm not sure. I don't feel right? I think?"

"Sir, can you take a few steps away from my car, please?"

The man did so, and not quickly. Cautiously, Walter opened his door and stepped out. He Banded and did a very quick, very illegal search of the man, but found no weapons other than a dull, chipped pocket knife. He looked around the area briefly, but found no obvious secondary threats. He returned to his original spot and released the Band.

"So, what's going on tonight?" Walter asked nonthreateningly.

"I'm not sure. I was at a buddy's house, and we were doing stuff with his girlfriend, like, drinking and stuff, and I don't know. I just ended up out here and I don't feel so good."

"Yeah? What kind of stuff were you doing?"

"Drinking and stuff, man, I don't know."

"Do you want me to call an ambulance for you?"

The man shook his head, still moving at a turtle's pace. "No, no."

"Do you want me to go to your buddy's house? Where does your buddy and his girlfriend live?"

"Just up there." The man made a vague gesture behind him. "It's not far. But they're okay, I think."

"You think? What was going on up there?"

"Drinking and stuff, man, I told you. Listen, I think I'm okay. I'm going to go home now."

"Yeah? Where's home?"

"This way." The man turned as if to leave, stumbled, righted himself.

Walter went and stepped in front of him before the man wandered into the road and got himself creamed. "Sir, I really think I should call an ambulance for you."

"I don't have insurance, man, I can't pay for that."

"All right. Can I at least give you a ride home, that way you're not wandering around in the road in the dark?"

The man grinned, his breath reeking of alcohol, and patted Walter's shoulder with a limp hand. "You're a good friend, man. I like you. We...should totally hang out some time. Have a beer."

"Maybe later." Walter steered him away from the road and back to the cruiser. "Why don't we get you out of the road and in bed?"

"Yeah, man, I don't feel like walking." He faced Walter again. "You're a good guy, helping a buddy out. You're a good cop. Thanks for not being a douchebag, man."

"Well, I try. Guess it's just because I'm old."

"Yeah, you're not one of those young gun tough nuts, are you? I like you, man. Helping a buddy out. Like I said, I really don't feeling like walking because I don't feel—"

His next word may have been "good" except it came with the added bonus of a full stomach of vomit all over the front of Walter's uniform. Stunned disgust made Walter freeze in place, and he was unable to react as the man collapsed into the grass. For a full two seconds, Walter just stood there, fighting his own gag reflex as the feel of it on his clothes and the smell of it choked him. Finally, he turned his head, spat once, took a breath, then knelt to check the man and get him on his side as he puked again. Then the man was still.

Shuddering with disgust, Walter gingerly touched his radio and managed to call for an ambulance. His only saving grace was that the man was breathing and had a pulse, so he didn't have to do CPR. He reached into his cruiser to grab a few napkins, but he wasn't sure how effective they were at anything other than getting the chunkies off his clothes.

The ambulance arrived just as the guy was starting to come back around. He spit a few times, threw up some stomach fluids, made a few unintelligible sounds, and passed out again.

"He's going to have one hell of a hangover," one paramedic said. "Any evidence of drugs?"

"Nothing in his pockets, no paraphernalia, arms are clean," Walter reported. "Doesn't mean he didn't do something. I think he was, but he wasn't admitting to anything other than the drinking, and I got nothing to tell me otherwise."

The second medic was several steps away, looking rather uncomfortable, as though he were fighting his own gag reflex. Walter knew he didn't smell the greatest still, and he wanted nothing more than to return to the station and grab a spare uniform.

With the man unconscious, he couldn't object to being taken in the ambulance, and Walter skipped out just as soon as he could, sitting forward in his seat and touching everything delicately, hoping not to spread the disgust. He didn't get five steps into the precinct before he was announced.

"Holy God, did something die?"

Arnold appeared from around a corner, expression scrunched up, eye twitching. He looked at Walter, let out a breath, and took several steps back. "God, Walter, what in the hell...?"

"Please, don't ask," Walter said. "I'm getting a spare."

He headed to the storage room, where extra and broken

radios, flashlights, tasers, and other assorted goodies sat quietly, including a few uniforms for emergencies such as these. The best he found was a size too small, but he wasn't going to go around smelling like regurgitated alcohol the rest of the night. Some might consider that a violation of the Eighth Amendment. But it might cut down on the arguing during traffic stops. Well, he didn't want to be stuck with the stench in his own nose all night, so he would change.

He got a garbage bag for his dirty uniform and managed to make the smaller replacement blues work. They would have to work, or else he would be making a detour home. He just walked out of the bathroom when Kate walked in from the garage. She stopped, her expression saying she'd caught the smell.

"Ho...ly shit. What the hell?" she asked, gagging and moving quickly in any direction to escape the smell.

"Sorry, it was me," Walter admitted, indicating the garbage bag. "Examining the contents of a drunk's stomach up close and personal."

"God, Walter, get that out of here." Kate made a shooing motion even as she hurried away from him.

He wasn't too keen on letting it fester in the back seat of his car, but there was little he could do about it. He put the bag in the trunk and went back inside. There was a little lingering smell, but it would be gone soon enough.

"Dammit, Walter," Kate said, exasperated. "Can I trust you with anything?"

"Apparently not. Would you like me to leave and find something to do out on the road?"

"Yes, please. As long as it doesn't involve getting puked on."

"I like it when we think on the same wavelength. Makes it easier to follow orders."

"Shut up, Walter."

Someone's been having a rough night, he thought, but he was wise enough not to say it out loud. Kate took a lot of crap, both politically and in the field. People thought that because she was short and slight that she was easy to intimidate. She didn't like bullies, and she was more than proficient in combat, if need be, with special commendations in gun-fu and kara-taser. Walter had a lot of respect for her for that, and the wisdom to know when not to tease her about it, especially when they were all having a bad night, it seemed.

He went back out, picking a quiet spot which was a decent road distance from several houses and popular with speeders and wannabe drag racers because of the twists and turns followed by a quarter-mile straightaway. Anyone worth their salt in racing wouldn't be able to slow down before he caught them. Even the poorest racers would still be going too fast to talk their way out of a ticket and a possible arrest.

It sounded horrible, but in a way, he was kind of hoping to catch Eli Shaw, younger brother to Tommen's friend Will Shaw. The kid was starting down the wrong path. Since learning from his brother's mistakes was out of the question—Will wasn't exactly a saint himself—Walter hoped that a little hands-on experience in the system might shake him of his misdeeds before they became dangerously ingrained habits.

He caught two regular speeders on that stretch before the real racers came out about one o'clock. He managed to maneuver two other officers into nearby locations before jumping out of their hiding spots in the bushes and breaking up the party. Some kids—ranging from fifteen to thirty years or so—scattered one direction, others scattered in another direction. With a little manipulation of Time, Walter managed to round up about ten kids, where Arnold and Ken nabbed half a dozen between them, calling for additional units for shuttling, as well as a couple tow trucks.

"So, Eli," Walter said, walking up to the—what was he, fifteen? Sixteen, max?—teenager where he sat against the cruiser, hands cuffed behind his back. "What would your brother say if he were here?"

"He fucking rat me out?"

"Watch your language, kid, he didn't tell me a thing. Don't go hating on your brother because he was smart enough to learn from his mistakes. I hope you are, too, because now your mother is going to know that she raised two delinquents. One wised up. What about you?"

Despite trying to keep a straight face in front of his friends, Walter could see Eli's bottom lip was trembling and his eyes were wet.

Walter took down the information for his catch, compared notes with Arnold and Ken, then separated the adults from the minors. Arnold and Ken watched the adults, while Walter started calling around to parents. It took some doing as he got voicemail after voicemail from sleeping parents, but eventually he got through to someone for each of the kids.

Kelly Shaw was naturally upset, her tone over the phone indecisive between utterly furious and absolutely terrified and on the verge of a tearful breakdown. In the background, Walter could hear a male voice, probably Will.

All pickups were to happen at the jail, which suddenly became very full.

"Racers are usually smarter than this," Kate commented. "Where was their lookout?"

"Criminals have to get lucky every time," Walter repeated sagely. "We only have to get lucky once."

"Well, make sure we do everything right so this doesn't come back to bite us in the ass. Nothing worse than bad PR with minor offenders."

"Yes, ma'am."

It—that is, ensuring that "everything was done right"—didn't actually make more paperwork, but going through everything was like walking on eggshells with a fine-tooth comb. Every i dotted, t crossed, every blank filled, box checked, signature signed, and filed in triplicate. The lawyers would be coming out in full force, Walter knew. No one liked it when a cop was accused of roughing up a minor, and he had a feeling that Eli Shaw was going to try and pull just that, to try and look tough with his friends by making a cop look bad, and maybe to spite Tommen in some way.

Hardly a year ago, Tommen was giving Eli a ride to school. The kid was a sophomore this year. He didn't even have a license. Walter wouldn't say he didn't like fast cars, but what was the appeal here? Where did he fall in the grand scheme of things? Was he a racer in training? Couldn't have been, because no self-respecting racer would let an unlicensed wannabe punk touch his wheels, and the flaggers were always women, as evidenced by the three women in bikinis that they hauled in with the rest of them. Other than a spectator, there was only one other thing a young kid like Eli could do...

Walter quickly returned to booking.

"Eli Shaw, where is he?" he asked one of the bookies quietly.

"In that one," the man, Norm, said, nodding discreetly toward one of the cells.

"Segregate him."

"And be accused of racism, no fucking way."

"He's a sixteen year old kid. He was their lookout. If he stays with the big dogs, they will beat him up something fierce."

"You sure about that?"

Walter sighed and went to the cell. "Eli. Come here."

The kid tried to maintain his tough facade, but Walter could see he was shaking.

"What you want now?"

"I want you to drop the act and answer a question. Were you the lookout?"

Eli barked a laugh. "A lookout? Nah, I know better than that. You wouldn't have gotten within ten miles of us if I was looking out. I was a mechanic."

"A mechanic? You don't even have your license."

"So? I've helped my mom sometimes, in the garage and stuff. I was there when she put herself through school. I know a thing or two."

"That's the story you want to stick with?"

"It's the truth."

"I hope so. Because if you were the lookout, how do you think these guys are going to feel about failure?"

Eli did not falter. "I wasn't the lookout. I'm a mechanic. And a damn good one."

With the kid maintaining his story, there was little Walter could do. He still had an uneasy feeling, but he couldn't justify separating Eli from the rest of them at this point. A failed lookout would be beaten before daybreak. A mechanic, though, held more esteem in the racing world. They would be protecting him. The beginnings of gang affiliation.

"I had the same thoughts," Norm said when Walter returned. "He says he's the mechanic. I can't see moving him until he's in danger. Sorry, Walt."

"All right, all right." Walter let out a breath. "Guess I should be going."

Only an hour and a half until quitting time, assuming nothing else major happened. But there were a few places he knew of where he could hide and have a minimal chance of running into anything catastrophic, at least by chance.

He could only hope. At the very least, paperwork could eat up some of his time, maybe carry him to the end of his shift.

Three words into his second report, his phone rang. When he checked it, he found that it was an international number. The only people who would be calling him internationally, theoretically, were other Time Agents. The only reason they would be calling him at this hour was because there had been an alien invasion, or because they knew he would be awake. There were only a handful of people who knew he worked third shift.

"*Bore da, Miach,*" Walter answered.

For a long second there was silence on the other end. Then, "You wound me, Walter. You wound me dearly with your use of such foul language."

"Beth byddach wneud arno?" (What're you going to do about it?)

"Aon ní fós," Miach replied. (Nothing yet.) "Because that's the least of our problems."

Walter sighed. "What now? And why are you telling me?"

"Because it only happened just recently and your Lieutenants are probably sleeping. Besides, it's only big news for those who are in the know."

"So it has to do with the Order."

"Yes and no."

Walter shifted in his seat. "You sound...exhausted, Miach. Exhausted but raring to go. What's—?"

"Micaiah's alive."

The silence stretched out so long, the Irishman ended up asking if the line went dead.

"What are you talking about?" Walter asked slowly, suddenly feeling like a hostage negotiator. "I was at the crime scene, same as you. Same as Kayla. Someone has to be playing a trick."

Miach sighed and ended with a yawn. "That's what I thought, too. Honestly, I don't even know if I believe it yet, and I've seen him."

"So what happened?"

"When Kayla found him in the office, he was still alive—clinically only; he wasn't talking or nothing—but she was too surprised and too hysterical to do much. She Slow Banded him, internally. That made him look dead. Then she had a friend of hers go ahead to the hospital, swap him out or something. Similar to how an advanced Harvester can give away traits, I suppose, or an Akari-bearer changed the Matter on another cadaver, just so it looked like him."

"He was shot three times. How'd they disguise that?"

"A few cuts, a few stitches, a few forged signatures to make it look like someone else already opened him up. Medical examiners are too overloaded these days to care much other than it got done, or that's what she told me. I don't think she's quite sure how they managed to pull it off, and I don't think she cares either way."

Walter still wasn't convinced. "So then where the hell has he been? If he could retake the Wheel with one good leg, the Akarin fortress and Borelian temple—"

"Walt, he might have been alive, but his body, more importantly his brain, was starved of oxygen for a fair amount of time. He wasn't even awake for the first few months. Just this side of brain-dead, or so Kayla told me."

He paused and considered that for a long moment. Then, "So how is he? Not his physical wounds, I'm sure those are fine by now, but how is he?"

Miach sighed again. "Aye, physically he's fine. And they're trying to—"

"Who is they?"

"Kayla and some of her friends. Some of her Tlingit friends are working on his physical recovery, and any who have any Akari experience are slowly trying to bring him back around mentally, using as much Energy and Matter manipulation as traditional cognitive therapy. They are literally going cell by cell, neuron by neuron, but the brain is so complex and unknown that they're afraid of doing too much at once and making it worse."

"But how is he? Does he remember you? His wife? Ireland? Any of us? Any of his adventures?"

"He knows me and Kayla, aye. It's clear that he knows that where he is, isn't home. He can walk, with someone on either side. But he's only just begun speaking, and..." Miach shuddered a sigh and covered up a sniff. "It's hard to watch, Walt. I can only imagine what it's been like for Kayla. I think she uses work with District Nine and the Krydik as a distraction."

"I'm sorry, Miach. Is there any way I can help?"

Miach sniffed again and seemed to come back to himself just a little. "No, no. Listening is enough for now, I think. Honestly, it's not even the reason I called, but...I just needed to tell someone." He scoffed. "Apparently Tommen already knew."

"How?" Walter knew the answer as soon as he voiced the

question. "His Books."

"Aye. Little tattlers, Godwin calls them."

"Godwin Lore? Rifun's right hand man?"

"The very same. But he's not wrong, and we're in a bit of a pickle."

"Let me guess, as much as Julianna is likely to go after those with Authored Books, she also reads them to gain intel, and it's only a matter of time before she figures out where Micaiah and Kayla are."

"I commend your detective skills, Officer Forbes." The joke was mediocre already, but Miach's fatigue killed what little humor remained. "Apparently, Rifun has...requested that his men keep an eye on those like Tommen, Micaiah and myself, and so on, maybe even actively defend us. But they have their own problems, too."

"Let me take another guess," Walter said. "They're willing to smuggle Micaiah and the others wherever they can, but you have to do some work for them in return."

"Correct again."

"What have they got you doing?"

"I'm investigating Haunstein, the doctor in Kentucky."

"The notorious Time Agent doctor."

"That's right." There was some background noise and Miach's tone changed again, now thoughtful. "I don't think the Miaramila are helping us out of the goodness of their hearts, nor just because Rifun asked them to. However much they respect him, they have their own issues."

Walter shifted in his seat and sighed. "What do you think they're up to?" Did he really want to know the answer?

"I think they're interested in Micaiah's recovery. There are very few Akari-bearers confident enough to touch the brain, and even fewer willing guinea pigs, however desperate. I think if Micaiah makes a recovery, they might try the same thing on Rifun."

Walter shrugged though Miach couldn't see. "All right, I can't say I don't understand. His blindness and seizures have only ever brought him trouble. I can see why he might be interested in the clinical trials."

"Well, it's not just the brain, though that's the most important part."

"Micaiah's leg?"

"Aye. As I said, neuron by neuron, cell by cell."

Walter shuddered. "I'm...I'm not going to think about that."

Miach made a strained sound of agreement. "It's not any easier to look at, believe me."

Walter let out a breath. "Miach, Micaiah was shot over a year ago now. I hate to ask the question, but do you really think he could make a reasonable, if not full, recovery?"

Now the Irishman made an incredulous noise. "Walt, I just found out that my twin brother has been raised from the grave. I don't know what to think. And on top of that, Tommen knew and didn't say anything."

"He probably didn't know how you would react."

Miach groaned. "Fair enough. How is Tommen, by the way? How is he holding up under the scrutiny of a pregnant girlfriend?"

Walter blinked, paused for half a second as he processed the change in conversation. "So far, so good, but I think the novelty is starting to wear off."

"Seven months to go."

"Oh, he knows. Although if you asked him, you would think the baby was coming tomorrow."

Miach laughed. "Poor kid. Shit, I remember when he wasn't much more than a kid himself who could barely speak English."

"Hey, I'm the one about to be a grandpa."

He laughed again. "Yeah, okay."

"How about your quest to move out of your great-great-great...grand-nephew's apartment?"

"Oh, you mean my cousin? Yeah, I'm moving out this weekend, which is just as well because I'll need some space to do my own thing for a while."

"Found a girl, did you?" Walter teased.

Miach sighed. "No..."

"Just want your own space?"

"Oh, absolutely, but it'll also serve as kind of a base."

"You're not moving across town."

"No. Now that I know, I have to help. I've never not been my brother's keeper, but...he does need me." Miach sighed. "I've got a lot of work to do, a lot of people to talk to. If it's not Cai, it's whatever work the Miaramila have for me."

"Do the Akarin know?"

"Walt, I don't even know where the Akarin are. Kayla is more focused on Cai and District Nine. Godwin and the Miaramila say good riddance. It is what it is. We have to get Micaiah moved before Julianna finds him, and I have to talk to Haunstein."

Walter nodded though Miach couldn't see. "All right. Keep me updated will you? And stop by on your way through to say hi."

"Oh, absolutely. I only got a few days to tease Tommen about being a new dad. I'll be sure to stop by and hassle him some more here and there."

Walter laughed. "You do that. He might take it better from you than from me."

"Come on, Walter. He knows you support him, right?"

"Yes, he does, but I'm still his old man. You're his crazy uncle."

"Damn straight. Listen, you've probably got a bunch of stuff to do yet tonight, so I'll let you go."

"Actually I don't, just a few reports, and it's almost quitting time anyway."

"So then you need to go to bed."

"I'll talk to you later, Miach. *Hwyl*."

"*Slán*."

Walter hung up with mixed feelings. On the one hand, he was always happy to get a call from a friend; for once, the time differences worked in their favor. On the other hand, he was just stunned. Micaiah was alive. Walter remembered seeing his body lying in its own blood in the office of the bakery. How could he still be alive? But then, with the little switcheroo that they did, considering how long he'd been left starving of oxygen, was he ever going to be the Micaiah that they all remembered? Would death have been kinder? And to think that it was going to take a whole team to rescue him, when he was rescuing whole teams not long ago.

And it all came back to Julianna. If it was just Tommen she was aiming for, that would be one thing. If they knew that Julianna was gunning for only his physical harm, that was a threat they could deal with, swiftly and severely. But revenge was not always about death; most times, it was about pain and suffering. How better to damage Tommen than by killing his new family, one he helped to create? After all his adventures so far and the pain and injuries he'd already sustained, that might be what finally broke him.

As much as Walter didn't want to tell Tommen, he also knew that he had to. They needed to be ready and stay in the loop, prepared to defend Becky and the baby at all costs.

It was an odd sensation, Walter thought. He wasn't just in this to defend his son, but his daughter-in-law and unborn grandchild as well. As much as it was the same ferocity as when he'd gone to rescue Tommen from the warehouse, there was also a certain sense of wisdom and experience that overcame him. Maybe he was overestimating himself, or maybe he was getting too philosophical with the whole grandpa thing, but it was different than merely defending his own offspring.

Add on to that the fact that Becky would have to remain blissfully unaware of the threats for as long as possible, being brought in only if absolutely necessary. It was as much for her own psyche as it was the health of the fetus. Being exposed to Time and the Akari and everything else was hard on a normal person. There was no telling what it would do to an expectant mother. And there was no way Walter was going to find out the hard way what effect Time could have on an unborn child. He wasn't going to risk his grandchild for a curious science experiment.

No. Becky had to stay out of it for as long as possible, completely unaware from start to finish as the ideal.

But where did it finish? It started with knowledge, but how would it end? Rifun had been relentless when it came to trying to recruit Tommen, and even that paled in comparison to what Walter's fears could conjure up for Julianna and her ambitions. What if she was relentless to the point that literally nothing short of death would stop her from trying to exact revenge?

Walter took a breath. He couldn't let his thoughts get away from him. Even if Tommen was a target, he wasn't much of a threat. He wasn't the most highly trained Akari-bearer, and he was alone. Plus he wasn't even on the run. He went to work, he'd be going to school, all very normal things, very routine. It wouldn't take but three days to track him—or her—and put a bullet in either of their heads from a thousand yards. Sad, but true. That alone might be what bought them the time they needed to act or react to the threat. Leave Tommen in his rut for a while, safe and sound, and go after more unpredictable targets in the meantime. Maybe that was why Rifun hadn't been murdered in his cell yet, easy enough to make it look like a suicide, especially in a suicide cell, or even start another riot and hope he got trampled in it this time. But as long as he was in jail, he was contained. Julianna could come back for him later once all his followers on the outside had been dealt with.

Say one thing for Julianna, she wasn't dumb. And she wasn't above using herself as a decoy or distraction. She'd done it once before, fleeing across the Atlantic with Cassius and spreading the lie that she, a poor woman, had been chased across the ocean by a madman. Her personal feelings and her image were nothing compared to the narrative at large.

And then there was the matter of the Time industry. Now that the Borelians were back in control of the judicial system, this time with ten times the power and one hell of a grudge, how were they likely to side? It wasn't likely to be an alliance with the Order, that was for sure. The Akarin were an unlikely ally as well. Would they side with the Time industry, seek to increase their own power and influence, take the industry for themselves? That was something to consider. What if they just sided with themselves, glory to Brelix, and tried to destroy the Time industry, get rid of that player completely?

Too many variables, and Walter was stuck on the side of the road with enough time to consider them all, or at least a good number of them. He had to stay focused on what mattered, and that was protecting his son and his son's family.

Damn, that was still a strange concept to consider. His son had a family now.

Of course, he couldn't just go rushing home to make a grand entrance like some middle-aged superhero. It was still only three in the morning. Tommen and Becky would be sleeping soundly, neither wanting to wake up to an alarm that would take them to work or school. Sure, Walter could wake Tommen up to relay the news, but was it really news? They'd both known that Julianna was an evil witch and she didn't like Rifun or his followers or the Akarin or Tommen very much. Was revenge really news?

No, but with the very real changes in his life, it would be easy for Tommen to dismiss everything else as half a fairy tale, a life he once lived but was no longer front and center. Just like it was hard for most Americans to care about woes on the other side of the world because they could not see them, so it would be difficult for Tommen to really consider Julianna a threat, not when he was up at two in the morning making a sandwich topped with boneless chicken wings and pepperoni, slathered in mustard. At that point, any extraterrestrial threats would be met with a harsh shushing as Tommen told them to keep it down because his pregnant girlfriend was having a craving in the middle of the night, he didn't want to upset her, and he just wanted to get back to sleep. And if they tried anything, they would be answering to her, and a pregnant woman is not someone you want mad at you.

Walter found himself smiling at that thought. Honestly, he thought that would be kind of funny to see. Becky was spit and vinegar on a normal day. Throw a few buckets of hormones in the mix and she could probably cow even Rifun. Pit her against Julianna and watch the fireworks. Popcorn, anyone? Now there was a thought.

He returned to the precinct in a little better mood than he'd left, though the uniform was still a bit uncomfortable. He promised Kate he would have it washed and returned in the next couple nights. She just waved a dismissive hand and told him that as long as his other uniform could be salvaged without stinking like vomit, they'd just call it good. He signed off on his last report, punched out, and left.

The plastic bag did a good job keeping his car from smelling like vomit, but that didn't mean he didn't catch a whiff here and there if he turned his head just right or if the air current in the vehicle changed slightly. He was loathe to turn on the washing machine at five in the morning, but he couldn't let his uniform cook any longer than it already had. Black could hide a stain fairly well, but nothing could disguise an ingrained stench like that. When he opened the bag, he nearly added another helping of vomit to whatever was already there. Eyes watering, he tossed the uniform in the washer by itself and ran it as a heavy soil load, making sure to add extra detergent and opting for a number of extra features, like a pre-wash and a second rinse.

The washing machine rumbled to life, and Walter half-expected either Tommen or Becky to come out and wonder what all the racket was. Neither of them did. In fact, when Walter checked in on them—still having trouble breaking the habit of looking when he got home from work—they were sound asleep. He let out a breath and backed away, silently closing the door and going into his room.

As much as Walter didn't want things to change, there were a few things in his life he could do without, such as constant impending doom over his head or his son's head. Things were easier before the warehouse, when he was just a Timekeeper Captain who oversaw his underlings, dealt with general Time politics, and oversaw the arrests of Runners. Things were easier when the Hands of Time were merely corrupt, but predictable and pretty easy to weather, being part of an

Unengaged society and all.

Rifun had taken a sledgehammer to that mirror of illusion, shattered what everyone thought they were seeing, and so unleashed a tide of death and mayhem. But, if Walter understood it correctly, this was not the first time that mirror had been broken. Eventually, the pieces got glued back together and everyone pretended that the cracks weren't there. Until the next madman came along.

Cassius, Rifun, and Julianna were the minds behind this latest series of events. Cassius was dead, Rifun behind bars and powerless, playing chicken with death over every seizure and every jailhouse fight. Julianna was the only one left to take out. And as it had been pointed out many times, they were only immortal, not indestructible. Just as Rifun should have succumbed to Kayla's knife in his chest, so Julianna could also be killed.

Hopefully, by the time the cycle began again and someone new decided to follow in their footsteps, Walter would be long retired, living on the beach somewhere. Maybe he would even be dead, or close to it. Living out a peaceful last life.

It was morbid to think about, but even as humans indulged in intermittent fantasies about having a longer life, there was also a part of them that craved death, craved a release from work and pain and suffering, that hoped their good deeds would earn them some sort of respite, whether it was a fluffy cloud and a harp, a private tropical island, an audience with God Himself, or some other iteration of a pat on the back from the universe.

Walter himself had dealt with his own issues of faith over the years. How did God feel about Time? Was it wrong to manipulate the physics that the Almighty Himself had conceived of and put in motion? What about the Akari, expanding those abilities to Matter and Energy, the Builders who could play with the very strings of Creation? What did God think about the Akari-bearers of either flavor and their worship of this Author? Was it idolatry? Blasphemy? If this Author gave them such great power, would God not be inclined to take it away from them before they did something really dumb?

Okay, giving a gangster a submachine gun was bad. But this was giving someone the power to change Creation itself. That gangster may as well have been a mouse with a needle for a sword.

And what about him, Walter? How would he be judged for his role in all of this? If Time was bad, would he be punished for being a Timekeeper Captain? Would he earn points for trying to save his son and stop Rifun? Would he lose points for not doing enough? How did that all work? Grace through faith was great and all, but how did he know? The Bible was sorely lacking on instructions for people who could manipulate the physics of the universe.

He was just about to get in bed when he heard Tommen's alarm go off. A minute later, the teenager wandered out of his room, trying to stay quiet. He did not even appear to notice Walter.

Walter waited up a few minutes more until his son was dressed and meandering his way out in search of food.

"Late night?" Tommen asked, slowly coming to life.

"Sort of. I would be prepared for a call from Will."

"Eli finally get caught?"

"You didn't hear it from me."

"Anonymous source."

"Naturally. Miach also gave me a call this morning."

"What's he up to?"

So Walter relayed their conversation in brief. Tommen did not interrupt, just plowed through three bowls of cereal and a slice of peanut butter toast.

"Has Rifun said anything to you?" Walter asked when he was finished. "Have you communicated at all?"

Tommen shook his head and force-swallowed his last bite of toast. "Nothing." His voice was hoarse and he got a glass of water before continuing. "He's been quiet on this front, but if dream-walking is an Akari thing, he won't be able to. And I haven't gone to him at all. Do you want me to?"

"Under any other circumstances, I would say no, we can handle this ourselves. But with Becky in the mix now, I don't think we can be too careful. Rifun hates Julianna just as much as we do, and he has the best wealth of inside knowledge."

His son nodded. "Agreed. It'll have to wait until tonight, though, because I kind of have to work and stuff."

"I understand. I just wanted to warn you."

Tommen grinned. "Funny how casual this has gotten. Yeah, there's someone out to possibly kill you and the people you love. Just thought you should know. Oh, and don't forget to pick up a dozen eggs on your way home."

Walter stifled a laugh. "I was thinking the same thing. Okay, kiddo, I'll let you get to work and I need some sleep."

And just as casually, they parted ways.

Chapter Four
Grainy Photo

Thursday night had been the latest in a series of especially tough nights for Tommen, beginning with the adoption box and leading into his session with Nathan, who was both his professional shrink and his mentor in Akari training. Since training together, Tommen had learned plenty about Time—similar to what the Time industry taught, but with more finesse and a hell of a lot more power. He'd also learned more about Matter, manipulating his DNA a little to work a Disguise, building a crude Disguise on someone else, popping out dents in his car, and being able to Feel people and objects. Feeling was perhaps the spookiest thing, when used on people. He'd literally been able to feel the food in his stomach, feel it digesting. He'd done it once when shaking hands with a stranger, and he'd Felt a small tumor on the man's left lung. His reaction probably hadn't made the best impression on the man, but it was startling.

And then there was Energy. He'd gotten better at his manipulation of Gravity, both himself and other objects, and it was something he use frequently at work to lift heavy items. Magnetism was also in his repertoire. Electricity was still a little touchy. Light he was getting better at, almost ready to start in on cool invisibility cloaks. Advanced concepts like Fire were still beyond his range, and his arm reminded him of that every time he even considered it.

The Akari was a powerful thing, and he was getting good at it. Nathan often told him so when they trained either before or after their normal session.

"You look like you need to talk," Nathan had observed when they met at Forbes Park. "And you're not normally one for canceling appointments out of the blue."

"Becky's pregnant," Tommen had blurted.

The silence had been long.

Nathan broke first with a congratulations and all the usual questions: How far along? How was mom doing? When was the due date? Was he excited? And so on and so forth.

Their session had gone long. They talked about all the changes that were going to happen, how Tommen felt about them, and what he considered the "normal stuff." That was the easy part, which should have said something about the second half of their session where they discussed if and how to proceed with his Akari training.

Time was a funny thing, and Timekeeping more so. In the Time industry, a Timekeeper could be afflicted by slowed aging, such as in the case of Walter or Miach or eighty-five percent of Timekeepers. The number of extra years a Timekeeper would naturally enjoy increased the more he used Time. The other fifteen percent were affected by accelerated aging, and their years decreased with their use of Time. Tommen was one of those. He'd been Suppressed, prevented from ever using his Timekeeping abilities in order to stave off the accelerated aging.

The Akari on the other hand only granted extended life, slowed aging. That meant Tommen had only a few options. First, he could bring Becky into the know, make her an Akari-bearer, and they could spend many extended years together. Second, he could continue himself but not bring her in, and he would watch her and their child and any future children grow old and die. Third, he could give it up completely, maybe enjoy some extended healthy years, but otherwise perish in a reasonably normal human lifespan.

The choice was not as easy as one might think, and Tommen felt guilty that he didn't immediately drop everything and cling to his family. Maybe it was because he enjoyed the extra power, the ability to mold the fabric of the universe. Maybe it was because he knew of all the threats out there, knew that his notoriety wouldn't slide under the radar forever, and he wanted to be able to protect his family.

There was no Suppression for the Akari except for the Akari-bearer to simply choose not to use it. Tommen and Nathan eventually came to an agreement to continue training on Thursday nights up until Christmas, then taper off until the baby was born when they would stop completely. Nathan suggested that a gradual transition would be better, provide a sense of normalcy for a while until all hell broke loose, that is, the actual birth. And if Tommen ever did need to defend his family, the Akari would be right there and waiting, and he would have the knowledge and training to back him up.

It was just as well that they came to that arrangement, since the next morning his dad told him about Miach's report. He knew Micaiah was alive, and the elder twin wasn't doing so hot. With the twins, Kayla, and at least a few Miaramila all in one place, it was looking like a jucier target than whatever stalemate the Krydik had forced.

Tommen dream-walked to Rifun that night. The brain was more active at night, and it was basically taking the Energy from his brain and connecting it to the Energy in Rifun's brain...but not in such a 60's hippie sense. There was science behind it somewhere. There had to be. The more you communicated with a person, the more easier it became to find their particular Energy and contact them. Tommen had dream-walked with Rifun several times, basically had him on psychic speed dial.

God, he sounded nuts.

He found himself in a concrete closet. No, not a closet. A cell. Six feet by six feet, a narrow metal shelf taking up just under a third of it, a dingy toilet-sink unit in one corner, a solid steel door making up most of one wall. There were no windows whatsoever, and the little light overhead was dim and covered by some kind of heavy plastic covering. No grate to tie off to. Claustrophobia quickly set in, and Tommen was not normally given to such a thing.

"Well, well. Look who decided to visit."

Tommen could hardly turn around where he stood, and he smacked his knee against the toilet, biting back a curse. Rifun lay on the metal shelf that passed as a bed. He was too tall to lie comfortably and his knees were bent. His dream self was not injured and he did not wear a cast, only the standard prison orange.

"Come to gloat?" Rifun asked, staring at the ceiling, not looking at Tommen. "I'm surprised you waited as long as you did. Or maybe I've lost track of my days. How long has it been?"

"Almost two weeks," Tommen answered, still trying to process being in a six by six by eight concrete box. Sixty seconds in and he wanted to claw his eyes out. Rifun hardly seemed to notice, and Tommen doubted the man had been broken so quickly.

"Hm," was all the man had to say.

"How much has Godwin told you?"

"The elder Durvin twin is physically alive, though hardly the man who once killed the Bat. Julianna remains in a surprising stalemate with the Krydik and may be turning her attention to other targets, such as said Durvin twin and his lovely nursemaid wife and brother."

"Is there anything else you can tell us? Did Julianna ever express—?"

"Look at you, being the little detective." Rifun chuckled. "I will save you the time and effort and say that I don't know anything more that would be useful. My final Book would reveal more from her perspective chapters. You may remember that I was a bit under the influence during that time; the Book remembers better than I do."

"Oh, come on," Tommen said. "Think!"

"You assume I spend my time doing other things. I do not."

"Miach said that Kayla and a few others are trying to help Micaiah, poking around in his brain and maybe even trying to regrow his fucking leg. You can't tell me you're entirely disinterested in that."

Rifun frowned. "All right, so maybe I am. What does it have to do with anything else?"

"You're a pretty juicy target yourself. And so am I."

"Yes, I did hear about that. Congratulations. I mean it. Once again, you have achieved something I could never hope to do. You stayed true to the Author and her purpose, opposed me while I perverted it. Now you have been rewarded."

"To quote my dad, I put my dick where I shouldn't have. No Author needed."

"You know better than that," Rifun cut in. "Fate is fixed, is it not?"

"And now they're a target," Tommen went on. "I am asking—I am begging you, do you know anything about what Julianna might be doing? Has she ever hinted at anything, does Godwin tell you stuff that he doesn't tell me?"

"Of course he does."

"Would Julianna really go after a baby or a pregnant woman? I mean, she's a woman, too."

"A childless hedon," Rifun stated. "Her barrenness only adds to her spite."

"She can have kids. I mean, I've heard that it's a little more difficult, but the Krydik get along just fine, so…"

"You are asking me to read her mind. I cannot. If I could, do you think I would be here?" He made a vague gesture. "Murder. Me, you and your family, the twins, Aklaq, the Miaramila, the Krydik, the Akarin, and anyone else who annoys her. As I have said before, she doesn't want to be a chosen one, she wants to be *the* Chosen One. Her specific plans, I cannot attest to."

"What about Godwin, swapping out Julianna's moles in the courthouse?"

"Then that would be a question for Godwin, don't you think?"

Tommen shifted his stance. Before he could speak, Rifun continued, "You are correct that I am interested in Micaiah's recovery. The fact that he is alive is a burden off my conscience. But until he is mentally restored, or until he has a brand new fleshly leg, and such results may be copied onto me, there is nothing I can do. Even if my fingers and sight were restored, my seizures cured, it means little without my Akari abilities. And until that day, if it ever comes, the Miaramila listen to Godwin Lore."

"And he just abandoned you after the trial?"

Rifun shrugged mildly. "We have an arrangement."

Tommen sighed and folded his arms. He wanted to sit down, but he wasn't about to sit on the toilet or the floor, even if it was only a dream. "Are you at least being treated somewhat well?"

"I'm in jail; it depends on how you define well. All they need to fulfill that statement is food and water three times a day and ensure that I'm alive every morning and every night. And that I don't cause trouble, which is fairly easy to do, even in this little box. On the days they remember my meds, they tell me it's quite possibly cyanide but to take it anyway so they can check me off on their little list for med delivery. They routinely tell me to kill myself, and sometimes they'll send in a piece of paper and a small pencil, under the guise that I asked for it, in hopes that I'll stab myself in the neck or try to cut my wrists or something. They really don't like it when I insist on living, and they hated it even more when I told them that I'm right-handed and it's really hard to stab myself in the arm with or through a cast. I think they might have wanted to beat me for that one if they didn't get called away to some other emergency right then."

"Fuck." Tommen shook his head. He wasn't sure which was more disturbing, that the jailers would treat anyone like that, or that Rifun was so calm about it.

"Oh, I can't wait to get to prison," Rifun went on, his sarcasm evident. "But at least a modern American prison will still be better than a Malagasy prison from French Imperialism. For one, there won't be pickaxes."

"Yeah, you'll be shanked with a sharpened toothbrush instead."

Rifun grinned but said nothing.

Tommen shifted his stance. "Well, I guess if you have nothing for me, then I have no reason to be here."

"You don't. But as I've said before, I enjoy our visits."

"Don't expect me to make the drive to Mt. Olive."

"No, of course not. Technically, I'm not supposed to have

contact with my victims at all, but who's going to believe this?"

"I'll see you at your sentencing."

"Write something nice in your victim impact statement."

Tommen ended the psychic call, slipping into darkness before being jolted awake by an alarm.

Work was normal, and Becky was slowly working out her school routine, figuring out what she needed to do to juggle her schoolwork and reopen her sewing business, which she still planned to do at some point in the next few weeks, hope to bring in the Thanksgiving and Christmas crowd. Over the weekend, she headed over to her parents' house, to her old room, and got everything cleaned and sorted and categorized and itemized and organized and ready to go. Her biggest project would be baby clothes, but she wanted to hold off until a genetic test could be done to determine whether the dwarfism gene was present.

Not a few times, as Tommen lay next to Becky, he considered Feeling her and the baby, but he didn't dare. Sure, he could poke around his own genes, make a few changes for cheap party tricks, but information about the Akari and its effects on the unborn was scarce to completely absent. Even if there had been some research, the earthquake and destruction of the Archives would have likely destroyed it. And even if it had miraculously survived, it wasn't as though he could just ask Julianna for a library card to go looking around for such information. He wasn't about to put his child at risk for his own stubborn curiosity that could be satisfied with proven medicine.

And it wasn't as though he had to wait long, either. The appointment with the OB/GYN was Tuesday. Becky teased him that he was more nervous than she was, and she was the one carrying. He again pointed out that she had a huge family with a lot of collective experience. He was completely new to all of this.

Tuesday morning, he got up for work, and her mom took her to class. At eleven o'clock, he left the job site and went to pick her up. She was waiting for him at one of the picnic tables and was packing up her books as he pulled into a parking spot. After the doctor, he had to bring her back for her afternoon class, then get back to the job site. It would be a long day for both of them.

"So how was school, dear?" Tommen asked mockingly.

"Ha ha, very funny," Becky said. "Class was fine. Apparently, I'm going to be the object lesson for when we get to reproduction. Our baby is already a celebrity."

"Does that mean that he or she will get an A for the course, too?"

"Hey, if it could carry over twelve years of schooling and knock off some future tuition costs, I am all for it."

"I don't think that's going to happen."

"Yeah, me neither."

The drive to the hospital was unremarkable except for Becky monologuing—hopefully to herself, because Tommen couldn't follow any of it—about some of the questions she wanted to ask about the genetic test, her own care, the C-section, and other things with long scientific names or else long acronyms which he did not understand. He hoped there wouldn't be a test because he was awash in alphabet soup right now. He was just happy he knew what OB/GYN stood for.

At the campus, Becky had seemed upbeat and alert. When they got to the hospital and got out of the car, Tommen saw she looked as though she'd run the whole way.

"Summer is not the time to be pregnant," she sighed. "It sucks. It's more work."

"Oh. You could have told me to turn up the A/C."

"It's not just that."

But she would not elaborate. Tommen told himself it was the humidity. Or maybe her incessant talking. Whatever it was, he couldn't change the weather. Besides, it was basically September; the weather would be cooling off soon enough.

They crossed the parking lot and entered the building. Tommen had no idea where he was going, but Becky apparently had a pretty good idea because she led the way with total confidence, as if she worked in the hospital and knew all the nooks, crannies, and secret passages. Actually, considering her parents worked in the hospital, she might actually know at least a few of those nooks, crannies, and secret passages. But did Audiology and OB/GYN really talk much? A year ago, Tommen never would have even considered questions like these, would have found them laughable.

The times, they were a-changin'. He said nothing, simply followed her down the hall, around a corner, down another hall, and through a set of double doors marked "Obstetrics and Gynecology." From there, it was a sharp right and down to a room which looked like any standard doctor's office.

Becky got them checked in, then went to a waiting area. One other person was already there, a woman maybe in her late twenties or early thirties, heavily pregnant, one toddler running around the play area while she struggled to focus on a magazine.

"I'd say you've been here before," Tommen commented to Becky.

"I came here once with my sister, but that's it," she replied.

"I thought this doctor specialized in difficult pregnancies?"

"She does. My sister had two miscarriages before, so she had almost weekly appointments to check for any problems and make sure everything was fine, do an emergency C-section if necessary once the baby became viable."

"Oh."

One couple emerged from the doctor's office and the other woman with the toddler went back with the nurse.

Tommen browsed through several informational pamphlets, each one convincing him more and more that something was going to go horribly, horribly wrong, and that he was not ready for this. Becky already had special needs of her own. Tossing a baby in the mix just scrambled everything in his brain. He found himself grateful for her large family and that they seemed to have everything together with enough experience to open their own clinic.

He texted his dad.

"I am not ready for this."

A minute or two later, his dad replied, "Sitting at the doctor's office, are we?"

"Yes."

"I'm afraid I can't offer a whole lot of advice other than women have been doing this for the whole of human history. It's why we have human history. And modern medicine is a wonderful thing. I think she'll be okay. So will you."

"Yeah, but..."

"Tommen, my wife did not have the luxury of a hospital or an OB/GYN. She had her female relatives and a midwife. And everything went smoothly for her. Becky has a huge family with lots of women, her mom is a nurse, and even ambulance crews are trained to assist in births, if it ever came to that."

"I know."

"As for you, there is exactly jack shit you can control about the situation. Your job is to be attentive, loving, supportive, and flexible. She is going to say and do things she wouldn't normally do. You just have to roll with it. Sorry to say, kiddo, but there isn't much that we as men can do when our women are pregnant. They seem to retreat into their own secret society from which we are barred."

"That doesn't make me feel better."

"Sorry, kid, I got nothing for you. Hang in there."

Tommen calmly put his phone away and picked up a magazine. There was no *National Geographic* or *Time* to be found here, and he found himself looking through *Parenting*, *Kidz!*, and *Focus on the Family*. He couldn't remember what he read, but he hoped he retained some of it.

The woman with the toddler returned.

"Becky?" the nurse inquired.

"That's us," Becky said, setting her magazine aside and walking over, Tommen trailing hesitantly. The door closed behind them and they headed down a short hall with only three doors: records and billing on the right, emergency exit at the end, and the actual office on the left.

"How are we doing today?" the nurse wondered, taking them into the office. Like most doctor's offices, there was the bed in the middle, a few chairs on one wall, cabinets, a sink, and relevant posters on the walls. He helped her onto the bed.

"Tired," Becky replied. "Sick. And I still have to go to class this afternoon."

"Okay. Well, I'm going to get a quick set of vitals on you, and then Dr. Whitmore will be in to talk to you."

Tommen didn't realize how wound up he'd gotten until the nurse got Becky's vitals and reported them normal, even her blood sugar. Then he felt exhausted with relief. Everything was fine. There was no emergency here.

But even so, it would be another eight weeks before even the beginning of viability.

His paranoia sat politely in the corner of his mind. At some point, his paranoia had taken on the shape of Mr. Snuffles, getting just a little closer every time he dared let his guard down, occasionally reaching out with a paw to tap on a particular thing to be paranoid about. So far he hadn't had any true, rabid paranoid moments, but he imagined they would be something like when Mr. Snuffles ran around on his crazy time, tearing up the house. Nothing was safe.

Tommen's first thought when Whitmore walked in the room was Lily Guile reincarnate, or resurrected. Light skin, jet black hair, great body. There were just two major differences: Whitmore was easily in her late thirties or forties, and her demeanor spoke of true concern and compassion for her patients. Lily had done her job just so she could Harvest entire lifetimes from her tiny patients and make a fortune at the auctions.

They shook hands and made introductions; Tommen hoped his shaking and sweating wasn't overly noticeable, or if it was, could be passed off as being from work which still clung to him as dirt and concrete dust. He suddenly felt inadequate, as though he were the filthy, reluctant baby-daddy who lived in a trailer, drank beer, got high, and wouldn't be sticking around long.

Self-conscious didn't even begin to cover it.

Whitmore interviewed them a little beforehand. When did they find out, how far along were they told, how had she felt during that time, any pain or trouble during sex either before or now. They answered honestly, though some of it made Tommen want to melt into the floor.

"I can see you're uncomfortable," Whitmore said finally, looking at him. "Is it just because it's your first kid, or...what's going through your mind?"

It was a long moment before he answered, "Y...eah. Basically. First child...I'm...an only child, adopted. I don't have a mom, or I haven't since I was eight. And...the...social implications. I think that's the right term."

"You're not married."

"Yeah."

Whitmore's expression was unreadable, but not unfriendly. "My job here is to ensure the health and well-being of mother and child. I leave the judgment part up to the Almighty. So know that as long as you're here, you're safe. Okay? And as far as your other concerns, I can see how being adopted and having only one parent might put a strain on you, and you might have some doubts. But I can recommend a number of excellent parenting classes, support groups, anything you need."

"I'm already seeing one therapist, I'd rather not see two."

This went way beyond self-conscious. Self-conscious wasn't even on the radar anymore.

She tried to reassure him again, then resumed her questioning. Most of it fell on Becky, going over her family history which didn't seem to matter as much as her personal history, for obvious reasons. Her dwarfism put extra pressure on her spine and she sometimes had to wear a back brace when she sat or stood for a long time, especially in her sewing. She also had malformed foot and ankle bones; that had been curbed by orthopedic shoes which she'd been wearing most of her life.

One of the biggest concerns was her narrow hips. There was absolutely no way she could have a natural birth; if she tried to push a baby out, she would break her pelvis, possibly damage her spine, and she would either bleed out or, with divine intervention, become paralyzed at best.

"Should we schedule the C-section now, then?" Becky wondered.

"Not yet," Whitmore told her calmly. "I want to wait and watch the baby's development, make sure everything is normal and see what's going on. As long as everything goes well, then in a couple months we can schedule the C-section. So, barring any complications, you kind of get to choose your baby's birthday."

Not something most parents could brag about, but interesting nonetheless, Tommen thought. March 10th was the official due date, so saith the ER doctors. That was a Thursday. Maybe shoot for March 11th. Fridays were always nice. It would give him the weekend off, anyway.

Another big concern regarding her small stature was the increased chance of an abdominal breach, where the baby tore through the uterine wall into the abdominal cavity. That probably scared Tommen the most because it involved internal trauma and massive bleeding, either of which could result in the deaths of mother and child. He was smart enough to keep his mouth shut, but he was pretty sure his fear was well-marked on his face with everything but the neon sign. Whitmore did her best to assure them that careful monitoring, good care, and no excessive consumption would be their best bet. Yes, Becky should expect to gain a little weight, but her stature was more sensitive to excessive weight.

They also had a talk about her diabetes. Tommen thought there were going to be a ton of restrictions, but Whitmore simply stated that as long as Becky kept herself in check, then everything should be fine. The trick was keeping herself in check through all the changes, hence why she'd passed out a couple weeks ago and so exposed their relationship. Most of the conversation was between Becky and the doctor, with Tommen getting the rundown on what to look for if something went wrong and what different symptoms could mean.

He felt woefully unprepared. He should have at least brought a pen and paper to write some of this down.

"All right." Whitmore said finally, grinning. "Now then, I'm sure this is what you're really here for. How about some pictures?"

Pictures? Oh, those pictures. The grainy little black and white things. Yes, he wanted to see pictures of his child, know that he or she was doing well.

The doctor set up the machine and smeared goop on Becky's belly, just starting to show, though her shirts could hide it still. The doctor flipped the monitor on and started rubbing the wand around on the goop, looking, looking...

And there it was. Tommen didn't expect to be so overwhelmed, and yet he found that his heart went to his throat and his stomach dropped at least into his ass and his brain began to float away. There was the head, tiny arms and hands, little legs and feet. Tommen thought he was going to fall off the stool.

"There we are," Whitmore said, grinning, still moving the wand a little here and there. "Hello, beautiful. And...here we go."

At first, Tommen couldn't understand what he was hearing except maybe a tap-tap-tap-tap-tap. Then he realized it was the baby's heartbeat, racing along like a speeding train. He felt Becky's hand squeeze his, but it took all his concentration just to stay upright.

"Easy there, big daddy," Becky giggled, evidently noting his disposition. "Sit on the floor before you pass out."

"No, no, I'm okay." He took a steadying breath. "Larger head, smaller body, does that mean it's dwarfism?"

Becky looked up at him. "All babies look like that at first."

"I don't know that."

"It's all right," the doctor told him. "It's a learning experience. Babies do have very large heads, proportionally speaking."

"Is there a test you can do beforehand, though, to know for sure?"

"Of course there is," Becky answered. "CVS at twelve weeks."

Whitmore nodded. "Very true, but I don't want to do a CVS. I would advise you to wait a few more weeks and then we can do a PM test. It can tell us more than a CVS, it's more accurate, and there is less risk to you and the fetus."

Becky did not like the sound of that, and she chose that moment to barrage the doctor with her more serious questions. Some of them, the doctor could answer without referencing the image, some she could point to this or that, and others she said it was too early to know. Tommen just kind of let it go over his head. This was Becky's fight and there was jack shit he could do about it.

In the end, it basically boiled down to, the fetus was twelve weeks old and perfectly healthy. Period, end of story, Tommen could live with that. He knew there was more to it, but the biggest thing was that everything was fine. For the moment. He could learn to live in the moment, with news like that.

Dr. Whitmore wanted to do regular check-ups every two to four weeks, and once the fetus reached eighteen weeks, they would do a genetic test to look for dwarfism and any number of other ailments, including the sex if they so desired.

She took three pictures and printed out a couple films of each, like those photo booth things in the mall or at amusement parks, three pictures to a strip to share. Becky tucked hers carefully away in one of the pamphlets she'd taken from the waiting room while Tommen put his in his wallet. These were pictures of his child. His—child. He couldn't explain it, but he felt a surge of overwhelming protectiveness, the need to defend Becky and their unborn child while simultaneously showing the pictures to anyone who would take three seconds to look.

This was his child. He couldn't wait to be a dad.

The thought gave him pause.

He couldn't wait to be a dad. He was terrified to the point of making himself sick, but he was excited, too.

How he wished he could talk to his pa, really have a talk, share memories, get advice.

And what he wouldn't give to talk to Teo.

The doctor gave Becky a few paper towels to wipe off the goo and excused herself to grab some paperwork and helpful literature, leaving the two of them alone in the room for a few minutes.

Before Becky could say anything, Tommen kissed her. She seemed stunned at first, then relaxed. When he pulled back, he found her laughing.

"Excited, are we?" she wondered.

"Why shouldn't I be?"

"Not saying you shouldn't. Just wondering is all."

He put a hand on her bare skin, about where he thought Whitmore had found the baby with the wand. "Just thinking about our life together."

"Well, don't let your imagination get in the way of real life. You still have to put up with my cravings and moodiness, and I'm not going to be the only one changing diapers."

"I'm trying to focus on the positive here. Let me have my moment."

She kissed him now. "Okay. You can have your moment."

Whitmore returned with a load of papers. Some were similar to the pamphlets in the lobby. Then there were the more in-depth guides concerning type I diabetes and pregnancy, dwarfism and pregnancy, preparing for a C-section (it was as much psychological as physical, the doctor explained, which was why they were getting the papers even before they scheduled the procedure), problems during pregnancy, when to call the doctor versus when to call an ambulance, and on and on. Tommen wasn't left out of the loop either, and there was a forest worth of papers for him to peruse as well, some of them oddly specific, such as help for foster and adopted children becoming parents of their own. Whitmore explained that as much as her job was to ensure the health of mother and child, she was a huge advocate for stable family units which contributed greatly to the physical, emotional, psychological, and spiritual well-being of children and the next generation as a whole.

Tommen could already tell that Becky and Whitmore were going to get along. Given half a chance, they would take their portable soapboxes, set up shop, and go to town on any issue they deemed halfway important to them. But that was good. It was good that they would get along. He wasn't sure what he'd do if they didn't.

Another appointment was made for three weeks, just as a health check. Three weeks after that would be the PM procedure, and the results would come three weeks after that.

Things would be happening in multiples of three, it seemed. Tommen hoped that was a good thing. Three was a lucky-slash-holy number, right? Maybe he could ask Chandler. But then, what were the odds the man would give him a straight answer about it? More likely the man would be a smart ass and give him some riddle relating to the number three, just to spite him.

It was a good thing, he decided. Maybe Becky's Catholic Judaism was at play here, God having mercy on them just a little, or having mercy on their baby, not punishing it for the sins of its parents.

This was getting too philosophical for his tastes. He needed to live in the moment, where everything was fine and he was excited to be a dad.

The strip of pictures was practically burning a hole in his back pocket, and he Banded so he could take them out and admire them again. Just a grainy little black and white photo, but it was the first picture of his child, the first of probably thousands or millions, right there in three three-by-three photos. Tiny feet. Tiny hands that he would hold. His—child.

He let out a breath and replaced the strip, pocketing his wallet and releasing the Band. Becky and the doctor finished up whatever conversation they were having, steps to take in the next few weeks to keep her blood sugar on track with fetal development, most of it explained in the papers.

Then they were out. They probably could have sat there and

had a conversation over the next six hours, but the baby wasn't due until March. Becky still had school and he had to get back to work, and that was just today. Still, they thanked the doctor and headed out the door, Becky stopping once to run—almost literally—to the bathroom. She'd been complaining about how she'd been told to drink a lot and have a full bladder so it was easier to find the baby in the ultrasound. Tommen was happy to have the pictures, so he wasn't complaining. Of course, he wasn't the one being told to keep a full bladder, so he wisely decided to keep his mouth shut. He was learning.

It was about two-thirty when he pulled into the parking lot nearest the science building of the college campus. Becky's class was at three. She'd been chatting happily the whole ride, her monologue divided between her excitement at seeing the baby on the ultrasound and her seriousness over some of the medical issues she had to contend with. Tommen had said maybe ten words total, but if she noticed, she didn't say anything about it.

She kissed him and headed inside, her bookbag almost comically large, but she wasn't about to get a children's bag with glitter and easily-ripped plastic. On top of that, her textbooks and notebooks wouldn't fit in a little kid's bag. She could almost get a suitcase and save herself the trouble of lugging a huge bag around, especially with her condition, and Tommen wasn't referring to her being pregnant.

He left the campus and returned to the job site, at least for a couple hours. The excavation was plodding along slower than they preferred. The trees were gone and they'd burned the stumps last Saturday, but the dirt work was not so smooth. If they were just digging a basement, okay, fine, no big deal. Burying half the house meant going deeper into the mountain, both down and in and there were a lot of rocks to contend with. Big ones. And they couldn't just yank out or blow up the boulders because then it could cause a whole rockslide which could be dangerous and deadly. This was about finesse.

It was so boring. As he found a spot to park, Tommen noted that most of the guys were standing around on smoke break while Chris and some of the more senior crewmen talked to some other guys who were pointing here and there and making gestures and this and that. Maybe they were trying to see if they could move the site five feet to the right or left without the homeowners noticing.

Tommen had thought the Victorian homeowners had been bad, nearly impossible to persuade to change their ideals until the site became a true hazard to life and limb. They were perfectly reasonable compared to these people, it seemed. They saw a picture in a magazine which inspired some beautiful plans and concept art and that was what they wanted. They wanted a picture perfect home to grace the cover of a magazine.

"Hey, welcome back!" Matt greeted as Tommen approached. "How are things at home?"

"Great." Tommen fished out his wallet and took out the strip of photos to show around. "About like that."

Ken nodded as he took a drag on his cigarette. "Yup. Looks like a baby."

"That's my baby, thank you. Twelve weeks along, perfectly healthy." Tommen replaced the strip. "And we intend to keep it that way."

There were various murmurs of congratulations mixed with sarcastic comments about mama being happy but daddy's going to find out the hard way how strong a pissed off pregnant mama could really be.

"All right, all right, what's going on here?" he asked, looking around and shifting his stance.

"This is it." Ken tossed away his cigarette butt. "Been this way for about forty-five minutes now. Got a big old rock in there somewhere that isn't coming out easy, but they're worried that if it does move, it could destabilize everything above it up to there." He pointed to an outcrop about a hundred yards from the mountain peak. "Maybe not today or tomorrow, but a good earthquake in Oklahoma could trigger a slide."

"What are they going to do about it?"

"That's what they're trying to figure out."

Unfortunately for the lay crew, that resolution was not reached that day, and they were sent home early. Early, meaning, four o'clock instead of five, and there was no exhausting clean-up. Tommen was okay with that, and he returned to the college campus to pick up Becky from class.

This time, Becky filled the drive with a detailed account of her class time, seeing how it was in the lab versus a classroom. Right now they were studying various organisms under a microscope, from bacteria and viruses, to plants and rocks, to various tissue samples like bone, skin, hair, and even organ tissue. When Tommen politely pointed out that the skin is technically an organ, he was treated to a five second pregnant tongue-lashing. This was her dissertation and he didn't need to be a smarty pants. Besides, they were simply recording everything, their observations, similarities and differences in the samples, observations about the microscopes themselves and how the different types showed each sample, and so on.

Tommen remained silent after that.

His dad had the night off, so he was home when they arrived.

"No dinner?" Becky wondered when she walked in and saw the empty, unused kitchen.

Walter glanced up from his book in his recliner. "I wasn't hungry, wasn't sure when you guys would be home, and wasn't sure what you would be craving."

That earned him a ten second tongue-lashing from Becky, but Walter shrugged it off, literally, with an amused grin. "I would suggest turning your wrath from me and onto the one who is supposed to be taking care of you."

Tommen gave his dad a look, but the man was unmoved. In Tommen's opinion, his dad was enjoying this a little more than he should be. If only there was some way to get back at him a little. Oh, wait, that was called babysitting.

Despite promising that he would make something for dinner, by the time he got showered and dressed in something clean, Becky was already busy in the kitchen. When he inquired after her, she told him she was fine and dinner would be ready as soon as possible as long as he didn't try to interfere.

"So, how's adulthood treating you?" his dad asked, still grinning, still reading his book in his recliner.

"Ha ha, very funny," Tommen murmured.

"How was the doctor's office?"

"Good...I think? Baby's healthy, mom's healthy, so that's all that matters, I guess."

His dad nodded, still not looking at him. "Indeed it is." He turned the page, read a few lines to the end of the chapter, then replaced the bookmark and set the book on the stand. "Did you get pictures?"

"Why should I show you? You've been making fun of me since we got home."

"Because you're the kind of kid, and I can see it in your demeanor, that the first thing you did upon returning to work was show all your coworkers the pictures because you're excited and you want the whole world to know it."

Tommen grumbled a little but nodded and brought out the strip of pictures. He handed it to his dad.

"Yup. Looks like a baby," Walter said. "How far along?"

"Twelve weeks."

"Do you know the sex? Can they tell?"

"Not yet. And even so—"

"I know, I know, you're not telling until Thanksgiving or Christmas and you'll already have a name and so on and so forth."

"Exactly." Tommen explained the timeline of appointments and the genetic tests.

"Well, it's not a bad idea to see what you're dealing with, genetically," his dad said seriously. "The most obvious problems being her dwarfism and diabetes, you've also got your colorblindness, plus a myriad of other things. Even if there is nothing you can do about it, it can help to know early so you can process it psychologically and be ready for it."

"I know."

"They may also want to test you to see what genetic problems and predispositions you have that you could pass on."

"Have you been researching—?"

"I sit on the side of the road for hours at a time," his dad cut in. "Yes, I may have looked up a few things."

In the kitchen, Becky burst out laughing. The men looked at her. She coughed and her skin flushed pink. "Ahem. Sorry. Something in my throat. Carry on with whatever you were talking about."

"Uh-huh," Tommen said. "Little eavesdropper."

He looked back at his dad who Banded the two of them. "And it would be interesting to see what your Time and Akari training may have done to your genes. I would be interested in comparing that test to the one on file in your adoption box."

Tommen folded his arms and nodded. "Yeah, that would be interesting, especially since part of the Akari is genetic manipulation. I mean, I'm at a level where it always reverts back to normal, but still..."

It sounded pretty cool, but it was also terrifying. What if he'd changed something he didn't mean to change? What if he'd accidentally made something worse? What sorts of things could he be passing on? If the tests came back that there was something wrong, was there any way to safely fix it? Maybe he would have to ask Nathan. The man was a Builder, capable of reshaping the physical universe and playing with things that were more sensitive than nuclear bombs; surely he could help out in the event of some kind of devastating news?

At the same time, how much did he want to risk? Even as much as he wanted to put Becky in a steel box and keep her safe and locked away for the next twenty-eight weeks, was there a line he was willing to cross, or maybe blur a little? Genetic manipulation was a serious moral and ethical conflict. Nathan had the power to do it on a whim, basically, and he could make genetic changes that were permanent. It was one thing to do it to himself, planets, plants, and things like that, and even Tommen was on the fence about genetically modified food. But a vulnerable, unborn child? Especially his own unborn child? He couldn't stomach it. But what if there was something truly, honestly wrong? Lethal, even? Was it still wrong if an abnormality was a death sentence anyway?

No, he couldn't get caught up in such uncertainties. They would wait until the genetic test came back, see what it said. It could be that everything was totally fine. No dwarfism, no diabetes, no color-blindness, nothing but a healthy, happy baby. The ultrasound was beautiful and the doctor had said that everything looked and sounded normal. Until such time as there was proof of worrisome imperfection, Tommen would hold on to the picture of that healthy, happy newborn.

When he asked Nathan about it that Thursday night, the Builder basically confirmed that point.

"And even then," he said, "I wouldn't touch your child unless it was a true do-or-die situation. I'm not a Tacagan. I don't see dwarfism as an imperfection. Or diabetes. Or autism. Or Down syndrome. Or any of that. Maybe not the ideal, but not an imperfection. It is human genetics doing what it does. Now, if it came across that there is Double-Dominant Syndrome in the mix, which is utterly lethal before two years of age, I may be persuaded to step in. But don't go getting any ideas. There is a line I will not cross."

Tommen nodded. "I can respect that."

"You say that now. Wait until the test comes back, see what it says, and then tell me what you think."

Well, that was still nine weeks away anyway. Until then, he just had to maintain the image of a healthy, happy baby. His baby.

Chapter Five
Allies and Enemies

His dad was right, Tommen was excited, and he did want to show off the pictures to anyone who would look. Unfortunately, his circle of friends outside of work was pretty small, and the one friend who was in the area was blind. Still, Will assured Tommen that he was happy for him and he was sure that the picture was beautiful. His sentiments were sincere, but distracted. Eli had spent two days in jail for the drag racing stint and was now under house arrest. When Tommen had visited, the younger Shaw brother had been holed up in his room with his music way too loud. Tommen tried to open a friendly door by showing Eli the pictures, but the sophomore wanted nothing to do with it and turned his music up even louder.

Meanwhile, Becky showed her strip of pictures to her family who was stunned with awe and love as if they'd never seen a baby before, despite having plenty of children of their own to go around. But it was good for Becky to see that her family hadn't completely abandoned her for straying from the straight and narrow. Even Dr. Polski looked like a proud soon-to-be(-again) grandpa. He was still obviously displeased with Tommen, but the two of them were civil. They had to be. Tommen had an appointment in his office at the beginning of January.

Tommen did not post the pictures online, but he took pictures of the strips and sent them via text to a few select friends, most notably Eric Brown. His once-best friend had returned to California for school shortly after the trial verdict.

"Congratulations," Eric replied to the picture. "It's a baby."

"Well, duh."

"What do you want me to say? It's an elephant?"

"Obviously not."

"So there you go."

"Jerk."

"Dad."

It was good to know that they still had enough of a friendship that they could trade jabs like that, Tommen thought, because his prospects for friends were about to go way down.

Lying awake Tuesday night, Tommen was suddenly hit with the realization that he would again be "that kid" in school, except now he would be in a social circle worse than just a freak or an outcast. He was a "baby-daddy" which was about one tiny step above "baby-mama" which was rock bottom of the high school social scale. Baby-daddy inched above it just for the fact that sexual activity was not exactly a secret in school, conquests were more public than teachers or parents wanted to admit to, and only the males of the equation could continue their sexual conquests without being bogged down by the responsibility of the pregnancy. The fact that he was sticking around to be a dad was what ostracized him.

Hey, he didn't say it made sense; that was just the way it was.

And there were still basement labels for those students even worse than baby-daddy or baby-mama. There was baby-killer, for the girls who had abortions or boys who beat up their pregnant girlfriends to kill the kid; and then there was the ever-increasing popularity of being a school shooter.

At least Tommen wasn't in the basement of the high school social system. He was pretty far down there, though.

The last few weeks, Tommen told himself that he didn't care. His first priority was Becky and the baby, everyone and everything else be damned. He was going to stick it out, stick around, and be a good dad. Among his adult peers, his dad, her family, his coworkers, and so on, this attitude was admired, and he was accepted as an adult. His start into adulthood was different than some, but he'd crossed that threshold. He had a job, was arranging a place to live, he was getting married, having a kid (not necessarily in that order), he was an adult who just happened to have two semesters of high school left. But then he was going to college, so it was all good.

The dynamics would be radically different once he was back in school. If he thought Rifun's trial had been heavy, now he would have the eyes and judgment of a thousand teenage peers and dozens of teachers and other staff. He was going to be the baby-daddy who hadn't even graduated high school yet, who had a demeaning job (because obviously construction was for dumb oafs who couldn't master STEM) that he would be working for the rest of his life and never amount to anything but common Appalachian trailer trash. And why not? He'd always been a freak. There was a certain threshold in the unwritten social hierarchy. Above the line, you had a chance to rise. Below the line, you could only go down. Eric was proof of that. He'd had to leave the state before being given a chance to break through that threshold.

Tommen thought about the conversation he'd had with Mr. Gillingham a long time ago, when the science teacher had gotten him into AP Physics. Gillingham had told him to ignore the others, do his best, let his talents shine, and one day the idiots would be delivering the pizza to his Nobel Prize acceptance party.

He'd ignored the others. He'd done his best and let his talents shine. He'd met Becky in AP Physics. Now they were going to be parents. Was a Nobel Prize out of the question now?

He rubbed his face and rolled over, jumping in surprise as Mr. Snuffles let out a muffled yowl and scrambled out from under him. The cat hissed at him and ran under the bed. Becky sighed and rolled over, still sleeping. The two of them had gotten more used to sleeping in the same bed, but the cat apparently hadn't. Nor was the cat pleased with the new accommodations as Tommen had to clean up several "presents" left for him under his bed. Mrs. Polski had mentioned several times that Mr. Snuffles was seen stalking around their yard during the day when he was out.

Tommen rolled over again and pulled Becky close. The bump

was still pretty hidden by her shirts, but it was noticeable to the touch. It made him happy.

To hell with the other students. Let them call him a freak, an outcast, the dreaded baby-daddy. Yeah, he was going to be a dad. He wasn't ready for it, but he was excited. He was going to be a dad, and a damn good one, too. He only had to put up with these morons for two more semesters. He was going to be a dad for the rest of his life.

He slept fitfully, but not violently, and woke up earlier than his alarm. He'd been completely prepared for his work alarm going off at five. His school alarm was set for six-thirty.

He got up quietly, turned off his alarm, and decided to just carry on with his routine, maybe at a little slower pace, maybe make himself a good breakfast. With as much as Becky was cooking these days, he almost needed to use Time and ramp up the accelerated aging metabolism again just to eat it all. But it was good. She had learned a thing or two from her mother. He would never want for school or work lunch ever again, he was sure.

His dad walked in the door about six, looking exhausted. He all but collapsed in the chair at the kitchen table and rubbed his eyes.

"Long night?" Tommen wondered.

"You have no idea," his dad sighed.

"Want to talk about it? My alarm doesn't go off for half an hour."

The joke fell flat.

For a long minute, it seemed as though his dad wouldn't answer, or had fallen asleep sitting there. Finally he answered, "Can I trust you not to say anything?"

"Of course."

"Is Becky asleep?"

Tommen Banded and folded his arms. "Better?"

It was still a few seconds before his dad would speak. "Well, the night started out bad enough when Vin announced that his wife was filing for divorce."

"Ouch."

"Yeah. I feel for him. I do. He's tried really hard to get his act together and be a real—well, I should say a useful police officer. But I think his wife liked it better when he was the idiot underdog who wouldn't let himself get caught in any difficult situation."

"That's too bad."

"Like I said, I feel for him. And that doesn't bother me so much as what he did later."

"He didn't...do like Dan, did he?"

His dad shook his head. "No, but almost as bad. He shot a suspect. Fatally."

"Okay..."

"Suspect was unarmed and surrendering, on his knees, hands behind his head. I was actually going up to him to arrest him when...I don't know, something spooked Vin—a cat or dog or something outside—and he fired. He actually grazed me—flesh wound only, I let the medics see it just so it was recorded, but I Banded it later. But it was a perfect head shot, execution-style."

"Fuck."

"I think Vin is about to lose everything. County is more understanding than city when it comes to officer wrongdoing, but I don't see this turning out well for him. He's going to lose his family, his job, he could be facing prison time, too." Walter shook his head. "So later today I have to go in and speak to Internal Affairs, give them my side of the story."

"That sucks. You're not on the hook for anything, are you?"

"I'm here, aren't I? Vin is spending the night—er, the day—in a holding cell."

"Good news for you, then."

"Yeah. But it's been a long night." His dad sighed and stood. "I'm going to bed."

Tommen released the Band and watched his dad leave. "Dad." He turned. "Ten months until retirement."

His dad nodded slowly. "Ten months until retirement."

"Seven months until grandpa."

Now his dad smiled. "Seven months until grandpa. Yeah. Good night. Or day. Whatever it is."

By the time Tommen finished breakfast and slowly meandered his way around getting ready for school—which didn't amount to much since it was only the first day—his dad had gone to bed, his bedroom door shut to keep out Mr. Snuffles. The gray cat was but a shadow in the hallway. The cat froze when he saw Tommen and slipped away stealthily as Tommen went into the bathroom.

There had been some debate over whether he should drive to school or take the bus. Becky and Will had graduated, and Eli wanted nothing to do with him, so it was just him in the car anymore. The economical answer appeared to be to take the bus so he didn't have to spend the gas. At the same time, school wasn't far away, his car got good gas mileage, and if anything came up he would need a quick ride out. Granted, he could Band, but there was something to be said for being incognito. He couldn't leave one place and arrive at another place at the same time. A car he could fudge believably.

He returned to the bedroom and kissed a sleepy Becky goodbye. Then he grabbed his keys and his phone and headed out the door.

The last few weeks he'd felt like an adult, like a man slowly carving out his place in society. Pulling in the parking lot of the high school felt foreign, the same way he would feel if he were to pull into the middle school lot. This wasn't his place anymore, he had no reason to be here. He should be going out to the construction site, meeting up with Matt and Ken and Pete and Jake, gearing up and going out to do whatever it was they were doing that day.

He sat there for a minute or two, taking it all in and trying to sort it all out. Everything about high school felt petty and useless. He thought back to two years ago when he was smoking and drinking, trying to get laid and goofing off with his friends. In those two years, he'd stumbled on a dead body, been kidnapped and held hostage, watched his father almost die, run off across the universe on an outlandish mission, survived a massacre, survived numerous housecleaning attacks, survived a massive fire with devastating scars, escaped from a dimension once believed to be inescapable, unleashed a madwoman from that same dimension, went to the funeral of one of his best friends and crazy uncles, survived a bombing, gone into battle, finally lost his virginity, gone into battle again, traipsed far and wide across the universe on a wild goose chase, gone into battle a third time to face down demons and their mortal instruments, survived a second coup, helped his former nemesis escape, helped put that same nemesis behind bars for a long time, learned that he'd fathered a child, become engaged, and also learned that the uncle whose funeral he had attended was actually still alive.

And he was going to walk into this government-run daycare where the freshmen were clumsily sorting out puberty, the girls were busy checking boys off their list of potential boyfriends for the next dance, the boys were more focused on sex than anything else, the academics were planning their glorious college futures, the jocks were talking all things sports, the freaks and outcasts were either talking about drugs or video games, and the one thing that linked everyone together was drama, drama, drama.

Tommen felt like an alien. He was beyond all this in more than one sense. He didn't know how he could survive, and he only had to go two semesters. Could he just skip to the third semester where he was off to college, please?

He was jerked from his thoughts as his phone buzzed. It was Becky.

"Good morning, my love."

"Good morning," he replied. "How's mama?"

"Rethinking her decision to take early classes."

They chatted back and forth for a minute or two until there was a knock on Tommen's window. It was a school safety officer, or that was what he called himself. New position they'd created over the summer. Similarly, there was a new policy where extended loitering in the parking lot, even or especially students, was prohibited. In case, you know, he was fucking his girlfriend in the backseat or texting some accomplice to carry out a school shooting. Inside or outside, no middle ground anymore. If he'd gone to orientation, he would know this.

No one except freshmen and overly-excitable academics went to orientation. The SSO did not appreciate that comment.

Things were changing, and Tommen felt that alien sensation creep up on him again. Nevertheless, he grabbed his backpack and got out of his car, feeling the SSO's eyes on him the whole way in.

Like every year, there were minor changes to be found. New paint, new carpet, old lockers being replaced. Cosmetic stuff, mostly. The sign on the door stating that all exterior doors automatically locked at 8:30 am and did not reopen until 2:30 pm was new. Did that mean no more open campus lunch? Probably. There was a doorbell-like apparatus on the door, another sign stating that it was a camera with a direct feed to the office. If you wanted in while the doors were locked, the office would see you, snap a picture, and then open the door if they liked you.

I'm in The Twilight Zone, Tommen thought, even as he knew it wasn't true. The world was a dangerous place, and there was a reason educational institutions were called schools: it would be like shooting fish in a barrel.

Muscle memory took him to his normal locker where his fingers deftly spun the dial and opened the door. He didn't even remember the actual numbers of his combination. Just spin, spin, spin, click, open.

The halls were filling up by the bus load as the big yellow bananas dutifully dropped off their cargo. No one called out a greeting to him. No one made a joke or tried a small prank. But perhaps most importantly, no one tried to stuff him in his locker, slam the door on his fingers, bash his head into the wall. No one made any rude, sarcastic, or leering remarks. No one called attention to him.

And he was okay with that. He was just here to go through the motions, sit and listen dutifully, turn in the assignments, and bide his time until March when he would head off to college. He wasn't here to engage in gossip and banter, wasn't here to settle a score or any of that. He was stuck here for the time being, but his real life was outside these walls where the doors would be locked from 8:30 to 2:30.

God, it sounded like prison.

Except, in prison, the inmates didn't have to pay three dollars for their meals.

Tommen folded his arms and briefly considered his day at school versus what he imagined Rifun's day in prison would be like. Being marched from place to place under the watchful eye of an authority figure, told what to do, when to do it, being allotted only a short span of time for bad cafeteria food, always under constant threat of being beaten up...yeah, school and prison were pretty darn similar. Difference was, Tommen didn't have to worry about getting raped, and he could go home and sleep in his own bed at the end of the day.

Still, the similarities were almost eerie.

He glanced at his schedule. First class was Pre-Calculus. Dammit. He did not want to do math that early in the morning. Time was, he would be totally excited for the challenge, ready to prove his math mastery because he was a science nerd. He was still confident in his abilities to do the work, but the glittering future he'd imagined...was no longer golden.

He stared at the back of his locker, empty save for his backpack. Thinking about it, he'd put a pencil behind his ear just out of habit because of work. He took the pencil and tossed it in his bag. He still didn't have friends to talk to or joke with, and he decided that he'd left way too early. Maybe it was because he'd just gotten up too early, but he could probably sleep in another fifteen, twenty minutes. At worst, he would just have to Band a little to get to school in time, but there was no reason to be here so early.

He headed to the office and picked up a parking permit sheet which he filled out and submitted with his driver's license to the secretary Mrs. Puifall. She was neck-deep in calls and paperwork and hardly looked at him as she processed everything and gave him a sticker to put in his windshield saying he could park in the lot. As he put the sticker in his pocket where he hopefully wouldn't forget it later, the principal, Mr. Layman, walked around the corner. He handed something to an already overworked Mrs. Puifall. Then his gaze settled on Tommen.

"Tommen?" he wondered, his expression conveying utter disbelief.

"That's my name," Tommen answered.

"What is up, man? You been working out or something?"

He shrugged and gave himself a once-over. "I work construction now."

"Holy cats! And what's up with the beard? You spit tobacco, too, or what?"

Tommen felt his face turn red, but it wouldn't be as noticeable as it used to be. After getting the ultrasound pictures, Tommen had decided to do things the old-fashioned way, just a little, and grow his beard out to signify that he was taken. He was a man.

"Um, no on the tobacco, for one."

Layman nodded. "Good for you. Terrible habit to get into, especially at your age." He shifted his stance and folded his arms. "So, how was your summer? Construction is a busy trade. And, if you don't mind my saying so, I saw your testimony in court—"

"Which one?"

"Both. I was in one of the overflow rooms."

Tommen took an even breath and nodded. "Yeah. It...it was a busy summer. Um...do you happen to have a minute?"

"Of course. I think you know where my office is."

Only too well, after a number of lectures and detentions over the years. It still looked like a cross between an advertisement for the Marines and the warning signs for Obsessive Compulsive Disorder. Layman took a seat and relaxed in his chair while Tommen skittishly took a seat in one of the slightly less comfortable chairs on the other side of the desk, taking his wallet out of his back pocket as he did so.

"Sounds like a busy summer," Layman began. "You were working construction at the beginning of the year, weren't you?"

Tommen shrugged. "Yeah, but it was weekend stuff. Summertime, I was working six days a week, eight or ten hour days, sometimes longer. Good money, but it was a lot. And then with the trial..."

"That was probably a whole new level of stress. Were you at least kept safe?"

"Oh, yeah, I mean, there was no doubt about that. I just didn't like it that they called me for both sides. I had to condemn and defend him."

"Did you tell the truth to the best of your abilities?"

"Yes."

"Do you think the resulting convictions and exonerations were fair?"

He took a breath and considered it. There was no doubt that Rifun had not been as complacent or manipulated as he'd made the jury believe, but between Rifun's Book and his own forgiveness, Tommen couldn't quite muster up the same hatred as everyone else. He had committed crimes that demanded justice, apart from Tommen's forgiveness. Even considering his deeper reasoning, trying to slay the dragon spirit, when the man himself admitted his own guilt in that department, justice still had to be served.

"I don't know," he answered finally. "Honestly, there's nothing I can do about it. The jury reached their verdict and now it's up to the judge to sentence him. No matter what, he's going away for a long time. Kidnapping alone is life, if the judge decides against the mercy recommendation which only brings it down to ten to forty years. Second-degree attempted murder of a police officer is ten to thirty years."

Layman folded his hands neatly. "In that time, do you think you can move on? Sometimes, the worst prisons are the ones we build for ourselves. What are you convicting yourself of?"

"See, that I'm not sure. I didn't have a choice about testifying for both sides; you can't just say no to a subpoena. And he is getting what he deserves, no question."

"Do you pity him, empathize with him?"

"That would make me a great candidate for Stockholm Syndrome, wouldn't it?"

Layman shrugged. "What do you think?"

Tommen sighed. "Honestly, I think we all got played. Hardcore. I think he is absolutely brilliant. I think it's a shame to let that talent go to waste in a prison cell. His actions need to be punished, but I think a great mind is being discarded. I think that maybe in another life, an alternate universe, he could have been one of if not the greatest mind of our time."

"So you feel bad that he threw his own life away."

"That's one way to say it, I suppose."

"You know, I felt the same way once."

"About me?"

"Mm-hm. You're a smart kid, and we could all see that. But the fighting, the drinking, the smoking...it wasn't going to lead anywhere good unless you got a solid wakeup call. I wouldn't have chosen the events that followed, but it got to you and you shaped up before it became a problem. And it could be that he never learns. Maybe he is a brilliant mind, but he chooses what he does with that mind. As long as he is focused only on himself and whatever goals he has, the world will never know that brilliance except as the face of evil.

"You, on the other hand, as I said, learned early. You shaped up. You decided to turn your intellect into productivity. You have decided to actually live up to your name of Chivalrous Welshman."

Tommen flushed again and opened his wallet. "Well, not exactly." He took out the strip of photos, not quite as pristine as they had been, and handed it to Layman. "I'm not as chivalrous as you all seem to think I am. Never have been."

Layman stared at the photos for a long minute, then looked at him. "Is this what I think it is?"

He nodded. "Ultrasound pictures of my child."

With one hand, Layman handed back the pictures. With the other, he shook Tommen's hand. "Congratulations, sir."

Tommen eyed him suspiciously. "Thanks...I think? You don't shake everyone's hand, I notice, when they say things like that."

"True, but you are maybe the second one in all my years of being principal who actually kept the pictures and showed them off. And I know we're not exactly friends. To me, that speaks of loyalty and love. You're sticking together."

"Yeah. Becky moved in a few weeks ago."

"How's she doing?"

"As of this morning, she says she is questioning her decision to have early college classes. Otherwise, she's good. Tired. Still carries her little soapbox around and is more than willing to give you a lecture for perceived slights."

Layman nodded, his expression amused. "How far along?"

"Thirteen weeks this week."

"And she just moved in with you? When did you find out?"

"I found out on my birthday. She found out a month before that but she was afraid to tell me."

Layman made a vague motion. "So the beard is the whole...I'm taken, I got a woman and a family, that whole thing?"

"Yeah."

"Are you planning on getting married?"

Tommen nodded. "Next summer after graduation."

"Very good. When is she due?"

"March, right after I'm done here. Her mom likes summer weddings, and she wanted to plan something really nice—she's a great party planner—plus she was all concerned about the wedding dress and this and that...I don't know."

"Sounds like summer was busy and it's not letting up any time soon. Life is changing for you."

"Don't have to tell me that."

"How does your dad feel about it?"

"He's...not fond of surprises. I thought he might have actually wanted to help her dad try and castrate me—that thought did cross my mind, and sometimes it still does worry me whenever I see Dr.

Polski—but at the same time, I think he's kind of looking forward to being a grandpa. He's retiring next summer, so he'll have a lot of free time on his hands."

"That is true. How is it with a woman in the house now? It's just been you and your dad for a while now, hasn't it?"

"Ever since I've lived with him, yes. And it's...different. I can't say just what exactly, except for a homecooked meal waiting for me most nights, but it's...different."

Layman's expression turned unreadable, but something close to amusement. "So with all your summer antics, coming back to high school must seem pretty strange."

"You have no idea."

"Well, we've made a few changes. You probably noticed a few on your way in. Your first hour teacher will explain some things more in-depth. But one thing that hasn't changed is that my door is always open. And I get the feeling that you and I will be talking more frequently than we used to."

"Wasn't I in here at least once a week freshman year?" Tommen wondered, looking around innocently. "I don't think we could get more frequent than that."

"Maybe not, but the offer still stands. You've got a pregnant woman at home in your bed. I think you might need a little advice in the future."

The conversation wrapped up quickly enough, and Tommen returned to his locker.

He couldn't say exactly why he'd decided to confide in Mr. Layman. Maybe just so the man knew, so if something came up or the rumor got out, then the highest power in the building would already know about it. Or maybe it was so he could have some advice from a decent authority figure who wasn't tainted with Time. Layman might know a thing or two about dealing with pregnant women without telling him to watch his back in case one of Julianna's murder squads decided to make a move. Sometimes, Tommen wanted a normal conversation.

The bell rang for first period. Pre-Calculus. Hooray. Because what else could he be doing with his life right now? Tommen glanced at the clock as he sat down. The guys would probably be having a smoke break about now while someone made a coffee run. Chris and a few of the guys and some subcontractors had worked out a tentative plan to remove part of the stone in their way and eek everything to one side just a smidge, not enough to be super obvious to the homeowners, but it would be the difference between a ten thousand dollar removal and a fifty thousand dollar removal with the added bonus of a rockslide in the very near future.

Tommen wanted to text someone, anyone on the crew and ask them how things were going. He refrained. Not only would he not likely get an answer, but it would seem childish to pester them so. He felt childish for even considering it, like a kid who asks his parents when Santa is coming, or the Easter Bunny. Just be patient. Santa always comes. So does the Easter Bunny. Just focus on what you're doing, go to sleep like a good boy, and all your presents will be there in the morning.

He found himself daydreaming while the teacher went over the course outline. Pre-Calc was only a two semester course, so their goal was to cover the first half of the book, yada yada yada...

"If you weren't here for orientation, you may have also noticed a few changes around the building," the teacher went on. "The school—all of the schools in the district are now on perpetual partial lockdown. The exterior doors lock at 8:30am sharp and do not reopen until 2:30pm. If you need to go out, your only option for reentry is through the door by the office."

Tommen glanced at the window. It had been replaced, he could see, and the new glass might have been thick enough to be bulletproof, but it was still cracked open to allow for a breeze.

"There will be no loitering outside in the parking lot anymore and no more open campus. If you are supposed to be here, then be here, inside. If you want to hang out with your friends outside, you need to be off school property.

"There are also more cameras inside in the halls and classrooms." The teacher pointed to one at the door. "They are now more actively monitored."

Because when Tommen and his friends had found the woman's body on the soccer fields, the cameras had been only passively monitored and consulted after the fact.

"Mr. Barrington is the new school safety officer. He will be patrolling inside and outside, and he will respond to any fights or other suspicious activity. He is not armed, but he does have the power to engage and detain if necessary."

Most of this would come as something of an annoyance if Tommen didn't have more to worry about. Although he knew that such measures were probably in response to incidents in other parts of the country, the fact that it was coming at the same time that Julianna was coming after him and Becky and their child was a little unnerving. Even if the new SSO were armed, it would be laughable in the face of Julianna's goons. At the same time, there was something to be said for having a little extra security. It might not mean much, but a door that was supposed to be locked and wasn't might draw more attention than a normally unlocked door.

How much of a scene would Julianna want to make? Would he just fall asleep and not wake up because she decided to use some kind of poison gas or maybe an injectible agent? Would she try to orchestrate something bigger, maybe invoke the terror of In Jezik again but with more specific targets? Would she hit them one at a time, or simultaneously so he couldn't help Becky, Godwin couldn't help Micaiah, and so on?

And with all of these greater worries, why the fuck was he sitting here in class? He should be doing something. He didn't know what, but something. He should be tracking down Julianna's agents and eliminating them.

Focus on yourself, the here and now, he heard Chandler whisper.

He didn't want to be reactive. Julianna had the upper hand, and he didn't like it. If she was just off doing her own thing, fine. Let her declare war on the universe. But coming after him and his family personally?

He had a headache. And it was only first period.

He received a number of compliments on his beard throughout the day. Some asked if he'd become a lumberjack over the summer. A few said it was only fitting for his job in construction. Still some mocked him, inquiring as to whether he'd become domesticated and had a wife at home. Because that was how things were done in the 1800's, right? Married at fourteen? He was practically a senior citizen by that standard.

"Well, I think you look rather dashing," Mrs. Reisig told him in class, fifth period 12th grade English.

"My dad says I look like my pa," Tommen said, bringing up on his phone the picture he'd taken of his parents' wedding photo.

Mrs. Reisig squinted at it. "By God, you do. Spitting image. Well, except for the beard since your pa was clean-shaven there, but as for you, I can certainly see the resemblance."

The late bell rang, thus signaling the beginning of another turn on the merry-go-round, the class outline. Reading, books, worksheets, essays, and repeat. Nothing new there. Tommen sometimes wondered why they bothered with the first day of school. It was a half day, and it was usually wasted on bullshit.

"So, I want to make use of this short time by getting you kind of in the zone for our first assignment," Reisig began. "We're going to go around the room and I want each of you to tell me something that is going to happen this year, this school year, that you think is unlikely to ever happen again in your lives. It could be political, social, or just personal in your own lives. I want you all to think of things that only happen once, usually, and impact us significantly."

"Katy?" Reisig started.

"During the school year...hm...it'll probably be the only time I'll go to Madrid over Christmas."

Oddly specific, Tommen thought, only because her family was rich enough to go anywhere at any time. But for the school year, yes, there would be only one trip to Spain over Christmas.

"Dan?"

"This year, there will only ever be one instance of it being October 15, 2015. And we will never see that date ever again in history," Dan replied smartly.

"Okay, wise guy," Reisig warned, her tone holding no malice.

And on it went, most of the seniors citing high school graduation, until she got to Tommen whose heart had taken up residence in his throat.

"Tommen, what about you?"

Tommen cleared his throat and sat up a little straighter even as he wanted to slouch more and maybe just slide into a hole in the floor. He didn't have to say anything about Becky; he could easily cite his early graduation. His only hangup was a little bit of advice his dad had given him when talking about the police and public relations.

"You can't control how the public will respond to the news, but you can control what news they hear as well as when and how they receive it."

Not a hundred percent foolproof, but a good guideline, nonetheless. No doubt the seeds of the rumors had already been started. Someone saw something somewhere on social media in the last few weeks, he was sure. He had to take control before things got out of hand.

He coughed once, fidgeted, and finally said, "During this school year, one thing to happen to me that will never happen again is...I'm going to be a first-time dad."

There was dead silence in the room. Someone's watch was ticking.

"So...how 'bout those Tigers?" someone said.

"And when is this happening?" Reisig asked, finally finding her voice.

"Middle of March," Tommen answered, surprised his beard didn't spontaneously combust from the heat from his skin. "Right after second semester is over and I'm off to college."

Her congratulations was not sarcastic or insincere, but it was halting, as if she were searching for some sort of punchline to a joke or other mischievous intent.

The rest of the students gave pithy answers to the original question, things that were unique to the school year, and the remainder of the class passed smoothly enough despite there not being a desk big enough for the elephant that had taken up residence and would probably stay in residence for the remainder of the year, following Tommen around like his pet.

But there. He'd admitted it. He had been the one to kick off the rumor mill, so now when the others asked him about it, he wouldn't be surprised or super embarrassed or otherwise caught off-guard. And why should he be ashamed? He wasn't ashamed of Becky. He certainly wasn't ashamed of their child. So his life choices were different than everyone else's, so what? It was his life. He was going to have a family and be a dad.

The bell rang. Tommen avoided being smothered by the other students and elected to just wait patiently until the mass had passed him by. When they did so, he found Reisig sitting down in the desk in front of him.

"You're not joking, are you?" she asked. "Because that's a huge rumor to let fly, and you know all about bullying."

Tommen fished out his wallet and handed over the pictures. "Not joking at all. Thirteen weeks this week."

"Oh, wow." Reisig expression changed into the warm affection of being a mother herself. She handed the pictures back. "Well, congratulations. Sounds like you're excited? Yes?"

"Yeah. Dealing with Becky is a little tough sometimes, but it's all good."

"Well, a bit of advice from the other side of the equation, it's tough dealing with yourself when you're pregnant. You ever been under anesthesia or anything?"

"A couple times."

"The things you say then make perfect sense in your mind at

the time, but not to anyone else. Being pregnant with the raging hormones, especially the first time, it can be a similar experience."

"My dad told me just to nod and say 'Yes, dear.' "

"Good advice. Most of the time. You'll get it." She stood. "Don't be surprised if Layman calls you into his office."

He stood and gathered his things. "No worries. I told him this morning so that when word did get around, he wasn't surprised."

"So this was all planned?"

"Not exactly, but the way I figure it, I have more important things to worry about. What's the rumor mill going to do to me, really?"

Reisig folded her arms. "What happened to the Tommen from a couple years ago who ditched class, got detention, and was always in fights?"

"Maybe that Tommen died in that cave up there, or in the warehouse when he held his dying father."

Now her expression turned unreadable. "Whatever the case, you've grown up. And I'm glad to see it. But just know, even from your own past experience, that the rumor mill can turn vicious, even physical. Like I said, that's a huge rumor you unleashed, and on the first day of school."

"What better way to start a fire than with gasoline?"

He headed out to his car, but sat there for a minute, keeping one eye out for the new safety officer. His chat with Reisig put him behind schedule and now he had to wait for the bus procession as it made its way to the middle school. Only then could he safely navigate onto the street and head home.

Becky was still on campus and his dad was still asleep. Gotten home at six, and now it was barely noon. Tommen tried to be as quiet as he could as he went down to the bedroom and tossed his backpack toward the bed. As the pack arced through the air, he saw the lump under the blankets at the last second. Panicking, Tommen Banded, took his pack out of midair, and released the Band. Then he calmly set the bag down nearer his pillow. The lump began to move, and Mr.

Snuffles slithered out of hiding and disappeared from the room without so much as a "How was your day?"

"Stupid cat," Tommen breathed.

He went out to the kitchen and fixed lunch, deciding to make a couple extra sandwiches in case Becky was hungry when she got home or his dad needed something to eat when he got up. His dad wasn't likely to be hungry, but food could do wonders for morale. No sooner had Tommen thought this than his dad appeared. He'd evidently Banded, to go from asleep to ready for work in only a couple minutes.

"I'm heading into the station, talk to Internal Affairs," he said, sounding as though he hadn't gotten nearly enough sleep, which he probably hadn't. "I'll probably be there all night after that for my shift, assuming they don't send me home."

Tommen hoped they sent him home. Still, he nodded and said, "Okay. Want a sandwich before you go?"

Walter looked ready to refuse, then reconsidered. He took one, thanked Tommen, then pulled on his shoes and was out the door. Not two minutes later, Mrs. Polski pulled in the driveway to drop off Becky.

And life went on.

Chapter Six
Covert Operations

There was still a spark of life within Micaiah, a ghost of his old self that demanded to be set free from the feeble prison his body had become. Miach could see it in his eyes when they locked gazes, could feel it when his brother forced himself to stand and pathetically stumble wherever he needed to go. Micaiah was still in there somewhere, and the day he made his way back to the surface could not come too soon.

Miach had never been especially buff. Physically fit, yes, but he didn't make a determined habit of excessive exercise like his brother. Now he was the larger of the two, and it was a little frightening to behold. Micaiah had easily lost over a hundred pounds and he looked at least twenty years older. It was not a good look for him, but at least he hadn't gone gray.

He sat on the couch going through an exercise routine. He was very slowly getting his strength back, and even more slowly recovering his cognition. As much as the therapist—and by therapist, she was a Tlingit woman who happened to be a nurse—put him through basic stretches and small weights like you might expect after knee or shoulder surgery, she also had Micaiah doing walking and talking exercises like a retarded toddler.

Miach tried to hold onto the hope that the spirit was strong, even if the flesh was weak, that Micaiah would one day break through. He wanted to believe that his brother was in there, still having complex thoughts, still formulating plans for revenge, could understand all the news that he and the others discussed. All he needed was the physical capability. Surely oxygen deprivation wouldn't destroy his memories. Surely he could examine those memories and piece himself back together.

It was hard, especially when the nurse rolled the walker over to Micaiah, helped him stand, then maneuvered him down to the bathroom so she could assist him like an elderly dementia patient in a nursing home.

Kayla, who had been silent thus far with an expression of forced interest and hope, let the facade drop as she slumped back in her chair.

She would not say exactly where they were, only that it was the mainland of the Northwest Territory. It wasn't a rugged mountain cabin with only two rooms, either; Miach was actually quite surprised by how modern it looked: open floor plan, large living room with huge windows that overlooked phenomenal sunsets; the kitchen was a bit small, proportionately; two bedrooms downstairs; full bathroom; a loft bedroom that was used more for storage. The electricity was run by solar panels in the summer and gas in the winter. They were situated near the ocean, so the currents made the winters pretty mild, even considering the alleged latitude.

"When we said we were going to escape together to live our lives for a little while, this isn't what I had in mind," Kayla sighed, staring at the floor. It was not the first time she had expressed such sentiment.

"I doubt it's what he had in mind either," Miach said, also not for the first time.

She looked at him, expression guilty. "I'm sorry. I didn't want to get your hopes up, and I really hoped he might be more recovered than this when you did find out."

He shook his head. "Why not tell me sooner? I could have been helping this whole time. Maybe I'd still be in Charleston running the bakery."

She shrugged. "I didn't know what to do. I didn't know what could be done, if anything. Like I said, I didn't want to get your hopes up."

Miach frowned. "And what about your hopes?" He shook his head again and let out a breath. "At least you tried. I was content to resign him to death."

"I don't know that this is much better." She wiped her eyes. "I want to believe he's still in there. Him starting to talk is really giving me hope." She wiped her eyes again. "I just wish it would happen faster because we could really use him right now."

Miach sighed and nodded as he turned to look out the window. "Yeah."

The trees obscured part of the view, but it was a grand sight nonetheless, the kind most people could only dream of waking up to. His attention was taken by movement to the southwest. He turned to see a portal just closing, Godwin, Nathan, and Haunstein walking up the path that served as a driveway. A moment later, there was a knock at the door. There were only two raps before the door opened. Godwin opened the door, but it was Nathan's posture that said he had been the one to knock.

"We don't have time for bullshit and formalities," Godwin growled.

"Nice to see you, too," Kayla said, Banding to compose herself before she stood to meet the three men. "He's in the bathroom."

Even as she spoke, the door opened and Micaiah shuffled out, followed by the nurse.

Miach Banded so he could judge his brother's reaction to the sudden company. To his eyes, Micaiah seemed very intent on walking. Difficult enough on one leg, but with the minor experiments on his stump, his prosthetic couldn't feel very good, Miach thought. Once out to the living room, Micaiah paused and looked up, studied the faces. He already knew Nathan, and Haunstein had apparently been making regular visits for the last six months or so. Godwin was the only new face in the last few weeks.

Come on, a Chai, Miach prayed silently. *Come on, talk to them.*

"Hu...hu..." Micaiah's posture looked like that of a man choking. Finally, "Hullo."

"Hello, Micaiah," Nathan began, friendly, if professional. "How are you today?"

"Beghur."

Miach sighed internally. His brother sounded like he had a palsy and was trying to swallow his tongue. His accent wasn't helping things either.

"I hope you're well enough to travel," Godwin cut in, "because that's what we're going to be doing here in the next few days or weeks."

Micaiah blinked, his mental processes slowly loading. Then, "Go where?"

"Away from here. Julianna is out for blood and you are one of the juiciest targets."

At the mention of Julianna, Micaiah's expression twitched. Miach knew it. He saw it. There was a definite reaction there.

"So why are you here now?" Kayla asked, trying to disguise her fatigue as boredom.

Godwin wasn't fooled. "If I have a chance to assess my escort beforehand, I will. I need to know what kind of arrangements to make."

"A portal. Here to there, no problem."

The mercenary shook his head. "Not that easy. We're taking extra precautions."

Kayla frowned. "I'm not blind to the danger we're in, and I'm not ungrateful for the help. I just don't understand why it's coming from you."

Godwin gave her a look. "Not me. Rifun. Consider this repayment for helping us escape from the fortress during Julianna's coup."

Kayla still looked uncertain. Haunstein saved either of them from having to speak more by making a motion and approaching the couch where the Tlingit nurse maneuvered Micaiah to sit.

"Whatever you're doing, we have a job to do as well," the doctor said, waving Nathan over.

Haunstein was not an Akari-bearer, only a Time Agent, but he was one of the few doctors anyone could go to for under the table care. He was the one who had Micaiah's medical records and could run hospital-level tests on everything Nathan did, give a direction on where to go next.

"Miach, come here," Nathan ordered. "I'm going to use you as my control sample."

Miach didn't need to be asked twice. He sat on the couch, the opposite end from Micaiah, Nathan between them. "That's why I'm here. You could have used me a lot earlier."

"Please, save your petty fights for later," Haunstein sighed, clicking his pen and opening up his folder. "You know why we didn't. Now shut up and do what he tells you."

"No need to be rude about it," Nathan scolded him. He put on hand on the back of Micaiah's neck, and the other hand on the back of Miach's neck.

From Miach's perspective, it just felt a bit like having a large spider in his hair, crawling around on his head. He knew it was just Nathan Feeling him, comparing his brain to his twin brother's, but it was still a terrible fight to resist the urge to scratch or swat at said invisible spider.

"If I remember correctly, from one of Rifun's Books, he found cancer in his girlfriend and had it cured in something like eight hours, Banded Time, barely a second in Base Time," Godwin said after about five minutes. "Why is this taking so much longer?"

"He cured it by destroying the cancer cells, breaking them up and turning them into common nutrients to be absorbed by the body," Nathan answered, his words halting as he did whatever he did. "Destruction is easy. Even turning the deadly cells into nutrients is less intensive because they are designed to be broken down and absorbed. Here...we are talking about brain cells, neurons, memories, motor pathways, and the core of consciousness that even advanced races cannot scientifically quantify. These are lasting elements, and also very finicky."

"And his leg?" Godwin made a slight, vague indication. "Looks standard enough."

"Your pseudo-Builder of a Faharoa had trouble enough with his own fingers," the Builder replied with a touch of acid. "We're working on it. And if we're successful, I'm sure he will gladly have you replicate the experiment."

That got the mercenary to stop talking. After another minute or two, he went outside to stand on the deck, probably very pleased by the natural watchtower the six-foot stilts afforded.

Miach did not know specifically what Nathan was doing, although he had a certain image in his mind from *Star Trek*, Data downloading into the computer and another android. Was Nathan making repairs and using him as a template, or was he actually trying to copy whatever he had in his brain into Micaiah? The only indication that the Builder gave of his work was the sweat at his hairline and his intense concentration. And the invisible spider on Miach's head.

After a couple hours, the spider retreated. Nathan's hands dropped to his sides and he leaned back into the couch, letting out a heavy sigh.

"That was longer than normal," Kayla commented. She approached Micaiah behind the couch and gingerly touched his shoulders. "How do you feel?"

Micaiah reached a clumsy hand up to meet hers and looked at her. His expression had changed. The palsy had ebbed just a little, enough for a shadow of a fifty year old Micaiah to bleed through. Still he looked like he was trying to swallow his tongue as he said, "I'm...bet...bet...bet-ter. I gan feel i'. I's ogay."

Kayla smiled and bent to kiss him, but Miach could see his brother was lackluster in his return. Was he uncertain or unable? Miach wasn't going to ask.

"Whatever you did seems to be working," Haunstein said, scribbling his notes. "There is some noticable improvement this time."

Nathan did not move. "It's helpful to have a carbon copy on

hand."

"And with all this alleged improvement, I'm hoping you regret not telling me about this sooner," Miach said bitterly.

"He was in a dead-to-rights coma for at least four months," Nathan replied sourly. "And unlike television would have you believe, you don't just wake up from them. It's a process. By that time, you had already closed up shop and returned to Ireland. Then Julianna made her move, and we didn't want to risk being found out. Then Rifun was arrested, and you had duties to perform there."

"Fuck Rifun's arrest and his trial. Not like I actually did much good there. You should have told me about this. This would have taken priority, and I'm already accomplishing way more than I did in court."

"What's done is done," Kayla sighed, resting her forehead on the back of Micaiah's head. "And since things look so promising, Micaiah may not need as much help as Godwin thinks." She looked at Nathan. "How soon can we do it again?"

"Now now, we don't want you two getting hasty and reckless," Haunstein said sarcastically, giving her a look.

She met his gaze, her own expression annoyed. "You know what I mean."

"If nothing else, I want him to get some sleep first, see how things get sorted out overnight," Nathan sighed, sitting up.

"What about his leg?" Godwin asked from where he sat in a corner chair, reading a book. "Furthermore, has he demonstrated any skill with the Akari?"

"We haven't even gotten to the Akari yet," Nathan admitted. "Basic cognitive function comes before the fabric of the universe."

"He's been wielding the Akari since he was five years old, if not earlier. Cognitive function has nothing to do with it." Godwin still did not look up from his book.

Nathan sighed again. "If nothing else, I need a break."

"And I will go over my notes from our last attempt," Haunstein said.

Miach stood and stretched. "Do you need my leg for that, too?"

Nathan shook his head slowly. "No. His good leg will suffice just fine."

"Then I'm going for a walk."

He left before anyone could argue, making his way down the steps to the ground. The land was cleared for about thirty feet around the house, and beyond was only thick pine. The only real trail leading up to the house was an old ATV trail, but even that was becoming overgrown in places. After a few minutes, Miach wondered if he was still on that trail or if he had wandered off onto a game trail. He paused and looked around. He spied what looked like a clearing and headed that direction.

It wasn't a true clearing, but the trees were noticably younger. A brush pile caught his attention. As he neared, noting the slope of the land, he saw it was not a brush pile, but a collapsed cabin. The supports had long since given way and the landing hadn't been gentle, but this had very clearly once been a home of some form. Most things were mossy or moldy, but he spied a few old pots and pans, some glass bottles, or fragments anyway.

A brief glint caught his eye. The best he could do was triangulate a general position, but it was a chore trying to figure out what exactly the thing was. Even when he found the glinting piece, he couldn't figure out what it was until he saw the old gun underneath. Old muzzleloader, like the kind from the old frontier. This place was definitely old.

Miach whistled to himself as he turned the gun over in his hands. It would never fire again, but clean it up and it might make a nice collector's item, something to display over the mantle.

He turned around and startled to find Kayla standing there, watching him from about twenty yards away. She closed the gap, taking her own sweet time.

"Godwin got worried, did he?" Miach laughed.

"I did," she answered simply.

Although she had darker skin, for her complexion and the current weather, she was quite pale.

"Why is that? Afraid I'd get lost?"

He tried to keep his tone light, but she just walked past him like a ghost, putting a hand on what used to be the side of the old cabin. She frowned.

"Something wrong?" Miach wondered.

Now she looked at him. "You know how most girls bring their boyfriends home to meet their fathers?"

"Yeah?"

She looked at the cabin again, running her hand over the old wood. "I brought Cai here years ago. To meet my first husband."

Miach blinked, mentally stumbling. "This…"

She nodded. "This is where I met Nika, where I had his children, and where I buried them all after the Russians murdered them." She glanced longingly down the slope, perhaps toward the old graves.

Miach cursed softly. He shook his head and tossed the old gun away, toward the place he found it. "Listen, I'm sorry. I shouldn't have come here."

"You didn't know." She stepped away from the old structure. "And this place, it means less than it used to. The cabin is gone." She made a vague gesture. "Their bones are resting."

"But if this place didn't mean something, you wouldn't have come back at all, and you and Cai wouldn't have built or bought this place so close to it."

She shrugged, looking as old as her husband. "I suppose you're right. Maybe I had hoped to redeem this place. To somehow show Nika that I was all right. Cai and I were going to stay here for a while, have children of our own…"

Miach could see she was fighting tears, trying to keep it together. As soon as he touched her, she lost it. Months of having to stay strong and keep it together poured out of her, and the most Miach could do was hold her and make sure she kept breathing. Right now she was acting as Micaiah's rock and anchor, just as he had done for her, but it was exhausting.

More than just months of being strong on account of Micaiah, this was years in the making. Fighting the Cult, being separated from her husband, the lies, the deception, all resulting in this.

Miach wished there was more he could do. In the books and movies, this sort of thing was usually followed by sex. As much as he might have wanted to get laid, he could not disrespect his sister-in-law like that, especially with his twin brother her husband back at the house.

At the same time, his twin brother her husband probably wasn't in much of a lovemaking mood or capacity right now. But he could be soon, if his more speedy recovery just now was any indication.

Kayla's sobs waned into nothing and she did not move. Even her grip around his midsection was weakening, slipping down to his waist. He jumped as her hands found the front of his shorts. Yes, there was the sex.

As she fumbled with his zipper, he put his hands on hers and took them away.

"No," he told her, meeting her eyes, red from weeping. "It's not what you want, and your husband is waiting for you back at the house."

She took a breath, closed her eyes, and simply leaned her forehead against his chest. She sniffed hard. "I know." Another sniff. "I'm sorry."

"Cai still loves you. For as fucked up as his brain may be right now, throughout everything that's happened, he still loves you. And I'll bet that once he gets his coordination back, he's going to be more than happy to stick it you-know-where."

Kayla sputtered a snotty laugh. "Oh, God, Miach, you're terrible. And probably right."

"I am absolutely right."

"Why, because you know you'd like to stick yours you-know-where?"

Miach felt his skin flush with embarrassment.

Kayla straightened and smoothed her hair the best she could, then wiped her face with her shirt sleeve. "Well, I guess we should get back before anyone starts wondering about us. Either that Julianna has gotten to us or maybe a bear, or maybe we've been out doing you-know-what."

She giggled stupidly at that, then turned and headed back the way they'd come. Miach followed a few steps behind, making sure to put his shorts back together.

"Do you know where Godwin intends to go?" Kayla asked as he caught up to her.

He shook his head. "I don't. He's got me on a slightly different mission right now."

"What's that?"

"Keeping tabs on Haunstein. Either making sure the good doctor doesn't sell us out to Julianna—voluntarily or otherwise—or else rescuing him if she decides to do some deep cleaning."

"You think she would?"

"She's already got it out for Tommen, and that includes Becky and their baby. Haunstein is nothing compared to that level of sadism."

Kayla sighed and shook her head. "I can't even fathom that kind of hatred. I spent years rescuing children from people like her." She glanced at Miach, expression grave. "If at all possible, tell me if you get wind that she's going after that baby. I will not let it happen if I can help it."

Miach nodded. "I'll let you know anything I learn."

They returned to the house no worse for wear. Godwin was back out on the deck, patrolling like a good soldier. He did not hail their return, merely paused in his routine pacing to assess their approach, then resumed.

Once inside, Nathan and Haunstein were arguing over something. Micaiah did not look as involved as Miach might have expected, but his countenance brightened when he saw his wife. He made a hasty move to try and stand. His first blunder was that he was not wearing his prosthetic, and this made any secondary blunders relating to poor balance and coordination difficult to judge. Whatever the case, the argument between the two doctors abruptly ceased as they worked to keep him upright. Nathan used Gravity while Haunstein scooted the walker over into the appropriate position.

To Miach's eyes, Kayla had looked surprised and delighted by this apparent display from her husband, but if she expected anything more, she was sorely disappointed. Micaiah did not hop his way over to her for a big welcome home kiss, nor did he say anything. He just stood there, hunched over the walker, goofy grin on his ragged face, watching her. If anything was different than last time, it was that he looked a little more enthusiastic for the kiss she gave him.

"No progress on the leg, I take it?" she wondered, helping Micaiah to sit down again. Miach noted that Godwin also entered the building, though he stayed by the door.

"Only as much as to render a prosthetic useless," Nathan sighed. "Bone, muscle, but…" He shook his head. "There is a lot that goes into human development in utero that is remarkably difficult to recreate in adulthood."

Haunstein made a wild gesture. "I keep telling him that if his Building is so awesome, if he can alchemically turn lead into gold, then just start with something simple. Form the shape of the leg using something simple and replenishable, like skin, and go in and change it later. It's no different than a sculptor framing in his work before chipping away at minute details."

"It is absolutely different. And pretending that I did agree to that method, where do you think I'm going to get all that Matter? It has to come from somewhere. His body does not have that kind of reserve, and anything else I would have to alchemically change the DNA. I can't just sew a couple of steaks to his stump and call it good."

Miach shifted in his seat. "What if…?" He sighed and tried to choose his words carefully. "So, some eight or nine years ago, a friend of mine had an accident. He fell off a ladder and shattered his foot. There was nothing to save, as far as the bone went because it was all in pieces. They used a pin and a cadaver bone in his foot, tying everything together until his own bone could regrow over it."

"Yes, but that is assuming the existence of muscle and skin as well," Nathan said as politely as he could.

Miach gestured to himself. "Use me. As frightening as it is to consider, compared to him, I have skin and muscle to spare. I don't know how you would specifically accomplish it, but you can't get much closer for a match as far as tissue donors go."

"And where do you suggest we get a whole leg bone, complete with foot and ankle?" Haunstein inquired. "I can fudge a lot of things, write off a lot of tests, but walking out of the hospital with a leg and ankle isn't one of them. There is also the matter of ensuring correct sizing."

"We have every reason to believe that Julianna is keeping tabs on you, Doctor," Godwin said. "You start walking around with a leg and foot, it won't take much to put two and two together, and she'll have ten agents following you right to him."

"Specific sizing shouldn't be much of an issue," Nathan cut in. "Get me in the ballpark and I'll take it the rest of the way. But surely you're not suggesting grave robbing?"

Godwin shrugged. "I mean, I could take it from a live subject, but I think you'll run into that same organ rejection problem with such fresh meat."

"You're sick."

"Practical. And anyway, if this is the best plan, should we wait on it? One gimpy escort is bad enough." The mercenary gestured to Miach. "I don't need two, if you suck him dry of all his useful muscles to refill him." He gestured to Micaiah. "Personally, I'd rather have smart but lame over physical but stupid."

The look on Micaiah's face, although a tad slow in coming, said he understood the insult.

"Use Nika's bones," Kayla said quietly after a moment.

"Who's that?" Godwin asked flatly.

Micaiah turned on the couch to look at her. "No."

Godwin raised a brow. "Oh, he does understand. Unfortunately, I don't."

"Nika was my husband," Kayla told him, "many years ago, before Time. He's buried just over the rise." She made a vague gesture in the direction of the old cabin. "I think he was a little taller than Cai, but…" She ignored Micaiah's incoherent mumbling. "In order to save one husband, I may have to enlist the help of the other."

She looked at her current husband. Micaiah huffed a frustrated sigh, as if he couldn't get out what he was trying to say. Slowly, deliberately, he managed, "Ah gant tooh hat."

Kayla's eyes were wet but she did not cry. "Saving you is saving me. Nika tried to save me once, and now he will."

Micaiah was still displeased.

"This is touching and all, but what is the timeline? The feasibility? I need to know," Godwin demanded. "We've determined that the twin brother can reboot his brain well enough. How much extra time for the body?"

Nathan rubbed his face and made a frustrated noise. "I'd like it if Micaiah rested for a bit, so we can see just how much progress we've made in his mind, where we need to go next."

"How much time do we have?" Miach wondered, looking at Godwin.

"Fuck if I know," the mercenary replied irritably. "We have maybe a dozen spies total within the Order, a dozen or so more if you count roundabout information, also known as hearsay, and gossip isn't always reliable. We haven't heard of any large-scale efforts other than the stalemate on Hlohi."

"Why would she make such a concerted effort, though?" Nathan wondered. "Keep it simple, keep it hidden, take us out quietly."

"Normal Akarin maybe. And likely she already is because of how scattered everyone is. But for you guys, all of you here with

Authored Books, you all talk. You keep up on each other. She tries one at a time, it'll tip you off." Godwin nodded. "I would be willing to bet that she's going to hit all of you at the same time, and it will be a large operation."

"So we may have a little time," Miach ventured.

Godwin gave him a look. "Don't take that as a green light. Yellow at best. I'm here as a favor, but we still have our own problems. Julianna might come after the Miaramila first, just to ensure you guys don't have any hint of backup."

"But we can call this good for the day and not have to try and rush something," Nathan concluded.

The mercenary just sighed, rolled his eyes, and turned away as if to mumble to himself. After a moment he turned back, speaking over anyone else who tried, saying, "Am I correct to assume, then, that you intend to do this again tomorrow, with his brain?"

"Yes," the psychologist said evenly. "Don't think I don't understand the time crunch we're under or that I don't take it seriously."

"Then I suggest you act like it," Godwin told him. "I will be coming by personally to bring you back here."

Nathan ignored the mercenary and instead turned his attention to the twins and Kayla. "It won't be right away that we try this idea. I want to think about it first, think about what I will need to do. What I need from you two—" He pointed to Miach and Micaiah. "Is a lot of protein. Build muscle, build fat, give me Matter to work with. Micaiah, you are far too skinny as it is. Miach, I don't want to incapacitate you, as Godwin mentioned."

"I can go out and hunt some game," Kayla promised. "Animals are gearing up for winter and hibernation, lots of fat on them."

"Perfect. I will leave that to you, then."

When there was nothing else, the doctors packed up and were gone soon enough, leaving Miach, Micaiah, Kayla, and Godwin. Micaiah was still sitting on the couch, the rest of them remained standing.

"Ah gan…" Micaiah began. He paused, expression frustrated. "Yah gant…goo…gant to…d-d-do gat. Yah…gant…d-do at."

Godwin cursed. "Do you know how many men I've seen over the years lose limbs? Plenty. You know how many wanted them back? All of them. You know how many got them back? None."

"B-b-but Niga—"

"Is dead. Long dead from the sounds of it. I respect you for respecting him as your wife's previous husband, but this is one of those times when you need to think about yourself. How are you going to best protect her?" Godwin went on, taking advantage of Micaiah's slowed thought and speech. "There is no nobility in touting wounds that can be fixed. But there is courage to be had and more to be gained by fixing them and getting back in the fight."

Micaiah sighed and turned it over his in head. Miach could see that he was trying to process it, trying to think it through. He just couldn't come up with the same snappy rebuttals he used to. Did he really understand what was going on, the big picture? How much was he still losing, and how costly was that loss?

"One…gund-dishun," he said finally.

Godwin shifted his stance. "I'll entertain it, seeing how we seem to be making some real progress, but I do not guarantee its acceptance."

Miach had a brief thought that the mercenary was being intentionally verbose, just trying to confuse Micaiah. Kayla's expression said she was having the same thought.

"Ooh gant…you gant…use…Niga's f-f-f—" Micaiah held up his hand. "—f-fingers…t-to…help Rif-fun."

Godwin raised a brow. "Is that all? That's easy enough. I accept your condition."

"You expect Nathan will help you, or are you going to be Rifun's surgeon?" Kayla wondered.

He looked at her. "I'm surprised you care. But I want to see this work first." He shifted his stance and prepared to leave. "I'll see you all tomorrow, then. Bright and early."

"Days are getting shorter quickly around here," Miach informed him snidely.

The mercenary was unimpressed as he opened a portal and departed.

"We should leave on our own," Kayla grumbled. "We don't need him to babysit us."

"Where...we go?" Micaiah asked.

"He won't say. Doesn't want to 'compromise security.'"

"Why...we go?"

Kayla's expression turned disappointed. Miach felt the same disappointment. Had Micaiah just been putting on a good show of understanding? Was he regressing in some way?

"Because Julianna is trying to kill everyone with an Authored Book," she explained.

"At ingludes...a gree o oos," Micaiah stated, gesturing around. "We af...we af foif boog. You haf a boog."

Kayla nodded. "That's right."

"Is it wise to leave on our own?" Miach wondered. "Godwin may not have the best bedside manner, but—"

"We can grab Nathan to come with us. He's a Builder—"

"So was Andrew."

"We don't know what happened to Andrew. And even if he is really gone, he was trying to protect a whole planet, or at least a whole society. Nathan only has to look out for us. And by us..." She sighed. "I mean Micaiah." She looked at her husband. Micaiah appeared attentive enough, but not what one might call involved. "At least until he can be fixed."

"And then what?" Miach asked. "We keep running? The four of us? There's another aspect to this I think you're forgetting."

"And what's that?"

"Nathan looks out for Tommen, too. Tommen has a family now. Are we supposed to take Nathan away from him? Tommen isn't known for being especially powerful or subtle. If Nathan were to travel back and forth, he becomes a liabilty if Julianna ever wanted to track us down. And if we disappear, if Julianna finds us, no one knows. No one cares."

Kayla gave him a look. "You really think Godwin is our best bet? There is a whole universe out there. We could hide in the wilds of Tacaga and those bubble-living bastards would never know it."

Miach sighed. "If nothing else, we should see what Nathan can do for Micaiah in the time we still have. If he can restore his mind and fix his leg, we'll be in a much better position to run. Whenever, wherever, and with whoever. If Micaiah can fend for himself, it can only help us."

She nodded. "You're not wrong there. And it sounds like we might have a little bit of time before we absolutely have to go."

"Oil get bet-ter," Micaiah chimed in. "B-bromise."

Kayla nodded again and went to give him a brief shoulder rub. "I know you will. And it sounds like part of that healing process is going to be meat, and lots of it. So, if you two want to hang out for a little bit, I will see what I can scare up."

In the brief time that they had lived together in Charleston, Miach had sampled some of the goods from her homeland and her adopted homeland. Maybe it was him, or maybe it was the specific animal being too old or something, or maybe it was the way it had been prepared, but he wasn't really a fan of everything she had offered. Now he was expected to eat it in rather large quantities.

"The things I do for you," Miach sighed, plopping into the recliner once Kayla had gone. She hadn't done much for prep, just grabbed her bow and walked out the door. With Time, what was the point of going out early, wearing specific clothes, tracking, lures, scents, bait, and all of that? Even the bow was unnecessary, but if that's what she enjoyed, then so be it.

"Y-you help me a lot," Micaiah stated.

"Well, I'm glad you recognize that anyway."

"Y-you...re good broter."

Miach leaned the recliner back a bit. "Don't go getting all

sentimental on me now."

"Oo are," Micaiah insisted. "You ta...tag gar a me. A lot."

Miach studied his brother. "How much do you remember?"

Micaiah shifted in his seat. "I rem..member a lot."

"Do you remember living on the streets? Do you remember St. Joseph's?" He went on before Micaiah could speak. "More than just whatever you might have read recently in our Books, do you actually remember these things?"

"I rem...remember. D...D...tere were t-two pigs. R-r-rory and R-riva."

Miach nodded. "That's right."

"R-r-riva ha ele-wen...lil p-pigle...pigle...piggies."

"Well, she had a lot more than that, but they definitely came in batches of ten or eleven or twelve, somewhere in there."

They lapsed into an awkward silence. Miach knew his brother wasn't an idiot. He wasn't stupid, he wasn't retarded, he wasn't slow. His brother was strong and brave and quick-witted and intelligent. Yeah, so maybe he'd taken a few too many knocks to the head when he was a prize-fighter, maybe he was a bit rash and impulsive, didn't always think things through, but he wasn't...this.

And what if he is now? a small voice nagged at the back of his mind. *What if this is the best he will recover to?*

I can't believe that. Nathan is a Builder. He can look at the Core of the Wheel, manipulate the fabric of the universe and rebuild it from the ground up. He can restore Micaiah. It might not be fast, because he doesn't want to make things worse, but it will happen.

But what if Micaiah is gone? What if that part of him perished with the oxygen deprivation? What if restoring his brain really is just copy and pasting you onto him? What if it isn't Micaiah who comes back, but you?

I don't believe that either. He still has his memories. Even if that is partially true, that maybe he'll imitate some of my mannerisms or lesser parts of my personality for a short time, his own memories and Kayla especially will ultimately set him back to rights.

Miach's thoughts were interrupted by Micaiah asking, "Y-you

really...t-d-ting...my leg gan be grown bag?"

Miach watched his brother feel around his stump, first with the sock and then without it.

"I don't know," he admitted. "It sounds promising, but then, it doesn't sound like it's ever really been tried. Any plan is going to sound promising and insane."

"Sh-shouldn' Nat-an know d-dis? What Builders learn?"

"I don't know. I guess if you're a career brain surgeon, your first aid skills could get a little rusty."

"Need m-m-more bearers. M-m-m-more p-profess...fess... fessionals."

Miach shrugged. "Little late to be saying that, I think."

Micaiah sighed, and for a moment, he looked almost normal. Then, "Gayla...do not wan...ooh go...f-far way. Not w-wan isolation." He raised his arm as if to gesture, but the best he could apparently do at the moment was a floppy, retarded wave. "Here...now...is n-necessary. B-but when sh-she was here...wi Niga an..." He struggled to form the next word, which Miach guessed to be "children." Finally he moved on. "Dey...murdered. W-would haf died alone. Begause n-no one knew."

Miach nodded. "I know."

"Sh-she doesn wan same t-to happen here."

His mind was there, or it appeared to be. But his physical impairments left much to be desired as Miach again wondered, *What if this is the best he's going to get?*

No, he scolded himself. *If one exploratory session, copy and pasting my brain onto him, can bring him back this much, then next time will be even better. Even if he doesn't get a brand new flesh leg, he functioned without it before, he can do it again. We just need his mind, if nothing else.*

"Well, you know what?" Miach said, shifting position. "You get a shiny new leg, you may not have to hide."

Before Micaiah could reply, the door opened and Kayla walked in with several large bags. Whatever she had gotten, she had evidently already processed it, at least somewhat.

"What you get?" Micaiah inquired cheerfully.

"Moose," she replied, trying to match his attitude. "Excellent protein, good steaks. Which cut do you want?"

Chapter Seven
Secret Guardian

Tommen's life up through tenth grade had been practically nothing but bullying, at least during school. His junior year hadn't been bad; actually, it had practically been heaven, considering his nights were spent training with Rifun and his psycho Cult. How it was that in the space of a year he forgot how ferocious a high school rumor mill could be, he couldn't even fathom. In a way, he was more ashamed of his own stupidity than anything the mill had to crank out about him.

Someone had, in fact, seen something somewhere on social media, so it wasn't exactly a secret-secret that he was going to be a dad, but his admission was like some silent cue to let the rumors fly free. As long as they were just strictly about him, he was good about keeping his mouth shut and just letting words be words. When the rumors involved Becky or the baby, that's when things could get ugly, such as the rumor that he'd raped her, but both their families were so old-fashioned that they still believed in the victim marrying her attacker.

Tommen may have redefined "attacker" for that particular junior who started the rumor. It earned him a detention, but his point was made. Layman then made the counterpoint that he was an adult now, and that was assault and battery; he ought to know this. Tommen admitted that he did. Dr. Polski had basically done the same thing to him. But he wasn't going to stand for malice like that.

Speaking of Layman, Tommen met with the principal once, occasionally twice a week before school for counseling and other life lessons. It was probably the first time Tommen had ever thought of the man as a human being and not just a jerk who was out to get him for every minor offense.

But with the counseling and something resembling a friendship, it made it easier to get excused absences, such as taking Becky to her next appointment. It didn't last long and there was nothing particularly special about it other than a confirmation that all was well. Whitmore wasn't going to take pictures, but Becky demanded them. As with many things, if Becky really wanted something, she would find a way to make it happen.

So Tommen returned to school with a new strip of pictures, stunned at all the changes in just three weeks. More than once during class, he would Band just so he could compare the films side by side. Then he would just stare at them in awe. This was his child. He still couldn't get over it. And did he really want to? He showed the pictures to Layman the following morning.

"And all is well?" the principal asked as he dug out his reading glasses and looked at them.

"That's what the doctor says," Tommen confirmed. "All is well so far. At the next appointment, they're going to take a sample of...I think she said it was the placenta, and do a genetic test."

"Are they going to, or is Becky going to insist on doing it herself?"

Tommen grinned. "As much as I'm sure she would want to do everything herself, they're going to do it. I don't know, maybe she can talk them into letting her watch or assist or something."

He didn't say that she'd already tried to do just that, and while Whitmore admired her determination and intellect, Becky would not be assisting in any way. But the doctor did promise to get the detailed results of the test for her to go over, seeing how she would understand it, or could use it to further her studies. Most people just got the basic rundown of things. Like Tommen. He would be looking at the one or two page explanation, letting Becky peruse the twenty-plus page detailed report.

Of his teachers, only Reisig was at all interested in how things were going, and she and Tommen would talk for a few minutes at the end of the day sometimes.

As for the rest of the teachers? Well, they were generally careful not to say anything where he could hear, but he could feel, at worst, disapproval and hostility, or at best, uncertainty. They knew his history, they knew him, they knew that a vast majority of high school parents didn't stick together and their children were just as dysfunctional. Maybe some of them were happy for him, but didn't want to get their hopes up too far. Who could know?

The lunch ladies were happy for him and adored his little strip of pictures, but then, they were happy about anything good. For a cynic, it could be annoying. Tommen had hated it for a long time. Oh, George got a C on his test when he normally got an F? Celebration! Missy got a sparkly new pair of shoes she'd been eying but cost a dreaded eight hundred dollars? Celebration! Lucas managed to get his drunk dad into bed last night instead of beating up on his equally drunk mom? Celebration! Carrie got her fourth straight A+ on an essay? Celebration!

Now, though, despite still being a bit of a cynic, Tommen liked the enthusiasm from the lunch ladies. If it made a student happy, it made them happy. For the well-to-do snobs, it meant nothing. For those of more modest means, it was a voice on their end of the court cheering for them. For Tommen, it was someone who could be happy for him without endless, hostile scrutiny or deep, thoughtful questions and contemplation. Just happiness and acceptance.

But other than those few exceptions, the strip of photos stayed safely in his wallet. Guaranteed that if he had them out too frequently, someone would come along and steal them or defile them or do any number of unspeakable things. Senior he may be, and it might afford him a little respect, but he was pretty far down on the social totem pole. Not a few students thought he should be transferred to the alternative ed school for delinquents and those who couldn't fit in in regular school, the pregos, the addicts, and so on. But he wouldn't. There was no reason he couldn't finish regular old high school. Besides, he only had a few more months and then off to college. Take that, bitches.

Ho hum, but it was still only September. There were days when it felt like the birth was just around the corner and somehow he'd lost track of the last few months of his life. Then there were days, most often during times when he was sitting in class, when time just slogged on and seemed to halt and life was going nowhere. Maybe that was a side effect of being able to perceive Time at smaller increments than mere seconds and minutes.

At the very least, Tommen thought while pretending to pay attention to the current lecture, Nathan was still a good sport. They were still training together, but most of their focus was shifting toward Tommen's new life as a husband and father. The past—the warehouse, the bombing, the battles—rarely came up anymore. Even the trial seemed a distant memory, or one set side for the time being, just waiting for the aftermath, the sentencing. No, these days it was all about Becky and the baby.

Well, that wasn't entirely true. There was some talk about Julianna, the Order, the Akarin, the Time industry, and all of those happenings, mostly just how to prepare for an attack, current goings-on, what to do if Becky started asking questions or was exposed to Time. They didn't spend a ton of time wrestling with these particularly difficult questions because, as Nathan stated more than once, it was going to be a lot of improvisation. It's hard to plan on how to improvise.

But there were some things that were known. For one, Julianna had stepped up her attacks on the Akarin and Miaramila. From what Tommen understood, the Miaramila, while small, once reorganized and now dug in wherever their secret base was, were scary efficient and wicked strong. They had little trouble defending themselves against the Order. With that thought in mind, they were no longer interested in helping or being helped by the Akarin. For the moment, the two had a ceasefire, but even Tommen knew that wouldn't last long.

As for the Time industry and the Borelians, both parties

seemed to be split. The Hands of Time saw an opportunity to be rid of the Akarin, but the Borelians, masters of war that they were, were more concerned with Julianna's strength and numbers as well as the Miaramila's strength and speed. They were running the odds of the two sides getting back together, the two sides remaining separate and both being powerhouses, the two sides being allies, being enemies. The Borelians learned to run these scenarios and calculate the odds when they were in secondary school, and with their rampant ethnocentrism, they would be going after the biggest threat to Brelix and the Borelian way of life.

Tommen was willing to bet it would be the Miaramila first. Rifun had attacked Brelix once. While conquest had never been an option, he'd still accomplished his main goal: breaking into a death temple, stealing an artifact, and causing as much mayhem as possible, including stealing Borelian ships. True, the assassination of the remaining council members hadn't gone as planned, but the mayhem definitely. Rifun's downfall hadn't really been in the military field, and his strategy and tactical knowledge was still a flowing fountain for his followers to utilize.

On the other hand, Julianna had the numbers, the strength, the stronghold, and the espionage. She'd been the mastermind behind the Zero Hour Revolution and then overthrown Rifun without him ever suspecting it. Could she have moles elsewhere? Who was in her pocket in the Time industry? Could she forge an alliance with the Borelians, take control of the Time industry, similar to how Rifun and Cassius had?

The Tacagans were also in on things, though to a much smaller degree, and it was uncertain just what their role was beyond providing information about humans and attempting to crack the secrets to wielding the Akari.

As for the Akarin...well, they were surviving. They had no known central stronghold, no known leader, and were purely reactionary to the whole thing. All their members had gone underground and it was next to impossible to track them down, which also left a lot of human Time Agents stranded, cut off from the Wheel.

There had been no specific mention of Tommen from any group. No one was threatening him, offering a bounty, equating him with Rifun or any of that. That didn't mean he wasn't a target; it just meant his enemies weren't being obvious about it. That was probably what scared him more. Rifun had always made a scene about following him, stalking him, manipulating him, using him; that had been unnerving, but, looking back, comfortably predictable. Julianna was being quiet about it. Tommen didn't like that, and there were times when he wondered how things might be different if he hadn't given away the secret to escaping from the in-between dimension. But then, that would mean he would still be stuck there in misery and wouldn't have a family to take care of. As Becky said, it wasn't about them anymore.

Tommen left the park that night, his mind whirling, as it usually was after talking to Nathan. Things seemed so simple the rest of the week, when he only had to deal with the things that were obviously in front of him. But all of those things were normal. There were other things out there, too, abnormal things. Strong and powerful abnormal things. It might not have been as bad if he were just some stupid teenager from an insignificant world, but he wasn't. He was well-known to the Hands of Time, the Borelians, the Order, the Miaramila, and the Akarin. He had to stay alert and stay ready in case of attack.

God, he sounded nuts.

His dad was home that night. Judging by the TV being off, Becky was already in bed. Between classes, restarting her sewing business, and being pregnant—especially being pregnant—she became fatigued much more easily and she had little time to pursue any outside hobbies. Once her mandatory work was done, so was she. When Tommen had asked how things were going to change as the pregnancy went on and the baby started moving, she'd given him a look and said nothing as she returned to her homework. He took that as a polite way of saying, "Well, it's not going to get better, so shut up, moron."

Still, he tried to be attentive and concerned. He asked about her classes, her classmates, her work, how things were going at her parents' house. Her classes were going well, very intensive, rigorous, exciting in an institutionalized-schooling sort of way. Her college classmates showed signs of much greater intelligence than her high school classmates. Work was going well; a lot of her clients had come back, and things were steady. Without knowing whether the baby was afflicted with dwarfism, or the sex for that matter, she wasn't making baby clothes yet. Things at her parents' house were fine. Her mom was a wealth of information and a warm blanket of support. Her dad was loving and supportive, of course, but he still kind of wanted to cut Tommen's dick off. Which was why Tommen generally stayed away from the doctor if he could help it.

As much as Tommen wanted to be attentive and supportive, he also wanted to know about weird goings-on, and not in the jealous boyfriend sort of way either...okay, not entirely jealous. He was always listening for signs of stalking, or scoping, someone looking to hurt him by hurting Becky or the baby. Was anyone following her, taking an unusual interest in her, being a creep in class? What was the mood on campus? After all, college riots were a big thing across the country now; was she safe? Becky assured him that no one was going to be bombing the college or toppling any statues or fountains; all was well. School was fine, work was fine, home was fine, she was fine, and the baby was fine, too. Stop worrying.

"I have to worry," he told her. It was Friday. "It's my responsibility."

"I think you are confusing defending with worrying," she sighed. "And worrying won't help you when you have to be alert and attentive on the job site tomorrow."

Was it his fault? If only she knew half the things that had really gone on in his life the last couple years.

He was just glad she hadn't found the Books, safely stashed away in the top of his closet. With her being too busy or too tired to do half the snooping she used to, he had a shot at keeping them a secret for a little while longer.

Dinner was a joint effort that evening, which was just as well. Becky's attitude toward food had changed drastically and it continued to change, though it remained a pretty steady gamble between weird cravings, morning sickness that lasted more than just the mornings sometimes, and a healthy diet. She'd always been good about her sugar and keeping it in check, but now she checked it religiously, before and after meals, between meals, between her between-meal checks, and she documented it all in a little notebook which she took with her to the doctor. It was almost scary. But Tommen wasn't complaining; it was for a good cause, after all.

He quizzed her on her schoolwork and she did the same for him. He was still self-conscious about still being in high school while she was in college, but there wasn't a lot to be done about it at this point. He just had to remind himself that there was no shame in dating—er, marrying?—an older woman, especially when the age difference was only about a year. It could be worse. There were couples out there where one was a decade older than the other. Like, hey, man, what are you doing after graduation? Oh, you know, I'm thinking about asking that cute second grader to marry me.

He managed to talk her into a movie that night. He settled into his dad's recliner and put Becky between his legs, resting his chin on top of her head until she finally shook him off. Still he put his arms around her, hands resting on her belly which was becoming more and more obvious. Life was good.

Tommen told himself repeatedly that he needed to be even more vigilant, do something more to keep her safe from whatever wackos were out there trying to harm her to get to him. Problem was, he didn't know what more he could do, feasibly, anyway. Work, school, home, everything was pretty standard. Short of going on the run like Bonnie and Clyde, he was doing the best he could with that secret life. And as his dad had pointed out, if he tipped them off—be they Order, Miaramila, Borelians, or whomever—that he knew they were onto him, it could launch an attack early when no one would be prepared. Better to keep going and make the enemy believe he was clueless even as he gathered his strength and made a plan.

Sun Tzu, he mused. *Rifun would be proud.*

He hadn't spoken to Rifun at all since the night he asked about Julianna's movements and alliances, and he had no reason to other than sheer curiosity. Tommen had, however, occasionally dabbled a bit with what he wanted to say at the sentencing. Because only the attempted murder and kidnapping had been served up guilty, only he and his dad would be giving victim impact statements. Tommen had a rough idea of what he wanted to say, but he was hardly a master of words, so he was taking his time and thinking about it—i.e., procrastinating. But he had until February, in theory.

Now his dad, well, that could be a whole different story. Tommen had asked his dad about his victim impact statement. His dad simply stated that he was thinking about it and jotting things down here and there. When he inquired as to the content of some of these statements, his dad would not elaborate. Tommen had great suspicion that even though it would be only his dad speaking, his speech would have the full weight and endorsement of the Charleston Police Department behind it, maybe even Kanawha County Police, the West Virginia State Police, Highway Patrol, probably the U.S. Marshals...

The movie ended. Becky was still awake but sleepy and wandered off to bed. Tommen remained where he was and found something else to watch quietly. He really probably should go to bed himself to he would be rested and ready for work in the morning, but he was still too awake for that. Some days, work seemed like the least of his problems, and he could comfortably skip an hour or two of sleep. The idiot box demanded his attention.

The next thing he knew, he was being prodded awake. In some dark recess of his mind, his subconscious was screaming at him to jump up and be alert; anything could be happening. Something could be wrong. But the majority of him was groggy and confused and wondering who dared to wake his blissful slumber.

"Okay, old man, out of the chair." It was his dad's voice.

Tommen sat up and stretched, blinking tired eyes and looking around. The TV was off and the only light came from the light over the stove in the kitchen. His dad was standing beside him, still in uniform.

"What time is it?" Tommen murmured.

"Almost time for your alarm to go off, and definitely time for you to get out of my recliner," his dad informed him.

"So protective of your recliner." Nevertheless, Tommen stood and stretched again.

"You haven't earned it yet." His dad headed down to his room.

Ten minutes later, Tommen was ready for work, and his dad was ready for bed. They converged in the kitchen, Tommen for breakfast, his dad for a glass of water.

"Long night?" Tommen wondered.

"Not as long as it could have been," his dad said.

"Any news on the investigation?"

Vin had been released on his own recognizance once Internal Affairs had gotten through with him, but his wife hadn't let him in the door. Filing for divorce was bad enough. Shooting a suspect execution-style the same night was worse. He'd been crashing on Arnold's couch, on administrative leave, at the beck and call of IA at all hours, day and night. Walter had been called in multiple times to answer questions and rehash the details of the incident. His story was consistent in its own telling and with the dash cam video. He was off the hook legally, but Tommen could still see it was taking a heavy toll.

His dad let out a breath. "Vin's going to be arrested today, formally booked and charged."

"With what?"

Walter rubbed his face, and Tommen knew he was wrestling with the logistics of it. His dad liked his work, knew that justice had to happen, but it still wasn't always fair. Those higher up on the ladder liked to play games, and police officers were their favorite pawns.

"You don't know this," his dad warned.

"Of course not," Tommen promised.

"He's going to be charged with second-degree murder, per the prosecutor. Most likely, unless he has some dumbass idea at the last second, he'll plead down to involuntary manslaughter. One-to-six, maybe a three-to-nine."

"Fuck." Tommen shook his head. "He's going to be murdered in prison. They do know that, right?"

"Out of my hands, kid, and it's pretty damn lenient if you ask me. Just watch the news and be glad they didn't sentence him to hang on the spot."

"They wouldn't. Your suspect was white."

His dad said nothing to that, but his body language spoke of disgruntled agreement. He finished his water, announced he was going to bed, wished Tommen a good day at work, and wandered off. A few minutes later, Tommen headed off to work.

The McMansion was coming along as well as could be expected. That is, it wasn't. The land had been cleared and excavated; there was a massive hole in the ground for the foundation. Then the problem came up that the concrete trucks that were needed to pour the basement walls and floor were having a hell of a time trying to get to the site. The loggers had ripped up the trail pretty well, and even Tommen and the others had to park their personal vehicles down on the main road. So it had taken a full day of grading and smoothing the trail-slash-future-driveway just to get the concrete up to the site, and then it was a creative dance to get them in a position advantageous to actually pouring the foundation.

Then it was time for the concrete workers and the masons to take over. Tommen stood back and played gopher as much as he stayed up front to watch and ask questions. He liked the poured concrete more than the blocks; the blocks he could never seem to line up straight or make ninety degree corners. Poured concrete was a little easier to work with, in his opinion. You just smoothed it out, feathered it level, and off you go. He kept these thoughts to himself, of course, because the masons took their jobs very seriously and would probably punch him for his comparatively frivolous attitude.

When it came to concrete, lunch was as fluid as the stone. Concrete didn't stop drying just because the clock struck one. Or noon, for that matter. It was almost two before they actually got to their lunch pails. Of course, that also meant it was almost two before they could get a bathroom break. There was exactly one portajohn on site near the construction zone, and their cars—and by extent, their lunches—were on the main road. One nice thing about this "mountain getaway" was the presence of a lot of trees, many of which were suddenly utilized.

Contrary to popular belief, dudes do not get off by watching other dudes go, and only in the presence of alcohol are there "sword fights." When available, a certain measure of privacy is expected. Of course, this also meant that Tommen had to go deep into the woods behind a grove of pines before he found any kind of privacy.

Tommen was just zipping up when a voice spoke behind him.

"Hello, Tommen."

He whirled around, half-expecting to see Rifun standing there. Instead, he found Godwin. The man did not look overly enthused, although whether this came from whatever he'd been doing previously or because he was now here speaking to Tommen, was impossible to determine.

"Fuck, dude," Tommen hissed, tightening his belt and shifting his pants back to a comfortable position. "What's wrong with you?"

The man did not flinch. "Places to be, things to do, sometimes social graces have to come second."

"So skip the handshake. I was peeing." Tommen did not bother trying to suppress a small shudder. "But you're here now; what do you want?"

"We have reason to believe Julianna is ready to make a major move against those with Authored Books. This is nothing new, of course; I hope you already suspected something similar."

Tommen nodded. "So what do we do?"

"Rifun currently has me repaying a debt to Kayla and the twins—"

"Where are they? How is Micaiah?"

Godwin gave him an annoyed look. "Such information makes you a liability, and I think you can guess his state. As I said, Rifun has me repaying a debt to them."

"I sense a 'but' coming."

"Rifun also still feels the need to protect you, considers your predicament somewhat his fault. Unfortunately, I can't be in two places at once, and, as you recall, Rifun has no Akari abilities to speak of."

Tommen shrugged. "So help them, and then you can help me. I can put up a fight for a while."

The man sighed and pinched the bridge of his nose. "Child, you may have fought in battle, but you know nothing of war. Julianna's most likely move is going to target all of you at once. She knows you're separated and weak, she knows the Miaramila are stretched thin; even my absence is cause for some consternation."

"What do you know about her plans?"

"We have some spies, but that kind of information is well above their paygrade. Julianna is keeping things very close to the chest. By the time anything specific comes down to them, it may already be too late to get out a warning."

"Okay, so...what do you expect me to do? What do you want me to do?"

"Not wandering off alone would be a good start. Not staying here in your predictable, vulnerable routine would be better."

Tommen blinked. "What? I can't do that. Becky—"

"Is even more vulnerable than you."

"She's Unengaged. Entirely unaware, not even suspicious. You think I should just drag her into Time and the Akari and all this bullshit like a bad action movie?"

"Your only alternative that I see is letting her and your child die like the beginning of an equally bad action movie, except you won't be able to avenge them because you'll be dead before act two." Godwin's expression was annoyed.

"I can't do that."

"Die, or leave?"

Tommen threw his hands up. "Either! Both! I don't know."

Godwin stepped forward. "Well you better figure it out fast. You might be young, but I hope you're not stupid. You can't expect Julianna to just let you walk away. She's targeting those with Authored Books, which you are. And your pregnant girlfriend is the sweetest leverage she could ask for."

Tommen stomped away a few steps, paused, then stomped back. "What do you want me to do? What do you suggest? I just leave right now, grab her out of the house, and have you whisk us away to your ship or your base?"

Godwin's expression turned smarmy. "Well, that would be one option. At least there would be some safety in numbers and experience. I don't know that anyone knows how to deliver a baby, but we could try."

Tommen scowled. Again he stomped away, and returned.

"I can't. I can't do that to her."

"You can, you just don't want to," the mercenary growled. "You want things to go back to the way they were 'before' and just carry on with a normal life. Well, that's not an option anymore. I'm trying to give you enough time to prepare yourselves and make a civilized exit. She could attack now, or tomorrow, or next month. How much do you want to be caught off-guard?"

This time, Tommen did not stomp away, but he did turn around, let out a heavy sigh, and run his fingers through his hair before facing Godwin once more. "Do the Miaramila or anyone else have any plans of their own? You're right, Julianna is a threat, and she won't stop being a threat just because we aren't in the kill zone at her desired time."

Now the mercenary frowned and hesitated. "Regrettably, the best we are able to do well right now is look after our own interests. We have spies, but we still don't have much capability for a true offensive strike. As I said, this is primarily a favor for Rifun."

"So the best you can do is just shuffle us from place to place to try and protect us."

Godwin gave him a look. "I don't like useless bodies. You need more training, to either help us or yourself. Probably your girlfriend, too."

Tommen sighed and rubbed his face. "And if you're having to help Micah and Micaiah, the Akarin probably aren't in any better shape." He groaned into his hands then let them drop to his sides. "I don't know. If it was just me, fine, but Becky…" He shook his head. "I can't do it, not right now."

"Well, don't take too much time to think about it. Slowest member of the herd gets eaten." Godwin dipped his head. "Stay safe on the job site."

Then he did something Tommen hadn't seen before. He opened a portal, but then he moved it. Rather than opening a portal and walking through it, he opened one and moved it so it enveloped him, without needing to break his statuesque composure. It was a small gesture, but enough to reinforce the point.

Sighing, Tommen looked around the clearing for anymore unexpected or unwanted visitors, then turned and started back toward the job site.

He'd never had any illusions that he was in the clear just because he'd escaped the fortress or Rifun had been found guilty in court. He just wasn't ready to face the real consequences that were coming for him. Rifun's trial had indeed been simply to buy time, and now that timer had run out. Worse, Julianna had probably used that time to concoct an even more heinous scheme to wipe out her most hated enemies.

He probably should have used that time to figure out what he was going to do. It might not be so difficult except for Becky. A breakup he could deal with, but he couldn't abandon their baby. He wasn't sure he could convince himself of an abortion either. She would never go along with a formal procedure, but he was known to be violent at night...

No. He couldn't do that. This spat with Julianna was no fault of the life growing inside Becky. He would abandon them—alive—before snuffing out that light. At the same time, he had no reason to think Julianna wouldn't have them killed anyway. His best option would be to stick by them and protect them, but was there any way he could do that without exposing them to Time and the Akari and all the garbage he'd been dealing with for the past few years?

Another thought popped into his head. Who was to say that Becky wouldn't like being part of Time and all that? Who was to say she wouldn't be good at it? She could put that same spunky energy into some Time or Akari abilities as well as anything else she'd ever done. Why was he automatically assuming the worst case scenario? Did he dare consider optimism for once?

Damn, this was confusing.

"You look deep in thought," Matt commented as lunch wound down. "And worried. The bears and lions almost get you out there?"

Tommen managed a small smile and shook his head. "Not quite. Almost, though. Turned out to be a rabbit."

That got the guys laughing and making jokes, but even as it had been a spontaneous response, it also gave him another option to consider, someone to ask who was indeed trustworthy and honest. His answers weren't always straightforward, but Tommen trusted him a hell of a lot more than he trusted Rifun.

He mulled over the situation as they finished up the last few hours of work, going over because, again, of the nature of concrete. By the time he got home, Becky was just putting dinner leftovers into containers and then into the fridge.

"You could have at least called and told me you were going to be late," she said coldly.

"I didn't know we were going to be so late, and on the site, I don't usually have my phone," he told her. "You know that."

"Even a text when you were leaving would have been nice, so I could have kept it warm a little longer, or at least known you weren't dead in a ditch somewhere."

She put the last container away, washed the spoon, and walked away. Tommen sighed as he untied his boots and slipped them off. *She's pregnant and saying things she doesn't mean. She's just concerned for you. You could have been dead in a ditch today, if Godwin had been less noble than he wants you to believe. That's all it is. Just let her cool off. All is well. She can't stay mad forever.*

Can she?

Regardless, he got out a container of leftovers and warmed it up in the microwave. By the time he got down to their bedroom, she was busy with homework. She pointedly ignored him as he grabbed a change of clothes. Only once he was clean and fresh from the shower did she appear calm enough to accept a kiss and the barest of conversation.

She'd spent her day at her parents' house, sewing, working away on several projects. Then she'd come home to make dinner, except he wasn't there.

Per his dad's advice, he apologized, even though he didn't feel it was necessary or even remotely his fault. *Keep the peace. She's under enough stress as it is; she doesn't want to butt heads with you, too.*

He worked on his homework for a little bit before they both decided that fatigued delirium did not work well for good grades. Tommen grabbed one of his sleeping pills and settled into bed.

"So, how's mama today?" he murmured in her ear.

"Exhausted," she mumbled. "How many more weeks of this?"

"Twenty-five, I think."

"That was rhetorical. Thanks for nothing."

She pulled the blanket tighter around her, exposing his backside to a draft. He shivered, but had only to wait a minute before she got too warm and loosened her grip. Then he politely tugged the blanket back over himself.

He hoped Chandler knew he wanted to talk, and he hoped the man would actually respond. True, he might not be a lackey, to come at Tommen's every beck and call, but pick up the phone every once in a while. Yeesh.

"I thought your generation hated talking on the phone?"

Tommen turned, murky blackness instantly forming itself into the familiar cave. He spotted Chandler at a small row of cabinetry, doing something or other. He continued, "Or, for that matter, I didn't think your generation knew what a phone call even was."

"Ha ha, very funny." Tommen folded his arms. "But seriously, was this so hard?"

"Not difficult for me, no." Chandler turned and headed to the fire, a large bowl in both hands. "But just as you do not want to rely on Rifun for information, so I do not want you to rely on me."

"I understand the whole thinking for yourself thing, but you have access to a lot more information than I do. A lot more authentic information, too."

Chandler put the bowl on a bed of coals at the edge of the fire. "Ah, yes. Whatever would you do without me?"

"Don't go speaking cryptic to me either." Tommen shook his head. "You worry me sometimes. Are you sure you're not going crazy in isolation here? You talk to animals, dispense riddles like a vending machine..."

"We animals are very good company, thank you."

He looked to his right and caught only a glimpse of white before he was forced to duck. The White Hawk glided through the air, wing feathers brushing over his head. He circled around and landed just a few feet from Chandler.

"You're feeling better, I see," Tommen commented. "Why are you still here?"

"He has to build back the strength in his wing, and he's still missing a few feathers," Chandler answered.

"And I am excellent company to keep," the hawk boasted. "But just as soon as I can, I will be free of this cage."

"Door is right there."

It sounded like an old argument, a comfortable argument between an elderly couple married for so long they had nothing to settle anymore. Tommen found it rather amusing.

"So," Chandler went on, "now that I have, in your words, picked up the phone, what is it you wanted to talk about?"

Tommen shrugged helplessly. "What do I do? I don't get it."

"What's not to understand? Surely you're not surprised by the consequences of your actions?"

"No, it's just...how am I supposed to handle this? Do I stay put? Do I whisk Becky and our child away to a life of intergalactic intrigue and shatter everything she thought she knew about the universe? Do I sacrifice myself and abandon them like a monster?"

Chandler nodded slowly, still looking at the large bowl. "This is not an unimportant decision, one you can really only make once."

"You're the one with the prophecy. What should I do?"

Now the man looked up, expression forlorn. "Prophecy does not say what you should do. Prophecy says what you have already done." He made a mild gesture. "Flip ahead one hundred, two hundred, three hundred pages, there you are, doing the thing or having done it already."

Tommen shifted his stance. "But I'm not one hundred or two hundred or three hundred pages ahead. I'm right here, and I haven't done anything yet. As far as I'm concerned, here on page...fifty or one hundred and fifty...I can still make a choice. Help me make the right one."

Chandler's expression was not even in the ballpark of reassuring. "Regrettably, this time, there is no right choice. There is only the end."

Tommen shook his head. "What do you mean? Are we all going to die? Are we heading for some intergalactic nuclear cataclysm? Is someone going to push the button in the fortress and blow up the whole universe?"

The man turned his gaze back to the fire. "The specifics are not mine to behold."

"But you have to have something, right? I mean, people have been preaching 'the end is nigh' on streetcorners for centuries. I consider you a little more reliable source."

Chandler managed a small smile, but there was little humor and no happiness within it.

Tommen huffed and walked over next to the man, aware of the White Hawk nearby as well as the White Woodpecker at the entrance to the cave, perched on a root. "Come on, Chandler, I need to know. As far as I'm concerned, if you've been given this information, it's because there is a road through the end. The end isn't the end. It might not be good, but it'll be the least bad, right? Isn't that what you like to say?"

Chandler took a stick and poked at some coals. "Most people associate a 'least bad' road with a minor inconvenience. Even a major inconvenience, so long as everyone still comes out the other side. Few equate death with a 'least bad' outcome."

"Death," Tommen state. "Whose death? When? How? Becky? The baby? My dad? Micaiah—again? Micah? Kayla? I need more."

The Native man took a slow, deliberate breath, and Tommen thought his expression looked thoughtful, even contemplative. Was he considering speaking more about this prophecy he'd apparently received? Was he silently conversing with the Author over whether to divulge such details?

"Whose death?" Tommen prodded gently after a moment.

Chandler sighed again and looked up. "Yours."

Tommen was silent.

Chandler patted the mat to his left, and Tommen sat meekly.

"You're taking on a lot of new responsibilities," Chandler told him sagely, "and you know more about life and the universe than the average person. You understand well that you are not invincible, but you are still very naive."

"Then tell me. Teach me," Tommen pleaded, fear knotting his gut. "How do I die? If it's saving Becky, I can accept that. If—"

"Selfishly," Chandler said quietly. "Alone and afraid."

Tommen felt his throat go dry even as he shook his head. "No. I refuse to believe that. You know me too well. Even if I die because of my own stupidity, it's going to be a grand spectacle in front of the entire universe." He spit a humorless laugh. "Probably start another intergalactic war somehow."

Chandler just shook his head.

"Come on, Chandler," he begged. "If there were no way out, there would be no reason for anyone reading this to keep going one hundred, two hundred, three hundred pages to the end." He again laughed anxiously. "You just spoiled the ending for everyone; don't you know that's a cardinal sin in the United States?"

"It's not looked upon too favorably here, either." Chandler's tone was unconcerned. "But sometimes, it is warranted."

Tommen looked to the hawk and the woodpecker for support; he found nothing but cold certainty. He returned his attention to Chandler. "How do I die? I don't mean my selfish disposition, I mean how? Where? Who? Most importantly, when? How much time do I have?" He felt tears break over his lower eyelid and spill onto his cheek. "Will I at least get to see my child?"

Chandler nodded slowly. "You will."

Tommen breathed a sigh of relief, but his stomach refused to untwist. "And Becky?"

The Native man nodded again. "She'll be fine."

Another sigh of relief and the knot began to loosen just a little.

"What — can — I — do?" Tommen asked deliberately. "There has to be something. This can't just be a full stop. I mean, even telling me the future changes it, right? Aren't those the rules?"

Chandler poked at the fire. "What little I've told you changes nothing. If I were to tell you too much more, well, remember that 'least bad' thing you suddenly love so much?"

"So, even if I die alone and afraid, I can still save the universe?" he wondered hopefully.

The man just shook his head. "You're not going to save

anything. Not until after you die."

Dread was at least partially replaced by confusion. "What kind of sense does that make?"

"The kind that can only be viewed from above."

"What about my dad? Is he going to be okay?"

Again Chandler nodded. "He'll be fine, eventually."

Tommen suspected that there was some small Shadow of Resentment buzzing around his ear, but he didn't bother to swat it away immediately as he said, "So everyone but me gets a happy ending?"

Chandler frowned. "It's not a good ending. Just the least bad." He turned to look at Tommen. "And your time is up."

Before Tommen could ask more, he was jolted awake by his alarm, which he fumbled to turn off. His stomach felt sick and his whole body felt cold. He got out of bed and found some decent working clothes. He wanted to pull on a bunch of layers, but he knew better. It would warm up a little during the day, and work would get his blood flowing.

Still, Chandler's sudden change in demeanor and cryptic parting message sent a chill through him.

It's not a good ending. Just the least bad.

He was going to die. Sure, everyone knew that in their heads, but to have it so certainly prophecied was deeply unsettling. This wasn't coming from some streetcorner naysayer or a preacher at a pulpit or even a doctor delivering bad news. This came straight from the man Tommen almost considered to be the in-text mouthpiece of the Author, the man who had confounded him with riddles time and again through war and political intrigue. He was destined to die, and it sounded like it wasn't going to be anything even remotely heroic. Just a little tidbit on the last page. And then he died, alone and afraid. The End.

But not today, he thought, looking at Becky's small, sleeping form. For the moment, he would just lament not being able to sleep in beside her, snuggle a little, maybe get in some morning sex before they couldn't do it anymore for five or six months...

He met his dad on the way out, in the driveway, both of them sitting in their cars, windows down. The man looked haggard. Yes, Vin had been arrested and would be formally charged and arraigned soon. He'd already said he was going to plead down. Going from minimum twenty-five years to one-to-six or three-to-nine wasn't a bad gig, really. Everyone knew a cop wouldn't last long in any prison, but there was no way he couldn't go to prison for murder. Guess they would just have to see what happened. Maybe he would get lucky and get sent to a minimum-security facility.

"Dad, are you okay?" Tommen asked. "I mean, I know it's a lot to take in and all...have you considered maybe dropping down to just part-time until your retirement? I know you're not much of a desk jockey, but..."

"I don't know, kid," his dad sighed. "Things just seem to weigh more than they used to."

"Well, think about part-time. After all, with both me and Becky working and going to school, we might need you as a full-time babysitter."

He meant it as a joke, but his dad still gave him a look. "All right, wise guy, you get going to work. I'll see you tonight."

"You're not working?"

"Not tonight, anyway. Kate arbitrarily switched my shift, said she would have given me the weekend off, but, well, suddenly we're down a guy. But at the same time, seeing Vin in a holder, it's hard. Anyway, I'll see you tonight, kiddo."

"Okay. Just let Becky know that I might be a little late tonight."

Something in his dad's expression said he knew and understood and was laughing internally. It helped to ease the knots in Tommen's stomach as he backed out of the driveway and headed to work.

Chapter Eight
Needles and Nuance

Tommen was never the victim of any explicit attacks, though he could never shake the feeling that he was being watched, studied. Maybe it was one of the Akarin or Miaramila making sure he just stayed put and didn't try to interfere. Maybe it was Chandler keeping an invisible eye on him. Maybe it was Julianna or the Hands or the Borelians watching him, deciding when to make a move. Tommen told himself he was just being paranoid and to focus only on what was in front of him; perhaps the most frightening part was that it was almost easy. It was easy to see his new life and forget all the old monsters in the closet. Problem was, the monsters hadn't forgotten him.

But for the moment, one chilly day in the middle of October, the monsters took a backseat. So did Becky, in a more literal sense. She was between her classroom and lab time for her biology class, and he'd gotten permission from Layman to leave early to take her to her next appointment, the one where, in addition to pictures, a needle would be inserted into Becky's womb to retrieve a small sample of the placenta for genetic testing. He wanted the pictures for sure, and he was a little anxious to see the genetic results. It was that in between part that got him nervous, that whole, sticking a needle that close to their child thing. The baby wasn't even viable yet, not for a few more weeks. If something went wrong...

He forced those thoughts from his mind. Sometimes he did have to rein in his paranoia. Until something was actually wrong, he couldn't let his mind tell him so. He had to believe everything was awesome until such time as contrary evidence appeared. That was hard. It went against his cynical nature.

"I'm nervous," Becky said from the back. "I mean, I'm used to my insulin pump and everything, but overall, I don't actually like needles. Especially big ones."

"You don't have to do it," Tommen reminded her, even as he was feeling the same thing and he did want to know the results. But then, he wasn't the one under the needle.

"I know it's not absolutely necessary, but it's necessary for me. For us. If dwarfism or any number of other issues are in the cards, we need time to plan for it."

"Did your parents have time to plan for you, or was that a surprise?"

"My mom says she wishes she would have known. Then she wouldn't have felt like she was scrambling at the starting line, trying to get her feet under her. She was used to normal kids. Suddenly, she had a not normal kid and a ton of normal kid stuff that instantly became useless. Some of it she could use, but everything was harder. If she had known, she could have planned better, been better prepared."

Tommen nodded. "I'm just letting you know."

"I know. And I'm actually a little more nervous about what the results might say."

"Afraid it's going to say that he or she is going to be exactly like you?"

She waved a hand. "No. I'm afraid he or she is going to turn out just like you."

"What's wrong with that? I mean, you can't improve upon perfection."

They arrived at the doctor's office in good time, and were again sent to the waiting room for the time being. Tommen felt a little more at ease this time, maybe because he wasn't dressed like a homeless carpenter.

He read through some of the available magazines, and actually read them. There were a lot of things to consider when it came to kids, even as babies. Babies might not communicate well, but they absorbed everything. What did he want his child to see, to begin imitating? First words were indicative of the environment, be it loving and nurturing, or not so much. Play dates, babysitting, all that stuff.

And that wasn't even considering the shifting family dynamics in the culture at large. His family growing up had been pretty cut and dry. His ma took care of the kids, his pa ran the farm. There was significant overlap, but ma and pa had a role. His dad had to play both. These days, holy shit. One group advocated for the traditional roles, another spewed forth the praises of the positive impact working mothers had on their daughters to develop strong, independent women of the future. Still another took a much gentler tone on the importance of fathers being in the lives of their daughters, or mothers in the lives of their sons. And that was just a more conservative sample. Looking around the office, Whitmore and her associates appeared to be as traditional as most of West Virginia, but with the grudging legal requirement to have everyone else's literature "available" as well.

He didn't want to think about it. This was their child, not society's. Their discussions thus far had been pretty brief, but while they were verbally agreed on traditional roles, Tommen knew that Becky's line of work would be the breadwinner at the end of the day, or the end of the week when paychecks came in. While he had no rational objection, seeing how the better job would pay the bills, and he would gladly raise their child, he kind of wanted to be the superhero. But what did that mean in the twenty-first century? People went to the store and bought their food, and heat came from propane, electric. Even wood-burning heat sources were far more efficient and required only a fraction of the wood compared to old fireplaces, like the one in the old cabin. Clothes came from the store, or at least the material was easier to come by. All the basic necessities of life were so accessible now, being the superhero breadwinner pretty much meant the nine-to-five and a paycheck.

It was a little disheartening.

"Becky?"

Becky made a noise as she got out of the chair. Being little made things hard. Being little and getting bigger every day made everything that much harder. Just under five months pregnant, while not huge, the changes in the weight and the balance and the center of gravity were hard on her frame. When Tommen asked about the maternity pants she made for herself, she simply said that short of putting metal plates in, there was only so much support the fabric could give. Her normal orthopedic back braces were out of the question, and only because of the cooling temperatures could she continue to wear her orthopedic shoes.

"How are you today?" Whitmore inquired, grinning hugely.

"Being pregnant sucks," Becky grumbled. "When can we schedule that C-section?"

"Well, believe me, after having kids of my own, I can sympathize with what you're going through. Today's a big day, though, and the results of the genetic test should give us an indication of what's going on and when we might be able to schedule the C-section."

Before any of that, however, Whitmore conducted an interview, probably the same one as last time. How are things going, how are you, any notable changes, any pain or discomfort, any spotting, and so on and so forth. Becky showed the doctor her little blood sugar notebook and they had a discussion about that.

As for Tommen, he answered a few questions about Becky, told the doctor things she herself didn't, corroborated some stuff, and answered questions about his own well-being, most of it psychological. The last time he'd been in was two visits ago when he'd been a nervous wreck, and dressed like it, too. This time around, yes, he was still anxious, but he was coming to grips with things, preparing himself mentally, making a plan in his own mind. Yes, he did have people to turn to, talk to, bounce ideas off of.

Whitmore praised his determination and sticking it out, preparing himself for fatherhood. She told him about the men who came in who assumed they knew it all and they had it all down. They had a plan. Well, babies didn't care much about your plans, she said. And those men were usually in for a rude wake-up call, often multiple times a night.

They talked a bit about some of the changes that were occurring, how the baby would be developing, how its and Becky's needs would change—mostly relating to her blood sugar. They talked about the changes that would occur once the fetus reached viability. A full, healthy pregnancy was obviously ideal, but sometimes it was safer for both mother and child to have an early C-section.

"I don't want to talk you into anything or schedule the C-section today," Whitmore reiterated, "not until the test results come in. I just want to make you aware of the option, the possibility. I don't want you to feel like you're jumping the gun or being bad parents if something happens and you need to have a C-section at, say, thirty weeks."

Both Tommen and Becky assured her that the thought never crossed their mind—about being bad parents for such a thing, that is. If the doctor said that they needed to have a C-section as soon as the baby became viable at twenty-six weeks, he would not argue. This was his child's life they were talking about. His own ego ought to have zero say in this.

What did that mean, then, for the possibility that he might have to take them on the run from a psychotic, intergalactic witch?

"Excellent. And I give you two props; you seem more with it than some other couples who come through here." The doctor stood. "Now then, why don't we take a few pictures, and then we'll take the sample, hm?"

Third time around, Becky was a pro and displayed no anxiety over the gel or the ultrasound. Tommen felt terribly sluggish by comparison as his mind shifted from conversation with a doctor to actually attending a minor procedure. He'd never witnessed one before; he'd always been the one under the knife, or the needle as the case may be.

He was still stunned at all the changes, even in just the last three or four weeks. When the doctor handed him his strip of photos, he laid out all of the strips. Twelve weeks, fifteen weeks, now a day shy of nineteen weeks. He was sure something showed through on his face, and the doctor seized on it once she had applied a numbing agent to the spot where the needle would go in.

"It's amazing what a difference a couple months makes," she commented.

"Yeah, no kidding," Tommen agreed dumbly. "Is it possible to tell the sex yet?"

"I could take a guess, but the test will tell us for sure."

He nodded. "Yeah, guess we'll wait for that."

Whitmore inquired as to the status of the numbing agent, and Becky replied that if it was supposed to feel cold, a little tingly, and make her kind of squirmy, then yes, it was working. Still, they waited another minute or two before the doctor brought out the needle.

Holy God, that thing looked huge, or maybe Tommen's fear was making it bigger than it was. He couldn't tell if it was his hand or Becky's hand that suddenly got tight. It was hers. His hand was going a little limp. He suddenly decided that he would rather be the one either under the knife or in the waiting room. Sitting here as a spectator was not his gig. Not at all. His stomach churned as the sharp end pierced Becky's skin and slid into her. Whitmore watched on the monitor, moving slowly and, as she said, not going any farther than absolutely necessary.

A million worst-case scenarios ran through Tommen's mind. In one, the procedure itself induced labor. The baby wasn't viable, and it died. In another nightmare, Whitmore was secretly one of Julianna's agents and she was injecting an abortion drug into the womb as much as taking a sample. The baby would die, and, oh, well, it was a high-risk pregnancy anyway. In yet a third nightmare, Whitmore was still an evil agent. She was working calmly now, but would suddenly ram the needle into the fetus, kill it, then run out the door while Becky screamed and bled and both she and the baby died. Then, in a fourth horrifying scenario—

"And there we are."

Tommen was brought slowly back to reality and he realized that the needle was no longer in Becky's belly. Whitmore was screwing the lid on a small glass vial and writing some notes on a label which she peeled off its backing and slapped on the vial.

"I'll get this sent up and then I'll be back," the doctor promised. She got a few alcohol wipes and a glass of water, which she handed to Becky. "Drink this, hon, make you feel better."

Becky just nodded and downed the water in just a few gulps. She let out a breath. "There. That wasn't so bad."

"Telling me or yourself?" Tommen wondered.

"Yes. Hey, you were just as nervous as I was."

"Well, if you're okay, I guess I'm okay." He took the wipes and wiped off the iodine and everything else as best he could. Becky tugged her shirt back down.

"Now my whole abdomen feels weird. Not bad weird, just...numbing agent weird." She giggled. "You looked so pale."

"Someone is putting something sharp into my pregnant girlfriend's belly, intentionally aiming for the baby. Is there a reason I shouldn't be a little nervous?"

"No, but it was still funny. Well, it's funny now that it's over."

Tommen nodded wordlessly and ran his hand through his hair. He could probably stand a haircut, he figured. Yeah, yeah, he was going for the whole, a beard means you're taken, but he didn't need to look like a grizzled old mountain man. He could keep trim and well-groomed. For his hair, that was a trim every month or so. For his beard, it was a trim every six hours, or so it seemed.

"All right," Whitmore said, walking back in the room, "so that's sent up to the lab. It's going to take about two to three weeks. We can make an appointment now, or I can just give you a call when they're ready and schedule from there."

They elected for a set appointment in roughly three weeks. Made it easier to plan and get days off from school.

"And you'll know the sex just in time for Thanksgiving," Whitmore said, trying to be optimistic.

"Oh, we're probably not telling until Christmas," Becky informed her. "We're not telling until we have a name picked out, that way we don't have to listen to everyone's opinions."

"People are going to give you their opinions anyway. Sometimes they'll give you opinions even after the birth. 'Oh, you should have gone with this name. Don't you think it fits them better? You really should have asked around a little more.' " Whitmore rolled her eyes, but she grinned anyway. "You do what makes you happy, guys. Don't listen to anyone else."

They thanked her and left the office, Becky complaining the whole way to the car that the numbing agent was throwing her balance because her whole center of gravity had been numbed. Tommen elected just to keep his mouth shut, and he delivered her safe and sound back to campus. He only had maybe ten minutes of school left in his day, so he decided to not even bother. Instead, they got lunch from the college cafeteria and ate together in front of the huge wall of windows overlooking one of the small parks.

When they were finished, Becky gave him a tour of the campus, inasmuch as she told him about everything they passed on her way to the lab building. The campus was still plenty big.

With her lab class being only an hour and a half, Tommen elected to just stick around instead of driving home and then having to turn round and drive all the way back. He made his way to the library, walking in and basically just keeping his head up, his strides purposeful, and his attitude saying that he belonged here, he was here to study, and no one needed to interrupt him.

He ended up doing some research on the genetic test, but everything was either overly simplified, or else overly complicated and more suited to the nearly-graduated med students. But everything he found said it was a safe test and would be able to tell them a number of things about the health of their baby. They just had to be patient.

His phone chirped and he quickly turned it down before heads began popping up everywhere. It was from his dad.

"How'd the test go?"

"They only took the sample today," Tommen replied. "It'll be three weeks or so before the actual results come back."

"Ah. Did they at least say if it's a girl or a boy?"

"No, we'll let the test determine that one, too. And besides, we're still not telling until either Thanksgiving or Christmas."

"There's a month between those, kid. What's the holdup?"

"Depends on how long it takes for us to decide on a name."

Tommen could imagine his dad's expression. "Uh-huh. Have you even started that discussion?"

"Some. We don't want to get serious about it until we know the sex."

"This is going in circles. Are you coming home, then?"

"No, I'm waiting at the college library until Becky's out of class, so I won't be home until after you leave."

"All right. Guess I'll see you tomorrow, then."

"Be safe out there."

"I always try."

Tommen put his phone away and continued reading. He was not interrupted until Becky got out of class and went looking for him.

"Learn a lot?" she wondered.

"I feel like I may have missed a few of the prerequisite classes, but I learned some stuff," he told her, walking her out to the car. "Still nowhere near as smart as you."

Becky raised a brow before ducking into the backseat. "You want to add some butter to that butter?"

He got in the driver's seat and asked innocently, "Whatever do you mean?"

"You know what I mean."

"I take it the numbing agent wore off?"

"Yes, finally, but now it feels weird and a little painful." She waved a hand. "I'll be fine by tomorrow."

Tommen navigated his way out of the maze that was the college campus and pulled into normal traffic. It wasn't a block to the bridge before he noticed a car following him. Every move he made, it made, changing lanes, speeding up, slowing down. When he decided to circle the block, it did as well.

He didn't know how to shake a tail, and he wasn't sure he wanted to call the cops either. In the back, Becky wasn't paying much attention, instead fussing with something in her coat. Tommen took a detour, watching the car behind him. It was a gold car, which told him two things. First, being the kind of car it was, it was nowhere near suited to Appalachian winters and wouldn't be out on the roads but for a few more weeks, max. Either the driver was not from the area, used it as a summer car only, or was poor — unlikely given that it was a newer car. The second thing, gold was an unusual vehicle color which made it stand out.

Whoever was behind the wheel wanted Tommen to see him, to know he was being followed. Problem was, the way the sun was in the sky, Tommen couldn't get a good look at the driver except to say it was a male, and appeared to be a well-muscled male at that. Could it be Godwin? No, posture said it was too tall to be the mercenary.

Finally, as Tommen circled back to the bridge, the car broke off. The point was made.

Perhaps what was most disturbing was that Tommen couldn't say when the car had begun following him. He didn't remember it being at the campus, but that didn't mean much. Probably not at the hospital. But whatever the case, the message was clear: you are being followed. Now the question became, was this a good thing or a bad thing? Every instinct said it was a bad thing. At the same time, a good bad guy wouldn't show his hand so blatantly. Julianna was smarter than that. Could it be someone working for the Hands? The Borelians? *Let's see...gold skin on a Borelian means...* He racked his brain. *Bone manipulation. That's it.*

Or maybe it wasn't that at all. Maybe it was just for the obviousness of the color, the attention-getter. Too many variables, too many enemies. He glanced anxiously in his rearview mirror as he crossed the bridge. No one behind him, and he didn't spot any gold vehicles anywhere. In the backseat, Becky was blissfully unaware and had in fact started another soapbox rant of which he was uncertain as to the subject matter. He let it go and pretended to listen.

Later on, he texted his dad about the incident. His dad promised to keep a lookout and even drove by the house a time or two as time permitted.

But over the next couple weeks, nothing of significance happened. No gold cars were spotted outside the city, no mysterious prowlers, no unusual calls or strange people. Of course, the strange people was pretty subjective. Shit, Tommen had spent his whole life in the Appalachians, and some things which might get folks in other states uptight and calling the cops was just an average Tuesday for him. Something had to be extra specially strange to get the attention of the cops for a "strange" person. As Becky had so eloquently put it, it was like Los Angeles, but with more moonshine and fewer rainbows.

Tommen again showed his pictures to anyone who would look, which, in school, was basically limited to Layman, Reisig, and the lunch ladies.

"Halfway there," Layman said, sliding the pictures back across his desk to Tommen. "When did you say is the due date? I understand you're having a C-section, but when is the natural due date?"

"March 10th," Tommen answered. "We're thinking about scheduling the C-section for Friday the 11th, if we can. It's after the due date, and Becky isn't too keen on going into labor and having to be rushed into the hospital in an ambulance. But we'll see what the doctor says when the genetic test results come back."

"Now, you're primarily looking for the dwarfism, right?"

Tommen nodded. "As far as size, yes. Becky's eager to start making clothes. She doesn't think it will be there. She gave me the long, genetic reason for it, but basically, dwarfism is the exception, not the rule. It's not as exact or predictable as, say, my color-blindness. But a lot of it will depend on the sex, too, if something is going to be dominant, recessive, or missing completely."

"Sounds like a good project for her."

"Oh, she's excited, no doubt about it. In between naps, that is."

Layman nodded sympathetically. "She's keeping up with her schoolwork and sewing work all right?"

"And she cooks dinner, too, most nights. I don't know how she does it."

"Welcome to married life. Almost. Basically. How's your dad?"

"I barely see him right now. I mean, for a few minutes between when I get home from school and before he goes to work, and on nights he has off, but I don't see him a lot. I mean, when I do see him, he's, I don't know, I guess he's good. About this whole thing."

"I saw on the news that one of his fellows was charged with the murder of a suspect. That's probably hard on him."

"Yeah. He's looking forward to retirement."

Tommen did not mention to Layman that his dad was considering dropping to part-time after the baby was born. Shit like what was happening to Vin was too hard on him anymore, and even the easy nights seemed to be a drag on him most times. He didn't want to move up the retirement date, but he could do part-time. Do a little road work, probably a lot of desk work, get out of the house, but have more time to spend with his new grandchild.

Walter never said it out loud, maybe because of pride or shame or because he thought he had a winning poker face, but it was pretty obvious that he was really excited to be a grandpa. Tommen offered to loan him his picture strip or see about getting another one the next time they got pictures. His dad had taken the most recent strip to the station one night and proudly showed them off, but waved off a strip of his own. They would only get destroyed, he said. Tommen countered that by saying that if his pictures could survive the construction site, they could survive sitting on the side of the road;

unless he got shot in the ass through his wallet, they would be fine. His dad said he would think about it.

It was about a week later that Tommen got home from school and Becky informed him that the doctor's office had called and the test results were in. Their appointment wasn't for a few more days, but at least they wouldn't have to postpone it.

It was a long few days. The results were in. Was it a boy or a girl? Which would he rather have? Did it matter, because he didn't have much of a choice. Was there dwarfism, or would their child grow up to be as tall as him? What about color-blindness? Would their son or daughter be in awe of a rainbow, or struggle to discern the colors of a stoplight? Would he or she be sticking themselves with a needle after every meal, or mowing down the buffet line?

The anxiety was awful, and it gave Tommen a headache. He could practically hear Chandler chastising him, telling him not to worry, the Author would take care of everything. But it was hard. The Author knew what the next page was going to say; he didn't know until he got there. Or did he know because his experience was dependent on the reader? *Fucking hell, here comes the philosophy.*

And let's throw some other moral and ethical dilemmas in there, too, why not? At what point do you ask Nathan for help? Anything that could be managed with modern medicine, he already stated he wouldn't touch. Only truly lethal things. Double-Dominant Syndrome, things of that nature. Tommen could respect that. But...what if? He wouldn't love his child less if there was something wrong, but they were in the twenty-first century now and had tools and resources available to them to fix problems and make life easier. What if there really was a way to genetically correct Down Syndrome, eliminate it prenatally, save the lives of thousands of children each year?

Once again with the philosophy. He really had to get it under control. Yeah, sure, tell that to his paranoia. His paranoia was still manifested in his mind as Mr. Snuffles. The real-life Mr. Snuffles must have picked up on this because the cat seemed to intuitively discern the moments when he most needed a heart attack, thereby zipping out from under the bed, jumping up on the bed in his face, entwining himself in Tommen's legs in the kitchen.

Becky wasn't immune to the anxiety either. Tommen reminded her constantly not to get too riled up for the sake of the baby, but he could hardly enforce a rule he didn't follow, and the whole ride to the hospital the morning of the appointment was that of shared anxiety.

They were the first ones in the office that morning and Dr. Whitmore was waiting for them along with another doctor.

"Becky, Tommen, this is Dr. Morico," she introduced. "He is a genetic counselor."

The new doctor was Mediterranean in ancestry, if not direct origin, late thirties to early forties, dark hair starting to highlight with gray at the roots. He was not particularly muscular and was a bit soft around the middle, but something about him gave off the vibe that he could still bench press a full beer keg if asked. Maybe it was just Tommen.

They all gathered round in chairs, ignoring the bed and the ultrasound machine completely for the time being. Tommen tried to read body language and decided that both doctors appeared fairly relaxed, so there wasn't anything too damning to report. Or maybe they went out and played poker every weekend. Or maybe their definition of catastrophic news was different than his, similar to Nathan. If it wasn't lethal, no cause for concern.

"So, I have the results of the prenatal genetic test here," Dr. Morico began, just a hint of an accent in his voice. "I understand you, ma'am, are a genetic student, so if you want to take them home, I would be more than happy to make a copy and give them to you. Otherwise, I also have the quick rundown."

"That's my copy," Tommen commented.

"What we're going to do is discuss the findings and a little bit about how to interpret them and proceed. Now, we place certain traits and diseases into a few categories: definitely present and showing, and definitely not present. And then there is a whole range in between based on whether the genes could be present, and whether the traits could also be masked. Some traits are also considered simply high, moderate, or low risk. Genetic testing has allowed for incredible breakthroughs, but it's not quite up to *Star Trek* hype just yet. We have maybe a decade or so to go.

"That being said, we'll start with the fun and easy question. Do you guys want to know the sex?"

"Yes," Becky said at the same time Tommen answered, "Absolutely."

Morico gave them a look. "It...is...a..." Pause. "Girl."

A girl. A daughter. Tommen was going to have a daughter. The color pink flooded his mind's eye. He didn't know anything about girls. He knew plenty about boys, but nothing about girls. At the same time, his protective instinct kicked into high gear as he imagined tea parties, princess dresses, and daddy-daughter dances. And hormones. Lots of hormones. Wearing makeup, crying over boys, and drama. Lots of drama.

No. They would have a no drama household. First rule. No drama.

Becky squeezed his hand and he returned the gesture.

"Now then, Dr. Whitmore mentioned some of the things you were concerned about, so I'll just give you the quick rundown and we can go back and cover everything in more detail if you so desire.

"First, dwarfism was determined to be definitely not present."

Tommen hadn't realized he was holding his breath until he released it. Even Becky seemed to relax to the point where she looked like she could walk out the door happy and not need to hear anything else. Morico gave them a moment before continuing.

"As for your other concerns: diabetes, certainly a high risk, but nothing present right off the bat, genetically; red-green colorblindness, present but may be suppressed; high blood pressure, present but may be suppressed; cancer, most likely present but may be suppressed.

"We also do some routine testing for other ailments, so I'll run through those quick: HIV/AIDS, definitely not present; autism, low risk; Down Syndrome, definitely not present; Alzheimer's, low risk; Celiac disease, low risk; autoimmune disorders, possibly present but most likely suppressed; heart disease, moderate to high risk; asthma, low risk."

With that, he handed them the quick overview paper.

"So what are we talking about with autoimmune disorders and heart disease?" Becky asked. "Can I see the full report?"

"I'll make you a copy, sure." Morico nodded. "Now, both those terms are very broad. Autoimmune could be anything from psoriasis to lactose intolerance. I believe..." He flipped through the report. "Yes, there were no definite results on any one particular aspect, which is why we believe it will be recessive, perhaps showing up in the future in her children."

"And heart disease?"

"It's only a risk assessment. Similar to the risk for diabetes, it could show up, it might not. The best course of action, always, is to live a healthy lifestyle and not give the body an excuse to slack off, as it were."

Becky held out her hand and Morico reluctantly handed over the paperwork.

"So what about the colorblindness?" Tommen asked. "Present but may be suppressed?"

"Colorblindness is typically passed on through the mother, and it affects half as many women as men. The second X chromosome is what typically masks it. She may pass it on to her sons, but it's unlikely to affect her. You're the only colorblind parent, correct?"

"That's right. My pa was colorblind. So is my uncle."

Morico frowned. "Then it is very possible that your daughter is colorblind, seeing how you are guaranteed to possess colorblind genes on both your chromosomes. Once again, we can't show you a hologram of your daughter and tell you exactly what's going to happen. This is largely risk assessment."

He nodded. "I understand."

"What's this?" Becky interrupted sharply, speed-reading

something in the report. "What's this about an 'abnormality' on chromosome 11?"

"That's related to the potential for heart disease."

"That is also where Beckwith-Wiedimann Syndrome originates."

"What's that?" Tommen asked dumbly.

"Put simply, it's where the organs are too large for the body."

Now Morico got a look on his face, one Tommen figured he could interpret fairly accurately as, *Great. Another first year med student who thinks she can diagnose everything after taking Bio 101.* He calmly replied, "Yes, that is true. But each chromosome is made up of numerous alleles, and it takes a lot of changes to just one in order to effect that kind of change. DNA is a chain reaction of traits. A little abnormality is not necessarily cause for concern. It's simply a note. Running it against everything else we test for, and it, along with other 'abnormalities' and factors, fit almost perfectly for a moderate to high risk of heart disease."

Becky huffed but grudgingly accepted his answer. Sometimes the more you knew about something, the worse it was because then you knew everything that could go wrong. For example, a stomachache in an older woman wasn't always just indigestion; it could also easily be a heart attack. Tommen learned that in his dad's medical first responder book.

There was some more back and forth as Becky skimmed through the report, then refused to give it back. Finally, Morico gave up and let her have it; he would print off another later if he needed to.

In the end, it all boiled down to a few simple facts. One, they were having a girl. Two, she wasn't going to be a dwarf. Three, she could very well be colorblind. Four, she could possibly have a few health issues, but then, wouldn't they all eventually? But otherwise, she would be a happy, healthy newborn.

His stomach leapt and his heart soared. He was going to be dad to a little baby girl. As much as he wanted to shout for joy and tell everyone who would listen, he also knew that they had to at least have a name first. Might be Thanksgiving, might be Christmas. But they were having a girl.

"Now, to that end," Morico continued, "the report also contains information to consider if you decide to have more children in the future, and it's based on the DNA samples we took from the two of you. It lets you know the risks for certain traits that could be passed on, such as dwarfism, diabetes, colorblindness, the whole nine yards. It's not to discourage you, but just for information. It looks like your daughter could dodge a lot of genetic bullets, but the cards always fall randomly, and you have a right to know what you might expect."

"In the event we have a child who's a colorblind, diabetic dwarf with an autoimmune disorder, Celiac disease, and heart problems," Becky said bluntly.

"Yes. Such as any of those things. But that is for you to peruse and discuss. As for this pregnancy right now, genetically, your daughter is very healthy."

"And with the way you've been taking care of yourself and everything looking good," Whitmore continued, "I foresee no complications at this time. So far, no reason to think that something horrible is imminent and we need to be planning for the worst every single day. Now, that could change. I won't lie to you; you're not coming to see me because you like me. I still want to see you every two to four weeks, but I really think everything is going to be relatively smooth sailing."

Becky grilled Morico a little more, but the man was eventually permitted to leave her vicious captivity.

Tommen was just reveling in the news, not just that they were having a girl, but that she would be healthy and even the pregnancy should be fairly normal. It was the best news he'd heard in a long time, and it was probably the first time in weeks he could really relax. Focus on the moment. Focus on his family. All would be well.

"So, since we're on the subject, let's talk C-section," Whitmore said once Morico was gone. "You're nineteen weeks along, due date not until March, no need to fix a date right now right away. Have you guys given it any thought?"

"Can we schedule it for the Friday after? I mean, date's on a Thursday, could we do the next day?" Tommen asked.

"Mm...that's kind of a gamble. We're pretty good at predicting due dates these days, and I'd rather not subject you, Becky, to labor if we don't have to because of the stress it will put on your body. I mean, we can do the day before, easily, or the Friday before. I don't want to do more than one week. A full pregnancy is a safe delivery, if at all possible."

They batted it around a little, but ultimately decided to put off the decision until at least the next appointment. Maybe the one after. Depended on whether they had a name. Then they could give their relatives the sex and the due date. Still debatable whether they wanted to give out the name once they had it.

"Well, I'll leave that all up to you," Whitmore told them. "But I do want to get a C-section date locked in around twenty-five weeks, and certainly no later than thirty weeks."

Tommen and Becky agreed, and then it was time for pictures. It had become Tommen's favorite part of the visits, when he could see his daughter, see how she was doing, see how big she was getting. Good Lord, comparing the twelve-week pictures to these newest pictures, it was as if years had gone by for her to get so big. He Banded so he could stare at them longer, stare at the ultrasound image itself. That was his daughter right there. Not even a mystery child anymore, but a little baby girl. His baby girl. Their baby girl.

He took a breath and released the Band. Life resumed. He pocketed his pictures and Whitmore turned the machine off. The next appointment was scheduled, and they were sent on their merry way.

"Okay, Miss Geneticist," Tommen said once they were outside and heading back to the car, "what's that report say? In English, please."

"I'm not that good yet," Becky told him. "I'll need a little time to look it over and make sure I have my terms straight. Plus I want to double-check a few things. But what I can tell you is that except for your colorblindness, you are very healthy, genetically speaking. You are going to live a long, healthy life, barring getting hit by a car or something."

Glad to know I didn't run into battle three times only to be foiled by a middle-aged heart attack. Or a teenage heart attack. "That's good, I think."

"Well, you're healthier than me. Most of the crap that could plug up the proverbial gene pool comes from me and my issues. Dwarfism, diabetes, Alzheimer's, Celiac, heart disease, autoimmune disease. Yeesh."

"And we'll deal with those if and when they come up."

They got in the car. He glanced back at her and caught her look. "What?"

"And what's that supposed to mean?" she asked innocently.

"What's what supposed to mean?"

"Dealing with those things if and when they come up?"

"Um...I just meant that, if, in the future, we decided to have more kids...then we can decide what we want to do about those things, if there is anything that can be done."

"Do you want more kids?"

Tommen paused and chose his words carefully. "I think I want to get through this kid first and see how things turn out. Might be that this is the only child we have."

"And you're completely against adoption," Becky stated smartly.

"I think this is the end of the conversation. You need to get to class, and so do I."

She made it in time for class, and he walked into the last half hour of second period. Only a few more weeks until exams, and then he would be down to his last semester of school. Last trimester. Of school. Last trimester of the pregnancy. Then the birth followed quickly by his first semester of college. The first chapter of his new life as husband and father. Or father, anyway. Husband didn't come until June.

Damn it. Story of his life seemed to be hurry up and wait.

It was a Thursday, which meant his weekly session with Nathan. As usual, they met at the park. With the onset of winter and the wind growing colder in the growing dark, they met in one of the small buildings, the one with a couple vending machines and nice bathrooms.

"So, you texted me that the test results were in," Nathan began after pleasantries. "What's the word?"

Tommen almost started his sentence with "she" and then thought better of it. "The baby is healthy."

Nathan grinned. "Still not spilling the beans on the sex."

"Nope. But it's healthy. The worst that I heard is a moderate risk for heart disease and a near-guarantee for colorblindness."

"So it's a boy."

"I did not say that. I have colorblindness across the board on my side, and I guess the way it falls, it's almost a certainty for either a girl or a boy. Becky drew me a little diagram, but most of it went over my head."

Nathan frowned but nodded. "All right. Obviously, I don't have the results, and I don't know anything about the situation, but if it's a near-guarantee for either sex...assuming you aren't bullshitting me to cover up your own slip of the tongue, then you've got me stumped still. But the overall good news, he or she is healthy. And that's what matters, right?"

Tommen nodded. "That's what matters. Doctor said no dwarfism, no autism, diabetes is unlikely. Going to be a happy, healthy little baby."

"You so want to tell. I can see it."

"I do," Tommen said tightly. "But we made our decision. Not going to tell until we have a name picked out."

"You know. I am your shrink. Nothing we say can leave us. If you so wished to confide in me the sex of your child, in the interest of your mental health..."

Tommen laughed but shook his head. "No. No. But you're

good. You are good. No, we made our decision and I will stand by it."

"Good man. Did you at least get pictures?"

He showed the shrink the pictures, laying out all four sets. Nathan looked them over more analytically than Tommen had, and he suspected the shrink was trying to make his own determination of sex.

"You're lucky, you know. Most healthy pregnancies only get two, maybe three strips of photos. You're getting pictures every three weeks. That's at least once a month."

"I know. But it's nice to know that Becky and the baby are healthy and doing well."

"It is nice to know," Nathan agreed. "Now how are you doing?"

"Fuck, I have no idea sometimes. I'm excited to be a dad. I really am. But...things are getting a little cramped. We've actually had to move some things over to her parents' house. We've got a ton of diapers already, most of them disposable but Mrs. Polski still has a supply of washable cloth diapers. Becky's siblings bring over hand-me-downs from their kids, mostly toys and stuff. Now that we know the sex and don't have to contend with dwarfism, they'll probably bring over clothes by the truckload. It's not bad. Don't get me wrong, it saves a hell of a lot of money. But sometimes it feels a little overwhelming."

Nathan nodded. "It can. It's a big change, no longer all about you, or just you and her. You're halfway through this thing now. It's not just a concept, Tommen, this is real. It's happening. These pictures prove it. Right now, you're living as 'the child is coming someday.' Well, one day you're going to wake up, and it'll be the day. And that baby is coming home with you. And he or she isn't going to be leaving for nearly twenty years. He or she is going to bug you every day of your life for a couple decades, and probably a little longer after that. And that's not even counting Becky."

"I know. Sometimes I wonder how much is real fear, and how much is just me psyching myself out."

"Is anyone's life in danger?"

"Um...no? I mean, Becky's, if she has complications or goes into labor."

"Fair enough. But once the baby is delivered, all is well. Is anyone's life in danger?"

"Um...no...?"

"Then I would say it's one percent real fear, ninety-nine percent psyching yourself out. There is nothing to be truly afraid of. Your child is going to look to you for everything. As a baby, he or she is going to have just simple needs: affection, protection, and the basic necessities of life. It's innocence and unconditional love at its finest. Cherish it. Worry about the drama later."

By the end of the session, Tommen was pretty convinced that most of his fear was not anything specific about being a parent, but mostly just fear of the unknown. He had friends and family around him for support, and he only needed to take things one day at a time. He didn't have to worry about his daughter's future phone habits or crushes while she was still only three weeks old and he was changing her diaper. At that moment, whether they were on Earth or off in the universe, he was offering her protection and affection.

He returned home. He did his homework on one end of the couch while Becky did her homework on the other end. It was ten o'clock before they crawled in bed. Tommen held her close.

"I love you," he murmured.

"Love you, too," Becky replied.

"We have a little girl." He gently rubbed her growing belly.

"Yes, we do."

"Do we have a name yet?"

"Well, I know we tossed around a few early on, you know, when it was either-or, but we only just found out for sure today, and we haven't really talked about it."

"True, but I thought women had their names picked out in secret, like, years before having kids."

Becky giggled. "Well, that's not entirely untrue."

"So what were your favorite names, Miss I-Was-Never-a-

Girly-Girl?"

"I always liked Penelope or Emily or Dani, things that could rhyme with Becky. I was a little kid when I thought about all of this. What about you?"

"Hey, every guy wants his firstborn son named after him, or someone in the family. It's just an unwritten rule. We don't give much thought to girl names."

"Well, I revisited my original plans and decided to scrap them for something a little more elegant."

"Her Highness Elizabeth Victoria?"

"Ha ha, very funny. Elegant, but more homey, along the same lines as your thoughts. What do you think about...Maisy Helen. Your mom, my mom."

Tommen felt his chest tighten and his throat close up, and it was a long minute before he forced a level, "I like it. It's...elegant. Homey, like you said."

"And if we're getting married in June, she'd have your last name."

"Maisy Helen Forbes," Tommen murmured. He shifted uncomfortably. "Yeah. I like it."

Maisy Helen Forbes.

Chapter Nine
Set Apart

Pretty soon, the attitude in school shifted from the mundane classwork, starting new chapters on Monday and taking tests on Friday, to getting ready for exams coming up the week of Thanksgiving. Monday would be exams for first through third period, and Tuesday would be fourth and fifth period exams. The week before exams was basically entirely review.

The good news for this was that it made Tommen's backpack considerably lighter as he turned in his assignments and didn't take on heaps more. By the Wednesday before exam week, he almost didn't need to take his backpack.

Tommen puttered around in the kitchen, looking for breakfast, when his dad walked in the door and Becky suddenly appeared from the hallway. Both men immediately inquired as to whether either of them had woken her. She sleepily denied it and said she was just getting a drink of water and taking a short walk after the baby woke her up. It seemed to be that since the baby was moving, she never stopped. That had been a suspicion at the last appointment where the ultrasound revealed small movements. Becky was pretty sure that at the next appointment after Thanksgiving, the ultrasound would show a party going on in there.

Still, she got her glass of water, gave Tommen a half-asleep hug, then wandered off back to bed.

"Since I know her standard answer, I'll ask you," Walter said, sitting to take his boots off. "How is she?"

"She's ready for it to be over," Tommen answered. "I mean, it's not just the kicking, her body has a harder time handling the stress."

"She's not that big; she hasn't gained a ton of weight."

"No, but her frame is smaller, more delicate though she'll never admit to it, not like that. If I gain a pound, I gain a pound."

"If you gain a pound, it's a miracle," his dad muttered.

Tommen gave him a look. "If I gain a pound, I gain a pound. If she gains a pound, it's an extra pound and a half to two pounds on her frame. She gains ten pounds, her frame treats it like fifteen to twenty. With the baby being normal size, there's a lot less room for everything internally, too."

"Is there any cause for concern?"

"Whitmore wants to up the appointments after Thanksgiving, make sure there's no danger of abdominal breach. If she thinks that there is any kind of internal damage going on, she says she's going to order an emergency C-section."

His dad nodded in understanding. "Very good. No reason to put either of them in danger."

Tommen frowned as he put a couple pieces of bread in the toaster. "I'm not too excited about the baby being in NICU, but considering the possible alternative, guess I can only hope for the least bad outcome."

"True, but I think you're being a little cynical. Everything has been going well so far. As long as that trend continues, there's no need to worry yourself over every situation your imagination can conjure up. Save your worrying for when you actually become a dad."

"Please." The toast popped up and Tommen went to work on the peanut butter. "At this point in my life, with everything that's happened to me, I am a pro at this, and I have more than enough cynical worry to go around."

Walter sighed. "That's what I was afraid of."

"What?" He took a bite of toast. "How's work?"

"Well, I don't think I'll be able to go to part-time after the new year. With Vin gone, we're already tight, and a couple of young yahoos are eyeing some openings in the city department. They can't stop me from retiring, but they don't have to cut my hours."

Tommen folded his arms. "What about Vin's rich uncle? Wasn't his endless wealth dependent on Vin being on the department?"

"Under normal circumstances, yes. Vin's actions and his impending prison time had nothing to do with the department or any of us; that was all on him. Could his rich uncle revoke his support? Sure. But he could have done that at any time. And even so, we still need guys to go out and run around. Might be that we have to play nice with city and get them to cover a little territory for us. I don't know. We'll find out soon enough, I guess."

"How long until grandpa?"

His dad sighed dramatically and looked at him. "Only because you keep reminding me and everyone else do I know this, almost down to the day: sixteen weeks. Actually, I believe it's one hundred and fifteen days. Damn you, kid."

Tommen grinned and took another bite of toast.

"How are things otherwise?" his dad asked. "Anything weird going on, anything that we might know about? To my knowledge, there's been no sign of your gold car."

He shook his head. "No, not really. My paranoia alarm goes off so much, half the time I don't know what's real and what's fake. That's enough to set off my secondary paranoia alarm that someone is doing that intentionally in order to lull me into a false sense of security before making a move, and then I don't know whether to entertain that notion or tell myself to shut up."

His dad raised a brow. "Did that genetic test say anything about schizophrenia? Do you hear voices?"

"It's only paranoia until it's true. Someone could actually be out to get me. A lot of someones. Has Miach said anything?"

"No, nothing. If anything is going on right now, it's not on Earth. Few dare to go to the Wheel, and even then, things seem to be normal." Walter shrugged. "Earth isn't a major player. Only because of Tacaga are humans really on the radar on a consistent basis."

"And Rifun and Julianna and me..." Tommen said.

Surprisingly, his dad shook his head. "Not really. Maybe at first, when they and you were up front and center, the outrage prompting prejudice against humans. But ultimately, it's less about the individual and more about the group, the ideology. Tacaga is who is keeping Earth from the Wheel technologically, but I would be willing to bet that if the Borelians didn't still have their declaration of war out for us in order to enforce the point, it wouldn't matter. As long as human Akari-bearers could still get through, we'd still be going to the Wheel."

"That...deflated quickly."

"It's politics. You've got thousands of species, a huge industry to maintain, politics to deal with, all the criss-crossing vendettas, the only thing that matters is the moment."

"Sounds like social media."

"Precisely. Give it a few more years, no one will even remember Rifun existed. Or you. If Julianna hangs onto her power, she'll still be prominent, but humans overall won't mean much, except to the Borelians."

"What about all these murder squads and the Hands and the Borelians getting involved and everything else?"

"With exception of the Borelian declaration of war against humans specifically, it's all ideology. One ideology against another. Order versus Miaramila and Akarin. Hands versus Order. Akarin versus Order with a temporary alliance with the Miaramila. The Borelians against everyone. A war of ideas, which is the hardest to fight and impossible to win." His dad stood. "And with that, I suppose I should get to bed and you need to get to school. Oh, and, uh, you've got some crumbs in your beard there."

Tommen brushed his beard free of the crumbs and reluctantly agreed. He wished his dad sweet dreams, then went down to his room to kiss Becky goodbye. She looked and sounded exhausted, but the baby wasn't letting her sleep. Then he headed off to school.

Light snow had fallen in the night, but it was supposed to get warm enough to melt it during the day. Tommen did a little slip and slide, saw where others did a little slipping and sliding, but otherwise made it to school unharmed. In the school parking lot, vehicles of all makes and models were starting to sport seasonal dents and dings. A damaged bumper, a little plastic missing from the grill, a missing headlight in extreme cases. For some, it was almost a game to see who could rack up the most minor imperfections. If you didn't get ticketed for it, extra credit.

Tommen did not care to play that game. Sure, he knew how to pop out his own dents now, but he could do without the mini heart attack that came with every one of them. And he certainly didn't want to risk anything really bad, anything that could potentially put his car out of service. If the pregnancy was healthy, he could borrow a car to take Becky in for the C-section. If there was an emergency, he didn't want to be stranded and wondering what was going on or trying to find a ride or a set of wheels to use.

He walked in the school and made for his locker. An obscene (and obscenely bad) drawing of him and Becky had been taped to the locker door. Nothing new, but wearying as they showed up about once a week. He simply took it down and tossed it in the trash.

He was above this. He was not part of that crowd anymore. He was in high school merely as a formality. Once March came around, he would walk out the door, not look back, and set off on his new life. High school didn't matter to him anymore. He tossed his almost-empty backpack in his locker and headed to Layman's office.

"If I'm right," the former Marine began, pushing some paperwork to the side, "you have new pictures to show off."

"Nope." Tommen shook his head and sat down. "After Thanksgiving."

"Ah! So close. I must be losing track of my days."

"I doubt that. Like my dad says, I bother him about it so much, he's got it down to the day. A hundred and fifteen."

"True enough. All is well, though?"

"So far. Becky was already up when my alarm went off. Got

kicked awake."

Layman nodded. "Yeah, babies can be inconsiderate like that. Kids can be, too, for a while."

They chatted for twenty minutes or so. It was surreal to think that for as long as Tommen had been in high school, he'd always hated Layman, swore the man was out to get him. Detentions, suspensions, and other creative discipline littered their past meetings, to say nothing of the time Layman suggested Tommen drop his AP Physics course. Or the time Layman thought Walter was abusing him. And now they were talking about pregnant wives and having kids and the bigger things in life.

"So, got exams and then one semester left," Layman stated.

"One trimester. In both senses," Tommen said smartly.

"Well, there is that."

"If I keep my grades up, do I still have to take what would be considered my last exams?"

"Oh, I might be able to exercise a little principal power and get you off there. You've been a good student, done good work, and they will be your last exams in high school, after all."

"Thanks."

Their conversation wrapped up and Tommen headed off to first period a few minutes early. Pre-Calculus, because mornings just couldn't get any more awful. Well, yes, they could. It could be full calculus. He thumped his book on his desk and sat down, bringing out his phone for his morning texts to Becky.

"Good morning, my loves," he wrote.

It was half a minute before she replied, "Well, at least you didn't call me beautiful because I sure don't feel like it."

"Aw, why not?"

"I can't tell if you're being sarcastic or just a sap."

"Let's go with the tree hugging one."

"Now that was sarcastic."

"Seriously, how are you?"

"Not much different than I was an hour ago. I'm exhausted,

sick, and I still have exams to get through."

"Yeah, but then you'll have a month off before the new semester. I still have to go to school."

He could imagine her expression. "I have to condense my winter semester into nine weeks or less, that is, unless I want to take the baby with me to those exams. So I'm going to have a huge workload right at the end of the pregnancy."

"Yes, but then you'll have months off of school, at least."

Becky had decided to skip her spring semester of school to take care of the baby, then pick back up again in the fall. She would still work, and when their child was six months old, they—that is, Becky and Tommen—would both be working and going to school and being parents. That would be hard. Real life sucked sometimes. But they would be a family.

Tommen sneaked a look at all the ultrasound photos. He'd photocopied them onto a single paper that he kept in his notebook, that way he could look without taking his wallet out all the time, and so the strips would stay in tact. The first strip was looking a little dingy. Usually the pictures were more interesting than the lecture.

But, my daughter is going to have a smart daddy, he thought. *He is going to be smart, educated, with a good job so she can have a good life. She's not going to be a trailer trash baby.*

He reluctantly opened his textbook to the exam practice questions and started copying the problems onto a sheet of paper. Enduring a couple of spitwads, he went through each problem line by line, showing all his work. Things was, he'd always been confident in his math abilities, up until now. Algebra I and II? Piece of cake. Geometry? Not his forte, but easy as long as he didn't overthink things, and working construction had helped him cement a lot of the concepts in his brain. Calculus? Well, he likened it to speeding down the freeway, looking for a particular exit, seeing no forewarning signs such as "Exit X in two miles," blowing past it completely, and having to figure out where and how to get back to that exit when there was no turnaround for another fifty miles and the lanes were packed. That was Calculus.

Becky had been tutoring him, of sorts, whenever he was hung up on a particular concept. She always claimed to have difficulty with math. In reality, she just wasn't very fast, but she was terribly methodical, almost to a fault. Once she understood something, it never left her, but that didn't speed things up in any sense of the word. All the same, watching her work through something and have her explain each step, the sequences, the variables, the methods, the symbols, it was pretty darn boring, but to her credit, she never had to explain anything twice.

She would probably be the one to help their daughter with her homework. Tommen wasn't selling himself short or anything; he knew plenty. Becky was just better at explaining things, meeting her pupil on their level. When he had once tried to help her with her homework, it had been a bit of a chore because he didn't know how to meet her at her level and speak her language, as it were. Becky said her talent came from having to explain things to young nieces and nephews and help them with their homework when she was babysitting.

Tommen had always just assumed that old families had a ton of kids just to help out on the farm. While that was a large part, it was also kind of preparing the kids for life, too, giving them a sense of family, community, helping each other out. And how Tommen still missed his brother. What he wouldn't give to have some brotherly advice about now. Becky's brothers were nice, but they were also his dad's age. Plus they had no shared history, no past antics or connection. He was alone. He was an adopted child in a single-parent household about to start a family of his own, having only faint memories of a life gone by to draw upon. He was woefully unprepared.

Dr. Whitmore had told them about some parenting classes that she recommended for their unique situations, but they ultimately declined. Parenting classes cost money. Becky had her family to talk to. Tommen talked to his dad, sometimes Mrs. Polski. Every so often, he would ask Dr. Polski a question, but he still had a healthy fear of the old man and generally kept a polite distance between them.

There was a lot that went into raising a child. Tommen laid his pencil down and rubbed his eyes. The math was easy compared to the daunting reality of parenthood. He flinched as something small and hard hit the back of his head; it was an eraser, one of the big pink ones. He shifted around and reached for it, setting it on his notebook next to his pencil.

"Give it back," Luke hissed, behind him and to the right.

Tommen gave him a look. "You threw it at me. I thought you were just trying to help me out a little with my math." He picked up his pencil and indicated the eraser on the end which was down to an almost unusable nub. He continued, "Thanks for the gift."

The next thing to hit him was a couple pieces of a broken pencil, striking him harmlessly in the shoulder. He ignored it and returned to his work. Could be worse, he supposed. He hadn't gotten beaten up or shoved in his locker, and his car hadn't been spray-painted with obscene words or images (one of the benefits of a school safety officer, he supposed). And even if any of those things had happened, it was hardly worth his attention considering everything he'd been through. He'd take having a broken pencil thrown at him over being caught in the middle of a war zone where a knife could appear through a microportal and slit his throat just as easily as any rifle from a thousand yards. Pencils and erasers sounded pretty darn tame. He concentrated on his work.

And anyway, he only had one more week of this semester, and then his last semester of high school ever. Then he was going to be a dad. These thoughts occupied his mind pretty much constantly, and he turned it over and over and over again in his brain. He texted Becky between classes but got no reply. Probably she was hard at work paying attention to her own lectures. Tommen envied her and eagerly awaited the day when he would sit in lectures he actually cared about.

Needless to say, his mind was anywhere but there in high

school. He just didn't care. He was going to do his best so he could get good scholarships and chip away at his tuition, but he was rather detached from the whole thing.

Second period was United States history. Senior history focused on the Vietnam War to the present, which, in their textbooks, ended with the upset election of Bush over Gore and 9/11. The last week or so had been independent research of the almost fifteen years since. That part hadn't been too bad, actually, because it was a project more than textbooks and worksheets. There was some stuff they had been required to find, and then they could look up and give a presentation on anything that interested them in that time period. Politics, war, religion, pop culture, anything.

Tommen had elected to study the changing nature of the family in America. Now, despite West Virginia still being vastly traditional, Charleston was still a city, a crossroads of opinions and ideas, and his opinions on the matter were not well-received by some of his classmates, and most of those who had glared at him and shaken their heads no longer called him by his name, but only "hypocrite." Maybe he deserved it, but was there no room for someone to change his mind, say he learned a hard lesson?

Didn't matter, he supposed. It was done and over with and now they were preparing for exams.

In a way, history was kind of surreal to Tommen. He'd skipped over a century of history, a whole century and a half, in fact. More than just not being alive for most of the history they were learning, he didn't have the same generational knowledge that got passed down in other families. This grandparent served in World War II, that uncle was in Vietnam, an older brother was in Desert Storm, and this classmate was an ROTC and heading off to bootcamp just as soon as he graduated. Or, when not speaking about wars, all the crazy antics that his classmates' parents got into in the eighties, or their grandparents in the sixties. One classmate's mom was literally named Starchild because her parents had been true, bona fide hippies.

Tommen didn't really have that. True, his dad had been alive through several generations and knew quite a bit about the culture, the politics of the time, and so on, but there was something far more intimate about having a whole family collection of knowledge and experience, a school of hard knocks, whereas his dad had gone dark and dropped out of the scene several times. He'd gone dark at least once to avoid the draft, though he probably wouldn't have been taken anyway, being older.

Things didn't get sticky until the late nineties, early thousands, when most of them would have been at least alive. Tommen hadn't entered the scene until 2005. He didn't remember 9/11 or any of that, though, to be fair, most of his classmates didn't really remember either. The age threshold was becoming older and older. This year's freshmen were only just born when it happened.

Mostly, Tommen just reiterated the point that his family had been poor and he hadn't even entered the school system until he was eight. Even then, it had been a kindly substitute teacher who'd visited four days a week while he was in the hospital until he was released and could attend regular public school. That had been ten kinds of a nightmare seeing how he could barely speak English at the time. But he didn't have the early education that his classmates had, didn't have the early exposure to the outside world and the ongoing political carousel.

While it made school a little awkward, Tommen was largely okay with this. He'd had a good childhood, not bogged down by drama and media and outrage and everything else. He kind of wanted something similar for his daughter. He wanted her to be able to run and play and enjoy life without worry, at least for a little while. Was that even possible in this day and age? Well, he would make it possible, one way or another. He would make the universe her playground.

He again texted Becky between classes, asking how class was. She responded a minute later with, "Yay. Finals."

"I know the feeling," he texted back.

"So we can be miserable together."

"How's mama doing?"

"She's asleep I think, so I can actually concentrate for a few minutes."

"Well, that's good. I love you, my dears."

"I think I speak for both of us when I say we love you, too."

He probably had an idiotic grin on his face as he wandered off to third period, but that was fine. He had every right to be happy. No one else had to like it.

Sociology wasn't a bad class, but the teacher had an obvious bias, one not shared by a majority of the students. Some had even filed complaints about it, but there was little to be done. By definition, he was teaching the course material requirements, and there was no guarantee that a replacement could be found for his classes, most of which were required. And then there was that whole union contract thing.

It might not have bothered Tommen so much except not everyone was as smart as him to be able to recognize a vast majority of the instructor's words were bullshit and fallacy. To his surprise, some of the kids on the debate team, a few of whom did share similar wacky ideas, did call him out on some of his more obvious logical flaws, but Tommen suspected it was more out of obligation than contradiction—correcting his grammar and punctuation as opposed to the actual content, to use an English analogy.

Not unusual for the man, the instructor had actually defended Tommen and his status as a baby-daddy, chastising the rest of the students for belittling him on account of their "outmoded sense of morality and the definition of family" (something he had belittled Tommen about in the past seeing how he was The "Chivalrous" Welshman). And honestly? Tommen felt disgusted. He'd straight up told the man in the middle of class that he did not want his defense, his failed logic, his support, his empathy, his sympathy, or anything else. Yes, he was the Chivalrous Welshman. Yes, he'd made a few mistakes. But he was going to make it right and go back to the traditional way of things, a way that had worked for thousands of years so far.

He hadn't spoken in class since. The teacher did not call on him to answer questions and barely acknowledged his existence at all except during roll call and assigning him to some group project, in which he always made sure Tommen did not get a chance to speak.

In olden days now gone by, Tommen had felt removed from school inasmuch as he didn't care, got in fights, smoked, et cetera, et cetera, ad nauseum (Ha! See, he had learned a few things). Maybe his only experience as feeling normal in school was his junior year, and most of that had come from his desperation at getting as far away from Rifun and his wars as possible.

Now, though, he felt like a true outsider. Not just in the sense of he was going to be a dad and he was going to have a little different post-secondary experience than the rest of them, but more in the sense that he was now looking beyond himself. This was school as he was experiencing it. How would things be when his daughter got here? What would she learn her first day of kindergarten? Of middle school? What would her high school classes be like? What if she wasn't good in school? What if she excelled? What if she wanted to go to a trade school instead of college? What if she didn't want to go to college at all, but be a stay-at-home mom? What if she wanted to be an exchange student and see the world? What if he was having to educate her himself because they were somewhere on the far side of the galaxy? What was he going to teach her then?

It helped to put things in perspective, Tommen thought, though he didn't like to follow through on all of his lines of thinking. If this sociology teacher was any indication, the future of terran education was bleak. And communist.

But it was almost over. Finals and then done. Boom. No more worries. Until his daughter got to school.

His daughter. Maisy. Maisy Helen Forbes.

Now he knew he was smiling like a moron, but he didn't care. Life was good.

Almost every day, he was set for lunch, taking leftovers from whatever Becky made the night before. Tommen knew he and his dad were being spoiled. His dad had once made the comment that maybe he, Walter, should have asked Laura to marry him because she was just as good a cook. Then Tommen made the point that, while that may be true, they would still only get a homecooked meal on a rotating basis, three days on, two days off, that sort of thing.

But, there were rare occasions when he did not have leftovers to bring, whether because there had been no leftovers or because Becky was too tired to cook. It was on these mornings that he was too scatterbrained to remember to make himself a lunch. He thought back to the time when he'd been Suppressed and considered that he'd had time then to make lunches, and he couldn't even Band. Then he figured that at that time, he hadn't been dealing with a pregnant woman who sometimes woke him up in the middle of the night to make her something to eat. When he got up, scattered and confused and found nothing in the fridge waiting for him, he just accepted it, didn't make himself anything because his brain told him Becky wasn't asking for anything, and hurried out the door without a second thought.

This was one of those days. Actually, it was one of those weeks. Becky had been studying relentlessly for her exams, so she was both busy and exhausted, to say nothing of her sewing business which she somehow managed to squeeze in there. When Tommen had once asked her how she managed everything, she'd answered, "Being pregnant is a constant, obviously. So I basically have a full-time eight-hours-a-day job, plus full-time schooling. I divide those two, throw in an hour for showering and eating, and just let the pregnancy happen on its own. It sucks sometimes, like trying to get through the day with a head cold, but worrying about it or fussing over it isn't going to change anything and can actually cause problems."

She'd said it so calmly, so matter-of-fact, that Tommen had a hard time believing she had any problems at all, though the strain was starting to really show.

Tommen moved through the lunch line, picking up this and

that and even making himself a small salad. He always kept one eye out for one-hit-wonder bullies, those who would never pick a real fight, but would run up, slap his tray out of his hands, and run away laughing. It had only happened once so far this year, but Tommen wasn't fooled; he knew someone would try something.

"Good morning, Tommen," Karen, the lunch lady on the register, greeted. "Any new pictures?"

He shook his head as he took out his wallet and handed over a five. He'd grabbed a few extra food items—more than just an entrée, a side, and a drink—and no change was made. Karen patted him on the back as he went by, always with a smile, and turned her attention to the next student.

His table was against the far wall, halfway between the large windows and the kitchen. The cafeteria had become extra crowded since open campus had been shut down, and the rest of the seniors still grumbled about it. Nothing bad was going to happen, they said. This was West Virginia, for goodness' sake. This was Charleston—not even Charleston proper, this was South Charleston. Why were they being treated as if they were gangbangers from Chicago, or crazies from San Diego or Dearborn or New York City?

According to the rumor mill, it stemmed partially from social violence across the country, and partially from Tommen's kidnapping and the incident at the warehouse, to say nothing of the trial. Everyone's favorite police chief, Casey Oldman, had been the one to lead the charge in school safety, and none of the neighboring departments wanted to be accused of not caring about school safety, so they went along with it. Some of the high school kids, especially freshmen, who had very young siblings, said that the elementary schools had seen some of the most iron-fisted changes and tempers were hot on all sides. The city council was taking a lot of heat and being accused of trying to implement some sort of lockdown, prison-style, martial law on the schools. Conspiracy theories took it from there, and West Virginians were good at nothing if not conspiracy theories.

Tommen mostly ignored it, but he kept an ear out just in case there was anything interesting he wanted to ask his dad about. Listening to the stories made him want to homeschool his daughter even more. Teach her the important things in life, let her play and be carefree, and don't worry about what the rest of the world is freaking out about. Not yet. It was like in theater; enjoy the play while it lasts, knowing that there is beauty in the play, but it is, ultimately, fake. He would let his daughter believe the world was good and perfect, just for a little while, before showing her the man behind the curtain. Ironically, that man had been him a couple years ago, doing *Alice in Wonderland*, all because he wanted to follow Becky around and get to know her a little better.

He texted a condensed version of his musings to Becky.

"You're so sweet," she replied a few minutes later.

"More sap than a sugar maple, I know," he said.

"Maybe, but it's still sweet. That's why I love you."

Well, at least she was in one of her good moods. Tommen had learned to take advantage of her good moods. Not in a bad way, but when a pregnant woman was in a bad mood, she wasn't giving an inch, and he could say and do nothing right, and it was just better to make himself scarce and wait it out. So he waited patiently until she was in a good mood to do nice things for her, tell her he loved her, all the sappy stuff.

He ate slowly, in no real hurry. He'd since lost pretty much every friend he'd ever had, even the more distant ones. In fact, the outcast table was so lonely that even those who sat there did not congregate. Tommen sat on one end, another kid sat on the other side at the other end, and a third sat awkwardly in the middle, switching sides every day so he wasn't mistaken as being friends with either of them. It was pretty sad, really. Sadder still when one considered that the bullies rarely preyed on this table for the simple fact that there would be no reaction. Half the fun of bullying was the reaction, and most victims banded together in their own little cliques based on the reason they were being bullied: the nerds, the sluts, the gays, and so on. Not the total outcast table. They wouldn't react. Because their table was not crowded, it was easier to see what was happening, too, so the chances of being caught went up.

Tommen surveyed the cafeteria. Most of the bullies around here were the social snob bullies, those who called kids names, maybe pushed them, started vicious rumors. They were generally harmless because they were just as fragile if anyone ever turned the bullying on them. There were very few real threats in the school, those who bullied physically and could not be intimidated, only encouraged or arrested. Tyler Freeman had been one of those. Last Tommen had heard, Tyler was running around the revolving door of jail. Maybe he'd been part of the riot that saw Rifun beaten almost to death. Ha!

Tommen did not see Ricky anywhere. Ricky Freeman was Tyler's younger brother, and he was a senior this year as well. He wasn't much of a physical bully, though he'd been known to throw a few punches or stuff a kid in a locker a time or two. He gave Tommen nasty looks in the hall or in class, but had never actually done anything to him. Even with the revelation of becoming a dad, Ricky hadn't gotten on Tommen or anything, basically left him alone. When Tommen asked Becky if maybe she knew about any goings-on, maybe Ricky or Tyler would target her to get to him, she'd chastised him for being so paranoid and not to think such stupid thoughts. It was one thing to bully a kid when he was a convenient target in school. It was a completely different thing to actually hate that kid so much that even after school, after not being locked up in the same building all day anymore, the bully would seek to harm him and go so far as to hurt his pregnant girlfriend. That went beyond bullying. She was no police officer, but she was fairly certain that was quite possibly first-degree murder, or something else very serious.

All the same, Tommen couldn't shake the feeling that he was somehow not in the clear.

And yet, some days he dared to hope, even entertain the thought that this was how things were meant to be. The Author wanted it this way. It started with Rifun at the warehouse and the humiliating defeat of the heroes, and now it was going to end with the bad guy going to jail, the police officer retiring comfortably, and the victim growing up and settling down into family life. And they all lived happily ever after. No one cared about the details of the politics, the economics, the social changes that inevitably followed the prince and princess marrying, though there certainly would be those things. No one cared about the kids they would have, the arguments, the make-ups, the little things, though they would certainly happen. All that mattered was that, in the end, they lived happily ever after.

Except for the part where you die, selfish, alone, and afraid. A lonely, selfish coward. What kind of happy ending is that?

Grudgingly he stood and tossed his garbage in the bin, taking the tray back to the lunch line and setting it on the dirty stack maybe twenty tall.

"So you're still not telling the sex," Karen stated as she approached to grab the dirty trays.

"Nope," Tommen confirmed with a smirk.

"Come on, you can tell us," Danny told him, elbowing him in the ribs.

"Yeah, and you'll tell everyone else. I know you will."

"It's like he doesn't trust us," Karen said, looking at Danny.

"I don't," Tommen laughed. "Not with that anyway. No, we're not telling the sex yet. Two weeks, after we've told everyone over Thanksgiving. Think you can wait that long?"

Karen folded her arms. "You're asking a lot of us, you know."

"Teenagers," Danny sighed. "So selfish. They want to keep everything for themselves. Mine, mine, mine, and you can't have any."

Tommen raised a brow. "Well then maybe I won't be telling at all and you'll just have to find out through other sources. How do you like them apples?"

"Sounds pretty rotten to me."

Their good humor was cheering. Nothing sinister, just fun back and forth. Kids who routinely socialized with the lunch ladies often got teased about becoming one themselves one day, but Tommen didn't care. They were nice, fun to chat with, and made him feel somewhat normal.

There was still some time before fourth period. In years past, most students liked to spend it socializing outside, at least during the fall and spring, and on nice winter days. Even on crappy weather days, students were free to roam the halls, play some pick-up basketball in the gym, bring out a few select board games in the cafeteria, or get on a few open computers in the library. These days, their options were limited to the cafeteria, the gym, and a handful of students who asked permission could go to the library. Without the ability to roam the halls or go outside, everything was pretty cramped, and tight space made for some unfriendly neighbors.

Of course, while teachers stood watch at the sacred passages into the hallways, some students knew how to get by them, whether it was by distraction or the old, "Can I go to my locker to get my homework?" shtick. Tommen had little reason to want to get past the teachers, except maybe for the claustrophobia. Sometimes, the cramped areas were a little too reminisce of the push and shove of the battlefield.

"Afternoon, Tommen," Mr. Robinson, the art teacher, greeted. "How's Becky doing?"

Two years prior, Becky had fixed or made dozens of costumes for the art department for use in theater. Ever since, Robinson had vowed to go to her for all his sewing needs, at least when it came to the costumes.

"Ah...she's doing good, I guess," Tommen answered. "She's tired, baby's kicking. But she's good. They're both good."

"And how's dad?"

That question always caught Tommen off-guard for some reason. Maybe it was because few people inquired after the father. Made jabs, asked if he was nervous or being a good, attentive, father-to-be to his wife, but few people really, seriously inquired as to whether the father-to-be was doing well. So it was a second or two before he answered, "I'm doing okay. I'd rather be working or going to meaningful classes than be stuck here. But...only one more semester to go. Then it all gets real."

"Hang in there," Robinson told him, clapping him on the shoulder. "Before you know it, your kid is going to be entering kindergarten and you'll wonder where the time went."

"Yeah, that's what everyone keeps telling me."

"It's true. Happened with me and my kids. I still can't believe how they're growing up. I'm going to be a grandpa before I know it. Look at this." He tugged on a lock of hair. "I've got gray."

"I think you've had gray for a while," Tommen said smartly, stumbling once as someone bumped into him. "I think that's what happens when you have or work with kids. In your case, it's both."

"Okay, wise guy..."

Before either could say more, Tommen was bumped again. There seemed to be a mass exodus from the cramped social scene. Tommen didn't remember hearing the bell ring, and, looking at the clock, it was too early for it anyway. Robinson looked just as confused.

Then, a freshman girl, hardly yay-high and make-her-a-sandwich pounds, slowly shuffled up to them, dragging her feet and looking confused. Her hair was blindingly bleach blond, her skin was pale, and she wore purple lipstick. Her mascara was running down her cheeks, making her look like a drowned raccoon. Her hands were folded over her stomach.

"Um, Mr. Robinson," she said in a small voice, "I think I have a problem."

That was when Tommen noticed the blood.

And then the shooting really began.

Chapter Ten
Isolation

On the surface, Haunstein was just another early middle-aged doctor who, despite having high hopes for a career in saving lives, had become jaded with the bullshit people came up with in order to go to the hospital, many of them hoping to get drugs to either get high or as a quick fix for chronic bad decision-making.

Underneath all that, when it came to the Time side of things, well, he wasn't all that much different. At least when dealing with Time-related cases, when something couldn't be mildly explained away as a household accident, things tended to be a little more interesting. Gunshot wounds, amputations, poisoning, head and brain injuries, things that actually needed a doctor's attention. This was probably the first time Haunstein would be involved in regrowing an amputated limb or reversing brain damage. Attempting them, anyway.

Godwin had said he would be escorting Nathan if Miach thought he could grab Haunstein. Miach had his suspicions about this arrangement. Godwin and Haunstein were completely onboard with this idea of using Nikita Balabinov's bones to try and regrow Micaiah's missing leg. Nathan, while he understood the principle of such a thing, was less convinced, despite his own, less-invasive, methods proving either fruitless or so slow to fruition as to be almost counterproductive.

The last time they had tried anything was two weeks ago. At the end of another session where Micaiah still did not have a functioning leg, Godwin had declared that they either make the attempt or else he was going to move them arbitrarily. He had it on good authority that Julianna's attack against those with Authored Books was imminent. Details of these rumored plans were sparse, but he wasn't keen on finding out those details the hard way.

As Miach stepped through his portal to Kentucky, in a secluded area down the road from Haunstein's house, he guessed that Godwin was going to have a short but pointed discussion with Nathan about what was going to happen at this session today. Miach approached the road across from Haunstein's subdivision, politely looked both ways, then jogged across the street.

After treating Rifun and learning about the coup within the Order, Haunstein had moved into one of those cookie-cutter subdivisions where the only way to tell the houses apart was by the color of the house and which side of the house the garage was on, in addition to any lawn decor. It might not have been a bad idea in theory, Miach supposed. If Julianna sent anyone to kill him at home who wasn't familiar with how local housing worked, any such attempts might come with enough forewarning to let him escape. The first minor hindrance for a hitman would be all the looped, winding streets. Miach thought there was just one road in a big loop; in fact, while there was one road in and out, there were at least five more subdivisions branching off of that road, which made things only more confusing.

Miach tried to pay close attention to the mailboxes, all of them neat and uniform and perfectly matching HOA standards, but soon, one number blurred into another. Then his calves started to hurt. He was fit, but he was no runner, and he had to have gone at least two miles by now. He slowed to a stop and looked around at the house numbers. 12513, 12515, 12517... He double-checked the address he'd written on a scrap of paper. 12571 Oak Leaf Lane, how quaint.

Reluctantly, he continued his jog, quickly locating the doctor's house, if only by number. It was a gray-blue color with no décor. The garage door was open, revealing a clean space with a nice car and some boxes that remained packed up from the move. A light was on in the kitchen, but Miach saw no movement.

Miach got halfway up the driveway when he heard a voice. He nearly came out of his skin, but it was just a neighbor sitting on her porch, a hot beverage in hand.

"Let me know if you need help!" she'd called.

Miach paused and turned to face her. "Why would I need help?"

The woman, maybe fifty years old, shrugged in her fuzzy pink robe. "Just in case. He came out like he was getting ready to leave like he always does, then he went back in…" She took a drink. "Haven't seen him since. Could be he's on the phone. But if you need anything, let me know."

Miach just nodded and headed for the house. Something about the conversation felt off, but he was more focused on grabbing Haunstein and heading to the cabin. He entered the garage and went to the door that led into the house. He knocked.

"Doc?" he called. He knocked again. "Doc!"

There was no answer.

Cautiously, he opened the door.

He found himself in a kind of utility room. To his right, the light on the washer indicated a load was done. On his left, the water heater ate up most of a space otherwise occupied by shoes, coats, and keys.

"Doctor Haunstein?" Miach called, stepping into the room and closing the door behind him.

Still there was no answer.

Past the utility room was the kitchen, and beyond that, the living room with one open door leading to an empty bedroom and another to an equally empty bathroom. Miach opened up another door which was closed, but found only a pantry. Yet another door led to the basement which was unfinished and devoid of life.

Miach returned upstairs, skin crawling. He headed to the door leading to the garage, put his hand on the knob, then stopped. A wrenching gut feeling told him no, don't open the door. If he did, something very bad was going to happen.

Miach wasn't one for intuition or gut feelings, but this one felt very compelling. He tightened his grip on the knob, listening for anything beyond. He didn't hear anything, but that didn't mean much. Finally, he let go, backed up a few steps, and decided to skip the formalities and open a portal straight to the cabin in Canada.

He ended up at the bottom of the steps. Taking the steps two at a time, he barged in the front door and was immediately met with the business end of a rifle handled by Godwin Lore. Behind the mercenary, Nathan and Kayla stood protectively in front of Micaiah on the couch.

"You better have a good fucking reason for spooking us like that," Godwin growled, relaxing only a touch but not lowering the weapon. "Where's Haunstein?"

"Gone," Miach answered, hands in the air. "Don't know where. His house was open, car in the garage, but he wasn't there. One neighbor was acting a little strange about it, and the whole thing was just...off."

Godwin cursed, moved the rifle barrel away from Miach, and went to the door.

"Was anyone in the house with you?" Godwin asked.

Miach slowly lowered his hands. "No, or not that I noticed."

"Where did you leave from, specifically?"

"The utility room. I was about to go back out into the garage, but...I just had an inkling that I needed to come here directly."

Halfway through the last phrase, Godwin headed outside, moving defensively along the wall on the wraparound deck, rifle at the ready. Miach and the others just watched, waiting for some kind of signal. The mercenary made two laps of the house before returning inside.

"No one's here yet, but they will be," Godwin announced. His rifle was lowered, but Miach could tell he wasn't going to be shouldering it any time soon. He looked at Kayla and Nathan. "We do this right here, right now, and then we leave whether he's ready or not. Once I get you out of here, you can do whatever you want."

"Fulfilling the contract and nothing more?" Kayla asked, her tone and intentions indeterminable.

Godwin met her gaze. "I have no reason to think the Miaramila aren't also under some simultaneous assault. Now then, I suggest you stop talking and start working."

Only then did Miach notice the lower leg and foot bones on the floor near the couch, looking remarkably clean. He himself was listed as an organ and tissue donor, and he gave blood regularly. He found it to be very altruistic. He'd heard several stories where someone's life was saved or a disease cured because someone who was dying effectively and literally gave of themselves in one last act of love.

Miach did not get those same warm, fuzzy feelings when he considered what was going on now. This was a leg dug up from a grave made over a century ago. What's more, it was from Kayla's first husband. There was so much wrong here, though it didn't feel nearly as creepy as what he'd experienced in Haunstein's house.

Haunstein. Damn it all, but it had to be today, didn't it? They couldn't have tried this sooner? Haunstein's kidnappers or murderers couldn't have waited another day?

Without the doctor present, it was basically all up to Nathan with a little assistance from Kayla. The original plan had been that Haunstein would put a cast on Micaiah's good leg, from hip to toe, effectively making a mold of his good leg. Then that cast would be taken off the good leg and reformed, using Matter, over the gimpy leg, placing the leg bones inside. Then, Nathan would use his Building abilities, with the cast and leg bones as a template, to put Micaiah's leg back together. Kayla had clearly been feeding her husband well over the last few weeks, and the excess weight would provide some of the Matter needed to, hopefully, form the skin, muscle, and other connective tissues.

Not having the cast materials wasn't the end of the world, but half the reason for it was just to protect the new flesh from outside contamination and buy time to do the procedure over a longer period.

Without that protection, this would probably have to be done in one go.

Kayla took Micaiah's hand in hers as Nathan unwrapped Micaiah's stump, lumpy and malformed from weeks of being poked, prodded, and experimented on. It had gotten to a point where he could no longer wear his prosthesis. With any luck, that wouldn't matter after today.

"Micaiah, just like every other time, I'm going to paralyze your whole leg," Nathan began. "Then I'm going to open up the stump, all the muscle and tissue, and get right down into the bone and nerves. I'm going to work on the bones and nerves first, and the ligaments to get everything attached. Then I'll see about the skin to keep everything contained and protected, and we'll work on the muscles and tendons last."

Micaiah just nodded, eyes huge as he stared at his stump and the dead man's leg bones that were unnervingly close.

"Anyone who isn't a fan of horror movies, I suggest you avert your eyes," Nathan announced.

Miach fixed his gaze on his brother's face. He wanted to look, he really did. He remembered when Micaiah was first injured, the bloody, gory mess his leg had been. Only the urgency of the moment had kept him sane, but he wasn't normally a blood and gore type of person.

His eyes darted down to where Nathan, through sheer Building prowess alone, split the skin of the stump, always choosing the existing scars to follow. Carefully, he peeled the skin back from the muscle, then gently began to finger the muscle around.

Miach looked away. Micaiah was leaning his head back on the couch, staring at the ceiling. Kayla was looking at Micaiah. Godwin was back making rounds outside.

"The good news," Nathan said, jerking Miach back to the present moment, "is that the DNA in the bones is degraded enough that it shouldn't be difficult to change to match yours, reducing the chance of your body attacking the new limb."

The Builder had his eyes closed, one hand on Micaiah's good leg, one hand holding the bones. Miach felt his stomach lurch, and he averted his eyes if not his ears.

"You thing I gan walg?" Micaiah asked.

"That remains to be seen, but it's a good start," Nathan answered.

"How much does DNA matter in bones?" Kayla wondered. "If cadaver bones are used to help others—"

"That is with the idea of one's own body growing new bone over the old. It's not an unimportant factor, just less of one. In this case, we're trying to fool his body and brain into thinking this is his actual leg. I'm working on threading existing nerves into new nerves. Giving the pathways the correct DNA is a little more important."

"Does DNA really degrade that quickly?" Miach inquired. "Haven't the police identified bones after, like, decades?"

Nathan nodded, eyes still closed. "Oh, sure, but remember that Nika has been dead for over a century. And when we're talking about modifying DNA permanently, there are two golden periods of doing so. The first is in utero, when everything is fresh and new and still developing, and the second is after death when the body itself is no longer functioning and can't fight the changes. That's how Disguises revert themselves after all; the body is constantly replicating cells, and when it finds that something isn't right, it fixes the malfunction."

Made sense, Miach supposed, not that he was an expert in genetics. He glanced outside and just happened to catch Godwin's eye. The mercenary made a motion for him to join. Miach nodded once and headed out, meeting Godwin on the deck, facing west.

"I've seen your Disguises, now how about any of your other skills?" the man asked, his voice uncomfortably low. "How are you in combat? Are you armed?"

Miach showed the mercenary his conceal carry, the pistol he had taken with him to Ireland. "One extra clip, all I got. As for anything else, I might not be a boxer, but I can fight. I still remember my combat training when I trained for Lieutenant Timekeeper."

Godwin nodded and looked out over the deck, westward, toward the old cabin. "They're out there. If I'm right, they're slinking around the old cabin now. Probably used her Book to triangulate their portal. They'll pick up a scent, then come here."

Miach squinted in the direction the man was looking. "How can you tell?"

"Sound, mostly. Smell, when the wind changes. These aren't humans coming after us. Something bigger, stronger, and, in this wilderness, it'll just look like an unfortunate run-in with wildlife."

Miach straightened, turning his body toward the house. "You want to leave now?"

"Not yet, but I want you to get them prepared for that eventuality. I'm going to go down and scout it out, see what we're dealing with. If it's too much for me and you to handle, I'll come back and we'll slip out."

"Me and you? What about Nathan and Kayla? They can fight."

"Nathan is in the middle of his procedure and I consider Kayla to be compromised; she's not going to leave those two. You and I are going to be running this show."

Miach didn't want to admit it, but the mercenary had a point.

Godwin made as if to leave, then paused. "And one more thing. I'm going to set a temporary Disguise over this house. It won't stop them from finding it in a methodical search, but it won't be a beacon from five miles away. Everything here is going to appear to vanish. Do not leave this plot of land or you won't be able to see it either to get back, unless you can navigate by feel. Understand?"

Miach nodded. "Got it."

The mercenary left, then, moving rather quietly for someone so obviously on a mission. Once he hit the ground, he paused and touched one of the house supports. Miach felt the slightest hint of change, like a sudden, very minor snip of vertigo, and as quickly as it came, it was gone. He guessed this was the Disguise over the house. Then he watched as Godwin donned his own personal Disguise, that of an apparent outdoor enthusiast with tall hiking boots and an enormous backpack, his rifle Disguised as a hiking staff, and headed into the woods.

When nothing happened for several long seconds, Miach went inside.

"How's it going?" he asked, trying to sound casual and not suddenly rushed and anxious.

"It's only been a few minutes," Nathan informed him. "I'm still working on the DNA in the bones. There are a lot of cells to go through."

"You couldn't have done this beforehand?"

"Miach, what's wrong?" Kayla asked, perhaps seeing something in his expression.

Nathan did not move from his position, but Miach could see that his attention was not fully on the task at hand.

"Godwin thinks Julianna might have a murder squad out for us, and they're snooping around the old cabin. He's gone to check it out, wanted me to get you guys ready to go." Miach made a gesture. "You Band him and stay focused on that. I'm going to keep an eye out for Godwin. If I break into your Band, just know that we're going, no questions asked."

Kayla nodded wordlessly, eyes huge. Godwin was right; she was too compromised to be an asset in this fight right now. Miach turned away and started for the deck.

Of all days. Today had to be the day when Haunstein disappeared, Julianna sent a murder squad for them, and Kayla with her mighty skill became useless. Miach's stomach lurched as he reached for the door handle. They were getting hit fast and hard and all at once. What did that mean for Walter? What did that mean for Tommen? Were they all right? Should he call them?

Maybe later, he decided, opening the door. He wasn't entirely confident in his ability to keep watch over the three inside the house; he couldn't add more people to the mix.

He'd just reached the deck railing when he saw movement in

his periphery. He startled and reached for his gun, but quickly recognized Kayla.

"Sorry," she murmured meekly.

Miach let out a breath and glanced inside. "Is he done?"

He could not see through the glass well on account of a minor glare, and he didn't want to risk using Light and possibly giving something away through the Disguise. From what he could see, Micaiah was still on the couch, and Nathan appeared to have taken up in the recliner. He was unable to discern the state of his brother's leg.

"He got the nerves in the bone and some ligaments formed, enough to hold the skeletal structure in place," Kayla reported. "He was also able to form a crude epidermis, just enough to hold everything and hopefully keep out infection and damage."

Miach still peered through the glass. He thought he could make out a flesh-colored plastic bag hanging from his twin's stump. "Won't it dry out? What about the rest of the muscle and stuff?"

She shrugged. "Nathan needed a rest. I decided to come and see about things here, then I'll go back and keep Banding." She looked out over the railing to the west. "No word from Godwin?"

Miach turned away from the house and shook his head. "Nothing yet, and I don't know when I should be worried."

Kayla straightened and stretched. "Well, while we have the time, we should use it. Stay vigilant."

He nodded and returned his attention to the greater landscape. Only after a moment or two did he consider that, Disguise or not, he was greatly exposed on this deck. Sure, it served as an excellent watchtower, but he was still exposed.

At what point should he be worried about Godwin? Was the mercenary using Bands at all? Were Julianna's goons? Was Godwin fighting them even now? Did he need help? What were Godwin's capabilities exactly? Miach didn't like not knowing, didn't like not having a real plan other than "Run." Even when he went along with his brother's asinine idea to request a Time Trial years ago, there had still been a plan. More importantly, there had been backup. There was no backup this time; no one was coming to save them if things went sideways. And if Nathan the Builder couldn't help them, no one could, short of divine intervention.

He paced back and forth on the deck a few times, hoping he might project an air of discipline and preparedness, and not confused anxiety. After his second trip, he again noticed Kayla emerging from the house. This time he got a glimpse inside where he noticed the flesh-colored plastic bag hanging off of Micaiah's stump had a definite leg-and-foot shape to it and didn't appear to be quite so limp. If it was a leg, it was severely atrophied.

"Looks like progress," he commented hopefully.

Kayla nodded. "There's a dermis under the epidermis, so the skin has better structure and defense, and it won't dry out. Nathan also built the first layer of muscle and tendons."

"Can Micaiah move it?"

She frowned. "Well, despite Nathan paralyzing the leg, once he let go of that paralysis…"

"His brain still doesn't know what to make of it."

"Nope. There was a fair amount of pain when the nerves were connected, and it didn't get any better this time."

Miach nodded and folded his arms. "So what does Nathan think? One more go? If he's got skin and basic muscle, should just be more muscle, right?"

Now Kayla hesitated. "Cai doesn't have any more reserves to use. Nathan would be stealing muscle from other parts of his body."

"He needs me."

"Right. But we need you out here guarding more."

Miach nodded. "If there's nothing more than Nathan can do for Cai right now, Band him for whatever rest he needs, then send him out here. We'll need him. And I don't think I need to remind you to stay close to Cai."

Kayla gave him a mild look, then ducked back inside. When Miach was halfway back to the deck railing, Nathan joined him. Judging by the man's appearance and the way his clothes hung more loosely than before, he'd been using his own "reserves" to help Micaiah, too.

"Seems we're at an impasse," Nathan commented. "We need you, but we need you."

"Why can't women ever say that to me?" Miach wondered aloud. "With them it's always, 'You're just a good friend' or 'I'm a lesbian' or 'You're my brother-in-law.' " He sighed dramatically and shook his head. "I don't get it."

Nathan grinned humorlessly. "One day, Miach. With this many lives to live, you can't be alone forever."

Miach frowned as they stared out into the wilderness. "You seem very optimistic about the situation. Do I have to pay you for this psychology session?"

The Builder laughed. "You either laugh or cry. I'm not giving up yet. We don't even know what we're up against."

Miach nodded. "So, are we about to make a massive breakthrough in reverse-amputation technology? Or am I making a big deal out of something common to the upper crust of the universe?"

"Starfish and lizards regrow limbs, and they're hardly the upper crust of the universe." At Miach's look, he added quickly, "But I understand what you mean." He shifted position. "It's just a matter of Matter. Yes, some species are able to do such procedures with advanced technology—"

"Why bother with the Akari, then, if technology can do the same thing? You don't have an in with some of these species?"

"That technology is, I've found, suited only to those species. Even if the Tacagans possessed such a tool, they have engineered themselves to be so different, I don't know that it would work." Nathan looked at him. "And what if that technology failed?" He shrugged and made a vague gesture. "We're out here in a cabin in the Canadian wilds and we're performing procedures that dwarf anything a hospital could produce. Just because some aspects of the Akari can be replicated doesn't mean they're superior."

Miach frowned and nodded. "Guess I shouldn't look a gift horse in the mouth."

Nathan chuckled. "At least when this horse breaks a leg, you don't have to shoot it."

Before either could say more, Miach spotted movement in the clearing. A lone figure which soon proved to be Godwin, jogging casually toward the cabin. Miach felt another minor snip of vertigo, suggesting the Disguise around the cabin was lifted as the man approached and hopped up the steps onto the deck. At the last second, Miach hit the man with Test; he checked out.

"You look like a mercenary who's just completed a contract," Nathan stated evenly.

"Please, don't thank me for saving your lives without a massive fight and hurried flight with just moments to spare," Godwin retorted. "I was right; they were Julianna's men."

"You took care of them?" Miach inquired.

"There were only three," the mercenary reported, "which means one of two things: she didn't know our numbers and expected a smaller or less-prepared party, or this was just a scouting group sent to discern and verify our location."

"Neither one is a pleasant option," Nathan mused, "but my bets are on the latter. Julianna has been frustrated too much to want to skimp on firepower against her greatest rivals, especially if she has any suspicion that I'm here."

Godwin nodded. "My thoughts as well. How's your patient?"

"He has a leg, though not a functioning one. His reserves are gone, and I had to use some of mine to get him where he is. Unfortunately, our position is not secure enough that I would feel comfortable trying to tap anyone else just now."

The mercenary frowned but nodded. "Understood. Once those scouts fail to report, more will be sent. And there's a good chance the Miaramila are under attack as well. We should leave now while we can."

Nathan made a noise like a resigned sigh. "Regrettably, I

agree with you. Where are we going?"

Godwin entered the house without answering, and Miach and Nathan followed. Kayla looked up from where she sat beside her husband, but Micaiah was busy staring at his leg.

"How many times did you tell me to not skip leg day?" Miach said lightly. He made a vague gesture. "What is this?"

Now Micaiah looked up. All color had drained from his skin; he was clearly in shock. "I have a leg again."

Godwin made a motion for everyone to stand. "Come on, up we go. There will be more coming, and I don't want to be here to meet them."

Kayla and Nathan got on either side of Micaiah to help him up. Clearly he had no idea what to do with this new appendage. The new leg might have had some muscle as a formality, but it didn't have any real strength required to hold him. Nor could anything be done to keep it out of the way so no one got tripped up by it.

"Does it matter what species the Matter comes from to build his leg?" Godwin asked once Micaiah was situated between his helpers.

"Human will make the process go fastest," Nathan answered, "but any living organism with appropriate muscle and fatty tissues could be used with some tweaking. In theory, any Matter at all could be used, but the less like him it is, the more work I have to do to change it, and progress slows way down."

Godwin nodded. "We'll see who we can get to volunteer."

Before anyone could ask what he meant, the mercenary had conjured a portal and was barking at everyone to get through. Miach went first to clear the way, then Nathan and Kayla with Micaiah between them, and finally Godwin.

They ended up in a room that was at once cheap hotel room and yet fine art museum. Furnishings like the bed, table, and chairs were slightly more comfortable than utilitarian, yet there were decorations that resembled no terran artwork Miach was familiar with. Glancing at a window, he saw only stars beyond.

"Where are we?" Miach wondered, venturing cautiously toward the window.

"*Runner's Refuge,*" Godwin answered, finally apearing to relax a smidge, "repurposed from one Captain Morain leRou Titik. This room specifically is mine."

Nathan and Kayla helped Micaiah to a chair, then the pair began meandering around the room, studying the art.

"Is this collection yours or Titik's?" Nathan wondered.

"Mostly mine." Godwin went to a computer console and started sifting through information. "Titik was too obsessed with money and currency to care much for art, though he had a few pieces he evidently fancied." Godwin straightened, relaxing a touch. "Some security reports, but nothing indicating immediate attack." He turned to face the group. "Now then, we'll get him fixed up and send you all on your way, as promised."

"What?" Miach asked.

Godwin gave him a look. "We're not a charity; we have too many problems to worry about cripples and freeloaders. I'm doing this as a favor for Faharoa. I brought you here because it's the hardest to track as far as portal travel is concerned. Most of the Miaramila is dug in elsewhere, but there is a skeleton crew here. A few volunteers should be able to provide the 'reserves' necessary to fix his leg. After that, debt paid, we part ways."

He did not wait for their consent, simply approached a panel which proved to be a comms panel, and called for several people to come to the room.

"We..." Micaiah began. "We gant leave."

"Unfortunately, at this time, only able-bodied members are allowed in this group," Godwin told him. "And able-minded."

"Oim not st-tupid."

"No, but you're not in fighting shape either. Even if you do get you leg fully restored right here right now, it's going to take time to retrain it to walk and run and fight. And being able to communicate quickly and effectively is more than you can do right now."

Now Nathan cut in. "If I were to stay and help with Miaramila with their injuries, would you consider letting them stay in some capacity?"

Godwin shifted his stance, expression visibly puzzled. "Why would an Akarin Builder help the Miaramila? We've already established this is simply a debt being paid. Or do you expect to hold us in greater debt to you?"

Nathan shook his head. "I expect no such thing. The matter is simply that we cannot afford to be isolated. Haunstein was picked off because he was alone. Even a small group like this is an easy target, and if something happens, who is going to know? Who is going to help?"

Godwin glanced around at the four of them. "You've discussed this already."

Nathan gestured to Micaiah's leg. "If anyone needs proof of my value, here it is. I don't know what Julianna is going to do to the Miaramila, but amputations may be the least of your worries. Kayla has proven herself well, and Miach is no rookie. That's three. Micaiah...I can't make any real promises, but you've seen his improvement."

"A babe learning to walk is an improvement."

"Having a Builder in your ranks is an improvement."

"Why come to us? Why not run and hide with your Akarin friends? I know you must have a few, and surely not everyone is a coward."

Nathan huffed irritably. "Will you accept us or not?"

Godwin eyed the Builder suspiciously, and this look continued even when the door opened and those he'd called for, a group of four, walked in the room. They were all humanoid, but none of them were human.

"You sent for us, sir?" one inquired.

Godwin did not answer for a long moment. At long last, he nodded slowly. "Yes. This is Nathan Wilde. He's an Akarin Builder."

Now the four newcomers shifted their complete attention to Nathan.

"He and the others are going to be staying a while," Godwin explained, "helping out on the base. Right now, Nathan needs a bit of help, and I expect you to make yourselves available to him. He knows the agreement. Once he's done here, I'll be taking them to the base."

"Are they all Builders?" one of the four asked.

"No—"

"Isn't that one an Akarin council member?" a second inquired, studying Micaiah.

"Populus only—"

"Isn't this one the one who tried to kill Faharoa?" a third wondered, stalking over to Kayla, its posture undeniably angry.

"And now she is obligated to help us," Godwin said. "And you are all under orders."

At the mention of orders, the stalking creature paused in its movements. It didn't look happy, but it obediently returned to the group.

"You will aid Nathan the Builder," the mercenary repeated coldly. "And when he is done, I will be taking them to the base where they will be assisting our forces. That is all."

The group assented, if only because, as Godwin said, they were under orders.

Cautiously, Nathan motioned them over, telling them to get comfortable.

"Why does a Builder require assistance?" the fourth member of the group asked. Miach was no judge of alien tone or body language, but he thought it sounded more thoughtfully genuine than the others.

"Well," Nathan began slowly, "here's what we're going to do..."

Chapter Eleven
A Match Made in Hell

Shootings had been happening since guns were invented; usually it was called war. School shootings were not a terribly new thing either, unfortunately. As the modern world understood them, they'd really started back in the eighties and nineties. What was new was the frequency of them and the motivations behind them. Used to be that it was once every few years because one or two kids got bullied and wanted to exact revenge in the bloodiest way possible. On top of the bullying and revenge, most of those kids had been anarchists in some way and wanted to enforce—violently—the law of the jungle.

Now, it seemed, there was a shooting of some form a couple times a year, one of them being at a school, and the motivations behind them were all over the board. It was no longer limited to just bullying, though that aspect remained. Now there were political and religious motivations to consider.

All of this crossed Tommen's mind in about the time it took for his gaze to dart from one person to another in the crowd that was just starting to panic, Banding to try and get a better look. Other thoughts crossed his mind, too.

For example, *What's going on?*

Is this real?

How do you know?

Is this happening here? This doesn't happen here. This happens in big cities far away. New York, California, places like that. Not in West Virginia. Yes, Charleston is a city, but...it's still West Virginia. We're all civilized people here. We make moonshine, not meth. We shoot game, not schoolchildren.

And still more thoughts crossed his mind as he looked from one student to another.

I was one of those kids who was bullied. I knew other kids who were being bullied. Did any of them ever express such a desire to kill? Did I ignore them when I got caught up in my own life? Could I have pissed one of them off because I made my life better when they didn't?

Was that a selfish thing to consider? Or was he simply being realistic? Some people couldn't stand the thought of other people bettering themselves, especially when they started out on roughly the same plane. But to this degree?

Well, shootings tend to take out a lot of people at once, if executed superbly—he winced at his own pun—but there is still a personal element to it. A bullied kid wants to wipe out half the school, but his main target is the kid who bullied him for years. He could wipe out the whole school except for one person, but if that one person is that bully, his mission still isn't truly fulfilled.

On the other hand, perception sometimes is reality. If someone feels bullied or slighted—most often by the faceless monster known as "society"—then that is what they will react to, regardless if there is intentional bullying going on from one specific person or group of people.

Problem was, bullying was not limited to the physical kind he himself had experienced for years. As Becky had explained, girls were masters of body language bullying, social engineering bullying, and every form of bullying that did not involve one person striking another. Women were psychological bullies, and sometimes that was the worst kind, because then there was nowhere you could go to find reprieve.

Even as he thought it, Tommen picked out two prominent bullies from two different social circles, pushing and shoving, side-by-side, trying to get through. One was a jock. He played all the high-intensity physical sports—football, basketball, soccer, baseball, tennis—was captain or assistant captain of most of them, and knew how to rig his teams so that his friends were more prominent, despite some of them severely lacking talent. By all outside accounts, he was a nice guy and did a lot of community service, but he ran with the popular jock crowd and rarely let those outside his social circle grab the sports glory.

The other prominent bully was the social engineer of the school, or so she fancied herself. She knew the who's who of the whole school. She set the trends, she set the style, she set the attitude. She knew all the gossip on every student and most teachers, and was the root of the rumor mill. If someone crossed her, it didn't matter whether they were even aware that they had slighted her, didn't matter if it was intentional, she knew how to destroy them. She was a master of psychological bullying through social constructs or deconstructs, and cyberbullying was another one of her specialties for those too stupid to ignore or block her on social media.

Now they were both running for their lives in the same crowd, both of them vulnerable sacks of flesh and blood, the bullets uncaring of their station in life.

But what if it wasn't about bullying? What if this was a religious agenda? West Virginia was majority white, majority Christian, even Charleston, but they still had their Jews, their Muslims, and Varad and his family had been Hindu. Who was to say that this wasn't religiously motivated? People liked to pretend that those things only happened in countries half a world away, or maybe in really big cities where white and Christian were only a slim majority or even a minority. At the same time, if someone wanted to kill a bunch of Christians, going to a predominantly Christian area meant that a wide sweep with an automatic rifle would take out primarily Christians.

Without even really knowing half the student body, Tommen knew well that less than half the school was truly Christian or had any idea what the Bible said or even was. And yet, being Christian was just kind of the thing, because they might go for Easter or Christmas or maybe they went to Sunday school with their grandma as a kid. It was just considered an inherited thing.

Political motivation wasn't impossible either. But what politics would someone be so upset over that they would want to shoot up a school? Another millage for the arts department? Tommen couldn't recall any especially controversial statements from any of the teachers or other staff lately. Sure, Mr. Ricks was half a lunatic and very outspoken about anything and everything, but he was a single teacher. Someone wanted to protest him, they'd off him in his car or at home, right? Besides, his last controversial class had been axed. Or maybe because it was axed?

Try as he might, Tommen couldn't come up with anything in the religious or political arenas that might justify opening fire on a mass throng of students during one of the busiest times of day. Okay, so there was never a good reason to massacre a bunch of students, but to do it now, at this particular time...

Pre-planned, then. Sure, mass-shootings were generally pre-planned to some degree, but whoever this was, they not only knew it was lunch time, but they knew the students would be penned up in large groups. What else did they know about the students and the school?

It didn't matter. They didn't need to know the students; they just needed to know basic human psychology. Human beings liked to be safe and secure. For these students, that would theoretically mean any of the dozens of classrooms where they had a plan for these things. They drilled constantly for fires, weather, and lockdown emergencies.

Ten years ago, a shooter might be caught off-guard by all the safety measures, but with how much the schools advertised their safety measures, especially with Casey Oldman touting everything, any idiot had to know that precautions were being taken. Bulletproof glass, tamper-proof locks and door handles, even panic buckets full of rocks and other heavy objects in the event that someone did manage to break in. The halls would be empty, and once a door was closed, it was closed.

So then, what was left? Once a shooter got in his initial attack on the herd, he had to know the herd would scatter and make for safety. Then he would be playing catch-up. This would be easy enough at the start because the herd moved slowly, but once the students started filtering into classrooms, it would get harder and harder, and by that time, the cops would already be here. Tommen would be surprised if there weren't panic buttons in the cafeteria, the locker rooms, the office. He would be surprised if the teachers didn't have panic buttons in their classrooms, the way things were getting these days. Point was, this should be over pretty quickly. But any good shooter would know that. Did he hope that this shooter was a moron?

No, he couldn't take anything for granted. In fact, in a worst-case scenario, the shooter would be a student.

He knows all the ins and outs, knows all the procedures. He can unleash the initial barrage of bullets, drop his weapon, and blend in with the herd. As soon as he's safely in a classroom with fifty other students, packed in like sardines, all he has to do is brandish another hidden weapon, kill everyone in the room, take the teacher's keys, and go door to door like a toaster salesman.

Cynicism might be a flaw, but sometimes it could save lives. Tommen had to make his way to the source of this chaos, take down the shooter himself if he had to. He had the power to dodge bullets, after all. And if he was destined to die alone and afraid and selfish, well, this didn't count at all. At least the alone and selfish parts.

The herd was thick, the narrow opening between the lunchroom lobby and the hallways packed with fleeing students. Everyone wore a panicked expression. Some were bleeding. Some were crying. Some were screaming. Some were white as a ghost. Tommen now knew what he probably looked like during the battle in the Akarin fortress, and again on Brelix. Thinking about those two instances almost made this something of a minor inconvenience.

He was going to have to drop his Band, just for a few seconds to let some of the students pass, hope for an opening in the crowd so he could get through.

As soon as he dropped his Band, someone bowled into him,

knocking him to the ground. Whoever it was did not stop, did not apologize, did not help him up. Tommen didn't get a chance to move before someone else stepped on him. Then another, then another, and then a third. He gasped as someone stomped on his knee and tweaked it the wrong way. Someone else landed right on his burned hand, and he couldn't stop himself from crying out. That cry was cut short as he got kicked in the face, his teeth clacking together and his tongue unfortunately getting caught in the middle. Another kick to the head almost knocked out one of his hearing aids. He flinched at the resulting feedback.

He couldn't let himself be trampled. Already he felt as though he were suffocating; he didn't need to add more injuries to his repertoire. Gasping for air and trying to keep himself from going into full panic mode, Tommen managed to roll over onto all fours before Banding, again bringing everything to a halt. He had to keep himself under control if he wanted to keep the situation under control. Aside from generally not wanting to die, he also had to consider that he had a family to get home to tonight.

So then maybe he should just hunker down with the rest of them, wait it out. The cops would be here soon to get everything cleaned up.

Even as he thought it, Tommen discarded the idea. He had the ability to bend Time itself, among other aspects of the physical world. There was no reason he couldn't resolve this before it got any worse. He was not going to die a lonely, selfish coward.

He pushed his way out to the common area. Students were frozen, mid-stride, as they ran into or out of the gym, the cafeteria, toward the halls, toward the library, anywhere but where they perceived the danger as originating. The unfortunate ones lay on the ground. Some were still trying to crawl away to safety, holding various wounds. For some, it was a graze, and they were already halfway to their feet. Others had penetrating wounds, embedded in flesh and bone. An arm was painful, but a leg slowed anyone down. Tommen saw where a couple students had another student between them, his arms around their shoulders, one leg limp and soaked in blood.

Still a few other students lay on the ground and did not appear to be moving much, if at all. One girl was crying and blindly reaching out for some kind of help. A freshman not ten feet away had been shot dead between the eyes.

Tommen did not know how long he stood there, staring, but it was long enough to make his eyes water and give him a headache. He forced himself to blink and close his eyes. He had to focus. He couldn't let—

Bloody battle in an open arena.

—anything—

Micro-portals opening here and there to kill from a distance, soldiers falling without ever seeing the faces of their assailants.

—get in the way—

Bodies piled up as much to keep them out of the way as to form walls, the enemy darting from one wall of bodies to the next.

—of what he needed—

Climbing up a massive staircase, packed shoulder to shoulder, can't breathe, can't get away, can only hope to remain unnoticed and just survive.

—to do—

Breaking out onto the next floor, swarming like locusts, swinging weapons wildly, wielding Time and the Akari as little more than small knives, just tools for killing.

—to stop this—

Rumbling, shaking, falling rock. Can't keep his balance to try and run away, watching as friend and foe are crushed under several tons of boulders, the staircase divided to separate the two armies.

—massacre.

Tommen found himself on the ground, contorted as if in pain from a live wire, yet nothing was touching him. As if someone opened a valve, air suddenly filled his lungs and he curled up in a fetal position, trying to breathe and clear his head. When he tried to sit up, vertigo took him back down. He was like a fish out of water, flopping around desperately.

He was not a warrior. He was not a soldier. He wasn't even a very good medic, truth be told. But there was no way he was going to be able to confront anyone in his state of mind.

Even just that realization and acceptance helped to clear his head a little. The military targeted boys his age because they believed themselves invincible. Tommen was very aware that he was not. But that didn't mean he was useless. Gradually, he got to all fours, closed his eyes, tried to breathe. He was not a soldier, but he was not useless. There was something he could do, but it wouldn't be confronting the bad guys. The cops had to be on their way, or they would be soon enough, and they would be the heroes today. Not him.

Breath.

Tommen had never really been a hero. He'd been kidnapped and held hostage. He'd started at least one, if not two or more, intergalactic wars. He'd been unable to save Saul. He'd severely injured himself and let loose a madwoman from her interdimensional prison. He'd been a straight up coward in one battle and could be rightly accused of aiding the enemy in another, actually in both.

Breath.

But all the same, he had found the cure for Borelian poison and crippled an empire. He had been able to protect his campers from the fire, though his role in putting out the fire afterwards was a little dubious. He had played a mole in a dangerous game. He had successfully broken into a Borelian death temple and defied their dragon god. And he had helped to put a bad man behind bars.

Breath.

He was not a hero. But he was not useless. His usefulness came in a different package than brute force.

Breath.

Tommen managed to stand, leaning against a wall until the vertigo had subsided. Nothing around him had changed. The students were still fleeing and many were wounded. Somewhere out there, a gunman was lurking, targeting them. But now his mission had changed. He was not here to confront the shooter or play the hero. He was not here to investigate. Leave that for the real heroes.

But the thing about the cops and their role was that their priority was safety. To that end, they had to play it a little safe, cautious. Looking around him, some of his classmates didn't have time to play it safe. There was nothing he could do for the freshman with a slug between his eyes, but the girl with a couple in her leg and one in her abdomen, that he might be able to do something about. He had to get the wounded out of here.

Tommen wasn't a medic in any sense. Any medical skills he had came from wilderness survival or things he had gleaned from his dad's medical first responder textbooks. Suddenly he wished he still had Laura's phone number at least, just to be able to call a paramedic and ask a few questions. But he didn't have that luxury.

He knelt down and took the wounded girl in his arms, pulling the Band tight to himself so she was not affected. All she would know was that she was suddenly somewhere else; it would be attributed to shock. Months of working construction had put some muscle on him, and he hefted her up with only a slight grunt of effort. He was careful not to touch any of the wounds directly, though he knew she would be feeling the pain of being jostled around.

Then he stood and looked around. He had her, now what did he do with her? Where did he take her? Well, the nurse's office sounded pretty logical, he thought, but how many could it really hold?

He didn't have time to bat it around, and neither did she. She needed help.

Tommen forced his way through the throng of students, now dispersed a little more through the halls as they packed into the first room they came to or maybe headed down the hall to one they believed was a little safer. Some made for the main office, as if Mr. Layman could protect them. At the same time, Tommen knew that Layman would die to protect his students, and today might just put that mindset to the test.

The nurse's office was part of the conglomeration of offices and other administrative rooms in the center of the school. News of the shooting hadn't reached this far yet, and the nurse was still eating lunch. Tommen laid the girl out on the exam table and paused. He would only get half a dozen students in here in any sort of comfort, a dozen if he wanted to really pack them in. But there was no way he could bring every single injured student to the nurse. With all the injuries and the chaos, the lesser wounded students wouldn't get seen to right away anyway.

The science rooms, then, he concluded, heading back to the common area. Easier to clean up, and because of some of the chemistry experiments, every science room had emergency bio kits and first aid kits.

He grabbed the next injury he found, the girl who had been shot in the abdomen and come stumbling up to Mr. Robinson. She was feather light, but dead weight was dead weight. Nevertheless, Tommen got her to the nurse's office.

It only occurred to him after he dropped off the third severely wounded student that the nurse was just going to turn around, still chewing on her sandwich, and suddenly find a bunch of critically wounded teenagers with no knowledge of what was going on. Indeed, the wounded ones were going to show up in her office before the rest of the student body even got to her to warn her. Well, she would be so busy, it probably wouldn't cross her mind again until much later. The counselors would help her make some sort of sense of it.

After dropping off the sixth student, this one with a minor wound to the arm and so a direct delivery to a science room, Tommen paused to rest. He'd been using Gravity as much as possible to help with the weight, especially with the bigger students, but it was still a chore, and his own little war demons were starting to creep back up on him.

Hiding in the bathroom, it was almost hard to believe that he was in the middle of a school shooting. He was moving so fast, the rest of the action had slowed to basically a stop. When he released the Band, at least half a dozen students would have suddenly vanished from one place and showed up in another, but the chaos would continue. It didn't stop just because he did.

He wished he could call his dad and let him know what was going on, but Time and technology didn't get along so well. Calling was tricky to maneuver in Bands. Texts were easier since he had to release the Band only long enough to get the text out. Problem was, it was the middle of the day and his dad would still be sleeping. He'd probably wake up to a prolonged ringtone from a call, but a little blip to indicate a text? He'd just roll over and go back to sleep, consciously unaware of anything.

He was on his own, then. Taking a breath, Tommen punched out a text and released his Band for the longest three seconds of his life. Outside the bathroom, he heard several more gunshots, screaming, panic, chaos. Before it shut him down again mentally, he threw up another Band, and everything went quiet.

Breath.

He had to stay focused. He had to get as many of his wounded classmates to safety as he could. Three seconds, that was long enough for someone to hit a panic button or dial 9-1-1. Help was on the way. He just had to stay calm and take as much time as he needed; he had the ability, after all.

Breath.

Despite being in a Band, Tommen still crept carefully out of the bathroom. He again navigated his way back toward the common area. Three seconds hadn't done much to get the students to safety — a crowd was still a crowd and did not move fast, especially when needed — but it had thinned just a little more, giving Tommen more room to get through and figure out who was wounded and who was not. Anyone who was already in a classroom, he did not bother. Anyone who was up and running well, he let go. He only took those who were struggling or unable to get away.

He moved another five students, one critically injured, four less so. The common area was still crowded, but no longer suffocatingly packed. The herd was moving, albeit slowly.

The cafeteria was pretty well hunkered down by now, and why not? When faced with disaster, people ran to where they knew there was safety. They'd only ever had lockdown drills in classrooms, so everyone naturally ran to a classroom when the shit hit the fan. Few considered the cafeteria a safe place, even if it was probably one of the safest places to hide.

In the gym, some of the smaller students got the idea to hide in the bleachers, but that was assuming that the shooter didn't get any ideas of his own. Most made for the locker rooms. Tommen did not see any major injuries here, and even so, sports was another place where risk of injury was high. There was a first aid kit in both locker rooms, in the storage closet between them, and in the sports offices. They would be fine.

In his mind, Tommen told himself everything would be fine. They were getting to safety and he'd helped his classmates get to the nurse's office or somewhere to get help for their wounds. The police would be on their way to wrap this up, and the ambulances wouldn't be far behind. With any luck, this would not end in utter tragedy.

All the same, if he wanted any of that to happen, he had to release his Band and let time move forward again. The thought of doing that sent Tommen's blood pressure through the roof once more and his palms began to sweat. Maybe he should go home first, Band his way home and tell his dad what was going on. Get some help from Time and whoever else, cut the response time in half.

He got another student to a science room with a leg injury.

He couldn't do that. As much as he wanted to, he couldn't just abandon his classmates and run away like a coward.

A lonely, selfish coward.

He had the advantage here, and he had to use it. He might not be able to be the hero, but he could direct the heroes wherever they needed to go. He could run around where they could not and tell them what was going on.

On the other hand, if he did that, he could just as well be accused of being the shooter, to have such intimate knowledge of what was going on, when he ought to be locked down with the rest of his classmates. Maybe he should run home.

Tommen ducked into the bathroom again and released his Band, this time for ten long seconds, which he intentionally counted out. He blocked out all the noise, or he tried to, and counted. *Un, dau, tri, pedwar, pump, chwech, saith, wyth, naw, deg.* And Band. The noise ceased and he emerged from the bathroom.

Ten seconds saw a lot more students in classrooms. Doors were being closed as rooms filled to capacity. The art room was closed, as was one of the history rooms. One of the drafting rooms was just closing its door. Students still flooded into the library. Several teachers stood just outside their doors, yelling and waving students in, telling them to hurry.

Tommen did a last sweep of the common area. He counted only three obviously dead students. He didn't make it past one before he threw up. But the injured students had all been moved, at least. All he had to do now was pick a room and huddle down with the rest of them.

Head still swimming, he forced himself to look away, look at anything else, until he got away from the common area. He was no hero. He was going to hide with the rest of them and wait for the cops to come and say everything was all right, it was safe to leave. Did that make him a coward? Maybe. But at least he would be alive.

Lonely, selfish coward.

He ended up in one of the English rooms before he released his Band. Mr. O'Kenny and Mrs. Ulborne were there, shuttling kids in and directing them where to hide. Tommen counted maybe fifty or sixty students before they shut the door and locked it. The lights went out. On the other side of the room, the window had been covered over with heavy black paper. The reasoning was so that gunmen wouldn't be able to see if there were students in the room. Tommen figured that the presence of the paper would be testament enough to that. After all, was someone out there in the school running from room to room putting up black paper on the windows? He didn't find that likely.

But there was little he could do about it now. He did what he could, and now he just had to wait with the rest of them.

"Put away your phones," Mrs. Ulborne hissed, her voice shaking. "Don't let them see the light from your screens."

It was a plausible explanation, but more likely, they didn't want anything going out on social media. The cops didn't need parents swarming the school, cutting off emergency personnel and putting themselves in danger. They also didn't need to find out that the gunmen were monitoring social media and just waiting for one idiot to post where he was hiding. Lockdown drills were great, and security was top-notch, but there was always a way in.

Tommen felt his phone buzz. He waited a second before Banding and bringing it out. It was his dad.

"I'm on my way," was all it said.

He put away his phone and dropped the Band.

Despite toothless warnings from the teachers about remaining silent, the room was not silent. The students whispered, a few wept quietly, a few whimpered prayers to any god who would listen. They huddled together as tightly as they could behind the teacher's desk which was out of view of the door. Some took up residence in tight corners between bookshelves or cabinets. Tommen was huddled in the corner behind the teacher's desk, squashed among sweaty, dirty, frightened students. After only a few minutes, the smell was enough to make him gag, and memories of the Akarin fortress swarmed his mind.

One student near him wore a watch that glowed in the dark and sat an angle where Tommen could mostly see the time. The minutes dragged on.

Outside in the hallway, the running and screaming gradually faded until it was gone completely, all the students tucked safely away in one classroom or another. Tommen wasn't sure which was worse, the noise or the silence. The noise was screeching and echoed in his head, but it was obvious, highly indicative of what was or could be going on. In the silence, the darkness, anything could happen, and his mind conjured up a thousand different scenarios, none of which were pleasant.

The watch ticked out another minute. The cops had to be here by now. Problem was, with the way the window was covered and the location of the classroom itself, Tommen couldn't tell if there were cars outside. There probably were, along with ambulances, maybe fire trucks, and almost certainly a helicopter from the news station. Probably there were news trucks from every major station in the area, all relaying the information to their parent news stations. If he thought he could get away with it, he might have gone online to look, see what the headlines were at NBC, CNN, FOX, and all the rest.

As it was, the best he could do was Band and fire off another text to his dad.

"Dad, are you here?"

He did not get a reply, but then, he wasn't expecting one. If his dad was here, he would be awaiting or carrying out orders, trying to shut this thing down.

Memories of the warehouse flashed through Tommen's mind, seeing his dad lying on the ground in a pool of blood, choking, unable to breathe, going unconscious. Seeing his dad in the hospital, dying but with no known cause.

Tommen could feel the sweat plastering his body. He closed his eyes and tried to focus. After a minute, he Banded again and texted Becky.

"I love you."

This time of day, she was probably just getting out of one class and passing the time until the next. A couple minutes later she replied, "I love you, too. So does baby."

Tommen felt tears roll down his cheeks and he hastily wiped them away.

The minutes continued to tick by. The students had settled into an uneasy not-quite-silence. The ones who had been crying no longer wept, though one still whimpered. The whispering had ceased, and the only ones talking now were those who still prayed. Tommen's phone buzzed again. It was Becky.

"Oh my God, what's going on?!"

He let out a breath and replied, "Um...someone decided to shoot up the school."

"ARE YOU OKAY?!"

"Yes, I am. I'm fine. I think the cops are just about ready to release us." It was an obvious lie, but there was no use in getting her stressed out.

"Oh my God, what should I do? I can't just drive over there or anything. Oh my God, I don't know what to do. I feel so helpless."

"If you want to do anything, start praying. It's the only thing you can do. And stay as far away as possible right now. Okay?"

It was another minute or two before she replied, "Okay. I just...I want to do something. I want to help. I want to know you're okay."

"I'm okay. Just relax. For the baby's sake."

"Yeah, sure, easy for you to say."

"Actually, it's not. Listen, I'll see you tonight. I love you. Make sure baby knows, too."

"I love you, too. Come home to me, please."

"I'll do my best."

Fundamentally, until he was actually home, safe and sound, or even at the hospital, his best was the best he could do. There were no guarantees. He sighed as his phone buzzed again, but now it was his dad.

"We're coming for you, kiddo. Hang tight."

"Did you get the guy?" Tommen asked hopefully.

"Not yet, but we're going to evacuate as many as possible. And keep your eyes and ears open; I suspect mischief."

Godwin's warning immediately came to mind. Julianna was gunning for all those with Authored Books, and it would be in her best interest to hit them all at once. Why not do something like this to take him out, and possibly his dad, too? They would be too busy with this chaos to worry about what was happening to the others. Were Miach and Micaiah and Kayla also being attacked in some fashion? Would he ever really know?

Tommen sighed and rubbed his face. Some days he wondered whether the fight was really worth it. Was the ability to manipulate the universe really worth some of the trouble it caused? It might be, if only other people weren't so stupid about it. On the other hand, he wasn't exactly a shining beacon of responsibility either. He'd basically thrown himself into the spotlight, and he'd pissed enough people off that he wasn't hard to find when it came to exacting revenge. If he'd just kept his head down and shut up, he might not be in this predicament.

But by that token, he probably wouldn't have a dad, either, and he would be the bitch of an intergalactic psychopath. It wasn't always about the good choice, but the least bad. But in the middle of a situation like this, how could he tell the difference?

Movement outside sparked some whimpers and uncomfortable shuffling. Mr. O'Kenny and Mrs. Ulborne hushed them and the students obeyed, but there seemed to be a collective deer in headlights mentality as they waited to see what was going to happen. There was more movement outside, too much for one or two gunmen. This had to be a police entry team, Tommen thought, and his heart soared. They were evacuating the students out the back door, so-to-speak. It was too dangerous to take them through the halls, but they could maintain formation around them outside.

Of course, that also meant that the shooter or shooters hadn't yet been found. If the cops didn't want to take the kids through the school, it meant that they believed the gunmen were still inside, waiting to play a little cat and mouse, or fish in a barrel.

Tommen tried not to think about that. His dad and his comrades knew what they were doing. They trained for this; they were professionals. All the rest of them had to do was shut up and follow orders. Don't try to be the hero or help in any way. Get to an ambulance or a police car or other designated area, sit down, and stay there. Wait for further instructions. That was all.

There was a dull thud from the next room over. Mr. O'Kenny and Mrs. Ulborne again hushed their students as more nervous shuffling rippled through the room. Tommen was pressed harder into the corner until he almost literally couldn't breathe. There was more movement outside, this time approaching their window.

A thud hit the glass and one of the girls shrieked.

"Charleston Police," a voice said, right before a hand ripped through the black paper, followed quickly by the barrel of a rifle. The hushing was ignored momentarily as the students began to panic.

They calmed down once the first officer climbed in the window. A second came in after him. Peeking over the teacher's desk, Tommen could see more heavily armed officers waiting outside and a line of students from the next room marching across the grass.

"Here's what we need you to do," the second officer began authoritatively. "Rule one, stay silent. Rule two, stick together. Rule three, keep your hands on your head. Rule four, move as quick as you can and go where we tell you."

She did not give any room for questions, instead making a motion and hurriedly shuttling the students out the window. The first officer's light darted around the room as students emerged from any number of nooks and crannies and other clever hiding locations. Students tried to be quiet, but they had to climb on the heating unit to get out the window, and the massive metal monstrosity was not built with the idea of being quiet. Some froze as they kicked it and it made a hollow clang, some tried to apologize to the officers. The female officer was polite but firm in her orders to keep it moving, get out the window, and get to safety.

Tommen took in several quiet gasps of air as the pressure was finally relieved from his body. The students moved away from him and he could breathe again. He did not move right away, instead waiting until he had ample room to get his legs under him. His feet had fallen asleep, as cramped as he had become, and he stumbled the first time he tried to stand.

"Are you injured?" the female officer asked as the teachers came on either side of him.

He dumbly shook his head. "No, I'm fine. My feet fell asleep is all."

He took half a second to stretch his legs and roll his ankles, trying to get some feeling back before he climbed onto the heating unit, the last one out. Momentarily blinded by sunlight, he groped for a hand outside which appeared after a moment. It was a gloved hand, and the man on the other end was one he never thought he'd be happy to see again.

"We need to stop meeting like this," Miles told him.

Miles O'Connor had been one of the officers at the warehouse, and the only survivor who still worked for the city police department.

"Is my dad here?" Tommen asked.

"Yeah, he's here. You just keep moving. Follow the others. Hands on your head."

Tommen obeyed, putting his hands on his head and following his classmates across the lawn. On either side of them, heavily armed officers in full tactical gear ensured their safe passage while smaller teams conducted a methodical search, classroom to classroom, rescuing students and looking for the shooters.

The whole block was swarming with cops from all around the county, and even the next county over. State, city, and county boys worked side by side. Fire trucks blocked the roads and shielded ambulances. Flashing lights were everywhere. Overhead, a helicopter made large circles over the area.

There were multiple staging areas set up, Tommen saw. One was for incident command, where half a dozen high-ranking police officers gathered information and doled out orders. He saw Casey Oldman was with them, as well as Dean Williams and a couple others he did not know personally but recognized as being important.

Another staging area was reserved for the wounded, ambulances quickly darting in to load up patients before retreating to a safe distance and ultimately departing for the hospital. Tommen did not see any of the critical patients he'd taken to the nurse's office, but it stood to reason that they would have been taken first. Even now, there were only a couple students there with minor wounds being attended to by medically-trained policemen.

They were directed toward the third staging area where they were counted and basic information taken. Layman was there with a bulk of papers and a clipboard, shuffling through them as he saw each student and relayed more information to the attending officer.

"Forbes, Tommen," Layman said as Tommen came up next in line. The principal gave Tommen a long look. "If you haven't already, you need to call Becky."

Tommen nodded. "I know."

"I saw your dad running around here earlier."

"I know."

He was released to a fourth staging area where students could call parents and let them know they were safe. Tommen brought out his phone and called Becky. He ended up getting her voicemail, which meant she was probably in finals. Still, he left a message.

"Hey, Becky, it's me. Just calling to let you know that I'm okay. I'm outside and stuff with the police. Um, I don't know how long I'll be here, but..." He took a breath and wiped his eyes. "I love you, babe. If nothing else, I want you to know that. But I'm okay, and I'll be home tonight with you and the baby. You just take care of yourself and our little bun and do good on your finals. Okay? I love you. Bye."

He hung up and put his phone away, wiping his eyes and trying not to get emotional. His heart was still pounding and he felt sticky and gross from how much he'd been sweating. Comparatively speaking, this was pretty tame compared to being in the thick of battle. At the same time —

"Tommen!"

He looked up to see his dad approaching. Tommen was barred from leaving the staging area, but his dad was permitted in.

With the bulk of armor his dad was wearing, it made the hug a little awkward, but it was welcome nonetheless.

"Oh, God, I'm so happy you're all right," his dad said. "Did you call Becky yet?"

"I just did. She's taking finals, though, so it just went to voicemail."

"Well, at least you told her. Does she know anything?"

"Yeah, she texted me about it. I told her I'm fine. Dad, what's going on? And you know what I mean."

His dad let out a breath and Banded the two of them. "Nathan texted me a little bit ago while I was sleeping, said that there was some trouble up where the twins are hiding. He didn't give any specifics other than it seems to be a coordinated attack by Julianna against those with Authored Books. He said that they were going to have to go into some deep hiding where cell phones don't work."

Tommen shook his head and folded his arms. "Shit. How many do you think we're looking at? If this is part of that coordinated attack, and if I'm the intended target..." He looked around. "I'm standing in a huge crowd of students right now."

"I know. Believe me, I do. I wish I had a good answer. Right now, we don't even know who they are, or even how many we're dealing with. If this is a murder squad sent by Julianna...whoever it is has the advantage and we may be playing by their rules for a bit. But the important thing is, you're safe where I can see you, and you're not exactly a lightweight yourself anymore."

"Great. So what do we do?"

His dad dropped the Band. "I don't know. We wait for orders. It's all we can do."

It was not something either of them wanted to hear, but it was all they had at the moment. Tommen watched as more students were escorted out of the school. First and foremost, the students had to be safe. All else was secondary, finding the shooters, apprehending them, all secondary to the safety and well-being of the students.

Tommen tried to listen to the radios, but the officers standing guard over the students either did not have radios or else wore earpieces to minimize what the students heard, try to keep them calm. The nearest open radio was a good fifteen feet away from the edge of their zone, and the general commotion of the scene meant that he really had to strain to hear. He could have used Sound, he supposed, but did he really want to know every horrid and mundane detail?

More rooms were evacuated, the number of endangered students dwindling, but still no sign of the shooters. Suspicion was now heightened that they may have been students who were now trying to blend in with the crowd and escape.

The last of the rooms was cleared, the students escorted out. Police did another thorough sweep of the building but found nothing. Whispers began circulating and students began regarding one another suspiciously. Tommen heard mumbled orders to start checking all the students one more time.

"That won't be necessary," a voice said over a megaphone.

Heads turned as two figures nonchalantly exited the school, heading toward them. Both had rifles in hand, one had a megaphone. But it was their identities that Tommen was more fixated with.

The one with only a rifle was Tyler Freeman, the biggest bully since the third grade and Tommen's personal tormentor for years. He was not a surprise, though Tommen was curious to know if there was any truth to there being Time involved and when and how that had happened.

But the second person...the second person...was Ryan Eugene Henderson, Tommen's old foster brother from Hell.

Chapter Twelve
Reluctant Partners

Work had gotten difficult since Vin was gone. True to form, he'd been charged with second-degree murder and pleaded down to involuntary manslaughter. According to a little inside rumor mill, his lawyer was looking for a two to nine sentence and the prosecutor wasn't disagreeing. They were merely arguing over where to send him. Minimum security wasn't harsh enough, but he would never survive at Mt. Olive, being a police officer. Nevertheless, Walter and the others had promised to visit him wherever he ended up.

But in his absence, the work got doled out even heavier on the rest of them, and a few of them, like Kate, were running six or even seven days a week before a day off. Walter, with his impending retirement and desire to cut back to part-time after the new year, remained on five days, but sixes were coming up quick, Kate had told him. In a nutshell, they just couldn't do it with the manpower they had, and they didn't have the funding to hire the personnel they needed. Vin would be replaced eventually, but it wasn't as though it would suddenly lift the entire burden. Priority was always given to first and second shift. Third shift was for newbies, punishment, and only a few volunteers.

Walter got off work later than his scheduled out time, but that was nothing unusual. Scheduled times were more of a suggestion, he figured.

He walked in door to find Tommen in the kitchen, pulling out bread and the toaster and preparing a pan for eggs. No sooner had he registered that than he saw Becky appear from the hallway. Both men immediately inquired as to whether either of them had woken her.

She sleepily denied it and said she was just getting a drink of water and taking a short walk after the baby woke her up. It seemed to be that since the baby was moving, he or she (still not telling) never stopped. She got her glass of water, gave Tommen a half-asleep hug, then wandered off back to bed.

"Since I know her standard answer, I'll ask you," Walter said, sitting to take his boots off. "How is she?"

"Um...she's ready for it to be over," Tommen answered. "I mean, it's not just the kicking, her body has a harder time handling the stress."

These days, Walter saw Becky more than he saw Tommen, and he would agree that Becky looked stressed, as in, physically stressed. She was demanding a lot of her body and there were concerns that even her sheer willpower wouldn't be enough to make everything go the way it was supposed to. Tommen mentioned that appointments with the doctor would become more frequent after Thanksgiving, but Walter still had his doubts. Maybe it was his own defensive instincts kicking in, to protect Becky and her unborn child at all costs.

"I think you're being a little cynical," Walter told his son, feeling not a little hypocritical. "Everything has been going well so far. As long as that trend continues, there's no need to worry yourself over every situation your imagination can conjure up. Save your worrying for when you actually become a dad."

"Please." The toast popped up and Tommen slathered on the peanut butter before cracking a couple eggs in the pan. "At this point in my life, with everything that's happened to me, I am a pro at this, and I have more than enough cynical worry to go around."

Walter sighed. "That's what I was afraid of."

"What?" He took a bite of toast. "How's work?"

He didn't give Tommen all the details. For one, there was nothing either of them could really do. It was just how things were going these days. Time to batten down the hatches and weather the storm, at least for a little while until he could finally retire. Tommen seemed to sense his discomfort and his exhaustion. He grinned.

"How long until grandpa?"

Walter sighed dramatically and looked at him. "Only because you keep reminding me and everyone else do I know this, almost down to the day: sixteen weeks. Actually, I believe it's one hundred and fifteen days. Damn you, kid."

Tommen grinned and took another bite of toast.

They talked a little more, glossing over all the developments in the Wheel, all these factions and alliances, declarations of war and murder squads. It was exhausting, and even as it was far away, it could also get very close, very quick. Walter had tried to maintain a policy of not getting involved. He was two hundred years old and had seen plenty of politics in his day, just in America. The Time industry couldn't be much different except it seemed to force itself on him or his son at every turn.

"With exception of the Borelian declaration of war against humans specifically, it's all ideology," Walter declared, wanting only to wrap things up and get to bed. "One ideology against another. Order versus Miaramila and Akarin. Hands versus Order. Akarin versus Order with a temporary alliance with the Miaramila. The Borelians against everyone. A war of ideas, which is the hardest to fight and impossible to win." He stood. "And with that, I suppose I should get to bed and you need to get to school. Oh, and, uh, you've got some crumbs in your beard there."

Tommen brushed his beard free of the crumbs and reluctantly agreed. He wished his dad sweet dreams and they headed down the hall, Tommen to his room to kiss Becky goodbye, Walter to his room so he could get some sleep. Indeed, he was out as soon as his head hit the pillow.

He knew he slept poorly, and he woke up earlier than he wanted. But he knew he would not be able to get back to sleep, so might as well get up.

Becky was already gone to class, so he had the house to himself, as he usually did during the day. It had been kind of nice at first, but now he was kind of missing the company of his son and future daughter-in-law. The cat certainly didn't count, and they eyed each other suspiciously as they passed in the hall.

He showered and got a quick bite to eat, just enough to taste. He returned to his room just as his phone was ringing. It was Sheriff Williams.

"Hello?" Walter answered, trying to hide the sleep still lingering in his voice.

"Walter, glad I got a hold of you." The man sounded absolutely panicked but absolutely resolute at the same time. "Get your ass down to the station and grab a car."

"Wait, what? What's going on?"

"Got calls for a school shooting at South Charleston High. Multiple calls, most of them frightened students, and social media is being flooded with some wild videos. Some shit's going on down there, Walt. I've already called in state boys and City PD for backup and some of the surrounding counties. We need all the manpower we can get."

Walter hardly heard him. He didn't really hear anything past "school shooting at South Charleston High." That was Tommen's school. Tommen was in school right now. Tommen was in the same building as a dangerous gunman. Something bad, something very, very bad, something deadly was going on right now at Tommen's school while Tommen was there.

"Walter? Walter!"

"Um, y-yeah, what did I miss?" Walter asked dumbly.

The sheriff sighed. "I know what you're thinking, Walter. I know it's your kid's school. If I didn't have to call you, I wouldn't, at least not now, and certainly not in this capacity. But we need help. Can you do it? You're not going to be on entry."

That brought him back around a little bit. "No, yeah, I understand. That's fine. I'll be there for whatever you need."

"Good man. You're not the only officer with kids there. I don't want any of you getting ideas. Understand?"

"Yes, sir."

"Good. Get down to the station, grab a car, and head that way. When you get there, report directly to Gonzales and he'll tell you where to go."

"Understood."

Click.

It was a full minute before Walter moved, and the first thing he did was look at his phone. There were a few texts from Tommen, and the last one was, "I love you, Dad. Make sure Becky knows I love her, too. And the baby."

Emotion and resolve warred for dominance in Walter's mind, similar to how he felt going into the warehouse. Like a mother bear protecting her cub. Something threatened the cub, and now that thing had to die. Furthermore, his son was going to have a child, and Walter would be damned before he let that child grow up fatherless.

He wouldn't say the clouds completely cleared from his head, because they didn't. He was still very emotional. But he forced himself to put it aside and focus on the task at hand. He could stand here and worry, or he could get his ass down to the station, grab a car, and haul ass to the school.

Walter sped the whole way to the station, on top of Banding, and he didn't care who saw. He wasn't even worried if someone called it in. All police presence would be diverted to the school right now, and no sane officer who wanted to keep his job or have any hope of promotion or recommendation would pull him over for any reason right now.

He arrived at the station just behind Kate. She grabbed a set of keys and tossed a second set to him. Neither said a word as they snagged a couple vests before heading out to the garage and grabbed the last two cars.

Lights and sirens and diesel therapy got them all the way to the high school, but a little creative Banding got Walter to the school five minutes before Kate. Under any other circumstances, she might have made some teasing comment about high-speed pursuits, but there was no room for humor right now. Once they crossed the threshold, slowing down as they passed the ambulances on standby and sneaking around the fire trucks blocking every road in a one-mile radius, there was only the job at hand.

An officer from another county directed them where to park and told them the location of the command post. Walter parked as quickly as possible and hurried to find Gonzales.

Captain Gonzales was at said command post, on the south side of the school, a pop-up canopy where City Chief Casey Oldman, County Sheriff Williams, and several others stood around looking serious and directing people here and there. Principal Orville Layman was also with them, providing as much information as possible: where were the students at the time, what special activities were going on, where would they have most likely gone for shelter? Because the shooting had started during lunchtime, everything was up in the air, and Walter suspected the perpetrator had planned it that way.

"Captain," Walter began formally.

Gonzales turned. "Officer Forbes, glad you could make it."

"I wouldn't miss this."

"I don't suppose you've heard anything from your son?"

Walter elected not to mention the heart-wrenching last goodbye style text. "No. He hasn't told me anything."

Gonzales frowned, but reflective sunglasses obscured half his expression. "Probably just as well then."

"Where would you like me, sir?"

"I want you over there with Lieutenant Warner overseeing Internal Team Two."

The captain directed Walter to another area on the east side. Cruisers were situated to form a protective barrier while a team of men in heavy armor with equally heavy weaponry awaited orders.

Lieutenant Warner actually worked for the city department these days, but did eight years with county, so he had an idea of how both departments operated. He had been one of the souls unfortunate enough to try and stay neutral during the hostile takeover at city when Walter was fired, but he appeared no worse for wear now. He waited only a few steps away from the team, speaking to a sergeant who appeared to be the master of the radios for the team.

"Lieutenant," Walter greeted formally, walking purposefully toward them but not injecting himself into the conversation.

"Cap—Officer Forbes," Warner said. "What is it?"

"Gonzales sent me to you."

"Good." He looked at the sergeant and held out a hand. "Go see to Ricardo."

The sergeant relinquished one of his radios and hurried off to find Lieutenant Ricardo.

Warner handed the radio to Walter. "I want you to be my relay between us and Winston while I coordinate with the other team leaders. We've got a team on the west side of the building, two on the north, and one ready to go on the south if need be, form a barrier for the command post until they can get to better cover."

"What's the situation?"

"Shooter sprung on them during lunch. Layman said that they were all heading for nearby classrooms, which means a majority of the students should be in the east wing, north side. No word on the shooters, description, number, whereabouts, nothing. We're dealing with a ghost right now."

"Any report on injuries?"

"School nurse is still inside the building. She and the teachers have been in contact with Layman somewhat. At least nine critically injured, dozens more with all sorts of lesser wounds."

Walter nodded and let out a breath. "What are our orders?"

"Perimeter team is verifying that we're secure and they're going to be our objective eyes in the sky. Our team is going to go internal from the east. One of the north teams will also go internal from the north. The second team will be going room to room getting the kids out of the classrooms and out to a safety area. The west team is going to be split into two and their whole job will be to head directly to the nurse's office and get the critically injured students out to the ambulances."

"How did the critically injured get to the nurse's office in the middle of the chaos?"

Warner shrugged helplessly. "No one knows. Or at least it's information I'm not privy to."

Walter knew instantly that Tommen had something to do with it. There was no other explanation for why students who had been critically injured would make it to the nurse's office, exactly where they would need to be in order to survive this chaos until help arrived. He felt a surge of pride in his son, and also fear that something could have happened to him while he was helping his classmates.

"Sergeant Bishop will be heading our internal team," Warner went on, pointing to the man. "Seven on the team including him."

Warner took Walter to the hood of one of the cruisers where a crude map had been drawn out on notebook paper. "They're going to be sweeping the cafeteria with North Team One in case any of the kids decided to hide there, and these hallways." Each one had a different label. "Initial mission will be solely to find the shooter if he is still active in the halls or any of the classrooms. Then they'll return. Once North Team Two has cleared the students out of the north classrooms, they will come around to the east rooms. Our guys will go back in while they clear these classrooms. North Team One will then assist West Teams One and Two in evacuating the west classrooms. Once that's done, one of the teams will evacuate the south classrooms while everyone else sweeps the school in full force, looking for the shooter, assuming he or they haven't been found yet."

Just running a few quick numbers in his head, that meant that there were upwards of fifty officers, maybe closer to seventy-five, running around here. The entire city department only had a handful over a hundred sworn officers. Williams had said he'd called in help from state and surrounding counties. The only people not here were the National Guard, but they would be next on the list in the event something went horribly wrong. But the point was, they weren't half-assing this. They wanted to get this cleared up and wrapped up quick, before the media wolves could interfere.

A helicopter hovered overhead. Too late. Warner swore, then shook his head.

"Shit. Well, they're up there and we're down here. We need to stay focused on the task at hand and wait for the all clear from the perimeter team."

Walter glanced around the area, tried to get a feel for his surroundings even though he'd been to the school a number of times for various reasons, most of them parent-teacher conferences or meetings with Layman about Tommen's behavior. Standing here now was almost alien, a whole new environment he'd suddenly never seen before.

He could just see the south side where Sheriff Williams and Chief Oldman had their tent set up, and it looked like more areas were being sectioned off as designated zones for one thing or another. To the north, one of the north teams milled about, seemingly oblivious but more aware than most people would give them credit for, and they could turn in an instant. He could not see the west team.

Another team came into view on the south side, the leader speaking to Gonzales. Walter was too far away to make out any small gestures, and certainly too far to hear any conversation. He considered Banding and having a look around by himself, but he refrained. He needed to stay in the moment and focus on his task. He had to trust his fellows to get the job done and not run around freelancing. That was how good officers got killed. He wasn't the only one who wanted this nightmare to be over, but they had to be smart about it or else it could turn into something far worse than just a nightmare.

Still, it wasn't easy. Walter wanted nothing more than to barge into the school, grab his son and take him home to his fiancée and unborn child. If nothing else went right, that was Walter's goal, to ensure his grandchild had a father.

"All teams, give me a radio check," Williams said over

Warner's radio.

Warner nodded to Walter who checked his radio with Bishop's. Both worked and communication appeared to be clear. Warner reported this back to the sheriff. As the rest of the teams checked in, Walter felt his phone vibrate in his pocket. He ignored it. It vibrated a second and third time in rapid succession. Gritting his teeth, he Banded and dug for his phone, desperate to see if it was Tommen. The first text was.

"Dad, are you here?"

Walter wanted to reply and hold a conversation, but he would have to Band every time he got his phone out, and he didn't want to be that distracted. At the very least, it let him know his son was alive, which was enough to calm his nerves just a little.

The second and third texts were from Nathan.

"Walt, I'm with the twins and Kayla. We're all right for now, but that could very well change in an instant. Julianna is targeting those with Authored Books, and we have reason to believe that she will try to hit everyone at once. We're going to go into deep hiding beyond the range of cell phones, but we will do our best to make contact as soon as possible to let you know we're all right. Keep an eye out for anything strange."

If only you knew, Walter thought grimly. He purposely ignored the text, put his phone away, and dropped his Band. Life resumed, though it was not resolving the situation any faster. At the very least, he knew Tommen was alive. Now to get him and the rest of the students out of the school.

Of course, the idea that this was far worse than the average school shooter, that this could be a targeted hit against Tommen by Julianna just made it all the more frustrating. Walter looked around at the dozens of men and women preparing for anything. Was this going to turn into another warehouse situation?

That was the other reason for the extra manpower, Walter realized. It had little to do with the media and everything to do with preventing another catastrophe. Except this time, there wasn't just one or two hostages, but hundreds of potential hostages.

"Team leaders, prepare for entry," Williams squawked on the radio.

Warner relayed the order and Walter watched as every man on the team shifted deliberately, adjusting armor, cracking necks, feeling up their guns. They were ready to go. Wanted to go. Nobody pulled this shit in their town and got away with it. Walter decided he felt better about the display of force and forced himself to relax, just a little. *Trust the teams and don't interfere unless you have to. Don't make things worse by trying to play the hero.*

"North Team One, are you ready?"

"Ready, sir."

"North Team Two, are you ready?"

"Affirmative."

"Prepare for entry..." Long pause. "You may enter when ready. East Team, are you ready?"

"Affirmative, sir," Warner responded at a nod from Bishop.

"Prepare for entry. West Team One, are you ready?"

"Yes, sir, ready," came the reply.

"West Team Two, are you ready?"

"Ready."

"You are clear for entry."

There was a pause.

Then, "Captain Amon, have you notified the ambulances of the situation?"

"Affirmative. They understand what's going on and they are prepared."

"You have teams ready to cover them if necessary?"

"That is affirmative."

"Very good."

"Command, we have twenty-four students and eight staff members exiting from the cafeteria," someone interrupted.

"Good work," Williams commended with an obviously stifled sigh of relief. "Escort them to triage."

Walter watched as East Team paused outside a door for just a moment before breaking in and moving with purpose, vanishing into the school.

A minute later, Walter saw the students and staff appear around the building, hands on their heads, looking as though they wanted nothing more than to simply make a run for it. But they refrained and were safely escorted to a designated zone on the south side of the building near the command post. He did not see Tommen among them.

"Tokyo Hall is clear," Bishop reported.

Walter relayed the information to Warner who went to the crude map and crossed out one of the halls. One by one, the east halls were clear: Tokyo, Beijing, Singapore, Delhi, Kathmandu. Through Warner's radio, Walter kept tabs on all the classrooms as North Team Two evacuated the students. Every so often, he glanced in the direction of the triage area, seeing if he could spot Tommen, but the zone filled up quickly and he couldn't make out one from another.

"Forty-three students and three staff coming out," the North Team leader announced. "And you can tell Sergeant O'Donnell her daughter is safe."

Walter could only imagine the relief the sergeant felt, if only because he was waiting for similar news.

Meanwhile, West Team Two had successfully extracted the critically injured students and were rushing them to the ambulances, tossing them in the back and getting the buses clear of the area before any sneaky shooters could fire at them. The ambulances didn't even run lights and sirens until they were out of the barricaded area past the fire trucks.

With their hallways reportedly clear, East Team returned. If Walter had to describe their demeanor, he might have said it was relieved that nothing bad had happened, but a little frustrated that it wasn't over yet.

"All north classrooms have been cleared," the radio said.

"Copy that," Williams acknowledged. "Pull back and prepare

to sweep the east rooms."

"Affirmative."

As they waited for further instructions, several people pulling small wagons approached them. They, too, wore vests, but they were not officers. Their wagons were full of cheese, crackers, beef jerky, cookies, bottled water, and the ever present coffee. In fact, there was probably more coffee than food. Walter took a cup, as well as a handful of snacks and a cookie. It was just nervous hunger, he knew, but he couldn't help it. He needed to eat and take his mind off the whole thing for even just a split second. The internal team, probably sweating in their heavy gear, were arguably the most grateful for the sustenance as they chomped down on jerky and cheese and guzzled the bottled water.

"East Team, are you ready?" Williams asked.

Bottles were dropped in favor of rifles and Warner gave the affirmative.

"North Team Two, are you in position?"

The extraction team was about ten paces north of them, and they did not look happy about having to pass up the snack wagon before going inside again. Nevertheless, they also gave the affirmative.

"Prepare for entry."

The next few seconds stretched on for at least an eternity, and Walter wanted to claw his eyes out.

Then, "Clear to enter."

Again, East Team entered the building while North Team Two began methodically going from room to room, opening windows and getting kids outside. From his vantage, Walter could see that most were in shock, faces white, eyes huge. Some had been crying. One had obviously wet himself. They all looked hot, dirty, exhausted, and ready to go home. Most weren't prepared for the chilly weather outside and Walter found himself hoping that there were blankets available in the triage area.

"Thinking about your son?" Warner asked.

Walter just nodded.

"Is he graduated yet? I don't remember."

"No, he's a senior this year. Graduating early, in fact. He's starting college in the spring."

"Good for him. Still a science geek?"

"He's good at it, but I think he's a little less sure of himself now. He might just be going for a general degree the first time around. He's already got a lot on his plate." Walter shook his head. "He's going to be a dad come March."

Warner shifted his stance and gave Walter a look. "You're shittin' me."

"Not even a little."

The lieutenant cursed, but he was grinning. "Well, tell him I said congratulations."

Walter took an even breath. "You can tell him yourself here soon, hopefully."

That cut the conversation short as they each took a self-conscious drink from their coffee cups. North Team Two continued to call out the students and staff as they were evacuated, once mentioning that Officer Michaels' daughter was safe and sound as well. Now all they had to do was mention that Officer Forbes' son was alive and well and then they could get moving, Walter thought sourly.

Still no sign of the shooter or shooters, though the actual gunfire had stopped. Walter hadn't heard anything regarding a description or any sort of pursuit. In all likelihood, then, the shooter or shooters were students. Start the shooting, scatter the herd, pick a few off. Then toss the guns and blend in with everyone else. Duck into a classroom, get evacuated with the rest of them, maybe go to the hospital for some self-inflicted wounds, and slip away. Say one thing for mass murderers, with the wealth of information on the Internet, they were getting smarter. Walter found it ironic that the ones who benefited the most from the endless archives of human knowledge were the ones who would seek to destroy humanity itself.

"West Team One, are you ready?" Williams called over the

radio.

"Yes, sir," someone answered.

"West Team Two, are you ready?"

"Negative, sir, we have a malfunctioning rifle."

"Copy that, Captain Furio will bring a replacement. Are you ready otherwise?"

"Affirmative, Sheriff."

"North Team Two, what is your status?"

"Four rooms to go, sir," was the report.

"Keep up the good work. West Team Two, has Captain Furio reached you yet?"

"Yes, sir, he just arrived. Rifles have been swapped and we are ready to go."

"Very good. West Teams One and Two, you are clear for entry. North Team Two, when you're finished on your side, you are clear for entry on the south side. When you're finished, hold position in the south hallways. North Team One, I want you to move internal and hold position in the north hallways. East Team, continue to cover for North Team Two. Once North Team Two has evacuated the classrooms, hold in the east hallways. West Team One, when you are finished, hold position in the west hallways. West Team Two, I want you to sweep the entire school, open every door everywhere, even the lockers and the bathroom stalls."

So the gunman still hadn't been located, Walter thought.

Everyone babbled their affirmatives and the radios went silent again.

Something wasn't right here, Walter knew, more than just the gunman being generally elusive. He was being more elusive than a shooter had a right to be. Some wanted to go down in a blaze of glory, but that obviously wasn't happening right now. It could still happen, but the dramatic timing seemed to be way off. Other shooters wanted to try to get away with it, which would involve hiding among the students, his peers, and being rescued with the rest of them. That was certainly a possibility. Still other shooters committed suicide, though no bodies had been found in such a manner.

Add Time into the mix and a whole realm of new possibilities opened up, possibilities which Walter did not want to consider though he knew he might have to.

Nathan said that Julianna was probably launching an attack against those with Authored Books. But she wasn't the only one out there. What if this came from the Time industry, the Tacagans flexing their muscles a little and going after anyone who wasn't strictly Time? What if this was the Borelians, going after Tommen who just kept undermining and thwarting them at every turn, to say nothing of his association with Rifun and the Miaramila? This war had more than two sides, and when multiple factions got involved, the potential for catastrophe increased proportionally.

Walter didn't want to think about any of this, but with memories of the warehouse flashing through his mind, he couldn't help but get a little anxious. For the first time in a long time, he felt pain in his three scars, where Rifun had shot him.

North Team One got in position in the school, holding the north hallways. North Team Two declared the east classrooms clear. East Team took up their position in those hallways, the different members of the team calling out their positions to Walter who relayed them to Warner who marked them on the map. North Team Two moved to the south side of the building and began their evacuations.

West Team One called out another classroom full of students and faculty heading to triage.

Walter grew anxious. They didn't have too many classrooms left. Where was Tommen? Surely they would have called him out, the same as they had for the other officers who had kids in the school. Tommen had texted him earlier, and there had been no evidence of gunfire or other mischief in the school. What was going on? Was he hiding in the very last room the teams were going to check? Maybe he'd hidden in one of the bathrooms. Maybe he'd Banded and seen himself out, which would be why no one had called him out. Maybe the teams just didn't know who he was, what he looked like. That was unlikely, Walter thought, but none of the city boys knew he'd grown out his beard.

He let out a breath, told himself to be calm. He had to stay in the moment and do his assigned duty, look out for his brothers in blue, no matter if they came from state, city, county, or somewhere else entirely.

"Fifty-one students and two staff heading to triage," one of the team leaders announced. "And you can inform Officer Forbes that his son is alive and well."

Walter stumbled back a step and almost went backwards if not for Warner grabbing hold of him. He just wanted to melt with relief. As it was, the best he could do was lean against the cruiser and try to breathe.

"Thank God," he breathed. "Oh, thank God."

"See?" Warner said, patting his shoulder. "Everything is going to turn out just fine."

"Oh, thank God," Walter repeated.

Blindly, he accepted a bottle of water and finished it off in a couple swigs. Everything came back into focus and he stepped away from the car.

"He's all right," Warner told him. "Your son is just fine. Now how are you?"

"A lot better, sir," Walter answered.

The lieutenant grinned and shook his head. "Don't 'sir' me. I chased your chevrons for years at city."

"Be that as it may, you're still in command for this team's operation and I answer to you. That said, permission to ditch my post and check on my son?"

"As much as I want to say yes, hold that thought for just a second. I think we're about to wrap this up." The lieutenant looked around the area.

Walter's heart sank but he nodded. "Understood."

About five seconds later, Warner made a sound and turned to look at him. "All right. Make it quick. Go there, see that he's all right, then come back. Got it?"

"Understood."

Walter handed over his radio, turned, and headed south to the staging area. He knew why Warner had changed his mind. Officers in good spirits worked better than ones concerned about other problems. By allowing Walter a short reprieve to check on his son, he was giving him a chance to see that all was well at home, and refocus his attention on the situation, that is, they still had a gunman on the loose.

The chaos only grew as he neared the south side. Multiple zones had been marked out here and there. One looked like a simple information area. As the students arrived from wherever they'd been rescued, Layman checked them off a list so they would know who they had and who was still missing. Injured students were separated and sent to another area where they were triaged and waiting for appropriate medical treatment. For some, this was a simple remedy that could be administered by a medically-trained officer. Others had to wait for the next available ambulance.

Students who weren't injured were sent to another area, this one heavily guarded by more officers, most of them the guys from the surrounding counties. Maybe they didn't understand Kanawha County or Charleston City PD or State Police protocols, but they could defend a bunch of school kids.

Walter went to Layman first, once the next batch of students had gone through.

"Officer Forbes," Layman greeted wistfully. It was the first time Walter had ever seen the man appear anything less than confident and in control. Maybe because he had no control over this situation. He had a school full of people to look after, and now a gunman threatened his haven of education, safety, and security.

"Has Tommen come through yet?" Walter demanded, maybe a little more harshly than he intended.

"Yeah, I saw him a minute or two ago," the principal answered, his posture clearly reverted back to whatever the Marines had instilled in him. "He got sent to the main zone there."

Layman pointed to the largest marked area, for uninjured students. Walter breathed a sigh of relief, even as he knew he wouldn't rest until he saw his son for himself. He thanked Layman and made a beeline for the zone.

"Officer Forbes, Kanawha County," Walter said, approaching one of the officers guarding the students. "I need to see one of the students."

The man said nothing and gave Walter no trouble as he stood aside. He stepped inside the perimeter, into the throng of students, and looked around. Tommen was a hair over six foot and had put on a lot of muscle since working construction. Pale as death and normally easy to spot, it did Walter no good seeing how his son was among a thousand of his peers. Time to start asking.

Or maybe not, Walter thought, as he thought he caught a glimpse of thick brown hair and a grizzled beard. Walter was surprised Tommen hadn't been taken aside for questioning by some of the officers who didn't know him; his beard made him look older, like he ought to have already graduated from college.

"Tommen!" Walter barked, pushing through the masses.

To his surprise, his son heard him, but was still unprepared for the hug. Walter couldn't help himself, really. He was too grateful to see his son alive and well to not show some affection. His vest made it a little difficult, but at least he was able to reassure himself that his son was real and really standing there.

"Oh, God, I'm so happy you're all right," Walter said, telling himself that relief was appropriate, but becoming overly emotional was not. "Did you call Becky yet?"

"I just did. She's taking finals, though, so it just went to voicemail."

"Well, at least you told her. Does she know anything?"

"Yeah, she texted me about it. I told her I'm fine. Dad, what's going on? And you know what I mean."

Walter let out a breath and Banded the two of them. "Nathan

texted me a little bit ago while I was sleeping, said that there was some trouble up where the twins are hiding. He didn't give any specifics other than it seems to be a coordinated attack by Julianna against those with Authored Books. He said that they were going to have to go into some deep hiding where cell phones don't work."

Tommen shook his head and folded his arms. "Shit. How many do you think we're looking at? If this is part of that coordinated attack, and if I'm the intended target..." He looked around. "I'm standing in a huge crowd of students right now."

"I know. Believe me, I do. I wish I had a good answer. Right now, we don't even know who they are, or even how many we're dealing with. If this is a murder squad sent by Julianna...whoever it is has the advantage and we may be playing by their rules for a bit. But the important thing is, you're safe where I can see you, and you're not exactly a lightweight yourself anymore."

"Great. So what do we do?"

He dropped the Band. "I don't know. We wait for orders. It's all we can do."

It was not the answer either of them wanted. It was not the answer anyone wanted. Human beings were not good at the waiting game, especially when it involved their lives or uncertainty that could very easily end in death. Human beings were quite adverse to death and pain, more so when they went together. No one wanted to suffer when they went, no one wanted to die in agony, and no one wanted to watch other people suffer and die in agony either. Well, mostly. In some cases, it brought out the best in people as humanity came together in friendships forged in fire and blood. In other cases, it only served to sow fear and panic as they were forced to wait and see how this drama played out, completely powerless to influence events.

His dread assuaged and his heart rate back to about normal, Walter returned to his post. All the holding teams remained in position, though from the chatter on Warner's radio, it sounded like there was some disagreement in management over whether to pull them out. Having them standing around like fish in a barrel wasn't good if they weren't turning up anything, and if the shooter was among the students, then they needed to have backup on hand in case things got ugly. Else they were just standing around looking heroic but accomplishing nothing.

"How's your boy?" Warner asked, handing the radio back.

"A little shaken," Walter answered, clipping the mic back in place. "But he called his fiancée to let her know he was okay. He just kind of wants to go home right now."

Walter did not know if that was true, whether Tommen wanted to go home. He imagined so. Really it was him that was ready to go home right now. Go home, take a long nap for the rest of the day, all night, and back around until he had to get up for work the next night. How many months until retirement? Seven? Eight? Too many in his opinion.

"I can understand that," Warner said, nodding. "I kind of feel like that myself." He listened in on his radio. "Sounds like they're getting ready to have the internal teams pull out."

"So the shooter is one of the students," Walter murmured.

"Looking that way. Question then becomes, which one?"

"Well, we only have a thousand or more to choose from. I think we can rule out the dead ones."

"No kidding. What about the cameras?"

"They'd have to put a detail on Layman to escort him into the building."

Even as he said it, there was some squawking on the radio, and it sounded like they were getting ready to do just that. Layman would have his own personal detail surrounding him more closely than Secret Service on the president, in addition to a full tunnel-like security wall formed by the teams as they exited the school. The teams leaving the school would form up around the waiting students, not with guns actively pointed, but if there was a killer hiding among them, there was no telling what more weapons he could have on him. Start shooting from the inside, there would be utter chaos as the students tried to run away and the officers tried to get in, not willing to fire into an unarmed fleeing crowd.

The thought of such a horrendous situation made Walter feel ill as he considered that his son may have actually gone directly into the line of fire, just by everyone doing exactly as they were supposed to.

Massive lies, built using only the truth. Everything going horribly wrong just for the fact that everything went perfectly right.

The rock of dread returned, settling uncomfortably in his gut. He didn't like this. Just taking the situation at face value, it was quiet. Too quiet. If he hadn't seen the wounded students for himself, he might have thought this just a very elaborate, hyper-realistic drill. He might have even been able to buy that story—and he and about a hundred other officers would have been absolutely pissed—except for the social media aspect of it. The students were the ones to watch. If it were a drill, they would complain about it being a drill. And they would have to know it was a drill because no one wanted to have this plastered on the news only to discover it was a set-up all along. You want to talk about bad press, that's how you make bad press. That would be one sure fire way to ensure Principal Layman, Chief Oldman, and Sheriff Williams all lost their jobs instantly.

More chatter on the radios as Layman's security detail prepared to go inside. Interior teams reported a secure avenue, enter when ready. There was probably more back and forth on the team radios, everyone making sure everyone else was ready. Then came the report that the team was entering, package secure.

It was like a military operation, Walter reflected, a team of highly-trained, highly-skilled special forces dispatched to deliver a highly-controversial political speaker safely to the extraction zone so he could be taken to a military base before being flown to wherever it was he needed to go.

Welcome to America, Walter thought sourly.

Package delivered, safe and sound, came the report.

It shouldn't take long to get to the appropriate camera at the appropriate time, Walter figured. He recalled a couple years ago when Tommen had found the woman's body under the bleachers. Layman had shown him how to look through the camera footage. Only because of Walter's lack of talent with technology did it take as long as it did to find what he needed. With the man himself zipping through footage, they ought to have their shooter or shooters identified fairly quickly.

As the interior teams pulled out and returned to their original positions, the rehab wagons came around again. Just running a few numbers in his head, they were going through dozens of cases of water, and God knew how many pounds of coffee.

An odd thing to think about, Walter mused, accepting a bottle of water and a package of cheap cheese and crackers. He wasn't really hungry, just anxious. He might have devoured more if he hadn't known Tommen had gotten out and was safe. How safe, however, was still a bit vague, and would be, until they knew the identity of the shooter and had him in custody.

Time ticked by in agonizing seconds, everyone waiting for something to happen. What was taking so long? Walter had heard no shots fired and nothing was coming over the radios. Maybe it was just his heightened perception of time, but he was about to go insane. Looking around, the rest of the guys seemed to have the same idea.

Then the radio chirped, squawked with some static, and then voices came through. Package is safely outside the building once more. Teams prepare for another sweep of the school, looking for two suspects. Suspect one is about six-foot-one, wearing black pants, black shirt, black coat, brown hair, clean-shaven, armed with a rifle. Suspect two is maybe five-eleven, wearing brown pants, a black shirt, a long brown coat, blond hair, and a blond beard, also armed with a rifle.

Two suspects, then, Walter thought. Well, it was a start. At least they had something to go after, or rather, someone. More orders were given, and the teams were again dispatched into the building. Walter manned the radios with a fervent desire to wrap this up.

The hallways and various classrooms were again investigated thoroughly, every cupboard opened, every table overturned. And again, reports came back negative. At first, this didn't bother Walter too much. It was a big school after all. But the reports kept coming in. Clear. Empty. No sign. Nothing. Moving on. He could see the irritation on Lieutenant Warner's face as well. They had to find the shooters. If they didn't, there was really only one more place to look for them. Among the students.

Nothing was found anywhere in the school, and the teams filtered back out, frustrated, looking for blood but finding none. This had gone from an intense rescue and engage operation to a game of cat and mouse, and no one was pleased about it. Walter was especially anxious. Any Timekeeper who had any idea how to control his Bands, even a half-trained probationary, could keep this game going for hours. Walter could handle a probie, but what if this really was one of Julianna's goons? How did he fight against something he'd long believed a myth?

The last of the teams returned to their positions. Williams came over the radio.

"Sandwich Team, prepare to search the students." He kept his voice low and neutral.

Sandwich Team had started as a bit of a joke that turned into something serious. If someone needed to ask for something discreetly —that is, law enforcement intervention—then he asked for a sandwich. On the force, Sandwich Team was reserved for those tasked specifically with protecting innocent bystanders.

"Perimeter Team, we're going to start locking things up here," the sheriff went on.

"Copy that," the perimeter guys confirmed.

"Copy, Sheriff, we'll begin searching," the Sandwich Team leader affirmed.

"Oh, that won't be necessary."

The new voice came from the south, over a megaphone, like the ones the fire trucks might carry. In fact, Walter wouldn't be surprised to learn that it was one of those very same megaphones. Might have been that they simply Banded and stole one of them to make themselves heard.

Walter could not see what was going on, but he did know the sound of gunfire. Harmless fire into the air if he judged correctly, and from the lack of panic and return fire.

"Now then, where is Tommen Forbes?" one of the suspects inquired. "Bring him forward."

"I need to go," Walter blurted out, fussing with the radio to hand it back to Warner.

The lieutenant grabbed him by the shoulders and held him fast. "No. You can't just go running over there. You don't know what's going on, and you can't just run out there like a neon target. For all you know, you're an intended target as well and they're just trying to get to you. Do you understand me, Walter?"

He took a breath and forced himself to relax. "I know. I understand. But—"

"Your son has already had to watch you die once. Don't make him go through that again. And that's an order. Wait. For now, play it safe. Play it cautious. Until we receive orders otherwise. Got it?"

Reluctantly, Walter nodded. "Got it."

"Good. Now stay here where I can see you. If you want, give me your radio."

He surrendered the radio and forced himself to stay put. He wanted to be over there. He wanted to see and know what was going on.

"Where is Walter Forbes?" the man with the megaphone screeched. "Is he here today? Why don't you come and chat with us, too?"

Not two seconds later, Williams was on the radio. "Officer Forbes, please come to the south side of the building."

"Roger that," Warner replied. "He's coming." He looked at Walter. "You take care of yourself. And your son. Think logically, and don't give in to emotion, whatever the situation."

Walter nodded and made his way around to the south side of the building. Memories of the warehouse flickered through his mind, seeing his son held hostage with a gun to his head. All hell breaking loose as vanilla humans engaged bona fide aliens they could not even hope to comprehend. Braving the dark to pursue a madman and rescue his son.

Facing down the barrel of a gun and feeling the pain of bullets tearing through his flesh.

But when he reached the south side, he found none of that. The Sandwich Team had been reinforced to protect the student body who appeared to be subtly siphoning out of danger one at a time. Only Tommen stood out, and he was on the right side of things this time. He was not held hostage, and there was no gun to his head.

It was the men he faced who gave Walter pause. Tyler Freeman he knew well. He was the suspect who was six-foot-one, wearing all black, brown hair, clean face, ready with a rifle.

The second suspect was a shock, but not a surprise. Five-eleven, blond hair, blond beard, rifle in one hand, megaphone in the other. Ryan Henderson, the boy Walter had fostered for eight months. The one he'd failed.

Ryan got on the megaphone again, grinning. "There he is. Hello, Dad."

Chapter Thirteen
Trifecta

The last time Tommen had seen Ryan, he'd only been about ten years old, Ryan fifteen or sixteen. Tommen lived in fear of his Foster Brother from Hell, yet they had no choice but to share a room. He'd come home from school one day to find Ryan packing a suitcase while simultaneously destroying everything else in the room, indeed, the whole house. Tommen hid outside for a little while, not returning until his dad got home and could intervene if necessary.

Ryan had ignored Walter for most of the evening, and only started yelling right before he left, when the social worker showed up. Walter had remained calm and did not yell in reply. Tommen remembered his dad sounding exhausted. Looking back, he would add regretful into that mix as well. His dad didn't want to give up on Ryan. He never wanted to simply pass him off to some other family, like taking a dog back to the pound. But he had to consider the safety of the son he already had. Ryan needed more than what Walter could offer as a single dad.

Clearly, he hadn't gotten it.

Ryan was six years older than Tommen, which would presently put him about twenty-four years old. He'd certainly grown into his manhood, finally shedding his baby looks and growing a beard in their place. His hair was not so much blond as it was straight yellow, and that was its natural color. His beard was the same way, though it looked white in a certain light. He'd often bragged about his state titles in jiu jitsu, and other accomplishments in various martial arts, and it didn't look as though he'd given any of them up. He looked like he could probably teach them now, as he had a lean, muscular build.

But there was a certain fire in his eyes that had remained the same. It was the drive to conquer, to dominate, to assert his place as the alpha male in any given situation. Tommen had seen this fire plenty of times and was usually on the receiving end of that desire to conquer.

As for Tyler Freeman, Tommen had always had a sneaking suspicion that merely parting ways because of graduation or expulsion was too good to be true. He'd always known there was something more in store for them, even as he told himself to not be so silly. That sort of thing was reserved for Hollywood dramas and...well, books. Maybe even Books. Had this all been orchestrated by the Author?

There was no way anyone in Time would know who these two were and their relationship to him, and both of them merely stumbling upon these abilities and then showing up here was far too coincidental. Anyone in Time who took the time to do that kind of research on one meager human had way too much time on their hands and needed a hobby. At the same time, a certain someone, a certain bitch with a serious bone to pick, might take a little time to craft such a scheme.

So then, where did that feasibly put their abilities? Julianna had been released from the in-between dimension only a year or so ago, and her treachery against Rifun's Order was barely nine months ago. Tyler Freeman had been out of school for a couple years now, so he was an Apprentice at the most, or the equivalent of an Apprentice. Without knowing what Ryan had been up to in the last roughly seven or eight years, he could be anywhere from a probationary to a Master, or whatever Julianna was calling her minions these days; Tommen doubted she'd stuck with vaovao, ambony, and the like.

Meanwhile, his Akari abilities were stunted at best, having received little formal instruction. Sure, he'd learned quite a bit under Berkloff and plenty from Nathan, but his training only amounted to...a year? Maybe a little more, if he wanted to count his haphazard introduction at the wildfire and that whole debacle with the in-between dimension.

Point being, he highly doubted that, if Tyler and Ryan were working for Julianna now, she would send them in untrained. She would learn from Rifun's mistakes at the warehouse and work to improve the odds for her lackeys. At the same time, he'd never run into these two while he was with the Order, and he was certain he would not have gone unnoticed, not with his intergalactic celebrity.

What a bitch, Tommen found himself thinking. What a royal bitch. Didn't she have anything better to do? Fine, so she was working on eradicating an enemy, as any evil dictator would. It was one thing when it was a clash of armies or else a metaphorical chess game with spies and cunning and espionage and double-crossing and whatnot. But he was in high school for God's sake. He was in high school, preparing for final exams, looking forward to college, getting ready to be a dad. Why go through all this trouble to take out one person who wasn't even much of a threat in the first place, who wasn't really trying to defy her and the Order, who, from the beginning, had never really wanted to be part of this whole ridiculous scheme?

Was it just a power trip of some form? Did she really hold that kind of a grudge against him? Well, considering what had happened at the coup, where she deposed Rifun, he might see how she could be a little sore. But all the same, of all the ways she could have had him taken out or otherwise threatened—going back to that whole bit about being a dad soon—why pick this way?

Or maybe she'd merely given Tyler and Ryan the ends and they got to pick the means. School shootings were all the rage these days, and with their long history of bad blood with Tommen, it would certainly be one to remember on all sides.

All of this passed through Tommen's mind in about the space of ten seconds. Ten seconds of tense, dead silence, as everyone processed the situation and sized it up, making their determinations for the next course of action. They'd been searching for these bastards all afternoon and now here they were. They had no hostages, but neither did it appear that they were totally surrendering. So then, what was going on?

Ryan answered the question soon enough, raising the megaphone to his mouth and asking, "Now then, where is Tommen Forbes? Send him forward."

"Hold position," Sheriff Williams barked over the radio.

"Sir, I have Tommen Forbes here," one of the officers said, not moving his head but casting a glance at Tommen sideways from behind reflective sunglasses.

"We're waiting," Ryan said. "I know he's here."

"I want every barrel pointed at these bastards," Williams growled. "If those two lower their rifles one iota toward him, turn them into Swiss cheese."

This was met with satisfied grumbles of assent, even eagerness. Probably most of the guys here would be happy to turn Ryan and Tyler into Swiss cheese with no pretext other than this horror unfolding before their eyes.

Gingerly, Tommen stepped out of the safety pen of students, an armed officer on either side of him, the rest of the officers cocked and loaded, and that wasn't even talking about their guns. Ryan grinned and lowered the megaphone, making sure to do it slowly so as not to spook the officers. Tommen stopped when there was about ten or twelve feet between them.

"Hello, Tommen," Ryan said. "Remember me?"

"How could I forget, Ryan?" Tommen answered. "I see you haven't made much of yourself."

And that was when his Foster Brother from Hell tipped his hand just a little, erecting an Akari Fast Band around him, Tyler, and Tommen. Tommen quickly recognized it as a Force Band, taught by Julianna and her cronies. While lighter and more airy than a regular Time Band, it was still distinct from the Faith Band that Tommen used.

"You were really holding out on us, Tommen," Tyler said. "Maybe you really were as chivalrous as you claimed to be, never

Banding in all the fights we ever had. How many years did I kick your ass? And you refused to use your power because..." He shrugged. "Of some moral code that you ascribe to?"

"Oh, but that can't be right," Ryan continued, smirking. "Chivalry involves honor and nobility toward fair maidens, protecting their honor and chastity. How can he be chivalrous if he's fathered a child out of wedlock?"

It wasn't exactly a secret, but it still bothered and even alarmed Tommen that they knew. Was there someone going after Becky even now? Was that why she hadn't replied to his texts, not because of finals but because of...? He forced himself to not react, merely focused on his breathing and sizing them up, looking for any sign of weakness.

"He's done a little growing up, I think," Ryan observed, appearing mildly amused.

He dropped the Band and raised the megaphone, again moving slowly so he didn't end up as Swiss cheese. Although, considering he'd just demonstrated his ability to Band and, consequentially, dodge bullets, Tommen was forced to wonder why he was even worried. Neither of them had ever shown any aversion to violence or blood.

"Where is Walter Forbes?" the man wondered. "Is he here today? Why don't you come and chat with us, too?"

Tommen had never really understood the term "pregnant pause," nor when to use it appropriately. It had always weirded him out, that a pause could be pregnant. But now he was fairly certain he found a very appropriate use for the term as they waited for Walter to appear, which he did quickly.

Ryan spoke again into the megaphone. "There he is. Hello, Dad." Pause. "Please, won't you join us?"

Tommen dared to turn his head to look. Walter Forbes moved as a police officer doing his duty, not a normal man, a father who had faults and regrets and feelings of guilt. He wasn't perfect. He regretted taking Ryan on as if he thought he could change him. He felt guilty for not being able to. But for right now, he was here on scene, on duty, and there was a civilian in the hot zone. He went up to stand beside Tommen, if not a step in front. If the shit hit the fan, he would shove Tommen backwards into the other two officers to get him to safety, providing cover fire as necessary.

"It's been some time," Ryan greeted.

"A few years," Walter acknowledged stiffly.

"But nothing has really changed, has it?"

"It appears not."

Before either Ryan or Tyler could speak, Walter sucked the four of them into a Fast Band, one of the strongest he'd done in a long time, and it knocked even Tommen off balance a little.

"Why are you here, Ryan?" Walter asked. He did not speak as an officer demanding answers. Now he spoke as a man who felt he had failed as interim father and role model. "Why are you doing this?"

Ryan frowned even as his eyebrows went up and he shrugged. "Gainful employment. Isn't that something you always lectured me on? Working for the Order is steady, it pays well, and it has great perks and benefits."

Walter shook his head. "No. Not that. Why this?" He gestured to the spectacle they had created. "If your mission was seek and destroy, your targets myself and Tommen, why do all this?"

"That was my idea," Tyler said, rather proud of himself Tommen thought. "A year and a half ago, Ryan and I ended up in the same jail cell. We got talking, figured out our common—I wouldn't call him an enemy; he's not much of a threat. Mutual acquaintance." Tommen wasn't sure Tyler even knew what those big words meant. "We got out of jail and an agent from the Order approached us. And what a difference it's made. Ryan wanted to just go straight to your house, but I had a few other things I wanted to take care of here. This is what we came up with."

"Did Julianna order you to kill us?"

"And what if we say yes?" Ryan wondered. "How are you

going to stop us and make it believable? In a Band, we'll only appear to drop dead. And if we don't make any aggressive movement, or even if we surrender, you are legally obligated to take us into custody; you can't kill us out of spite."

"I don't want to kill you at all," Walter told them. "I will if you force my hand, but I would much rather avoid it. The problem is, I think we both know that you have a few more tricks up your sleeve than can be contained by mere walls. Everything you're doing right now is a show, an act."

"What is it that you want, anyway?" Tommen cut in. "Or what does Julianna want? Does she think I give a damn what's going on in the Order or Time or any of that anymore? I might keep up on the recent news, but I have other things to worry about, better things. I haven't wanted to be involved since I got started."

Ryan shrugged nonchalantly. "Oh, just a little housekeeping. Years of chaotic and disparate violence under Cassius; years of fretting, planning, worrying, and trying to make peace with the enemy under Rifun. It's time to be rid of it all. No more talks, no more negotiations, no more pretending that the universe is big enough for everyone and their stupid beliefs. Time to burn it down, starting with the heretics that started it all. And when you're taken care of, the news will spread, and the choice will come. Join or die."

So that was the reason for the spectacle. It would make national news and capture headlines while rumors would quietly circulate among those undecided Time Agents and other recruits that one of the victims had been a somewhat prominent Timekeeper and Akari-bearer. Behold the might of the First Order. No one is safe, and the perpetrators will get away with it. Coming soon to a town near you, that is, unless you swear your loyalty.

"And I know what you're going to say," Ryan went on, cutting into Tommen's thoughts. "Stop, there's a better way. Don't make the same mistakes I made." He gave Walter a look. "I know your story, Owain. And...my God, it really just made me hate you more."

"Let me guess: hypocrite?" Walter stated.

Ryan shifted his stance. "You know, it's not so much about all your actions and lectures and everything else, as it is that you never owned up to them. You never told. You hid them, hid from them, and pretended to preach from a clean pulpit."

Tommen half-expected his dad to be worn down by Ryan's words, so he was mildly surprised and a little pleased when Walter simply squared his shoulders and said, "Would it really have made any difference? If it's an apology you're looking for, then, yes, I'm sorry. I'm sorry I gave up on you and passed you off to the next family and the next and the next. I'm sorry you got a rotten hand in life. If there were a way to go back and change things, I'm sure we would both take it. But we can't, and it's no excuse for what you're doing here today."

"Pretty speech," Ryan said, apparently unmoved. "So what do you plan on doing with us now?"

"You're going into custody of some form, one way or another. Police custody would certainly satisfy justice and wrap things up here, but I don't know that it would hold you very long. Turning you over to the Grandfathers may be the only option, as loathe as I am to pursue it at the moment. But it may be the only way to contain you."

"Contain? You only wish to 'contain' us?"

"I would very much like for you to be rehabilitated into honest, productive members of society, but it has to be as much your choice as any form of punishment. Some have to be taken even to the point of death, as I was."

Now Ryan looked at Tommen, one brow raised. "You buy this bullshit?"

"Actually, I do," Tommen told him.

"I thought so. You always were a bit of a daddy's boy. Of course, it all makes sense now that I understand the big picture. As I said, you were really holding out on us."

"It was necessary," Walter said.

"Why? Because we're bad guys? Because we're evil? Who makes that determination, Walter? You? The Hands? The highest honor in one culture is the greatest blasphemy in another. Who decides who gets to have this gift? Who decides who gets to know about the bigger universe?"

"Not you," Tommen growled.

"I think everyone should decide for themselves," Ryan said, very matter-of-fact.

"As long as they decide in a way that you like," Walter finished. "Hence why we're here, because your employer wants everyone to side with her."

"Very good. Now we're getting somewhere. I love it when a plan comes together."

"What plan is that?"

"The one where you figure it all out, just before you lose."

Truthfully, Tommen hadn't really figured anything out, nor did his dad appear to have had any sort of revelation, but he did have a momentary flashback to the night he confronted Rifun and Cassius at the boat launch after following them from the museum. Rifun had made a grand display of not telling Tommen anything that way he had nothing to give the police. No information, no plans, nothing. It made him useless, but also not a liability.

Ryan and Tyler had never been the brightest bulbs in the box; they weren't smart enough to pull off schemes like that, eluding the authorities and making even eye witnesses all but useless. They could do the force, planning a school shooting and whatnot, but the underlying political maneuvering was not their forte. They probably wouldn't even know what that meant.

So either they were total morons who hadn't really planned this far ahead, once they actually got to the meeting with Tommen and Walter—evidently expecting to just shoot them dead and vanish back to the hole they crawled out of—or else there was some other angle they were trying for, something Julianna wanted to accomplish. She really could have picked better messengers, Tommen thought. Something was supposed to happen here, or else the shooters thought it was, but it just wasn't happening.

"It's too bad," Tyler said finally. "You really had great potential."

His ripped his way out of Walter's Fast Band. Rather than try to fight it, Walter let the Band dissolve. Life all around them, all around the school, resumed. Movement, sound, everything came roaring back to life.

"Nothing changes, it seems," Ryan stated.

He may have moved as if to aim his rifle at the two of them. Tommen jumped as gunfire erupted all around them, officers following orders to turn the shooters into Swiss cheese if they made a move against anyone. The problem was, the shooters were not turning into Swiss cheese. Instead, they were pulling a *Matrix Reloaded* move, catching all the bullets in midair, holding them in place within a Band and dissipating the Energy. When the Band was released, the bullets dropped to the ground harmlessly.

Dead silence filled the schoolyard. Tommen didn't need to look to see the officers glancing nervously at each other. What just happened? Had they just seen what they thought they saw? Was it a trick? A trap? Should they keep shooting? Even the radios were silent, command ops just as stunned.

This is going to turn into another warehouse situation fast, Tommen thought, *or worse.* His dad looked like he was thinking the same thing. They had to do something. The problem was, Tommen was the only one who stood a chance against them.

Bullets began flying again, but not from the police. Tyler and Ryan remained rooted where they were, surrounded by hundreds of rounds of free, live ammunition. Gravity would provide the track and the direction. Combined with Time and a few other nuanced Akari elements, and they didn't need a gun to fire off the rounds. With their Gravity tracks, they could also maneuver the bullets into all the little vulnerabilities in the officers' armor.

Tommen watched his dad try to use Time Bands of his own to either stop Tyler and Ryan or else save his fellows, but his success was limited. Tyler continued to effortlessly fire off rounds while Ryan simply kept Walter's feeble Time Bands at bay. Several officers went down with wounds of varying severity.

Time was no match for the Akari; whether it was Force or Faith, it was just simply superior. Tommen was the only other Akari-bearer here, and he couldn't just stand by like a frightened civilian and watch a massacre happen while he did nothing. No one was holding him hostage this time, and he wasn't powerless. He was not a lonely, selfish coward.

Sending up a silent prayer to God or the Author or whomever that he would be able to see Becky and the baby at the end of the day, he took a breath and launched himself at Ryan, tackling him. His Faith Akari Band penetrated anything Ryan tried to throw at him with Force, and they went to the ground. The rifle and the megaphone tumbled from Ryan's hands and skidded across the sidewalk.

Tommen recalled all his years of fighting Tyler, how he'd never had a chance of beating him physically. Ryan wasn't much smaller than Tyler. But then, Tommen was working construction now. He'd put on some muscle. He could land on Ryan and made it stick, make it hurt, even. He could hear the sudden vacuum of air as the wind was knocked from Ryan's lungs. Still, his foster brother recovered quickly and tried to heave Tommen off, up or to the side, didn't matter. But Tommen had a little trick. Most people used Gravity to make things lighter, like how he used it on the job site to lighten loads he had to carry. Now he used it the opposite way, to make himself heavier, so Ryan couldn't throw him off. He sat on Ryan's chest and held the man's arms down.

"Stop this!" Tommen said, listening to Ryan wheezing beneath him. "Don't keep doing this. Let everyone here go. Walk away from Julianna."

"Why would I do that?" Ryan rasped. "You think I want to live your petty life?" He grinned and shook his head. "No. Not even close. The Order gives me an opportunity to do everything I ever dreamed of doing."

"Like shooting up high schools? That's all you ever want to

amount to?"

"Travel. Power. Authority. Enforcing my will on others. Commanding respect."

"Giving orders isn't the same as commanding respect," Tommen told him sagely.

"Maybe not, but you want to know something I am good at?"

"What's that?"

"The art of distraction."

Only a Reflexive Band saved Tommen, stopping the bullet before it could break the skin of his temple. Letting go of his hold on Gravity, he rolled away, off of Ryan, sprawling out for a moment before landing safely about ten feet away. He saw his dad on the ground, mid-acrobatic as he dodged a few bullets of his own. He no sooner processed this than he felt a shove on his Band and suddenly Tyler was there in front of him. He delivered a fierce blow to Tommen's face, then, instead of pulling back, grabbed him by his hair and smashed his face over his knee.

Dazed, Tommen stumbled back a few steps and fell to the ground, blood pouring from his nose. In an oddly lucid moment, he noticed the sun's reflection off one of the nearby cars, the chrome on the bumper or something. He reached for Light and amplified it, blinding Tyler long enough to buy himself a few seconds of time which he stretched out for several minutes in a Band.

He wasn't going to talk them down or convince them of any ideological changes, that much was for sure, but how much force did he really want to use here? He had no desire to kill, and he wasn't sure he would be able to stomach killing in self-defense. All the same, they were here specifically to kill him and his dad. That was the end goal. Anything else would be a bonus to them, a show, flair, fireworks at the end of the exhibition.

How, then, was he going to stop them? There was no way Earth-side justice could hold them, and while the Time industry and the Tacagans and Borelians were less than friendly toward humans right now, well, they were less than friendly toward humans. There was no way Tommen could deliver them to justice without risking arrest and punishment himself. On top of that, he had to assume that anything he could do, they could do also; he would let himself be pleasantly surprised if he could do something they couldn't. It was a nice thought to be able to open a portal to Brelix and push them through, but they could open portals themselves and come right back.

There had to be a way. Was there such a thing as Akari Suppression? If he could accomplish that, his dad could deliver any remaining Time Suppression and render them powerless.

Somehow, that didn't seem likely. The Akari was a thing unto itself from the Author and couldn't be Suppressed by the mere will of man, regardless if it was Faith or Force.

So then what?

Still safely in his Band for the moment, Tommen made his way over to his dad, pulling him into the Band as well and getting him safely to the ground.

"This is a young man's game," his dad said, breathing heavily as he recovered from his bullet-dodging acrobatics. "How many months until retirement?"

"Too many, I think," Tommen told him.

"So, we know I'm pretty useless. What's your plan?"

"I don't have a plan. I was kind of hoping you had one."

"Tommen, I don't know their abilities. I don't even fully know or understand your abilities. This is way out of my league." His dad gave him a look, and it wasn't a comforting one. "I can't do anything. You're going to have to take the lead."

That was what Tommen was afraid of. He took a breath and looked around, trying to quickly assess the situation before Tyler and Ryan caught on and broke into the Band. "I don't want to kill them."

His dad nodded. "I understand. I agree, but only in principle. It may honestly come to that, because I can't think of a way to stop them and hold them, with the abilities they possess."

Tommen frowned. "I know."

"You're going to have to decide quickly what you're going to do, because we can't run around here all day."

His clothes were sticky with sweat and he could smell himself. He could feel his heart thudding in his chest, and his hands were shaking. Tommen clenched his fists, closed his eyes, and tried to breathe through congealed blood. When he opened his eyes, he nodded. "Okay. I think I have an idea."

"All you, kiddo."

Tommen had no desire to kill, but he also had no doubt that Tyler and Ryan weren't going to stop trying to kill him and his dad. Maybe they were defeated today, but they would be back. Julianna was too much of a bitch and they were too intent on besting their adversaries to simply give up. If it was just him and his dad, Tommen might have gone for mere defeat and figured something else out later. Problem was, it wasn't just them, and if the pair were merely defeated and took off, he knew exactly where they would be going: Becky and the baby.

Walter got in position, ready for anything, his job simply to protect his fellows and the remaining students. It was all he could do. Tommen was going to be doing all the heavy lifting in this engagement. Taking a breath, he stepped up to the plate and released his Band and everything else he'd been hanging onto.

Once more, life resumed. Light and sound and movement, all of it saturated with confusion and disbelief. What was going on here? Were they all crazy? Was there some sort of toxic gas in the air making them hallucinate? Did these people somehow have superpowers? What was happening?

And for the first time, Tommen was in control. He was the one calling the shots. He wasn't being held hostage. He wasn't hiding behind his dad either in Timekeeping or the police force. He wasn't being pushed around a battlefield at the whim of a madman. He wasn't weak and alone. He was the one facing off against the bad guys this time. He was the one with a plan. He was the one everyone was depending on, even if they didn't realize it. True, this wasn't how he might have chosen to spend his day, but at the very least, he had some say in how this all turned out.

It took half a second for Ryan and Tyler to figure out what had happened, as they were still in their previous positions of attack, but they regained their composure easily enough.

"All that time, and he didn't have it in him to cut our throats," Tyler said. "He just keeps running away."

"I don't want to kill you," Tommen told them. "Honestly, I don't even really want to hurt you."

"Well, aren't we all domesticated?" Ryan purred, taking a step forward, completely unconcerned with the police officers still surrounding the area, their weapons still trained on him. "But I thought part of domestication and being a family man meant protecting your family? Now, what's to stop us, once we're done here, from going and taking out your precious family, too?"

"Honestly? Nothing. In fact, I would expect you to do that."

Ryan grinned and shifted his stance. "Well now, this sounds like the beginning of a plan. Distraction? Stalling? A feeble attempt at persuasion? What's he thinking? Where is this line of thought going and why?"

He sounded so much like Rifun, it was almost terrifying. Had they trained under Rifun, even a little bit? Nevertheless, Tommen kept his composure and, with his heart hammering in his chest, said, "You're here to kill me. So here I am. Kill me."

"A sacrifice? To what end? You fancy yourself a noble savior, do you?" Ryan backed up to stand beside Tyler again. "I don't buy it."

"So then, what's next?" Tommen challenged. "You want to kill me, but you won't accept a sacrifice. Do you want me to run? Beg? Fight for my life? Is it the thrill of the chase you want?"

"It does make things more interesting."

Tommen folded his arms. "Well, I'm not running."

It was Tyler who spoke now, shifting his rifle. "Standing target is easier to hit anyway."

Not even bothering to Band his rifle, Tyler lowered the weapon and fired, several times at Tommen, and several times at

Walter.

Multiple things happened at once, in that space of about half a second, or the time it would take about a thousand rounds of ammunition to leave the barrels of their respective guns and fly toward their intended targets.

First, as soon as Tyler began lowering his weapon, all the officers again started firing at him, continuing to follow their orders of turning him into Swiss cheese, even if they were less than confident now in their ability to do so.

Second, Tyler and Ryan again attempted to slow down the tiny projectiles, using Time, Gravity, and a few other abilities.

Tommen was not going to stop them necessarily, but he was going to make it harder for them to pull off the same trick twice. With his dad Banding the bullets heading for himself and his son, Tommen was free to pull off a trick of his own, using Sound. He took the sound of the gunfire, all the dozens of guns going off at once, all of them aimed at the perpetrators, and, like using Light to blind Tyler, amplified it. The pitch and the frequency both dropped, turning it into what amounted to a near-subsonic shockwave.

The wave knocked Ryan and Tyler off their feet, breaking their concentration on the bullets. Tommen heard them shriek, but could not immediately tell if they had been injured. Behind them, all the windows on the south side of the school shattered and the fire alarm went off inside.

Bullets still hung suspended in mid-air, courtesy of Walter's Band to save himself and Tommen. They were only suspended in Time, but their velocity remained in tact within the Band. Tommen defused the ones heading for his dad, but reached out and kept the ones for himself handy for the moment. Just in case.

Several officers rushed forward, taking advantage of Tyler and Ryan on the ground, taking the chance to try and arrest them. Tommen heard Sheriff Williams bark an order to approach with extreme caution and to not let their guard down.

Ryan and Tyler were still shrieking and rolling around on the ground, though Ryan appeared a little more dazed. Both had their hands over their ears, and Tommen found himself wondering if the shockwave hadn't ruptured their eardrums. He found himself feeling a twinge of guilt over it as he suddenly became conscious of his own hearing aids.

No. He couldn't let feelings get in the way. They were still armed and dangerous, and he wasn't referring to the rifles.

Two officers confiscated the rifles, snatching them and taking off to the command tent. Four more officers, two for each shooter, roughly manhandled Ryan and Tyler and got them onto their stomachs so they could be cuffed. A ring of officers surrounded them, weapons trained on them in case they tried anything.

The officers on either side of Tommen suddenly grabbed him and started forcing him backwards, away from the scene, but also away from the rest of the students. His dad joined him, also slightly less than voluntarily, and they were secured within their own ring of bodyguards.

Tommen could not see well beyond the wall of armor and muscle, but he was able to loosely track the movements of Ryan and Tyler and the officers arresting them. He knew from experience—voluntary experience, his dad giving him a demonstration—that there was no comfortable way to stand if you got cuffed behind your back, especially if you were on your stomach at the time. Human shoulders just weren't designed to move quite in that way. As such, it took a few extra seconds for the officers to get Tyler and Ryan to their feet.

The pair could not walk a straight line, even with officers on either side. They weaved this way and that, stumbled, fell to their knees several times. Tyler was shouting incoherently while Ryan looked too out of it to process what was going on. As they got closer, Tommen could see both had been struck by weapons fire. Tyler had taken at least one in the leg, a couple in his shoulders and collarbone area. Ryan he could not see well. Nothing to the chest or abdomen on either of them, but those bullets had probably been neutralized first. These were the haphazard shots that got lucky once the pair's concentration had been broken and they were thrown backwards by the blast.

Tyler saw Tommen first and lurched. Ryan followed suit, though he still appeared dreadfully dazed, unable to comprehend his surroundings.

The first jerk against their captors, the police simply jerked them back. The second time, Tyler managed to wrest one of his arms away, the cuff falling harmlessly to his side. More shots were fired, but Tyler was still coherent enough to get up a Band and defuse them. He got his other arm free. Ryan, starting to come back around, jerked against his captors as well.

Tommen had one last trick up his sleeve. He still had the bullets they had meant for him, still encased in tiny Bands where they were still quite lethal.

He used a trick he had learned from the siege on the Akarin fortress, something he had been terrified of. Sometimes he still had nightmares about them. They were micro-portals. Just big enough to stick a knife through, or see an arrow to its target without having to worry about trees or other obstacles. In this case, he opened up a couple micro-portals just big enough for a couple bullets.

He told himself that it was effectively Ryan and Tyler killing themselves. He told himself it was no different than the officers around them shooting them dead. He told himself it was self-defense. He told himself that there was no way anyone would know or even believe that he had done it.

It didn't make him feel any less sick as the bullets struck true even before the micro-portal snapped closed. Two rounds each, both to the back of the head.

He would never forget Tyler's face, that split-second of surprise, his eyes going wide for just a hair of a second before the light died within them. Every muscle turned to water and he went down, twitching once before going still.

Ryan had a look of resigned confusion. He wasn't sure what was going on at the moment, but he was accepting his fate, accepting that Tommen was the author of his fate.

There was one time when Tommen and Ryan had actually gotten along and had a good time. It was about a month into Ryan's stay, and they had gone out to the mall for the afternoon, just the two of them while Walter went to work. It was a Saturday, so everyone else was out, too. They had just gotten ice cream when something caught Tommen's attention outside. He couldn't even remember what it was anymore. He just knew that as he was heading that way, Ryan suddenly grabbed him from behind and pulled him out of the way of a car meandering its way through the parking lot, the driver not paying attention.

"You saved me," Tommen said.

"Of course I did," Ryan told him. "We only have each other. We have to look out for each other, right?"

Tommen nodded. "Right."

It had been the early days, when Ryan was still trying to butter him up and get him to turn to the dark side. But in the moment, they had been brothers.

That shadow crossed Ryan's face in the last moment of his life, before the light faded from his gaze and he dropped to the ground.

Tommen got sick.

He didn't remember a lot in the immediate aftermath. All he could think about was that he'd just killed two men. Two battles, multiple skirmishes and close calls, and it was here that he had broken his no-kill vow. It didn't matter that they had been trying desperately to kill him, his dad, and his family. It didn't matter that they'd had the power to defy anything and everything Earth-side justice had to throw at them. It didn't matter that they had been bitter enemies for as long as they had known him, and he them. All that mattered was that he had taken their lives and cut them short.

They had fully intended on returning to their beds tonight. They had fully intended on having dinner later this evening. They had fully intended on doing other things with their lives.

Maybe Tommen had just saved a million people.

But he'd just killed two men.

At some point, his dad sat down beside him.

"You're a lover, not a fighter. Always have been."

Tommen did not reply, just wiped his eyes and his nose with his sleeve, smearing tears, snot, and crusted blood. He looked around. Somehow, he'd ended up sitting on the bumper of one of the fire trucks. Ryan and Tyler's bodies were gone. The fire alarm in the school had been turned off. Cops swarmed everywhere still and the command tent was as active as ever.

A long line of cars was moving one way down the road as parents picked up their children. Many cars were parked on the shoulder, parents and children hugging and crying.

All the ambulances had gone.

"*Gwnes i ddim eisiau fo,*" he said quietly (I didn't want to.)

His dad nodded. "*Dw i'n gwybod. Ond oedd o angenrheidiol.*" (I know. But it was necessary.)

"*Sut fedru i agweddu Becky heno a mynegu bod lladdais dau dyn? Lladdwr dw i.*" (How can I look at Becky tonight and explain that I killed two men? I'm a murderer.)

"*Dydych chi ddim lladdwr,*" his dad told him severely. (You are not a murderer.) Continuing in Welsh, "You are not a murderer. I am a murderer. I killed six men in cold blood. That's murder. What I just saw was not murder. It was self-defense, to protect yourself, to protect me, to protect everyone here. More importantly, you protected your family. I'm not saying it's not difficult, but no one would fault you for it. Besides that, I don't think anyone here even knows what you did."

Tommen wasn't sure if that statement improved things or not. On the one hand, he couldn't be arrested or charged for the crimes. On the other hand, no one else would be able to officially tell him that what he'd done was justifiable.

"Have you called Becky yet?" his dad asked, mercifully changing the subject.

His phone had been going off for a while now, but he hadn't

paid it any mind, lost in his own little world. He checked it now, finding dozens of messages from Becky, the latest one stating that she and her mom were coming to get him.

"Apparently she's coming to pick me up," Tommen stated, his throat dry. He pocketed his phone without replying. "Can they do that?"

His dad shifted position. "On the one hand, you're an adult now, so you don't need me to sign you out. Speaking on the police side of things, I think it would be the best thing for you, get you out of here and away from the trauma for a while."

"Do you need an official statement or anything?"

"You already gave one."

"I did?" He didn't remember.

His dad nodded. "It was brief, but enough for the time being. Seeing how Ryan and Tyler won't be going to trial, I think this is going to be pretty open and shut. At least as far as you're concerned. Regardless, for the time being, I do think you need to go home. Eat some junk food, watch some stupid TV, get Becky on her soapbox, do anything but think about this. Try to get some sleep tonight. In the morning, I want you to try and call Nathan and talk to him. You can always talk to me—you know that—but he's the professional and he knows more about this Akari business than I do. Got it?"

Tommen sighed and ran a hand through his hair. He was still shaking, and he could feel the sweat dried to his body. He felt disgusting, in more ways than one.

"Tommen," his dad said, his voice seeming to echo in the distance. "You're going to call Nathan tomorrow, right?"

After a second of consideration, he nodded. "Yeah, I'll do that."

His mind felt a thousand miles away. A thousand light years, in some distant galaxy. Maybe farther than that, more like some god or other higher being looking down upon the meager marble of creation, this little speck of dust known as Earth, the subatomic particle called Charleston, West Virginia.

And yet the whole incident, for the time being, was Tommen's entire universe. Nothing mattered outside of this plot of land. Homework didn't matter. Thanksgiving break didn't matter. Business and politics and intrigue and backstabbing didn't matter. The only thing that mattered was this horrific tragedy, and the fact that he killed two men.

He hadn't even been able to let Rifun die, and he hadn't been the one to stab him. But here he was with two bodies at his feet. Bodies of his own making. Directly. Not by action or inaction, not because of war or anything else. Direct action. Action and consequence. Cause and effect. He had put the bullets in their brains. And they were dead now.

It was a victory. Somewhere in his brain, he knew it was. Him or them. Further catastrophe avoided. His nemesis thwarted for the time being. This battle went to him. Tommen: 1, Julianna: 0. Hooray.

But he couldn't do it. He couldn't enjoy it. He didn't want to enjoy it. If he enjoyed his victory, he became them. But then, what did he do with it? He couldn't enjoy it, couldn't ignore it. He was stuck with only the memory of the last few hours going round and round his brain, distorting just a little more with every replay until he couldn't remember what was real and what wasn't. Guilt twisted his stomach and he felt nauseous.

Something was pressed into his hand and he instinctively grabbed it. Looking down, he found a water bottle. He glanced at his dad.

"You need it," his dad told him. "Drink."

Tommen could find no will or reason to argue, and he chugged the bottle. Getting something in his stomach brought his body back to life a little, and he was made aware of several needs, not the least of which was the need to pee. By the time he returned from watering a tree, his stomach had gone from nauseous to hungry. He wasn't sure how he felt about that. Why was he feeling hungry? Could he really eat after an event like this? And at what point had it gone from a shooting, to an incident, to an event?

"Becky and her mom are here," his dad informed him. He gestured to an approaching vehicle which turned out to be Mrs. Polski's van. "You go home."

"What about you?" Tommen asked.

His dad sighed, hands on his hips, looking around. "I expect I'll be here a while longer yet. After that, I don't know. They might send me home early on account of what happened." He looked at Tommen. "But you don't worry about that. You worry about yourself. Got it?"

Tommen nodded absently, entirely unprepared for his dad's embrace, not a little awkward around his vest and other armor. "I love you, Tommen. And I'm proud of you." His dad let him go. "Go home. Sleep it off."

With that, Walter sent Tommen on his way. Tommen tried not to look too sullen as he made for the van. As soon as Becky spotted him, she jumped out of the vehicle. Between her orthopedic shoes and being pregnant, she could not run fast or gracefully, but still she moved quickly, throwing her arms around him and holding him tight.

"Oh, thank God you're okay," she said. When she looked up at him, tears were streaming down her cheeks. "I was so worried. You weren't replying to my messages—which, I mean, I guess I was sorta mad at first, but then I figured the police probably didn't want you guys texting and posting and whatever—and we had to get all our information from the news, but that was just so...ambiguous and frustrating." Tommen got her to release her grip enough that he could kneel in front of her. She was still talking. "And then we had to play twenty questions with the perimeter officers who weren't letting anyone in quickly, as if an old woman and a pregnant dwarf could be conspiring with whackos to blow up the school or—"

He cut her off with a kiss, maybe more forceful than originally intended, but it shut her up. Three seconds in, he had to break it off so he could put his head on her shoulder and cry. Actually, "cry" was too polite of a word. He bawled. Like a baby. Like their baby would be doing in just a few months. He wept in fear, in relief, in hurt, in exhaustion, and in love. He was so happy to see her again, and there was no other way he could think to express it.

And she would never know what really happened, the depth of his emotion or guilt, the rest of the reason why he was crying.

Becky just held him, not saying a word. She let him cry, not saying anything about ruining her shirt or making a scene, because everything right now was utterly immaterial. And he cried.

It felt like forever before he stopped weeping, but he continued to shake all the way home. He sat in back with Becky, leaning over so his head was in her lap—though just barely because of her small lap and growing belly. Internally, he felt a small smile at the thought, but it could not find its way to his face. His head felt heavy, his mind empty except for that last moment, the look of surprise on Tyler's face, the resignation on Ryan's.

Tommen had never liked either of them, and he would be lying to himself, if no one else, if he said he hadn't fantasized about their deaths on more than one occasion. Maybe they were hit by a random passing train. Maybe they got shanked in jail. But never had it crossed his mind that he might be the one to do them in. He felt sick for having to do it, and shame over all his past fantasies.

Vengeance is mine, saith the Lord.

Now Tommen understood why. Because mere mortals could not stomach what vengeance really entailed. It wasn't just about pulling the trigger. It wasn't just about pointing an accusatory finger at someone. It was about facing the fingers pointing back.

Mrs. Polski dropped them off at home, saying to call if they needed anything.

"Do you want something to eat?" Becky asked quietly as he sat to take off his shoes. "Or I could make you some tea."

Tommen just shook his head. "No. Thank you. I just kind of want to go to bed."

She did not stop him and he ambled off to their room. It was only late afternoon, but in late November, night came early. With the mountains providing extra shade, the room was well dark. Although, he could have been at the North Pole on the longest day of the year with the sun blasting in every window for twenty-four hours and he still could have gotten to sleep.

He slept fitfully for a while, having trouble getting past more than a heavy doze before tossing and turning this way and that. A few times he remembered having sluggish thoughts that he should probably move to the couch or even his dad's bed in order to not endanger Becky and the baby. He never did, and he woke up again when she finally got in bed.

It was after that when he finally got to sleep, and the only reason he knew this was because he knew the cave he woke up in.

The steam was so thick it was almost like being underwater. Tommen could hardly see his hands in front of his face, but he could see the glow of the coals and followed that to the main living area. He could not see Chandler, but he could hear him, muttering prayers and adding more water to thicken the steam even more.

Tommen took his place on the rug, folded his legs, and simply waited. He wasn't sure if he ought to offer up some prayers of his own. Would the Author approve of the Lord's Prayer? He didn't know any others, and he wasn't the best at improvising. In the end, he decided to keep his mouth shut. If the Author—or God, or whomever —knew his heart and his needs, then they could act on them and his nebulous wails of woe without him trying to blunder his way through a stunted prayer.

He didn't realize the steam was beginning to thin until he could make out Chandler's form across the fire, or the coals anyway. He'd ceased speaking his prayers aloud and merely sat, legs folded, eyes closed. He might have been mistaken for a statue if not for his deep, deliberate breathing. Tommen did his best to emulate.

The last time he'd been here, Chandler had told him that he was going to die. Selfishly. Alone and afraid. Tommen had found that rather insulting. If he was going to die, at least have it mean something. Well, today would have meant something. He would have been a hero, saving his fellow students. Except now he was wondering whether heroism was all it was cracked up to be. A real hero probably could have talked them down, gotten them to surrender. The best hero would have found a way to stop it before it even started.

He glanced at Chandler. Couldn't he have gotten a little warning about Tyler and Ryan? A heads-up as to their plans? Maybe a way to stop it before it happened, an anonymous tip to lock down the school so the cafeteria hadn't turned into a shooting gallery? Could there have been a way to talk them down, even, a way to save them before Tommen was forced to kill them? Or maybe a little guidance in those last moments, an alternate course of action? Had it really been necessary to kill?

"That which is necessary is not always easy," Chandler said, as if reading his thoughts. He did not open his eyes.

"Why did this have to happen?" Tommen asked, his voice hardly more than a whisper. "People died today. I had to kill two people."

"Old things ending, new things beginning."

"Enough with the bullshit!" Tommen stood suddenly, angrily. "I want to know!" He ran his hands through his hair and sank to his knees which had suddenly turned to jelly. "I'm so confused."

For a long moment, there was silence in the cave.

"Things are about to change, but in order to do so effectively, some elements of your past needed to be dealt with and finished up."

Tommen stared at one of the rocks around the fire pit. "So this was all about Tyler and Ryan and me."

"And you and Becky and your baby."

"You told me that I'm going to die. What things could honestly be changing for me that it somehow means more than that?" He struggled to put his thoughts together coherently. "What am I supposed to do? Julianna is trying to kill everyone. Today failed, but she's not one to give up. She's going to try again." He looked at Chandler. "You said I die a lonely, selfish coward. I tried to be the hero today. I lived, but at the expense of others. What does that mean?"

Chandler's expression said everything, and he spoke not a word.

Tommen sighed and looked away. After a second, he glanced around the cave, becoming more and more visible as the steam dissipated, condensing on the walls of the cave and streaming down in small rivulets. "Where is the hawk?"

"Well recovered," Chandler replied, his tone neutral but on the glad side, finally being rid of an annoying roommate. "He is out soaring once more and preparing for a new mission from the Author. To hear him tell it, it's going to be quite lengthy and dangerous."

"What is it?"

"He won't say. He said the only reason he told me about it was so that I would not worry when he suddenly disappeared for a while. As if I could dissuade him from one of the Author's missions."

But Tommen's attention span was severely limited at the moment. His gaze darted away again, though he could feel Chandler still watching him.

"There was nothing you could have done, Tommen," the Native man said.

"What about the students who died?" he asked quietly. "Just a little forewarning—maybe not telling me why, but just telling me where to be, how to make small changes to ensure that at least the student body wasn't decimated. Butterfly effect, you know? Did they really have to die so that I could turn a new page, start a new chapter, or whatever? Was it really that essential for them to die? Is it going to provide some sort of closure to readers?" Tommen shifted his position. "And for that matter, are there readers? If there is an Author, it would stand to reason that someone would read what she writes. With the Books appearing on my bookcase and stuff, does that make us the readers? To what end? Why would the Author write books, write everything within her creation, only to send those books into her creation? It's just...it's multiverse fuckery."

"It's also beyond what your mind can comprehend, and I'm not talking physics or philosophy," Chandler told him severely.

Tommen rubbed his face. "What do you want me to do, Chandler? Tell me. What is it you expect from me?"

"I expect you to do exactly what you are supposed to do. No more, no less. Leave the rest to the Author."

"You want me to blindly trust that things will turn out just fine? I watched classmates die. I wasn't sure if I was going to join them. Chandler, I killed two people today. I—killed—them. Me. My actions. My hand. I couldn't even let Rifun die. I betrayed my own species, my friends, to save the man who tried to kill me. And now..." By now, tears were snaking their way down Tommen's cheeks and his voice was little more than a pathetic whimper. "I don't know what to do. I don't like not knowing. How am I supposed to keep my family safe if I don't know what's coming, if I don't know what to do? What if they had killed me? There would be nothing to stop them from going after Becky and the baby."

He wiped his eyes and nose on his sleeve and stared at the coals through blurry eyes.

Chandler poked at the glowing orbs a bit and added some sticks, gradually coaxing life into the fire. "Trust is a hard thing. It doesn't come naturally to many people. It is difficult to build, easy to destroy, and nearly impossible to rebuild in some instances." He looked at Tommen. "You're right. It's not fair. According to our standards and narrow view of things. It's difficult to see the silver lining in all of this. Did you just save millions of lives? How would you know if you had? Does it really make you feel any better when you see their bodies at your feet? Was there any other way, some other means to accomplish the same end? What is it about this that it had to happen this way in order to set up for something in the future?"

"You mean I might have to kill more people in the future?" Tommen scoffed and wiped his eyes again, looking away. "Great."

"I don't know. Sometimes the best course of action is only the least bad. As I said, it's not fair and we don't always see the silver lining. But we have to trust that things will work out."

"Not everyone gets a happy ending, though. They didn't. Apparently I'm not going to. The Author is directing everything, anyway. So then, what's the point?"

Chandler did not reply. Tommen closed his eyes and sighed. He felt consciousness slipping away from him even as he felt it simultaneously returning. Confusion overcame him initially as he knew instinctively that he'd overslept his alarm. Panic set it for half a moment. Then he remembered. How could he have forgotten? Then he figured that there would be no point to having an alarm. School wouldn't resume until after the scheduled break. Happy Thanksgiving, kids, have some extra time off.

Becky was asleep beside him. He reached over, wrapped an arm around her, and pulled her close. She sighed and murmured something.

"I love you, too," he whispered.

"That's not what I said," she murmured.

"What did you say?"

"I said your beard is tickling my ear."

He moved his head away and she rolled over, tucking herself under his chin against his body as best she could. He kissed the top of her head.

"Oh, God, I'm so happy to have you here and be able to hold you," he whispered.

"And I'm glad you're okay," she mumbled into his chest. She wiggled away so she could kiss him. "I love you. And I don't want to lose you."

He kissed her back, and things just went from there.

Chapter Fourteen
Sensation

The only reason Tommen left the house that morning was to give Becky a ride to class. Otherwise, he lay on the couch in the living room and watched TV with the subtitles on; he didn't even bother with his hearing aids.

Five hundred channels and he watched the news. The incident hadn't even been declared over before the pundits came slithering out of the woodwork and the weeds to give their opinions. He saw the incident from a dozen different angles: the news chopper, a couple drones, a couple reporters standing outside the yellow tape around the area, and not a few eyewitness videos from students who were too scared to do anything but whip out their phones and capture the chaos. It was surreal and maddening at the same time. *Don't bother to help your fellow man, maybe fight back if you get the chance. No, get it on camera and be a sensation.*

But even as Tommen looked, he did not see much. At least having subtitles and not wearing his hearing aids helped to keep the memories from becoming too vivid as they raced through his mind. He flipped from station to station, the same story told six different ways, all with the same footage.

And through it all were the same tired issues being batted back and forth. Gun control and mental health. Gun control and mental health. No one really had an informed opinion or a persuasive argument about anything at any end of either spectrum. Tommen figured they just liked yelling and talking over each other, and he who shouted the loudest somehow won the argument. It was the only thing he could come up with.

"You really shouldn't be watching that."

Tommen looked up just as his dad reached down, took the remote, and turned the channel to something else, something not the news. Tommen shrugged. "So?"

"So...it's not good for you. Have you called Nathan yet?"

"No."

"Why?"

I forgot? "I don't know."

"Do it. Check on the twins if nothing else." His dad turned and headed toward the kitchen. "Are you hungry? What do you want to eat?"

"Not hungry," Tommen told him. He was slow to get his phone out of his pocket. Even the thought of moving was exhausting, and he was loathe to see the opinions of the rest of the world vomited out upon social media. Gun control and mental health. Medication for everyone to make them normal and compliant, but take their guns away anyway. Everyone was crazy in their own way, but the functional crazy people couldn't be trusted to defend themselves against the dysfunctional crazy people. Simply make every aspect of humanity a textbook disease and lock up everyone in the asylum. And who would be the wardens of this asylum? Well, what's good for thee is not good for me. Welcome to communism, comrade.

That was a depressing line of thought, Tommen mused, absently scrolling through his contacts, suddenly confused about who he was supposed to be looking for. Right. Nathan. His shrink. Who was also on Julianna's hit list. He hesitated for a second or two before calling.

In the kitchen, he could smell the bacon cooking, even if he couldn't hear it. His mouth watered and his stomach rumbled.

"Hello?" Nathan said, answering on the third ring.

"Hey, Nathan, it's Tommen."

"Stop me if I'm wrong, but I suspect you're calling about what happened yesterday? I saw it on the news."

"Yeah."

"Well, we have our regular meeting tonight at seven. You want to bump it up a little? I think you might have a few things to say."

"Yeah, that would be good."

"How about we meet at five? We'll grab something to eat and then head out to the usual spot to talk."

"Sounds good."

"Good. Just remember, it's only a plan. Plans can be changed. If you need to talk or feel like you're in crisis, call 9-1-1. Got it?"

"Yeah."

"All right. I'll see you later."

"Bye."

He hung up before Nathan could respond, then resumed watching TV, another *Law & Order* rerun. By now, the whole house was filled with the smell of a hearty breakfast: bacon, sausage, biscuits. Eggs didn't have much of a smell, but he was sure they were in the mix, too. And hashbrowns.

He pulled himself off the couch and slogged his way to the kitchen where his dad was just bringing down a couple plates.

"How you feeling, kiddo?" he asked.

Tommen shrugged. "Dead. I don't really feel anything."

"You're still in shock."

"Figured that much."

His dad handed him a plate. "Sleep all right?"

Another shrug, and Tommen helped himself to a little bit of everything. "I guess. When did you get home?"

"Well, we left the school about nine-thirty. Returned to the station to work on the truck load of paperwork. The Powers That Be disappeared into meetings. The counselors got there about eleven o'clock. They wanted to talk to me first, but because of the magnitude of the call, it was done in more of a group setting. We didn't get out until about one, and I was ordered to go home. I got home some time between one and two."

"And what did you do?"

"Tried to read. Ended up falling asleep in my recliner for a few hours. Got up about six and got into my own bed."

It was just before two o'clock now.

"Do you have to pick up Becky from school?" Walter asked amiably.

"Um, no," Tommen answered, momentarily unsure. "No, she already had plans to go out with her mom today. I told her to go ahead and go."

"What are they doing?"

"Some sort of hand-me-down, child stuff swap meet thing at the church. Parents give their kids' things that they've outgrown to poorer families in the church. They're going to look for baby stuff."

His dad nodded thoughtfully. "Not a bad idea. Pink or blue stuff?"

Tommen managed a small smile. "Still not telling."

"Give me a break, I had to try."

"You can't even wait one more week?"

"Thanksgiving, then?"

"Yeah."

His dad gave him a look. "All right. I'm holding you to it. Gender reveal, next Thursday."

It seemed an odd thing to talk about, even though Tommen had really had little else on his mind during the whole standoff. He'd just wanted to be able to see Becky and his baby. First and foremost, he'd wanted to get home to them. But now that he was, his mind couldn't leave the standoff. Even as he felt dead, his body was still on high alert. A sluggish high alert, true, but alert nonetheless. If something extravagant were to happen at that moment, his body would react before his mind could comprehend what was going on.

He nibbled on some bacon, acutely aware of his dad's gaze upon him.

"Are you working tonight?" Tommen asked, not looking at him.

"No. I have tonight and tomorrow night off."

And why wouldn't he? He'd been involved just as much as Tommen. They couldn't just throw him back on the roads, not knowing what could happen or how he might react. He had to process everything for a couple days and give himself a little reprieve, a chance to spend time with his son.

Tommen knew he was in the same boat. He needed to rest, relax, spend time with his family, and have a couple days of normalcy. He ought to talk everything over with his therapist, lay everything out there, and work through things. He'd finally been able to wrap things up in his mind with the warehouse and that chapter was coming to a close; the door would finally shut and lock once Rifun's sentence had been officially delivered. He could move on from tragedy and rough times, he'd done it before. He might have to do it a little quicker this time, though, because he wanted to be one hundred percent better once the baby came. That would take up quite a bit of his attention, and between work and school, too, he couldn't afford to lose more of himself to invisible demons and Shadows.

He chased a few hashbrowns around the plate, scooping them onto toast with some egg and sausage. It sounded nice, but it was damn hard to do. It only took half a consideration for Tyler and Ryan's faces to flood his mind. He closed his eyes as if he thought it might help, even as he knew it wouldn't. There they were, surprise and resignation, and then the light fading from their eyes.

Tommen jumped at a hand on his shoulder. It was only his dad.

"You're okay."

Not, "Are you okay?" or "What's wrong?" Just a simple statement of fact. You are okay. He was okay. He was safe at home. He was fine, his dad was fine, his family was fine. Everyone was fine. Everything that had happened was in the past. He couldn't change it and he couldn't stay there. He had to come back to the present.

He finished his breakfast, washed the dishes, and returned to the living room to continue watching TV, or flipping through the channels anyway. Any time his dad caught him watching the news for longer than three seconds, he came in and changed the channel arbitrarily, telling Tommen not to watch such things.

He did not check social media or look at his phone for any reason, though he was sure someone had probably texted him about what happened. Maybe Will would have called, left a message. Maybe Becky was innocently asking for an opinion on something for the baby and it had nothing to do with what happened. He did not look.

Well, on second thought, maybe he should look and see if Becky was looking for an opinion on something. She might understand that he didn't want to be bothered. On the other hand, she might suspect something terrible had happened to him and could be stressing out over nothing.

But still. That meant getting up and going back to his room. Sure, it was just around the corner, a short jaunt down the hall, but it felt so far away. The effort to get up and around...he may as well run around the block enough times to make a marathon. He sighed and shifted position on the couch, which was about all he was good for right now.

About ten minutes later, his dad walked in from the garage. He went down the hall, and Tommen heard the telltale squeak of his bedroom door. Then another squeak. A few seconds later, his dad returned and held Tommen's phone out to him.

"Becky's been texting you," he said. "When you didn't answer, she started texting me." Tommen took the phone and his dad went on. "She's worried about you. And she wants your opinion on something."

With that, Walter returned to the garage.

Tommen sighed and waited a few seconds longer before checking his messages, deliberately ignoring all of them that were not from Becky.

She indeed wanted his opinion on something. She wanted his opinion on a lot of somethings. She was also lamenting how hard it was to find stuff without giving away the gender before their planned reveal. Cribs and strollers were pretty universal, but when it came to clothes, well, she couldn't just pick out a whole bunch of little dresses, could she? It would be far too obvious. Clearly they should have waited to have this event until after Thanksgiving.

"I'm sure someone will get fired for not consulting with you on the appropriate time to throw a massive hand-me-down baby shower event," Tommen told her sarcastically.

"Well it's about time you responded," Becky texted back almost immediately. "I was worried. I thought something might have happened."

"Nothing's happening. Believe me. What do you want an opinion on?"

She'd made a few executive decisions while waiting for him, but there were plenty more items to go around. First they tried calling and talking things out. Then they tried video calling, but the signal was so poor that it was impossible to hold more than a stunted conversation. Finally Mrs. Polski suggested that Tommen simply meet them there and avoid the whole issue.

Tommen really didn't feel like going anywhere, and he said as much. Mrs. Polski lightly chastised him, told him he needed to get out of the house, get out of his well of dark thoughts. Becky said she understood, but she wasn't going to let him sulk around for too long. Today, sure, but don't let it linger, she warned.

Eventually, they came to a compromise. Becky would send him pictures of items she was debating between—a couple strollers, a couple of these, a couple of those, whatever it was—and Tommen would simply send her his vote. He mentioned that because she was present, she could pick whichever she wanted. As Mama, she would probably overrule him on many decisions in the future and render his votes null and void.

For the moment, he really didn't care.

He spent the better part of an hour texting Becky and sending his votes on this or that, occasionally giving commentary on something she suggested. He wouldn't say it didn't help his mood, as he did feel a little less like roadkill for the duration of the conversation, but it was still the present moment warring with the endless reel of memories from the day before for occupation of his brain and attention. It physically hurt, and by the time Becky declared that they were finished and out of the church, he had a headache bordering on a migraine.

Some of the stuff they were storing at her parents' house for the time being, just in the interest of saving space and having everything mostly ready whenever they needed it: clothing and diapers in larger sizes, more mature, age-appropriate toys, and so on. For the moment, the only thing they were keeping at their house — that is, Walter's house — was the stuff for a brand new newborn. The good news was, at least where clothes were concerned, they were pretty darn small and Becky was able to easily stuff them in the dresser drawers. Toys were beginning to migrate into the living room, and Walter had made an off-handed comment about having to teach the adults to clean up their toys before trying to get the kid to do the same.

A new hour rolled around, the show on TV ended, and Tommen again went channel surfing, being careful to avoid the news. His mind was a muddled mess, but he roused from his daze at the sound of a vehicle pulling in the driveway. Glancing out the window from the couch, he could see it was Mrs. Polski's van.

Tommen hauled himself off the couch and headed outside, somewhat stunned by the chill wind that greeted him on the other side of the door. Of course. It was November. Nearly Thanksgiving. Obviously it would be chilly. Why had he thought otherwise?

Had it been warm yesterday? He couldn't remember. Maybe it had, but he hadn't been able to feel it with his blood pounding through his veins as he fought for survival. Because that was what he had done. He'd fought for his survival and his dad's survival. Us or them. Tyler and Ryan had intended to kill. There had been no other way out. Survival. Of the fittest. Or the cowardly. Some days, Tommen wondered what the difference was, if there was a difference at all.

He hugged and kissed Becky, though it was more mechanical than emotional this time. Then it was the simple task of unloading the van. She'd gotten some clothes, which she took in herself. The toys, Walter and Mrs. Polski took in to the living room. Then came the crib. Presently, it was disassembled. Tommen still didn't know quite where they were going to put it. His biggest fear was that it was going to end up in the closet and he would have to do some cleaning in there to get it to fit well. Might be that Becky would do that. She had a knack for cleaning and organization, knew where everything had to go and how to make everything just so.

His dad was right: having a woman around the house was pretty nice.

When everything was unloaded from the van, Mrs. Polski wished them all well and headed back down the street to her house. Tommen, Becky, and Walter ducked back inside to the safety and warmth of the house.

"Looks like shopping went well," Walter observed, mildly amused.

"Oh, please, it's cutthroat competition in there, almost as bad as one free Gucci bag on Black Friday," Becky said waving a hand dismissively. "Catholics like to have kids, and I can use my mom as an example. Well, procreation works on a multiplicative factor, but hand-me-downs only work on a linear factor, if you get where I'm going with this. Most of the stuff there was all the stuff people deemed insufficient to pass on to their own kids having kids. The stuff that was decent, well, pregnant women are a scrappy pack of dogs."

Walter cleared his throat. "No comment." He looked at Tommen. "All yours, kiddo. Keep your scrappy little dog under control."

He escaped, but not without a few words to his back as he returned to the garage to work intently on whatever project he had going.

Tommen spent the rest of the afternoon and evening helping

Becky assemble toys, sort clothes, and make plans. Well, to be more specific, she did most of the technical work, anything that required thinking and concentration, and he just did the mindless assembly and heavy lifting. Whether she noticed his demeanor was unclear, but he wasn't going to interrupt her just to let her know that he wasn't exactly peppy or feeling the greatest. It wouldn't accomplish anything. And what did he expect her to do, anyway? Pick out the best wall for him to stare at?

The tasks probably did him some good, but he would leave that determination to Nathan. Tommen briefly mentioned his usual shrink session, and Becky did not stop him as he grabbed his keys and headed out the door. He hated doing it to her, felt as though he were running out on her, but he really did have an appointment to keep.

He met Nathan at a fast food joint where they each got an order of fries and chocolate milkshakes to dip them in, taking them to the park and sitting in the enclosed pavilion to eat. Neither said a word, though Tommen could feel Nathan's gaze on him as he dipped his fries three or four at a time into his shake.

Then, "So."

Tommen gave him a cursory glance. "La."

"La?"

"No, you're supposed to say, 'Ti.' "

Nathan considered this for a second, then nodded. "Ah. I get it now. Scales. Do re me fa so la ti do." He spoke, rather than sang, the notes.

Tommen just nodded.

Nathan took a long drink of his shake. "Well, at least we've established that you haven't completely lost your appetite, and your sense of humor appears to be somewhat in tact. That said, what's on your mind?"

Tommen bought time by taking half a dozen fries, loading them up with ice cream, and stuffing them in his mouth. Nathan was still scrutinizing him, no doubt taking mental note of his stalling technique. Finally Tommen answered, "I can't get their faces out of my mind, how they looked as they died."

"How did they look?"

So he described it again. Tyler, surprise. Ryan, resignation. By now, it had all boiled down to a single image and a word for each of them, but Tommen knew that those images and words were like concrete now, cemented in his brain (his mason coworkers would probably skin him alive for using the terms interchangeably).

"I betrayed a lot of people by giving up the Borelian poison so Rifun could live and I could buy Kayla time to escape," he finished. "But I killed two men in cold blood yesterday."

"Cold blood?" Nathan questioned.

"I know it really wasn't. I know it was self-defense. And if I hadn't done it, someone else would have. But I did it. I know I did it. No one else knows, no one else really understands what happened. And for all the years I wished for both of them out of my life..." Tommen studied his hands, still around his milkshake, the cup now empty. "I only wanted them gone. Even if I did want them dead, I didn't want to be the one to do it." He scuffed his foot on the ground. "My dad says I'm a lover, not a fighter."

"I would agree with that. Speaking of which, how is Becky handling it?"

"Better than I thought she would. I mean, I can imagine she would have been freaking out, but she still completed her finals for her class and she went shopping with her mom today. She blew up my phone wanting to know my opinion on a bunch of baby stuff, and I got done assembling a bunch of stuff before meeting up with you."

Tommen knew that Becky was able to stay strong for him in the beginning, while the event was still fresh in everyone's minds, but if he didn't find a way to knock it out and move on, learn to function again, it would start to wear on her, too, and their relationship. Nathan confirmed as much.

"What do I do for it, though?" Tommen asked. "The warehouse, the coup, the fire and the Land In Between, the fortress attack, Halloween, the attack on Brelix, now this? I'm starting to lose track of it all."

Nathan shifted in his seat. "When you go home, I want you to do something. Draw up a table with three columns and however many rows you'll end up needing. Write down all of the things you just listed, plus any more that you can remember, in the first column. All these things that have happened and are weighing on your mind. Write down the event. In the third column, write down what you learned from it. The warehouse, you learned External Bands. The Land In Between, you learned more about the Akari. The attack on Brelix, you learned courage and keeping yourself together in the midst of chaos. In everything, you learn something.

"Then, between them, in the second column, I want you to write down whether the event is finished or ongoing. One of those two words, finished or ongoing. I don't mean the effects or the consequences, because those can last for some time, just the event itself.

"When you're done, cut off the third column. Tape it to your wall, put it in a notebook, whatever. Keep it with you. Then take the rest and cut out each row individually, which would be the event and whether it is finished or ongoing. If there are any that are ongoing, bring it with you next week and we'll go over it. Anything that is finished, get rid of it. Burn it, flush it down the toilet, whatever, just dispose of it. Once and for all. Keep only what you have learned. Does that make sense?"

Tommen nodded, still a bit sullen. "Something a little more absolute than just removing my glasses or my hearing aids or whatever."

"That's right. It was only an aid, but I think it needs to be tweaked a little bit because you keep bringing up old things. You seem to move on, but when something new happens, you take the weight of everything from the past and heap it on your shoulders again. We need to get rid of that habit. A dog returning to its vomit, as the saying goes."

"I know it."

"That's your homework for the week. You think you can manage it?"

"I think so."

Tommen drummed his fingers on his cup, still not looking at Nathan. "How are the twins and Kayla? How bad was your attack?"

"Godwin took care of the initial scouting party, and then we fled to another location. We have no reason to think we're in the clear, but it bought us some time, enough time that Micaiah has his leg back."

"Really?"

Nathan nodded. "Physically, it looks and should function just like his leg did before. His brain still needs a little convincing after so long without it. Then we can focus more on rehabilitating his mind."

Tommen made an intrigued sound and nodded. "That's good."

They continued talking for a while, which helped to ease Tommen's troubled mind, and he returned home in a better mood. He greeted his dad with less sulk, and was able to put some feeling into his hug and kiss for Becky.

"So talking to a therapist does help?" she asked. They were alone in their room.

Tommen nodded. "Yeah. It's not an instant thing, but it's a work in progress."

"As long as progress is being made. You feel all right, though? Pretty okay?"

"I guess so, yeah."

"Can I talk you into rubbing my feet?"

He did so without fuss, and was pleasantly surprised when she gave him a hand job in return. They'd reached the point where sex was not a good option, the previous evening notwithstanding. She was frustrated by it, but at least he could still get off. Or that was what she said, with the caveat that she better be the reason he was getting off. He was just surprised he was capable at all, given the last twenty-four hours. Maybe his mind wasn't as far gone as he thought, or else his shrink session really was that helpful. He chose the former reason, preferring to think he was still relatively sane.

They stayed up for a bit, though Tommen couldn't recall that they did anything of importance. He knew they didn't talk about what happened, but he also couldn't say that he helped her with any of her studying for her last exam, nor could he say for sure whether she had mentioned anything about her exam. For just a little while, it was the two of them, almost like they were just dating again. Tommen half-expected his dad to open the door to ask if they were being good. One look at Becky now, and it was obvious they hadn't been good. But they were making it right.

Becky was the first one to mention sleep, if only because of school. One more exam, she said. Then they could spend all weekend and all next week doing whatever they wanted. Tommen almost protested, saying that he still had a few more days, then paused and reconsidered. Would they still have school for all of two days next week? Or would the Powers That Be just say heck with it, no need to drag the kids back into school where their classmates died right before a holiday weekend. Give them a little time to relax and recoup and enjoy Thanksgiving with their families. Then bring them back afterwards to the school where their classmates died and ruin them for Christmas.

Tommen did not sleep especially well that night, but he was not wrestled to the floor by his dad, so he considered that a good thing. He again gave Becky a ride to school and then returned home. He watched TV for a bit. The news was still awash in pundit opinions of the shooting.

The attackers had been identified immediately. Their motives, not so quickly. Theories and opinions floated around, spinning wild threads, dragging as many buzzwords as possible into the conversation. Gun control. Mental health. Foster care. Abusive parents. Gun control. Absent parents. Addiction. Mental health. Obvious criminal record. Warning signs and red flags. School intervention. All of this sprinkled liberally with gun control and mental health.

He was quick to change the channel when he heard his dad stir. It was harder for Walter to keep up his third-shift routine when he had multiple nights in a row off, and it was only eleven in the morning. He made his way to the bathroom first, then back to his room, then out to his recliner in the living room.

"Good morning, Sleeping Beauty," Tommen said.

"Yeah, you can talk," his dad said, yawning and indicating Tommen's hair.

"I brushed it this morning. Besides, I've been up for a while and laying on the couch."

"So I gathered. What else are you doing today?"

Well, that was the question, wasn't it? Taking a day to calm down, collect his head, and talk to his shrink was perfectly reasonable. Expected, even. He could probably plead off for another day, but to what end, and for how long? Should he just jump up right now and knock out a to-do list? Could he do it? Physically, there was no reason he couldn't. He just didn't have the willpower at the moment. All the same, he was feeling better and might be able to get a few chores done. It would be good for him, he figured. Sighing, he stood and made his way out of the living room.

He had just finished cleaning the bathroom when his dad announced that he was going out. He would be hitting a few of the home stores and the hardware store, try to check off a few items on his own to-do list, seeing how he had the time and all. It was Friday and he'd been told that he was returning Monday night. He had only the weekend to get stuff done. Tommen wished him well and put the cleaning supplies away.

Tommen knew most of the guys on the construction crew loathed housework, and so did plenty of his classmates. Tommen never had a problem with it, probably because it was only him and his dad. Sure, they weren't exactly jumping at the opportunity to clean the toilet, and usually the job was left up to chance in a game of rock-paper-scissors. But when it came around to Becky, who had certainly injected a feminine touch into their decidedly masculine household, Tommen still had no problem cleaning the bathroom because she was unable.

He peeled off the nitrile gloves (courtesy of the local ambulance, though they didn't know it) and tossed them in the trash, making his way back to the living room.

Tommen had left his hearing aids out again, so he could only conclude that whoever was at the door was knocking to the point of breaking it down. Thinking it might be the police or a well-meaning neighbor who feared the worst for his eighteen-year-old neighbor involved in a shootout earlier in the week, Tommen hurried to the door and opened it.

If he'd just looked out the window first, he would have ignored the reporter instead.

"Hi!" she greeted, just a little too cheerfully in Tommen's opinion. She held out a slender hand, but when Tommen reached to take it, she slipped a business card into his hand. "My name is Kristy Lowe, from—"

"*The Charleston Tribune*," Tommen read off the card. "That's nice. We don't subscribe, sorry, and have no plans to. But if you have Girl Scout cookies, then we might be willing to talk."

Her smile got only bigger somehow. She was probably five-six —or five-three or so, with a few extra inches from her heels—with blond hair swept up in a bun, makeup that made her look almost as pale as him, and bright blue eyes. She wore a nice business outfit, nice shirt, jacket, and a skirt to her knees with only thin, black tights. If Tommen were feeling gentlemanly, he might have offered to let her in for a moment, out of the cold. But if he didn't, then she would be less inclined to just stand there on the stoop for an interview.

"Believe me, I wish I had some Girl Scout cookies," she said. "Terrible for you, but so good. Actually, I'm here to talk about—"

"I know why you're here," Tommen cut in. "The initial investigative gag order is lifted after twenty-four hours, so you and everyone else at every other news outlet is canvassing the crowd.

Someone is talking to Casey Oldman, someone else to Dean Williams, and so on and so forth, getting every angle you can. I know how it works."

Her thoughts were tough to gauge, but he was fairly certain that he saw her expression waver just a touch. She shuffled her feet just a smidge on the porch, disturbing the snow dust.

"I know you're just doing your job, and I know you have a job to do. Everyone does—"

"What was your relationship to Tyler Freeman and Ryan Henderson?"

Tommen paused and frowned. After a second, he told her, "It's not polite to interrupt people. And I'm not answering your questions at this time. I'm sorry."

"When would you be willing to sit down for an interview?"

"When would you be willing to stop asking questions?"

Her expression was rather taken aback. He went on, "I'm sorry. It's been a rough couple of days."

"I understand." Now her tone was hesitant. "Well, you have my card. Feel free to give me a call."

That offer would last the weekend, at most. Regardless of how sensational the story was, there were more stories happening every day that vied for the attention of reporters. He just had to wait until his story was no longer sensational.

He returned to the living room, mood crushed, and watched TV once more. He turned it to the news. He didn't know why, necessarily. Probably he was a glutton for punishment.

For the moment, the pundits had abandoned the school shooting in favor of other things, like a report from NASA on the Safe Earth Defense System—known to a few as the Tacagan shields—the latest companies to be hacked for financial reasons, some report about a string of identity thefts encompassing not just the United States but multiple countries around the world, and the usual political BS, now served up extra hot and spicy with less than one year until the 2016 elections. And then, just for kicks and giggles, the fun and obnoxious stories about people seeing aliens and UFOs and everything else. Tommen was a touch skeptical about the UFOs, but aliens...well, he'd seen a few in his day, so he would just keep his mouth shut about that.

What would happen if Earth were suddenly and dramatically exposed to Time? He thought about those who had been enslaved while In Jezik was still operating. Somehow he imagined that many committed suicide, or tried to. But on a less scary, more planet-wide scale, what would happen? Total meltdown of organized religion. Jockeying by world leaders to be the first to welcome the little green men and be seen as the supreme leader of Earth. Jockeying by other world leaders to blow up the little green men and so prove the mighty firepower of the human race. Mass cultural upheaval. First world citizens may seek knowledge and friendship. Third world citizens, well, they would likely see it as a form of colonialism. Would they be enslaved in some form? Could the little green men really come in peace?

On the other hand, Tommen mused, what if there was a way to make it a slow introduction? Little bits here and there, so that one day, people just woke up and thought, Oh, hey, I need to make a run to the marketplaces in the Wheel to buy some Time. Where the secret was so obvious that people had already integrated it into their lives even before world leaders made the "official announcement." Was that possible? Maybe on the alien side of things.

Now throw in a little Time.

Better yet, throw in the Akari.

Then chop it all up into various warring factions. Ta-da! It's just like Earth, but on a much larger scale! Yeah, all that hope and peace and going where no man has gone before? Ha ha, sucks to be you. Flush your dreams down the toilet because that stupid future doesn't exist.

Tommen turned off the news and dragged himself to his room. He should probably at least get started on the homework assignment from Nathan. He needed to get rid of all this garbage floating around in his mind, this vomit that his inner dog kept returning to. Better to do it now while he was alone.

It was harder than he expected, honestly. Not the part about writing down the events; those he could call up in an instant. He even added a few that he hadn't originally considered especially significant, like his trip into the salt cave in the first place, when he was eight years old.

The expected difficulty was figuring out what he had learned or gained from each one, be it literal, like learning how to Band externally, or more metaphorical, like courage or perseverance. Eventually, he got at least one thing for each event, finishing off the last one when the bedroom door opened and Becky walked in.

"Hi!" she said, grinning and looking rather pleased with herself.

"How'd your final go?" he asked, trying to sound amiable.

She waved a hand dismissively. "Hardly worth the effort it took to study. First one done. Corrected them in class, only missed one."

"Hardly worth the effort to study and you still got one wrong, hm?"

"Please, it was a trick question. I wasn't the only one who argued it, but it doesn't matter. I passed with flying colors."

"That's good." He reached over and pulled her onto his lap. She hadn't gained a ton of weight in her pregnancy, but it was still cumbersome trying to maneuver her, even more when she fussed against his grip. She spotted his paper.

"What's this?"

"Ah, just some homework that Nathan wanted me to work on. Talk about it next week and stuff."

"Oh." Her eyes got huge as her expression turned serious. "Do you want me to leave? I can entertain myself for a while."

As much as he wanted to tell her no, he ended up saying yes, just for a little while. He was almost done. As she could see, he only had one column to fill in and he only had two choices when it came to the word he would write there. She told him she didn't need to know the details. Then she kissed him, slid off his lap, and meandered her way out of the room.

He stared after her for a moment, then glanced at his paper. And back at the door. And back at the paper.

He wanted to spend his life with her, and he wanted to be a good father to their child, but he couldn't just ignore this other part of his life. It had caused plenty of trouble and gotten countless people killed one way or another. This same secret life had also saved countless lives, and those lives didn't even know it. Time held the secrets of millions of people from millions of species and the answers to a million more questions. How many problems could be solved if Earth had access to such superior technology? Disease, famine, those were good things to eradicate. People envisioned the end of poverty and war, but that wasn't going to happen. Even so, there was good to be found out there.

Knowledge saved lives. It could have saved the lives of all the police officers at the warehouse, and maybe Dan would still be alive, too. It could have helped the soldiers on the ground dealing with In Jezik on the battlefield, or the police with the domestic terrorism. It might have helped Tommen when he was stuck in the in-between dimension; instead of wasting resources tracking him over hill and dale, more focused efforts could have been made.

But most importantly, he wouldn't have to lie to Becky and cover up half his life. He wouldn't have to pretend like he was being hugely affected by only a few things. She would be able to know that he was carrying the weight of a lot of things, battles on distant planets, fighting aliens who couldn't even be touched.

He leaned back in his chair and rubbed his face. Was it possible? Maybe. Was it ethical? Was it right? Was it not better to simply let humanity progress on its own, in its own natural order? Who made that determination?

And what were the dangers? Sure, it might be nice to be recognized for who he really was and what had happened, not have to hide his abilities. But history was rife with examples of people being exiled or killed for being different. Sometimes it was as superficial as skin color. Sometimes it was because of religious or ideological reasons. Sometimes it was for genetic defects of one form or another. Why shouldn't he consider the possibility that some government agents in New Mexico might want to try to experiment on him? Even if he got away, what would they do to Becky and the baby? If he fled and took them with him, could she adapt to life on the run, maybe even life not spent on Earth? Would they go for her family? Could she live with that possibility? Could he take them all with him? Where did it end? Her family was huge with tons of siblings, grandkids, marriages, and every marriage brought into consideration a whole new family, and so on.

What happened when families became divided? God forbid, what if Becky left him because of it? What if she feared him? What if she considered it evil or demonic? How would it affect her worldview? Her little sphere of safety where humans were alone in the universe but for God and His angels, as well as the other guy? Religious and political meltdowns were fine when they were abstract concepts on TV and a thousand miles away, but this was personal.

"Why do you care now?" Rifun had once asked him, when Tommen proposed the idea of allying the Cult, the Akarin, and the Hands against the Borelians. "Why haven't you cared when it's been going on for a while now, this war? Is it because now it's personal? It's not just on TV or in a land far away that you'll never see. Now it's in your backyard, and it threatens you. So now you care."

And in that, Rifun had the right of things. The failure of the ideal had also become obtrusively evident when the Cult conquered the Akarin, lost to the Borelians, was divided itself, and now the power balance in the Wheel was sitting precariously across the shoulders of the Borelians, the Tacagans, and only a few of the original Hands. All of them had their own agenda, their own interests in mind.

Tommen sighed and stared at the ceiling. Earth would make its way into the larger universe. There was nothing to be gained by forcing it there any sooner than it needed to be. War was war. Poverty was poverty. Politics were the same the universe throughout.

But was Godwin right, that he should grab Becky and run?

He looked at the piece of paper, filled in the second column, then cut out the words as Nathan had told him. He put the third column in his school notebook. Then he grabbed a lighter and took the rows one by one and burned them in a metal tin. Salt cave, gone. Ryan's stay, gone. Tyler's bullying, gone. Warehouse, gone. All the way up to the school shooting.

It was the only event he hadn't labeled as either finished or ongoing, mostly because he couldn't decide. On the one hand, that single incident was done. But if it was part of a worldwide coordinated attack, and considering Tyler and Ryan had failed, there was no reason to think there couldn't be another attempt of some form.

He stared at it a second or two, then folded it and put it in his pocket. He would wait and see what happened over the next few days. Or maybe he would wait until after Christmas or New Year's. If the Author was still writing his life, she seemed to have some vendetta against holidays, especially Christmas. He nodded to himself. Better to wait on that one.

With the papers burned—himself having done a few tentative tests with Energy on the small flames, with no catastrophic results—Tommen stood, stretched, tossed the ashes in the trash can, then went out to the living room. Becky was in the kitchen making something for dinner, which was just as well since his dad was just pulling into the garage. He walked in and took a deep breath of the delectable food smell, a gesture that made Becky blush hard.

Life went on, Tommen thought. But which direction was it going?

Chapter Fifteen
Politics as Usual

Tommen managed to wait out the reporter over the weekend. Actually, he waited out several reporters as various people from various newspapers, TV shows, and aspiring hit blogs made the rounds and came knocking on the door. By Sunday afternoon, Tommen just ignored them; he didn't even care if they could see him right through the front window staring at them. He was not speaking to the media.

That wasn't to say that others shared his sentiment. By the Saturday after the shooting, he'd gotten up the nerve to look at social media. His profile was littered with people asking what happened, how he was doing, if he needed anything to just ask. Similarly, there were those who wanted to know his opinion on the whole thing, often citing his relationship to Tyler and-or Ryan, and the fact that he had been called out specifically, along with his dad. Still others wanted to know his stance on all the issues—that is, all the buzzwords—that had come to the forefront since the shooting.

Gun control and mental health. Bullying. Addiction. On and on the list went. Studies and impromptu research papers popped up alongside or in tandem with random, disconnected anecdotes and armchair refereeing. Tommen had been silent. His classmates had not. And like all victims of crime, they suddenly became world-renowned, Nobel prize-winning experts on all aspects of every issue being debated. Didn't matter that they were still in high school and only had a rudimentary knowledge of the real world, they were the current leading authority on gun control and mental health. And bullying and addiction and everything else.

It made Tommen's stomach churn and feel ill, and he put the phone away. He had half a mind to avoid the vigil planned for that evening, but he went anyway. He knew that if he didn't, there would be rumors, either that he had something to do with it or that he would soon be joining the victims they were gathering to mourn.

There had only been three deaths in total so far, the safety officer outside who had first confronted the shooters, and two students whom Tommen had known were dead as soon as he laid eyes on them. But every single student that he'd managed to get to the nurse's office had pulled through. Well, they were alive, anyway. Two were still in worrisome limbo.

It made him feel good to know that he'd helped to prevent a much bigger tragedy. It made him sick to think that no one would ever know. Reportedly, the school nurse was still reeling from having so many injured students suddenly appear in her office. Some of the lesser wounded students whom he'd gotten into the classrooms were also still a little freaked, but they were less worried about it since memory became fragmented in the chaos. They must have blocked it out in the stress, or maybe from pain, they said.

Half the cops in the county must have showed up to the vigil, Tommen thought as he stood next to Becky in the crowd. Someone had begun singing "Silent Night," but he did not feel like joining the chorus.

The hour-long vigil ended with the civilians lining up to shake the hands of the police officers who had come. The impromptu nature of the gesture was a little sloppy at first as it caught the officers off-guard, and then they were moving along. Most were handshakes, but there were a few hugs that Tommen saw. Honestly, he didn't feel like joining, but he knew it was the right thing to do and it would be rude not to.

Afterwards, people were still slow to break up and leave, and they congealed into small groups to speak quietly. Tommen and Becky did not intend to join, but they got sucked into a group involving Mr. Layman and Sheriff Williams.

"Your dad doing all right at home?" Williams asked Tommen.

"Well, having a few days off is messing with his sleep schedule, but he's all right," Tommen answered with an uncertain smile. How much humor did he want to bring to a vigil? It was one thing to lighten the mood at a funeral, but this was the site of a near-massacre. *Have some respect for the dead, Tommen.*

"And what about you?" Layman inquired seriously.

"I'm all right."

This earned him a severe lecture from both the principal and the sheriff, but his attention was elsewhere on a nearby conversation from another group. It was comprised of all officers, all present at the shooting but off-duty now. They spoke in low tones about the bullets freezing in mid-air and falling to the ground. Yes, they had all seen it. They couldn't all be crazy, right?

"Maybe it was magnets of some kind," one suggested. "Electromagnetism."

"But they didn't hit anything that I saw," another said. "And to have that kind of complete coverage, no flaws, no weak spots, no boundaries. I mean, that sort of technology ought to be used by the military in some fashion. I've never seen anything like it."

"Lot of weird stuff going on the last couple years," a third officer said seriously, folding his arms. "At this point, I don't think it would be strange for cats and dogs to start talking or aliens to come down in flying saucers."

This was nervously laughed off.

"Tommen?"

Tommen blinked and came back to the present. "Huh?"

"You all right?" Layman asked. Both he and Williams were looking at him.

Tommen blinked again and rubbed his eyes. He yawned, only half-deliberate. "Yeah. No, yeah, I'm fine. I'm just tired."

"Please," Becky said. "I'm the one who's pregnant."

The way she said it told Tommen it was intended for a laugh, a way to ease the tension of the conversation. All the same, he took it as a cue for an out. They said their goodbyes to the principal and the sheriff—both men telling him that if he needed to talk or anything, they were more than willing to listen—and returned to the car. Walter had also come to the vigil, but he'd driven himself and was still speaking to some of his fellows.

Tommen and Becky left the school.

"All in all, it wasn't as bad as it could have been," Becky said in the back seat.

"That's true," Tommen agreed.

"But it's still a little odd that all of the severely wounded students got to the nurse's office. I mean, it's a good thing. Seriously, it is. I'm glad they made it. But how could they have gotten there in the chaos and confusion and all that?"

"Survival instinct?"

"Maybe. I don't know. It's pretty bizarre, but I'm not complaining. Maybe angels came down and swept them away to safety."

"Guess you'll have to ask them."

"The students or the angels?"

"Either. Both. I don't know."

They arrived home and found several business cards of various reporters taped to the front door or wedged in the frame. If they'd still had a landline and answering machine, Tommen was sure it would have been full of messages asking for comments and interviews. Tommen had blocked half a dozen numbers on his cell phone. But for the moment, the house was quiet.

Tommen did not go to Mass with Becky the next morning, despite her stubborn insistence. She said he needed a sense of community. He said he wanted to be alone. She said he needed to talk to God. He said he didn't want to make a scene if the conversation got heated. He only had to hold out until the last second before she absolutely had to leave with her mom, and he did. He wouldn't say he didn't question his decision and consider going anyway after a few minutes, but he remained where he was.

His dilemma was not with God, why He would let such a thing happen, all the usual things, though he wouldn't say those thoughts didn't occasionally dance around his mind. After all, he who did not occasionally question the nature of evil was probably living in it and therefore could not see it. But that was a little more philosophy than he wanted to think about at the moment.

His thoughts actually veered more toward whether it would be more beneficial for humanity to step into the Time industry, and how to go about it relatively safely, with as little bloodshed as possible. The two biggest things to consider were the two things never discussed in polite society: politics and religion.

This was not a new consideration, obviously, as he'd wrestled with the idea many times over the years, his arguments on either side growing more refined as he got older and could appreciate the consequences of such a dramatic change. His dad had also admitted to toying with the same ideas and questions but was unable to come up with anything feasible. There were just too many unknowns, and with the world the way it was, it probably wasn't the smartest thing to try.

But what if there was a way? Maybe it wasn't about talking to world leaders, presidents or Popes, but common men. Start small. Take an aspiring astronomer to Aleis, a human world millions of light years away. Ask him to identify the constellations and watch the look on his face as he realizes these aren't his stars. Take a ship's crew to Dorigis and watch them navigate foreign waters to new lands. Take the physically disabled and other freaks of nature to Sakaria II and introduce them to an entire world dedicated to being a proud freak. Once humanity accepted portals and far off planets, then show them Time. Show them the Wheel and the vast array of alien species found elsewhere in the universe. Maybe things would turn out all right.

His phone buzzed, the ringtone telling Tommen it was Miach. They hadn't spoken since days before the attack.

"Only have a couple minutes," the text read, "just letting everyone know we're okay. How are you?"

"Fine," Tommen replied. "How's Micaiah?"

"Instead of being gimpy on one leg, he's gimpy on two. But he's definitely getting the hang of it. Should be walking and running just fine in the next few weeks."

"What about his mind? I haven't even seen him since he apparently rose from the dead."

"Well, unless you want to follow Godwin, I don't think that's much of a possibility in the near future."

Tommen sighed. "He tried to talk me into taking Becky and my dad and running, probably with you. I should have done it. But I still can't bring myself to do it. I don't know how Becky would react."

"Life and limb, kid. I can't force you, but I would definitely suggest it. What are you doing for Thanksgiving?"

"We're going over to have dinner with Becky's family."

"Big gender reveal?"

"Yup."

"Do I get to know, too?"

Tommen managed a small smile as he replied, "Sure. After everyone else, unless you happen to be there at the same time."

"Damn," Miach said. "Well, give a guy credit for trying." Pause. Then, "Anything else on your mind or does Becky keep you on a pretty short leash?"

Tommen hesitated for a minute before answering, "Do you think there could be a safe way of doing it, or safer, anyway?" Tommen briefly relayed his ideas. They sounded fanciful now that he got them out in written form. He considered deleting the text, then sent it anyway.

It was a long few minutes before Miach replied, "Interesting thoughts, and I appreciate the approach. Bottom up instead of top down. Once again, I don't know if or how it would work. All the same, I've never been particularly ambitious. But are you asking about humanity, or Becky?"

"I have to keep her safe, Miach. Her and the baby. I don't know that I can do it and still keep her in the dark. But I don't want her to hate me for exposing her either."

"I don't have any authoritative advice to give you, kid, and I wish I did. I don't know that Cai or Kayla would either since they were both in Time when they met."

"Maybe, but Micaiah kept you in the dark about the Akarin for decades."

"I know, the jerk. But the big difference there is that I was still part of Time. I was already acquainted with the idea of aliens and universe-bending physics. The Akari and the Akarin were just one more aspect of that. It's the aliens and the universe-bending physics that are the major stumbling block."

"Becky has a stronger faith than I could ever imagine. I don't want to shatter it, but I don't want her to die because of that."

Even as he sent the text, he felt foolish for it. Chandler had said Becky would be fine. The baby would be fine. His life was the one that would end. Maybe this slothful indecision was the reason he would die a lonely, selfish coward.

"Well, you know how to run if you have to, with or without them," Miach replied. "If Godwin visits you again, I suggest you accept his offer, whatever it is. But I can't make that choice for you."

They chatted back and forth for a bit longer before Miach mentioned that his time was up and he had to retreat back to whatever interstellar hiding spot they had found.

Tommen set his phone down, leaned back in the recliner, and rubbed his face. He hated the fear and uncertainty. He hated sneaking around and having to cover everything up, explain it all away. It was getting harder and harder to do that, like putting bandaids on a leaky dam. Eventually the bandaids would fail and the dam would burst and everyone who lived downstream would be caught by surprise. Was there no pressure relief valve he could utilize?

On a whim, he called his friend Eric. Eric had been exposed to Time during a hostage negotiation gone south. He wasn't a Time Agent, but neither was he Suppressed. He knew just enough to keep Time and Bands from sneaking up on him, enough to defend himself a little if the shit hit the fan and he needed to make a quick getaway.

"Tommen, you do realize we live in different timezones now, right?" Eric answered sleepily.

"It's eleven o'clock here, so it's only eight o'clock your time," Tommen said.

"It's also my first day off in six weeks. No school, no work, no alarm."

"You're the one who picked up the phone."

Eric sighed. "What do you want, Tommen? Is something happening?"

"You didn't hear about last week, then."

"I haven't heard anything outside the damn restaurant, and I haven't been on social media much lately, or at all this last week. Why?"

Tommen relayed the events of the previous week, glad that he did not necessarily have to omit the parts about Time. He skimmed the political details. When he was finished, he could tell Eric was awake by the way he cursed.

"That's just..." Another curse. "Fuck, dude, are you all right?"

"Getting there," Tommen answered wearily.

"I mean, shit, I heard passing mention of some kind of shooting somewhere, but I guess I should have paid more attention. Fuck, man, I would have called if I would have known."

"Nah, that's all right."

"No, it's not. Look, shit happened between us, but I'd still consider you my friend. Okay?"

Tommen smiled even though Eric couldn't see. "Thanks."

"You tell me what you need, man."

"Actually, I called because I'm looking for an opinion. Someone who's an outsider but has just enough information to know what's going on."

"Knowledge of the Time industry and stuff but isn't part of it?"

"Right."

"Well, I am in California, and everyone here has an opinion. Hit me."

"Knowing what you know, and considering how it happened —at the airport and all—do you think there would be any soft or gentle way to introduce humanity to the Time industry? Is it even a good idea?"

There was silence on the line for a long moment. Finally Eric said, "Someone's been staying up at night."

"I've heard something similar. What do you think?"

Eric hesitated. Tommen could picture his expression and stance, frowning, thoughtful. Then, "Well, I don't think it would be wise to do it en masse, and I certainly don't think it would be a smart move to involve any world leaders on any scale except at the very end. Humanity isn't known for its unity and wisdom when it comes to wielding massive power. But, you take small pockets of balanced, intelligent people and gradually bring more and more people in, it might be slightly less traumatic than a nuclear bomb."

"Would you give it to everyone or just a select group?" Tommen pressed.

"Well, my first instinct as an American is to say everyone, make it fair, but that really could just be California talking. They're bleeding into me, and I don't like it. I don't think everyone would want Time, and I definitely don't think everyone could handle it. But then, who gets it, who doesn't, and who makes that determination? I don't know. That's all way above my pay grade, though it sounds like it's kept you up a night or two."

Tommen sighed. "I'm just wondering if more people wouldn't have been saved if they at least had the knowledge of it, knew it existed. Standing there stunned like a deer in headlights is just enough time for a bullet to kill you."

"You're not wrong there. But as I said, I don't know the answer. It might be that there is no good way to do it, if indeed it came to a point where humanity must know."

"Maybe the best we can hope for is the least bad," Tommen

suggested.

"Exactly, as terrible as it sounds."

They talked for a bit longer, catching up on old times and shooting the breeze until such time as Becky arrived home and Eric commented about being hungry and needing to get up and around. He promised to call at some point when he was slightly less than swamped with work and school. And maybe he would do it when it was eight o'clock at night for him but eleven o'clock at night for Tommen. Ha! How did he like that? Tommen just laughed and hung up.

He went to meet Becky, giving her a hug and a kiss and carrying off to the bedroom despite her protests.

"Someone's in a good mood," she observed, adjusting her position on the bed so she could look at him. "What did you do this morning?"

Tommen shrugged and sat down beside her. "Just called a couple friends. Talked. That's all."

"Must have been a good conversation."

"Philosophical stuff."

"Oh?" She raised a brow. "Like what?"

"Like, if humans had the power to control Time, would it be a good idea to use it on a larger scale?"

"So these are serious questions."

"And, if Books suddenly started appearing on your bookshelf, and they were Books detailing your life with total accuracy, even things you knew were hidden, as if God Himself wrote the Book just for you and about you, what would you do?"

Becky shifted position. "That is an interesting proposal. Any particular reason these were today's topics?"

He shrugged again. "I don't know. Guess I kind of wish I could go back in time and change some things. You know, what if someone did read about my life, all of the stupid and embarrassing things I've done, all the little details I would have rathered kept hidden, or just not happened?" He shifted. "What do you think?"

"I don't know. I'd have to give it a little thought. What did you come up with?"

"Well, in controlling Time and using it on a larger scale...I don't know. It might be good for the average person, but world leaders? Can you imagine the ability to manipulate Time while on the battlefield?"

"Sure. Easy. It's called *Doctor Who.*"

"Then you know what I'm talking about and why it would be a bad idea."

"You just said you weren't sure."

"Well, you just made me more sure."

Becky sat up and moved a pillow behind her to lean back on. "I don't know. What if bad guys got their hands on this power? How would good guys defend themselves against it?"

"But that just brings back the point of, is it wise to use it on a large scale?"

"Come on, Tommen, you know this. It's the same argument for or against guns; it's just a different weapon."

"Is Time a weapon?"

"It could be, I guess. The same way guns can be tools of survival, or recreational sport. If the weapon is here, there's no point in wishing it wasn't, and paranoia ultimately only breeds tyranny. The better approach would be to learn about it, understand it, and use it safely. And if someone decides not to use it safely, then chop their head off."

"So you would argue for this mass use of Time."

"Looks that way."

"But how would you introduce it? Changing the physics of the universe is...pretty heavy."

Becky nodded. "Oh, definitely. So to that I would say one person at a time. Do it en masse and you'll only cause widespread panic. As it was once stated, 'A person is smart. People are dumb.' Just do it a little at a time so that everyone who is aware of and uses this power is highly intelligent and emotionally stable. It's hard to make vilifying accusations stick when the one being accused is an upstanding citizen, if you get my meaning."

"I don't know, have you been on social media lately?"

"All right, point taken. But you get what I'm saying."

"Oh, I do."

Becky grabbed a second pillow and put it behind her, shifting uncomfortably. "Now, as to your second philosophical question of the day, about a book appearing detailing the events of your life as if God Himself had written it...how detailed are we talking?"

Tommen hummed. "Not necessarily a minute-by-minute or second-by-second account, but a fairly detailed series of events. This Book just randomly appears on your bookshelf one day, and inside there's a date telling you when it will be available on the general market."

Becky's eyebrows went sky high. "Oh. Wow. That does change things a little, I think. Because then it's not just being quietly called out on something—you know, if that's the intent—it's letting you know that everyone else is going to know someday, too."

"What would you do about it? And assume that there could be more than one book in the future."

For a long moment, Becky did not speak. Her eyes were huge, but her mouth was open and no words were coming out. Finally she shook her head and said, "I have no idea. I suppose, if it was from God or even just entirely factually accurate, that I would want to clean myself up a little, knowing my thoughts and actions were out there. It sounds terrible, because I should already be living that way, knowing God is always watching, but that obviously isn't true a hundred percent of the time." She looked down at her baby belly and patted it twice. Then she looked at Tommen. "What about you? What would you do?"

"I'm right there with you. I don't know what I'd do. Now, if it was a real person doing it, I'd sue them for stalking. It's a little harder to tell God to do or not do something."

Becky laughed. "You're not wrong there."

There was a knock on the door, then a pause before Walter pushed it open. With a woman in the house now, he made an effort to be more presentable than just an undershirt and boxers, and as such, he stood in the doorway in sweatpants and an old plain T-shirt. He yawned dramatically. "Young'uns have no respect for their elders."

"Sorry," Tommen said, still grinning.

His dad waved a hand. "Nah, you didn't wake me. But it's good to see you smiling again, kid."

Tommen felt his ears turn red and he looked away. "Yeah."

"At any rate, are either of you hungry?"

They both declined and he wandered off, closing the door behind him.

"Your dad can be so weird at times," Becky commented.

Tommen nodded deliberately. "I'm coming to this conclusion as well, after many years of living with him—ow!" He made a scene of rubbing his arm where Becky had lightly punched him.

"I can see where you get it." Becky climbed off the bed. "Come on, let's do something."

"Like what?"

"I don't know but I'm bored, baby's active, and I want to get out and do something before being snowed in for six months."

"It won't be six months," Tommen sighed dramatically, following her out of the bedroom and to the living room. "Get it right; it'll be at least eight."

Becky just shook her head and made for the kitchen to pull on her shoes. Walter raised a brow and looked at Tommen who shrugged but dutifully followed suit. She headed out to the garage, outside to Tommen's car, and climbed in her usual seat in the back.

"So, where are we going?" Tommen asked, opening the driver door and getting in.

They ended up going to see Will. The blind man was working on some college work and was all too happy to have visitors to distract him. His service dog, Sydney, was happy for a new playmate to throw her ball. The other dog in the house, a dachshund named

Graham Cracker, was also happy to have a lap to sit on. While Tommen, Becky, and Will went outside to play with the dogs, Mrs. Shaw made them all lunch. Eli remained shut up in his room, still angry at all of them over the street racing incident. He blamed his brother for telling Tommen who told his dad. Will was more than happy to let him stew, and instead enjoyed the late fall afternoon with his friends.

"Well, no matter what, I'm glad you're all right," Will said, tossing the ball and listening to the dogs take off across the leaf-covered lawn. Becky laughed as leaves kicked up from Sydney's massive paws showered over her.

"I'm glad I'm okay, too," Tommen said smartly.

"Yeah, you sound like you've been through some shit with your hearing and your arm and everything else. It's about time you got a break."

"A break. Yeah, that's what it was."

Will shook his head and opened his mouth, but could not speak before the dogs came scampering back. Tommen threw the ball this time. Leaves and dirt went flying, Graham Cracker barking hysterically, probably telling Sydney with the much longer legs to slow down.

"I didn't mean it like that," Will said.

"I know," Tommen told him.

"How's college going for you, Will?" Becky asked.

"Not bad, actually. My instructors think I'm an audio learner. My English grades have been great, just listening to stuff, you know? I don't have to read a bunch of stuff, look at tables and a bunch of words on a page. Just listening to it, I get it. And I'm like a speed reader in braille now, which is cool."

"Come and get it, guys," Mrs. Shaw called from the front door.

The dogs knew what that meant, and they reacted quicker than the humans. Despite being farther away, they moved faster than the humans, too, and got to the house first, nearly taking out Tommen in the knees and ankles as they stormed past and clambered through the door, Sydney tripping over Graham Cracker and causing a small pileup right in the entryway.

"Sydney, come!" Will snapped as they crossed the lawn.

The German shepherd jumped to attention and went to her master like a heat-seeking missile, standing faithfully by his side to guide him into the house. Tommen and Becky followed, both still laughing from the furry collision.

Lunch was sandwiches and potato salad. The three of them spent the afternoon talking about work and school, as it related to Will and Becky being in college. While Tommen knew this was a deliberate attempt at avoiding mention of the shooting, it also made him feel left out and, if truth be told, a little inadequate, like a child sitting in at the grownup table. He was still in high school. He still plodded along with everyone else in the same schedule five days a week. Half the school couldn't drive yet and drama covered everyone and everything like a fast-spreading disease. And here his friend and his fiancée — his fiancée! — were discussing classes and schooling on a much higher level, leaving him behind.

He said none of this out loud and only occasionally added his thoughts and opinions to the conversation, pretending to be immersed in the food and even asking for a second helping when he really wasn't feeling it. Getting rid of Time and using more of the Akari had set him back to rights on slower aging and a slower metabolism, though it would be short-lived until the baby arrived.

Tommen and Will talked school and work while Becky and Mrs. Shaw talked kids and family. In a moment of clarity and reflection, Tommen suddenly realized that he was an adult. He didn't give two shits about who was dating who in school, who was cheating on who, some frivolous upcoming test, his future plans as if they were still a distant thing, this teacher or that teacher was being so mean lately, or any of that. He was an adult talking about work and family and, yes, school, but on a practical level, not a dramatic one. It was oddly refreshing.

In one of his Books, Tommen read about some past thoughts

he had about those who had graduated being such snobs toward those who were still in school. They weren't necessarily snobs. They just had more important things to worry about, like whether a paycheck was coming in, if they could afford both food and a badly needed brake job, and whether things would be calm enough at home to have some semblance of a relaxing night. It was all so simple now, he thought.

After lunch, they played with the dogs a little more until it began to rain. Tommen and Becky returned home. From there, it was pretty much free reign. It was odd to consider that there would be no school the next day, though Tommen had a tough time convincing himself that it was just an extended Thanksgiving vacation. To help calm some of his anxiety over it, Becky gave him a back rub plus a little more. Tommen found himself lamenting that their schedules were finally falling in such a way that sleeping in and morning sex would be possible...except that was out of the question now. No more until after the baby way born. Months after the baby was born. Tommen's groin was not pleased with this idea.

But he was pleased to wake up beside Becky the next morning, Monday morning, and just lay there for a while. Cuddling, kissing, touching, he was okay with that, and Becky didn't complain either. In fact, the only reason they got up was because she got hungry. The smell of breakfast brought Walter out of hibernation, too. The three of them had pancakes and sausage, then headed into the living room to watch TV. It was raining out, and Tommen and Becky were just happy to finally have a day without school. Sure, she could go down to her parents' house and work on her sewing, but she declared she was taking a vacation day. As the boss of her business, she could do that; who was going to stop her?

Not Tommen. He was just going to enjoy a slow day, drown himself in fantasy television, not think about last week, look forward to Thanksgiving on Thursday, and make today a very forgettable day.

His dad left for work around three, but it didn't change anything for Tommen or Becky. The pair had alternated between TV and the Internet for entertainment, with occasional bouts of reading.

Tommen's boss, Chris, asked him if he wanted to work Tuesday to pick up some extra hours, seeing how he'd had last weekend off. Tommen considered rejecting the offer, but agreed at the last minute. He needed to get back to work and do something real to take his mind off all the bad things. TV was a bandaid, but some hard work would do him good.

He got up the next morning just as his dad was getting home from work.

"How are things at the station?" Tommen asked, flipping on the light over the stove.

"Not bad at all," his dad reported, sounding relieved. "Every single one of the kids—or, you know, those who weren't DOA—they all pulled through. Even the critical ones turned the corner over the weekend and are expected to make a recovery. That helps a lot, it really does."

"That's good."

His dad leaned back in the chair and used his heel to slip his other boot off. "And, of course, everyone has an opinion on the politics of the situation."

"Gun control and mental health?"

"You know it. Gun control, mental health, abuse, addiction, security, the whole nine yards."

"What's the sheriff got to say?"

His dad gave him a look. "You want the PC answer or his personal thoughts?"

"Which one do you think?"

"He says that Tyler and Ryan had been getting off way too easy, Tyler a more recent example of school administrative authority not being allowed to go far enough to discipline truly dangerous students."

Tommen folded his arms. "Oh, tell me what he really thinks."

"Well, now that the chaos is over, he and Casey Oldman and school administrators are at odds over how to prevent future tragedy." He made a point of adding sarcastic emphasis to the last two words.

"Why is Oldman involved?"

"Because he was there, and he was the one who was literally spear-heading all of the new safety measures for this school year, safety measures that obviously failed. Now all of the school districts are on edge. Since what happens at one affects the rest, at least in terms of events like this, the Powers That Be think it would be beneficial for all or most of the schools to be on the same page, that way all of law enforcement is generally caught up on procedure and protocol."

It wasn't a bad reason, Tommen thought. It just meant that people had to play nice with each other, and not everyone was willing to play nice when it meant letting the other guy call the shots. Egos could be set aside in the midst of chaos, but when they had time to think about it, ego usually won out. In this case, you had the grizzled old-timer of the county mounties pitted against a retired Coast Guardsman and New York City cop who was now in charge of a city police department. There would be plenty of measuring going on, and that was even before school administrators, city councils, and county government got involved. Welcome to politics.

"Any other news floating around of the non-local variety?" Tommen wondered, unsure if he really wanted to know the answer.

His dad looked thoughtful for a moment. Then, "Well, seems pretty cut and dry. Julianna sent out her murder squads against the Akarin and a slightly larger force against the Miaramila. If rumors are to be believed, the Borelians are a little upset that they didn't get invited to the murder spree, or attempted murder spree, against the humans involved, and are harping on the Tacagans to figure out a way through the shields or else unlock the Akari. Those are the highlights from the eastern front."

"Any indication that she could try again in those areas she failed in?"

"What do you think? I just got the evening news report from Miach who got it from someone else. I'm sure there is plenty more going on in the battle tent, but if you're not going to be a part of it, then don't go knocking."

"I didn't ask for Tyler and Ryan to come shoot up my school," Tommen said hotly. "I would love to be able to just walk away from the battlefield, except now the battlefield seems to be coming to me."

His dad just nodded graciously. "I understand that. But that's why you're still training with Nathan, isn't it? You learn what you need to protect yourself and your family, but you're not getting overly wrapped up in the larger politics and the mayhem." With a grunt, Walter got to his feet. "I'd like to think it's a bit like myself."

"How so?"

"In police work. I've learned enough to protect myself, my family, this community, but I don't get involved in the politics, and I'm not out fighting a war. Bad things happen, but I deal with them. See where I'm going with this?"

Tommen let out a breath and nodded. "Yeah, I guess so."

"Do what you can, where you are. Same as I'm about to do. I'm about to go to sleep, in my bed."

Tommen grinned and moved so his dad could get past him.

He got himself some breakfast and packed a lunch, leftover meatloaf from the night before along with some potato salad, a bag of chips, a couple cookies, and a fruit drink in addition to his regular water bottle. Safety was Chris' number one priority, and that included staying hydrated, even in the winter. Then he returned to the bedroom to kiss Becky goodbye.

"I love you," he murmured.

She smiled sleepily and he wondered if she would even remember this when she got up later in the morning. Then she mumbled, "Only a couple more days."

"Until what?"

"Until we can finally tell everyone the sex. Then we don't have to keep up this charade."

"Yup." He kissed her again. "Only a couple more days."

Then she pulled the blankets up farther and rolled over away from him.

Tommen crept out of the room and headed out to the garage. The ground and roads were still wet from the day before, the temperature hovering around forty with thick fog resting in the low areas, but they were supposed to see a pretty good dip over the holidays. If things didn't dry out before then, they would be looking at some serious ice. This wouldn't normally be a problem as Tommen considered himself a decent driver and he didn't normally have too far to go. It would, however, be a problem trying to get to their current construction site, both in terms of driving and walking. The driveway was a long, steep, winding thing that most big trucks could not make easily or swiftly. Once the ice and snow hit, there would be no delivery trucks of any size going up to the house. Even most small vehicles probably wouldn't make it (hardly a problem since the owners were only seasonal snobs anyway). Tommen's car was getting pretty iffy about it, and it was a treacherous climb without cleats on his boots.

He wasn't the only one disgruntled with the choice of venue, but they only had to build it; they didn't have to live in it.

At the very least, all the outside work was done and the furnace was installed and working, which meant they could work comfortably and not freeze their asses off.

Since going back to school, Tommen only worked weekends, or an occasional after school gig for a few hours. He'd worked basically all day every day over the summer and been a major part of the team. Only working weekends kind of made him a grunt, a helping hand of sorts. He got everything on a need to know basis.

It was a little strange to walk on the site on a Tuesday, but the guys welcomed him back and put him to work. The electrical and plumbing had just been approved by the inspector, so now it was a sprint to the finish line. Drywall, flooring, then small stuff. With any luck, they would be done by Christmas. If that was the case, Chris said he would give everyone that whole week off, from Christmas Eve through the weekend after New Year's, with a holiday bonus check. It was pretty good motivation, say it that way, but only if they got it done fast and got it done right.

The problem really wasn't the project itself, whatever it may be, but the sheer size of the house. Tommen's house could fit on each story twice and then some. And it wasn't just throw the drywall up, slap some flooring down, but everything was infuriatingly complex and detailed. Nope, couldn't just lay down wood floors. They had to be herringbone pattern. Same with the tile. Not just squares, not just rows, but detailed patterns and pictures. Complex and tedious.

The guys were really coming to hate this project and the homeowners. Only because of the generous paychecks did they keep their mouths shut, or in check, anyway. But with the end in sight, they were happy to plow ahead.

Tommen got put on mud duty, mixing up the mud for the drywall. One team went through to cut and slap panels while another team came behind them to mud and sand the drywall. It was dusty and dirty, and soon Tommen's clothes were covered in drips and drywall dust. The sinks weren't installed yet, so he had to make do with the garden hose to wash his hands before lunch.

The guys asked general questions about Wednesday's shooting—Was he all right, how was he, was everything all right, everything calmed down yet, were all the wounded going to pull through—but the only one who pressed him at all was Matt. It was after lunch as they wrapped everything up and took bathroom breaks, all of them infinitely glad that the toilets had been installed at least. Matt caught up to Tommen as they were just heading back to work.

"Are you all right?" Matt asked, his tone telling Tommen that he wasn't referring to any indigestion or other bowel problems.

"Yeah, I'm fine," Tommen said dismissively.

"I'm not talking physically, though it is good to hear."

Tommen gave him a look. "I'm fine. I'm alive. I got to go home to sleep next to Becky. Everyone who was only injured is going to pull through."

"I'm not asking about everyone else, though. You talk about going home, but did all of you come home?"

"I doubt it. You don't just walk away from shit like that. Same with the warehouse or the Halloween bombing or anything else."

Matt dipped his head. "It takes a brave soul to acknowledge that. Now what are you doing to restore yourself? You're right, all of that stuff breaks you down, wears you out. Is there anything you would like to say, get off your chest? Talking alone can do well to restore a man in the short-term."

He was probably looking for the usual, "Why does God let bad stuff happen" shtick. Thing was, Tommen was past that. It seemed a question for small-minded people. His thoughts ran more along the lines of, How much more did he have to endure before he finally got the prize so earnestly promised to him? Run the good race, my fellows. But why did it feel as though his race was more like a super ultra marathon through a minefield with heavy artillery fire while others got off easy with the 5k downtown?

"No," he said finally. "But thanks for the offer."

Matt just nodded graciously. "Up to you. If you need an ear, I'm here."

Tommen thanked him again and they returned to work. No more was said about it.

By the time they called it quits, Tommen was covered in drywall dust and dried mud, and it felt as though they hadn't made any progress. The house was enormous. The drywall panels went up with little problem and made the whole place look almost done, but the mudding and sanding was so slow and tedious. Well, at least it wasn't like their last house where it had a ton of teeny little niches and alcoves that had to be precisely measured and and finagled here and there and they still wouldn't fit. There was something to be said for open floor plans.

He returned home. His dad was gone. Since he had the forethought to text Becky when he was leaving, she had dinner going by the time he walked in the door. By the time he took a shower and changed his clothes, she said, it would probably be done. He kissed her, tossed his dishes in the sink and made his way down to the bathroom.

Warm water felt pretty darn good, he thought, standing under the shower head. It still made his burned arm sting a little, but otherwise, it was nice to watch the dust and mud slide off his skin and clean it out of his hair. Construction was tough and dirty, but at least he could get rid of his work down the drain and not have to carry home a huge briefcase full of papers or other extra work that needed to be done.

Feeling a hundred times better than when he walked in, Tommen toweled off and went to find a change of clothes. Becky was trying to talk him into getting a set of pajamas to throw on after he showered off from work—just something comfortable to wear for the evening, she said—but he didn't see why a normal change of clothes couldn't work. Problem was, he knew that someday a custom-tailored set of pajamas was going to show up on the bed or in a Christmas present. Well, he figured, a present was fine. He just wasn't going to go out of his way to buy a set of pajamas.

He pulled on a T-shirt and some light sweatpants and called it good. When he turned to head out the door back to the kitchen, he noticed something on his nightstand. It was a simple card, tented on top of the stand. He knew the handwriting on the face almost instantly. It was from Chandler.

With some trepidation, Tommen reached for the card. Was it a warning? A message? Could the ghost man simply be wishing him a happy Thanksgiving? He opened it up.

You are not safe. Don't let your guard down. -Chandler

Tommen's heart jumped into his throat, but his body did not move and his mind did not react. On the one hand, it was almost laughable. Of course he wasn't safe. Not only was it nothing new, but the man had already told him that he was going to die. What could top that? He'd been through so much shit, gotten rid of his two greatest adversaries to no real effect, what more could possibly be asked of him except his life?

It was his own thoughts that made his blood turn to ice. He'd gotten rid of his two greatest adversaries. Gotten rid of them. Disposed of. Been victorious over. Killed.

He'd crossed a line. It wasn't just about going into battle, being a failed medic, or aiding the enemy. He had killed. Julianna had forced his hand so far as to ensure he could never be Batman. He had broken his no-kill vow. He had killed. He could kill. He would kill. And now that that wall had been torn down, what else was she going to unleash on him? What else would she try and make him do? Push him hard, incriminate him, maybe, isolate him, certainly. Get him alone, separate from the herd, and go in for the kill. A lonely, selfish coward. The shooting had certainly been a plan with a specific goal in mind. But if that failed, it didn't mean that it had all been for nothing. The shooting hadn't been as unproductive as most might make it out to be.

You are not safe. Don't let your guard down.

Tommen swallowed, took an even breath, and got out a lighter so he could burn the card. Maybe Julianna's ploy wasn't going after Becky directly, but turning Tommen into the very bad guy he feared. And who was a man's worst enemy but himself?

Chapter Sixteen
Giving Thanks

Tommen watched the news for any mention of an Earth-side link between the half a dozen attacks confirmed to be Time-side linked back to Julianna, but none was revealed, which was to be expected. A school shooting, a fight in a dark alley—which no one would have seen because of the use of the Akari and Time—a Mt. Everest hopeful falling a hundred and twenty feet and miraculously surviving, a sudden and unprecedented shark attack off the coast of Australia, a surprise jaguar attack on a group of tourists in Guatemala, and an attempted mugging in Rome. There was no way any casual observer was going to link all of those incidents together.

Miach mentioned that the Miaramila claimed to have intercepted plans for a dozen more attacks on Earth Akarin and others sympathetic to the Akarin and Miaramila. Between those intercepted plans and the other foiled plots—or not so foiled, as the shark attack victim proved to be—a dozen Order operatives had been captured and were being interrogated. Tommen did not expect any information to make it as far as his doorstep, though he was willing to bet that Julianna was not pleased with her dismal success rate.

You are not safe. Don't let your guard down.

Chandler did not visit that night or the night after. Thanksgiving arrived. Tommen was fully prepared for some catastrophe in true poetic form, right in line with everything else the Author had done so far, beating up on various holidays until they were nothing more than temporal torture chambers on the calendar.

That preparedness only lasted about the first two minutes of wakefulness, until Becky stirred beside him and moved his hand to feel the movements inside her from their child. Their daughter. And by the end of the day, everyone else would know that it was a girl, too. Then maybe they could get some peace and quiet and stop with all the backhanded attempts at weaseling out the information. Then they would have to listen to everyone give them suggestions about names.

They had decided to keep the name in reserve until the birth. Let them guess, let them suggest, and then let them be amazed. A little over three months, they could deal with it.

She kissed him. "So, what are you thankful for?"

"I am thankful for you," he murmured. "And our daughter. And I'm thankful to be alive today. What about you?"

"I can't answer that without sounding like a lame copycat. But, aside from all of that, I am thankful for my family and your family, that they still support us even if we've been less than angelic."

"I can agree to that, definitely." Tommen let out a breath. "Yeah, I'm thankful for that for sure. And for having a job and the chance to get an education so we're not trailer trash parents. For still being physically healthy enough to hold a good job." He flexed his left hand for emphasis. "There's plenty to be thankful for."

"There's always something." Becky kissed him again and sat up. "For instance, modern plumbing." She got off the bed. "And other people's cooking."

She meandered her way to the bathroom while Tommen stretched, all the way from his head to his fingertips to his toes. It was a good day, he thought. He still didn't feel quite right since the shooting, but putting a little temporal distance behind him helped to soften the burden. He relaxed for a second, then forced himself to sit up and acknowledge the existence of the outside world.

Thanksgiving. A day for eating too much, telling the same stories as last year, remarking on how big children were getting, and so on. It was almost like dress rehearsal for Christmas, except Christmas involved presents.

As for the two of them, it would be another day of everyone

wanting to know how Becky was doing, how was the baby (and, by the way, what was the sex again?), were they ready, and on and on. Except this time it would be the entire family. Her entire family. All her brothers and sisters and their kids—well, the older ones. The same questions asked a dozen different times a dozen different ways.

Really, Tommen was just going for the food. That was half the point of Thanksgiving, after all. It wasn't that he wasn't thankful for things, but he was just more...aware of it lately, so much so that having a dedicated holiday almost felt unnecessary. He was very thankful, very grateful to just be alive. Now pass the mashed potatoes.

Actually, the odds of having mashed potatoes at this particular Thanksgiving were pretty slim. Becky's family didn't do things the same way other families did, normal families. The dishes that they passed around had names that sounded more like sneezes or something out of a Dr. Seuss picture book. Turkey wasn't just turkey, and there was no such thing as just plain old potatoes or common biscuits.

Becky had made up a Polish dish the night before and made the whole house stink, so Tommen cooked up some Welsh stew to drive away the smell and replace it with something far more appetizing. Once they were ready, they'd just walk down to her parents' house and join the fray.

Walter would not be joining them. The night before had been long, and he expected another long night tonight. He was taking all the sleep he could get.

"Have fun without me, kids," he'd told them the previous afternoon before leaving for work.

Tommen suspected that even if the former weren't true, his dad probably still wouldn't be enthusiastic about the prospect of dinner with Becky's family. They were a nice family, but Walter wasn't much of a people person. A group of adults, sure, but toss in a dozen grandkids and great-grandkids...even Tommen wasn't thrilled at the idea except for the part where he was going to have a kid here soon. He was going to have to get used to stuff like this.

It was a daunting prospect.

Becky finished up in the bathroom and Tommen took his turn, making sure his grooming was impeccable. There was no such thing as a casual dinner with her family either. Tommen could not recall any instance where her dad wore jeans or cargo pants or even shorts. Always good clothes. Her mom was a little more relaxed, but then, she wore scrubs at the hospital and she had numerous grandkids at her house at any given time, so jeans and a nice blouse probably was her idea of getting dressed up.

True to form of what would be expected, Tommen wore his good clothes, dress pants and a button-down shirt. Becky had arranged his clothes in chromological order, and his color-correcting glasses certainly helped things, but he kept the pins on the sleeves anyway, denoting which shirt was which color. Today he chose purple.

He brushed his hair again, figuring he was about as good as he was going to get, and headed out to the kitchen. He'd barely crossed the threshold when his pot of stew was pushed into his hands. Becky grabbed her dish—still reeking despite the plastic cover—and looked at him expectantly.

"I still have to get my shoes on," he informed her, setting down his pot and reaching for his shoes.

"My goodness," Becky said, her tone making it difficult to judge whether she was being playfully exasperated or if she was actually annoyed with him. With her pregnancy hormones, sometimes it could be hard to tell. Nevertheless, Tommen elected to Band just a teeny bit to speed things up so they could be on their way.

Initially, Tommen had offered to drive the quarter mile to her parents' house, citing the cold, the possibility of ice, and, of course, the pregnancy. Becky had harshly informed him that just because she was pregnant did not mean that she was suddenly made of glass. She could handle a short walk. In fact, in might actually be good for her. For both of them. Tommen simply put up his hands in surrender and said it was her call.

It was hard living with a pregnant woman. He'd engaged in a few jokes here and there relating to it, but now that he was actually living it, he understood. He understood very well, and he was finding that there was very little that could be exaggerated too much. She was emotional. She was moody. She was stubborn. And there was no way she was going to ask for help. So it was that Tommen did not ask if she wanted him to take her dish that she was carrying, but he simply shortened his stride, manipulated Time just a teeny bit once more, shifted his own pot, and took her dish from her. She grumbled a protest but did not fight him. The going was a little slower after that as he carefully juggled two dishes, but they made it to her parents' house no worse for wear.

Becky's brother Danny met them at the door and took the dishes, handing one off to his wife. Tommen was grateful for the reprieve, knowing he would not be able to slip his shoes off and balance everything with the number of children running around and playing games in every room in the house, including the entryway.

It was the first major holiday that Becky was spending as a guest in the house. She couldn't just sneak away to her room to hide (although she probably could and would later on), couldn't just run to grab this or that from her room, and she hadn't had to get up early with her mom to cook and get everything ready. Put simply, it was her first major holiday as a grown adult. Nothing was unusual about it to Tommen, coming over, but he could see the shift in Becky's demeanor as she greeted her brothers and sisters and other assorted family members. Hell, she had nieces and nephews older than her.

Tommen received multiple compliments on his beard. The men called it ruggedly handsome, the women called it thick and luxurious. Tommen decided he liked the former better.

And while it wasn't unusual for him to walk into the house as a guest, the general attitude toward him had changed. He was no longer just Becky's boyfriend, her latest one from high school that she wanted to show off to everyone. He was family now. He was the father of her child. He was in this for the long haul. As such, conversation turned from pithy questions and answers about high school and other superficial stuff, to work, parenthood, future plans, higher education, political leanings, and religious beliefs. As one of the brothers put it, polite society said that politics and religion should never be discussed. But for Catholics, Jews, and Muslims, there was no discussion except politics and religion.

With the elections coming up in less than a year, opinions were hot and heard around the house, whether they were requested or not. Everyone had something to say about the candidates, the platforms, the proposals, and all the doom and gloom and the end of the world that would inevitably ensue should one person or the other win.

The family certainly gave Tommen a run for his money. He liked to think he didn't come across as ignorant himself as he proposed some very odd theories, using his experience with the Author and the Akari and especially the Books to, in a roundabout way, mine for possibilities and answers and other political and theological challenges. The conversation wound this way and that, tying them all up in theological and scientific knots until they hardly knew which way was up. Personally, Tommen thought it great fun, but even he had to admit he was exhausted from the debates and growing rather hungry.

Children ran to and fro with various toys playing a multitude of games. Conversation was often interrupted by a child approaching mom or dad, asking for this or that, or crying for them to settle a dispute in their favor. Tommen had largely ignored all of this activity in holidays past, but now he paid attention. How was he going to respond to his child asking for this or that? How would he handle disputes with other children? If they had more kids in the future, how would he handle sibling rivalry? Obviously he wanted to be fair, but it was just a fact of life that everyone wanted to make his side of the argument sound the most plausible and sympathetic, even if that meant adding or omitting a few details, and children were no different. Whoever reached Mom or Dad first always had the toy first and the other child wasn't sharing or was being bossy or annoying or whatever the case was.

"So, when are you finally telling the sex?" Uri, the oldest Polski child, asked after he successfully mediated another dispute.

"After dinner," Tommen informed him.

"You're just making everyone wait as long as possible, aren't you?" Danny chuckled. "Masters of suspense."

"Not quite. If we were masters of suspense, we wouldn't tell you at all and make you wait until the birth."

"Well, all the same, you are terrible people. Clearly Becky has corrupted you."

Tommen just grinned.

"All right, you gossiping hens," Mrs. Polski said from the kitchen. "Dinner is about done, so go get washed up."

The men were slow to get up and actually get around to washing their hands and finding a place at the table. Seats were claimed with jackets and drinks, but no one actually sat yet. Dr. Polski and his Jewish clan had to say their prayers, and Mrs. Polski and her Catholic kin bowed their heads for their recitations. Tommen still found it all a bit strange and maybe a little off, but he respectfully said nothing, simply waited for everyone to be finished and the feast to begin.

Unlike most places where the children were fed first in order to shut them up long enough for the adults to grab a bite to eat, the Polski family did everything by descending age. Dr. Polski, being the oldest, got his food first, followed by Mrs. Polski, then the children and the grandchildren and on down the line. A few children complained about being hungry or it being unfair, but most of them were actually very well-behaved and understanding of the whole thing. Tommen wondered whether they understood the significance of their place in line. The closer they got to the front, the more people ahead of them had died, and the closer they themselves were to death. It was a morbid thought.

It was an entertaining thought to consider how things would

be different if they went by actual years. Tommen would end up being ahead of Dr. Polski, having a good eighty years or so on him. Or there was Walter at a solid two hundred years old, or thereabouts. Now that would be a Thanksgiving dinner line to have, taking a bunch of Time Agents or Akari-bearers and lining them up for dinner according to actual age. Ha!

Tommen sent a quick text to his dad, asking if he had changed him mind about coming down. His dad did not reply. Probably still sleeping then. He would wake up just in time to go back to work for another long night. Well, at the very least, Tommen could bring him back some leftovers; there would be no shortage of those, despite the dozens of mouths getting ready to chow down.

He himself would be back for seconds, mostly because there was too much food, too many choices, to fit on just one plate. He only took a little scoop of everything, child-sized portions that almost made him feel disrespectful, until he considered that two bites of everything eventually added up to a full plate. Or two or three, in the case of the Polski Thanksgiving.

He paused for just a moment, considering. He'd learned that concept from the twins. Micah and Micaiah. It felt like so long ago, the four of them sitting at the dining table in the twins' rather luxurious home. Tommen didn't even know who'd bought their house. Had they made any changes or simply left everything as-is? There was certainly no real need to undertake any major remodels, at least, not for the same reasons Walter had updated his house. The twins had lived in a fairly posh affair. Only a rich person concerned with the latest styles of the season would be so rude as to rip anything out.

On the other hand, maybe Tommen was just being sentimental. There were days when he wondered what life would be like if he'd never found that body in the soccer fields. If the coup had never happened. If he just lived a normal life as a normal teenager. Would he still be here, having Thanksgiving with Becky's family, about to be a dad in just over three months?

He'd had a chance to be normal once, right after the coup

when his dad Suppressed everyone. He'd whined and complained and said he couldn't do it. He hadn't really taken the time to enjoy life as a normal person. Well, he thought, looking at Becky and her swollen belly, it looked like he was about to get a second chance.

You are not safe. Don't let your guard down.

He sighed internally. Would he receive a postcard in the mail telling him when the threats had stopped and life could resume, when he could breathe a sigh of relief and move on with his life? Maybe he would get a phone call? Or maybe he would finally receive his last Book, the one that ended with, "Happily ever after. The end."

No. Because there was no happily ever after in store for him. A lonely, selfish coward.

He forced his thoughts away from his brooding and back to happier things, trying not to let his wild imagination and paranoia ruin a nice holiday. At the same time, the Author had ruined so many holidays for him in the last couple years, could anyone really blame him for being so cynical?

He took a bite of food, trying to bring himself back to the present. He needed to find a conversation or something to focus on in the present, something to anchor to and be a part of. Becky was talking to one of her nieces who was actually a couple years older than her. The men were still discussing politics and religion.

You are not safe. Don't let your guard down.

Yeah, thanks a lot, Chandler. I probably could have figured that out on my own. Now how about giving me a few clues on what to watch out for? Places to avoid, people to avoid, things like that. Hey, if you see this person, run. Hey, there's going to be an attack on this day and time. Or, if you go this place, then it will set events in motion that lead to an attack at a later date. Things like that. Telling me stuff I already know doesn't really help things.

He took another bite of food.

"So, when is the gender reveal?"

Tommen turned to see Aaron approaching, plate of food in hand. He was Becky's nephew and also a junior this year at school.

From what Tommen understood, no one knew their relation, so Aaron managed to skate any bullying by association.

"Between dinner and dessert," Tommen informed him.

"Well, at least that's a little more specific than just 'today' I guess," Aaron mused.

"What exactly do you guys think is going to miraculously change just from this announcement?"

"Nothing. But at least everyone knows."

Tommen gave him a look. "Do you really care that much, or did someone put you up to this because we go to school together?"

Aaron shrugged. "Mom and Grandma may have put me up to it. Hey, they said I'd get twenty bucks apiece if I managed to get the information out of you."

Tommen whistled. "That's a pretty easy forty bucks right there."

"So what do you say? Help me get rich today?"

"Not a chance. But—" Tommen raised a fork in mock toast. "—I commend your efforts." And he took a bite of food. "See if maybe they won't go for half price for at least trying."

Aaron shook his head, but he was grinning. "All or nothing deal, I'm afraid."

"You people," Tommen sighed, tsking light-heartedly.

"It's a big family, what can I say? Big Catholic and-or Jewish family. Everyone's in your business and everyone's interested in the latest gossip, especially when it involves kids and pregnancies."

"Isn't there a Bible verse warning against gossip?"

Aaron waved a hand dismissively. "Bah. Details. Besides, where's the line between harmlessly exchanging information and gossiping? Otherwise the evening news could be considered gossip. And anyway, I'd rather see the gossip out in the open, you know, being talked about, than wonder what people are thinking. In case you haven't noticed in the last couple years, or the last couple months, it's not hard to figure out what people in this family are thinking."

Tommen raised a brow. "I don't know. Dr. Polski still spooks me a little. What?"

Aaron was laughing. "You're, what, a year older than me? He's my grandpa and your father-in-law. How f-ed up is that?"

Dr. Polski had great-grandchildren older than this newest grandchild who hadn't even been born yet. Tommen hoped Becky was right, in that the Church and the synagogue kept impeccable family records, because future generations were going to look at this and say, "Huh?"

At least they hadn't made him go through baptism or confirmation or anything like that, at least not yet. There would probably be something of the sort at the wedding. As long as it wasn't circumcision, he could suffer through whatever ritual they wanted him to partake in.

Damn. Wedding. He was going to be getting married here in, what, six months? Seven? They hadn't even talked about it for a good six weeks. Most of that stuff got put on the backburner in favor of baby stuff which was coming up much faster. Tommen knew less about weddings than he did babies, and that was saying something. Mostly he just figured that women had their future weddings planned out from the first time they heard the words, "Happily ever after." All he had to do was show up. He was probably being fanciful, and Becky would surely inform him of that and let him know just how ignorant he was of the whole thing.

But that was neither here nor there as Tommen got himself another plate of food. Aaron had wandered off and evidently informed those who commissioned him to needle information out of Tommen that the gender reveal would be between dinner and dessert. And Tommen had just gotten himself another plate of food, which meant that the reveal was being pushed back, stalled for an indeterminate length of time.

Becky had wanted to do a number of wacky ideas for the gender reveal, things having to do with balloons or a scavenger hunt or just blowing up a block of colored chalk infused with Tannerite. Tommen wouldn't say that he hadn't taken to the Tannerite idea, but he wasn't sure how he would react to the explosion, given the events of Halloween, something Becky admitted she wasn't quite one hundred percent over yet either. PTSD was something they had to contend with now, and it was frightening to consider. Tommen also cited concerns from the neighbors as well as ensuring that her parents didn't keel over from a heart attack induced by the explosion, both of which she reluctantly conceded.

So, for as much fun as it would be to blow stuff up, they decided to forgo the Tannerite. Instead, they went with something a lot safer, though it still involved colored chalk.

Tommen made sure to drag out his eating as much as possible. He knew he was probably mentally exaggerating everyone's interest in the reveal. Most of those gathered were immersed in their own conversations about a variety of topics, and only a couple seemed to have any sort of dedicated interest, at least to the extent that they were giving him dirty looks, no doubt willing him to hurry up and finish so they could get it over with.

Only when he delivered his plate to the dishwasher did Becky announce that the gender reveal would commence posthaste. All they needed was a garden hose.

The family gathered outside, or the adults did, anyway, facing the sidewalk at the end of the walkway. Uri brought a garden hose around and gave it to Tommen.

The night before, he'd come out and painted on the sidewalk with a fairly durable paint. Then he colored over it with at least a thousand pounds of sidewalk-colored chalk and a little concrete dust from work. He swept the nozzle back and forth over the colored over area, revealing "It's a" painted deviously in blue. Becky had the idea for the second part. It wouldn't take but three seconds to identify the curve of a "g" or the straight lines of a "b" and half the surprise would be ruined, to say nothing of his hard work. So instead, she got a little cheeky, instead telling him to use chromosomes instead. Everyone had an X, and it wouldn't be until the last moment that everyone would see the second X. Tommen had the idea of making the whole thing blue except for the second X which would be pink.

Everyone thought they had it figured it out, then, as the water washed away the first X, still colored blue. Then the smiles and the cheers died down to confusion as the blue suddenly gave way to the pink of the second X. And there it was. "It's a XX" on the sidewalk. Then the smiles and cheers came back, even as a few faded and a couple people shook their heads and commended the couple on a creatively deceptive reveal.

"What's XX?" one of the grandkids asked, about five or six years old.

"That means it's a girl," his mom said.

Mrs. Polski hugged her daughter and said something in Hungarian. Becky's smile was huge and she replied, matching whatever sarcastic comment her mother had made.

"Very clever," Dr. Polski said, walking up behind Tommen. "You really had my hopes up for a second."

"Hoping for a boy, were you?" Tommen asked.

"Every man hopes for a boy, if he is honest with himself."

"Well, my family has a history of having only two boys and a multitude of girls. I'm proof of that, my dad, his dad. So, we'll see what happens."

The doctor raised a brow. "Already planning on more?"

"Ah...we're waiting to see how this goes."

"Good answer." Dr. Polski patted Tommen on the shoulder and moved off to speak to Becky.

And there it was. Finally out there. They were having a girl. Bring on the dresses and the flowers and the name suggestions.

Tommen took a picture of the sidewalk and sent it to his dad and Miach. Miach did not reply, but that was to be expected. His dad, though, replied within sixty seconds.

"Congrats, kiddo! Get ready for pretty princesses and tea parties!"

"What if she's a country girl?" Tommen replied, grinning.

"Pink camo and racing her Jeeps against the boys?"

"Works for me, long as she wins."

"I'm sure you'll teach her how to do that. Can I spread the news around or is it still classified information?"

"No, go ahead, tell the guys."

"Do I get a name with this or is that still pretty hush-hush?"

"We're debating on Christmas, but for now, hush-hush."

Tommen could imagine his dad dramatically rolling his eyes. "Sheesh. You'd think the information would start a war if it got out."

"Considering some of the things I've started wars over, I wouldn't joke about that," Tommen replied.

"Very true. You do seem to have it down to a science."

"Dad..."

"Hey, congratulations, kiddo. It's a girl! I'll see you in the morning, all right? Save me some leftovers."

"How many tons?"

His dad did not reply, but looking at the time, he was probably at work actually doing stuff. Might be he was running through the office, shouting, "It's a girl!" to everyone within earshot. Nah, not likely. But he would still mention it to everyone who had ever asked him over the last couple months, and it would spread from third shift to first shift and then to second, and from county to city. And by Monday, every police officer in the county would know that Walter Forbes had a granddaughter on the way. Not just a grandchild, but a granddaughter.

Tommen put his phone away and headed back inside where Mrs. Polski was checking the pies in the oven. Like all the other food in the house, nothing was store-bought if it could be helped, and pie and dessert was no exception. Special desserts were made for Becky to accommodate her diabetes, and these were set aside, away from grabby little hands.

"I thought for sure I would have seen you out there painting that," Mrs. Polski said, glancing at him while she pulled out the pies. "When did you do all that?"

"Last night." He shrugged. "Guess I'm just that good."

"You must be." She shook her said and muttered, mostly to herself, "I thought for sure I would have seen something. Or maybe not..."

She set the pies out to cool for a few minutes, but once the word was out that dessert was ready, a line just mysteriously formed. Tommen grabbed his desserts and snagged a few things for Becky as well from her specially-made goodies, delivering them to her at the dining table.

"Whew. Glad that's over," Becky said, taking a bite of cake. "Now maybe everyone will stop pestering me about it."

"Same here," Tommen agreed. "Except now we have to listen to everyone's suggestions on names and clothing and everything else. My dad's already bugging me about the name, too."

"Believe me, I know. But suggestions are only suggestions. They're open-ended and we don't have to listen. The name, well, yeah, that's kind of secret information, but...I don't know. I just feel better getting it out there that it's a girl."

He wasn't going to disagree, though he would express his dismay that they didn't even get to finish dessert before the suggestions started coming in. Mostly it was names, mostly for various family members. Name her this for your sister, that for your aunt, this for your great-grandmother's goat's first kid. All right, that last bit was exaggerated. Tommen was asked — politely, if skittishly — if he remembered having any sisters when he was younger, and what their names were. He lied about not remembering his sisters' names. Then he was asked about his mom's name, his grandmothers' names. Oh, Maisy was adorable. Gwyneth was simply darling. And Harriett? Such a classic!

By the time they were getting ready to leave, Becky had figured out that if they took every suggestion that people had come up with, their daughter would have sixty-eight possible first and middle names, and that meant hundreds or thousands of possible combinations.

"Oh, let's just name her all of them," Tommen said. "Then we can say we took everyone's suggestions, and we don't have to remember any single name, just call her whatever we feel like at the time."

He laughed and didn't bother to dodge a swat on the arm from Becky. No, she informed him, they were sticking with what they decided. When asked about what they decided, they quickly shut down all the curious inquirers.

Really, it wasn't all bad, Tommen reflected, walking home with ten tons of leftovers. He was probably overthinking things, exaggerating it in his mind how much people were bothering them for the gender, the name, all this and that. Life still went on, and other conversations were had, most notably, politics and religion. And there were other goings-on in the family. It was just that his and Becky's relationship and turn of events were less than...traditional, so they got a little more attention, a little more gossip, a little more scrutiny. But people weren't exactly falling over them as if they were movie stars, dying to know everything about them and the baby.

They went inside. Becky made for the bedroom, and Tommen looked for room in the fridge for all the leftovers. Mrs. Polski was very generous, but she didn't seem to grasp that not everyone had a massive refrigerator in their house for feeding endless swarms of grandkids.

It was a quiet rest of the evening as they both recovered from Thanksgiving food coma, Becky checking her blood sugar religiously and writing it down in her little notebook. It was only because of the holiday and the overeating, Tommen knew. By morning, she would be fine and back to her regular routine.

Despite being Thursday, due to the obvious holiday as well as the string of attacks, he counted it fortunate that he was able to get in a session with Nathan the following day. Tommen politely inquired as to Nathan's holiday. The man shrugged.

"I don't have any family anymore, and I can overeat just looking at food," Nathan told him, taking a seat.

It was one of the few times when Nathan showed himself to be a real human being with thoughts and feelings of his own. He generally tried to remain aloof of himself in order to focus on his client—Tommen—but he was not a robot. Tommen appreciated the times when Nathan let his guard down just a touch, let him know that he wasn't speaking to a psychopathic serial killer with no emotion.

"But, if I recall correctly," the shrink went on, coming back to himself and closing that door of emotion, "yesterday was Thanksgiving, which means gender reveal time. So then, out with it. Boy or girl?"

"It's a girl," Tommen answered. "Princesses and pink camo, I know."

"Congratulations! About to be an even match in the household, then, two men and two women?"

"At least until my dad leaves. Then I'll be outnumbered."

Nathan nodded, but his demeanor was such that it said he wasn't fully there.

Tommen shifted in his seat. "I'm no psychologist, but your expression says you want to say something, but you don't want to say it now because you don't want to interrupt me."

The man frowned, expression puzzled and thinking, Was it that obvious? Was I so worried that it actually showed through? This only served to worry Tommen. After a while, at least a century or two, few things really bothered Time Agents. What was going on now? Furthermore, where did shrinks go for mental health and help, especially when it involved Time?

Finally Nathan dropped the charade and the multiple expressions warring for dominance on his face. "I was going to save it until later, but..." He hesitated. "I'm afraid this will have to be our last meeting, all other things being equal."

"What do you mean?"

"Godwin considers it a security risk, this jumping back and forth. I've done it, Miach has done it, Kayla has done it. Given the recent attacks, it's been grudgingly permitted, but, regrettably, no longer."

Tommen blinked. "What does Godwin care? Unless..." He shifted in his seat. "Are you with the Miaramila now? Or have the Akarin and Miaramila joined forces? What's going on?"

Nathan tried to shrug it off. "Circumstances demanded negotiation. There was no coercion; Godwin didn't even want to take us in at first. But as it stands, we are under his orders for the time being, and that means cutting some ties. Hopefully it's only temporary, but you never know."

"I'm guessing you can't tell me where you're hiding."

"Tommen, I don't even know."

"So we can't keep meeting and training."

"I have an inkling that Godwin is going to approach you once more to try and convince you to join us. If that were the case, we could absolutely continue meeting and training."

Tommen frowned and shifted again. "I don't know if I could do that to Becky. And even if I could...Nathan, she's a high-risk pregnancy. How much do you know about pregnancy and prenatal care? Could you keep an eye on her? Could you perform a C-section out in space? Does Godwin want a newborn around?"

The shrink nodded slowly. "You've clearly given this a lot of thought, and there is no easy solution. I admit, I don't knot a lot about pregnancy and prenatal care. I don't know a lot about newborns. Could I perform a C-section? Probably, seeing how I just reattached a new leg onto Micaiah's stump; effectively doing the opposite shouldn't be difficult.

"Tommen, you are going to have to make that decision, to come or stay, with or without Becky. There is fast-approaching a time when there will be no third option, and I think you will have to commit to that decision with little or no time to think about it. You need to decide before that time comes."

He didn't want to. Problem was, no one cared what he wanted. Wanting something or not wanting something was not going to change the choice that had to be made.

"I don't want to make the wrong decision," Tommen stated

quietly. "I don't want to jeopardize them."

Even as he said it, he felt the hypocrite. Chandler had said they would be fine. True, in the moment, whatever that moment entailed, he might have some doubt over whether everything would turn out all right, but while Chandler could be infuriating with his riddles and mystique, he was not a liar. If he said Becky and the baby would be fine, Tommen had every reason to believe they would be fine. Agonizing over it was only for theater and it was costing him sanity.

Perhaps it was the thought that this was their last session that stopped him from confiding Chandler's prophecy about his death. He wasn't even sure what he would say about it, or what he thought the shrink could do about it. But it would take more than tonight's session to work that out. Maybe he should take up Godwin's offer.

Nathan nodded slowly. "I completely understand. Now then, did you do your homework?"

Tommen pulled out his list of things he'd learned from all his traumatic experiences. In the case of intangible items, like courage or perseverance, he was made to give an example of how he had used it since and how he could use it in the future. In the case of tangible items, such as External Bands, he had to demonstrate these abilities. By the end of the list, Tommen was feeling a little better about himself, that maybe not all was lost. He wasn't a bumbling probationary pretending to be a hero; he actually had some skill to back up his bravado. Although he wasn't feeling especially brave, he would have to be if he wanted to avoid dying a lonely, selfish coward.

Then they came to the last item, the only one he hadn't been able to classify as being "finished." The shooting. Tommen explained his reasoning, about being unsure if there could be a follow-up attack.

"I can understand that," Nathan said, nodding slowly. "But here's the thing. The shooting itself is over. You're not at the school, you're not facing down the gunmen. In fact, you won't have to face them ever again. You will never again have to look over your shoulder and wonder whether Tyler is going to shove you in a locker.

You will never again have to wonder whether Ryan is still out for blood, yours or your dad's in particular. That chapter in your life is officially closed."

"Tyler had a younger brother who's in my grade. I don't know what Ricky knows. Does he know about Time now, the Akarin and the Order and everything else? Or did Tyler keep Ricky in the dark? I can't imagine he would. How can I go back to school on Monday, wondering like that?"

"The same way you went to school for years under threat of Tyler. At the very least, I expect you will know whether or not Ricky knows about Time. Otherwise, you will only have a lingering, nebulous fear following you for many years to come. Knowledge is power."

"What if he comes after me, though, for his brother's death?"

Nathan gave him an odd look that somewhat resembled sympathy and pity. "Tommen, was Ricky part of the shootout in any way?"

"Just because he—"

"Yes or no?"

Tommen let out a breath. "No."

"No. And there are a thousand ways he could still do bad things, I'm sure. I can conjure up half a dozen right now, and you can probably think up another dozen if I gave you but two minutes. But for the purposes of this exercise, right here today, is the school shooting ongoing or finished?"

After a few seconds of grudging silence, he answered, "Finished."

"Good. At some point this week, I want you to burn this the same way you burned the rest of the incidents. I can tell by your voice that you don't believe it yet, but I think you will. Once Monday rolls around and goes by without incident."

Tommen reluctantly agreed.

They spoke more of home life then, Becky and the fast-approaching birth, his graduation, college, work, a wedding they had barely planned for, a whole new life beyond childhood. Again, they went past the normal one hour allotment, but that was all right. Tommen was glad for the talk.

"But you know none of that will even matter if we have to go into hiding," Tommen said, sighing.

Nathan nodded slowly. "I know."

"You really think I should take Godwin up on his offer?"

"I can't promise that you will be much safer. Julianna is coming for all of us, regardless. She just has to find us, and you are very easily found. At least with us, there will be more eyes, more hands, and a little more skill to keep you safe."

Tommen let out a breath. "Yeah. Rifun commented a lot on how easy it was to find me, predict where I'd be, what I'd be doing. Guess that's never really changed. The routine helped to push away the crazy shit that I was getting into halfway across the universe."

"It did. But now, you'll need to figure out a new routine."

Tommen nodded, then paused. "I want to do it, but I want to wait until after the baby is born."

Nathan blinked. "Whatever for?"

"However spunky she is, Becky is fragile and this is a high-risk pregnancy. I want her in the care of doctors who specialize in that, who know more than you about pregnancy and childbirth, who can intervene if something goes wrong and who can diagnose a problem faster than you. Plus, we don't really know the effects of portal travel or space travel on pregnant women, and I'm not going to volunteer her as a guinea pig."

For a long moment, Nathan mulled over his words, expression contemplative and understanding. Slowly, he nodded. "I understand. I don't have to fully agree, but I understand and I respect you for it. Godwin isn't going to like it, and I doubt he's going to authorize any kind of security detail, but at least it's an answer."

"Once the baby is born and everything is cool, then..." Tommen took an even breath. "Then I guess we get to start a new life somewhere else in the universe. Or try to."

Nathan nodded and stood. "I'll try to check in as often as I can, sneak away when Godwin's back is turned. And we should make a plan ahead of time."

Tommen wordlessly agreed, and the two of them returned to the parking lot. There, they shook hands, got into their respective vehicles, and departed.

The weekend passed uneventfully. Well, except for Pete stepping off a ladder wrong on the job site and breaking his ankle. That was an event with great amounts of profanity and fists pounding on the floor. The rest of them took their lunch break while Chris took Pete to the emergency room. But otherwise, the weekend was unremarkable.

Monday morning, Tommen was awake long before his alarm went off. He'd lain in a cold sweat half the night, utterly petrified of going to school. Ricky's reaction was but one part of the fear, yet it was the only fear in focus. The rest of it was ambiguous terror, memories of the shooting racing through his mind, mixing with images from everything else he'd endured. He didn't want to go. He wanted to call in sick, tell them to just mail his homework to him. He had a sneaking suspicion that there would be a great percentage of the student body absent today. What was one more?

Then his alarm went off and he dragged himself out of bed. Shower, trim the beard, clean clothes, empty backpack on account of the new semester, his last semester of high school ever. His last first day of class, repeated five times in one day. His last semester of going to the same classes every single day. His last semester of dealing with the same people, the same students, the same teachers every single day. His last semester of a lot of awful things about high school. Then it was on to college. There was life beyond the dull conveyor belt of public education, and he could see the light at the end of the tunnel.

Thinking about it helped him to relax some as he went out to the kitchen on stiff legs, looking for food. There was still a good amount of leftovers from Thanksgiving, and he tossed a couple in his lunchbox. Eggs and peanut butter toast made up his breakfast, and then he was out the door. Even just the routine and the drive to school seemed to help, at least until the school came in sight.

Flashing lights whirled in his mind, dozens of police officers swarming here and there, all in tactical gear.

Tommen blinked and pulled into the parking lot. It was pretty empty for the time of morning. He glanced at the bus drop and noticed that there were decidedly fewer students getting off the buses than normal. When he got inside, he would say maybe only sixty percent of the student body was present, seventy percent at a high estimate.

People were hurting. People were scared. Tommen felt more conspicuous than ever as he made his way through the halls. Once upon a time, he'd found a body on the school soccer fields. But no one had really been there to see it outside of the police. Once upon a time, he'd been kidnapped and held hostage for two weeks. But no one had really been there either. This time, he'd been called out in front of the entire student body. More than that, freaky, fucked up things had happened, and he had been right there associated with it. Maybe the details were lost because of the Bands, and maybe the counselors had managed to explain things in such a way so as to assuage the immediate fears, but the human brain is not always so easily fooled. Fucked up things had happened. They all knew it. And Tommen had been front and center for it.

He reached his locker, spun the dial. The lock clicked and the door swung open. He was lucky. When the police went searching the school, they'd been instructed to pry open all the lockers looking for the shooters. Not all of them had opened gently, and more than a few had cock-eyed doors, or the doors were missing completely, stacked against a wall with busted hinges. Not a few students had to double up for the time being.

He glanced toward the office where it looked like the secretaries were busy answering calls, dozens of parents excusing their kids for the day. A sudden flu epidemic right after a school shooting. apparently, although even that was a hollow excuse after

Borelian flu-monia claimed several lives the previous year. Layman was just visible from Tommen's vantage point, and the man looked absolutely haunted. His demeanor was dark and imposing, but he was deathly pale, his expression haunted. How many years a Marine, how many tours overseas, and it was a stateside catastrophe that broke him.

Tommen had just tossed his backpack in his locker when he heard the voice he'd been dreading all weekend.

"Tommen."

Ricky Freeman.

He turned.

Ricky Freeman probably couldn't top six feet but on the very ends of his tippy toes. He probably couldn't beat a Girl Scout in arm wrestling. And he probably couldn't win any beard growing contests. His clothes had always been dark and baggy, falling somewhere on the spectrum between goth and gangster.

Today, he wore light jeans and a T-shirt, making him look almost normal. He'd gotten a haircut and started a thin beard around his jaw. Actually, Tommen wouldn't have recognized him except for the voice.

"I'm sorry." The words were out before Tommen could call them back. Funny thing was, Ricky said the same thing at the same time. They stared at each other for a long moment before Tommen asked, "What did you say?"

"I said I'm sorry," Ricky sighed. He frowned, his gaze darting here and there. "I'm sorry for all the years of hurt Tyler did to you. All the beatings. Truthfully..." He took a breath. "Truthfully, he wasn't much better at home. He hurt me, he hurt our mom." He shifted his weight here and there some, chewing on his lip. "After he graduated —or, you know, got expelled—he landed in jail. When he got out, he started hanging around some new friends. Worse friends than I had ever seen before. He got worse, and he got weird. He showed me things." Ricky continued to chew on his lip and bounce on his toes, and he ran a hand through his hair. Then, suddenly, he stopped. "I know. I know what he knew. About Time and all that. He showed me."

"And?" Tommen wondered.

"It scared me. It scared me even more, what I saw, two weeks ago. I didn't want to believe it. He tried to teach me some, but he was only a beginner himself and a bad teacher anyway. Plus he was too wrapped up in himself and his new power...he got drunk on it, left me out to dry. But...the more I thought about it, I guess some things started to make sense."

Ricky made a noise and shook his head. "I guess what I'm trying to say is, I'm sorry. I'm sorry for what he did to you. I'm sorry for not speaking up and trying to stop him over the years. But, knowing what I do now...know that I have greater respect for you, that you did have tremendous power and could have used it to really hurt Tyler, but you didn't."

Tommen frowned and shut his locker. "Just tell me one thing. Did you know what they were planning?"

"No. I swear to you, I didn't. Like I said, Tyler got all hyped up about his power and his new friends, and he just...left. Never really looked back. I don't know, maybe I should have guessed this was coming, said something. But what could I do?"

"Do you really want that answer? Do you want to learn more?"

"I don't know. It was scary enough the first time."

"Then do yourself a favor. Lay low, keep it to yourself. And maybe get yourself gone before people start coming after you." Tommen continued before Ricky could speak. "I want to believe you, that you're innocent in all of this, and that you are truly apologetic. I do. I want to believe good in people right now. If all of that is true, be a better man than your brother ever was. Be a better man than Ryan my foster brother ever was. I'll try to do the same. And we'll just stay out of each other's way."

Ricky's expression turned wounded, but he dipped his head. "I understand. Thank you."

Tommen burned the school shooting incident that night.

Chapter Seventeen
Notice

Unlike years past, the attitude in school, at least that first week back, was very muted. Distracted. There were a few empty seats in a few classes, and they would remain empty permanently. There were a few classes where the teachers had to bundle up assignments and send them off with parents to their child still in the hospital or at home recovering. There was far less rough-housing and shenanigans in class, and a few of the wannabe tough guys snapped out of their defiant phase. Even a few of the true bullies and pseudo-gangsters looked repentant and motivated to take a new path in life.

Not everyone, of course. There were still a few out there who seemed to think the entire shooting deal had been a game, a spectacle, as if they hadn't been running in fear with the rest of the student body. But there was nothing to be done for them if they did not want to change. Lead a horse to water and all that.

So it was that the return from Thanksgiving vacation—an extended vacation, though no one celebrated the reason—and the lead up to Christmas vacation was met with near silence.

Monday morning, as soon as the late bell rang, Mr. Layman had the entire student body assemble in the gym to hold a moment of silence for the three people who died, and to finally talk about the shooting. It was a tragic event, but they all did exactly as they were supposed to do. They didn't try to play the hero or do anything stupid. They hunkered down and waited for the police.

There was also a talk about grief and suicide, resulting maybe from the deaths of the students or just the sudden trauma, the realization that bad stuff could happen to anyone, the loss of control and the feeling of security. Bullying and mental health was also addressed, citing statistics, and mentioning that counselors would be at the school for the next two weeks. Any student could leave class at any time to speak to a counselor and not be penalized for it.

Tuesday was the first of December. It was a bit surreal to consider that 2015 was nearly over. Christmas was coming, and then New Year's. Welcome to 2016. Just another day. Another year.

Tommen was still trying to sort out his feelings about Ricky and their encounter. It didn't hit him until the middle of second period that maybe they were both victims of terrible older brothers. The difference was, Ricky couldn't get rid of Tyler. He'd been stuck with him, day in and day out, with no reprieve. Maybe he went along with the bullying a little, maybe he indulged here and there in miscellaneous antics, but maybe that wasn't who he wanted to be. Maybe his change in style and attitude wasn't just about staying somewhat incognito in the halls, not being recognized at a single glance, but it was his way of finally getting out from under Tyler's shadow. How often had Tommen feared Ricky after Tyler's expulsion, not because Ricky had done anything to him, but simply from association?

The rest of the student body seemed to sense some of this as well, when Tommen approached Ricky at lunchtime. Would the Chivalrous Welshman exact revenge on the younger brother of the kid who had bullied him incessantly for nearly a decade? With a certain look of resignation, Ricky stood from his lonely spot at the lunch table to meet Tommen.

For a long few seconds, the two of them just stared at each other, each acutely aware of the curious stares and a loose circle forming around them, spectators wondering if there was a fight to be had today.

Then Tommen held out his hand.

"Thank you."

Ricky stared at him, looked at the hand, looked back at him, and gingerly took the peace offering. "For what?"

"For coming up to me and talking to me. I think we both know what we actually thought was going to happen. Took guts. And I respect you for that. Thank you. And despite past misgivings, I don't hold you responsible for Tyler's actions."

The younger Freeman brother gripped his hand tighter and looked his straight in the eye. "Thank you. That means a lot."

Tommen released his hand and clapped Ricky on the shoulder. "Live the life you want, not what your brother told you to do."

Then he went and sat down to eat his own lunch.

It was after that brief exchange that Tommen got a circle of friends again at the lunch table, spearheaded by Ricky who came over about halfway through lunch. Wednesday, one of Ricky's friends came to join them, if only out of curiosity. By Friday, there were six of them sitting together, including the other two outcasts at the outcast table.

Tommen wouldn't have said that they were really friends, in the sense that they were going to go hang out Friday night or could play a friendly game of pick-up basketball, but they were civilized, friendly acquaintances. They could hold a conversation, get a few laughs, share a few problems, and stay safe from the occasional roaming bully. It was a good feeling, to not be left out.

"But I think what's even better, really, is forgiving Ricky," Tommen said to Chandler that Friday night.

Chandler looked up from where he was stirring his stew, his brow raised. "Forgiving him for what? What did he do to you?"

"Well, nothing, but all these years that I thought he was going to be as bad as Tyler..."

"Sounds like the change came from you, not him. In fact, it had nothing to do with him, not really."

Tommen shifted position where he sat on a mat a few feet away. "I guess so, I mean—"

"Forgiveness is moving past a wrong that someone has done to you. But don't confuse being wronged with merely being offended. Offense typically only affects one party, and that party chooses to be offended. You may not choose to take a punch or be cheated on a deal, but you do choose to react to it in a negative way. Similarly, Ricky never did anything to you. The change came from within you, to alter your perception of him, see things in a new light, and shift your thinking. It wasn't about forgiving an offense, but maturing yourself. If anything, Ricky ought to be the one forgiving you."

The man ladled out some stew into two bowls. Tommen took his but only stared at it. He sighed. "Then I guess I owe you an apology, too."

"What for?" Chandler took a bite of stew.

"I've been rude and short-tempered with you, demanding and ungrateful. You just do your best to do what the Author tells you."

Chandler nodded, still chewing, and swallowed hard. "Apology accepted. And believe me, you're not the only one who is frustrated."

"What do you mean?" Now Tommen took a bite of his own savory stew. "You can't get annoyed with the Author. She's the Author. She'd...I don't know, erase you?"

The dark-skinned man laughed. "Of course I get annoyed with her. I am a human being, the same as you. I get annoyed, confused, frustrated, angry, depressed. It is simply that my well of trust runs deeper, so I am able to move past it. It does not mean that I do not get caught up in the storm, it simply means that my hull is reinforced and has a better chance of surviving.

"I do get annoyed when the Author shows me only part of the story. I get frustrated when she shows me the whole story and tells me to be silent on most of it. I get angry when I don't understand or I don't agree with what's going on. I get depressed when things go horribly wrong. But then things go right again, just as the Author plans, and I am content. And I chastise myself for ever doubting. I then take that experience and add another layer to my hull. As such, the Author shows me more and more and entrusts me with more knowledge."

Tommen gave him a look. "But you can't speak a word of it,

can you?"

"Not a lot, I'm afraid."

"Then what's the point?"

"To give just enough to give more. Once, the Author gave me enough water for one plant. I did my job dutifully. Then she gave me enough water for two plants. More water, yet each plant continued to receive its same amount. Then five plants, then ten, and so on."

"Do you speak to others? Who?"

"That is not for you to know. And as each plant does well, it receives more water in turn."

Tommen scoffed. "I must be a pretty poor plant, that one that's constantly wilting no matter how much water you give it."

Chandler's expression turned coy. "You are more like the plant that is part sun and part shade, and I never know where to put you so you do not scorch but you do not wilt. You move here and there and it never seems to be the right mix. Or you go in the sun when you need shade, and you stay in the shade when you need sun."

Something in Chandler's expression changed when he spoke that last sentence, but then it was gone and he took another bite of stew. Tommen wanted to ask him about it, then decided against it. Apologies had been made and he felt appropriately chastened. If Chandler had something to tell him, then Chandler would tell him.

Instead, he asked, "Is Micaiah all right?"

The sudden change in subject almost seemed to catch Chandler off-guard, which was odd in itself. Still, he composed himself and answered, "He is alive and whole again, physically, but this much you know. What do you really want to ask?"

As if the man couldn't guess. "Will he ever be the way he was? I don't know how he is, but if Miach was any indication, he isn't really Micaiah."

Chandler frowned. "A chain is only as strong as its weakest link. For all the great power of the Akari, the weakest link is always our own frail humanity. Our need for sleep and sustenance, however intermittent, the migraines and physical exhaustion that come from extended or repeated use, simple lack of knowledge and understanding of how things work, and, sometimes, an inability to make things happen the way we want."

"So the Micaiah we knew isn't coming back."

"He will get stronger, sharper, but the shadow does not control the man."

Tommen mindlessly fiddled with a loose string from the mat he was sitting on. "Will he be all right?"

Chandler nodded slowly, scraping together the last of his stew. "He will."

There were more questions going around in Tommen's mind as he finished off his own food, but before he could ask any of them, his alarm was going off. Up and at 'em to work. Hooray for him. Another day on the job site.

It wasn't all bad, really, except for the part where he had to park way down at the bottom of the hill and walk up this godawful driveway. There was some debate going on over whether a small delivery truck could make it up the driveway. If not, should they get the appliances now and just store them in the garage for the time being, or wait until spring when the homeowner returned from Florida and wanted everything sparkling new and turnkey?

The drywall was almost done, and painting crews had been through to paint the walls that were completely finished. Tommen was put on the flooring team, throwing down plank after plank of solid cherry flooring. That went a lot faster than the drywall, even for the herringbone pattern or when they hit walls or corners or butted up against the tile flooring in the bathrooms, it wasn't a nightmare. Just measure, mark, cut, set, nail, boom, done.

It was nice to finally see the house come together. It wasn't just a plan or a dream or a drawing on a piece of paper. It was here. It was concrete and wood and electrical and plumbing and colorful walls and gorgeous flooring. As they finished laying the wood in the living room, Tommen could just imagine the furniture that was going to be brought in. He was no longer seeing measuring marks and OSB, but a place where grandkids would run around playing games, where little appetizers might sit on a plate at a fancy dinner party, where a couple might argue over what movie to watch on a Friday night. It was a home.

Granted, it was a monstrous home, far too large for just two people, but a home nonetheless. Tommen stood and wiped the sweat from his brow, rather pleased with himself. With everything he'd learned and would continue to learn working this job, maybe he could build his own house for his family. Scrap the over-expanded miner's shack and build a real house, enough to accommodate them with a little room to expand and grow, if they so chose.

If only.

Sunday was more of the same. The drywall was officially finished, so the flooring could be finished. Then it was time to work on the baseboard and cabinetry. Seeing how building custom cabinetry was an art form, Tommen had no part in it, though he did watch the craftsman a bit whenever he came by to take measurements. He would build everything in his shop, then have it delivered when finished.

But, could he get it up the driveway, that was the question. No one felt like hauling heavy appliances up the hill, and cabinets weren't exactly on the list of things they did want to haul uphill. Hauling their lunchboxes was about the extent of it.

At least with all the electrical done and the outlets working, they could bring in the microwave and use that to heat up their food. They had to test out the microwave and make sure it would work for the homeowner, after all. Who wanted to spend over a million dollars on a home, only to find out the microwave didn't work?

Thankfully, lunchtime conversation had returned to normal. No one mentioned the shooting or anything of that nature. It was back to the usual, griping about the homeowners and the project, griping about something from home life, griping about school for Tommen occasionally, and poking fun at Tommen over his impending fatherhood and later wedding. There had been plenty of joking when he finally told them it was a girl, and there was more than one occasion of him being called upon—usually someone yelling in a faux high-pitched voice from the opposite end of the house, calling for Daddy—to read a girly bedtime story or kill a teeny weeny spider.

When Tommen told Becky of these antics later that evening, she got a real kick out of them and laughed hard, nearly knocking the pan of food off the stove. His dad was a little more polite with his laughter, but he laughed nonetheless.

"It's not always about the big things," his dad told him from where he sat in his recliner, reading a book. "Sometimes the devil is in the details."

Tommen just rubbed his face and made an exaggerated sound of exasperation.

"I don't know which is worse to deal with, a baby or the rest of my family," he said mockingly.

"The rest of the family," Becky told him, very matter-of-fact. "Babies are loud, but they're really just trying to get your attention for a basic need. It's when they develop that free will thing that it gets complicated."

"Speaking from experience?" Walter inquired lightly.

His back was still turned, so only Tommen could see Becky doing a mock flick of her stirring spoon at him. He snickered and tried to cover it up with a cough.

"I can see you," his dad said, still not looking up from his book. "There's a reflection in the window there."

Now Becky made an obnoxious coughing sound, still grinning, and returned to her cooking. Looked like fried chicken night with homemade onion rings. She seemed to accept that Walter did not eat much, if at all, though she still found it puzzling, and did not go out of her way to make a huge plate for him. She did, however, continue to make teenage-boy-sized portions for Tommen, which he often split between dinner and lunch the following day. Becky had been offended in the beginning, that her food was not devoured, but the men assured her that it was fantastic. They just didn't want to get sick or fat.

It was a pretty quiet evening. He and Becky stayed in the bedroom, talking and looking at random things on the Internet. It was a perfectly lazy way to spend a weekday evening, something everyone needed from time to time. They deliberately avoided any talk of the baby, both of them wanting to keep their separate identities, and instead did some wedding talk.

As expected, Becky quickly had Tommen convinced that he was totally ignorant of the whole affair and to leave ninety percent of it up to her. Well, her and her mom. Who better to plan a party than the best party planner in the family?

Tommen let her gush about all the different plans she had made, the things that would work well together, the things that wouldn't, the decisions she had to make, and it was all so exhausting. Meanwhile, he internally fretted about what he was going to do. What was he going to tell her? How was he going to break the news that he was essentially an intergalactic fugitive and they needed to go on the run?

He pondered this over the course of the week, sitting in class. She would probably laugh at him first, make some cheeky comments about an overactive imagination, maybe tell him that he should write it down as a story in one of his notebooks. All of it perfectly innocent and charming, and he wished that was how it could stay.

But it couldn't stay fanciful. He was going to have to show her. He was going to have to demonstrate all the things he could do: Banding Time, manipulating Matter, toying with Energy. He was going to have to show her that he could rip open portals to other worlds. He was going to have to show her legitimate alien races. In short, he was going to have to shatter her entire preconceived notion about the universe.

The bell rang, announcing the end of second period. It was Wednesday again, the ninth, no longer tiptoeing into December but striding confidently through it, marching ever onward to the new year. A new year, a new life, Tommen figured. Forget resolutions that depended on sheer willpower alone, his new life was being forced upon him whether he wanted it or not. Forced upon Becky, too, and she certainly hadn't asked for anything that he was about to thrust upon her. How was she going to deal with all of it? The younger a person was at exposure, the easier it was to accept. Tommen wondered how religious devotion played into that. For Becky, everything in that realm was simple and predictable. How was she going to reconcile this?

Third period passed in much the same way. Basically listening, mostly daydreaming, going through the motions as he had to. Counting down the days to everything. Christmas, New Year's, Valentine's Day, baby's birthday, going on the run as an intergalactic fugitive with a woman and newborn...

And then class was over. Just like that. The bell rang and they were off to lunch.

He and Ricky weren't really friends, per se, but they still sat together with a loose group of friends at the lunch table. Truth be told, the rest of the student body wasn't sure how to treat them. Ricky hadn't been involved in the shooting, and Tommen's involvement was dubious at best. He hadn't done anything wrong, yet he'd been called out. One of the shooters had bullied him for years, the other was once his foster brother. Where did he stand in all of this, then? And why was he making friends with the younger brother of his archnemesis?

"Doesn't matter much to you," Ricky told him. "You're graduating, busting out of here, going to be a daddy, start a whole new life away from this hellhole. I still have one more semester, and then I have no clue what I'm going to do with myself."

"Not going to college?" Tommen wondered.

"Hey, Tyler was the dope dealer, not me. I don't have that kind of money, and my mom isn't sharing either. College is way far out of my reach."

"You working?"

"Short order cook on weekends and sometimes fill-in after

school."

"You like physical work?"

And so it was that Tommen introduced Ricky to Chris Thursday after school. Friday, Ricky quit his short-order cook career. Saturday, they were working together in the massive mountainside mansion. Different tasks, of course, because they couldn't have two rookies on the same project. When Tommen protested his rookie status, Chris politely reminded him that he was not certified in anything, not presently in school for anything in the trades, and he only worked full-time for a few months. Maybe if he went full-time, or at least more than weekends, after high school, then he could start to think about being not a rookie.

Tommen wouldn't say it wasn't awkward, being friends with Ricky after years of fear and imaginary intimidation. And he wouldn't say there weren't times when he wanted to yell at him and vent over the unfair treatment from Tyler. It always came back to one principle, well, maybe two. First, Ricky was not Tyler. Every man had his own free will. Second, there was every chance that Ricky was as much a victim as Tommen, just as Tommen had been a victim to his foster brother from Hell, Ryan.

And, if he wanted to be honest, forgiveness was good. It was freeing. It brought some life out of the tragedy, a little bit of hope. It lifted a burden that he hadn't even been aware of, that blind fear by association. Now it was gone. The chapter with Tyler and Ryan had officially closed, and he was moving on. They were both moving on.

They rarely spoke about the freakier aspects of the shooting, that is, Time and the Akari and the strange powers that they wielded. Ricky himself had been exposed to Time and knew a little bit about Banding, both in Time and the Force Akari. Tommen managed to explain a few things, take the magic out of what Tyler and Ryan—and Tommen and his dad, for that matter—did during the standoff. Gravity, Energy, Time, Light, Sound, just your casual Wednesday manipulating the physics of the universe.

It turned Ricky almost as pale as Tommen himself. He

declared that he'd seen enough for the time being and did not want to learn more. Tommen advised him to lay real low, saying that if anyone knew that Tyler had taught him, even a little bit, they could come after him for recruitment next. Ricky readily agreed.

"And so, new life springs forth from the ashes," Chandler said that night as Tommen took a seat in the cave.

"Is it going to last, though?" Tommen inquired. "Or am I just dragging someone else into my problems?"

"If he was exposed before you befriended him, he was potentially in danger long before you knew about it. And without some measure of friendship and guidance, he would still be walking around in No Man's Land between the trenches." Chandler gave him a look. "I'm saying you did good."

Tommen put up his hands. "Wait. So, this is a good thing that's happening? Like, this involves Time and the Akari and whatnot, and something good is happening here? Holy shit, this is a rare occasion. I should mark it on my calendar, maybe designate it a holiday." He shifted position. "Okay, so what bad things are going to come tumbling down now? I mean, there has to be something."

"Does there?"

"There always is. Is this a direct catalyst for my death?"

Chandler moved into a cross-legged position, a particular one that he got into before imparting some nugget of wisdom. "Do good and evil work in balance, or do they simply work according to the soil into which they have been sown? If a man finds only success in his life but does evil with it, is it good or bad? If a man finds only misfortune yet retains a pure heart and clear conscience, is that good or bad? Or what if a man finds only success and does immeasurable good? Must there be a man out there also who finds only misfortune and does unspeakable evil? If evil may be reworked into something good and true, bringing about a thing that could never have happened otherwise, how is that supposed to balance?

"Good and evil do not sit idly on scales trying to balance each other out. Indeed, they continuously war for dominance. I am not the counterbalance to the Dragon. Nor is the Author, else that would imply that the Dragon also has the power of creation. It may appear as though the Whites and the Shadows may be foils of sorts, but they do not sit on scales. They fight. They war. And there are many factors to consider when trying to predict the outcome of a battle. And sometimes, the best outcome is only the least bad. Sometimes, retreat may be the best option in order to effect a better outcome in the war down the road."

"More Sun Tzu," Tommen stated.

"Something like that, yes. If a man is the battlefield, his attitude largely determines the outcome of the battle, acting as the environment. Sometimes, it is an easy victory for the Whites. Sometimes more easily for the Shadows. And sometimes, it is better for the Whites to retreat for a time, that there may be a greater victory later."

"Do the Whites and Shadows influence men like that? I mean, I know I've seen them in the in-between dimension and whatever the forest is, and I've encountered them in dreams, but..."

"You have seen them in real life, Tommen."

He paused. Then, "Tujor." The Borelian god of death, the Dragon.

"Precisely. The Shadows take many forms. Do not think that because one does not appear the same as the next that they are not the same in nature."

"Like the Whites being different animals. Different strengths and weaknesses, but all Whites."

"Indeed."

They sat in silence for a long moment. Chandler poked at the fire a bit. Tommen shifted position. "How is the hawk? He was supposed to go on a mission for the Author, wasn't he?"

"He is preparing to leave very soon. He's actually quite antsy and raring to go." Chandler grinned. "He needs only the signal and he'll take off like a rocket."

Tommen laughed at this. "Sounds like him, and I can't say I

know him well." He nodded. "So, good things are happening? No pretense? No fine print? No ominous warnings?"

"Nothing new, I'm afraid," Chandler sighed. "You'll just have to make do with the ominous warnings I've already given you."

"Darn. I like to throw in something new every once in a while to keep my paranoia and sense of danger alert and fresh, otherwise I might go noseblind to the constant smell of one particular danger."

Chandler managed a small smile, but his expression was a little fearful and a lot knowing. He knew something, but he wasn't saying what. Tommen felt a stab of frustration, but did not say anything. He couldn't have if he wanted to. The cave started to fade, and he got that funny feeling when he was drifting out of his dream and back into his own body. He'd physically visited Chandler in the cave before, when he'd been trapped in the in-between dimension, and he wasn't always sure that he wasn't physically going there at night still, transporting between dimensions while he slept. At the same time, Becky was up a couple times a night to go to the bathroom, and she'd never said anything about him disappearing.

It was another day on the job. The cabinets were far from finished, but Chris decided to make the hard decision to get the appliances and see if the trucks couldn't make it up the driveway. The box truck managed to sneak its way up the treacherous slopes and the tight turns to deliver the washer and dryer, but the semi driver carrying the kitchen appliances outright refused. Thus they, the crew, were forced to haul the massive fridge, double oven, and dishwasher up the driveway to the home. By the end of the arduous task, thirty degrees outside felt pretty good.

"So, are you going to stick around for a bit?" Tommen asked Ricky at the end of the day. "Or did the driveway scare you off?"

Ricky waved a hand dismissively. "Please. What's a little mountain climbing?"

"It won't be this way forever," Chris told them, walking up. "Our next project after New Year's is much easier access, a parcel in a new development just outside the city, nice, flat piece of property.

Smaller than this castle, and the homeowners sound like very reasonable people."

They all wished each other a good night and headed to their respective vehicles. Tommen noticed Ricky and Matt standing around talking. Maybe the kid whose older brother shot up a school was seeking some words of wisdom. Tommen got in his car and headed home.

Monday came around again, as it always did after Sunday. Again he went through the motions in school. It was eleven days until Christmas, fewer until Christmas vacation. While the shooting had dampened the mood some, Christmas cheer was slowly filtering back into the school as garland and baubles and other assorted decorations began appearing, a little late, but understandably so.

Instead of doing Secret Santa exchanges in class, the entire school had decided to have a fundraiser for the families of the those who had died, even the safety officer, families who were probably still grieving and too scattered to even think about having a holly jolly Christmas. Information had been gathered about the families, who was in the immediate family and their ages. The first day would be for handmade cards and handwritten notes and letters. The second day would be a gift collection day for them. The third and final day would be a cash and gift card collection. On Friday, Mr. Layman would present all of the gifts to the families and have a few other staff members with him to sing carols and film the reaction. Then Tuesday, the day before they let out for Christmas break, they would gather in the auditorium to watch the videos.

Tommen turned in a handwritten letter for each of the families that Monday morning. Becky had helped him with it, to get his thoughts in order and correct some of his more egregious grammar and spelling mistakes.

At lunchtime, Ricky was busy bragging about his cool new job. A thousand times better than a cook, he declared. He could do it all day long. He'd found his calling, a career in the trades. Tommen smiled politely even as he knew Ricky's opinion would change once he really was working all day in hundred degree heat in the middle of August.

Overall, it really wasn't a bad day. Just another Monday, just another day of school.

He arrived home and had a sudden moment of confusion, momentarily thinking that he had to work a shift at the bakery. It felt like so long ago that he'd worked side-by-side with the twins, or even one twin. He shook his head to clear it and went inside.

Both his dad and Becky were gone, so he had the house to himself. Judging by the arrangement of things, and the presence of his dad's work boots in the kitchen, he'd gone out earlier and would be back soon to hurry up and get ready for work. Nothing was on the kitchen table, and the junk mail in the trash was from Saturday.

Tommen went out and got the mail. As he was looking through it on his way back in, his dad pulled in the driveway.

"How was school?" he asked amiably.

"School," Tommen said, still flipping through the mail.

"Anything interesting there?"

They made it through the garage and back into the relative warmth of the house. Tommen pulled out a couple envelopes, identical save for their intended recipients.

"Yeah," he answered, knitting his brows. He handed the appropriate envelope off to his dad. "A notice from the courts."

"Great, maybe we get to go into Witness Protection," Walter murmured. "Save me the trouble of going dark."

"But if that were the case, wouldn't that mean something bad has happened?" Tommen wondered.

"Hm...you have a point there. Well, let's find out."

They ripped open the envelopes and unfolded the papers within.

It was a notice, informing them that the date of Rifun F. Ndolo's sentencing hearing had been moved to December 23, 2015 at 10:15 am. As victims in the case, for whom a guilty verdict had been rendered, they were entitled to draft a victim impact statement and read it before the defendant and the courts at the hearing.

"I thought it was supposed to be in February," Tommen stated.

"So did I," his dad said lowly, clearly displeased. He brought out his phone. "Let me make a call."

Courteously enough, the letter also included a phone number to call in case they had any questions. It took some doing, and Walter had to get short with a few people, but he finally got through to the prosecutor himself. Walter put his phone on speaker.

"Gary Calhoun speaking," the man said.

"Mr. Calhoun, Walter Forbes."

"Ah, so you got the notice."

"Yes. Care to explain? I thought this was supposed to be in February. Has something happened?"

"Nothing dramatic or terrible, I assure you. The reasoning goes like this: Judge vanHouten is retiring at the end of the year due to his Parkinson's. As you may have heard on the news, I lost my race for reelection, so I'm out of here at the end of the year, too. We judged it best that the sentencing ought to be delivered by and in the presence of those who were there for the trial. The presentence investigative report is nearly complete, will be by the end of the week. His lawyer isn't fighting it, so we're going ahead with the change. I understand the notice is a bit short, but nothing really moves quickly around here."

"Indeed," Walter mused. "And you're not blowing smoke here, right? Things are all going well and secure on that end? He hasn't tried anything, hasn't said anything? Rants, threats, anything like that?"

"Not a peep. From what I've been told, he's a bit like a mouse. You don't know he's there until you go looking. The biggest problem they have with him are his seizures. Otherwise, it's like he doesn't exist." Calhoun made a sound. "I know. It's probably not what you want to hear, but he is going away for a long time. You and I are probably going to be dead and gone before he sees the sunrise again."

Not likely, Tommen thought. Calhoun might be dead and gone, but his dad would still be living off his Time-induced youthfulness, and Rifun could outlast any sentence they gave him. That was assuming Rifun decided to wait and play by the rules. He might, for a time, to keep a low profile and out of Julianna's immediate sights. But once he got bored, got a plan in his head, he knew how to disappear, and Godwin would probably help him do it.

"So, as the letter says, you will have the chance to address him in a victim impact statement," the prosecutor went on. "It can be as long or as short as you want. The only thing you can't include are tangible threats. You can tell him to burn in Hell for all eternity, but you can't say that you're going to track down his wife and kids and kill them—assuming he had them, but you get what I mean. Other than that, this is your opportunity to speak directly to him."

"I've been present for one or two in my time," Walter told him.

"So you basically understand the premise."

Walter confirmed the time and date, thanked the man, and hung up.

Tommen and his dad moseyed their way into the living room and each slumped into a seat, Walter in his recliner, Tommen on the couch.

After a moment, Walter said, "You know, I'm less irritated about the sentencing moving up, than I am that it's going to be a long week next week and that is right in the middle of my sleep schedule."

"You say that as if I don't have the ability to manipulate Time and give you more sleep," Tommen said smartly.

"Cheeky kid."

"Well, it's true. Honestly, I don't know why it bothers me as much as it does, except that I'm going to have to take time out of school."

His dad raised a brow. "Because that's ever broken your heart before?"

"It's a disruption in my day."

"Well, think of it this way. It'll be the last time Rifun disrupts your day for, with any luck, a very long time. And this time, you can tell him how much you dislike it and he can't do anything to you. And I'm not just talking about the handcuffs."

It was an odd vote of confidence that Tommen found himself reveling in. Just as he'd been a match for Tyler and Ryan at the shooting, he was now able to really defend himself against anything Rifun might try. Even if Rifun had magically regained his Akari abilities, Tommen was no featherweight. He'd trained and honed his skills under the tutelage of a Builder for crying out loud. There was still a lot he could learn, but he was no longer a helpless probationary or vaovao recruit.

"All right, Mr. Ego, I can see your head inflating from here," his dad said, cutting into his thoughts.

So maybe he'd indulged a little, so what? Tommen felt his ears and face burn hot. His dad laughed, hauled himself out of his recliner, and headed off to get ready for work.

Tommen watched him go and did not leave the couch until his dad returned and headed off to work, pulling on his knit hat as he walked out the door. Only then did he slide off the couch, stretch mightily, and go down to his bedroom.

He'd no sooner opened up his laptop than he heard an engine in the driveway. A second later, the door opened and he could hear the heavy clunking of Becky's orthopedic shoes. Two minutes later, she was in the bedroom, her tiny form taking up most of the room. She had several bags in hand.

"I know it's really cold outside, but it actually feels pretty good," she declared, not for the first time that week. She crawled up on the bed and dumped out the bags. Dozens of sets of baby clothes tumbled out.

"Been sewing away, have you?" Tommen wondered.

"What gave it away?" Becky asked in mock surprise. "I was already working on some of these, and decided just to keep them all stored over at my parents' place for a while. These are newborn to three month sizes. They may have to be adjusted depending on how big she is when she's born and how fast she grows."

"Well, I know that in animals, a baby animal will typically grow at the rate of the father."

"Grow like a weed, got it."

"I don't know. I was pretty small up until thirteen, fourteen years old. I didn't even hit a major growth spurt until I was fifteen. I thought I was doomed to be five-foot-five forever."

Becky put her hand to her forehead and fell back on the bed in a dramatic swoon. "Oh, the horror! The shame of it all! Being five feet five inches..."

"Ha ha, very funny. It's important for a guy to be tall."

"Why?"

"Isn't that what all the girls want? Tall, dark, and handsome, mysterious and slightly bad boy optional?"

Becky sat up and studied him. "Well, you've got the tall and handsome. Dark, not even close."

He raised a brow. "Gee, thanks a lot. At least I've got two of the three going for me."

"As for the optional features...if mysterious and slightly weird can be used interchangeably, then you've got that going for you. As for bad boy, that I can do without. Usually that leads to drama, with abuse and jail time in the more extreme cases. I can do without all three of those. So you've got three out of the four, which is good." She shifted position. "Now do me. What do guys look for, and how do I rate?"

Tommen raised a finger. "Even I'm smart enough to know that's a trick question. Therefore, I am refusing to answer."

She grinned. "And you're smart. I think that makes up for missing the 'dark' in 'tall, dark, and handsome.' So you're back to four out of four."

"Good to know."

He turned back to the computer and brought up his word processor. Becky climbed off the bed and stood beside him. "English homework?"

"No..." Tommen explained the notice in the mail. "So now I kind of have to work on my victim impact statement."

"You don't have to," Becky said. "You can always just tell him, 'I have nothing to say to you.' That in itself can speak volumes."

"I know, except...I do have something to say. I just don't know how...I want to say it or how to make it flow together. I want it to sound strong and confident, not like an idiot high schooler."

"Survivor, not victim?"

"Something like that, but I don't want to use terms that make it sound like he raped me, either."

Becky nodded. "Fair enough." She craned her neck to study the paper. "So then, what do you have so far?"

A series of disconnected thoughts and statements, but it was better than nothing. He worked on it a bit that night with Becky's help, then moved on to his other homework while she went to make dinner. They finished the night watching TV before bed.

Tommen lay awake for what felt like an eternity. He hadn't dreamwalked to Rifun in months, after Godwin's first warning about Julianna's murder squads. He hadn't heard a peep from or about him. It was almost starting to feel as if the whole thing had been a bad dream and maybe he could move on. At the same time, silence could be very suspicious. Silence from Rifun was certainly unusual and not a little unnerving. Should he dreamwalk to him, find out what was going on, if anything was going on?

But wasn't that also still allowing Rifun to have a little power over him, to be that concerned over it? Tommen couldn't allow himself to live in fear of Rifun. Just as the shooting had been the final page, closing the chapter with him and Tyler and Ryan, so this sentencing hearing had to be the final page in the story between him and Rifun, their paths diverging as Chandler had once said. And it had to be treated as an afterthought, an epilogue, something to sum it up, a little cherry on top to finish it off. He couldn't keep putting his nose in where it didn't belong. Rifun's path was Rifun's path now, and

Tommen would not be a part of it.

Even as he thought it, more ideas for his statement started formulating in his mind, bringing his rough outline into a smoother, more fluid work of art. Maybe it wouldn't make the man cry, maybe it wouldn't be studied in English classes or Criminal Justice classes for years to come, but it would effectively end this chapter. It would shut the door, lock the handle, the deadbolt, and barricade it against a hurricane.

It felt good, he thought as he drifted off, to take charge of his life and do a little housecleaning, getting rid of all the evils he had known through the years. Maybe he really would be able to start off family life in the spring with a clean bill of health.

Just in time to die.

Chapter Eighteen
Statement

It felt strange to sleep in on a Wednesday, Tommen thought, lying there in the dark. Instinct had told him to be ready long before dawn, but the most he'd managed was simply waking up. In the gloom, he could see Becky still asleep, her breaths slow and even. He'd learned to let her sleep when she could. According to her, there was no sleeping when a little parasite was trying to claw its way out of her body from the inside. When he asked if she'd explored any ancient tombs or played with any aliens lately, she'd swatted him playfully.

He lay there, watching the light grow brighter as the sun came up, lightening the sky by proximity only, as it would be a while before it peeked over the mountains.

Then, at eight-thirty, an alarm went off. But it wasn't his. Becky jolted, then sleepily reached for her glasses and her phone. She punched off the alarm, then rolled over to kiss him.

"What's the alarm for?" he wondered.

"So we don't miss the hearing." She still sounded half-asleep.

"What makes you think you're going?"

"What makes you think I'm not?"

"I don't want you to go."

She blinked a few times, then got up on one elbow. "Why shouldn't I go? I went with you to the trial."

"Yes, but I don't want you at the sentencing. I don't want him to see you."

"Why?"

"I want him to think maybe we broke up, maybe we're not together anymore. I want him to think you're gone. I don't want him to know about the baby. The rest of those lunatics are still out there somewhere, and I don't want them coming after you."

"A little late for that, isn't it? If anyone is going to intimidate a witness, it's going to be at the trial while you're testifying, not four months later, after a guilty verdict, at the sentencing."

Tommen let out a breath. "I still don't want you to go."

She shook her head. "You still haven't given me a satisfactory answer why not."

Because he fully expected Julianna to be there, whether in Disguise or out in the open. She was going to be there, and Tommen suspected that she was going to try something. Her first target would likely be Godwin, assuming he was still masquerading as a bailiff on occasion. After that, most likely Rifun, given their animosity and the fact that the man was now helpless to defend himself. Once they were taken care of, Julianna would turn her attention to Tommen, and he didn't want Becky involved. Chandler only said Becky would live; he didn't say that nothing bad would happen to her.

"Because I say so," he said finally, his words holding no authority.

"Mm...nope. Still not good enough."

With that, Becky kissed him again, then rolled herself over one more time and slid off the bed. She meandered her way to the bathroom while Tommen lay in bed a moment longer. Maybe he could Disguise her, just long enough to get through the hearing. Julianna would see a different girl, think Becky was out of the picture, and all was well. At the same time, other people would see a different girl, too. That could start some vicious rumors that he'd been seen with another girl, and only confuse Becky where she swore that she had been there with him. Tommen had little doubt that there would be reporters and photographers in the courtroom, and he would never be able to explain a Disguise.

Maybe he could Disguise her just enough that she wouldn't look pregnant. Julianna would see her, know that they were still together, but not know of the baby. No, that wouldn't work. Ryan or

Tyler had mentioned the pregnancy out of wedlock, and if they knew, Julianna probably knew. All the same, he had to keep her safe.

But where would be safer than the courthouse? There would be cops there, for sure. No way CPD was going to miss it, even if they hadn't gotten the guilty verdicts they wanted. On top of that, he and his dad would be there, with their Time and Akari abilities at the ready. If Julianna tried something, Tommen knew that Rifun held little love for her. He might not have his Force Akari anymore, but he was still a Warden Timekeeper and could throw a few punches.

And on top of all that, at least if Becky was with them, then they could protect her. All things considered, it might be safer for her, rather than leaving her alone to be picked off. Yes, Tommen's paranoia was in overdrive today.

He got out of bed just as the toilet flushed and was dressed before the bathroom door opened. A minute later, he heard his dad's alarm go off, and the grumpy bear came out of hibernation. Tommen suddenly recalled that he was supposed to have Banded him to get more sleep, which was why Walter's alarm was set for fifteen minutes later than his. Oops.

Still, when Tommen met him in the hall, his dad just gave him a look. Walter returned to his bedroom to look for nice clothes, and Tommen headed for the kitchen to look for breakfast.

"As I recall, this was only supposed to be a two-person excursion today," his dad said, coming out to the kitchen a minute later. "Becky looks like she's getting ready for Mass. Except it's mid-morning already and two days before Christmas."

"She won't be kept away," Tommen sighed. He quickly Banded the two of them and explained his reasoning. His dad looked unhappy, but did not dispute. He dropped the Band.

"He might have had a better chance at keeping me away," Becky said as she crossed the living room toward them, "if he hadn't sprung the restriction on me, you know, this morning. And if he'd used nicer excuses, like, 'You need your beauty sleep' and not just, 'Because I say so.' "

Walter gave Tommen a look. "Never a good reason to use on a woman."

"Thanks, Dad," Tommen growled.

"Besides," Becky went on, "you were just a convenient hostage at the time. I don't know why anyone would come after you. Plus you testified for him, too. And against. Both sides." She crawled in one of the seats at the table. "And it sounded like he wasn't exactly in the group's good graces, anyway, and they were planning on finishing him off a long time ago. Going into a courtroom with a gun —if you make it that far—you'd only get probably one shot. Between you and him, who'd want to off you? Like I said, just a convenience thing. He'd be the real target I bet."

"You're not making me feel better," Tommen told her, sliding some eggs around a pan.

"Nor me," Walter agreed. "I would very much like this to all go smoothly, in and out and be on our way."

"On our way back so you can get more sleep?"

"Precisely."

Tommen ignored the look he knew his dad was giving him. Yes, yes, he would Band him so he could get his beauty sleep. Sheesh. Did his dad Band him every morning before school? No...Tommen had to get himself up. Sometimes they met on his way out the door, sometimes not. One morning of interrupted sleep wouldn't kill him. And he didn't have a pregnant girlfriend to watch out for. Well, maybe he did. Becky was rather indiscriminate when it came to an audience for her soapbox rants or her tongue lashings for an offense. Well, his dad wouldn't be around a whole lot longer for it, once he went dark. Then he could safely send them off whenever he wanted.

That was something Tommen hadn't really given much thought to, and it disturbed him a little as he doled out the eggs and bacon. He hadn't really mentioned any of this running away bit to his dad. It came up a few times as a hypothetical, but never as a serious course of action to persue. How would his dad feel about it? What would he think about taking Becky and the baby?

"How long is a sentencing hearing?" Becky asked.

"The bare bones of it, not long at all," Walter answered. "The real wild card is the victim impact statements."

"Mine is finished," Tommen commented. "It's not super long."

"Neither is mine. I can't imagine R—Ndolo—" He caught himself before sounding too familiar with Rifun. "—will say much when he is given his chance to speak. We won't be there for long. I think the introductions and formalities will take longer."

"Why does he get a chance to speak?" Becky asked, tone sharp. "Shouldn't he have done all his talking at the trial?"

Walter shrugged. "It's part of the proceeding, a final farewell between parties. On more than one level. VanHouten is retiring. Calhoun is looking for a new position in the courts since being ousted as prosecutor. New year, new changes."

Becky shifted in her seat. "Why did Calhoun lose the election? He still got Ndolo put away. I mean, I admit I didn't vote this year because nothing exciting was really going on. Not like the presidentials next year."

"He got Ndolo put away, true, but he lost all the murder charges. Those were cop murders. Not a lot of people were happy with that, myself included. I might understand it, but I didn't like the way he handled the case. He was pushing too hard, focusing on the elections more than the case and the justice. I'll admit, I didn't vote for him."

Tommen kept silent. He didn't vote this year mostly because he'd forgotten. Hey, it was his first time being eighteen. After years of being told he couldn't vote, had to wait, he just kind of tuned it out. And as Becky said, there wasn't really anything exciting on the ballot. The president and the governor, well, that was a different story.

By the time they finished breakfast, Tommen hadn't come up with any viable excuse to keep Becky home. She was fully intending to go, and he couldn't and wouldn't stop her. He was still debating Disguising at least the pregnancy, though he was leaning toward not bothering. Tyler and Ryan already knew he'd fathered a child, so

Julianna would, too. No need to go through the hassle of hiding something that everyone already knew was there.

He washed the dishes and pulled on his shoes. He elected to drive, but again, they used his dad's car. It was nicer, and the heater worked better. His dad gave him another look as he got in the passenger seat, but did not argue. Becky clambered into the back.

"All right, let's go!" she exclaimed. "I want to see this son of a biscuit get put away for a good long time, how about you?"

It was the closest she really got to swearing, and it only served to amuse Tommen as he backed out of the driveway.

By mid-morning, the plows had already come through, but more snow was falling and coating the roads again. Tommen could look in his mirror and see the flakes filling in his tracks. Another reason he liked his dad's car more, better tires and better brakes. Once they got closer to the city, the sheer congestion of people kept the snow melted. As they crossed the bridge, the river was still flowing strong, though snow was accumulating at the banks. Christmas lights adorned the bridge, including a huge light-wreath on the side.

Two years ago, Tommen remembered looking at the bridge as he jumped in Rifun's boat heading away from the launch. He remembered the lights reflecting in the dark water as he fought for his life, swimming to shore, clawing his way onto the icy sand. It all felt so far away now. Nine or ten Books ago, at least. And now it was finally coming to a close.

He considered something then. Did that mean that his Books were ending? Was this really going to be his end? It started with him and Rifun, now it would end with the two of them going their separate ways, one victorious, the other not. But was it really a victory if Tommen was destined to die? How was that supposed to come about? He had at least a few months until the birth.

At the same time, Chandler had never actually said just how long after the birth Tommen would die. It could be two days, could be two years. Was Chandler's prophecy simply a means of providing closure to readers, a way of telling them what happened to him without actually following his every move until that time? How many more Books were there?

He slammed the brakes as someone cut him off, an SUV in a desperate rush to get into his lane right now. Maybe it was his fault, maybe not, but at least he didn't hit them. Becky made low growling sounds and his dad gave him a look. Tommen let out a breath and cautiously let off the brake, easing on the accelerator.

"To be fair, that would have been his fault," his dad mentioned.

"Unless you're a teenage driver," Tommen said.

"Unless your dad is a cop and a witness and a former employee of the police department whose jurisdiction you're driving through."

Okay, so there was that. At the very least, it helped to calm Tommen's racing heart some. He glanced in the rearview mirror. "You okay?"

"Fantastic," Becky growled. "Warn me next time."

"Tell him to use his blinker next time, and give me more than three inches to work with."

In his peripheral vision, Tommen could see his dad smiling.

Traffic only got worse as they reached the far side of the bridge, landing in the city and all its congestion. Two days before Christmas, which meant all the last-minute shoppers were out and about, taking advantage of ever more desperate deals. Forty percent off. Fifty. Seventy. December 26th, everything would be ninety percent off. The perfect time to stock up on Christmas candy and non-perishable supplies for next year. Ten rolls of wrapping paper for the price of one, or so it seemed. Why bother to buy beforehand when it was smarter to buy after the fact? Tommen would never understand the life of impulsive shopaholics.

Pedestrians were also swarming everywhere. Most were considerate enough to stay on the sidewalks. Some were polite enough to wait for the appropriate traffic signal or use good judgment at a crosswalk. Others were assholes who didn't care because pedestrians automatically had the right of way. Didn't matter that they were essentially jumping out in front of traffic from between cars parked too closely on the side of the road; they needed to get to the sale across the street, damn it!

But they arrived at the courthouse no worse for wear, and with no new dents, dings, scratches, or bodies stuffed in the grill, or none that he was aware of.

"I'm not even going to look until we get back," his dad said, as if reading his thoughts. "As long as we make it out of town alive, I guess that's all we can hope for."

"Bet you're glad you don't work for the city anymore, right?" Tommen said, getting out of the car.

"I'm glad I don't have to deal with the traffic. The county has its own set of problems over the holidays, thank you."

"What's the weirdest thing you've encountered over the holidays?" Becky asked.

Walter chuckled. "Ask me January 2nd, and I'll tell you. They seem to get weirder and weirder every year."

The trial had been rather sensational in the area, and every day of the trial, the parking lot of the courthouse had been full to overflowing, civilians parking in employee parking, police department parking, across the street in a strip mall that became a tow truck driver's best friend for the duration of the trial. People parked anywhere they could find a spot. Inside the courthouse, overflow rooms had been set up and they ended up having to turn people away due to security concerns.

The sentencing...was not so sensational. For one, it was the Wednesday before Christmas, and who wanted to sit in a courtroom when there was shopping to do? Barring that, people were out of town, and it was winter now which meant braving the cold and snow. Besides, everyone knew he was getting put away for a long time. Who really cared whether it was forty years or four times forty years?

That wasn't to say the parking lot was completely deserted. They were able to park in the court lot, but just barely. The employee lot was just visible from the front of the building, and Tommen thought there were more civilians than employees here today. Might be that this was the only thing on the docket today, a way for Judge vanHouten to end his career with a bang, right before Christmas. *And for my final trick, I shall make a violent criminal...disappear! For twenty-five to life.*

It was much less of a hassle trying to get through security this time around. One of the guys greeted Walter by name and gave him directions to the specific courtroom.

Once past security, the courthouse was nearly deserted except for a bailiff here and there, a lawyer or someone else important-looking striding purposefully down a hall. Tommen spotted a photographer disappearing around a corner, and a man with a headset pack on his belt headed into the bathroom. While he'd fully expected that media of some form would be present, he had been more envisioning newspapers, aspiring bloggers, and a few photographers. Why would they need cameras? Was it just standard for every case that went to trial, follow it and get it on camera from beginning to end? Was it just standard, CYA for the courts in the event someone tried to sue them for...judicial malpractice? Was that a thing?

Becky ducked out from under Tommen's arm, breaking off to go to the bathroom herself.

"Think I should wait for her?" Tommen wondered, looking at his dad.

"I think it might be a good idea." That was what his dad's mouth said. His dad's overall expression said, "Why are you even asking?"

So he waited. He leaned against a wall and brought out his phone. There was no public Internet here, and Tommen knew that extended cell phone use would start to make the security officers anxious, the time before one of them asked him to put his phone away dependent on a particular officer's paranoia level that a civilian was secretly going to activate a bomb or give the signal for some other mischief.

The bathroom door opened and Becky walked out, looking much relieved. Tommen put his phone away and went to her.

"I am so ready for this to be over," she said, not for the first time, or even the first time that day.

Tommen was ready for this case to be over. Guilty verdict down, time to deliver the sentence and haul Rifun away. Then it was a hop, skip, and a jump to happily ever after. The end.

They found the courtroom easily enough. Even if they hadn't been given directions, it was the only one open today. Briefly Tommen wondered whether everyone was supposed to have had the day off today except vanHouten wanted to deliver this sentence and today was the only day it could be worked into the schedule. Well, if the old man was retiring, it wasn't as if anyone could really do anything about it or say anything.

A clerk opened the door for them and they slipped inside. Tommen spotted his dad immediately in the front row. Even before he could move, Calhoun the prosecutor came out of nowhere to stand beside Tommen.

"You'll sit in the front row there," he said quietly, putting a hand on Tommen's shoulder and pointing to where Walter was sitting. "Do you have a statement to read?"

"Yeah, I do," Tommen answered.

"All right. Well, it's not rocket science. Just wait your turn."

Tommen nodded and he and Becky joined his dad. The old church pew creaked noisily.

"Oh, for heaven's sake," Becky huffed. "I haven't gained that much weight."

"Blame it on me for having that extra bacon this morning," Tommen told her.

He shifted position and looked around the room. It was full, but not overly packed, and they were about ready to begin. On the surface, nothing seemed especially out of the ordinary. Mostly it was older adults, in their forties or fifties, those without kids or who didn't have any last-minute shopping to do. One elderly couple had a few grandkids with them, three of them ranging from maybe eight to about fourteen, the youngest on his knees on the pew looking at the back of the room. There were a few characters Tommen might have marked as suspicious, in that, they didn't look like they had a squeaky clean record themselves.

He also spotted several police officers, all of them out of uniform. He located Miles O'Connor sitting next to Sean Tanner. Casey Oldman was in the back in civilian clothes. Standish was also present, sitting next to Steggmann. A few others he recognized but could not name were scattered here and there, all of them intent on Rifun's sentence.

Then Tommen Banded, bringing everything to a halt. He looked at each person intentionally, looking for anything obvious. Finally he sent out Test on each person. If a person was who they said they were, they would remain as they were with a bit of an ambient glow about them. If someone wasn't who they said they were, there would be a bit of a shadow over them and their true self would be revealed. It was a way to punch through Disguises and temporary DNA changes, but it would do nothing for those skilled enough in Matter and DNA who could permanently alter their DNA and so themselves. Nathan was one such person. If he altered his DNA and changed his appearance, Test would not reveal anything about it; everything was exactly the way it was supposed to be.

Tommen scanned his half of the room first, going pew by pew, person by person. A clean Test only took about one to three seconds. If it found something not quite right, it could take up to five seconds to reveal the person beneath the Disguise.

It wasn't until the final row that his Test hit a snag. His heart jumped and his paranoia alarm went off. To his surprise, it was not Julianna hiding there. Rather, it was Godwin. Tommen brought him into the Band.

"So, you found me," the mercenary stated.

"You weren't who I was looking for, I admit," Tommen said,

trying to match his bored demeanor.

"Julianna."

"That's right."

Godwin jerked his head to one side. "Other side, fourth row back, the lady with the black hair and the green dress. She was here for the whole trial, too, but she played it smart and stayed in the overflow rooms. Now then, what do you plan to do with that information?"

Tommen shrugged, trying to stay nonchalant and not give away his nervousness. "I don't know, but it's good to know in case something happens, wouldn't you say?"

"I would."

"Are you the only one here?"

"We are spread thin and have matters of greater importance to attend to. I'm the only one who could come, if only as moral support."

"But you can't tip off Julianna because she's still hammering you guys," Tommen concluded.

"Her attacks were not limited to the Akarin, nor to Earth," the man confirmed evasively. "And this brings me to my next question: are you fucking stupid?" When Tommen blinked, he went on, "I can take the three of you out of here just as soon as we clear this place. If you want any decent chance of having a wife and child at all, you'll take me up on that offer."

Tommen opened his mouth, but the mercenary kept talking. "Nathan gave me your bullshit excuse. You want witch doctor medicine when we have a fucking Builder and other Akari-bearers. If you think you can hold out for however many weeks or months, fine. Their funerals are on you. Assuming you're still alive after the kid's birth, maybe I'll re-extend the invitation."

Tommen locked gazes with Godwin for a long moment until the man ripped his way out of the Band. Life resumed in the courtroom. After a few seconds, he erected another Band, this time with just him and his dad.

"Julianna is here."

"Where?" his dad asked, deliberately not moving.

"Other side, fourth row back, lady with black hair and a green dress. No sign of mischief yet, but just thought you should know. Win is here, too."

"Godwin?"

"One of Rifun's followers, now one of the commanders of the Miaramila. He was Disguised as a bailiff during the trial. He's Disguised so he can hide from Julianna. He means no harm."

"He told you this?" His dad raised a brow.

"Implied."

"And you trust him?"

"No more than I trust Rifun. But if Rifun's followers are anything like him, he's a man of his word. We may not always like his words, but he always tells the truth."

"Just not all of it. But there's nothing we can do until there's a situation. Guess we'll just have to play it by ear and pretend like everything is just fine and we're excited to see Rifun put away."

Tommen nodded uncertainly and dropped the Band. He looked around again, this time in the more casual, more curious sense, and not so much nervously looking about and waiting for something to happen. He quickly took stock of his surroundings, made note of the exits, where everyone was, who everyone was, all of that. He felt conspicuous and paranoid, but he couldn't help himself. He deliberately tried to avoid settling his gaze on the lady in the fourth row, but not a few times he was sure she was looking at him. Did she know he knew? Did she know that he knew that she knew that he knew? Was there an agenda to be had here today, or was it simply to watch the final nail in the coffin of her greatest adversary? If she knew where he was being sent to serve his time, would she plant a correctional officer to watch over him, make sure he didn't cause trouble, maybe give him a good beating from time to time? Or would she just wait for the sentence, then kill him herself?

The doors at the back of the room swung shut. At the front of the room, a side door opened and Calhoun walked in. He had only a thin briefcase with a few papers, the last of his caseload as the county prosecutor, before he was demoted to a common lackey. He walked straight and tall, a man on business, but he'd lost his glowing pride that he'd had at the trial, the certainty that the world — and the verdict — was his to command. In a way, Tommen actually felt sorry for him. So maybe he'd rushed things a little — not entirely his fault given Julianna's moles — maybe looked at the polls and the elections a little too much, but he'd also been given a case where half the information was missing. Take out Time, and Rifun could not have lost except for his overindulgence in his flair for the dramatic, holding a teenager and a cop's son hostage at gunpoint and then shooting said officer in front of said son. If not for those little cherries, he would have won. Misdemeanors didn't even really count in a case like this.

Behind the prosecutor came the lawyer, Kevin Bartlett. The man was fat and crabby, but he was a damn good lawyer. Any man who could get a child pornographer and a murderer off almost scot-free certainly earned his keep. He had a slightly larger briefcase with a couple yellow legal pads poking out the top. Tommen smiled to himself, remembering Miach commenting on having to buy them a dozen at a time to try and keep up with everything that was going on. He'd gotten a glowing letter of recommendation for it for his next "exchange student" adventure, but he'd ended up shredding it, feeling too guilty about being on Rifun's team and not doing more to actually get a guilty verdict, a more helpful mole on the inside.

Then the side door opened again and Rifun Ndolo was led into the room in handcuffs. He looked better than he had at the end of the trial. The night before he was supposed to testify in his defense, he'd been beaten almost to death in a riot in the jail. Multiple broken bones, broken face, internal damage. He'd had to give a recorded testimony from a hospital bed which was played later for the jury. Walking into court now, all the bruising had gone, all the swelling. He did not limp or appear to favor any hidden injuries. The only noticeable things were the scar on his right cheek, a long surgical scar down his right arm, and his two missing fingers. Judging by the way his right arm looked smaller than the left, Tommen guessed he'd only recently gotten his cast off.

Rifun did not say a word as he was marched up to the witness stand and made to sit, his cuffs attached to a lock under the lip of the stand. His expression was unreadable as he took in his surroundings, scanning the room from wall to wall without really settling on any one thing or person. Tommen recalled that the man was slowly losing his vision on account of his seizures. What could he see from his position, sitting perhaps twenty or thirty feet from the audience? Could he make out the faces in the crowd? Was he able to see Tommen and Walter? How useful would he really be if Julianna decided to cause a huge scene?

As curious as he was, Tommen forced himself not to dwell on it. Those were all Rifun's problems. This door was closing, and their paths were diverging. Maybe for a time, maybe forever, but this was where they separated. He would not dwell on it, he would not become enslaved to it. He was not a Stockholm Syndrome victim.

"Why is he up there and not sitting with his lawyer?" Becky asked aloud.

"It's so we can address him face-to-face as it were," Walter answered, "look him in the eye and tell him what we think of him."

The bailiff stepped forward as the judge's door opened. "All rise." Everyone stood. "This court is in session, Judge Cecil vanHouten presiding."

"Thank you, Marty," vanHouten said, stepping up to his seat. He sat, saying, "You may be seated, thank you." Tommen noted how the man's hands twitched more noticeably than they had at the trial. "The only case we're hearing today, the last before my retirement. How exciting." Polite chuckles from the audience. "Sentencing for the case of the State of West Virginia versus Rifun Ndolo." He looked around as if to ensure that everyone who was supposed to be present was indeed present. Rifun did not move or fidget in his seat, nor did he look at the judge when the judge looked at him, just looked here and there at nothing in particular, no longer than ten seconds at a time, almost like a blind man's stare.

The judge managed to get his glasses on his face as he looked over some papers before him. "Mr. Ndolo, you were found guilty of attempted murder of a police officer of the second degree, kidnapping with intent to use as a hostage with the recommendation of mercy by the jury, breaking and entering, petty theft, evading and eluding, and illegal possession of a firearm. Do I have that quite right, Mr. Calhoun?"

"That is correct, Your Honor," the prosecutor replied.

"Good." He removed his glasses—more to the point, he shakily knocked them off his nose. "I would hate to think I'd become senile in my old age." More polite laughter from the audience. "Any disputes from the defense?"

It was probably just a question of formality, Tommen thought. Nevertheless, Bartlett stood. "No disputes, Your Honor." He sounded rather cowed, compared to his boisterous personality during the trial. Or was he simply distracted? No doubt he had or was going to draft dozens of appeals on this case.

"Very good. Moving right along, then. The attempted murder and the kidnapping both warrant the privilege of a victim impact statement from said victims. Mr. Calhoun, do your victims wish to give statements?"

"They do, Your Honor." Calhoun turned. "Officer Forbes, would you like to go first?"

Walter stood. "I suppose I could be persuaded."

A clerk brought the rolling lectern to him as he stood between the prosecutor and the defense, angled so he could face Rifun. He dug out a folded piece of paper and smoothed it on the lectern. It was a long moment before he began.

"I've never been good with words, so I'll get straight to the point," Walter read. "You shot me. And you had the nerve to deny it, try to blame stress or age or faulty memory. You willingly took my son hostage, held him for two weeks in a cave I knew not where, and you put a gun to his head to try and force my hand. And you had the nerve to play the victim yourself. You willingly associated with a group of freaks, murderers, and terrorists. And you had the nerve to claim fear and ignorance, though you seemed to know enough about the justice system to be able to elude it for a year and a half.

"I see a lot of bad things in my line of work, and I deal with a lot of bad men. Bad men like you who have no regard or respect for the law until they seek to exploit it for their own gain, taking advantage of a system that is meant to be fair and bring justice for all. I am looking at justice, as I stand before you a free man, while you take the punishment for your crimes against me. And even if you die and rot in prison, the families of the officers killed will not have the same feeling that I have here today, because you escaped that punishment. You will not have that weight upon your shoulders.

"Instead, I shoulder that weight, as I think about every man and woman who died that day. I remember their faces, their resolve and determination that day as we left the precinct, all of them for the very last time.

"I also remember two more faces. One of them is yours as you stood over me, revolver in hand. I remember your last words to me. 'Goodbye, Walter.' That I will never forget, and it sickens me that you denied it. The other face I remember is that of my son, holding me as I was dying in his arms. When people say they want to die with their family around them, I don't think that's what most people have in mind.

"I don't know whether you were the ringleader of that particular operation, but I sure as hell know you weren't a victim. Quite frankly, I would rather you own up to that than try to pretend to be the meek and mild, which I think we both know you are not. There's hope for a man who is honest about what he is. But I don't know that there is hope for you."

Walter stared at Rifun a moment longer, then folded his paper and returned to his seat. Tommen noticed that over the course of the reading, Rifun's expression went from unreadable and almost passive, to more focused and even determined. For a moment, Tommen expected him to Band so he could personally address Walter's statement, but it never came.

"Mr. Forbes?" Calhoun prompted.

"Um, yeah." Tommen stood. "Right."

Gingerly, he made his way to the lectern, fumbling with his statement that had turned into almost a speech assignment for English class. He smoothed it out and looked at Rifun. Rifun looked at him expectantly, curiously, eagerly. They hadn't spoken in months, and the man wanted to know what he had to say. What was he going to read from that paper, and did he have anything more to say in a private Band? Did he write something nice? Tommen broke the stare first and looked at his paper.

"Two years ago today, you held a gun to my head and demanded that my dad turn over Lily Guile. It was my life or hers. Later, I held my dad in my arms as he bled from three bullet wounds that you personally delivered to him. Still later, I was told that those bullets had been poisoned by an associate of yours and that my dad was going to die." Tommen paused. "Let me tell you, that was the longest day of my life, the longest week.

"Because of the warehouse shooting, I now have to wear hearing aids, I have nightmares, and I talk to a therapist regularly. I'm learning to put the past back in the past, but it's not easy. A victim impact statement is meant to provide an opportunity for the victim to address his attacker, speak the candid truth to him without fear, whatever is on my mind that I want to say." He nodded. "And I do have something I want to say to you." Tommen paused, took a breath, and looked Rifun right in the eye. "I forgive you."

Rifun blinked.

Dead silence in the courtroom, except for the shutterclick from an overeager photographer.

"I forgive you," he repeated, looking back at his paper. "Believe me, it's not an easy thing to say and it's even harder to do. But it must be done. Because harboring hatred and bitterness does not hurt you as much as it hurts me. And as much as everyone might point to a reason for me to curse you, I find that I couldn't do it if I tried.

"I have to disagree with my dad in one respect. I do think you are a victim, but not in the way you tried to portray. I think you are a victim of evil ideology, deception, and poor judgment. We all long for a higher calling and a greater purpose. I think you honestly believed you were doing something right, that you wanted to do something right. But this wasn't it. I think you now find yourself adrift, lost, alone, and confused, not knowing where to turn.

"I do believe that you ought to serve appropriate time to satisfy justice, but I would be lying if I said I wanted you to be idle and rotting during that time. Because it's going to be a long time. I wish you conflict of conscience, guilt, regret, remorse, all those things I don't think you've quite grasped yet. I wish you depression and agony of the soul. But I wish you growth because of it. I wish for you to find genuine hope and acceptance and happiness not dependent upon rules and outward ideology. I don't know what it is you're looking for in this life, whether it has to do with some shaman's curse or some other hidden agenda. But whatever it is, I hope you find it in such a way as to make other people happier and better for it."

Tommen met Rifun's gaze once more. His expression was mixed. Surprise, confusion, suspicion, and a few others Tommen could not readily name, all pulling at him. Finally, Tommen folded his paper, calmly put it back in his pocket, and returned to his seat. He took Becky's hand and squeezed it. His heart was racing, and he was sweating.

The courtroom was still quiet, everyone trying to process what had just happened. Two victim impact statements, vastly different. Walter, the veteran cop, stating that he didn't think there was any hope for the man on the stand. Tommen, the kid who'd been held with a gun to his head, forgiving his captor, wishing him both agony and hope. More pictures were taken, reporters scribbling madly in their little notepads.

Tommen glanced at his dad. If he had to hazard a guess,

judging by his expression, his dad was feeling a little guilty himself, that he was unable to forgive while his son was. Nevertheless, his dad gave him a small smile and an almost imperceptible nod. You did good, it said. I'm proud of you.

Up front, the prosecutor, the defense, and the judge, were all taking notes. A couple clerks whispered to each other. One broke off and went to retrieve the lectern. After a minute, vanHouten spoke.

"Thank you, Officer Forbes, Mr. Forbes, for your statements." Even his tone sounded a bit bewildered by the experience. Sentencing could sometimes be influenced by the victims as they read their statements, if they were emotional wrecks, shaken to the core by their ordeal, or if they were calm and forgiving. Now he was faced with two victims who seemed to oppose each other.

VanHouten whispered to his assistant to write something down, then spun in his chair to look at Rifun. "Mr. Ndolo, you may also speak, if you wish."

For a minute, it looked as if Rifun would not speak. Several cameras shuttered in rapid succession. Tommen saw two brief Band flashes—regular Time Bands, Fast Bands with an orange wake. Then there was a third, right beside Tommen, encompassing his dad. When it was released, Tommen had just enough time to register the frustrated look on his dad's face before he, too, was snagged by a Band of Rifun's making.

"How much of that did you mean?" Rifun asked.

"I meant it," Tommen told him. "I forgive you. Honestly, I forgave you a long time ago. That's why I helped you escape Julianna. But it doesn't mean I'm going to help you escape other forms of justice."

"Always so noble. So chivalrous. Except the part about you fathering a child out of wedlock, I see."

"Don't make this about me."

"Of course not, for today is my day of reckoning, is it not?" It was tough to judge his demeanor, but Tommen guessed that he was all bark and no bite today. The man on the stand sighed and looked around a moment. "I suppose, then, that this is where we part ways."

Tommen nodded. "Looks like you've healed well physically, anyway. I do hope you find other healing. Got nowhere to be for a while, I think. Gives you plenty of time for reflection."

"Yes, of course, isolation is good for the soul." Rifun dipped his head. "Keep up the good attitude, Tommen. It will serve you well in life."

And that was it. No threats, no sarcastic remarks, no hints at evil plans, no pleas to visit him either in person or in dreamwalks. Everything simply was. Rifun dropped the Band, studied his hands for a second, then said, for the benefit of the court, "I have nothing to say, Your Honor."

Whispering and murmurs of frustration and outrage from the audience, all except four people: Tommen, his dad, Godwin, and Julianna. They sat quietly amid the growling, all watching Rifun, confused and a little suspicious of his meek and mild disposition. But then, as everyone liked to point out, the trial was over. The guilty verdict had been rendered. He wasn't fighting for his freedom here, as it had already been taken away. With the Tacagan shields still up and his Akari abilities gone, he was simply whiling away his time in a suicide cell. Even in the most strong-willed men, that kind of isolation started to wear.

Even vanHouten looked disappointed as he gave Rifun an additional five seconds to change his mind. When the man said nothing, the judge nodded.

"Very well, that is your decision. Now then, concerning the charges and the penalties. We'll start from the bottom up, understanding that there is no prior record on any of the charges.

"For the breaking and entering, I sentence you to thirty days in jail, credited for your time already served. For the petty theft, I sentence you to another thirty days in jail, again credited for time already served. On the evading and eluding, you ran from the police for five hundred thirty-three days, and so you will make up that time to them, a sentence of five hundred thirty-three days, less time you have already served."

It was the only justice the officers would see. Looking around, Tommen could tell the officers present were less than thrilled. Ten officers dead, and Rifun was essentially getting only fifty days apiece.

"Moving up the ladder, then, we have illegal possession of a firearm. For this, I sentence you to two years. Next we have attempted murder of a police officer, second-degree. This is a definite sentence that can range from ten to forty years. Based on the facts of the case and what I have seen here today, I sentence you to thirty years."

Similar to when the guilty verdict came down, Rifun's demeanor did not change significantly, just enough to show he was displeased. Tommen wondered if anyone else caught it. The cops probably did, because they knew what to look for, but the lay people? Not likely, he thought.

"Finally we have the charge of kidnapping with intent to use as a hostage," vanHouten said. "A kidnapping conviction by itself is typically enough to warrant life without parole. A recommendation of mercy by the jury, should I choose to honor it, can bring it down to a definite range of ten to thirty years. Based on the facts of the case, and, more heavily, what I have seen here today, I am going to choose to honor the recommendation of mercy."

As he paused, there was more disgruntled murmuring in the audience, most of it from the police officers in attendance.

"However, I am also going to impose the maximum allowable sentence at thirty years. You ought to be thanking your hostage, Mr. Ndolo, because his mercy may have just saved your life and kept you from dying in prison." VanHouten gave Tommen an unreadable look, then continued, "Your sentences will be served consecutively. Because of the heinous nature of the crimes, they will be served at Mt. Olive Correctional Complex. Because there was use of a deadly weapon, one third of your total sentence must be served before you are eligible for parole, with a minimum of ten years for the attempted murder alone. Furthermore, you are not to have contact with any of your victims in any form. If contact is made, further action will be taken."

That probably didn't include dreamwalking, Tommen figured. But with Rifun out his Akari abilities, he couldn't make contact that way anyway; Tommen would have to deliberately go to him. He had no intention of doing so.

Running the numbers in his head, Rifun was looking at sixty-three years in prison, and he would serve at least twenty before he could even think about parole. If he was never able to reclaim his Akari abilities, and if Godwin or the Miaramila were unable to break him out, that was a long time to sit in a cell. Hell, Tommen's daughter would be grown up, maybe off to college or moved out of the house by then.

"Quite frankly, Mr. Ndolo, I don't know what to make of you," the judge went on, getting in the last word. "Even your victims are divided over your degree of involvement and how much responsibility you should bear. I am, however, inclined to agree with both of them in part. When I die, I want my family around me, but not because I'm bleeding to death from a bullet wound. No one should have to endure that. I do believe that your actions there were of your own free will, that they were not only willful but malicious, evil actions as only an evil man can do.

"Similarly, I also agree that you are a victim of an evil ideology. We see far too much of that in this country these days, but I don't believe that we can simply lock it up, out of sight and out of mind and merely hope it goes away. I, too, desire for you to see the error of your ways and change. But that must be your choice. And change does not absolve you of your sins, nor does it mean you can escape the justice due these people.

"Like Officer Forbes, I, too, have seen many monsters in this courtroom over the years. Many of them rely on intimidation, fear, and brute force to accomplish their terrible goals. But it is men like you whom I fear more, who are highly intelligent and more than capable of doing whatever you set your mind to. But when you marry intelligence and capability with evil ideology, well, we call that terrorism. But there will be no terrorism within the walls of the prison, and I hope you find a way to put your intelligence to good use. As I said, you should be thanking your hostage for possibly saving your life. You may have a chance at seeing the sun again. But if you walk out of prison the same way you go in, then you are the only one responsible for wasting several decades of your life." He paused to let that sink in. "We're done here."

He swung the gavel, and that was that. VanHouten descended the steps from his bench and disappeared through the same door he entered.

Just ahead of him, Tommen heard Calhoun tell Bartlett, "Should have taken my offer, Kevin. Forty years and he could have been out in ten to fifteen."

The lawyer said nothing to that, simply rose and went to meet Rifun as the bailiff unlocked his cuffs from the stand. Bartlett was speaking, but Rifun did not look at him. Finally Rifun sighed and said something to his lawyer, cutting him off. They continued to exchange words all the way out the side door, the convict looking ever more annoyed with his attorney.

It was the only event on the docket that day, which meant the courtroom had to clear out afterwards, but it turned out to be slow going. Everyone wanted to stay and chitchat, discuss or grumble about what had just happened. Older folks got together, the cops congregated in a corner, and so on. Being at the front of the room, Tommen and the rest of them had a tough time getting out, the last ones to leave once the bailiffs and clerks got everyone shooed out. The throng snaked through the halls and slithered out into the chilly winter weather beyond. Part of the crowd dispersed to their vehicles, but small groups still formed here and there in the parking lot, around this or that person's car.

Tommen looked around but did not spot Godwin or Julianna in their Disguises. Were they duking it out in the back halls, trying to kill or free Rifun? Or were there more sinister plans going on? Did he really want to know?

No surprise, Walter was drawn to the covey of cops standing around Steggmann's vehicle.

"Well, it's obvious you two didn't collaborate on your statements," the former chief chuckled.

"My kid continues to put me to shame," Walter sighed.

"You said what you meant, Walt," Standish told him. "No one's going to fault you for it."

"So what did you guys think?" Becky asked directly. "I don't think he got enough. If kidnapping is for life, he should have gotten life."

"Well, it's going to be for my life," Steggmann said. "Or close enough. Twenty years, I may or may not be around."

"And that's assuming he even makes parole," Casey reminded them. "One of the big issues over the trial was that he's a foreign national. Combined with his evading and eluding, they're not going to want to grant him parole because he'll just run off again. I wouldn't be surprised if he did thirty or even forty years, or maybe just his whole life. How old is he, thirty-something? I don't know too many eighty or ninety year old prisoners. Sixty is pretty up there in maximum security. Seventy is ancient. He won't be coming out."

Tommen had his doubts, and he could see his dad did, too, but Becky appeared appeased for the time being. She would probably have a soapbox rant on it later.

"What about you, Tommen?" Miles inquired. "Did you really mean all that? It sounded like you're the reason he didn't get life. I mean, basically you had the power to see him put away for good."

I had the opportunity to kill him and I didn't take it. "I meant it," Tommen told him. "I forgive him. I forgave him a long time ago. And you know what? He's still in there, and I'm still out here. But I'm not hurting. Anger wouldn't have fazed him one bit, but it would have killed me. I have bigger things to worry about now, so I can't be concerned with him or anything that happened, because it's all over now."

"You're wise beyond your years, Tommen," Steggmann said

severely. "And I commend you for it. Hell, you make all the rest of us look bad for it."

Tommen blushed and he hated himself for it.

The sun was out, but it was still cold, and the conversation wrapped up quickly. Tommen, his dad, and Becky ducked into Walter's car and were on their way soon enough. Once they were on the bridge out of town, Tommen spoke to his dad. To protect from Becky's prying ears, he not only used Welsh, but he also put up a Sound barrier, basically an invisible sound-proof wall between the front seat and the back. He made it one way, so that she could not hear them, but they could hear her if she decided to get on her soapbox.

"What did Rifun say to you?" Tommen asked.

"You know, he actually apologized for shooting me," his dad answered, shifting uncomfortably.

"Was he sincere?"

"Partially. Not soul sincere, as in, he was sorry for trying to kill another human being. Maybe a little bit, but the majority of it, I think, was...logistical. He was sorry he tried to kill me, it wasn't really supposed to happen, it wasn't part of the plan, it was a flaw in the heat of the moment. Like apologizing for causing a minor car accident. You might be sorry, you might be sincere, but there's little real weight behind it because the incident itself is more or less inconsequential. Know what I mean?"

"I think so. Did he say anything else?"

In his peripheral vision, Tommen said his dad give him a look, one he couldn't interpret but he couldn't just look over to study either. "He also said you're a good son. I'm lucky to have you and I should be proud of you." His expression changed. "He said it was unfortunate that things turned out the way they did, referring to Julianna's coup. He had a lot more planned for you."

Tommen wasn't sure what to make of that.

"What did Rifun tell you?" his dad wondered.

Tommen repeated the conversation as best he could

remember, short and sweet.

"He's a leader with no followers now," Walter stated after a moment of silence. "But I would be lying if I said I wasn't a little anxious about what he could accomplish in twenty years in prison, never mind forty or sixty.

"The thought crossed my mind, too," Tommen agreed. "But it's out of our hands now. Maybe he'll sit there for a while, or maybe Godwin will break him out in a few months. The Author will write his ending as she sees fit."

"So much for free will."

"Who knows? All the same, I would have loved to have heard what he said to Win and Julianna."

"How did he know they were there if they were in Disguise and he couldn't Test them?"

Tommen ran his tongue over his teeth. Then, "I don't know. Maybe they had some arrangements already made, him and Godwin? Godwin tells Rifun that Julianna is there, where she is, and he strikes up a conversation with her? Maybe Godwin has a Disguise that he always uses, one Rifun would recognize? I don't know. Honestly, I don't care. I don't. I'm trying to push it at least to the side. It's not my main concern anymore. If the Order and the Miaramila want to fight, that's their problem. Not mine. My problem is sitting in the backseat right now."

His dad nodded. "Good answer."

"You think this might be the end of my Books? The conflict between hero and villain ends, the villain is sent off to jail, hero gets the girl, the day is saved, happily ever after?"

"Well, I think it would be a nice end. Are you still getting Books?"

"I have eight so far, and it doesn't sound like they're ending any time soon."

"What does eight cover? Or where does it end?"

"It ends with the attack on Brelix and Julianna's coup. The Akarin and Rifun's followers helped each other to escape, and then

Kayla and I went to a funeral for another Builder."

His dad mulled this over. "Have you done anything exciting since then?"

"According to the front of the Book, the next one is called *Turning Point*. I don't know what it could be about. Rifun's trial was the most exciting thing to happen up until a month ago, but I don't know if *Law & Order* drama is exciting enough to make a whole Book about it."

"Guess you'll find out when it appears."

They arrived home safe and sound. Walter went to bed, and Tommen Banded him for at least a few extra hours. He then followed Becky into the bedroom where she sat on the bed with a huff.

"I still don't think it's right," she said, in the manner she got when she was about to get on her soapbox. "Forgiveness is great, but he still should have gotten life, just to make up for all the charges he skated. I mean, if he is as intelligent as everyone seems to think, he's not going to just sit idly in a prison cell. If he still buys into some twisted ideology, he's going to spread it to other prisoners. That's how terrorism breeds. At the very least, keep the mastermind behind bars, know what I mean?"

"He got sixty-three years," Tommen stated. "And like Casey said, they're not going to let him go the first time he goes before the parole board. He fled police once, and he's a foreign national. They don't want him to flee a second time because he'll most likely leave the country."

"You think so? How many times have you seen on the news where a dangerous inmate is released, goes out, and immediately commits another heinous crime? But they let him out because his original crime 'wasn't that bad' or maybe because 'he was a model prisoner'? The way I see it, Ndolo spends twenty years in prison, spreading his terrorist ideology and winning converts. But he always follows all the prison rules, makes friends with the officers, and is essentially a 'model prisoner.' When he gets out, because of him, the number of terrorists in the area goes from one—him—to possibly dozens or hundreds."

Tommen shifted his stance. "All right. What would you do to him, then?"

Becky folded her arms and huffed. "I'm not sure. That's the problem with mass incarceration. It's a breeding ground for disease and depravity."

"He's already in a suicide cell in jail because of his seizures. They'll probably stick him in solitary in prison. He's not talking to anyone."

"Great, so he'll be insane by the time he's released. Highly intelligent insanity."

"Insane. And old. I think you're making it bigger than it needs to be."

Tommen tried to sound like a calm voice of reason, tried to make it sound like he was really trying to move on. And he was. But he would be lying if he didn't admit to himself that he had similar misgivings. Rifun might go insane in prison, if he spent twenty or more years in solitary. He might have an army if he spread Time and the Akari to the other prisoners. Either way, he would come out only more dangerous than when he went in. But he most certainly would not be old when he got out. In fact, he could serve the entire sixty-three years and age only five years, maybe, at the high end, depending on how much he used Time to Slow Band his way through the years.

Becky wasn't done. "Yes, but—"

He put a finger to her lips, then kissed her gently. He looked her in the eyes. "By the time we need to worry about him, our daughter is going to be all grown up, graduated high school, maybe even off to college or moved out. There is a lot of time in between now and then. Okay?"

She grumbled a little but sighed, nodded, and kissed him. "Okay. I guess you're right. We have a lot of milestones to cover before we need to worry about him."

"The biggest milestone is just having the baby." Tommen poked her in the belly. "We haven't even gotten there yet."

She giggled. "Yeah, yeah, you're right." She sighed. "Still, something about it today just feels...hollow. Like a victory that wasn't really a victory."

He raised a brow and poked her again a few times. "Aren't you the one who just loves to quote at me, ' "Vengeance is mine," saith the Lord'?"

"Yeah, so what? But if this is the Lord taking vengeance, shouldn't we feel a little better about it?"

"I have no idea. I can't speak to that end. But it seems to me that I feel a little better about it than you do. I'm the one he held hostage, and I'm the one who managed to forgive him. Maybe the peanut gallery can learn to forgive, too?"

She growled a little more. "Yeah, yeah. Okay, fine."

"You don't sound convinced."

"I'm working on it."

He laughed, stood back, and stretched. Two days before Christmas. He smiled at the irony. *Now how's that for a Christmas gift, Rifun? Two years ago, you hurt me and tried to kill my dad. Last Christmas you took me into a battlefield with a nuclear weapon at the center. This year, I'm going to be celebrating the right way, and you're going to be alone in a suicide cell.*

He went out to the living room to watch TV.

Chapter Nineteen
Festivities

While nothing really changed or even happened between Tuesday, the day before the sentencing, and Thursday, the day after, Tommen found himself walking just a little taller, a little lighter. Life—was—good. It really was. He really felt as though the door leading into the dark depths of the past two years had finally been closed. Not just closed, but locked, deadbolted, and barricaded. It was over. He wasn't waiting for schemes, training, war, battle, politics, backstabbing, or pop-up coups. He was waiting for food, family, and presents.

His dad didn't have Christmas Eve or Christmas Day off. The reasoning went that he was retiring next summer, and then he would have all the holidays off. The other reason had to do with being short-staffed.

So instead, the three of them—Tommen, his dad, and Becky— had their own mini-Christmas on Christmas Eve before Walter had to head to work. Becky made meatloaf as one entrée, and barbecue ribs as another. With it were all the more traditional sides one might expect to find at Christmas or Thanksgiving: mashed potatoes and gravy, green bean casserole, baked beans, pasta salad, homemade coleslaw, and homemade biscuits that Tommen insisted on making himself. No store-bought biscuits in this household, thank you. She also made a small cake for dessert. This she made fresh after dinner so it would still be warm with their ice cream.

"So, what do you think?" she asked as they loafed in the living room, finishing up the dessert.

Walter looked at her, glanced at Tommen, looked back at her.

427

"He doesn't deserve you."

"I'll second that motion," Tommen said from where he lay on the couch, ready for a nap.

"Aw, you guys are so sweet," Becky gushed. "But if you really do like it, all you have to do is say so."

"I say so," Tommen said, lazily raising his hand even as his dad raised his fork, mouth full.

Walter set his empty bowl and fork on the stand near his recliner and leaned back. "Ah, damn. Now I want to take a nap."

Tommen obliged by Banding his dad so he could take a nap that lasted a little over an hour. His dad didn't even seem to realize he'd fallen asleep until he woke up. He momentarily panicked until Tommen assured him all was well.

"I needed it," Walter yawned.

"You're welcome," Tommen told him, dropping the Band.

"Ah, so where were we?"

"You and Tommen were just about to lapse into food comas," Becky reminded him.

"Right. Presents. My thoughts exactly."

They didn't put up a tree or hang stockings or any of that. The small pile of gifts sat against the wall near the TV.

"Who wants the honors?" Walter asked. "I'm old."

"I'm pregnant," Becky said.

"I'm..." Tommen couldn't think of anything. " —handing out presents, I guess."

He got down on the floor and rummaged through the presents. None of them were especially big, and he would be lying if he said he wasn't excited to see what his dad got him. Two years ago, he'd gotten a Time watch that could show the local date and time of anywhere on any planet in the universe. Last year, it was a pair of glasses that not only corrected his common vision like any ordinary glasses, but they also corrected his color-blindness. On top of that, they had a lot of cool modes, so he could see in night vision, X-ray, thermal, and others. Plus, for his birthday this year, his dad had gotten him his own gun, taken him to get certified and everything.

"Stop hogging the presents and hand them over," Becky complained.

"All right, all right," he sighed.

He'd divided the presents into three piles. His dad got the fewest in number, but also the biggest. Becky got a lot of small gifts, but the most in number. Tommen was right in the middle on both accounts.

Becky's number one gift that she gave was sewing crafts, as one might expect. For Walter, she made him a full suit. Pants, shirt, vest, and jacket. He tried it on at her behest and found that it fit perfectly.

"How did you do it?" he asked. "I don't recall going to a tailoring session."

She grinned and shook her head. "No, I just watched what you wore and made mental notes. Then, when I went through and sorted laundry, I started taking measurements of your clothes and making adjustments."

Walter stared at her. "You scare me sometimes. But thank you."

He changed out of the suit into his work clothes, but commented that he would stick around for the rest of it, if they could hurry it along. His second gift from Tommen was a pack of gift cards and certificates, one for a local mechanic, one for a parts store, one for a hardware store, and one for a restaurant.

"Why do I need a restaurant card when we have our own in-home chef?" he wondered, indicating Becky who blushed.

Still, he thanked both of them sincerely, telling them to open their gifts from him first. Then he could leave and they could gush over their presents from each other in private. Both Tommen and Becky blushed at that.

Becky received two gifts from her future father-in-law. The first was a voucher for the bookstore at college, enough to cover all the textbooks she would need for her next semester (certainly no cheap investment). That got her emotional. The second gift was two-fold. On top was a subscription to a parenting magazine. Under that was a full printed copy of a research paper in the latest developments in genetics, including genetic therapies and manipulation and the latest in utero technologies. That gift sent her sky-high and she thanked Walter profusely.

Next was Tommen's gift from his dad, and he tore into it eagerly. It was a small box, but the smallest things packed the biggest punch, after all, right? Well, no. Even the laws of physics disagreed with him there. Inside the box...

"Hearing aids?" he wondered, confused, disappointed, hurt, and desperately hoping there was more to them than met the eye. They looked basically like the ones he wore now, behind-the-ear style, a little slimmer maybe on the outer piece. As for color, the inner ear piece was so clear it was almost invisible, and the outer piece was a sleek jet black.

His dad Banded, and Tommen allowed himself a measure of relief. So they weren't just run of the mill hearing aids.

"They're made by the same guy who did your glasses," his dad told him. "Generally speaking, they function the same as your hearing aids now, right down to the quiet mode, which is that switch there. But, I also had him swipe a little technology from the Wheel, specifically, the language program. Yeah, you found it, the second little switch. You can turn it on and off so you're not overwhelmed, which I thought was important. When it's on, it basically functions as a universal translator. If a language is recognized by the Time industry, it'll be translated in your ears. I had him set the language to Welsh, in case you were worried.

"Furthermore, there is also a feature, again with an on-off switch—yes, that one on the other one—where the hearing aids will actually vibrate if they detect noises normally too high or low for humans to hear. So if you're at the dog park and have that feature turned on, if anyone used a dog whistle, they would vibrate. Or if you were out in California and there was some subsonic rumbling right before an earthquake, it would pick that up, too. Fast vibration is high-frequency, slower vibration is low-frequency.

"Furthermore, these things are also said to be able to last for a century."

"This guy makes a lot of hearing aids for humans, does he?" Tommen asked cheekily.

His dad shrugged. "No, but he is a meticulous craftsman, if your watch and glasses are any indication."

"Sweet," Tommen said, grinning. He made as if to swap them out, but his dad stopped him, reminding him that they were still in a Band and Becky was right next to him.

"Remember to look sullen," his dad told him, smirking.

Tommen did his best, but it was hard now that he knew just how awesome these things were. He coughed, cleared his throat, took a breath, and finally nodded. After a second, his dad dropped the Band.

"I may have done a little looking around," Walter said, responding to Tommen's initial dismay. "Not just hearing aids, but fancy shmancy, handy dandy bluetooth hearing aids that will let you listen to music without needing a big stereo or uncomfortable headphones." He Banded again. "Supposedly, they can actually do that, too, but the how is lost on me." And away with the Band.

"Did my dad tell you about these?" Becky wondered, taking the small box. "I don't remember him saying anything about this kind of technology."

Walter shrugged. "A little Internet search. I don't know, it could be a terrible investment. I try."

Tommen swapped out the hearing aids and was momentarily stunned by the clarity. The ones from Dr. Polski had been good. They'd restored his hearing to what amounted to 20/20. These new ones went beyond that. If he focused, he could hear the smallest, quietest noises, distinct from the general din around him. He could hear the high-pitched whine of a power strip that was turned on. He could hear the fibers of his dad's clothes rubbing against each other and the recliner. He could hear what may have been a mouse in the wall.

"Thank you," Tommen told his dad.

"No problem, kiddo. You're welcome."

His dad made to get out of his recliner, but Tommen Banded and stopped him. "Thank you. For the hearing aids, the glasses, the watch. These are...they're not just last-minute, find-a-good-deal-on-something-nice gifts. They're not only thoughtful, but they're tailored. And with the Wheel the way it is right now, the hearing aids couldn't have been easy to acquire. Thank you."

Now his dad nodded. "You're welcome. I was hoping to try and do my best before we had to part ways, wanted to give you something that might travel with you for a while and remind you of me, wherever your future journeys take you. It might be the stars if you are forced to go on the run. But, at the same time, your great adventures might just be around here. And that's all right, too. Sometimes, the best adventures are the ones you take every day." His expression was kind.

Tommen released the Band. His dad wished them well and a merry Christmas, promising Becky he would bring back plenty of weird stories for their enjoyment on the 26th. Likely they wouldn't even see each other on Christmas Day. Then he went out to the kitchen, pulled on his boots, and departed.

"Your dad is getting sentimental, I think," Becky said.

"He's getting old. I'm growing up and starting a family of my own," Tommen told her. "I think he's entitled to a little sentiment every now and then."

"Yeah, but it's more frequent for him."

"He's a cop. Any day could be his last, as much as no one wants to admit it. He's got retirement in sight and he wants to make it. He wants me to make it, without all the crazy shit that's been happening the last couple years."

Becky couldn't disagree. "Yeah, okay, I get it. Still, he does get sentimental sometimes. It worries me. He needs a woman of his own,

I think. What ever happened to Laura?"

"Ah, her dad died, she ended up moving back to Minnesota, and she reconnected with a high school sweetheart."

"Ouch. Well, your dad needs a woman anyway, or he's going to get too lonely. Once, you know, we're on our feet and moved out and stuff. I think there might be a period of time after the baby's born that he's going to want to kick us all out of the house just so he can have some peace and quiet."

Tommen laughed at that, but it felt kind of hollow. His dad was going to have to come with them when they ran away; there was no way he could defend himself against the likes of Julianna or her minions. He was active, yes, but he was old, and he had no Akari abilities whatsoever. His only chance would be to come with them to wherever Nathan and the twins were hiding. Then he wouldn't probably wouldn't have much of a choice but to learn the Akari. Tommen didn't know Godwin well, but he suspected that the man ran a tight ship and did not tolerate freeloaders. Walter would have to learn and contribute. Becky would have to learn and contribute. Even their daughter would probably have to learn at a very early age and contribute.

It was a sobering realization, one that he managed to push aside as he and Becky opened up their gifts from each other. He opened his gift first. Like his birthday gifts from her parents, she also got him a couple of books. The first was a complete guide to the expectations of college grammar with a secondary companion going over basic grammar concepts and terms, and how they were applied in the English language.

"Trying to say something?" he wondered, raising a brow.

"It'll be important in college," she insisted. "I want you to get good grades and stuff." She gave him an innocent look. "Open the other one."

He found another book, *The Big Book of Dad Jokes.* Becky giggled and said, "Just in case you needed some inspiration or something new that your dad hasn't already come up with."

"I'm not sure how to take this," Tommen admitted honestly.

The third present proved to be a set of custom-made pajamas. Two, in fact, one fleece for winter, the other light cotton for summer. The winter ones had reindeer on them, the summer ones sharks swimming around small islands. He laughed, unsure if that was the appropriate response. Nevertheless, he thanked her and told her to open up her gift now.

She only got one from him. Even as she unwrapped the newspaper wrapping, she seemed to know what it was. And why not? Ring boxes have a very distinct shape, after all. Though her expression turned puzzled when she opened it up and found three rings inside.

"I don't know that I'm quite ready for that leap into a threesome," she said, her tone making it difficult to judge her mood, though Tommen was betting on sarcastic.

Of the three rings, he took the odd one out. It was titanium with cut-out crosses and laser-engraved designs. He got down on one knee. With her on the couch, he was just below eye-level. "Since I never got to ask properly before, I'll do it now. Rebecca Elizabeth Polski, will you marry me?"

Becky squealed with delight, which he took as a yes. He put the ring on her finger, breathing a small sigh of relief when it slid on and fit well. They'd talked about it a little, measured for ring sizes, but that had been about as far as it got. Now it was official. Officially official.

"And these are the rings for the actual ceremony, right?" she guessed, looking at the other two which were basically plain silver, a nice bevel breaking up the monotony.

He nodded. "Yeah. I wasn't going to, but there was a Christmas sale going on and stuff."

Becky rolled her eyes though she was still smiling. "Leave it to men. Can't buy a gift for his lady unless it's on sale."

Tommen decided not to say anything to that. Once she was done inspecting the ceremonial rings, he took the box, along with his new high-tech hearing aids, and went down to the bedroom. The hearing aids he attached to their charger and put on his bookshelf next to his other charger. The ring box he stuffed in his sock drawer, right in the corner. Originally, he'd considered the closet, but then figured that the chance of losing the box was too great. At least in his sock drawer, there was only so far it could go.

He made his way back out to the living room. Becky was still admiring her new engagement ring, examining the design carefully and probably taking mental notes.

"You know, I might be able to draw this out and input it on my embroidery machine," she said, not looking at him. "It's a gorgeous design, and I think it would look really nice on, like, a skirt or something, you know? Something that goes all the way around. Or maybe like a waistband on a dress." She looked up, a shine in her eyes as she just got a great idea. "I know! I'll put it on my dress! Right around the waist. It'll look fabulous."

"Happy to help?" Tommen offered.

Now she looked at him. "It's great!" She got off the couch and latched onto him at the waist. "I love it. I love you."

He wiggled free of her and got down on his knees to kiss her. Fuck, he wanted her. He thought it had been bad before, when he was a horny virgin. That was nothing compared to actually knowing what real sex felt like and not being able to have any. Four more months of celibacy at least? How was he going to stand it?

The two of them cleaned up the wrapping paper and other miscellaneous garbage from presents and dinner and whatnot, then settled in to watch TV. Christmas Eve meant Christmas movies. Every channel was full of them, and Becky lamented that all her favorites seemed to overlap. When Tommen asked what her favorites were, she answered, "Only all of them!"

She finally called it about eleven o'clock, citing fatigue and a big day the following day. Tommen would have stayed up longer except for that last point. Christmas break and they had to get up early so they could go somewhere. How was that fair? Oh well, it was only one day.

He slept well, he thought, except for the part about having to set an alarm for Christmas morning. On the other hand, he thought as he got himself around, Christmas morning would have an alarm clock for at least the next ten to twelve years, if not longer. Except it wouldn't be a phone or other alarm clock, but kids. Kids begging Mom and Dad to hurry up and wake up so they could open presents.

That is, assuming he made it that far. He still didn't know how much time he had between his daughter's birth and his death, but Chandler wasn't one for long-term prophecies.

Tommen had never been big on birthdays or holidays, but something about the prospect of this being his last Christmas, maybe his last Thanksgiving, his last birthday, put a rock in his gut. The last, the last, the last. What was he supposed to make of it? How was he supposed to process it? Quietly for the moment, he figured, at least until he and Becky were somewhere on the other side of the galaxy.

Sitting up and looking outside, Tommen could see his dad wasn't even home yet. He texted him real quick to make sure everything was all right. His dad replied that everything was fine, just a little scattered. He was probably going to punch out here real quick.

They skipped breakfast, though Becky grabbed a quick snack, and headed down to her parents' house. Mrs. Polski would undoubtedly have something there to eat for a light breakfast while she worked on her lunch-slash-dinner masterpiece. It forced Tommen to wonder why they needed to get there so early in the first place, but he wasn't arguing.

As they walked down the sidewalk, Tommen spotted his dad's car down the road. A minute later, Walter pulled to a stop beside them and rolled down the passenger window.

"Swear ossifer, I only had one," Tommen said, putting his hands up a little and pretending to be drunk, nearly slipping and falling in the process.

His dad looked too exhausted to react in any fashion. He looked too tired to drive, even, but the house was literally only a few driveways down.

"Very funny," he said, breaking out in a huge yawn halfway through. He sighed. "Damn it. I'm getting too old for this. New Year's isn't going to be much better."

"Maybe, but it'll be your last one," Tommen pointed out.

"That is true. Still, it's cold comfort when you've had the night I had."

"Got any weird stories?" Becky inquired, peering in the passenger window.

"Oh, Lord, girl, do I ever." Walter rubbed his eyes. "It'll have to wait until tomorrow. Or the next day. Whatever day I manage to crawl out of my bed for something other than work." He yawned again. "Okay, kids, you have fun today. I'll see you...later."

They waved him off and he pulled away.

"He looks exhausted," Tommen commented.

"I'm excited for the weird stories," Becky said, grinning.

"The ones from New Year's are better."

"Oh, I'll bet."

She fell silent, but Tommen could see the wheels turning in her mind. God only knew what she was thinking. Maybe she was imagining all sorts of weird stories that his dad might have.

They arrived at her parents' house, glad to get out of the chilly wind. Despite her insistence on walking and that the cool air helped to make the pregnancy just a little more tolerable, Becky was grateful to curl up in one of the comfy recliners with a cup of specially-prepared hot chocolate. She was also more than happy to show off her new ring. Tommen figured that he must have done something right because she got a lot of compliments on it even though it didn't have any diamonds.

"Diamonds are overrated anyway," she'd told him. "They're a dime a dozen in Africa where they're mined with slave labor, but they're just the ritz here in the first world. It's pretty much just a money grab. I would rather have one that is beautiful and has a lot of thought put into it. This one is simply marvelous!"

No one disagreed with her, Tommen noticed, or made comment on the lack of diamonds. He was a little ashamed to admit to her dad that he'd just ordered it online, but Dr. Polski just made some remark about how online shopping made things so much simpler and yet so much harder when it came to jewelry. When he was younger and he and Helen were due to be married, he either went to the only jewelry store in town and paid their outrageous ransom or else improvised. He was forced to improvise for fifteen years before he found the ring he believed was worthy of the finger it still sat upon.

"Hey now, are you two-timing me?" the doctor suddenly asked.

"Huh?" Tommen wondered, heart rate going sky-high.

"Those don't look like the hearing aids I prescribed you."

"Oh. No. They're not. My dad got them for me. Ordered them online and stuff. Says they're supposed to bluetooth connect to my mp3 player and stuff."

"Uh-huh. Well, it's a nice gesture, but don't expect them to last very long. Cheap Chinese garbage is all that is, a marketing gimmick."

"It was the thought that counted. And actually, they seem to work pretty well."

Dr. Polski grunted but did not look convinced. Actually, the hearing aids worked phenomenally, both in terms of sound, clarity, and they were indeed bluetooth compatible. Tommen was very happy with them, and he could still keep his old pair as a backup, just in case. Still, he said nothing of this to the doctor who wandered off to meet someone at the door, one of his kids who brought a whole troupe of grandkids.

Tommen thought Thanksgiving was bad in the Polski household with the kids, but he'd forgotten about Christmas. Thanksgiving was just food and playing with other kids. Christmas had presents, and the kids wanted to open them. It didn't take them half an hour to have the gifts already sorted under the tree, everyone's presents in neat, separate piles, just waiting to be devoured.

Conversation kind of flowed over him, but his alarm bells started screaming in his mind when his phenomenal hearing aids picked up a term he'd hoped was behind him. In Jezik. He pinpointed the term as coming from a conversation Mrs. Polski was having with a couple of her daughters and one son-in-law.

"I heard about that," one daughter was saying. Nomi was her name. "Yeah, they're becoming more active in Europe and stuff, maybe in parts of Australia."

"Real low profile, though," another daughter, Charity, commented. "Like, some of the stuff you wouldn't even know was connected. A knife attack on a group of tourists, maybe. But a random burglary in someone's apartment?"

"Maybe it's not In Jezik," the son-in-law, Kyle, suggested. "Not as they were. Maybe it's people claiming to be In Jezik, make a sensation of themselves."

"In Jezik hasn't been defeated long enough for that," Nomi said, shaking her head. "Even when a terrorist group has been 'defeated' all they really do is split into smaller and smaller cells and go underground for a time. Wait it out a little bit, wait for the heat to pass, then come back. I'd be willing to bet that the knife attack was the main group, and the burglary was some stupid teenager trying to get their attention, pledge loyalty."

"But the one defining feature of In Jezik, the core of the group," Mrs. Polski said, "was their use of horned helmets of some kind. And poisons, chemical agents, nerve gas, things of that nature. None of that has been spotted with these attacks."

"Maybe they're reforming themselves," Charity suggested with a shrug. "The horns made it kind of easy to tell who's who, and they didn't last very long. Figure out their mistakes, make a comeback."

Tommen made his way to a seat and tried to sit down as naturally as possible. So In Jezik was back, or the name was circulating again, anyway. Were they the Borelians' human supporters, trying to make a comeback? Had the Borelians gotten through the shields somehow? Could it be Julianna's agents, looking to cause trouble and make the Akarin panic, think there were more foes than there really were? Maybe they were using the In Jezik name and causing trouble to try and keep the Miaramila at bay, afraid of vengeful Borelians.

So many politics, so many possibilities. Tommen took a breath and quietly wondered if it really was wise to wait so long to run. He wanted Becky to be in the care of doctors who specialized in her situation, but would it matter if something happened before then? Chandler said she would be fine, but he hadn't said that she would be fine on Earth or some other planet. Maybe she would be fine in Nathan's care; the man was a Builder after all. Two and a half months was a long time for Julianna to try something, and if she was stirring up In Jezik, well, that was a little bigger than a school shooter.

Lunch was ready about one o'clock. As usual, it wasn't a spread of food found on most American tables. About the only thing Tommen recognized right off the bat was a whole roasted chicken, but it was probably covered in a blend of spices he'd not tasted before. Per the Jewish side of things, there was no ham anywhere in the house. There hadn't even been any bacon at breakfast.

Prayers were said, and the line formed. It wasn't as long this time as some of the Polski kids had gone to their in-laws' for Christmas. Danny and his kids and grandkids were gone, Eden, Andrew, and their clans were absent. That wasn't to say it wasn't still a huge gathering, but they didn't have enough people to form an impromptu flash mob.

Dr. Polski came back to ask Tommen more about his new hearing aids. While there was a lot of jealousy in the doctor's voice, there was still a hint of curiosity, wondering where hearing aid technology was going. Tommen wasn't sure how much he wanted to tell the doctor. Did he want to mention that his hearing aids could also act as translators? Would that be too weird? Earth-side technology was certainly advancing in that direction.

And maybe it was part of that slow exposure to Time he'd been considering lately. Show an astronomer the stars of Aleis, a seaman the oceans of Dorigis. Show an audiologist the technology that already existed in the universe, help him help his patients. Show an optometrist — or ophthalmologist? — the wonders of his glasses, the vision correction, color correction, and all the different modes. Show a separated family, a parent with children overseas, the watch so they always knew what time it was wherever their children were.

He refrained from mentioning the translation power for now, telling himself to save it until a later time, maybe his next appointment when it would be just the two of them in a quiet office and not a whole, house full of people.

After dinner came the presents. While the children had to hand out the presents to everyone else first, there was no rule stating who had to open the gifts first, and once they were doled out, the kids tore into the paper, getting ninety percent of their presents unwrapped before Tommen had even really finished unwrapping one gift.

Becky's parents were the only ones who got him any gifts, and it was more than he expected. There were two gifts. The first was something of a guide to fatherhood for first-time dads. One only had to look at the cover to know it was religiously-based. The second gift turned out to be a gift card to the local home building supply store, good for a hundred dollars, so he "could buy good tools and be prepared for anything on the job site," Mrs Polski told him. He thanked her, but did not mention that any good tools typically started at a hundred dollars apiece. Just a decent measuring tape was twenty-five, thirty bucks. A really nice drill? Forget it. All the same, it would prove useful, and he squirreled it away in his wallet.

Becky's gifts from her parents were almost exclusively in the realm of baby things, or gift cards to get baby things. Tommen saw only one sewing item, but he surmised that it, too, would be used to make baby things. More questions were asked about the pregnancy and the baby, specifically if they'd picked out a name and what it was.

They fleetingly mentioned that they had decided on a name, but they had also decided not to tell until the birth. This statement opened them up to a new flood of name suggestions—some the same, some different from Thanksgiving—but neither paid attention. They'd talked about it some and decided to not be swayed. Their daughter would be named Maisy Helen.

The children ran off to play with their new toys and whatnot. The adults, with their gifts being far less fun, settled in for another round of conversation before dessert. Tommen never knew people could talk so much, but then, in such a large family, you couldn't get to all the gossip in just one sitting. Now that he and Becky were slightly out of the center of attention, they had to get around to the rest of the rumors in the family that had gone unattended.

Tommen kept his ears open for any further mention of In Jezik or similar news, but that conversation had moved on to other things. Eventually, all of the conversation turned toward the elections next year. Everyone had an opinion. Tommen noted that the Jewish side of the family was more apt to vote one way, and the Catholics the other. While there was no yelling and all tempers were kept in check, that didn't mean the conversation was nice, polite debate. There were accusations and cutting words on both sides. Tommen did his best to stay out of it, though there were times when a particular comment almost demanded a reaction. Usually, if he waited three seconds, someone would deliver a response similar to his own thoughts. All the same, it was hard to keep quiet sometimes.

"Come on, Tommen, you don't have anything to say?" Kyle asked at one point.

"I would rather not get caught up in the debate," Tommen replied meekly. "I'll keep my political leanings to myself."

"And let the country be overrun by those who seek to force their views and policies on everyone else?" Eden's husband Josh questioned, his words still a little heated from the conversation.

Before Tommen could respond, Mrs. Polski saved the day by announcing that dessert was ready whenever they were. Tommen took the out and got up for a slice of pie and a scoop of ice cream.

"I agree with both of you, unfortunately," Mrs. Polski said, carefully maneuvering a slice of pie onto his plate. "I would much rather everyone simply kept things to themselves, but then, how would we understand each other if nobody spoke? How would we be exposed to new ideas? All the same, there is a polite method of discourse, which many people are not doing these days."

Tommen did not respond except to thank her for the pie and ice cream and retreat to a chair at the empty dining table. He just wanted to relax and ignore the stresses of life for a while. Politics was not conducive to such things.

Dessert helped to calm things down for a while. With everyone laden with sugar, carbs, and everything else from dinner, conversation drifted back toward the finer things in life, such as sports. Tommen wasn't big into sports, but it was a conversation he was more inclined to partake in, if necessary.

He and Becky left the party about six o'clock, after leftovers from lunch had been served for dinner. She carried the gifts, and he carried the tote of leftover food. It was dark by now, and the going was a little more treacherous than it had been that morning. They arrived home in one piece, happy for the relative warmth.

"There," Becky said, setting all the gifts on the bed for the time being. "We made it through the holidays. All is well."

Tommen wished he could be as optimistic. This would be the first major holiday in two years where something catastrophic hadn't happened, and he didn't trust his good luck. The Author hated Christmas too much to not ruin it for a third year in a row.

They watched more Christmas shows that evening. Tommen tried to relax, but it was hard. Between a shitty track record for Christmas and Chandler's warning and the gossip from Mrs. Polski, he couldn't help but mentally bet on something terrible happening.

It was a bet he was glad to lose. He and Becky went to bed that evening and woke up the next morning. That in itself was a plus. The second good thing was that everything appeared to be fine. The electricity and running water still worked, and people weren't gathered outside wearing tin foil hats and pointing up at the sky. His dad was in bed, sleeping soundly. It was all too quiet, too nice. Something had to be wrong somewhere.

He turned on the news, expecting to see some terrible event. A bombing. A mass shooting. A hijacking of the airwaves by the Borelians, telling all Earthlings that they had exactly seventy-two minutes to surrender peacefully or be obliterated. He found virtually none of that. There was mention of In Jezik, a panel of so-called experts debating whether the terrorist group was returning, or if someone wanted to make it seem like it was. Otherwise, it didn't look like anything out of the ordinary, or nothing catching his attention, anyway.

He turned off the TV when he heard the bathroom door open, then got up and went to take a shower. The massive mansion had gotten completed, everything short of the cabinetry. But their work as the construction crew was finished, which meant they got the whole week between Christmas and New Year's off, with a holiday bonus check. For the first time in years, Tommen had the holiday week off. He wasn't building, baking, or running around an alien planet.

Something was bound to happen.

Breakfast passed without incident, and he and Becky went about something resembling a routine. The magic of living together had sort of worn down into routine, settling in, like breaking in a new pair of shoes. They had another appointment with the OB/GYN the following week, another checkup and more pictures. Just over thirty weeks along, if there was even the slightest hint of danger, Whitmore said she was ordering a C-section. Better to do it that way while a living baby is viable rather than get hit with terrible news that the baby had died, or get caught up in a medical emergency of some form, thereby putting Becky at risk as well.

Otherwise, the C-section was scheduled for March 11th.

Walter lumbered out of his den around one. As soon as he emerged from the bathroom, still only semi-conscious, Becky pounced on him, almost as fearsome as Mr. Snuffles.

"So what kind of weird stories do you have from Christmas?" she begged.

"Good grief, girl, let an old man wake up first," he grumbled. "Go out and get comfortable in the living room. I'll tell some stories once I get out there."

Becky cozied up to Tommen on the couch and waited.

"Why are you so intent on getting weird stories out of him?" Tommen wondered.

"Because I bet they're awesome, and I want to hear some weird stories," Becky informed him. "Do I need a reason?"

Her tone told him the question was rhetorical. Even if he wanted to say something, he couldn't as his dad made his way from his bedroom to his recliner, plopping down as someone who hadn't gotten nearly enough sleep the last few days.

"Well, first of all, if I haven't told you, everyone says congratulations on having a girl," Walter began.

"You told us that already, after Thanksgiving," Tommen said.

His dad just yawned in reply.

"Did you chase down any bad guys?" Becky wondered.

"Speeders, plenty. Car accidents, more than I care to count. I don't know that a whole lot of 'weird' stuff happened."

"Come on, Dad," Tommen said. "You can't tell us that nothing of interest happened. What about office gossip? What sort of pranks did you guys pull on each other to try and lighten the mood a little?"

Now his dad faltered just a little, usually an indication that he'd been the victim of a prank and didn't want to tell. He hummed and hawed a bit, then finally nodded. "All right. All right. I will admit to one thing that happened. So, Greg from second shift volunteered to cover part of third last night, just to help us out a little. He is a bit of a prankster, sort of like Dan but with less glitter." He swallowed nervously, then continued. "At the start of shift, he's just doing little things. Jumpscares from doorways, whoopie cushions, things that are better suited for fourth graders—so saith Kate to get him to stop. To be fair, she got pranked more than I did.

"Anyway, we get called in for backup for Arnold, says he's got a drunk driver fleeing an officer and he's in pursuit. We go out, box the guy in, he gets arrested, no one's hurt. It was about as perfect a call as you can get for that type of thing, which was really nice. Greg's first prank came after Arnold got the guy in the back of his car. We're chatting for a minute or two, listening to the drunk yell and holler in the back of the car and just letting him stew. Greg goes off like he's going to talk to the guy and tell him to be quiet. So Arnold and I are talking. Arnold sneezes and we just hear this huge thump! Kind of like if someone had thrown a rock at one of our cars, you know? We originally thought maybe the guy was trying to kick the doors or something.

"We look around, and Arnold's car is covered in snow, and the drunk guy inside is screaming like he's being mauled by a bear. As it turned out, Greg had taken a rope and thrown it around a branch of the pine tree the car was sitting under. Give the branch a little shake and all the snow came tumbling down. He said he was originally going to try and get the drunk guy to help him a little, but Arnold's sneeze was too good of an opportunity to pass up.

"We return to the precinct to book the guy and file paperwork. Well, obviously it's cold out and we're all wearing our hats, gloves, sweaters, and so forth. We take them off when we get back, kind of set them out to dry a little on the heater."

"Let me guess," Becky interrupted. "He switched all your nametags, so when you came back to get your coats, yours was really small, someone else's was really big, and nothing was right."

Walter nodded. "Exactly. He did exactly that."

"Where did Greg get the rope for the pine bough?" Tommen wondered.

"Glovebox of his cruiser. We keep a lot of basic supplies in the cars. Never know what you might need or when you might need it."

"Like shaking a foot of snow onto your fellow cop's cruiser?"

"Not nearly a foot, only a few inches, but Arnold made the

mistake of keeping his windows open. That was Greg's excuse. He claims there has yet to be an open window that he hasn't pranked. I told Arnold to let me know if Greg was ever walking through my neighborhood so I could make sure all the windows were shut."

Tommen grinned and shook his head. Then he grew serious. "How's Vin doing, do you know?"

His dad frowned and shifted in his seat. "I went to see him last week. He's still sitting in the jail, awaiting transfer. He's not adjusting well and he genuinely fears for his life and body. Not a few guys in there know his face. Prison is only going to be harder, so it sounds like his lawyer is pushing for some form of protective custody arrangement. Personally, I don't think he'll get it."

"That's too bad."

"Did nothing interesting happen?" Becky cut in grumpily.

"Not especially, sorry," Walter told her. "I'm sure there will be plenty of interesting stories over New Year's, though, so ask me then."

She promised to do so. Actually, she guaranteed that she would do so. Therefore, he better make sure he had some interesting stories to tell. He assured her that he would do his best.

Overall, nothing of interest really happened that week. Tommen kept one eye out in the real world as he went here or there, sometimes shuttling Becky around wherever she wanted to go. He looked for anything suspicious, anything that might indicate mischief of the Time or Akari variety. He also kept one eye on the news, looking for anything that might indicate larger schemes or evil plots. The pundits were undecided on the validity of the claim that In Jezik was back in action, though they did agree that it might be better to play it safe so no one got blindsided.

It was the day before New Year's Eve when Tommen finally got a text from Miach.

"Congratulations on having a girl."

"Where have you been?" Tommen demanded. "It's been over a month. How was I supposed to know if you died or something?"

"You would have heard. How are things going there?"

"Fine. Did you hear about Rifun?"

"No, what? Has he escaped?"

"No, he got sentenced. VanHouten is retiring and he wanted to be the one to sentence him. Sixty-three years in total."

"Oh, wow," Miach replied. "Of course we both know it still won't be enough. Even if he doesn't have the Akari anymore, he still has Time and he can outlast that sentence, either by Slow Banding or just because of the slowed aging. Assuming Godwin doesn't just bust him out."

"Has Godwin or anyone from the Miaramila said anything about that? It's not like Rifun is an insignificant figure to them."

"I haven't heard anything, but I doubt they'd consult my opinion on it. How long do you want to bet they'll wait before trying?"

Tommen paused and considered that for a minute or two. Finally, "I give him five years."

"That long?" Miach wondered. "Shit, I was going to say six months, a year at most."

"No. Way too soon with Julianna gunning for him. It's in his best interest to let her succeed in her own endeavors and forget about him, that way he can sneak out the back door. Or, if she fails, then she fails, and he is free to go without having to worry about her."

"You may have a point there. Still, I wouldn't give him more than three years. He took control of the Wheel in a matter of months, conquered the Akarin in just over a year, then went after the Borelians. If Julianna is half as clever, she'll have a firm grip on things within a couple years, and he'll be nothing more than a footnote. Then he can, as you said, sneak out the back door."

"And all of this is assuming that he gets his Akari abilities back, or else the shields would have to go down."

"I still don't buy that he's been stripped of his abilities. Saying that he has helps his case and keeps a low profile, but I don't buy it."

Tommen would be lying if he said he didn't have doubts about it as well. But it no longer mattered, because their paths had diverged. "Maybe. But for the moment, he is safe and sound and out of the way."

"What do you think he said to Julianna?" Miach wondered, and Tommen could imagine his conspiratorial tone. "Or, better yet, what do you think she said to him? Godwin mentioned that Rifun had Banded the two of them but was a little offended that the content of their conversation remained undisclosed, even to him."

"I'm not a hundred percent sure," Tommen said, "but I think she may have said something along the lines of 'neener neener neener' and he could have said something like, 'I'll be back.' Except I'm not sure about that last part. He was still looking and acting pretty depressed."

"Well, serves him right. Maybe now he'll be able to understand a little bit what you may have gone through, seeing your dad in the hospital. Or me, seeing Cai in the hospital. Empathy is a wonderful thing. So is a guilty conscience."

"That is true. I hope he discovers that at some point in his prison stay, preferably before he plans to break out." Tommen nodded even if Miach couldn't see. "So, what's going on with you? Where are you? What's going on?"

"Just trying to lay low and help Cai as much as I can. He's able to walk again, which is great. We're working on getting him back to his usual physical fitness. Nathan is really happy to have me as a blueprint to try and fix his brain, but...it's not going quite as hoped. He can talk, knows English and Irish. He can recall a lot of facts about things, past events, but it's like he's reciting the life of another person. He just isn't connecting that he is the same person he is talking about."

"Damn. I'm sorry to hear that. But at least he can run and maybe learn to fight again. I heard that In Jezik might still be lurking around."

"Just their human supporters," Miach said. "Assuming it is them. But I have it on good authority that the shields are still in place, still defending you, and no Borelians or other common Time Agents can get through. The Borelians are pissed, the Tacagans are pissed, but neither can do a damn thing about it."

Tommen breathed a sigh of relief. "Well, that's good. Puts my mind at ease a little. Are you back for a while or just checking in?"

"Just checking in; Nathan is indisposed at the moment but he still wanted to keep an eye on you, pull you out if necessary."

"Believe me, I've been giving it some thought, but with Becky...I don't know if I can bring myself to do it. Two and a half months is a long time for an attack, but she's over thirty weeks and literally anything could happen that could require an emergency C-section. I don't want portal travel to be one of those things."

"I understand. That's why I'm checking up on you."

They talked back and forth, catching up on all the excitement from the last month or so. Their conversation ended on a high note, and Tommen felt relieved. His friends were still looking out for him, regardless of Godwin's grumbling.

The morning of New Year's Eve, Becky again pounced on Walter as he slogged out of bed, demanding interesting stories. This time, he had a couple to tell, though they would be nothing compared to what he got tonight. But for the moment, they worked. Most of his stories were about trespassers and all the clever and weird excuses they tried to use as to why they were not where they were supposed to be. Some said they were just out for a walk. Others claimed it was state land when it obviously wasn't. One couple tried to pull a lost hiker shtick.

"Don't people already have their party places picked out by now, though?" Becky wondered.

"Sure, for the main hub of the party," Walter told her. "But these were all couples and smaller groups scouting out places where they could do drugs and have sex. The party around the fire might be legal, but that doesn't mean that it ends at the treeline."

On top of that, he explained, some people were out pre-partying, testing their drinking abilities the night before the big drinking party, doing the drug deals the night before so the cops didn't catch them later, that sort of thing.

He finished up his stories and explanations. Tommen thought Becky's expression was absolutely hilarious.

"You put up with a lot of crap," she said at last.

Walter burst out laughing. He was still chuckling when he finally said, "Yes. Yes, I do put up with a lot of crap."

"How do some guys last twenty, thirty, forty years? I'd get tired of seeing the same offenders over and over again, tired of stupid people doing stupid things."

He shifted in his recliner, laughter reined in, though his expression and posture was still amused. "Oh, I know. I get it. That's why I'm retiring. As for the guys who stick around for thirty years, they usually have rank, which means they can choose to sit at their desk and let the grunts handle the heavy lifting. Or they have a specialty so they don't have to deal with every little thing that comes up. That...that was kind of where I was at with the city. These days, I'm just one of the grunts."

"At least for six more months," Tommen stated.

"For six more months, yes."

"Tommen said you plan on moving over the summer," Becky said. "What about the house?"

"If you want, I'll sell it to you. It'll be in both your names—or however you want to do it—and you will be responsible for everything. Or I can keep ownership and rent it out to you. It's not paid off, but I am more than willing to sell it to you for the remaining balance. I can tell you now, no bank is going to give you a decent deal on a loan. You're teenagers, only just adults, among other factors. Your better bet would be renting, but then I would charge you. I'm not financing two homes all by my lonesome here. I'm sorry." Walter went on before either of them could speak. "I'll let you two talk about it between yourselves for a while. You let me know what you want to do."

That cut that conversation short. Tommen knew it was a form of forcing them to grow up and make their own decisions. Micaiah had phrased it this way, the difference between asking for permission and expressing a desire. True, it had been in reference to Tommen trying to negotiate getting his job back in the event he got the counselor's position at the summer camp, but he thought it could be applied here just as well. Daddy wasn't going to tell him what to do; he had to make his own choices and live with the consequences.

None of them did much that afternoon, except for Walter who went to work. He told them not to worry about him unless he wasn't home by two o'clock the next afternoon. If that happened, call the precinct first, make sure he wasn't napping in the storage room. If he wasn't there, then they could be worried.

Becky made dinner shortly after he left, and Tommen flipped on the TV. Seven hours to go until the new year, and the countdowns were out in force. Top ten new movies and TV shows, top ten celebrities, top ten politicians, top ten political events, top ten new scientific inventions, top ten cat and dog breeds, top ten baby names, top ten this, top ten that. It wasn't always necessarily ten, either. Depending on the list, it could be anywhere from five to twenty-five.

"You know," Becky said, "I could understand the hype if New Year's was, like, the first day of spring or something. Because then everything does feel new and fresh and a time for new beginnings. Having it right after the winter solstice, though? Things are just going to get worse. More snow, more cold, more dreary. People would be a lot more motivated to keep with with their resolutions if the daily forecast didn't look so bleak. I mean, when you have nothing to do except sit and eat and watch TV, how can you hope to meet your weight loss goals?"

"If you can do it in the tough times, you can do it in the easy times?" Tommen suggested.

"But you need the easy times in order to start and keep a habit and establish yourself, get some motivation, before the hard times hit. Know what I mean?"

"Yeah, but it comes around the time of the winter solstice, so, you know, at least the days are getting longer."

"But it's still winter. It needs to come in summer. It would make the school calendar much easier, too, I think."

He shrugged. "Works well for Australia, then, I imagine."

She waved a hand dismissively, then snuggled in beside him to watch the ball drop.

Chapter Twenty
Last Go Round

Walter hated New Year's. If he wanted to be honest, he really, really hated it. He hated working it as a cop because of all the stupid drunks and other shenanigans. He hated it as a civilian on account of the noise of the fireworks; he was no veteran, but he was still sensitive to the gunfire-like noise.

But it was his last New Year's out on the beat, and it could not come too soon. He'd always thought that things in the city were bad, and they were. County wasn't bad, per se, but stupid people could be clever when they wanted to be.

He started his shift at four o'clock, actually ten to four, and the afternoon guys were running around like headless chickens. Walter noticed that even a few of the first shift guys were still on the clock, slaving away at their desks trying to finish up paperwork and go home.

"Glad you could make it to the party," Kate said, slapping him on the back as she walked by. "Feel free to jump in anywhere. No shallow water here."

Walter didn't like the sound of that as he punched in and filled his thermos. Jump in anywhere. You'll either find sharks or snakes, take your pick.

He pulled a report off the printer and looked at it. A roll of the dice and his first call of the day turned out to be...a bunch of teenagers trespassing on someone's land, the property owner saying they were probably drunk, the way they were acting. At the very least, they had a bunch of spray paint canisters with them, so they couldn't be up to any good.

It sounded easy enough, and Walter took it, sneaking out of the precinct before too many people noticed he was there and asked for his help with something.

He had no trouble getting to the residence, and from the moment he stepped out of the car, he could hear the young people in the woods. The homeowner was waiting for him in the doorway, arms crossed, frown rapidly turning into a scowl, evidently displeased with the whole situation.

"They're still here," the homeowner stated stiffly as Walter walked up.

"I noticed. Do you know roughly how many there are?"

"Eleven. They told me as much. 'Eleven of us and one of you. What are you going to do about it?' they said."

"Have they made any threats or been aggressive in any way?"

The homeowner shrugged. "Not especially, unless you count the threat to party like it's 1999. I don't know that these kids are even old enough to know or appreciate what that means. I mean, I partied like it was 1999...in 1999." He waved a hand dismissively. "Darn kids, anyway."

"Do you know if any of them have any weapons?"

"No knives or guns that I saw, just spray paint."

Walter inquired about the man's property lines and was told to "look around. It's mine. And if it's not mine, it belongs to someone who appreciates this far less and is far less likely to call the cops to handle it. I'm being nice."

He gave the man a light verbal warning about possible threats, but went to investigate the noise.

His first thought was to sneak up on them. But stupid and juvenile offenders were like deer. Spook them and they run. If he announced his presence and made himself seem like a blundering idiot—a stupid pig, to use a sixties reference—then they were more likely to stand around laughing at him. Joke's on them because then he could count them and work their faces into his memory and the body camera.

He got his opportunity when he looked down and saw an empty spray can. Blue, as evidenced by the cap next to it and the blue painted trees in the nearby vicinity. He saw movement just up ahead through the trees. Judging his distance, he kicked the empty spray can.

The laughing and talking and carrying on dwindled down but did not completely die as the can bounced along through the trees. Only when Walter emerged did the kids really stop to look at him.

There were indeed eleven of them, and a quick Band sweep of the area did not turn up an elusive twelfth man. The oldest couldn't have been more than eighteen or nineteen, the youngest thirteen or so. Of the eleven, two had six-packs in hand; three more had alcohol of some form, a can or a bottle; eight had spray cans of varying colors, and some had two cans, one in each hand. All of them were intoxicated.

"Aw, man, shit got real," one of the older kids said, grinning and pointing at Walter. "Old man called the cops on us."

His apparent second-in-command was not so amused as he nudged the ringleader in the ribs. "Yeah, and who do you think he's after? Us! Come on, dude!"

Three of the youngest ones took off. Walter did not move at first. He let them get out of sight before Banding, bringing everything to a standstill. He only had two pairs of cuffs, but he was going to save those for the older kids. The rest, well, who was going to prove breaking and entering, really? So he returned to the home and found some rope in the garage, most of it clothesline taken down for the winter. Then he calmly walked up to each of the escapees in turn. He brought each kid into the Band, enough that he could physically catch them and hold them. Then he fashioned rope cuffs from the clothesline and marched them back to the house. With any luck, they were too intoxicated to think about how he was able to catch them all. He tied off one end of the line to the porch and sat the kids down. Once they were secure, he released the Band.

It took some time and some creative Banding, but Walter got

all eleven kids on the clothesline chaingang. By the time he got the older kids handcuffed, Trevor from second shift showed up to help ferry them back to the station.

"I hope their parents give them a good paddle," the homeowner grumbled. "My parents spanked me and I'm just fine." He spat to one side. "Undisciplined brats."

The smarter ones would be out later, Walter wanted to say, but bit it back at the last second. They would be out later with more spray paint, more alcohol, drugs, and probably fireworks, too. All the same, the homeowner thanked them, told them to be safe that night, and watched them leave.

With eleven kids, a third car had to be called in. The three officers squashed three or four kids into the backseat of their respective cars and headed back to the station. Walter ended up with two girls and two boys. The girls were crying and imagining all the ways they would be punished. The boys were arguing over whose fault it was that they got caught. All of them were only fourteen or fifteen, and only one even had a driver's permit.

"How did you catch us so fast?" one of the girls blubbered drunkenly. "Like, you got us and I don't get it. It's like you stopped time or something." She sniffed and managed to regain semi-composure. "I've read about that, you know. On the Internet. The government's doing experiments in time control and time travel. And the two guys who shot up the school last month, they were like test dummies or something, but they escaped." Now she got mad. "It's all about control! They're fucking fascist, man! And you're going along with it! You're just a pawn, you know!"

"Do you even know what fascism is?" Walter questioned.

The girl seemed taken aback and sat back in the seat, muttering, "I read it on the Internet."

They dumped the kids at the station and went out on their next respective adventures.

Walter picked up a car accident, a two-vehicle collision where someone making a left-hand turn misjudged the speed of oncoming traffic. The vehicle that had been that oncoming traffic was irate, not least because his custom paint job on his custom truck was now all jacked up. The vehicle making the turn was panicking because she was too poor to afford to fix her car, but swore up and down that the truck had been doing at least twenty over the speed limit, and she gave the man a lecture about his own safety doing high speeds during the winter. This did not help the man's disposition in any way.

There were no other witnesses to the accident, which meant Walter had to look for clues. The most obvious one was the damage to the woman's car. There was a big difference between an impact at forty and an impact at seventy. Seeing how it was a fairly straight stretch of road, the truck could have gotten up to speed. At the same time, the man's tracks leading up to the accident were steady, and he had very little weight in the bed of his truck which in itself was dangerous.

While Walter did his brief investigation, the two continued to bicker, and it escalated. Finally he ticketed them both—her for pulling out in front of him which would be reckless driving, him for going too fast for conditions—and told them to wait in their vehicles until the tow trucks arrived.

He didn't like giving out tickets to both drivers in an accident, but they were annoying him and he really did believe they were both at fault in some way. Let them take it to court.

He hid out for a few minutes on a deserted two-track, as much to deter any ne'er-do-wells who might decide to look for a secluded party place as to take a minute to breathe and relax and have a drink of his coffee. At some point, his phone had buzzed and he hadn't even looked to see who wanted him.

To his pleasant surprise, it was Miach, crawling out from under his rock, wherever he'd been hiding.

"Happy New Year!" he'd written.

Walter texted back, "We still have a few hours to go, there, Miach."

He didn't expect a reply, but he got one a few seconds later.

"Congratulations, Grandpa. Hear you got a little granddaughter coming."

"Yes, that's true."

"How are you taking it?"

"I...choose to see it as a second chance of sorts. For Victoria."

"You coming with Tommen when they make a break for it?"

"He's mentioned running, said something about Godwin and the Miaramila, but there haven't been any serious plans that I'm aware of. Has he told you something I don't know?"

"No. Honestly, I was kind of hoping you might have been able to talk him into going, the sooner the better. I understand that the pregnancy is difficult, but he can't waste time."

"I'm not disagreeing, but would it really be any safer?"

"Julianna is one of those who isn't going to stop hunting him because he gives her the slip. If anything, after the school shooting, she's only more determined."

"I know," Walter admitted. "And whatever happens, it's not going to be pretty."

"At least with us, he'll be with us. The Miaramila can provide some protection, and Nathan and Kayla—especially Kayla—can oversee Becky's pregnancy."

"I'm not the one you need to convince."

"Well, you see him a little more than I do these days. Honestly, Godwin doesn't know I'm here or else he'd shit bricks; Nathan helped to smuggle me out."

"I understand security, but are things really that bad?"

"Godwin runs a tight ship. The Miaramila are not a social or religious movement, they are a military unit. Technically, I'm AWOL."

"Just say you went out to find a woman."

"Very funny, Walt," Miach said. "You need a woman more than I do, I think."

"I need to get back to work is what I need to do. You take care of yourself, Miach, whatever you're doing."

"Thanks, Walt. You, too. Congrats on a granddaughter. If I don't make it to the birth, send me pictures. I am Tommen's crazy uncle, after all."

"Will do. Talk later."

Grudgingly, Walter put his cruiser in gear and crept out of hiding. He managed to catch one speeder, two drunk drivers, and one high driver just in that trek back to the station. It gave him plenty of paperwork which gave him an excuse to stick around the office for a minute or two.

Well, Becky, he thought, *you may get your weird story yet.*

While he'd always enjoyed telling Tommen about some of the antics that he got into, he told them because he knew Tommen could keep a secret. He was more careful about what he told Becky. He just assumed that anything he told her would get out eventually. Therefore, he could say nothing that the general public could not know. The evening news edition, as it were. It made him feel bad because he was having to cut back on what he told Tommen, too, until he could determine how much Tommen was telling Becky. Probably if Walter told him to keep a secret, he would do so, but he decided it better to just avoid the situation completely.

"It's a beautiful day in the neighborhood," a wretchedly bad voice was singing as he walked in. "Won't you be my neighbor?"

"Aw, come on, man, make it stop!" another man whined.

It was Arthur who was singing—in an obnoxiously bad voice that Walter had a hard time deciding whether it was intentionally or naturally bad—while escorting a man in handcuffs through the station down to booking.

Had to find humor somewhere, Walter figured, signing off on the last of his papers. The secured inbox was already full, and a stack of completed reports was forming on top. He added his to the pile and went to the printer. He thumbed through the papers like a magician about to reveal the card the audience participant had drawn earlier, finally snatching one out and looking to see which lottery prize he'd won.

A complaint only eleven minutes old, breaking and entering at a residence. Sounded about as good as anything. Walter grabbed his keys and headed that way. It was a little over an hour until midnight. Right now they were dealing with trespassing, noise complaints, and a few more serious crimes like the breaking and entering. After midnight, they would get all of that but tenfold, plus a sharp spike in drunk driving incidents. And they would probably all come down at the exact same time as people left their New Year's parties. The ball would drop, people would kiss, have a drink, snort a line, have sex, then all drunkenly depart for home.

But for the moment, he would deal with the breaking and entering. By now, the thief had probably been scared off by the homeowner and was long gone. Walter would get a description of the incident, a description of the suspect, take an inventory of damages and losses, pass it along to the same cluttered pile of "be on the lookout" and move on to the next situation, just trying to get through the night.

But of course, this was West Virginia. This was the sticks of West Virginia. A homeowner didn't just scare off a thief, he met him head on with a twelve-gauge.

When Walter arrived, he found the homeowner with the would-be thief on his knees facing the garage door, hands behind his head, a sawed-off shotgun ensuring the thief's full cooperation.

"'Bout tahm ye showed up," the homeowner growled into his mustache which was far bushier than Walter's. He lowered the shotgun. "Mah arms was gittin' taird." He indicated the thief, still on his knees. "Styupid jeckess thaw he was gonna brek inda mah hahs. Wew, nah t'naht, sahn."

Walter sent the homeowner a short distance away and turned his attention to the thief. "So, what happened tonight?"

The man wasn't more than twenty-five, smelled like booze and weed, and he'd been crying. "I swear, I thought it was my house. I just got the wrong house. I swear, I thought it was mine and I just didn't have my keys so I was going to get in through a window or something. Please, sir, I didn't mean it."

"Well, why don't we sort this out later after the night's worn off?" Walter suggested. He broke out the handcuffs and the Miranda rights, sitting the guy in the back of the cruiser while he started a report, talking to the homeowner some more and stumbling through a thick mountain accent.

By the time Walter thanked the homeowner and returned to his cruiser, the thief was still blubbering and insisting he thought it was his house. He'd wet himself and was now starting to nod off.

"All right, kid, here we go," Walter said, getting in the driver's seat.

The man perked up a little. "I swear, man, I thought—"

"I know. I heard you. Maybe it's all a misunderstanding, but for the moment, I need to at least separate you two. Then you need to chill out and take a break for a while, maybe take a nap."

"How old are you, man? Did they even say 'chill out' when you were a kid?"

Walter grinned though he knew the man couldn't see. "As a matter of fact, no."

"Yeah, that's what I thought. You're what, sixty? Shouldn't you be all sittin' nice in an office or something? The hell are you doing out here?"

"I ask myself the same thing sometimes. Then I remind myself that I'm retiring in six months."

"Shit, man, I got arrested by my grandpa."

Walter got a kick out of this, and it was all he could do not to break out laughing. Instead, he settled for, "Not quite, I think."

The ride to the station was uneventful, though the urine smell was really starting to get to Walter. But it was an excuse to stay at the station for a few extra minutes to give the car a quick carpet clean and a new air freshener. Then it was off to the races once more. The closer they got to the ball drop, the more shenanigans they had to respond to and the more idiots they had to deal with.

Most of them were probably pretty nice people on any given

Tuesday, Walter thought. Good people who worked long hours at thankless jobs, who just wanted to let loose for a little while, go out to a party without the kids and pretend to be young again for just a little while. Problem was, they weren't young anymore and they couldn't party like it. Plus, they ought to have been old enough and experienced enough to know better. The younger idiots, well, they were getting their higher education from the School of Hard Knocks. Some of the courses they would be paying for the rest of their lives, in jail time and in reputation.

Statutory rape, for example, would mess a guy up for life. Walter found himself breathing a sigh of relief that Becky was older than Tommen. There was no doubt in his mind that her father would have pressed every charge he could if it had been the other way around, if he had been nineteen and she seventeen when she got pregnant.

Other crimes that would haunt some people included drug possession, and lots of it. Possessing, doing, distributing, and selling to minors, tobacco and alcohol included. The best ones—with a heavy sarcastic emphasis—were the ones who were so cracked out that it took eight officers to bring the situation under control. Thankfully, Walter was only a backup on that particular call, though he was no less worn out for it.

Vehicular homicide was also pretty damning and could make future career prospects difficult, as a drunk driver struck and killed a drunk bicyclist on the road, both of them leaving the same party.

Walter never even really noticed when the clock struck midnight and the five turned to a six at the end of the year. It was all the same hectic night for him as he rounded up the people like cattle, stuffing them into the cattle car known as his police cruiser, prodding them along with handcuffs and the threat of his cow prod taser, penning them up in the holding cells which were crowded, filthy, and had the poor keepers gagging. The only time he got a break was when he had to take five minutes to clean up vomit and other bodily fluids in the backseat.

By the time he really looked at the clock, it was quarter after two in the morning. Parties were still going on. Noise complaints abounded, sometimes interfering with more pressing issues, but mostly ignored. That is, until the callers started getting smart about it. Then the cops just got even more annoyed. One man called in for a breaking and entering, suspect with a knife. Walter got there and the man said he just wanted to report a noise complaint, but knew it would get pushed to the bottom of the pile, so he had to amp it up a little. Hardly in a mood to stand there and lecture, Walter just arrested the guy and took him in, saying he was going to get time for 9-1-1 abuse. Walter had no intention of pressing charges and would be happy to let the guy go in the morning, but the guy didn't need to know that.

It would probably come back to bite him in the ass, maybe in the form of police misconduct, but at three in the morning, after the night he'd had, he was in no mood for games. He'd been running around and dealing with more bullshit in just this one night than he would in the entire month of January and February combined.

Sometimes Tommen had the right of things. He hated holidays.

He delivered the annoying homeowner to the holding cells amid much protesting, then made his way back out, running into Kate on the way.

"Have you eaten yet?" she asked.

"I haven't had time to think about food or anything else. I haven't even had time to look at the clock until about half an hour ago. I don't even know that I've had to refill my thermos. I don't even know that I've taken more than one drink from my thermos."

Kate put her hands up in surrender. "Easy there, big guy. It was just a question. Don't take it out on me. Sit down, take your lunch. Unless we get another mass shooting incident, don't let anyone distract you for at least twenty minutes. That's an order. Stay sane for us, okay?"

He grunted, sighed, and nodded. Twenty minutes of

uninterrupted downtime sounded pretty good, as long as he didn't fall asleep in the middle of it. Wouldn't that be just lovely? He didn't think anyone would blame him for it, but that didn't mean he wouldn't get some sort of disciplinary action.

He made his way to the break room and sat. Just sat. He tried to relax, but it would not come without completely falling asleep, so he refrained. After a minute or two of just enjoying the feeling of not having to run everywhere, he got up and grabbed his lunch out of the fridge. He didn't always bring a lunch, but given what day it was, he deemed it appropriate. They were still eating leftovers from Christmas dinner at the Polskis' and he tore into it.

Mrs. Polski was a good cook who knew her stuff; Walter would not deny her that. He wished he could have been there for dinner and tried everything fresh.

He had a brief, passing thought of Laura. He missed cooking for her. He missed her cooking for him. He wondered what she was up to lately, though he already knew the answer. She was as busy as he was, except her job was carting all the stupid drunks to the hospital instead of the holding cells. If a drunk was smart, he'd feign illness and call for an ambulance, that way he could spend the night in the emergency room instead of jail and maybe save himself a little embarrassment.

Walter was just finishing up his food when Harold, who normally worked second shift, walked in.

"Are we done yet?" Harold sighed.

"Please," Walter said. "You're a young man, only a couple years out of the Academy. Don't you stay up until four in the morning on a regular basis?"

The younger officer raised a brow as he refilled his thermos. "Please. I work the twelve to twelve because I have classes all morning. I sit in my cruiser doing homework. I don't get to think about retirement for another forty or fifty years, assuming retirement even exists in the future. Either way, I don't have enough time in my day to go out and party, or do anything at all, really."

Walter shifted in his seat. "Well, while I'm a proponent of general R&R, I'd stay away from the partying. You can obviously see where it leads."

Harold waved a hand dismissively. "Please. The holding cells are far less terrifying than what my wife would have in store for me. I'd end up like Vin." He noted Walter's expression and faltered. "Sorry. That was poor taste. Vin really didn't deserve that. Just wrong place, wrong time, I think."

Walter nodded distantly. "Yeah. Wrong place, wrong time."

He stood, rinsed his dishes, tossed everything back in the fridge, and headed out. So it had only been eleven minutes out of the twenty Kate had ordered him to, so what? Judging by the general demeanor around the precinct, things were starting to slow down just a touch. They were no longer running around non-stop; they had time to pause and breathe and remember which planet they were on, which county they were in. Although, looking at the holders, Walter wondered if there was even anyone left in the county to arrest. Only the absence of Tommen, Becky, and her family told him that other people still existed outside these walls.

Quarter after three. Typically his shifts ran either four pm to four am or five to five, the out times being mostly just suggestions. Given that it was New Year's, his out time would more likely be some time around eight or nine. First shift ran four am to four pm or five to five, second shift or swing shift, did the noon to midnight. Seeing Harold still here did not give Walter hope. On the other hand, maybe things would just magically taper off and they would all be sleeping in their cruisers by six o'clock.

This kind of hope was utter folly before five am of course, especially when New Year's fell on a Friday or Saturday. Any other day, things might not be bad because people might still have to go to work the next day. Weekends, all bets were off.

Even before Walter was ordered to take lunch, the guys in holding were begging the officers not to bring in any more, if at all possible, and still no one could honor this request, no matter how much they wanted to. Walter would have been happy to let people off with a warning, except he really couldn't do that for drunk drivers, high drivers, domestic abusers, rapists, or any of the other terrible and stupid people he ran into.

It was seven-thirty, three and a half hours past his scheduled out time, before he was able to walk into the precinct again and sit down without having to run out on patrol, chase a call, or back someone else up. This time of day, people were reported missing after parties, people were waking up where they shouldn't be, all the clean up after a huge festive bash. Walter was about to go out again when Dean stopped him.

"You're not going out again today, Walt," the sheriff told him. "All us good-for-nothing first-shifters can handle the mop up. You had a hell of a night. You third-shifters are real troopers, and you don't get near enough appreciation. Finish your paperwork and get out of here. You got tonight—or maybe you think of it as tomorrow night—you got it off, don't you?"

"Yes, thankfully."

"Well, get you some sleep. I'll see you in a couple days."

Walter thanked him and went to sit down and finish his paperwork. He was several hours behind on the paperwork, and it was nine o'clock before he was able to punch out. He'd seen the sun go down the previous day and watched it rise again. He was dead on his feet as he slogged out to his car and sat for a minute while it warmed up.

He really should get going before it warmed up too much. He needed to get home and not fall asleep at the wheel. He would never hear the end of it from the guys. At the same time, they would probably understand completely. But they would still give him a hard time about it.

Reluctantly, he put the car in gear and nosed his way out to the road. Snow had fallen most of the night in big, fat, wet flakes. It had since ceased and the plows had gone through, but Walter was still leery of driving as tired as he was. He played it extra safe, looking for traffic, Banding to buy him more time. But the Banding itself took a small toll, using energy he did not have in reserve. He was running on fumes. Coffee fumes. The events of the night swirled through his mind in snapshots and half-remembered snippets only a few seconds long.

He remembered the guy who broke into his own house and a neighbor called in...wait. Was that what happened? No, couldn't have been, because he'd been held at gunpoint. No, he broke into a house he said he thought was his, and the homeowner had him subdued for the cops to haul away. That's right.

Then there was the party where half the attendees got taken in for drugs of one form or another. The initial call had been for an overdose. Walter and Kate had arrived first and at the same time, their first priority to get the girl breathing again. Because of the chaos of the night for all forms of first responders, they'd had to do CPR for almost eighteen minutes—enlisting the help of a few bystanders and other officers so they could rotate positions—before an ambulance got there. Then they went to work on the arrests, not feeling very good themselves after doing CPR for so long.

And there were plenty of drunk drivers to go around. At the precinct, someone had started a rousing chorus of "99 Cars with Drunks on the Road" and even went so far as to start a tally on the whiteboard. Someone else started another tally for the number of drunk, ambling, aimless pedestrians they had picked up and given courtesy rides to, just to get them off the roads in the middle of the night in the cold.

All of this wasn't even considering the usual riffraff they might get on a Friday night, someone sliding into a ditch through no real fault of their own, a car hitting a deer, a teenager texting and driving. That one had been fun because the kid tried to pull the "don't you know who my dad is?" shtick. Turned out, the dad wasn't anyone special, but he was hoping that the question itself might spark a little hesitancy, a little leniency. Instead, it just got him in bigger trouble.

Tommen had never tried that. He knew that if he got in trouble, everyone would know who he was, who his dad was, and there would probably be some form of punishment at home on top of whatever citation he managed to get. He knew that if he ever did pull the "don't you know who my dad is?" then his fines would probably be the maximum allowable and any punishment at home would be doubled.

That wasn't to say that he hadn't ever pulled the "you're not my real dad" card in years past, once he became a teenager and the hormones kicked in. There had been times when Walter considered telling him about their relationship, that they were uncle-nephew. But he always refrained and instead came up with some other clever ploy to make Tommen rethink his stance. Sometimes they were more emotional, sometimes more aggressive, but Tommen learned real quick not to play that card. And, Walter liked to think that Tommen had learned that it didn't matter whether or not he was his "real dad" because he loved him all the same.

At least Tommen wouldn't have to deal with that. His child would be his own, and he would be there every step of the way. From birth and first cry, to first steps and first day of school. First bra and first boyfriend. First rebellion and first break up. He would see it all. He wouldn't have to play catch-up like Walter had.

A sudden change in trajectory jolted Walter back to wakefulness and he only just managed to avoid hitting the tree head-on. Instead, he opted for something of a corner and side impact of the passenger side. It might not have been so bad, except he still had enough momentum to hit another tree, this one head-on. He didn't think it was that bad, but the airbags did.

His first thought was, *Sheriff's going to kill me.*

His second thought, *Now Tommen's going to be all worried.*

Third thought, *I'm going to have to borrow his car now. How ironic is that?*

Fourth, *Am I still alive?*

As the airbag slowly settled and the snow and dirt and debris cleared, Walter took stock of himself. He didn't think he'd blacked out, at least not in the crash. He knew he was going to be feeling this in the morning, but for the moment, he wasn't aware of any immediate aches and pains. No broken bones or busted knees.

His saving grace was that this was only a small ditch and not one of the many cliffs that plagued West Virginia roads. Cars that went off cliffs tended not to have survivors.

Next thing, then. He had to get out. Get out and radio it in. Gingerly, he started moving, unclenching his hands from the steering wheel and slowly moving his arms, his wrists, flexing his hands and fingers. He tested the door handle. It gave, and the door popped open.

He hadn't realized how badly he was shaking until he went to move and get out of the car. He had virtually no fine motor control, or even major motor control, and he went face-first into the snow. When he got his arms under him, his hands slipped on wet slush. As he was dragging his legs out behind him and trying to stand, the snow began reflecting flashing lights.

Shit.

"Walt!" The sheriff himself. Even better.

Dean Williams got out of his cruiser and rushed toward him, nearly slipping and falling himself. He got to Walter just as he managed to stand and keep his balance in the icy slush.

"Walter! Shit, what happened? Are you all right?"

Only adrenaline kept Walter awake at this point, but there was still an undercurrent of fatigue wreaking havoc on him. Despite the harrowing event, he still yawned and rubbed his face. "I don't know. I think I fell asleep at the wheel."

Dean cursed. "Damn it, Walt. I knew you third-shifters think us first-shifters get off easy on New Year's, but you don't have to go and make more work for us." He shook his head. "Shit. Well, I already got an ambulance on the way." He went on before Walter could protest. "It's a precaution. Take it. I won't make you go to the hospital, but at least let them check you out."

Walter sighed, rubbed his eyes, and nodded. "Fine. They'll probably get here before the tow truck anyway."

"You want to sit in your car or the cruiser?"

He considered this for a moment before answering, "Might as well stay in my car. That way they know who the patient is. Otherwise the ambulance might think he ran off or something."

"Very funny. If it's all the same to you, I'm going to go back to my coffee and start this report."

Walter waved him off as he got back in the driver's seat and tried to relax. What a start to the new year. New year, new deductible on his car insurance. Damn. Well, at least he would be covered for the rest of the year if anything happened. Still, this was not how he wanted to start off the new year.

"Walt? Walter!"

He jerked back to wakefulness again, and it was getting more and more difficult every time. He needed sleep something fierce. He put a hand up to block a flashlight beam. "What?"

Looking around, the fire department and the ambulance had arrived. One of the medics and the sheriff were looking at him.

"You think you can get out and up to the ambulance, or do we need to get some guys down here?" Dean asked.

"I can get up there," Walter told them. "Just don't put one of those damn collars on me. I'm not a dog."

He quickly discovered that he'd stiffened up, sitting there in his car. He had to force his legs to move, and his arms and face were stinging from the airbag. Once he got outside and upright, it was a chore to keep balance on the slush and the waxy leaves beneath.

"You called your boy yet?" Dean wondered as they finally broke out of the snow onto the pavement.

Walter sat down on the ambulance cot in a heap. "No, not yet."

"Want me to do it?"

"Just don't tell him I'm dying. I'm fine."

The sheriff gave him an odd look, but stepped aside for the medics.

The ambulance crew was all concerned that he'd hit his head and had a concussion, due to his persistent fatigue and lack of memory about the events leading up to the crash. He tried to tell them that he'd had a long night — surely they knew all about that from the overnight ambulance crew? — fell asleep at the wheel, and went into the ditch. It could have been worse, but he had managed to mitigate the damage somewhat. Bottom line, he was utterly exhausted and it wasn't getting any better.

The medics got their report. Because he was still conscious and lucid, they couldn't force him to go to the hospital, and he signed the waiver. Then the fire department needed their report. Finally the sheriff returned, and Walter knew all the paperwork that was going to go into his report. The only saving grace there was that Walter hadn't been on duty at the time.

"Your kid's coming to get you," Dean reported. He sighed. "I'm not going to write you a ticket, Walt. I know what you guys went through last night. I can appreciate a simple accident. Besides, your car repairs are going to be punishment enough, I think."

"No, having to borrow Tommen's car is going to be punishment enough. At least he got rid of the old Cadillac."

Dean laughed at that. "So, I take it you're not going to the hospital?"

"Nope."

"All right. Well, how about you come sit with me and we'll let these guys go?"

It was akin to going to the principal's office, Walter thought, but he agreed nonetheless. The ambulance left the scene, leaving the fire department for basic scene safety — not a difficult thing since the scene was off the road in a ditch — and the cruiser.

The tow truck showed up about five minutes later, the man a grizzled veteran of the towing business. He did not ask for help, did not appear to need help as he examined the car and the wreck, then wordlessly went to work.

"You got everything you need out of there?" Dean asked.

Walter nodded soundlessly.

The wreck was simple enough to deduce, but the icy slush

presented a bit of a challenge. That, and the fact that Walter had managed to swing sideways instead of continuing head-on, thereby eliminating the easy-in-easy-out rescue. The driver was just starting to get the car budged when Walter saw Tommen's little silver Honda pull up in the opposite lane. The fire engine was blocking the road, but he was able to get through on foot.

"Dad, are you okay?" Tommen demanded from about thirty feet away, closing quickly.

"I'm fine," Walter sighed. "Just exhausted."

"Yeah? Your head okay? Did an ambulance crew check you out?"

"Yes, they did." In his peripheral vision, Walter noticed Dean's smirk. "I'm fine, Tommen. I've been up for over twenty-four hours at this point, worked an eighteen-hour shift with non-stop stupidity. I'm exhausted."

"Sheriff said you fell asleep at the wheel."

"Hence the meaning of the word 'exhausted.'"

"You sure you're okay? You have tonight off, don't you?"

"Yes. I intend to spend most of my day sleeping."

Tommen glanced back at the car, slowly creeping back up the embankment. "You already call the mechanic?"

Walter gave him a look. "I left a message. It's a weekend and a holiday; they're not in. Once he's on his way, then we can go home."

"Hop in the back, Tommen, it might be a minute," Dean told him.

Walter saw his son was slightly leery of the prospect, unsure if there was a joke in there somewhere, but he did so after a minute of consideration, keeping one foot in the door just in case. Walter found it amusing, and he could see Dean did, too. Nevertheless, after a second, Tommen was on his phone doing something or other.

"Have to report to Becky all your coming and going?"

"Well, considering you were just in an accident, she wanted me to text her and let know that I wasn't in an accident, too. That way, if I was, she would know and could send in the cavalry."

"Who would that be? Her mom?"

"Most likely. With her right there beside her, ready to chew me out or else worry over me."

"Hm, wouldn't know anything about that," Walter mused.

"Hey," Tommen said sharply. "It's one thing if you call me to say you've been in a little accident and it might be a few minutes before you get home. The sheriff himself calls me to say you've been in an accident, I take that a little more seriously."

Walter shook his head, even as he was secretly flattered. He'd raised a good kid. Young, naive, and with plenty more mistakes and stupid decisions to make in the future yet, but a good kid.

He dozed off again waiting for the tow truck. Then it was a bit of a haze as he vaguely recalled walking from the cruiser to talk to the tow driver, then to Tommen's car. As soon as he sat down and felt the heat, knowing that it was all over and he was going home, he was out.

He could only conclude that Tommen must have Banded him a little bit. It wasn't more than fifteen, twenty minutes to get home in current conditions, but Walter woke up feeling at least mildly rested, enough that he wasn't in danger of falling over at any given moment, though he was certainly going to sleep for a good long time.

"Are you okay?!"

The question blasted Walter even before the door was fully open. Becky stood there in the path between the kitchen and the living room, arms folded, looking far bigger and taller than her modest three-foot-nine.

"Yes, Mom, I'm okay," Walter answered.

"Hey. Don't give me no backtalk. You are not allowed to go and worry your son like that. You've done that a little too much the last couple years. Now he's going to be a dad of his own and he's going to need you around a bit. Regardless if you're moving or whatever you're doing, he needs to be able to call someone at least."

Even from across the tiny kitchen, Walter could hear the shake in her voice. She'd been just as worried about him as Tommen, if not more worried. He sat to remove his boots.

"In other news," Becky went on, her tone shifting. "Do you have any good stories? You must have at least one good one."

"I'm sure I do, but I don't remember any of it right now," Walter sighed. "Let me get some sleep and give my fried brain a chance to reset."

"Fair enough. But, seriously, are you okay?"

He rubbed his eyes. "Yes, I'm fine. I just need some sleep."

With that, he made his way down the hall to his bedroom. His first instinct was to throw himself on the bed and pass out. He forced himself to undress, peeling off his grubby uniform. After a moment of consideration, he took a detour to the bathroom for a quick shower, or at least a rinse. From there, he made a beeline to his bed. He didn't even remember getting in.

Walter had every intention of sleeping the day away. He got in bed sometime around noon or twelve-thirty, and he promised himself that he wouldn't wake up until the clock read midnight or twelve-thirty in the morning. That did not happen. As a matter of fact, when his bleary brain dragged itself back to consciousness, he felt as though he hadn't slept at all. When he moved his heavy head to look at the clock, it was only five-thirty.

He rolled over and pulled the blanket up over his head, willing himself to go back to sleep. The best he got was a heavy doze that lasted for about an hour or so. At seven o'clock, after several minutes of laying there with his eyes closed, he admitted defeat and got up. A quick trip to the bathroom, then out to the living room.

Even just getting out of bed, he was feeling the accident. Everything hurt. Every joint ached, every muscle throbbed. He felt stiff and about ten years older than he claimed to be. Problem was, he didn't know if it was just from the accident or his hectic night, too.

He made it out to his recliner, about the extent of his adventures for the day, he decided. He closed his eyes. Time slowed one's aging tremendously, but it never truly stopped. He'd been in his forties when he'd started using Time. Now, he looked about in his fifties. Getting up now, he felt in his seventies. Looking back, he found himself silently thanking God that none of the last night's shenanigans involved Time or any other faction. He really didn't know if he could handle it.

A minute later, he heard the telltale squeak of Tommen and Becky's bedroom door. His son appeared in the hall.

"We were trying to be quiet," he began.

"Wasn't you," Walter told him. "I don't know what it is, but I just couldn't sleep anymore. But that's all right. I can stay up tonight and go to bed at a decent hour in the morning."

"If you're sure. I mean, I know your recliner is comfortable. Wasn't sure if you were just looking for a change of venue."

Walter waved a hand. "Nah. You're fine. Do whatever you need to do."

"You feeling all right? Since this morning?"

"I'm feeling it all right, but nothing of concern. A little stiff, a little achy, still a little tired. But I'm fine."

Sitting there relaxing actually helped to wake him up some, and he had to remind himself that he wasn't a spry young man anymore who could just jump out of bed on a whim and two hours of sleep and be ready for the day. For him, it took time. He could see his son wasn't completely convinced, but accepted it anyway.

A few minutes later, Becky also appeared from the bedroom. While she no longer looked overly worried, she still had a certain stubborn determination about her as she approached.

"Are you sure you're okay?" she demanded.

"I'm fine," Walter told her.

"You're absolutely sure? I can call my mom and have her check you out if you don't want to go all the way to the hospital. She'll do it."

"I have no doubt about that. And I thank you for the offer, but I'm fine. Really."

For a long moment, it looked as if Becky would call her mom anyway. At the last minute, she relented and accepted his answer, saying, "Okay, fine. If you're sure. But if you change your mind, she works nights, too, so she'll be up all night. I already told her what happened, so it won't be a surprise or a bother or anything. Okay?"

"Yes, Mom."

"You're darn right."

And Walter thought he'd had a case of Mother Bear Syndrome with Tommen. Becky didn't have Mother Bear Syndrome; she was the mother bear. She was the mother bear with everyone.

"So, other than busy," Tommen said, sitting on the couch with what looked like an egg salad sandwich, "how was your night?"

"Busy."

"I said other than busy."

"The amount of stupid never ceases to amaze, and the guys in holding were begging us to stop bringing people to them. I don't blame them; it didn't smell very good in there midway through the chaos."

"Ooh, so that means you have to have at least one good story, right?" Becky said, crawling up on the couch beside Tommen.

Well, he'd opened himself up to that one, didn't he? He sighed and sorted through his memories from the previous night. Now that it was all over, it was almost as if it never happened. All the little stuff, the simple stuff, that got filtered out. He knew he'd had plenty of traffic stops, but he couldn't remember hardly any of them. That part of his memory was more taken up with the bigger things like the thief at the wrong house and the parties and everything else.

And besides, what could he tell her? He wouldn't tell her anything that couldn't be known to the general public. Problem was, just simple drunken stupidity wasn't enough to really warrant a story, and the things that might warrant a story might end up going to trial, and that all had to stay pretty well under wraps.

"Well...?" Becky prompted.

Finally Walter nodded. "All right. I might have one good story. Let's wait until Tommen finishes his sandwich so I can demonstrate what happened."

Walter watched his son's eyes get huge and he stopped chewing for just a moment. He cautiously finished off his sandwich and took the saucer to the sink, stalling by washing the saucer and the few other dishes there. At Becky's prodding, he returned.

"All right," Walter sighed, pulling himself out of his recliner. "Tommen, stand here. No, just right here. Now relax, but pretend you're some tough guy, Mr. All-that. Yeah, like that. Okay, so we get called out for a noise complaint..."

Chapter Twenty-One
Home Stretch

It was a good thing Tommen didn't have to work that weekend, because he didn't know how he and his dad would have juggled their work schedules. At worst, he thought, he would have to call up one of the guys and ask for a ride.

School, however, was a different matter. Tommen's schedule was fixed. His dad's was not. There was no way they could hope to balance it out. Considering the holiday and the fact of it being winter, mechanics and body shops were swamped. Walter was told he would have to wait two weeks before his car even got looked at. Judging by the damage, it may end up totaling out, anyway. If it didn't, or if he was really set on keeping his car, it would probably be another two weeks for repairs. A whole month of father and son having one vehicle between them.

It ended up that Walter drove Tommen's car to and from work. If he made it back in time to pass it off to Tommen for school, then that's what they would do. Tommen just had to book it back home after school to give the car back so his dad could book it to work. Not much of a problem for them with their ability to Band, just more of a nuisance. It was like not having a license all over again, not being able to go anywhere on his own.

For those mornings that Walter ran late, Mrs. Polski would pick Tommen up, along with Becky on days that she had class, and take them both to their respective schools. It was still a little embarrassing that he went to high school while she went to college. Then he would either get picked up by his mother-in-law or ride the bus back home. Or, if Chris needed him on the job site, one of the guys would swing by to pick him up, then drop him off later. The weekend routine was pretty easy, being picked up and dropped by the guys.

They'd managed to wash their hands of the mountain mansion. As much as they'd all been ready to not climb the driveway anymore that winter, it was a damn fine house, and they were proud of it. Yet they sallied forth to the next project.

Compared to the mansion, this new house they were building in a little development subdivision seemed to go up twice as fast with half the effort. It was almost a surprise when the end of the day finally came around.

"How's your girlfriend doing?" Mike asked as he took Tommen home one Saturday evening. It was about two weeks after New Year's.

"She's ready for the pregnancy to be over," Tommen answered. "Eight weeks to go, so am I."

Mike laughed. "Just remember. If you ever get it in your head that you want more kids, you still have to put up with the forty weeks before."

"I've thought about that, believe me."

They pulled up to the curb. "Here we are. See you in the morning."

Tommen thanked him and got out, shuffling into the house as fast as he could as another chill wind buffeted his coat. It had felt good just coming off the site hot and sweaty, but now it was freezing.

"Please tell me you're getting your car back soon," Tommen said, kicking off his shoes.

His dad looked up from his bowl of chili. "Actually, the guy called me last night while I was on shift, left a message saying it would probably be a couple more weeks. He offered to have it towed to another mechanic."

"Are you serious?!"

"It's winter, kid. It's busy."

"What kind of excuse is that?" An idea popped into Tommen's head. "Have it towed here."

"Why? I can't fix it."

Tommen glanced down the hall. The door was open and the light was off, which meant Becky was still out with her mom. He looked back at his dad. "No, but I can."

His dad raised a brow. "You, who called up Will's mom that one day because your gas light came on?"

Tommen felt his face turn red. "Hey, I was tired, okay? And I had a lot of things on my mind. And I'm not talking about the engine and stuff. I can do the body work. Matter. Nathan showed me how."

"Great. I'll have a car that looks good but still won't run."

"But if it looks good and all the panels are good, it won't be so difficult to get to the mechanics of it. They won't have to rip your car apart to get to a single nut and bolt."

His dad ran his tongue over his teeth. "Well, there is that, I suppose."

"Panels, frame, get it structurally sound, and the rest should just fall into place, right?"

"I don't know. I suspect you don't know either, really." Walter sighed. "All the same, body work ain't cheap either."

"Come on, Dad. I can't make it any worse."

Now his dad gave him a look. "You talk about manipulating Matter at the molecular level, and you think you can't make it any worse. Now that is a first world problem if I ever heard one." He shook his head. "All right. Fine. You do make a point about the cost and just trying to get to any damaged parts and systems. I'll call the guy back on Monday and have him tow it home."

Tommen pumped his fist. "Yes!"

"Now here's the other question," his dad cut in. "How are you going to explain to Becky how my car is getting fixed?"

"Uh..." Tommen let his hands drop to his sides for a moment. He folded his arms. "Hm."

"Yeah."

"What if I found out Becky's plans for the week? If she's going out with her mom at some point and she'll be gone for a while, you can have the car towed here. I can fix it—probably in a Band—and then when she gets home, it looks like new. She doesn't need to know it doesn't run. If nothing else, it worked to get it home, but then something else got messed up, it's not starting, whatever, have to get it back."

His dad leaned back in his chair, expression thoughtful. "Normally, I wouldn't condone lying to your bride-to-be. I am also disturbed and impressed at your ability to come up with a clever lie to cover up Time and the Akari, almost on the spot. At the same time, I don't have any better excuse to suggest." He went back to his chili. "Well, I can't do anything until Monday anyway. Maybe you should take the time and go look up the specs for my car that way I have a better chance at having a car once you get through with it. The same car. I don't want you reforming it into an SUV by mistake."

Tommen put a hand to his chest. "Your lack of faith in me—"

"Is not entirely unfounded," his dad finished, indicating Tommen's arm. "It's for everyone's safety and sanity. I just want you to be careful and not make things worse."

Okay, so he might have had a point, but did he have to rub it in? Tommen headed down to his bedroom where he grabbed a change of clothes—the fleece pajamas Becky had made him were pretty comfortable, actually—and went to take a shower, washing off all the fun he'd had at work, digging up cold and frozen ground and trying to make things perfect so that when they got their little window break in the weather to get the basement done, they could get it done in one shot with as few delays as possible.

Once he was dried and dressed and feeling clean, he opened up the laptop and got online, looking for all the specs and manuals on his dad's car. And, hey, maybe he could figure out a few things and do some repairs that were more than cosmetic. He'd never been mechanically inclined, especially when it came to all these newer cars that were better serviced by computer repairmen, but he could learn.

He'd only just opened up the manual online when he heard Becky walk in the door. A few minutes later, she entered the bedroom. Thankfully, she did not have an armload of clothes or other sewing projects. She was good at organization, but their room was only so big and could only hold so much.

"How was dinner?" Tommen asked.

"Good," she answered, climbing on the bed. "We had to wait a few minutes for a table to open up, but it was good. The food was ridiculously expensive, so I'm glad I wasn't buying."

Becky had become more fiscally conscious lately, as she and Tommen talked about some of the changes they would have to make after the wedding, especially if they were going to buy or rent the house. While she'd always been good about managing her business, the word "budget" seemed to have finally entered her personal vocabulary.

"What are you up to?" Becky wondered. "Something wrong with your car now?"

Tommen looked at the screen. "Ah, no. No, just looking at the manual for my dad's car."

"Getting a little antsy about it?"

"Something like that. I swear, they milk the clock any way they can."

Becky made a sound of agreement.

"Are you doing anything next week with your mom? Or anyone else? Going to be gone in the afternoon or evening?"

She looked thoughtful. "Um...not really, that I know of. Well, hang on. I have a special science lab I have to go to on Tuesday, part of me trying to squish my classes down into a tighter schedule. Why do you ask?"

"I was going to go out with my dad that night. You know, sort of a thank you and stuff. Being kind of sappy and all that. I figured that if you were busy, if he had the night off, then—"

"You don't need my permission to be nice to your dad," Becky said, looking rather offended. "I mean, you're obviously not a clingy daddy's boy or anything, and I think it would be great if it was just the two of you. Why not tonight?"

"Kind of a last minute thing. Plus I had to work, and I didn't know what time I'd be off."

"Yeah, no, it's fine. Do whatever."

Tommen nodded and went back to looking at the manual, at least for a few minutes before Becky began spouting off her four-star review of the restaurant she and her mom went to.

If he wanted to be honest, he did feel bad about lying to her. His dad raised a brow when he told him of what they were allegedly doing while waiting for the car to arrive on the tow truck Tuesday afternoon.

"So, if you are planning to Band to fix this, then you do intend on going out afterwards, right? Because you know she's going to want to know where we went and at least what we thought of it. Restaurant, she wants to know how the food is; movie, she wants a review, all of that." Walter shifted his stance. "So, what are we doing?"

Tommen was saved from having to answer by the arrival of the tow truck. His dad's car got dumped in the driveway. The driver confirmed that the mechanic paid for it, Walter signed, and the tow truck departed.

For a long moment, the two of them stared at the car. The side didn't look at bad as Tommen remembered, a bit of a side scrape impact from a tree. The quarter panel was nearly undamaged, but both doors were unusable. The front may not have been so bad. Everything looks worse in the initial accident, after all. It was the mechanics of it that scared Tommen.

"Well, let's see if it starts," his dad sighed.

It started after a minor cough, and the dash quickly let them know everything was that wrong. But they got it in the garage easily enough. Tommen stared at the car a minute longer, fully aware of his dad watching him.

"Okay, kid, work your magic."

"Yeah. Well, Band or not, it's still cold. Can we close the door?"

His dad agreed and closed the door. Aside from the cold, Tommen didn't want anyone to witness both the change that was about to happen, be it a miracle fix or something going horribly, horribly wrong.

His heart was racing as he studied the car. This was kind of like when he'd fixed the dents in his car, except this was him working solo. Nathan wasn't here to teach or correct him, and his dad certainly couldn't do much. This was all him. His talents, his learning, his skills, his time.

"Just relax and think about the problem," Nathan had told him once. "Your brain knows something is wrong, now what is it? Even if you can only come up with an abstract answer at first, it will help you to refine things down until you find the solution."

He started with the passenger doors, figuring those would be the easiest things to fix. Fewer mechanics. It was just a door, right?

The rear door was the least damaged. It was scratched and dented. That was the problem. The fiberglass was no longer smooth. And he knew that every crease, every deviation from that smooth surface was a flaw, a weak spot, in the overall integrity. He had to rework the fiberglass, get it back smooth and strong. The paint he wasn't sure he could do anything about, but he would worry about that later. One step at a time.

He touched the panel. He Felt it. He felt the paint, the fiberglass overall. He felt where it bent and creased, twisted and warped. He felt each strand within the fiberglass, felt the ones that were strong, the ones that were bent and weak, the ones that were broken completely.

Then he started moving his hand, as if playing the piano or the guitar, making tiny movements, Touching the fiberglass and making it move, reform. He almost felt as part of the car, and each movement was like ultra super intense hot yoga for beginners. It was invigorating and exhausting, feeling everything coming back together the way it should be.

He ran into a few snags as he worked. He could reform what

was there, but he could not create. If a chunk was missing, a chunk was missing; he could not manufacture new fiberglass. Or new paint, for that matter. He cheated it a little, stretching out some of the fiberglass and paint over the thin areas. It would be weaker than the surrounding material, which wasn't good, but it would still look all right, anyway.

The fiberglass was the easy part, but cars were more than fiberglass. He had to work on the frame, too. Inside the door, avoiding the excessive number of airbags, the hinges and the overall frame itself. Tommen quickly discovered that the denser the material, the more demanding the work became. By the time he completed just the passenger doors, taking about an hour or so just because he kept going back to check and double-check his work, he was soaked in sweat and ready to sleep for a week. Holding an intense Fast Band wasn't helping, either.

He released the Band and went to sit beside his dad on the garage step.

"Looks the same from here," his dad said. "You look like you've been working hard."

"For about an hour," Tommen told him. "Check out the passenger doors."

His dad got up and went around the other side. He whistled, then tested the doors, opening and closing them with no trouble whatsoever. They locked and unlocked, and the windows even worked.

"I'm impressed," Walter said, sounding genuine. "You're not going to charge me double for this, are you?"

"How about you buy dinner and we'll call it even?" Tommen suggested, wiping his face.

"Fair enough. Want me to Band you for a nap? You look exhausted."

"No, I want to get this done. Now that I have an idea of what I'm doing, I don't want to lose the momentum. But if you wanted to hold the Band, that would be very helpful."

His dad nodded and returned to his spot on the step. At Tommen's cue, he erected a Fast Band.

Moving around to the front of the car, Tommen fixed the hood first so he could pop it up and see what he was dealing with on the inside. While he'd always been fascinated by cars and had learned plenty from Mrs. Shaw about how things worked and how to fix them when things went wrong, he was still somewhat lacking.

The impact hadn't been terrible, enough to set the airbags off and rattle things a bit under the hood, but otherwise, not as bad as it first appeared. Tommen felt a little better about the situation and his ability to remedy it. He wiped his face again, then Banded and set to work.

Few things were actually missing, the worst offender being the front grill. As for the internal stuff, most of it was just crinkled. Knocked a few sensors out of whack, maybe broke something here or there, but overall, not bad at all. As long as he got it looking good, knowing that it had the capability to run, his dad could have it taken to a mechanic for the rest of the stuff, or maybe Tommen could call Mrs. Shaw about it. If he could learn more, he could do more. Gain useful knowledge, save time, save money, all those good things.

Three hours later, he was ready to drop dead. Nathan could make this sort of thing look like magic. A wave of his hand and whoosh! Everything fixed! And to think he had reattached a functioning human leg and might be involved in a C-section in space! For Tommen, this inanimate stuff was more like trying to wear smooth a walnut shell. It would happen, but only with a lot of effort as he Felt the different materials, the systems, how they interacted, what they were like presently, what they needed to be, how to get there, plus the actual effort of getting those materials to cooperate.

Nevertheless, it was done. Well, it looked better, anyway. The panels were all nice and smooth, the paint and fiberglass stretched thin in some spots to cover the damage. The frame was all remolded, just the way it was supposed to be, nice and tight and strong. The front, well, that was a little tricky to get around the missing bits and pieces from the grill and the broken headlight. The headlight he managed to stretch the plastic thin just so it looked like a solid piece, but it would definitely have to be replaced. The grill, well...

"I'll just say I wanted the economy service," his dad said when Tommen presented to him his dilemma. "I can replace a grill or a headlight or any of the small things. Obviously, I couldn't do what you just did." He gave Tommen a serious look. "Thank you. More than just saving me money, thank you for doing me this service."

"I was doing myself a service, too," Tommen said breathlessly. "I want my car back."

His dad laughed and patted him on the shoulder. "I'm sure you do. Now what do you say we go to dinner? My treat?"

"Only if I can get a shower first. Yeesh."

His dad agreed and let him go.

A shower made Tommen smell better and also perked him up a bit, but he was still ferociously tired. Manipulating the physical properties of the universe really took it out of you.

He pulled on some fresh clothes and went to meet his dad in the garage.

"How about we take your car for tonight?" his dad suggested. "Just in case we get stranded."

Tommen waved a hand. "Sure, whatever."

"You okay?"

"I'm tired." He went on before his dad could speak. "Yes, I'm sure I still want to go. It's your night off, and Becky is going to want a play-by-play, or at least a review. Let's go. I'll even drive since your car is supposed to be out of service."

They went out and got in Tommen's car. At least driving would help keep him awake, if not the act of driving, then simply trying to maintain his speed and trajectory as he navigated treacherous roads. Or, if that didn't work to keep him awake, then trying to predict and react to other people's driving certainly did the trick.

"The good news is, if something happens to your car, you

know how to fix it," his dad said cheekily.

Tommen waved him off, but only briefly.

"How are things going with Nathan and the twins?" his dad asked.

"I really haven't heard lately," Tommen answered. "I know that Godwin was annoyed by my refusal to just pack all of you up and whisk you away across the universe."

"I can't say I blame him."

"If Becky wasn't around, or if her pregnancy wasn't so high-risk, I would probably be less hesitant. I know, I know, Nathan is a Builder and he just gave Micaiah back his leg; he should be able to handle a little high-risk childbirth. But..."

"You're still not sure how Becky would react to it."

Tommen nodded. "If I don't take her, I could be condemning her and the baby to death. If I do take, there's no guarantee that we'd be safe from Julianna anyway, and I don't know if I could handle it if she decided she just wanted to leave. What if she did decide to leave and Julianna went after her anyway? And the baby is obviously helpless in this whole thing. How do I keep them safe?"

His dad sighed. "I have no good answers for you, kid, and being this close to the birth isn't making that decision any easier, I'm guessing."

"I don't know. The smart thing to do would be to go with Godwin to whatever safe location he's found for Nathan and the twins and the Miaramila. There, at least, we would be among those who have the ability to resist whatever Julianna dishes out. I just don't know if it's the right thing to do. I can barely even conceive of abandoning them in the name of safety, because I have no reason to think Julianna would leave them alone. I mean, if it didn't work for you, it wouldn't work for me, right?"

As soon as the words were out of his mouth, Tommen knew it was the worst thing he could have possibly said. In his peripheral vision, Tommen could tell his dad was looking at him, daggers in his eyes. "You want me to answer that question honestly?"

Tommen sighed. "No. I'm sorry. That wasn't fair."

They rode in silence for several tense miles before Walter broke it with a stiff, "Still think you're closing in on your last book, the one with 'happily ever after. The end'?"

"I don't know. I would like to think of the sentencing as 'happily ever after. The end' for the simple reason that this started with me and Rifun, and that's how it's going to end. Once again, bad guy goes away, hero gets the girl, ride off into the sunset. Therefore, that would make this post-happily ever after. Considering that, barring endless sequels, no one really knows what happens after 'The end.' Does that mean that we're completely freestyling now? Absolute free will, beyond the scope of the Author and her words? Does that make this some sort of limbo between the end of the book and death? Is there really death for us, if all we are is words?"

"Kid—" Walter interrupted. "—I feel like if you got your degree in Philosophy, you would go the way of Hippocrates."

"Poison hemlock?"

"Exactly. You're too thoughtful and too paranoid for your own good. Or anyone else's good, for that matter."

"Oh. Thanks. I think."

His dad just shook his head.

"So what about you?" Tommen asked.

"What about me?"

"What's the first thing you're going to do when you are officially retired?"

"Get my sleep schedule back to normal, for one. I can't do this all-nighter business forever. The next thing that I want to do is rip down the road at full speed and dare any of them to ticket me. Problem is, I'm pretty sure they would since they know I couldn't pull officer privilege. Other than that, I'm not sure. What are you guys going to let me do, since I have a great suspicion that I will be called upon as a babysitter?"

"You can do anything you want," Tommen told him. "If you're moving, we can't rely on you too much for babysitting; we'll have to figure something out."

His dad shifted in his seat. "Well, when you put it like that, I don't know that I would do anything, at least not until I move."

"Why not?"

"Because I'm moving. We both know the reason. And if I'm going to have to stay separated from you, then I want to spend as much time with you and Becky and my first ever grandchild as I can."

Tommen gave him a look. "You're such a sap."

"But an honest sap," Walter told him. "I figured that it might just be you going off to college, me retiring, and if anything like this ever did happen, then I could start over again and have more time, ten or fifteen more years instead of just six months. It just...didn't work out that way." He shifted position. "On the other hand, if we do have to go into intergalactic witness protection, we could be spending plenty of time together still. We'll just have to see how this plays out."

Tommen Banded himself and looked at his dad. Despite having plenty of time left from the slowed aging, he did look as though he'd aged some from the time Tommen first saw him. Time in general, stress caused by a myriad of events just in the last two years, and the fact that he didn't overly use his Time abilities, his dad really did look his age. He had one more life in him, two good ones, maybe three if he really needed to, but he was coming to the end of his mortal life. The train might be moving slower, but it would always arrive at its destination.

Nothing frightened Tommen more at that moment, the thought of seeing his dad off to retirement and never seeing him again, or maybe that whole once or twice a year for Thanksgiving and Christmas, an impersonal call for Father's Day. Or, maybe worse, being with him for another century in hiding and watching a painfully slow decline. It wouldn't be so bad, if they were all moving on the same plane, but they weren't. Becky was one hundred percent vanilla human. Tommen had only rudimentary training in Time which caused accelerated aging and more extensive Akari training which slowed it down, so things could pan out either way in the future.

Walter had a century of Time usage but was still marching faithfully toward death.

"You're getting sentimental over there," his dad said, cutting into his thoughts. "I can tell by the way you suddenly get quiet, dark, and broody." He looked at him. "It'll be okay, Tommen. You focus on your family now. They are the focal point of your life. Not me, not you, not your job, not your education. You do what you need to do to keep them safe. Just as I tried to do with you. All right?"

Tommen nodded wordlessly. They hadn't even made it to the restaurant yet and things were getting emotional. That was not what he'd had in mind for this trip. He hadn't even really had anything in mind for this trip except as a convenient excuse to make sure Becky was out of the house so he could magically repair his dad's car. Where had all this come from, then? Was he really that sentimental about it? Normal people dealt with this stuff all the time. Except, maybe, for that intergalactic witness protection thing.

He pulled into the parking lot of the restaurant. In winter, parking was kind of a do-it-yourself deal as all the lines were covered. As such, some spots were narrower than others, while others were almost big enough for two cars but not quite. Like everyone else, Tommen made his own parking spot. Then it was a mad dash from the warm car to the warm restaurant through the frigid cold in between.

The restaurant wasn't packed, but it was full for a Monday night. Cabin fever, Tommen thought as they were shown to their table. Everyone was happy for the change of seasons and Christmas and all the fun stuff. Then reality set in, the knowledge that the crappy weather was here to stay for a few months.

"Okay," Walter began once the waiter had taken their drink orders, "if memory serves me right, you guys had another appointment with Dr. Whitmore yesterday."

"Your memory hasn't failed you yet," Tommen said, digging out his wallet.

Thirty-three weeks along and the little blur on the ultrasound had turned into a full baby. In just a few weeks, they would get to meet that little blur live and in person. Tommen was anxious and excited and not a little fearful. Becky just wanted it to be over.

"So did that fancy DNA test tell you who she's more likely to take after, or what she looks like?" his dad wondered.

"It could give us basic details, but it wouldn't tell us anything. Becky and I both have brown hair and brown eyes. We're both white. She may or may not be colorblind, but Becky is happy she's not a dwarf. The rest, well, we'll see." He put the photo strip back in his wallet and gave his dad a mischievous look. "A little excited yourself, are we?"

His dad shrugged, though he did turn a little pink. "What can I say? I'm going to be a grandpa." His expression twisted. "That's still a weird thing to consider. It was tough enough trying to think of myself as a father to you, now I have to deal with everything that comes after."

"I'm sure Dr. Polski could give you a few pointers."

"Please. Dean's already been giving me grief about it, and plenty of advice. The rest of the guys, too. Even Kate's giving me advice, and she doesn't even have grandkids. I don't even think her oldest is a teenager yet."

Tommen grinned. "And what advice do you get as grandpa versus dad?"

His dad shifted position. "Well, I believe it can be summed up as 'Give them sugar, take away their toys, and send them home.'"

"Oh, gee, such great advice."

"I might be laughing, except they seem to forget that I'm living in the house, too, at least for a little while. By the time she gets old enough for that sort of thing, well, things could be very different."

The awkward moment was relieved as their drinks arrived. Tommen and his dad both Banded to quickly peruse the menu, Walter telling him to keep his choice below the cost of car repairs. That wasn't hard; it wasn't a super fancy restaurant. Nor was Tommen dealing with the accelerated aging from Time anymore, and the side effects of that had worn off months ago, including an insatiable appetite.

They ordered and the waiter departed.

"Have you guys talked about what you want to do about the house?" Walter inquired, his tone suggesting that this was more of a cover conversation.

"Well, like you said, no bank is going to give us that kind of loan," Tommen mused. "I don't even have a credit card. Neither does she, though she's talked about it. We're kind of sunk there, anyway, when it comes to credit. We're going to have to rent."

"I thought so, but I wanted you two to come to that conclusion yourselves."

"Yeah...we figured that."

"Well, as long as I'm living there, I won't make a fuss. You two need every advantage you can get. But once I move out—"

"Rent to you, utilities in our name."

"Precisely."

They spoke more on a variety of subjects, pausing only when their meals came. For Tommen, a giant bacon burger with all the fixings that leaked out over his fingers and onto the fries. For Walter, a nice juicy steak with both fries and buttered vegetables, topped off with a buttery roll.

"Indulging a little, are we?" Tommen teased, indicating the steak.

"Living a little, yes," his dad said, meeting him. "Not as concerned with my girlish figure."

"No new women in your life, then?"

His dad shook his head and did not answer. Tommen frowned. "You think, in the future, if you knew it was going to be your last life, you think you would date, find love, settle down?"

Walter sighed and swallowed his bite of food. "Ah, kid, I've asked myself that more times than I care to admit."

"And? What did you come up with?"

"She would have to be a truly unique woman. The last thing I would want is to live my last life and have it be so miserable that I would wish to be dead." He went on before Tommen could speak. "I know, it's rather cynical."

"Just a little," Tommen commented.

"I guess I still haven't quite gotten over Laura. We didn't date long, but it was the first time in a very long time for me. And the way it ended..." He shook his head. "Bah. Doesn't matter now, I suppose. She's happy. And I would have outlived her anyway."

"Maybe someday."

"Maybe. But I've learned to accept that the consequences of my actions are far-reaching. Some things just can't be changed."

Tommen raised a brow. "Now who's the dark and broody one? What actions are you referring to that would prevent you from finding a woman? You already found one. Doesn't matter the how or why she left. You found a woman who you really liked, maybe even loved. Just because she wasn't 'the one' doesn't mean that there is no hope for you." He leaned back in his seat. "Good grief, now I sound like you."

That got a good chuckle from his dad. Walter sighed. "Maybe you're right." He stretched where he sat and returned to his food with a little more pep. "I guess it's just something I'll have to get over. It comes around again every so often, the idea of me finding love. It used to be an abstract concept, before Laura. Losing her, I guess I've been afraid that I lost something I would never be able to find again."

"Give it time," Tommen told him. "You've got plenty of it."

And the conversation moved on from there. It wasn't until the waiter took their plates that Tommen considered that this outing was different from ones in the past. This time around, they were conversing as two adult men. Father and son, yes, but two adults. Not a dad asking his teenager about school or girls or finding a job, but two men talking about buying homes, retirement, family, careers, and other adult things. It was kind of nice, he thought, to be considered an equal of sorts. About the only thing that really killed his mood was the consideration that he still had to go to high school in the morning. Couldn't that just be over already? He wasn't going to fail anything, and he had more important things to worry about, like how to balance college classes and a full-time job and possibly think about running away across the universe.

"You look like you have something on your mind," his dad said, digging out his wallet. He picked a card and set it in the book the waiter had left.

"Oh, just thinking," Tommen said. "The last two years have been just non-stop adventure, usually of the bad kind. Now it's almost like it never happened. And the jump from where it all started to now...a lot's changed."

"You've grown up, and I think that's the biggest change. I still don't know about these Books of yours, but just from my personal observations, you have matured a great deal. Maybe this is your happily ever after. I hope it is, because you deserve it."

It took forever for the waiter to return to collect the bill, and another half an eternity to get back. Tommen heard his dad grumble about keeping an eye on his bank statements because the waiter probably took down all his credit card information while he was gone and passed it around to the rest of the staff. Tommen offered up a cheeky comment about leaving a nice tip so as to discourage the waiter from using the information. His dad gave him a look and said nothing.

They left the restaurant and returned home, the roads becoming ever more treacherous in the growing dark and cold. Tommen was pleased to see that all his hard work on his dad's car hadn't magically come undone. He wasn't sure how or why it would have, but it had been a tiny, lingering fear in the back of his mind that the repairs wouldn't actually last and that it would revert back its previous damaged state.

He went in the house to find his dad staring longingly into an ice cream container.

"Tell Becky that if she's going to raid the ice cream, then take it all. Don't leave the last bite in the tub," he lamented, showing Tommen what amounted to one or two spoonfuls of mint chocolate chip ice cream.

"Um, that wasn't her," Tommen said meekly. "That was me. I left the last two bites for her so she could taste it without getting her sugar completely out of whack." He noted his dad's expression. "What? You almost never touch the stuff anyway. Why were you intent on this, anyway? We could have gotten dessert at the restaurant."

"Please. Three dollars for a sundae or five dollars for a tub. I understand that you pay restaurants to prepare food for you, but I think I can scoop my own ice cream just fine."

"Want me to run and get some from the store?" Tommen offered.

His dad sighed, waved a hand, and returned the tub to the freezer. "Nah. It's dark, you're tired, and you have school in the morning. Besides, I think I've indulged enough for one month. This will just keep me honest."

"If you say so."

Tommen headed down the hall to the bedroom. It was starting to feel super cramped. Actually, the whole house was feeling cramped with all the baby stuff floating around. As much as he loved his dad and hated to consider the terms of his leaving and what it all meant, Tommen was definitely ready to move into his dad's room and give the baby her own nursery, a place she could use and grow for many years. Then he and Becky would be able to keep everything separate. Having their things together made space tight, but adding a third person to the mix hadn't helped anything.

Even as he thought it, he heard the door open. Words were exchanged between Becky and Walter. Tommen couldn't make out the conversation, but he thought he heard the word "ice cream" mentioned a time or two. Probably his dad letting Becky know there were two spoonfuls of ice cream left just for her. He was probably also telling her that if she didn't eat them soon, then he would. Staying honest and worrying over a girlish figure aside, Tommen knew his dad could have a vicious sweet tooth when he was in the mood.

The conversation ended and Becky made her way down to the bedroom where she threw open the door with a grand flourish. Tommen knelt to give her a hug and kiss and pick her up and put her on the bed.

"How was school?" he asked.

"Oh, I love the lab," she told him, starting right off on her speech about what they learned, what they did, and how awesome it was. Tommen considered himself pretty knowledgeable about science things, both in general and because of his Akari insight, but he also knew that she was quickly outpacing him in the terminology department. He could temporarily change his DNA with only moderate difficulty, but he couldn't explain how he did it, not in the way she was speaking. To him, it was damn near magic.

A wild thought passed through his mind. A century ago, or maybe two centuries, the Akari and Time would have been seen as magic, its wielders gods. But what happened when technology proved to be able to do everything that magic could? What happened when the magic went away? There were species out there in the universe who wanted zero part in the Time industry because there was nothing the industry could offer that they could not do themselves, speaking in broad terms.

Earth was only considered Scientifically Advancing, but what happened when they became Advanced? Superior?

Tommen mentally shook his head. That was a long ways off. Earth was more likely to become part of the Time industry first before blindly stumbling upon Scientifically Superior status. There were too many Time Agents and Akari-bearers and too many shenanigans for it to happen any other way.

"Your dad said you went out to eat," she said, changing topics so fast it gave Tommen mental whiplash. "How was it? Must not have been very good if you had to come home for dessert."

"No, it was good," Tommen said, still reeling from the sudden change in topic. "He just didn't want to pay that much for a little sundae or something. He thought he was going to have a bowl of ice cream. Except I kind of ate the ice cream already."

"Yeah, he said you left a couple spoonfuls for me. How was the food? What did you have?"

So Tommen gave his official review of the restaurant. Yes, the wait staff was friendly, but they took forever and his dad was all worried about them stealing his credit card information. Tommen didn't see how it was any different from any other restaurant that took the cards back to the serving stations. Obviously, other waiters were just a little faster at stealing customers' information. The food was definitely good, and Tommen would recommend them for anyone looking for a good burger, though the price had been a little much in his opinion. His dad appeared to enjoy his steak quite a bit. Yes, he did eat his vegetables. And the fries, too. Yes, the place was clean.

He could just as well have written a review online and just had her read that, he thought. Except then he would have had to sit there for an hour while she corrected his spelling and grammar before actually submitting the review.

"Did you guys have a lot of father-son bonding time?" Becky inquired sweetly.

The straight answer was yes, but it just sounded so sappy when she put it like that. So Tommen amended his answer for a, "Yeah, I guess so."

She rolled her eyes. "Good grief. It's not like men are emotionless, sex-driven Narcissists. You can say a simple yes." Then she made another hairpin turn in topics. "Hey, I saw your dad's car in the garage. Looks good."

"Looks good, but the mechanics of it are still way off. My dad's not too happy; he's going to have to take it to another mechanic."

"Well that sucks! What's wrong with it? I'd sue their pants off! Mechanics aren't cheap, you know, especially when it comes inspection time. And to have to take it to a second guy to fix the mistakes of the first...it's not right. It's really not. I'd say the first guy is just taking advantage of your dad and how busy they are because of the season."

Tommen just shrugged. "Who knows? I told him to get a hold of Will's mom, see if she could do anything for him."

"Great idea. I like it. Hey, maybe you could go and help her. You've done it with your car before, so you've learned a few things. Learn a little more and you'll be handy both around the house and in the garage. That'll be important in the future, you know, being able to fix all your own stuff so we don't have to hire someone."

"I suppose you want me to buddy up with an electrician and a plumber next, too."

"You work with them on the construction site, don't you?"

"Well sure, but they can be kind of cranky and protective of their work. Trade secrets and all that, I guess."

Becky rolled her eyes again. "Sheesh."

"Relax," he told her. "Let everything happen in its own time."

She barked a laugh. "Ha! You're telling me. Why did I let you talk me into waiting so long for a C-section? God, this is misery. It really is. And seven more weeks? Unthinkable! If we decide on more kids, we're adopting. I am not going through this again, I can tell you that. We can adopt. Save an unwanted baby from death and still make the other woman go through all the hassle of pregnancy. It's a win-win, I think."

When she got like this, the most Tommen could do was nod and go along with it, and try to keep the smiling to a minimum lest it enrage her further. All the same, it did get pretty funny sometimes, the things she ranted about.

"All right," she huffed after a couple minutes. "You guys went to dinner, but I went to school, and I'm starved. Maybe I'll just make something quick, a sandwich or something like that. You want anything?"

"I'm good."

"Fine. Well, I want something."

"Don't forget to eat those last two bites of ice cream," Tommen reminded her as she headed down the hall.

She turned around and stuck her tongue out at him.

Chapter Twenty-Two
Countdown

Tommen had heard somewhere that November boasted the most birthdays out of any month of the year. Tracing everything back, mostly it had to do with a lot of couples having sex on or around Valentine's Day. Anniversaries were spread out the year round, but Valentine's Day was pretty much the single universal day of love and sex.

Unless, of course, your girlfriend was thirty-seven weeks pregnant and on an absolute rampage.

From what Tommen understood, it had to do with something said either during or after Mass that morning, whether it was the priest and his sermon, or one of the gossip circles. He had been at work at the time, so he wasn't sure except for what Becky told him. In a nutshell, evil things would happen because of their sin. Didn't matter that they were making it right and getting married in a few months, the fact that it happened at all had doomed all three of them, plus any future children. It was just a fact of life.

Thinking about it now, Tommen decided it had probably come from one of the holier-than-thou gossip circles. They'd been giving Becky subtle grief over it since the pregnancy was announced. When she was ranting and wondering why they picked now to do something so awful and public and humiliating, he said that it was probably because it was Valentine's Day and they knew they weren't going to get any from their husbands, so they had to pick on someone else to distract from that.

While it had kept any direct heat off of him, he still felt the radiant heat from her seething anger. He hoped that a day at school the next day would be enough time for her to cool off, at least enough that she couldn't melt ice just by her mere presence. His hopes proved to be quite in vain, and he spent that evening listening to her rant about everything under the sun, and occasionally gnawing on his bones for something, too. Like how she didn't want him gone for twenty hours a day. Didn't matter if it was school or work, she wanted him home some of the time to raise their daughter and be a presence in her life, not merely an ATM. Not being trailer trash was all well and good, but she would rather be poor and happy than rich and miserable. Tommen then made the mistake of opening his mouth and asking why they couldn't be rich and happy.

So, Tuesday, he did something terrible. He lied to his girlfriend and told her Chris wanted him to work out on the site for a couple hours. He knew it was a bad thing to do, and he promised himself he wouldn't make it a habit. It was just a little relief for him. Becky was pregnant and cranky and just wanted the whole thing done and over with. He could understand that. But he would give her some space until such time, thereby saving his own sanity. Things would be better after the baby was born.

Instead, he went to see Will at his house. Mrs. Shaw met him at the door and gladly welcomed him in.

"How's your dad's car running?" she asked, raising a brow when he helped himself to some snacks in the fridge.

"Great," Tommen answered. "Better than it was before."

"You think flattery is payment enough for those mini-quesadillas you're stealing?"

Tommen felt his face burn with embarrassment even as she started laughing. He was saved from having to say anything by claws scratching on the linoleum, and a huge, wet tongue made a grab for the quesadillas. Tommen jerked his hand out of the way just in time and made a point of eating one of the quesadillas.

"Sydney has taught Graham Cracker a lot about being a service dog and learning commands," Mrs. Shaw observed. "But I think she's learned just as many bad habits from him."

"Long as she gets me around and doesn't push me in front of a speeding train," Will said, coming down the hall. He had his white cane, but Tommen suspected it was more of a formality than a real need. He knew the house like the back of his hand. Probably it was to see where all the dog toys were currently scattered.

"What's up, man?" the blind man said, grasping Tommen's wrist. "You a dad yet?"

"Three weeks."

"Shit. What the hell are you doing here, then? You should be at home seeing to your lady and baby. Or did your gas light come on again?"

"I was tired, okay? No, my car is fine." He described the situation.

Will whistled. "Sounds like you got a problem. Well, you're welcome to hide out here for a little bit. Just know that this might be one of the first places she comes looking."

"I told her I was at work." He put his hands up and went on before Will could speak. "I know, I know. I'm a terrible human being and a worse boyfriend, and it's a bad habit to get into. But I need to get away for a while."

"Hey, you're the one who has to live with her. Forever."

Well, there was that.

But would he really? Comparatively speaking, this was just one teeny little white lie. What happened when he had to pull back the curtain on the even bigger lie about the other half of his life? How was she going to react to Nathan and Godwin and the Time industry?

On several occasions over the past week, he had come just short of hitting "send" to officially send the text to Nathan to set up a time when they would escape. The nice way to handle it would be a few preliminary meetings to try and gently explain everything. Unfortunately, it was more likely to turn into a sudden, singular, irrevocable displacement.

"Eli still mad at everyone?" Tommen asked as they walked down the hall and he noticed the younger brother's door was closed.

"Hell if I know," Will replied apathetically. "I think so. Says he got an after-school job and that's why he's almost never home. Well, even I know that he can't be working that late or that much. Child labor laws won't allow it. So either he's working for some shady people, or he is a shady people."

"You sound unconcerned."

"What do you want me to do? Lecture him again? Obviously he hasn't learned from my mistakes. I don't know what's going through his head, but he's tuned me out. And I know for a fact he's not likely to get within half a mile of you with your dad being a cop and all. That alone is enough to tell me he's not working at McD's after school." Will sat down on his bed. "Come on, man, find something else to do or talk about because you're killing my mood."

So the subject of kids came up, almost inevitably, primarily focused on Tommen's impending fatherhood. Will seemed surprised by the news of Walter moving shortly thereafter.

"It's just to give you guys your space, right?" Will said. "Your house is pretty small, and it can't be fun to be cramped in your little room. Where's your dad moving to, down the road, different neighborhood, retirement home?"

"I think my dad would kill himself before going into a home," Tommen laughed. "As for where, I don't know. I don't think he knows. He's had this planned for a while, a few years actually, but...being a grandpa is kind of throwing a wrench into those plans."

"I can see that, and I'm blind."

"For a while, he thought about going back to Wales. If he did that, he'd never see his granddaughter. I mean, he could probably travel and see her, but we couldn't."

When the conversation flip-flopped and turned to Will and his future family plans, the blind man said he'd sworn off dating for a while. If nothing else, he'd sworn off dating in the Charleston area. Too many crazy bitches, he said. Maybe it was just him, that he couldn't see to understand the amount of crazy he was getting into. Maybe some of them thought they could defraud him or insurance in some way. Maybe they had the idea that he was some sort of sugar daddy. Whatever the case, he was done for a while. Maybe after next Christmas, take a whole year off to refresh himself and figure out how to approach the dating scene being a blind man. Tommen expressed his sympathies, but Will waved him off.

"It's hard, don't get me wrong. We all want someone to care for, protect, we all want to be respected and looked up to as a man. That does hurt. At the same time, I go out to eat, I can go wherever I want, wear whatever I want, and eat whatever I want without someone criticizing me for something."

"But, if you have to get a ride, aren't you always going out with someone?" Tommen wondered.

"Not always. Sometimes I just ask for a ride into town. My mom will drop me off, and she'll pick me up a few hours later. I'm not completely helpless, and people are always willing to lend a hand if I ask politely. A couple of my favorite restaurants know me well enough that they're no longer afraid of me when I come in. If I go someplace new, you know, I ask them to read the menu or tell me the daily specials and I swear some of the waiters or the hostess or whoever just vanish into thin air. Poof. It's like, what's the matter, can't you read, either? I'm blind. What's your excuse?" He shook his head. "Nah, but some of my frequent places are cool with it now. I have a couple of the menus basically memorized."

"Becoming a regular restauranteur, are you?"

"Damn straight. And an entrepreneur. You know, I'm actually working on a project at work—my own thing, not a commissioned project—to make braille menus more accessible. Because, you know, restaurants change their menus from time to time, and solo blind patrons just aren't common enough to warrant new braille menus for every change, assuming they have them at all. I'm working on a menu that you can, like, piece together however you need it whenever it changes. True, you might not be able to label the full Jumping Jack's Jammin' Buffalo Bacon Burger Surprise, but if you can piece together something that says: Burger, quarter pound patty, cheese, bacon, buffalo sauce, mayonnaise, it would make life simpler for blind people like me, and you wouldn't have to sit there and read me the menu. And all the ingredients would be separate tags that can be rearranged, so if Jumping Jack decides to scrap the mayo, you don't need a whole new menu. That would be super awesome."

"Power to you, man," Tommen told him. "I actually think that's really cool."

"I've talked to my boss about it a little. He says to refine my idea some more—in my own time, downtime on the machine, you know?—and if I get some of the local restaurants to buy into it, then he'll help me with whatever I need to get it going."

They decided to end things on a high note. It was six-thirty, a reasonable time for Tommen to be leaving the job site. After swearing Will to secrecy, he headed home.

So then, Will was doing well at work and finding purpose in a potential business investment kind of thing. He was doing well in school, and things were looking up, minus brother drama which he seemed to have written off.

Eric was out in California living it up in the restaurant world, learning lots and, according to social media, advancing very quickly. He could probably open up his own place, except he was just a little reserved and not ready to take that leap yet. He was going to wait another year or two before making that decision. He wanted to think it through. But on the whole, things were looking up.

And here was Tommen, lying to his pregnant girlfriend, awaiting the birth of his first child who might not even grow up on Earth. She might be the first terran child to grow up with aliens as playmates and teachers. Maybe she would learn the Akari at an early age, early enough that using it would be as natural as breathing. Maybe Tommen would have to deal with the sudden drama of her wanting to date an alien. How was he going to handle that one? And the most that anyone here would know was that they all just suddenly moved away after the birth. Few, if any goodbyes, no real further contact. Just gone.

Tommen was jealous of Will and Eric. Was anyone jealous of him and his family and the life they thought he lived? They congratulated him and wished him well, but did anyone look at him and say, "Gee, I wish I could be him. I wish I could go back and do things like he did." About the only friend he was doing better than was Varad. But then, any homeless guy on the street was doing better than Varad if they weren't engaging in religious terrorism.

Three more weeks, he told himself as he pulled into the driveway. Three more weeks until dad.

It wasn't until he turned the car off that he considered that he was still pretty darn clean. Even in the middle of winter, and even if he'd only been doing a little grunt work, he should at least be a little dirty, grungy, sweaty for sure. Hanging out with Will wasn't exactly hard work.

His only saving grace when he walked in the door was the fact that Becky wasn't home. With him "at work," she'd gone over to her parents' house to do some sewing. This gave him time to shower and pull on his pajamas. Just for good measure, he also started a load of laundry. To cut down on suspicion, seeing how she'd been the master of the laundry — even Walter's — since she moved in, he also started something for dinner. He was trying to be nice. Yeah, that was it. Trying to give her a rest and apologize for anything he may have said or done to offend her the last few days.

It made his stomach sick to think about the lengths he was going to in order to conceal one small lie. He found himself praying that Becky would be in a good mood, thereby making him feel at least a little justified in his schemes. He was going to need to build up a lot of husband credit in order to pull off the big reveal.

She returned just as Tommen was bringing the biscuits out of the oven. Fried chicken, mashed potatoes, green beans, biscuits, it was enough to make the colonel jealous. When she questioned him, he explained that he wanted to do something nice, to take the burden off her shoulders, and to apologize for any offenses the last few days. He still did not own up to going to see Will instead of going to work.

At any rate, her mood was already better than it had been, and his gesture of good will made her melt, especially since she'd been craving something fried pretty much all day. He put the cherry on top by offering a foot and back rub, which she readily accepted.

"Okay, what do you want?" she asked sleepily as Tommen rubbed her neck. They sat on the couch, watching TV.

"Can't I be nice to my girl without my motives being questioned?" he wondered teasingly.

"No. What do you want?"

To cover up for my little white lie today? Possibly ease into the biggest shock of your life? "I do want to help you and try to make things easier. But if you really want to know, and if you're really offering..."

He could just imagine the eye roll as she sighed. "Of course. I take it the neck rub is over, then?"

He was willing to go another couple minutes in good faith, but eventually his excitement won out.

"At least pleasuring you doesn't take as long as a back or foot rub," Becky mused afterwards.

"You sound like you resent it," Tommen stated, frowning.

"Only inasmuch as I'm jealous." She closed her eyes and sighed. "I love our daughter. I do. I'm excited to meet her and start a family. But I kind of want to go back to the way things were before between us. At the very least, I just want to not be pregnant, and I want to have sex again."

"Well...things are going to change here pretty soon. We should take them as they come."

She grumbled a bit but could not argue.

The only thing Tommen could think about that night as he lay in bed was that he'd gotten away with it. He'd gotten away with his little lie, though he still hadn't told her about the escape. It wasn't that he took any pleasure in it necessarily, but things really seemed to be okay again. He'd hung out with a friend for a while, and his actions to secretly make amends to himself had helped to calm her down and brush away the last of her bad mood. If he could keep things squeaky clean for the next few weeks, then maybe they would get through the escape in tact.

"Your thinking is so short-term."

Tommen was walking forward toward the fire before his brain or his consciousness or whatever caught up. As he sat down, everything came into focus. "Hi, Chandler."

But the man did not appear to be in a jovial mood, or even calm and content. His posture was rigid, expression a mixture of severity and distress with just a touch of panic. Tommen didn't like it. He was sure Chandler could see his reaction, but he forced himself not to speak for a long moment.

Finally, Tommen got up the nerve to say, as evenly as possible, "Long time, no see."

"Indeed," the Native man said, his voice sounding as strained as Tommen felt, trying to remain calm. "And I fear it may be the last time for a long while."

"Why is that? You're kind of scaring me right now, man. What's going on?"

Chandler blinked and it was like night and day, like watching the storm be calmed with just a word. The fear dissolved, the panic fled, and the rigidity in his posture relaxed. And he just went about his normal routine. If Tommen had to compare it to something, he might have likened it to watching his dad come flying out of his nightmares, the stark difference between the roaring bear and the tired man. Perhaps it was similar with Chandler. Perhaps the Author had shown him something terrifying, and Tommen just caught him at a bad time, that moment between storm and calm.

"I have seen your path, where it leads," the man said, just as calm as he had ever been. "Your work is not done yet."

"What more do I have to do?" Tommen demanded, throwing up his hands. "My daughter is being born in three weeks. Are you talking about our escape, or what?"

But Chandler shook his head. "Beyond that. Far beyond that and through such darkness as I have never seen."

Tommen made a loud, frustrated growling sound. "Really?! Are you fucking serious?! You've given me nothing to work with! The last time you gave me anything substantial, you said I was going to fucking die. Alone and afraid and selfish, I'm dead. How much fucking more could there really, possibly be? How long do I have? What do I have to work with? Are you actually going to give me an answer, or just more fucking riddles?" His last question came out more like a whiny toddler about to have a temper tantrum, but he didn't care.

Chandler waited patiently for him to relax a little. Then, "I cannot tell you what I see, except that it is fixed. All that remains is when it will happen."

"Then what does it matter whether I know it or not?"

"Because of the events that follow. If it happens sooner, there is a certain sequence of events. If it happens later, another sequence."

"And you're the one who chooses which sequence happens, is that it?"

"Ultimately, it is on your shoulders. As for me, the Author has shown me what will be."

"You're a lot of help, aren't you?" Tommen rubbed his face. "I know, I know. We talked about this last time. But if I'm speeding headlong into such vast and terrible darkness, why won't you be there with me?"

Now Chandler's expression turned into one of sorrow and longing and pain, one Tommen could imagine him wearing as he watched his people cross the threshold into life on Hlohi, half a universe away. And he said, "Because you will not want me to be."

The cave vanished before Tommen had a chance to reply, and he woke up as if coming out of a nightmare. He rubbed his eyes, momentarily confused about where he was and why and what that annoying noise was. Then it occurred to him that it was his alarm, and he had to get up for school.

For the better part of the day, he actually couldn't remember his dream, though he knew he'd spoken to Chandler. That in itself was enough to spook him, since he'd never before had a problem recalling his visits. And when he finally did remember, he was less than thrilled with the message.

If there is going to be such darkness, why won't you be with me?
Because you will not want me to be.

Why would Tommen not want Chandler to be with him? Sure, the man could be frustrating with his sagely wisdom and non-answers and weird sense of humor, but he was a human being like the rest of them with his own quirks and faults. Tommen couldn't fault him for being human. So what in the world would cause Tommen to not want this man, whom he considered a spiritual guide of sorts, to not, well, be his guide? Just how lonely would his death be?

Maybe there was going to be some betrayal of trust. Tommen did trust Chandler to a significant degree, and he would be devastated if the man betrayed that trust. Such a thing could also cause a sort of mental or spiritual darkness. Maybe Chandler was trying to lessen the blow by subtly forewarning Tommen of this betrayal. It was inevitable, he said, just a matter of when. Maybe this was the path of the least bad option.

At the same time, he said that it all rested on Tommen. Was Tommen going to have to betray Chandler in some way? Or could it be something totally different that had nothing to do with trust or anything like that?

Tommen sat in his car as it warmed up and stared at his phone.

"We need to make plans to escape," he'd written to Nathan. "The C-section is March 11th. If all goes well, I think we can leave within the week. If you can use Matter to heal Becky some more, that would be even better."

He hadn't sent it yet. He'd been putting it off, pretending that ignoring the problem would make it go away. It wouldn't. Becky and the baby's vulnerability wasn't going to solve itself just because of the birth. Maybe they should have already fled, he didn't know. But he had to make the decision while he still could.

He hit send.

There was no reply, but at least the message would be there whenever Nathan got back to Earth next. Hopefully it would be soon.

The notion of the whole thing bothered him deeply over the course of the week, getting worse as Nathan remained silent, and even following him to the job site that weekend. Work was slow-going in the winter, but at least the basement got done. Now they were pre-fabbing the walls in the shop in town during the week and taking them out to the site on the weekends. Studs, OSB, wrap, siding, all included in the panels they made and installed, more than ready for whatever winter had to throw at them. A few open spots of siding were patched in on site and the windows and doors were installed during set-up. Once they got the roof on, it would be nothing to finish it all off inside.

It was about two o'clock on Sunday when there was an accident with one of the saws. The blade broke and twisted and got jammed in the mechanism. The first indication that anything was wrong was Pete's shrieks as his hand got caught by the broken blade and jammed into the mechanism as well.

Once everything got carefully untangled and disassembled, with Pete on his way to the ER, it was determined that something in the saw itself had broken, and the machine was no longer safe to use.

"Ricky," Chris called, "you and Tommen, take your truck, take this saw back to the shop, grab the other saw."

"Roger that," Ricky said.

Together, the two of them got the busted saw in the back of Ricky's truck, then hopped in and made for the shop. It was mostly just a warehouse with all their stuff, plus an attached office, more of an afterthought, for all the official paperwork and stuff.

Tommen still wasn't sure that he would consider Ricky a friend, not like he thought of Will or Eric as friends, but they worked well together, could laugh together, and generally got along at school, too. Ricky often thanked Tommen for getting him the job and had declared that he was going to go to school for the trades. General contracting to start, but he might consider being an electrician.

"What about you?" Ricky asked, pulling into the warehouse once Tommen opened the door. "You were always a science nerd. Still going for, what was it, chemistry?"

"Physics," Tommen corrected, "and...I don't know. I mean, I enjoy construction, and it pays good. Physics...it's hard to get excited about theoretical physics when they're not theoretical, at least not to me."

"Talking about the Akari thing?"

Ricky was still leery of Time and the Akari, and there was certainly a wall that went up whenever it came up in conversation. Tommen had demonstrated its uses around the site, usually involving Gravity to help with the heavy lifting. Ricky could not deny that it had good uses, but his brother's actions were still too fresh in his mind.

Tommen nodded in answer to the question. "Yeah. I mean, ooh, let's see if there are any aliens out there. Well, there are. I've seen them, fought with some, fought against others. Moving on. Traveling across the universe? Been there, done that. Expanding the human race to distant moons and planets? We've already got half a dozen colony worlds. Come on, guys, come up with something original."

"Doesn't mean you can't learn something new, or learn how to apply the things you know in different ways. You might be fluent in conversational English, but you suck at spelling and grammar. So you go to school to learn how to refine your talents and develop them in different ways." Ricky turned off his truck and got out.

"True," Tommen said, climbing out of his seat, "but I don't want to have to pay for it for years and years and still only scratch the surface. But if I wanted to pursue anything else, anything real, I'd have to give up family. I can't do that. Earth is still Unengaged, and I'm limited in my options."

Ricky shrugged in a way that said he was generally dismissing the conversation. He was done and moving on. Tommen was grateful for it. Back to work, then.

That wasn't to say that, now that they were alone, Tommen

didn't use Gravity to basically telekinetically lift the saw out of the truck and set it on the ground, thus saving both their backs and avoiding any more injuries that day.

"I feel like, if you put on a cape and a goofy hat and went to Vegas, you'd have a killer show," Ricky commented.

Tommen just nodded and said, "Probably." There probably were a few Akari-bearers in the Vegas show business. He would be more surprised if there weren't at least one.

He got the saw moved out of the way and Ricky fetched a red tag marking it as broken, out of service, do not use.

The shop saw was a little bigger and more cumbersome, but still movable. It was hardly a chore for Tommen to use Gravity and get it in the back of the truck. Then they tied it down securely and took a few steps back.

"Should we grab a couple extra blades?" Ricky wondered, looking at the saw.

Tommen frowned, then shook his head. "Nah. We're only going to be on site a few more hours, and then it'll have to come back. Tomorrow, their first priority will be fixing the other saw and making sure it's safe and good to go. We'll be fine."

Famous last words, he thought, climbing in the truck with just a touch of trepidation. Things had been going too well lately. First Chandler told him he wasn't safe and to not let his guard down. Then the man said that some rift would come between them and Tommen would be left adrift in darkness. Between the birth, the escape, and this new warning which he fully believed had something to do with his death, something was going to happen.

They did not go careening off the road in a tragic accident on the way back to the site. They did not hit anyone or anything suddenly crossing the street or jumping out in front of them. They weren't suddenly taken out by a sniper rifle at a thousand yards. Absolutely nothing of note happened on their return trip.

They unloaded the saw and continued about their work, installing pre-fab panels for their pop-up house. If all went well, they could set trusses within the next couple days and get the roof underway. Everything was moving along just swimmingly. Because this was one of the first houses in the development, Rock Construction would have a leg up on advertising, showing off to potential homeowners just what they were capable of.

Ricky took the saw back to the shop with a few of the guys following, but Tommen was permitted to go home. While he knew it was the guys being considerate and highly recommending he be close to Becky the next few weeks, he couldn't help but feel a small twinge of jealousy. He'd been here longer. He'd been the one to recruit Ricky. And they seemed to like him better. Was it because he'd proudly declared himself a trades major while Tommen still wasn't sure? Was he just imagining things?

"Ddiwedd."

The presence of a new voice in his car nearly sent Tommen through the roof. Had he been driving, he might have gone screaming into a ditch. As it was, he'd just been waiting for his car to warm up and the rest of the guys to leave and was about to take off himself, the last to go. Alone.

He looked over at the passenger seat, unsure if he really wanted to know who this was or what was going on.

He did not recognize the man at all. He was of Asian descent with hair to his shoulders and almost clean-shaven except for the thinnest of mustaches, as if he had forgotten to shave that area this morning. Tommen would guess him to be about five-eight in height, maybe five-ten, probably a hundred and sixty pounds. His clothes were clearly not from the local department store, instead looking like he was about to be an extra in a kung fu movie set in ancient China or something.

"Um, who are you?" Tommen asked.

"Ho Chu ydy fy enw," (My name is Ho Chu.) was how it came across, though Tommen could see that the sound was not matching up with the man's lip movements. He touched his hearing aids and found the translator switch on.

"You touched my hearing aids," he stated lamely.

"We have no language in common," the man said, indicating his own translator.

"Okay, fair enough. So your name is Ho Chu. As in, Ho Chu doin'?" The man gave him a puzzled look and Tommen felt his whole face turn red. The joke went over the man's head, but Tommen was still embarrassed, and he elected to stick with Welsh instead. "Where are you from, um—family name comes first, so your given name is Chu, right? Where are you from, Chu?"

"I am from Vin Lay, a town called Birds by the River."

Tommen guessed that it was the literal translation of the town name. "Cool, cool. Um...why are you here? Which faction are you with? Akarin or Miaramila?"

"We have no name, for we are not a faction guided or misguided by a particular philosophy or religion," Chu answered. "I am here to help you and those like you."

"Those like me who?"

"Those who wish to stop hiding and running. Those who do not want to choose between their Time duties and their shadow lives. Our goal is to bring humanity into knowledge of the Time industry and its agents."

Tommen nodded. "Nothing like a lofty goal. Why approach me?"

"We only recruit those we believe have motivation and a desire to see this goal achieved," Chu said simply. "You have motivation. Others do not. Because we understand the debate is heated, our situation is precarious, and we must choose our recruits wisely."

"You picked me because you know I'm straddling that gap, and it's getting wider every day."

"Precisely."

He considered this for a minute before putting his car in gear and pulling onto the road. "I can't just sit here all night. Ride and talk. What do you hope to achieve? Who's involved?"

"The group is headquartered on Vin Lay, and we have members on Dorigis, Sakaria II, and Earth. Aleis was regrettably cut off, and the only colony world we have not persuaded is Hlohi; they wish to remain separate and distance themselves from Time. The idea is to bring humanity fully into the Time industry and reunite the people. Vin Lay is the most active of the colony worlds with many Asian peoples still fleeing there in secret, and many families remain separated. This is unacceptable. Give humanity full access to the knowledge and tools that the universe has to offer, reunite families."

"Okay, I follow so far. How are you going to get over or get around massive political and religious upheaval? I mean, I don't want to sound insensitive, but Asia, Southeast Asia has usually gotten the short end of the stick when it comes to global wars and religious persecution. How are you going to avoid making things worse?"

"No transition will be perfect," Chu said honestly. "Even in the best of circumstances, there will be fighting. Humans value control, whether it is personal or political. We fully expect that some of the more reverent of the religious may commit suicide or convince others to do so. We fully expect that world leaders will see to expand themselves into places they do not understand and have no business being. It is only the way of things. If you wish to help, this is a fact you must accept."

Tommen let out a breath. "I understand. Believe me, I do. I just kind of wish it wasn't so."

"As do we all. Everyone wishes that war could be won without any fighting, but then it would not be war."

"You ever hear of the Cold War?"

"No."

"Well, it was won without fighting. Mostly it was just fear and intimidation until one side backed down. On the other hand, if it had gone into fighting, Earth probably wouldn't have much of a population left by now."

Chu grunted. "But you understand my point."

"Yes, I do. I would be lying if I said I hadn't been thinking about this sort of thing a lot the last few months, which, again, is why you're here. But you never answered my question. How are you going to do this so it's the least bad outcome?"

"How do you get a donkey to move? By convincing the donkey that it wants to move, that it was the donkey's idea to move. We seek to achieve this in small ways, through personal interaction and utilizing current events. On Earth, the three major events are the planetary shields, computer hacking for financial and identity theft, and—"

"In Jezik," Tommen finished.

"Exactly. Our agents speak to those people who are faced with these problems every day, slowly feeding them information and ideas, showing them things when they are ready."

"In doing so, you're hitting three major sectors of human industry across the planet: scientists, especially those concerned with planetary safety and extraterrestrial communications; banking and finance, which controls the stock market and whole global economy; and the military, those charged with keeping everyone safe from things that go bump in the stars. You are specifically excluding any political offices, so that when those who have the power find out about this stuff, their underlings are well-informed and know what's going on, and they can make informed decisions and recommendations."

"Exactly. You're a smart kid."

"Do the Tacagans know about this operation? How long has this been going on?"

"We have been operating since the end of the Great Strife, what you might consider the mid-80's, but it was primarily an endeavor to reunite families after many wars and limited to Vin Lay and Asia. It has since expanded to other colony worlds, minus Hlohi, and Earth as a whole. Because of the Tacagans' reputation as a bunch of Narcissistic assholes, as well as their disdain for humans and desire to engineer themselves away from *Homo sapien*, we never brought them into the operation. It is unclear whether they know of it anyway, but we doubt it."

"Why is that?"

"Because of their hatred for humanity right now, especially Earthlings. If they can't get through the shields to destroy you, then starting another massive global war would be the next best thing, let you destroy yourselves and save their own resources. My guess is, the only reason they haven't done that is because of the Borelians."

"Yeah, what about them, anyway?" Tommen wondered. "If Earth is brought into the Time industry, then the Tacagan shields would have to come down in order for humans to get to and from the Wheel. That just opens us right up for invasion. And for that matter, what about you? How did you get through the shields?"

"I only said we were not guided by a particular philosophy or religion, but that does not mean we do not have members from other factions, Akarin, Miaramila, and Order alike. I myself am not affiliated with any of them, but an Akarin member brought me here today. Our only requirement is that our members are human and that they have a vested interest in seeing humanity united and open to the universe."

"That doesn't solve our impending invasion problem."

"Well, as you said, in utilizing the threat of In Jezik, we gain access to military entities and are slowly bringing them into the knowledge and ability. It is slow going already, and the events of the last couple years on Earth have set us back some. This is not meant to be an overnight campaign. It will take time. We acknowledge that it will not be a bloodless transition, but we also wish to do it with the least harm."

Tommen nodded. "I understand." He paused. "Why doesn't Hlohi want to be part of this? Wolf Clan's whole job is to keep an eye on Earth and see if and when it might be safe to return to their ancestral lands. And there are still plenty of Native Americans on Earth who could benefit from free contact with the Krydik. District Nine might get their official recognition because of it."

Chu shrugged. "It is what they have chosen, to move away from such a thing. We always keep the door of communication open if they wish, but we do not push. Their conflict with the Order is consuming most of their time and resources now."

Tommen turned a corner. They'd been running around in aimless not-quite-circles throughout the whole conversation. He needed to get home at some point tonight.

"Let's pretend I'm interested and I want to join up with you guys, sally forth into knowledge. Great. Awesome. What do I actually do? You're right, I have a vested interest. Problem is, that vested interest is going to take up a lot of time, going to work, going to school, changing diapers, babysitting, the whole works. I don't have time to go running off on more adventures. I might actually be going into hiding here soon."

"The good news is, Earth is far more advanced than the rest of the colony worlds, and you have incredible means of communication," Chu told him. "Your biggest tool would be the Internet. Maybe you're not a soldier or a scientist, and maybe you don't speak to anyone of importance. But you have the ability to disseminate information quickly to the masses."

"You're talking about, like, blogging?"

"The agents of Earth know more about it than I do, how everything works behind the scenes. I would put you in contact with one of them, and they would get you set up. They would give you the information to spread at certain times, and it would be up to you to decide how it got out."

"Conspiracy theory blogging, then. Awesome. Do I get my own tin foil hat and T-shirt?"

Chu shifted in his seat. "We have found that Earthlings are becoming more and more gullible to stupid things. While embarrassing for the rest of us, it also provides an opportunity to speak to them and lead them into the knowledge."

"I don't know how I feel about that," Tommen said.

"That would most likely be your assignment, based on your circumstances. If circumstances change, you may do something else."

"Is it paid or volunteer only?"

"Volunteer, which is why we only choose those who have an interest in this succeeding. As it becomes more successful and makes real headway, then we may be more flexible about our membership, and there may be pay in the future. I make no promises."

Tommen nodded. "Fair enough, I guess. Mind if I ask what your vested interest is in this?"

"My family was separated during the Vietnam War. My parents still remember Earth. They love Vin Lay and wish to remain there, but they also wish to see the rest of the family and travel freely."

"Makes sense."

He Tested Ho Chu then. The man had been nothing but polite so far, but Tommen wouldn't put it past Julianna to try and give him exactly what he wanted most in an effort to lure him into some kind of trap. But the Test came back clean for any Disguises, which meant he could only take Ho Chu at his word.

"Now that we have spoken of this," Chu went on, "I ask only that you keep it a secret. Do not tell your friends. Do not tell your father—"

"Why not tell my dad?" Tommen cut in sharply. "My daughter is his granddaughter, and he has to go dark soon. You think he doesn't have a vested interest in being able to be a grandpa? We might all be fleeing ourselves here, too."

"I am making this offer to you. Not to him. That does not mean he could not be considered in the future, but for now, it is for you and only you."

"What if I tell him anyway?"

"Then that is your choice, but consider this: Our work is precarious and must be carried out with delicate precision. Every offer we make is a potential vulnerability and could result in the collapse of our operation from those who wish to keep Earth and humanity at large Unengaged or simply vulnerable to attack. You have a vested interest. Do not risk our success because you don't like the rules as they currently stand. They could change in the future."

Tommen sighed but could not think of any witty comebacks.

Finally, Ho Chu gave him directions to where he was supposed to meet his ride back to Vin Lay.

"How do I contact you if I'm interested and want to help?" Tommen asked.

"I will give you nine days to think about it," Ho Chu said, getting out of the car. "Then I will give you the information of one of our members here on Earth. You may contact them at any time."

There was nothing more to be said or done. The offer was made, and the ball was in Tomen's court. He either accepted or rejected. Ho Chu thanked him for his time, wished him well, and headed inside the little cafe to either speak to or wait for his intergalactic rideshare. Tommen pulled away from the curb and eased into traffic, eventually getting around the block and making for home.

Had all of that really happened? Had someone actually just told him that there was a movement to bring humanity fully into the Time industry and bring all the colony worlds back together? It was like a dream come true! At the same time, it kind of meant someone had been stalking him and knew of his predicament. The thought sent chills up and down his spine, but then he told himself that the information wasn't exactly a secret. Probably every human Time Agent, Akari-bearer and whatever else on all the colony worlds knew that he was going to be a dad, thanks to Tyler and Ryan and their little adventure. Why wouldn't it get this group's attention?

He wanted to go home and talk it over with his dad, or call him and chitchat about it for a while. He wanted to call Nathan or Miach and get their thoughts on the matter. In theory, though, he couldn't.

He didn't like the thought of not being able to tell anyone. While the reason might have been understandable, it presented itself as manipulation. Tommen didn't like being manipulated, having spent years being manipulated by psychopaths, and he harbored a suspicion that Ho Chu was actually a Miaramila agent, and this was some sort of test. Maybe this was orchestrated by Win, with or without Rifun's knowledge, just to see if he was capable of keeping a secret and actually laying low before letting him know where the Miaramila were hiding.

Or it could be an agent from the Order, trying a more subtle approach to killing him. If he contacted this alleged operative in nine days and went to meet them, who was to say he wouldn't be met by Julianna herself, or one of her murder squads?

Or it could be a legit organization with a legit mission and they were trying to keep things on the down low.

How could he know without being able to discuss it with someone else, someone he trusted, and ask more questions? Sure, he could wait the nine days, get the contact information, and ask questions of a more knowledgeable, more local agent, but he wanted to talk about things now, figure out what just happened and what to do with the information.

Would they spy on him, to see if he was talking to others about it? If he did speak, would Ho Chu not give him any contact information in order to protect his agents? It would be the smart thing to do, it seemed, for a small organization that wanted to stay secret.

Something about it still felt fishy, or incomplete at the very least. Even Tommen had to reluctantly admit that there probably would be no bloodless transition. Humans were volatile and resistant to change, and they especially enjoyed the feeling of control. Spin someone the wrong way and watch them spin out of control. No matter which way you sliced it, people were going to die. This really was an instance of trying to effect the least bad outcome. Therefore, it had to be done carefully, with utmost precision as Ho Chu said. Working with individual people in strategic positions in order to build a sturdy, knowledgeable base.

Tommen's job would be concocting and promoting conspiracy theories. Not the ones with little green men who had ray guns and anal probes, but the ones just plausible enough to get the attention of the masses, the ones intermixed with verifiable facts and current events. An idea, the hardest thing in the universe to kill. Plant an idea. A work of fiction that was not a work of fiction but seemed like it was.

Part of it sounded thrilling, being part of a secret organization within a secret organization whose job was to make the larger secret organization no longer a secret. Sitting on a computer, late at night, feeding carefully prepped information to the masses, watching the herd of sheeple move this way and that, but always guiding them toward the end goal, the knowledge of the Time industry and the universe at large, and reuniting Earth with its colony worlds. It was like a spy movie or a TV drama or a suspense novel.

If it happened, if humans were exposed, he wouldn't have to hide half his life. His dad wouldn't have to move, or not go dark anyway, and he would be able to be a presence in the life of his granddaughter. Time Agents all around the world could move about freely. And who knew how many problems might be solved with knowledge of Time? Anyone concerned about the planet could use portal travel to bounce from place to place, no more fossil fuels and no more traffic jams. Anyone concerned about poverty and hunger around the globe had only to glimpse the Food Court and know that those problems could be solved permanently and inexpensively. And, as Ho Chu pointed out, humanity could become one entity again. The Asians separated by wars spanning from Genghis Khan to Vietnam would be whole. Those seeking the simple life could learn so much from the Aleisi, if there were any left.

Tommen pulled into the driveway, his head still in the clouds. Those clouds quickly cleared when he got inside. He took in a huge whiff of the delicious dinner spread on the table, hugged and kissed Becky and put a loving hand on her belly, feeling the baby give a mighty kick.

How would Becky react to such news, such a realization? More than that, there were great dangers out there in the universe. The Borelians were the biggest threat, but by no means the only one. The Tacagans had quite a bone to pick with Homo sapiens, after all, for turning the tables on control of the shield generators. Opening up humanity to the universe would be like blowing up a dam. Ho Chu and his group thought they could dismantle it brick by brick, release the water a little at a time, but there would come a point where the water pressure could not be held, and it would collapse.

This was already happening. They were already working on this, long before he'd shown up in the twenty-first century. And they would keep plugging along, with or without him.

So all it really served to do was drag Tommen back to the same questions he'd been debating for the last couple years. Was it smart, and was it safe? The threats were already out there, and they were gunning for Earth and humanity in general. Things were happening that no one could rationally explain. Should they expose humanity? Should they keep trying to bandaid the dam? Should they seal themselves off entirely, as Hlohi was attempting to do? How did he break this to Becky?

These questions were extremely distracting as he tried to finish up his homework and make sure he had everything ready for school the next day. Less than three weeks until the birth meant less than three weeks of high school left, and Layman had arranged it so he didn't have to take his final exams, which meant he had Wednesday, Thursday, and Friday off, Friday being the day of the C-section. Chris had already promised him the next week off after that, which was good because he started college classes that week, assuming they weren't on an alien planet.

It was going to be hectic, say it that way. Becky was stressing out a little, too, having to condense her classes so she had the week of the birth off.

So they sat in the bedroom, him at the desk, her on the bed, working on their respective homework.

"Do you think God created aliens?" Tommen asked suddenly.

Becky looked up from her textbook. "As in, little green men kind of aliens?"

"Any kind. Just aliens not from this planet."

"I don't know. I wouldn't think so. We are created in His image, the pinnacle of Creation. Seems like it wouldn't be right that He would make highly intelligent aliens not in His image. I think it would be insulting, and a great excuse for racism."

"Why do you say that?"

"Because it was used for centuries to justify any form of slavery. Sure, you could make arguments about phenotypes and all that, but any two given humans are still ninety-nine-point-nine-nine-nine-nine percent similar. But space aliens? The differences would be more significant, I think. You get people who place humanity at the top of the pyramid, the little green men don't stand a chance."

"So, if a flying saucer were to land, say, tomorrow, you don't think it would turn out well, long-term?"

"Not at all. If the aliens were less advanced than us — which I don't foresee if they are capable of space travel — then humanity wants to maintain its position at the top of the pyramid. I would see slavery at worst, war at best. Where did this topic come from?"

He shrugged. "I don't know. Just my mind taking some topics from the news and running off with them into parts unknown."

"Obviously."

Thus ended the conversation. The two returned to their respective homework and study assignments.

It was four days before Nathan replied to Tommen's text. Ultimately, they decided that one week after the birth, Nathan was going to whisk Tommen, Becky, the baby, and Walter away, point blank, to *Runner's Refuge* for a sort of transitory period. It would be harder for Julianna to track them, they wouldn't get in the way of Miaramila operations on the ground, and it would provide a controlled environment for Becky to come to terms with the larger universe.

March 1st marked nine days after Tommen's conversation with Ho Chu. As school got underway again during the week, he didn't give their conversation much thought. Even when the information showed up in the form of a postcard in the mail — which he got to first, thankfully, so Becky didn't find it — he set it aside for the time being. The offer was interesting, but he just didn't think it was going to work well if he had to go into hiding.

If nothing else, he thought, hiding it in one of his Books, he would wait until after the birth and see how things worked out.

Chapter Twenty-Three
Jolt

March was a month of tentative hope, Walter thought. December, January, February, those were all the dark, cold, dreary winter months that just sucked all the fun and hope out of everything as the weather forecast day after day after day of freezing cold, rain, and snow. But when March came around, it was like everything shifted. Sure, there might still be day after day after day of cold and rain and snow, but there was hope in the air. Temperatures turned over from below freezing to above freezing. From there it went from so cold a cop didn't want to pull you over because he didn't want to get out of his car, to a manageable walk from his car to yours in a comfortable sweatshirt and coat. Then came the break when temperatures stayed above freezing, when the sun came out and it felt warm.

Walter liked those days. The only problem was, he rarely saw them when he was working nights. Make no mistake, he was glad for the longer days, when it was no longer dark when he went in and dark when he punched out. The sun stayed in the sky for a few more hours, which certainly helped his mood and the moods of his fellows. But he still longed for the day when he could wake up to a sunrise and enjoy the day, the whole day, not just a couple hours and then descend back into darkness.

With the warmer weather also came more calls. It wasn't much fun to go out and graffiti someone's house when it was ten degrees and the paint wouldn't cooperate and the cops could follow your footprints. But when it got to be a little warmer and the sidewalks were clear and people's driveways were clear, well, it was an opportunity for a little mischief after a long winter.

Walter punched in, pleased to find that it was pretty darn slow for a Wednesday night. No one was running around like a bat out of hell, the phones weren't ringing off the hook, or at all in fact, and it looked as though everyone had a pretty relaxed attitude. It was going to be a good night, as long as no one moved too quickly or spoke too loud or said any of the First Responder Swear Words, words like, "Quiet," and, "Slow," and "Easy," and so on.

"Afternoon, Walt," Kate greeted. "Last night as a grandparent bachelor, huh?"

That was the term the guys had chosen to describe his impending state of becoming a grandparent. Seeing how he wasn't a grandparent yet but had one on the way, he was a grandparent bachelor.

"Well, technically second to last," Walter told her. "But since I have tomorrow night off, the next time you guys see me, yes, I will be a grandpa."

He'd taken a few days off so he could get his sleep schedule adjusted a little and be able to make it to the hospital to meet his granddaughter. The procedure was scheduled for Friday, but he wanted Thursday off as well. He also had the weekend off, "to act as a backup once Tommen and Becky realize just what it means to have a baby." And to help out a little with chores while Becky recovered from the C-section. It wasn't just about the baby being born, after all.

"We want pictures; you know that, right?" Kate said.

"I know, I know." Walter waved her off. "You want to see if I can fit a tiny newborn into my big hands."

"Hand. One hand. I bet you could. I want to see."

"They given out the name yet?" Allan wondered.

"Nope, keeping that pretty close to the chest. But I think I can manage to wait a couple more days to find out."

"Hey, at least they told you the sex, so they're not keeping you in that suspense."

"You're not wrong there." Walter shook his head. "You know they're already talking about what color they want to paint my room once I move out and they take it over? I just painted it a year or two ago when I remodeled the whole house. I don't even get a thank you."

"What color?" Arthur wondered.

Walter sighed. "Dark blue. The room they're using now is going to become the nursery—"

"Painting it pink?"

"Nope. Becky has declared pink a hideous color. Yellow and light green, so it's bright and cheerful."

"Not a bad idea," Trevor said. "My sister did yellow and white in her nursery. Supposed to be all yellow, but the baby came early and they had to stop, so the white was technically just primer. It still looks good, though."

"Well, I guess I can't have too strong of an opinion, seeing how I won't be living there much longer," Walter mused.

"Got all your stuff packed?" Kate wondered.

"I'm...getting there."

"You don't even have boxes, do you?"

"No. I'm procrastinating. I'm really just waiting until after the baby is born to start in on that, or anything major at this point."

Kate gave him a look. "You don't have to go, you know."

Walter nodded. "Ah, yes, I do. I might not be going to the Bahamas, but the house is not big enough for the four of us. It's not going to be big enough for them either if they decide to have more kids. So, yes, I will be moving."

"You just don't know where."

"Not at this point."

If only they knew, he mused silently. Tommen had finally negotiated an escape plan with Nathan. One week after the birth still left them open to an attack from Julianna, but at least it was something. Walter wasn't sure about the whole thing, had a number of objections and general misgivings, but he could not in good conscience suggest that they just ignore Julianna's threats and hope they went away. Whatever her reasons for not quickly following up on the school shooting, they all knew that she would try again.

One week after the C-section, the four of them would meet up with Nathan and possibly Godwin, if the cranky mercenary could be convinced. One portal, one trip, make it as simple and painless as possible.

This would be little trouble for Walter, of course; his biggest gripe was that he would be bowing out before officially retiring and having to leave all of his stuff behind to be claimed and redistributed by the courts. For Becky, though...Tommen had come to the conclusion that there was little point in trying to be gentle or subtle about it with roundabout conversations. The only way to do it was to do it, so that's what they would do.

It was unfair is what it was, and Walter would be lying to himself if no one else if he didn't acknowledge it. It wasn't fair. There was no reason for any of this except Julianna was a vengeful, vindictive witch on a power trip.

He let out a breath as he hopped in a cruiser and made his way out onto the roads. This wasn't how he expected to go dark. He felt terrible about just disappearing one night, probably ending up on an episode of *Unsolved Mysteries*. He couldn't say he wasn't frustrated that he wouldn't get to actually retire. But he couldn't ignore the possibility of Julianna using him to get to Tommen. If a plan worked, why not do it again?

But this had been a good life, Walter thought, one he could look back on and be proud of. Whatever Godwin or the Miaramila or anyone had him doing while in protective custody, he could look at himself in the mirror and be okay. He could look at his son and his son's family and be proud. Things were going to be okay.

Maybe he was just getting sentimental, but that was all right. He was two hundred years old, after all. He had every right to look back on the things he'd seen and be a little sentimental. At least he hadn't turned into an old hermit yelling at neighborhood kids to get off his lawn. At least he was still on this side of the criminal justice system. At least he was still on this side of the grave. For a little while longer yet, anyway.

He found a place to park and hide and wait for speeders and other ne'er-do-wells. Drunk driving was so nineties. These days, driving under the influence of drugs—especially the opiate and prescription kind—was all the rage.

Walter remembered when he had been addicted to painkillers. It was not an experience he wanted to relive, and he considered himself very lucky that he'd gotten help the way he did, saving his reputation and career. Bad enough to be rank-busted; he could have lost his job entirely, including all the benefits that went with it.

More than once, as he sat here on the side of the road, he wondered about ways to help those he caught. He knew the demons of addiction, knew the stranglehold they could have on a person, not just their body, but their soul as well. Jail was not effective. Simple rehab was not enough. It had to be a systematic, societal shift in thinking. Problem was, those kinds of shifts typically only inspired those on the hilltop, who were in no danger whatsoever of these demons. But pithy slogans made poor rope for those struggling in the tar pits and quicksand.

He didn't know the answer. Probably never would know the answer. Humanity had been dealing with these problems for thousands of years, and they still couldn't make it better. The best he could do was help contain it.

His first problem of the night proved to be a common speeder. Not texting, not a teenager, not anything special. The driver didn't even really have an excuse other than he must have just lost track of his speedometer. In a fairly good mood, Walter was willing to let him off with a warning. The man thanked him profusely and promised to do better.

The next speeder he caught was not so lucky, mostly because even if he hadn't been drunk, he still acted like a jackass. Even as Walter was walking him back to the cruiser in handcuffs, the man was promising to call the mayor, call the county commissioner, call the sheriff, call the attorney general, call the governor himself! This was police abuse! Misuse of power! This was damn near communism! If he'd been black, the cops wouldn't touch him because they knew they'd get their asses chewed up and down the national news!

Walter just turned up the radio in the cruiser to drown out the yelling as he returned to the station. He kept a few preprogrammed stations handy for such occasions, when he needed to calm himself down or else annoy the hell out of his unwilling passengers. Country was one channel, specifically for those who considered themselves gangsta. There was another station that played old gospel and church music; that was probably his favorite station to flip on when someone was giving him lip. The third and fourth stations were talk radio on opposite ends of the political spectrum; those were especially fun when someone tried to pull stunts like this guy was here, saying he was going to call the governor and everyone else and rake the cops across the coals.

It didn't take five seconds of one-sided conversation to learn the man's political stance, so Walter turned on the opposite talk radio station. That got the guy really pissed off and he continued to yell, but Walter just tuned him out and kept driving, smiling to himself the whole way. There were nights when the job really wasn't that bad.

He got a decent break after that, far cry from what he'd experienced over New Year's, with the drunk morons right and left. Certainly better than Valentine's Day which saw a sharp spike in domestic assault and rape. They'd even gotten an attempted murder call that night. It had been a messy situation, but everyone made it out alive and it helped to eat up some time on shift.

People sometimes called Walter crass and cold-hearted when he thought of intense situations merely as a bridge between punching in and punching out, but if he didn't think of it that way at least part of the time, he would go insane. He couldn't afford to get emotionally invested in every single call that came down the line, no matter how tragic. Just experiencing one tragedy could mess a person up for life; the warehouse was proof enough of that. Having to respond to and investigate dozens or hundreds of those situations over a few decades could drive a man insane.

He sat on a side road, drinking coffee, listening to the scanner and the regular radio.

Walter's first and only real big adventure came about eleven o'clock with a break-in at a local convenience store. Kate and Arthur got there first while the guy was still inside. He took off out the back door where Walter just pulled up in his cruiser. With a little creative Banding, he made it so it looked like the guy ran out of the store and straight into the back of the cop car, Walter holding the door open for him like a gentleman. The spectacular fail was caught on the security camera above the back door and produced a good many laughs when they finally got back to the station.

"Who says chivalry is dead?" Walter said, shrugging nonchalantly.

"A regular public serviceman right there," Arthur laughed.

Other than that, his night was spent drinking coffee and sitting on one road or another waiting for antics and shenanigans. Speeders came by every once in a while; a call for a loose dog that he ended up taking to Animal Control (he spent a few minutes at the station after that cleaning drool off his seats and windows); some kids with nothing better to do but stand around smoking at a grocery store that was long closed; an older woman in a robe and curlers calling to complain about her drunk upstairs neighbor who was talking to himself...and answering. Walter prepared himself for some kind of fight on account of a police officer being called, and was relieved when the guy agreed to just go to bed, passing out on the couch.

Only a few more nights of this, Walter thought, watching the clock tick faithfully toward four o'clock. It had been a slow night, so he might actually get out on time.

He thought about his life in retirement, this dream he still couldn't fulfill. He thought about how he would interact with people. He would be able to go to parties and social gatherings, without having to consult his work schedule or his son's work or school schedule or any of that. He could do something because he wanted to do it.

And he would tell people that he was a retired police officer. People would ask him questions like, what was the weirdest thing he saw? The saddest? The dumbest? Who was the one guy who he knew belonged in jail but could never pin anything on him? Who was the guy you knew was innocent but unfairly locked up?

Well, he knew the answer to that last one.

Visits to the jail typically had to be scheduled in advance, and the guys were very good about following the rules. But sometimes they could be persuaded to look the other way, as long as their kindness wasn't abused.

So it was that Walter punched out at four o'clock, went home to sleep for a while, then went to visit Vin in jail about two.

The man was a ghost of the officer Walter had once worked beside, and he couldn't help but feel partially responsible for his predicament. Vin had been a bit of a duty-dodger, always able to wiggle out of any tough or dangerous jobs, and he was usually relegated to fluff tasks just to keep him out of the way. Walter hadn't realized that this was intentional by the department, so when he complained and got Vin kind of forced into the mainstream of things, well, maybe it hadn't been the best place for him.

For just a while, Vin had come alive as he realized what it meant to be a police officer, and Walter thought he'd begun to enjoy it. Then his wife filed for divorce, and then he killed someone on the job. That turned into prosecution and now he was heading to prison.

"How are they treating you, Vin?" Walter asked.

Vin shrugged. "The officers seem pretty divided over whether I'm a dirty cop or just wrong place, wrong time. The rest of the inmates, well, yea though I am locked and barricaded in the valley of the shadow of death..."

It was a variation of one of his standard answers. The man looked haggard, as if he hadn't gotten much sleep, and Walter thought he could safely assume that most of Vin's food got "reappropriated" to other inmates as supply and demand—emphasis on the demand part—dictated.

"This is probably going to be the last time we talk here, Walt," Vin told him. "I'm supposed to be transferred on Tuesday. Going to my new home for the next two to nine."

"Come on, Vin, we both know you're a good guy. You're an upstanding officer and a good man besides. Sentence lengths are just a guideline, a way to make people think twice, but they don't mean a whole lot when you can get out on parole that much sooner. You'll be out in no time."

"Where will I live? Andrea's lawyer is pushing the divorce papers through, and I have no right to contest. I will literally have nothing."

"You have friends who will bend over backwards for you. You need a couch, just call and ask. The world isn't going to end while you're gone. And on top of that, you're still getting credit in here. Less than two years, you'll be back."

"I kind of wish the world would end while I was away. I don't know how I feel about it moving on without me."

Walter nodded. "Believe me, I know what you mean. I'm going to be a grandpa here before the week is out, and I'm moving over the summer. That kills."

"Yes, but you don't have to. Okay, fine, maybe move to a different house in the neighborhood, but you are free to move and go here and there. I don't get that." Vin sighed and rubbed his eyes. "I'm an idiot. I never should have become a police officer."

"Don't talk like that. You were—"

"A patsy," Vin cut in. "I was a nice little puppet. I was the dog of the office that no one liked but they had to keep around in order to secure funding from my rich uncle." He sighed again and licked his lips. "You know, when I first got hired into county, I didn't know that was why they hired me. I thought it was because I did good in the Academy and they liked me. Okay, I knew that police departments everywhere were hurting for people and resources, but I guess I never expected them to..." He cut himself off and looked away. Then he looked back at Walter through the glass. "I like you, Walter. I hated you at first because you pointed out my faults and everything with the funding and whatnot, but then I realized that you were the most honest one there. You called it like you saw it. It was a first-shift captain who finally told me why I was there, and the way he said it, it was so dismissive. Like a dog. And then I was sent on some meaningless errand boy task.

"I wish I would have known, Walter. Maybe I could have done more with myself. Maybe I would have been smart and left the force entirely, saved everyone the hassle and the grief and the embarrassment. Maybe I wouldn't be here."

"You feel betrayed," Walter stated.

Vin bit his lip and nodded. "Damn right, I feel betrayed. And because of it, my whole fucking life is going to be screwed up, even after I get out of prison, assuming I don't get killed first."

Walter started to say something, but Vin hung up and signaled he was done with the conversation. Walter sighed, gave Vin a brief wave, mouthed "Good luck" to him, and left. As he went out to his car, he couldn't decide how much of that conversation and emotional outburst had been raw emotion and the core of his thoughts, and how much was jail rubbing off on him. Inmates talked a lot about respect and betrayal, but Walter couldn't say that Vin was entirely wrong when referencing the department in a similar light.

He returned home, walking in the door to find Tommen looking like he was about to head out. Or just coming in.

"Where you going, kid? Thought you didn't work today?"

"I'm not," Tommen said, grinning and tying his shoes. "The guys are taking me out for like a bachelor party sort of thing."

"Which guys?"

"From work."

"No alcohol, I hope?"

"Dad, I'm not old enough."

Walter raised a brow. "Because that ever stopped you before."

Tommen blushed. "Maybe, but no, there's no alcohol involved. Or strippers."

"I think you would have more to fear from Becky than me if there were."

"Pretty much we're just going to, like, a sports bar and getting all-you-can-eat wings. I'm grabbing Will, too."

"Is Becky out with her mom, then, or what?"

His son shook his head. "No, she's taking a nap. Rough night last night, so she just wants to take it easy."

"Fair enough; I'll try to be quiet." Walter caught himself. "Wait a minute, why am I not invited to this shindig? You know I love wings. It's because I'm your dad, isn't it? You don't want me embarrassing you."

His son turned even redder as he stood and shrugged. "Well...kind of."

"You weren't supposed to agree. You were supposed to lie to me, maybe ask if I wanted to go, too?"

Tommen threw up his hands. "You're as bad as Becky, you know that? You tell me to be honest, then turn around and say, 'Lie to me.' Make up your minds. Are you two in cahoots or what?"

Walter laughed. "No cahoots here. All right, kid, go enjoy your bachelor party. But make sure to bring me back some good wings."

"That sounds like a challenge. It means I am going to have to sample every single flavor and every single sauce to find the combination I think you would like the most."

"Do you get a T-shirt for that or something?"

"Considering how many different combinations you can make —we're talking in the hundreds—I definitely think there should be if there isn't one."

Walter patted him on the shoulder. "Go get 'em, kid."

Tommen grinned and grabbed his keys. "I'll see you later."

And he was off. Walter watched him leave from the kitchen window.

The house was quiet. Feeling in a rather good mood, Walter decided to help Becky out a little, grabbing the clothes from the dryer and rotating the rest of the laundry through. He took the dry basket down to his room to start sorting. The door to Tommen and Becky's room was closed, and the light was off.

It had been at least six months since Walter had done laundry, and he almost forgot what it was like to do it himself. True enough, Becky spoiled them. Laundry, dinner, cleaning as much as she could, and still she found time to go to school and work. Now a newborn was going to be tossed into the mix.

He thought back to his days as a father of a baby, miserable though he had been. Despite his drinking and constant fighting with his wife, there were a few days he could recall where he wouldn't have had it any other way, when he couldn't stand the thought of ever putting down his child, as if to do so was to invite tragic misfortune. Well, maybe it had been, considering he often put her down so that he could pick up a drink.

Gritting his teeth, Walter forced himself to think about the happy days for just a moment longer before pushing such thoughts from his mind. It was over a hundred years ago that all that happened. What was it about him or the situation or anything at all that wouldn't let him get over it emotionally? He needed to be ready for this baby as much as his son did, because Walter knew for damn sure that he would be called upon for babysitting duty. He couldn't be found lying next to the baby in his own fetal position.

Maybe that was a bit of an exaggeration. His wounds were healed into scar tissue now, a little more sensitive than the rest of him, perhaps, but otherwise back to normal. Or he liked to think so.

A sudden memory flashed through his mind, a little girl lying dead in a ditch. She'd been riding on an ATV with her dad or her uncle, and he'd been drunk. There was a car crash. She was killed instantly, or so the thinking—and hoping—went. He remembered her face, the way she'd lain there, head cocked at a very unnatural angle. He remembered asking the ambulance for a sheet to pull over her.

Walter almost went to his knees thinking about it, even as he couldn't understand why. He'd seen plenty of gruesome stuff in his time as a cop, and he'd seen worse during his time at City. What was it about this one, except that it was a little girl and he'd been thinking about his little girl, and the girl his son was about to have? Was that all it took? Could a cop get PTSD like that? Was he doomed to spend the rest of his life—however many lives he lived—heaping more and more soul-crushing memories upon his psyche and reliving all of them? If that was the case, he would certainly go insane, given enough time.

It was not a happy thought, and Walter muddled through the rest of the laundry, telling himself to focus on that, deliberately trying to remember how Becky had everything organized by person, color, size, type, she had her own system. Walter just separated the clothes by their owner and stuffed his clothes in his dresser. The only thing he paid attention to was his uniforms which he carefully hung up. Not a few times, Kate would make an officer take off his shirt and iron it before going out; she'd brought in an iron and ironing board for just such an occasion.

He took Becky's and Tommen's clothes out to the couch so he could reclaim his bed, then returned the basket to its usual spot. He glanced at the clock. Just after five. He wanted to be around and semi-conscious for the birth in a couple days, but he didn't want to completely throw off his sleep schedule so that he couldn't return to work. Well, he could go to bed early—early for him being three or four in the morning—and just muddle with his sleep a little instead of throwing it completely off-kilter.

He watched the evening news but found little of interest. New research on the Safe Earth Defense System, seeing what other capabilities the technology held, what it could be used for in the military and civilian life. An increased effort to locate and destroy any In Jezik sleeper cells throughout the world. The 2016 elections which were just over seven months out. Walter just sighed, internally rolled his eyes, and turned off the TV. Sixty percent of the commercials now were political ads. Once they hit summer, that would be up to seventy-five percent. Come the new school year, easily eighty or ninety percent of all commercials would be political. Fighting, lying, cheating, backstabbing, and they wondered why trust and turnout was so low.

Down the hall, he heard the bedroom door squeak open. Then the bathroom door shut. Ah, the thrilling life of pregnancy, Walter thought.

He got up and went down to his room to look for a book. He hadn't gotten to the library lately, so he was forced to choose from his tiny personal collection, most of it work-related. He still had his textbooks from Police Academy, already outdated seeing how he graduated before 9/11 when the bureaucracy increased a hundredfold; several editions of *West Virginia Penal Code and Automobile Handbook*, getting bigger every season as more teeny tiny laws were put into effect; his Medical First Responder textbook, easily a decade outdated since Lily Guile had been his testing proctor and had recommended Micah and Micaiah as Lieutenants during that time. He also had an assortment of fiction books, most of them mystery novels or true crime stories. Looking over those, he frowned and mentally pushed them aside. It wasn't much fun when you already knew the twist at the end.

Maybe he should consider having a garage sale before they escaped. It might be one last fun hurrah in the neighborhood. And if he was retiring from the police force, the textbooks did no one any good. They barely did him any good anymore. Maybe have a garage sale, make a little extra money, take Tommen and Becky and the baby out to dinner one last time before they departed. That sounded like a good idea. Maybe a little idealistic, but it would be his one chance to —

"Um, Walter."

He turned to see Becky standing in the doorway of his room. Even just glancing at her, he could tell something was definitely wrong. For one, she was pale. She was pale enough to make Tommen look tan. She had one hand on the doorframe to support herself as if she might fall over, and the one hand under her belly.

Then he saw the blood.

"Oh, shit."

He didn't even have to make one long stride to get to her, immediately scooping her up and placing her on his bed, grabbing an extra blanket from the end of the bed to put under her.

"When did this start?" he demanded, grabbing his phone and punching in 9-1-1.

"Um...I don't know." She sounded tired and confused and, if Walter was any judge, very afraid.

"9-1-1, what's your emergency?" the dispatcher answered.

"This is Officer 629, requesting an ambulance at 5555 S. Deering Rd. I have a—how old are you? You're still nineteen, right?" Becky nodded. She lay back on the bed, eyes closed, tears streaming down her cheeks. "Nineteen year old female, forty weeks pregnant, first pregnancy, high-risk, heavy vaginal bleeding. She is breathing and...mostly conscious I would say."

"Copy that, 629, I have an ambulance en route to your location. Is the patient in active labor?"

"Ah..."

Walter looked at Becky. She could very well be in labor; today was the predicted natural birth date. They'd just been hoping to be able to put it off another day. All the same, she wasn't screaming in pain or anything, and he hadn't heard a peep out of her all evening. He turned his attention back to dispatch. "I don't know. But it would be really bad if she is because she is physically unable to have a natural birth."

There was a little more back and forth before dispatch hung up. Walter put his phone down and took Becky's hand in his. She did not open her eyes, but she squeezed his hand. Tears were still rolling down her cheeks and she was still bleeding.

"You're going to be okay, hon," Walter told her.

"It's not me I'm worried about," she sniffed.

"I don't know what's going on inside there, so you have to tell me. You don't look so good, so if something happens, I need to be able to communicate with the medics."

She took several shallow breaths and squeezed his hand again. Based on stories he'd heard from other men, he judged that she couldn't be in labor because she wasn't breaking any bones in his hand. Yet. He was about to say something more when she spoke, saying, "I didn't sleep good last night. It's not uncommon, I know, but I just had a really hard time. Today was just miserable. It didn't hurt, it just...it was so heavy and uncomfortable, like trying to carry around a bag of rocks or bowling balls. I thought a nap might help, just to get me through until tomorrow, you know? I woke up because I had to pee, and then there was just...so much blood."

"So you were bleeding before you went into the bathroom? Or that's where it started?"

"Um...it might have been a little bit before, but it all just...suddenly released. I mean, it felt okay at first, a lot of the pressure being released, losing the rocks and bowling balls, but now it just feels like needles and it's getting worse so that it's starting to feel like knives."

"Knives where? Abdominally, vaginally?"

"All over." She choked a few sobs.

"When is the last time you ate?"

"I ate a little bit this morning just because I knew I had to, but that's it. I just haven't felt hungry."

Walter nodded and looked around. There was absolutely nothing he could do. If she tried to deliver, it would shatter her pelvis and she would bleed out. She needed to get to the hospital. Where was the ambulance?

"Is Tommen out with his friends?" Becky wondered, sounding faint again.

"Yeah. Listen, once the ambulance gets here, I'll call him and get him on the way to the hospital. Right now, I'm just keeping an eye on you."

He put his fingers on her wrist. He had no trouble finding a pulse, for it was very strong, but also very slow. With her other hand, Becky made a fist and weakly hit the bed.

"He said he was going to bring me home some wings," she complained. "A good last meal before the birth."

Walter couldn't help but laugh at that. "He told me the same thing. Maybe he can get them to go and bring them with him. Then it'll be a good first meal to recover from the C-section."

She shook her head loosely. "I don't think they let you do that. I'm going to be on a liquid diet."

"You and the baby both?"

She weakly swatted him away. At least she wasn't completely gone yet.

In the distance, Walter heard sirens. They cut out abruptly, but he could still see the reflection of the flashing lights. Briefly he tried to think about the day and time. Thursday, and it was evening. There was a fifty-fifty shot of Becky's dad being home and seeing the ambulance. Considering what happened the last time an ambulance stopped at this house, if he saw it go by and knew where it went, he was probably already on his way over.

"EMS!" someone called.

"Back here!" Walter shouted back.

A minute later, the medics appeared outside the room. Groaning, Walter stood, saying, "Medics are here. They'll take care of you."

"Will you call my mom, too?" Becky asked, making a grab for his hand. "Do you have her number? I know she's at work, but she got permission to have her phone on her so she knew if something like this happened so she could go to maternity."

"I think your dad can make those calls."

"Is he here?"

"Not yet, but I imagine he will be soon."

He stepped aside for the medics, excusing himself from the room for a second so he could make a call.

Tommen did not answer his phone, and Walter sent him half a dozen texts in rapid succession, hoping to get the point across. As he was doing that, sure enough, Becky's dad showed up.

"Is she all right?" he demanded.

"She's bleeding, but she'll be fine," Walter answered, trying to stay calm and make it all sound less terrifying than it actually was.

The audiologist got an upset look on his face as he folded his arms and grunted. "Her mom and I both told her—both of them, actually—to schedule the C-section the week before. But no, try to do it the day after. Hope that nature doesn't take its course." His words were grouchy, but tears were leaking from his eyes and he was shaking.

"Why don't you go ahead to the hospital and find your wife?" Walter suggested. "By that time, Becky should be arriving soon and, I would imagine, going into emergency surgery."

Dr. Polski shifted on his feet, looking rather antsy, but ultimately relented. Walter took him down to the bedroom where the medics were talking to Becky.

"Becky? Sweetie? It's Dad."

"Hi, Dad," Becky said from somewhere in the midst of medics and machinery.

"Sweetie, I'm going to go ahead to the hospital and get Mom. We'll meet you there, okay?"

Becky agreed, and the doctor was off like a racehorse. Walter watched him go, then turned back to the medics. "Is there anything you need from me?"

"If you could just hold the cot steady so we can get her on, that would be golden," one of them replied.

He braced himself between the hallway wall and the cot, holding it steady while the medics picked up Becky, blanket and all, and placed her on the cot.

"Is Tommen on his way?" Becky asked.

"Yeah," Walter lied. "He's on his way. Everyone will be waiting for you at the hospital."

"Okay." She relaxed a little, and the medics took her away.

Come on, Tommen, answer your damn phone!

Nevertheless, Walter ran around looking for a few things

before grabbing his shoes and running out to his car. Damn it he wished he had his cruiser so he could run lights and sirens like the ambulance. At the same time, every cop in the county, including Charleston PD, had heard the call go out. They knew it was his house, and they knew what was going on. Let them try to pull him over and not commit career suicide. Walter would be on them so hard and so fast that whichever officer it was, whatever their rank, even if it was Casey Oldman himself, they would be busted down to bike patrol for the next decade.

He grabbed his phone and dialed Tommen again.

On the fourth ring, his son picked up.

"Hello?" he sounded totally oblivious.

"Don't you check your phone?" Walter asked, sounding more like a pissed off cop than a dad.

"Whoa, hold on. Chill out. Sorry, there was this trivia thing that we were doing and we weren't allowed—"

"Becky's in labor and she's in an ambulance heading for the hospital."

Dead silence.

"What?" Tommen's voice broke.

"Your fiancée is on her way to the hospital, which you should have been, too, when I called you five minutes ago. Now get your ass to the emergency room so you can meet your newborn daughter!"

Walter hung up and tossed his phone in the passenger seat. It wasn't that he was angry necessarily—it wasn't Tommen's fault that this was happening, though Becky would probably be blaming him for it, as all women did in labor—but he was afraid. If he wanted to be honest about it, he was truly afraid. For Becky, for the baby, for Tommen. He didn't want to see this hope of new life and a new family suddenly evaporate at the eleventh hour. He didn't want his son and daughter-in-law to experience the same pain he had in losing a child.

He wouldn't say he didn't Band and speed on his way to the hospital, but he felt it was justified.

He pulled into the hospital parking lot, immediately spotting the ambulance in its bay. It took forever for him to find a spot, or so it felt. Every time he tried to claim a spot, someone else got there just a few seconds sooner. Since when was the hospital so busy on a Thursday night? Was it a full moon? Was there some event he didn't know about? Was it just a crazy day for the medical field?

At long last, he found a parking spot. Then it was a long march into the building, the sidewalk stretching out long before him. Maybe it was just his perception, his adrenaline still running high.

"Evening, Walt," Dina greeted in the emergency room. "Not in uniform, so what brings you here? You all right?"

"Here for my daughter-in-law, just came in," he said, looking around absently.

"Daughter-in-law? This is new." Her expression said she wanted more details later, once it became convenient. "I think I know who you're talking about."

"Nineteen year old in labor?"

She nodded as she printed off a visitor tag for him. "Yup. Her dad's already here."

Walter took the tag and stuck it on his shirt. "Tommen should be here shortly, if you could get him through, too."

"I can direct him. She's heading to the maternity ward, if she's not there already."

"Thanks."

He was already walking away. It wasn't until after he walked down the hall and turned the corner that he realized he had no idea where he was going. He'd been in the emergency room more times than he cared to count, and he made rounds to a few other departments as needed, mostly for coworkers in for one reason or another. But never had he gone to the maternity ward. He'd never had a reason. He wasn't even sure where it was. Maybe he'd passed it from time to time, going from one place to another, but he couldn't quite remember just how to get there.

He paused at a map and studied it. The good news, the maternity ward wasn't far. It made sense; you didn't want to rush a mother in labor up six flights of stairs and through three different wards from the emergency room to the delivery room. Actually, the maternity ward was just around the corner and down the hall.

Taking a breath and reminding himself that he wasn't going to be permitted in the delivery room anyway, Walter forced himself to walk at a normal pace down the hall, turn the corner, and down another hall to the maternity ward.

The nurses here did not know him whatsoever, and they were very protective of their charges. He was interviewed when he first walked in, and he had to admit that he was impressed. Half of the nurses would make great interrogators; he was feeling the heat.

Eventually he got past them, though not without a brief thought that he was heading to jail or something. He shook off that feeling and proceeded down the hall to Room 2C, C standing for C-section.

The Polskis were already there, looking a mix of fear and joyful anticipation.

"Where's Tommen?" Mrs. Polski wondered. She was still in her scrubs and looked like she was having a long night; probably she was grateful for the reprieve.

"On his way," Walter answered. "His coworkers decided to take him out for a bachelor party."

Even as he said it, he also heard a, "I'm here, I'm here."

He turned to see Tommen making long strides toward him. He smelled like chicken wings but looked otherwise presentable, if harried.

"Is Becky all right? What happened?" he demanded.

Walter explained things as best he could.

"We haven't heard anything since," he finished. "I just got here."

Tommen looked at his in-laws who shook their heads. Nothing. He was obviously displeased with this knowledge vacuum.

Walter sat but his son did not. Tommen stood and paced without pacing, moving here and there and trying to make it seem nonchalant. A few minutes later, the door opened and a nurse walked out.

"Tommen?"

"Yes?" Tommen snapped to attention in such a way that it would make a drill sargent proud. "That's me. How's Becky?"

"We're ready to begin the procedure, if you would like to come in?"

Her tone said that this was not really a suggestion.

"Wait, like, you mean, watch the C-section?" Tommen wondered. Walter watched his son turn pale.

"Yes," the nurse said calmly. "We'll get you dressed up in a gown and everything, then you can stand by her side."

Tommen hesitated for only half a second before nodding. "Yeah. Okay."

"Great." The nurse stood to the side, holding the door open. "Come on in."

With that, Tommen followed the nurse into the room on stiff legs. Walter and the Polskis watched the door close and were left alone.

Chapter Twenty-Four
Maisy Helen Forbes

Tommen had eaten one full order of wings before the trivia game started. Phones were not allowed whatsoever, not even to call for help. His team was eliminated in the third round, and they returned to their table where he devoured another order of wings. He was well on his way to tasting every possible combination of wings and sauces when his phone rang.

"Is that your dad telling you which wings to bring him?" one of the guys joked.

Far from it. His initial reaction was to jump out of his chair and fly to the hospital, but his feet got tangled up in the mess of chairs that they had created and he ended up on the floor.

"Dude, what's wrong?" Will wondered.

"Becky's in an ambulance," Tommen said, getting back on his feet and grabbing his coat. "She's in labor and it doesn't sound good. I have to go."

He didn't give anyone an opportunity to respond as he bolted out the door and made for his car. Somewhere in the back of his mind, he wondered how Will was going to get home, seeing how Tommen had been his ride. Well, the rest of the guys had their phones, so Will could call his mom. With a brief whisper of an apology misting in the back of his mind, he pushed all that aside and started the engine.

They'd really been hoping that they could put everything off until tomorrow, but nature had to take its course, it seemed. Everyone advised against scheduling the C-section after the natural due date, even the doctor, but no. No, it had to be on a Friday, that way they could have the weekend off and whatever other bullshit excuses

547

they'd conjured up. Fucking hell, if something happened to them—not because of Julianna or the Borelians or any other hostile entity, but because of him—Tommen could never forgive himself.

Fear knotted itself in his gut as he Banded his way to the hospital. Now that they were well into March, the roads were not so treacherous, and he felt more comfortable with the gas pedal. Combining the two, he pulled into the hospital parking lot within five minutes of leaving the restaurant.

Unsure where to go, he elected to start at the emergency room.

"Oh, Tommen, your dad was just here," the receiving nurse said as he walked in.

Tommen had not been an unknown visitor to the ER when he was younger and getting in fights with Tyler Freeman, but it still spooked him that the nurses knew him so well. He suspected his dad had something to do with it, showing off his yearly school photo whenever he had to come by for official police business.

Before he had a chance to speak, she was handing him a visitor tag and saying, "She was taken to the maternity ward. Down the hall, make a left, follow the signs. Just tell them who you're looking for and that you're the dad."

"Yeah. Thanks."

He stuck the tag on his shirt and numbly followed her directions. This was actually happening. This was actually—literally—happening. The baby was coming and he was about to be a dad. He was going to go in there and meet his daughter for the first time. He was going to walk out of this hospital with a newborn infant.

He stopped. Shit. Did he have the carseat installed correctly? He'd put it in the car last week, and his dad said it was good. The cops did random carseat checks sometimes, so his dad ought to know, right? Still, how could he be sure? Maybe he could ask one of the nurses to check before they left.

He shook his head and kept going. Step one, the baby had to arrive. That was happening, but it sounded like far less than ideal circumstances.

Down the hall and to the left. Huge letters over enormous doors read "Maternity". Seemed like a logical place to start, Tommen figured.

Upon entry, it was almost like being arrested and taken in for interrogation as a nurse stopped him. Just out of sight down the hall, Tommen noticed a security guard standing by, trying to look casual about the whole thing.

"Can I help you?" the nurse wondered, words polite, tone and gaze anything but.

"Um, my girlfriend just came in on an ambulance," Tommen said. "She was in labor and there was bleeding and problems. The ER nurse said she'd been brought down here. Becky, er, Rebecca Polski."

The nurse gave him a hard stare, then ordered him to stay put while she tapped away at a keyboard and looked at her computer. Despite being momentarily annoyed by this delay, Tommen also felt oddly reassured at the level of security here. If anyone was going to try anything—and by "anyone" he was referring to Julianna or someone similar—they would be stopped and some sort of commotion would at least get his attention, alert him to mischief, before being surprised. Hopefully.

Finally she nodded. "All right. I will let the doctors know you're here."

She directed him down the hall to a smaller department, and from there to Room 2C. Room 2 out of five total that he saw, C standing for C-section. His dad and the Polskis were already there. Becky's mom was still in her scrubs. She and her husband were sitting, looking equal parts anxious and excited. His dad was standing, looking as though he'd just arrived.

Tommen heard his name mentioned, probably them wondering where he was.

"I'm here, I'm here," Tommen said, striding toward them purposefully. He hoped he looked as concerned as he felt, and not like he'd just come from a drunken bachelor party. There hadn't been any alcohol involved, but he wasn't sure he didn't look like it.

"Is Becky all right? What happened?" he demanded.

His dad explained things as best he could. She'd been sleeping, got up to use the bathroom, and then suddenly blood. Some women claimed their water broke, but she claimed her blood broke. So she went to him looking for help. He got her on his bed and called an ambulance.

"We haven't heard anything since," he finished. "I just got here."

Tommen looked at his in-laws who shook their heads. Nothing. How could they not know anything? Privacy concerns aside, this was her family. More to the point, her mom was a freaking nurse. Her dad also worked at the hospital. Couldn't they get anything out of the doctors, pull a few strings, call in favors? Why were they being left in the dark like this? Was something wrong? What was going on?

Walter sat down in one of the chairs across from the Polskis, but Tommen elected to remain standing. Aside from all the usual worry, he was also mentally kicking himself for letting stupid idealism get in the way of the health of his wife and unborn child. Had it really been that important for him to get the weekend off? Did he really think Chris wouldn't have given him an extra day off, or that Layman wouldn't have understood if he wanted to skip school? For fuck's sake, they were about to bolt halfway across the universe, school and work be damned. He rubbed his face. God, he was an idiot. He was a total fucking idiot.

Fear turned to dread in his gut. If anything happened to either of them, he could never forgive himself. Was this what his dad meant when he talked about not letting his own selfish ego get in the way of his family? Because it kind of felt like he'd let his own selfish ego get in the way of his family.

Tommen hardly noticed when the door to the room opened and a nurse poked her head out.

"Tommen?"

"Yes?" Tommen snapped to attention in such a way that it would make a drill sargent proud. "That's me. How's Becky?"

"We're ready to begin the procedure, if you would like to come in?"

Her tone said that this was not really a suggestion.

"Wait, like, you mean, watch the C-section?" Tommen wondered. He felt the blood drain from his face and his knees turn to jelly. He'd been anxious enough about the procedure in the first place, putting a knife that close to his daughter. Now they wanted him to watch? He didn't know if he could handle it.

"Yes," the nurse said calmly. "We'll get you dressed up in a gown and everything, then you can stand by her side."

It was the right thing to do, Tommen knew. He got Becky into this mess, in more ways than one, so he should be there to see how it all turned out. And if Julianna wanted to try something, he would be there to stand in the way. Still, he hesitated for only half a second before nodding. "Yeah. Okay."

"Great." The nurse stood to the side, holding the door open. "Come on in."

Heart thundering in his chest, Tommen walked toward the door, toward the nurse. This was really happening. This was the moment of truth. He was going to be a dad. He was going to meet his child for the first time. All those fuzzy pictures were about to become real. His stomach twisted and lurched as he entered the room and the heavy door closed behind him. With no other options now, he followed the nurse.

It wasn't actually the resting or recovery room that the nurse came out of, but another door leading to the operating room. The nurse took him to a side room with a large window. Becky was already there, though he could only just see her amid a waterfall of blue, doctors and nurses in their gowns and gloves and nets. Tommen was unprepared for the package of sterile items the nurse shoved in his hands. He hastily dressed in the gown, pulled on the gloves, and let the nurse help him with the hair and beard net. Was all of this really necessary? Still, he wasn't going to argue when it came to the safety of his newborn daughter.

Satisfied that he was squeaky clean, or at least modestly so, the nurse motioned for him to follow her, which he did obediently. He was parked at Becky's bedside.

The last time Tommen had been in any kind of surgery, it had been for his burned arm, and he had been unconscious. It was a little different being in the operating room and seeing what was going on. It was also surprising to see Becky awake and looking at him.

"You made it," she said, sounding a little drugged up.

"Yeah, I made it." He took her hand. "I am so sorry about this."

She drunkenly waved him off. "It was as much my fault as yours. But that's okay. Just means her birthday will be March 10th instead of March 11th."

He forced a small smile and nodded. "Yeah. Guess so."

Becky was naked under the bright surgical lights, only her chest covered by thin, blue, sterile sheets. Her belly was orange where the doctors had marked where they wanted to cut. Her legs looked like they had been cleaned up, though there were still blood smears on the inside of her thighs.

"Did they give you something?" Tommen asked, unsure exactly what that something was or would do.

Still, she nodded sleepily. "Yeah. It helped to stop the bleeding and the pain, and it made me sleepy."

He looked around, unsure what the doctors were waiting for. A minute later, familiar goop was smeared on her belly and a nurse laid down an ultrasound wand. After a second, fuzzy images appeared on a monitor. There was talking and pointing, and one of the doctors used a blue marker to indicate the exact position for the incision. Tommen felt his stomach do a backflip.

More talking and pointing. A nurse laid out a few more utensils on a tray. The ultrasound moved this way and that. Finally a doctor nodded. The wand was taken away and the goop wiped off.

"Okay, sweetie, we're going to begin," a nurse said on Becky's other side. "How are you feeling?"

Becky yawned hugely. "About like that."

"Good. You shouldn't feel a thing."

"Is it okay for her to be this...out of it?" Tommen wondered.

"She's at the low point of the drugs, which is what we want," the nurse told him. "It won't harm the baby, and when she comes back around, she won't remember a thing."

"How long does it take?"

"Not long, assuming everything goes well."

Before Tommen could ask what that meant, one of the doctors said, "Ready. And...here we go."

Tommen didn't know a lot about childbirth to begin with, except for a very awkward movie they had to watch in health class in middle school. All the same, that had been a natural birth. No one ever liked to talk about C-sections. It was like it was a cursed method of delivery, as if a baby delivered by C-section was less...born or something. Of course, C-sections were typically reserved for high-risk and emergency situations, and who wanted to watch a video of what could be a harrowing life-or-death experience?

For the second time that day, assuming the first time wasn't just carrying through, Tommen felt his knees turn to jelly as the doctor made the first incision. He didn't normally flinch at small cuts and wounds, but the delicate precision combined with the knowledge that his daughter was right there at the tip of the blade...

Becky wasn't exactly sleeping, but she was pretty out of it. The most reaction she gave to the scalpel slicing her flesh was an eyebrow twitch, like the one she sometimes got when inserting her insulin needle somewhere on her body. Other than that, it wasn't anything more significant than a mosquito bite as far as she was concerned.

Tommen deliberately looked away from the doctors as they worked, not desiring to see any part of the procedure. He was here to be moral support for Becky and to see his child when it was all over. He could do without the part in between. Did that make him a coward or a bad father? No. Because he was going to whisk them away to safety once everyone was in the clear.

Tommen had read about and heard on numerous occasions that it wasn't uncommon for surgeons to talk about their favorite restaurants or movies or music or anything at all during surgery. Surgery was an intense and sometimes scary thing for the patient and the patient's family, and they didn't want the surgeon to be thinking about anything but the life they held in their hands. For the surgeon, though, it was like having a pleasant conversation while putting together a thousand-piece jigsaw puzzle.

Still, it was hard to ignore the intensity of the situation. Considering the rather demure attitudes of the medical staff present, Tommen guessed that this was a little more mentally taxing than a jigsaw puzzle or a routine shoulder surgery.

Somehow, he had always envisioned a C-section as a little cut here, maybe a small slice there, peel back the skin, and voila! There's the baby! While fundamentally true, it was a little more intricate and delicate than that. There was a lot of blood and a few organs they had to watch out for, too.

"What's the matter?"

The question made Tommen look away from where he stared at Becky's drugged up expression and toward the surgeon. All eyes were on the surgeon, and his expression—what little could be seen amid the sterile blue coverings—was not reassuring.

"The baby's breached the uterus into the abdominal cavity," the surgeon said. "That's the cause of the bleed. We need to open her up more, get the baby out, and stop this bleed."

Suddenly, a scary but somewhat routine C-section turned into a real problem. Tommen tightened his grip on Becky's hand. She weakly responded in kind, but did not appear to have registered the situation. Was that from the drugs or the blood loss? He knew his heart rate skyrocketed at the doctor's words, and he was feeling some serious indigestion. Damn chicken wings anyway.

A hand on his arm broke his attention, and he looked to see a nurse gently pulling on him.

"What?" he questioned dumbly. "No. I'm not leaving her."

"I'm not asking," the nurse told him. Her words were firm, and he could see she was not happy about having to tell him to leave, but this had gone from a simple birth situation into something far worse.

He put up a little fight, just so they knew he wasn't happy, but followed the nurse back out of the operating room. He stripped off all the gowns and gloves and everything else.

"Can I at least watch?" he asked.

The nurse's look was pained as she answered, "I'm sorry, no. Go back out and wait with your family."

Tommen pointed at the window. "That is my family."

She said nothing more, just returned to the operating room. She lowered the blinds, totally obscuring Tommen's line of sight.

He could have Banded and gone in there. He could have done a lot of things. He toyed with the idea of trying to save Becky and the baby himself. But he didn't. He didn't trust himself. He didn't trust his skill or his emotional and mental stability. He didn't even know what he would need to do. And if he was a little squeamish just about the first incision, things probably wouldn't go so well once he actually looked inside her body.

He stood there for a long minute, batting it back and forth in his head, though he wasn't entirely sure what "it" was. He couldn't go in, didn't want to go out. He didn't want to have to explain to the others what was going on. He didn't know if he could. He didn't want to explain if he didn't know how it was going to turn out.

Had Julianna or one of her minions actually tried something? Was this their doing? Had they somehow pushed the baby into Becky's abdomen, tried to cause her to bleed out? Or had they just decided to sit back and wait for what was basically a natural consequence of her short stature and the already high-risk pregnancy?

After a few more agonizing seconds, he turned and went out the way he came in. It felt longer this time around, but maybe it was just him. Maybe he got lost. He did his best to navigate his way through and picked the door he thought was the right one.

Thankfully, he got the right one.

A couple of Becky's sisters had shown up, and now there were six people in the waiting room. They all looked at him expectantly. He ran a hand through his hair and sighed, which was evidently a cue for fear and panic.

"What's happening?" Mrs. Polski asked. "Is she all right? Is the baby okay?"

"Um...the baby broke out of the uterus into the abdomen," Tommen answered numbly. He looked at his dad. "That was the cause of the bleed. They think the baby is just fine, so now they're working on her."

It was a lie, and he wasn't sure where it had come from. Maybe it was something he just wanted to believe. He didn't know. Reactions from the rest of them were mixed. The baby was okay, which was good. She wasn't doing so well, which was far cry from good.

"Do they know how long it might be?" Nomi asked.

"They didn't say anything to me, just took me out." Tommen sat in a heap next to his dad.

Knowing all of this didn't make things any easier as they sat and waited. Everyone wanted it to be over, but no one wanted a quick visit from the doctor. Such a situation demanded time and attention, and a fast return would only mean bad news. Similarly, if it took too long, that meant things were bad for an extended period of time and the news could go either way. There was a delicate balance of what was going on and how long it ought to take to fix, in such a way that the news would be good. Maybe Tommen was just overthinking things.

Shortly after sitting down, he got up again to run to the bathroom, almost literally. The stress of the last couple hours had put his body into fight-or-flight mode, and his bowels were certainly taking flight. He would just blame the chicken wings.

When he returned to the waiting room, nothing had changed. He looked at his phone, found a few texts asking him if everything was all right, congratulating him on being a dad, and so on. He ignored these and leaned back in the seat.

"At least you only have to go through this once," his dad offered, his voice sounding loud and echoing in the large, silent room. When Tommen looked at him, he clarified meekly, "I don't think you'll be having more kids. Sorry to say, but I highly doubt it."

Tommen sighed. "Yeah. Probably not. Becky already said that if we did decide to have more, then we were adopting because she did not want to go through this again."

"All women say that," Mrs. Polski said gently. "I said it after every single one of my kids. Then the endorphines kick in and you forget all about the pain—at least for a while, long enough to say, 'Let's have another.' " She frowned. "But, in light of this, she may not be able to have more. In that case, adoption is always wonderful."

While optimistic with a slight hint of realism, there was also a shadow of fear on her face, one that worried whether her daughter would even be around to have more kids, period. Tommen would not deny that his thoughts strayed there from time to time, even as he told himself repeatedly not to go there. Stay optimistic. There was a time for cynicism and pessimism, but this wasn't it. He had to stay strong for Becky and the baby. He couldn't let himself slide into a depressive mood, not when this was supposed to be such a happy day.

Tommen had arrived at the hospital some time around six, he thought. He'd been kicked out of the operating room about six-thirty, maybe closer to seven. The door opened again about eight o'clock.

"Tommen?" the nurse asked. "Is he still here?"

"Why wouldn't I be?" Tommen wondered, yawning. He'd been relaxing, or trying to, anyway. He must have dozed off a little. Passed out, more like it.

"Would you like to come in?"

Her tone now was gentle but much more optimistic. Everyone in the waiting room caught on. So things had gone well. There was a silent, collective sigh of relief. Tommen agreed without question.

So it was back to the operating room. Actually, once the door closed, the nurse took him to a recovery room of sorts, stopping at an alcove just outside the door. He did not need to dress up in blue paper linens, though he was made to wash his hands and face before entering, just as a precaution.

"They're okay now?" he asked hopefully.

The nurse nodded. "They're okay."

She pushed open the door and Tommen slipped into the room. He hardly made it three steps before something small and pink was pressed into his hands. It was a baby. His baby. His daughter.

"Congratulations, Dad," a second nurse told him.

He stared at the thing in his hands. She was sound asleep, not bigger than a loaf of bread and fitting neatly in both his hands, wearing only a diaper and a little pink hat. Though he did notice a wheezing sound as she breathed.

"That's not uncommon for C-sections," the doctor told him when Tommen voiced his concerns. "Babies have fluid in their lungs while in the womb. Normally it gets squeezed out during birth. With C-sections, it has to be drained. She'll be all right in a day or two."

"And Becky?" He looked at where she was completely conked out in bed.

"She'll make a full recovery, though it will take several months. I'll be happy to go over everything with both of you once she wakes up. But, to that end, because she's out, we never got a name." The doctor indicated the baby in Tommen's hands. "What did you guys decide?"

For a second, Tommen completely drew a blank. What *did* they decide? They'd gotten plenty of suggestions. Common names, popular names, unusual names, older names, Biblical names, stupid names. Finally he said, "Maisy. Maisy Helen Forbes."

He spelled it out for them.

"Maisy Helen Forbes, it is," the nurse said, entering the information on a computer. "Lovely name."

"It's my mom's name," Tommen told her. "Well, Maisy was my mom. Helen is her mom."

Suddenly he felt Maisy being taken from him. His first instinct was to grab and pull away, fend off whoever was attacking, but he stopped himself at the last moment. The nurse took her to a small glass box at Becky's bedside and laid her inside on a soft blanket, sticking a couple monitors on her.

"We want to keep an eye on her," the doctor explained. "C-section is traumatic enough, but we want to make sure she didn't suffer any harm from breaking into the abdominal cavity."

"How long will they have to be here? When can we go home?" Tommen asked.

"I want Becky to stay here for a few days at least. She suffered the greater trauma, and I want to be sure that she can handle taking care of a baby while she's recovering."

It made sense, but it didn't make Tommen any happier. But at the very least, they were alive and on their way to a recovery and a happily ever after. That was all that mattered.

Tommen sighed in defeat. "How long before she wakes up?"

"Half an hour to an hour, I'd say. Would you like to go back out or wait here? I don't want everyone in the room until I can assess Becky's health once she wakes up."

"I'll stay here."

He spent the entire time staring at the baby in the box. His baby. His daughter. Maisy. She slept, tongue sticking out, still wheezing a little, fingers and toes curling. This was his. He still couldn't wrap his mind around it. This was his child. He'd helped create it.

Once upon a time, when Tommen was still struggling with the reality of being adopted, on top of the raging hormones of puberty, he had gone on a rant that if people were really so concerned about the welfare of children, especially those with huge families, then all natural procreation should cease until such time as every child on its way to an abortion clinic or already in the foster care system was adopted.

Now he understood. This was life he'd helped to create. This was mankind's act of creation, something so powerful that it was normally reserved for God Himself, coming down to touch humans. Now he got it.

The box was not a true NICU box, designed to protect premature and at-risk infants from all diseases and germs and provide growth and nutrition. This box was simply to keep her warm and safe while Becky slept, sort of like a crib, but with vital sensors in the blanket and the little sticky nodes on her chest and stomach. The top was open, so he was free to touch her.

For a long time, he didn't dare. She was so small, and he didn't want to disturb her sleep.

After a good ten minutes, he couldn't stand it anymore. He stood and put his hand in the box. He looked like a giant, he thought. He touched her whole hand with just one finger. Her little fingers brushed his but didn't quite grab. All the same, it was like a bomb went off in his chest, the way he wanted to hold her and defend her and show her the world, the whole universe.

It was about forty-five minutes after Tommen walked in the room that Becky stirred, and another twenty minutes before she was lucid enough to hold a decent conversation. As soon as she came to herself, she demanded to see her baby. A nurse disconnected the sticky nodes for a minute and handed Maisy to Becky.

If Becky could have melted into a puddle on the floor, Tommen was sure she would have. An expression he had never seen before crossed her face as she held the tiny bundle. As she relaxed, the nurse tried to take Maisy and put her back in the box. Despite the surgery and probably still under the influence of drugs, Becky nearly came off the bed and bit the nurse's head off.

"You're still recovering from major surgery," the nurse told her. "She'll be right here by your side at all times."

"If she can be right there, she can be right here," Becky hissed.

And that was where she stayed, at least until the doctor could be brought in to explain what had happened and what they had to do to fix it. Yes, Maisy looked fine, but they still wanted to monitor her vitals and keep an eye on her to ensure she was as in the clear as she looked. Becky was still skeptical, but she allowed her newborn to be taken from her and put back in the box.

"It'll be okay," Tommen said calmly. "She'll be right here, and it's an open box, so you can still touch her."

"Easy for you to say, O Tall One," Becky growled. "I'm sitting here like a child. When can I get up and moving?"

"In the morning," the doctor said. "I want you to stay in bed for now. Rest, relax, recover. No moving, no working, nothing. Just stay put."

"But what about the bathroom? I am not using a bed pan."

"Tonight you are."

The doctor left, ignoring her spitting words and arguments that she launched at his back. Tommen saw the doctor say something in hushed tones to the nurses. Probably letting them know that Becky was going to be a difficult patient and to keep a close eye on her. He smiled to himself, then quickly turned his attention elsewhere. He still couldn't take his eyes off their daughter. With Becky's outburst, Maisy had sleepily woken, blue eyes looking around dreamily at the big, wide world.

Only after that was the rest of the family permitted to come in and see the newest addition. There was much ogling and tons of pictures, and Tommen found himself across the room next to his dad.

"Maisy Helen," Walter stated.

Tommen blushed. "Yeah."

"I like it. I think your pa would be proud."

"Thanks, Dad."

"Did the doctor say when they can come home?"

"A few days. They're more worried about Becky than the baby at this point."

His dad nodded. "Understandable. But at least everything is turning out all right."

"Happily ever after," Tommen said, trying to put some authenticity behind his grin.

"Exactly. Happily ever after. The end."

Becky's sisters left first, giving her gentle hugs and big congratulations. Then her mom had to return to work, telling them that she was going to brag it up to all of her coworkers for the rest of the night.

Dr. Polski left next, citing his need for sleep and having to prepare for Sabbath.

"*Lehitra'ot*, Becky," he said, kissing his daughter on the forehead.

"*L'itra'ot, Abba*," she replied, sounding tired once again.

That left Walter as the only visitor left, and he made as if to leave, saying, "Well, kids, I work the night shift, so I could stay here all night. But I think you want to be left alone for a while."

"I'll text you in the morning," Tommen told him.

"Make it the afternoon. I'm going to stock up on my beauty sleep since I have a few extra days to do so."

Becky had a few things to say to that, but they were half-hearted and laced with sleep. Walter wished them well, congratulated them profoundly, and left. Tommen went to sit on the edge of the bed.

"This was not how I planned to spend my day," Becky said grumpily.

"Me either," Tommen agreed. "But look at it this way. It's all over now. Baby is born. We're a family."

She smiled. "Yeah. We're a family. Now I just have to bust out of here and we'll be golden. Riding off into the sunset on our happily ever after. Or closer to it, anyway, since we still have the wedding and all."

Tommen faltered. When did he want to bring up the escape? Not now, he decided. Instead he went with, "Maybe. But let's forget about the wedding for just a second and marvel at this moment here. Maisy is here. She's only a few hours old."

Maisy was back asleep. Tommen stared at her, still impressed, still unsure what to think or even do. What did he do with a baby now? She was just born, so she wasn't walking or talking or getting into mischief yet. What did he do with her? When he looked at Becky, he saw that she was studying the tiny monitor hanging from the box. She held her arms out.

"Bring her to me. Let me hold her."

"I don't think the wires are long enough," Tommen said, standing and studying them.

"Then disconnect them. Come on, it's not complicated. You saw the nurses do it."

"I don't want—"

"You won't hurt her. It's just while I can't hold her or do anything. It's just for a minute." When Tommen did not move, she added impatiently, "I want to hold my daughter before I go to sleep for the night, dammit!"

Her use of mild profanity was what got him to move, though he was still careful about disconnecting the sticky nodes. He half-expected a whole chorus of alarms to go off and a SWAT Team of nurses to come barging in, demanding to know what was going on and who was responsible. But none of that happened. The machine made a small blip, but Tommen noticed that Becky pushed a button on the box, probably to silence it—probably something she saw the nurse do, too.

Tommen did not give up Maisy right away; he wanted to hold her, too.

"I think she looks like me," he declared, finally handing her off to Becky who was getting antsy. "She has my eyes."

"But my nose," Becky said, though her tone wasn't one hundred percent...in it. She wasn't really engaged in the banter, and it wasn't because she was just a little sleepy.

The way she held Maisy and the expression on her face made Tommen glad there weren't sticky nodes on his body reading his vitals. No doubt it would have shown his heart heading straight for the moon and beyond. Still, he tried to remain optimistic, sprinkling in a little sarcasm. She was a new mom and she wanted her first baby to be absolutely perfect. Every teeny tiny thing that wasn't perfect was a catastrophe, until it wasn't.

"Tommen, something's not right," Becky stated.

"The doctor said that her breathing might be a little wheezy because of the fluid still draining," Tommen told her. "It's part of being a C-section delivery."

"No. Tommen, listen, something is wrong."

He took an even breath. "What am I listening to?"

She directed him to a spot on Maisy's chest. He could hear her tiny heart beating a hundred miles an hour. He could hear her breathing. It sounded wheezy, but also strange. Not that he knew what constituted normal or abnormal. He straightened and said, "Your mom's the nurse. I don't get it. What do you hear or not hear?"

"Now listen here," she ordered.

He put an ear down a little lower on Maisy's chest. After a second, he straightened again. "I don't hear anything."

"Exactly. This is where her lungs are supposed to be. But there is nothing there."

"Are you sure it's not because she's a newborn and her body isn't developed yet?"

"Her lungs may not be fully developed, but they should still be in the same place as an adult's. Furthermore, she doesn't have a strong, developed diaphragm which means she's a belly breather, and she should be using her stomach muscles instead. I should be hearing something, but I'm not. Tommen, I am telling you, something is wrong."

Carefully, she poked a finger in Maisy's mouth. She still slept with her tongue sticking out, which Tommen thought was adorable. Becky evidently did not find it quite as adorable, and she gently opened the baby's mouth and looked inside. After a second she murmured, "Macroglossia."

"Macro—what?"

"An enlarged tongue, the other reason she can't breathe."

"I thought babies already had huge tongues?"

"They do, but they're not occlusive." She held Maisy in one arm and rubbed her face with her free hand. "I knew I should have pushed harder."

"Harder for what? What's wrong?"

"That abnormality on chromosome 11. It's Beckwith-Wiedemann Syndrome." She rubbed her face again. "Oh my God." She blinked and shook her head. "We need a doctor in here now. Like, now. Before she suffocates."

"Is her tongue getting larger?" Tommen wondered, reaching for the help remote.

"No, but she's just not getting enough oxygen. That's why her stats are low. It's not just because of the fluids from the C-section. But because of this, those fluids can't drain, which means she's getting even less oxygen."

"Okay, okay, I'm calling."

A nurse was in the room within three minutes.

"She needs a doctor," Becky stated forcefully, sounding just like her old self, as if she hadn't had a harrowing experience just hours earlier. "She has Beckwith-Wiedemann Syndrome." Before the nurse could object, Becky went on, "She already tested positive for an abnormality on chromosome 11. Her tongue is abnormally large, and her organs aren't exactly where they should be. You can hear it in her lungs. They're squished! I don't know what you have to do, what tests or...I don't know. But she needs something before she suffocates."

The nurse still looked skeptical. She did not immediately run out looking for every doctor and the cavalry. Instead, she tried to calm Becky down. She took Maisy in her arms and did a little look and a little listen for herself. She used her stethoscope and listened all around Maisy's chest and abdomen. Tommen noticed that while she had started off with a certain amount of skepticism and pity, maybe even amusement, her expression changed as she did her little examination, growing more concerned, more worried.

After a long couple of minutes, the nurse handed Maisy back to Becky.

"Let me get a doctor in here to check her out," was all she said before she left the room.

"Wait," Tommen said, looking at Becky, "so, what's the treatment for Beckwith—whatever Syndrome. What do they do for it?"

Now Becky's expression twisted into something so agonizing that it made Tommen's heart stop.

"A lot of times, it's not fatal and it will sort itself out," Becky said, though she did not look heartened by the prospect. "But it still poses an increased risk for childhood cancers. A lot of it depends on the symptoms. Macroglossia can be fixed with surgery, but if her organs are enlarged, they'll crush each other."

"Isn't there anything that can be done?"

"It depends on what they find. I'm hoping it's just the tongue and this birthmark here on her neck and head. But she's so tiny. She's like me. There's only so much room in a body, and it doesn't always fit right."

The doctor came. His first test was a simple ultrasound to try and locate all of Maisy's organs and make sure they were where they were supposed to be. They were, and they weren't. Everything was generally in the right place, but as Becky had suspected, they were squishing each other, too large of organs fighting for too little of space. An MRI confirmed the same.

"So what do we do?" Tommen asked.

"Start praying, and start packing," the doctor told him. "I'm going to have her transferred over to NICU at the children's hospital."

"I'm not leaving her," Becky said. She was shaking even as she held Maisy close to her chest. "You can't keep me here and send her there."

"And I won't, I promise. You'll be going with her to their maternity ward. I don't know that they will have you in the same room, but you'll be in the same hospital and they'll let you see her more."

Becky was clearly unhappy with the idea, but she had to let

her baby go in order to let the doctors do their thing and try to save her.

Suddenly Tommen looked at Maisy like he might look at a ticking bomb. She was only just born. She was so tiny and innocent. Did her life really have an expiration date already? How was that fair? Just yesterday he was anxious about being a father and unsure just what he was going to do once she was born. Now he couldn't imagine life without her. Was their time together really going to be cut short before it ever got going?

Suddenly, all the things that he imagined would happen were called into question. First boyfriend and first break-up. First fight and first make-up. First bra and first time out with friends. First day of school and first friend. First tooth. First word. First steps. Would she even see her first birthday? Would she even be able to make the escape? This was only her first day of life itself and it was off to a rocky start.

"I'll let you stay here and hold her," the doctor said, addressing Becky. "Since she is in no immediate danger, I'll see if she can't ride with you in the ambulance, too. They'll get you transferred over to the children's hospital, and the doctors there will take over."

"What about me?" Tommen wondered. "Can I drive over there and meet them?"

"Yes, but have your ID ready. Security is pretty tight over there. I would wait five or ten minutes just to be sure. I'll fax the papers over there and include you on the permitted guest list, but it may not be an instant thing for you. Understand?"

Tommen nodded. "I get it."

The doctor left and an army of nurses took his place, getting things arranged just so in order to make the transfer as easy as possible on Becky and Maisy.

"Um, you should call your dad and let him know," Becky said, wiping her eyes and trying to stay strong. "After they take us out of here, go down and find my mom. Tell her what's going on. She'll probably call my dad, but let him know, too, just to be polite. That should be a good five or ten minutes, right? Then you can come over and see us."

"I wish I could go with you."

"Yeah, but then, how would you get home? Your car is here."

"I would walk back here if I had to."

"Sap."

"More than a sugar maple, I know."

She smiled, but tears rolled down her cheeks. She sniffed. "Tommen, I'm scared."

"I know." He gave her a gentle hug, mindful of her surgery and Maisy between them. "I am, too. But you know what?"

"What?" She wiped her nose on his shirt sleeve.

"She's a Forbes. And a Polski, too. And we Forbes and Polskis are nothing if not stubborn and determined, right? She'll pull through."

Becky smiled at that but swallowed nervously.

Then the nurses came and took Becky and Maisy away to an ambulance waiting down in the ER bay. Tommen stood there a moment longer before turning and going back out the same way he came in. First he would find her mom, then he would call his dad.

Mrs. Polski lit up when she saw him, but her expression faltered when he could not share her joy.

"What's wrong?" she asked.

Tommen could not explain the details because he did not understand them himself. He decided that she would figure it out if and when she got over to the children's hospital and could exchange medical-speak with the doctors. Instead, he just told her that something was wrong, and that Becky and Maisy were being transferred.

"Oh, goodness!" Mrs. Polski exclaimed. She dug out her phone. "I—I have to call Ioshua." She put it up to her ear. "I don't know that I could leave a second time tonight, but what are they going to do, fire me? Ha! I will retire first." Her determination was decidedly muted. "Ioshua?"

While she talked on the phone with her husband, Tommen went outside and called his dad. There were times when he was glad his dad worked third shift. It meant he would be awake to take late-night emergency phone calls.

"What's up, kiddo? Want out of fatherhood already?" he teased.

"There's something wrong with Maisy and she's being transferred over to the children's hospital," Tommen blurted.

Beat. Then, "What do you mean, something's wrong? What's wrong? Is it Julianna?"

"I don't know the details real well, but basically it comes down to, her organs are too big for her body. She's not getting enough oxygen and her lungs are crushing her heart."

"Is Becky staying there?"

"No, they're going together."

"Do you want me to come? I will if you want, but I also know security is tight there at the children's hospital."

"Not right now." Tommen shook his head though he knew his dad couldn't see. "No, they're going to want to do a bunch of tests and stuff first, so we won't know too much right away."

His dad made a small sound. "Tommen, I love Maisy, too. But I'm not asking if you want me there for her. I'm asking if you want me there for you."

That made Tommen stop for a second. Finally he answered, "No. Not right now. Maybe in the morning once I've slept it off. Who knows, maybe this is just a bad dream."

"We can only hope." Even over the phone, his dad didn't sound entirely convinced.

Tommen hung up and stood there for a minute. His whole body felt numb, rigid, like a statue. He didn't know how to process it. Too much had happened today and he could hardly take a minute to breathe and wrap his head around it. He'd just become a father and just as quickly been told that his newborn daughter could die. He didn't know how to think about that or what to do. He wanted to do something, and just standing around or sitting around wasn't part of that desire.

A couple years ago, Lily Guile had been the NICU director. He might have gone to her for help, asked, begged her to save his child in any way possible. But she was gone, and Harvesters were a snooty bunch when it came to helping others.

He called Nathan, praying the man was on Earth.

"Hello, Tommen," his therapist greeted. "If I'm right, your daughter should be here soon. Are you ready for the ensuing escape?"

"My daughter is going to die," Tommen said. "I need your help. Like, right now."

"Hold on a second. What are you talking about? Is this Julianna's doing?"

Once again, Tommen explained the situation, noting to himself that each telling got more and more condensed. He hadn't understood the medical terminology to begin with, and it was only becoming more confused in his mind with each passing minute. When he was done, Nathan was silent for a long moment.

"Come on, Nathan," Tommen begged. "You were volunteering as a midwife not long ago, and this is something way beyond my abilities, even if I weren't emotionally compromised. You can change your own DNA permanently in your Disguises; you can fix whatever genetic abnormality this is."

Nathan took an even breath and let it out slowly. "All right. At the very least, I will come and take a look. I make no promises."

"But you—"

"We'll talk more when I get there."

"Are you coming now?"

"I'll be there in the morning." He went on before Tommen could protest. "I want them to run their tests first and do what they need to do. I want to know what the tests say so I have an idea what I'm working with, where I might need to start tinkering. Can you understand that?"

Tommen sighed and rubbed his face. "Yes, I get it."

"Good. For right now, you need to stay calm and stay strong for both Becky and Maisy. Do you understand me? You need to be the rock."

"I understand."

"I'll see you in the morning, Tommen. I know it's going to be difficult, but I want you to try and get some sleep."

And he hung up.

Tommen stood there a minute longer, shaken, confused, and wailing internally about the unfairness of it all. But he had to be strong. He was of no use to Becky or Maisy if he was curled up in a mental fetal position. He had to do it for them. It didn't mean it was going to be easy.

Chapter Twenty-Five
Morning

It was a long drive from one hospital to the other, and it was an even longer wait to get in. Even once security had him verified, he was stopped and questioned at every department. Maybe that was too strong of a description. He wasn't tackled and dragged away to a small room to be interrogated, but he was stopped frequently by doctors, nurses, two janitors, and a security guard. When that wasn't happening, he noticed security guards everywhere, watching him. Was security that tight, or was he that suspicious? Maybe it was the beard. Had to be the beard. The only other option was that every person who stopped him was one of Julianna's agents keeping tabs on things, ready to attack and kill all of them if they tried anything.

He found Becky in the maternity ward, though she mentioned that they intended to move her to a NICU room with Maisy. She said only that when they arrived, a nurse came by to check their vitals and a doctor walked in with the reports faxed over from the general hospital. He did a few things, then took Maisy for testing. Tommen was welcome to come and watch and everything, but Becky was still set on bed rest. Her bed had sensors in it, too, so if she decided to get up or try anything, it would alert the nurses.

"Do you know where they took her?" Tommen asked.

Becky ran a hand through her hair. "Not specifically, no." She sighed. "I'm so tired, but I'm afraid to sleep."

"You should try to rest a little. I'll figure out where she is."

He kissed her, then got up to start searching.

In the general hospital, it was pretty easy to find people or things once you knew which department they were in. Having an entire hospital dedicated to children, well, that could be a different story. NICU was a huge department with a ton of specialized equipment, and it constituted easily one fourth of the entire hospital.

He found Maisy more by happenstance than intent, and it was on her way back from all the testing.

"How is she?" Tommen asked, falling in beside the nurse as she wheeled Maisy along in her glass box.

"The doctor will come by to give you the specific results, but she is doing better than she was," the nurse said gently.

Relief flooded Tommen and he felt a sliver of hope break into his chest. The nurse took Maisy to what seemed to be a semi-normal hospital room. Becky had been moved there already and was waiting anxiously. Apparently something must have shown on Tommen's face because she relaxed a tiny bit when she looked at him. Maybe things weren't as bad as they seemed. Mama's paranoia and education spotted a problem before it became a catastrophe, but that didn't mean it was the end of the world.

Tommen felt his gaze drawn to a nearby janitor who was watching them. They could only hope.

Maisy was given a tiny oxygen line and she still needed a few sticky nodes, but there was no reason she could not be held by her anxious parents. By now she was awake and looking around, making small, haphazard movements. Tommen had never felt more proud, nor more fearful of losing everything he loved.

Hopefully, it wouldn't be as bad as they thought.

Hopefully, Nathan would be able and willing to help out however he could.

Hopefully, she could be healed and they could escape tonight if they had to.

It was an hour before the doctor showed up to talk to them.

"You are a very perceptive young woman, Miss Polski," he said. "I commend you for it."

"So I was right, then," Becky stated. "It is Beckwith-Wiedemann."

"Yes. The tests from the general hospital as well as the genetic tests from your OB/GYN were faxed over, and it is confirmed Beckwith-Wiedemann. You probably know, then, that each case can present in slightly different ways. In this instance, the macroglossia, the enlarged tongue. It sounds like that was one of the things that alerted you to the possibility, as well as the difficulty breathing. The blotchy birthmark on the back of her neck and head is one minor indication. Her stomach, liver, lungs, and kidneys are enlarged, and they are essentially squishing the rest of her organs, including her heart. This also makes it difficult to know if there are any tumors, but we did not find any in the preliminary tests. Because of your stature and the nature of the delivery, a few things were pushed aside in favor of your lives, but it is known now that she is a large newborn. That may be what caused the uterine breach, just running out of room. That is another sign of Beckwith-Wiedemann, but as I said, between your stature and the situation at hand, the details were not attended to."

"She looks so tiny, though," Tommen said, looking at Maisy.

"You're six feet tall, everything looks tiny to you," Becky told him.

"She's not the biggest baby we've ever seen, but she is abnormally large," the doctor said calmly. "Significantly larger, when we consider proportions." He nodded to Becky again. "Again, details that got overlooked."

"So what do we do?" Tommen asked. "Where do we go from here?"

"The first thing that we can and must see to is her breathing. Her tongue is significantly restricting her airway. What we can do is minor surgery to remove some of the tissue and bring it down to normal size. It will restore her breathing and it should head off any difficulty eating or swallowing. I don't want to do anything until then, because if and when we have to do any abdominal surgery, she needs to be able to breathe."

"When do you want to do that?" Becky wondered.

"We can get started within two hours."

"That soon?"

"We gain nothing by waiting. Your daughter needs to breathe."

"How long will it take?" Tommen asked. "Are there any risks? What if we don't do it?"

"It'll take less than an hour. There are no special risks other than what I call standard risks associated with surgery. It's not unique to her, just—"

"If the anesthesiologist messes up," Tommen cut in, a little more sharply than intended.

"Yes. If you don't do it..." The doctor shifted in his chair. "Her tongue isn't swelling, it's not getting any larger. Which is good. She is physically breathing. Not doing it, she will continue to have breathing issues, she'll have trouble feeding, swallowing. She may need to be on oxygen." He shifted again. "In the best cases, Beckwith-Wiedemann resolves itself usually around puberty, just by nature of hormones and the transition into adulthood, the adult body. But childhood could and would be more difficult. I want to push for this surgery because of the enlarged organs. We won't be able to do major surgery well if she can't breathe, and that's not going to change in a month or a year or two years. With her lungs in the position they're in, they're already going to pose a challenge for intubation. Am I making sense?"

Tommen rubbed his face. "Too much of it, I think."

"I understand. It's all coming hard and fast, and she was born literally today. I wish there was an easy, one-step fix, but there isn't. It's a process. Step one is going to be fixing her breathing."

"Do it," Becky said, her voice strangled. "Do what you can to save our daughter."

Thus, things were set in motion. Becky continued to hold Maisy, but Tommen took the baby in his arms when Mama began to doze off. He was just as exhausted, but he told himself to stay up, stay alert. Don't fall asleep while on watch. An hour and twenty minutes later, he followed the doctors as far as he could to the operating room, reluctantly handing over his child. Not even one full day in the big, wide world and she was already under the knife. It terrified him.

They told him that there was a place where he could watch if he wanted. He wanted to be strong and oversee everything that went on, be on alert just in case. He also didn't want to get sick. He hadn't exactly handled Becky's operation with a calm stomach.

In the end, he accepted. He was taken to a little observation room—where he could observe the backs of the surgeons—and given a chair. Ten minutes in, he was out.

He jolted awake as someone shook his shoulder.

"Mr. Forbes?"

He straightened in the chair, yawned, rubbed his face and eyes, and slowly came around to see a nurse staring at him. A second later, the doctor walked in. The nurse stood and stepped to the side.

"The surgery was a success," he reported. "Everything went just as smooth as you could hope for."

Tommen relaxed so much, he half-expected to melt into a puddle on the floor.

"She's being taken back to the room, so she'll be with you and Becky. We ask that you please not pick her up or touch her face for a few hours, just so she can recover."

"Fair enough," Tommen said. "I think I'm going to be asleep for the next few hours anyway."

"We'll get something set up for you in the room," the nurse promised.

With another yawn, he stood, stretched, and returned to the room where Becky was asleep. Maisy was asleep in her box next to her bed. A cot with pillow and blanket was brought for Tommen. He laid it out, got comfortable, and fell asleep.

Tommen kind of hoped to dream about Chandler and talk to him about what was going on. Then again, he wasn't sure he wanted to. He didn't know what he himself would say. He could complain about the unfairness all he wanted, but it wouldn't change anything. Chandler couldn't do anything about it. Nor could the wise man tell him anything he didn't already know. Words of wisdom were great, but Tommen wanted results.

He woke up feeling alone and confused. As his mind came back to him, he saw that it was well into the morning hours, sunlight streaming in through the blinds. He also took stock of the room, now that he wasn't of a one-track mind.

One wall was painted bright yellow, but the rest were like scenes from children's picture books. Green hills with trees and flowers, stick people and amateur animals, clouds in the sky, and a bright yellow sun. Several common hospital instruments were decorated with stickers or covered in puppet characters. A toy chest sat in one corner, the lid closed.

Becky was awake and had Maisy in her arms, bouncing her a bit and making soft noises. When she saw Tommen watching her, she managed a small smile. He stretched, stood, stretched again, almost fell, and finally righted himself.

"How's she doing?" he asked.

Maisy looked up at him with large eyes.

"She's breathing better," Becky reported. "She was able to feed. Not a lot, but she did. The nurse came in and said everything was looking good."

"That's good, right?"

"It's a step in the right direction. But because she's breathing better and getting more air in her lungs, it's putting more pressure on her heart."

"Is that why she's all bundled up in a bunch of blankets?"

Becky nodded. "Her heart is working harder, but her temperature is still low."

But she was awake and active, and that was all that mattered. She cuddled up against Becky's chest and stayed there. When Tommen peeled back the blankets enough to touch her hand, she instinctively gripped his finger. Hope and fear warred for dominance in his mind.

"Did the doctor say what the next step would be?" he

wondered.

She shook her head. "Doctor's gone home for a while. Nurse said he left right after the surgery and should be back around noon or so. If something happens, there are obviously other doctors here, but for now, just keep her warm and comforted and let her know she's safe with us."

Tommen kissed the top of her head. "And how's Mama doing?"

Becky let out a breath. "I'm feeling it. I'm definitely feeling it. The pain meds wore off in the middle of the night and I admit I had to hit the magic button. Wouldn't you know, it only gives child doses."

"You normally get child doses for medicine, though, don't you?"

"Yeah, well, I was in adult-sized pain. Back off. But I'm okay now. Better than I was."

There was a knock on the door and a woman walked in with a tray. "Breakfast for Polski?"

"That's me," Becky said.

Tommen took Maisy while the food service worker got Becky's birthdate and handed over the tray of food. Mickey Mouse pancakes with strawberries, two tiny sausage links, a tiny cup of milk and a tiny cup of orange juice, both with long bendy straws. Being facetious, Becky twisted and twirled the straws and tied them up in knots together. Then she had to take a drink from each one to figure out which was which.

"The only thing up here is the kid's menu," Becky informed him when he gave her a look. "All the adult stuff is in the cafeteria downstairs, except I still can't go anywhere because of these stupid sensors. I tried to go to the bathroom last night and was almost assaulted by three nurses."

"When did this happen?" Tommen asked.

"About four-thirty or so. You were out. Like, totally out. I don't think you would have woken up for a nuclear bomb."

"I don't think so either, but for different reasons."

Despite his own hunger making itself known, neither of them wanted to let go of their infant daughter who was watching everything with huge eyes. So Tommen waited until Becky was finished with her breakfast before handing Maisy off to her and mentioning that he was going to get something to eat.

"Bring something back for me!" she told him.

"Chicken on a rotisserie, got it!" Tommen replied smartly.

The cafeteria in the children's hospital was something truly magnificent, clearly designed to be a haven or a retreat from the rest of the hospital. And the rest of the hospital was already designed to be welcoming and comforting and less scary than a regular hospital. This was a place of food solace, and it reminded Tommen of the Food Court in the Wheel.

He got a tray and looked around at the different sections, reminding himself that he still had to pay for all of this, so he couldn't just go grabbing everything as it looked good.

To his surprise, the cafeteria even served bacon. He couldn't think of any good reason why except for sheer comfort food. It was fatty, greasy, salty, and contributed virtually no nutritional value except maybe protein. Or was it fake bacon? Non-pork bacon that was supposed to be healthy? God forbid, could it be veggie bacon?

"Is this real bacon?" he asked a worker who came up to deliver a fresh tray of food to the warmer.

"As real as it gets," the worker replied. "Sizzly, crispy, crunchy, delicious bacon."

Tommen grabbed a portion. As he went to explore his entree options, leaning heavily toward the sausage gravy and biscuits, someone came up beside him. Looking, it was Nathan.

"I figured if you weren't upstairs, this is where you would be."

"Not sure how I feel about that," Tommen stated. "Am I that predictable?"

"Naturally. Most human beings are, and I'd say I know you pretty well." Nathan grabbed a banana and an apple, making Tommen feel like a bit of a slouch. He guiltily grabbed an orange.

Nathan went on, "So, how is she doing?"

"They did surgery on her tongue last night so it didn't block her airway. It worked out great and she's breathing a lot better, but her lungs are already enlarged, and the extra air is putting more pressure on her heart. Doctor also said her stomach, liver, and kidneys are enlarged."

Nathan grunted and frowned. "So it's not a mild Beckwith-Wiedemann."

"No. And the doctor said that because of the enlarged organs, it makes it more difficult to tell if there are any tumors in there, too, I guess."

The shrink nodded. "Beckwith-Wiedemann is a rather tumor-happy disease. Cancer-happy, too, if I remember right."

They paid for their meals and went to find a spot to eat. This time of morning appeared to be peak service time, and there were no truly private tables. This was no problem for the Akari-bearers as they sat and simply erected a Sound barrier around them. It was basically a manipulation of the air around them, thickening it in order to dissipate sound waves, preventing other people from hearing what they were saying.

"Sounds like you were up there already," Tommen said.

"Only looking for you," Nathan stated. "I didn't want to do anything without you present."

"Thank you. Do you know anything more about this, how to fight it, cure it, any of that?"

The shrink made an uncertain, hesitant sound. "It's not an easy, overnight fix. Okay, it's one thing to change eye color, hair color, whatever. That's easy. You can do it. It's manipulation on a very small scale. But this is more advanced than any common Akari-bearer. This falls in the level of Building for the simple fact that it is fundamentally transforming tissue." He shifted in his seat. "I don't think you realize just how complex the human body is, especially in its embryonic and fetal development, how many things have to go right at just the right time in order to make everything, well, right. Something going wrong at various stages of development results in missing or deformed limbs, physical and mental disabilities, it is all very astounding to think about.

"It's one thing to correct something that has simply gone wrong. For example, a baby whose hand grew out the side of its wrist instead of the end. Oops. It's a malformation. The correction is painful as hell, but it can be done, like stitching a new leg onto Micaiah's stump. At the root of it, it is tissue only.

"Beckwith-Wiedemann is a defect at a much deeper level. Every copy of her DNA that is made in every single cell of her body carries this defect, and it will continue to carry this defect. It can resolve itself when she hits puberty and her body gets big enough to accommodate larger organs, but that doesn't mean that it's not still present at the chromosomal level."

"What are you saying?" Tommen asked. "Can you do it or not?"

"What I'm saying is that is would be complex and time-consuming. Right now, her organs are enlarged. If I mess up, and if I'm working on, say, her kidneys, and something goes wrong, her kidneys shut down and she dies. Almost instantly. Or if something goes wrong with her lungs, she suffocates. I'm not saying I can't do it. I just want you to understand what could happen. I'm a psychologist, not a surgeon. I don't do miracle healings on a regular basis. I have never done this before."

"You've never healed someone with the Akari before?"

"Healing tissue is not the same as fundamentally altering someone's DNA. If you get stabbed, I could heal you, because I am simply manipulating the processes your body already has in place to heal itself, and working a little magic with the soft tissue. This is not that. This is on the same level as me permanently changing my DNA. And I will tell you that doing so is tedious and not a little painful. I will also tell you that I have only ever done it on myself and maybe a couple other people way back in Builder training when we were just learning about this stuff."

Tommen leaned back in his seat and rubbed his face. He took several deliberate breaths before returning to the conversation. "My daughter's lungs are crushing her heart. I can't afford not to do anything. She can't afford for me to not do anything. Is there anything you can do, even just small steps, something discreet, that would help? Just a little at a time to make her better? We'll call it a miracle surgery, a miracle drug, or a just plain miracle, I don't care. I just want my daughter to live. And live without fear that something bad is going to happen to her because of something out of everyone's control. But ours."

Nathan sighed and picked at his food for a minute. Finally he looked at Tommen. "I cannot and will not promise anything except that I will do my best."

"Thank you."

"To that end," the man went on, "I'm not just going to run up there and start poking around in your daughter's cells. As I said, I'm not a doctor. I know the basics, but this hospital, these doctors, this is their life. This is what they do. Do you understand? They know a thousand times more than I do."

"Okay. Fair enough."

"Did the doctor say what their next planned step was?"

Tommen shook his head. "Just to see how the tongue surgery went and how it improved her breathing. Doctor went home after the surgery, won't be back until this afternoon."

"All right. When the doctor comes back and he does his exam and whatever else he needs to do, once he has a planned course of action, let me know. Their plans will at least give me an idea of where it might be safest to start. Does that make sense?"

"Makes perfect sense."

"Good. I understand you're frustrated, but you'll be more than frustrated if I make things worse. I don't want to do that."

Tommen nodded. "I know. I'm sorry."

"Don't be sorry. You are doing exactly what you should be doing, which is looking out for your family. And to that end, I'm going to put you on security detail while I work."

"Julianna."

Nathan nodded. "More than a few Order agents snooping around. I'm guessing they're under orders to not attack directly, but that doesn't mean they can't still do damage. They will come for you eventually. When they do, I am going to advise you to simply grab Becky and Maisy and run. Rip open a portal to anywhere and run. I'll come get you later."

"I understand."

They finished their food and parted ways. As he left the cafeteria, Tommen noticed a few people watching him. Had they noticed the odd way in which he and Nathan had conversed but no sound came from their lips? How even their utensils made no sound? Would someone blog about it later, just another tiny clue that things were not always as they appeared? Was he just being paranoid?

He returned to the room, pleased to find that everything was exactly as it had been. It bothered him that nothing was getting done, but they had to do things carefully, not always quickly. They would have a plan by this afternoon.

Becky remained in bed, looking frustrated. Maisy was still in her arms.

"You okay?" Tommen ventured.

"I need to pee," she growled. "But I don't want to be tackled by a bunch of nurses, and I'm not using a urinal."

"They only tackle if you try to escape. Ask nicely and they might be more understanding."

She grumbled about it a little, then finally hit the help button. A nurse came in. Becky handed Maisy off to Tommen and went to the bathroom. While she was in there, Walter came in the room, poking his head in before walking in all the way.

"This place is a maze," he commented.

"Just one of their many security features," Tommen told him.

His dad took a minute to admire the little pink bundle. Maisy looked up at her new grandfather. Even as a baby, Tommen knew that expression. She didn't know what to make of this big man with the bushy mustache.

"How's she doing?" he asked.

"Tongue surgery last night or early this morning, whatever it was," Tommen sighed. "She's breathing better and she can feed now. But with all the extra air, her lungs are crushing her heart even more."

"What are they going to do for it?"

"We won't know until this afternoon."

His dad frowned, then shifted his stance, evidently trying to lighten up a little. "Well, she does look a lot better, not that I'm any expert in babies."

"Neither am I, but I feel like I'm going to become one here very quickly." Tommen shifted and lowered his voice. "I talked to Nathan earlier."

"About?"

"He's a Builder. He can fix Maisy's problem at the DNA level. Permanently."

"Does he know what he's doing?"

"Well...not precisely. He says he's willing to try, but he wants to know what the doctor wants to do first." He went on before his dad could interrupt. "Her lungs are crushing her heart, and it's not going to get better. If something doesn't get done..."

Emotion flooded him like a breaking dam and he bit off his words.

His dad frowned and sighed. "I'm hardly one to tell you not to use all the resources you have available; I just want you to be smart about it. Okay? These doctors have years of experience and know what they're doing. Let them do their work and try not to sabotage it. Make sense?"

"It does make sense, but I don't want to sit idly by."

"I don't want you to. I just want you to be smart about it. Okay? I'm on your side, kid."

Tommen sighed. "I know. And I appreciate it. I do. Really."

"It'll be okay. Just a nervous first few days."

Tommen could see his dad was having a hard time believing his own words. Still, it was nice to know the support was there.

The bathroom door opened and Becky emerged.

"You know what would be awesome right now?" she asked of no one and everyone. "A freaking pair of pants. And a shirt. I'm not the patient here, and I'm sick of this gown. They cut my clothes off in the ambulance, probably got rid of them. And these hospital underwear are embarrassing."

"Want me to run home and grab you a change of clothes?" Tommen asked as she crawled back into bed.

"Please. And take a shower while you're at it."

He was loathe to leave Maisy behind, at the mercy of all the agents milling about the hospital. But he really did need a shower. His dad agreed, and the two of them left the hospital together.

"Do you want me to tell the guys at the precinct about all this, or just leave it at the baby being born?" Walter wondered.

Tommen hesitated. As much as he wanted to keep it all to himself and suffer only with those who needed to know, he also knew that it wasn't the best route for any of them. And if this dragged on for any length of time, people would eventually find out. Then the questions would start coming.

"You can tell them," he said finally. "Just not the details."

His dad dipped his head. "Understood."

In a way, going home helped to ease Tommen's thoughts a little. Showering, changing into clean clothes, grabbing a small snack from the fridge, all of it very normal fare. He was still anxious, but getting out of the hospital managed to strain out the worst of his fear and anxiety. He could think a little more clearly, and, he told himself, would only make him more effective in a fight.

He grabbed some clothes for Becky, enough for a few more days at least. While he was at the dresser, he also grabbed a tiny outfit for Maisy, the one Becky had intended to dress her in and bring her home in for first pictures. It was red and white and trimmed with fur —from one of Tommen's exploits, no less—and looked simply adorable. It even had a matching hat and socks.

When he returned, Becky's parents had come to visit. Becky was pleased with the clothes he got for her and simply delighted that he had thought to bring Maisy's little outfit. Tommen had never seen her so happy as when she carefully put the little dress on her newborn daughter, being mindful of the oxygen line and sticky nodes.

With Maisy all dressed up in her little outfit, it was apparently picture time. They must have spent half an hour or more taking pictures, at least until the little baby, the star of the show, got fussy. Lunchtime, apparently. Becky and her mom stayed in the room to chitchat, and Tommen and his father-in-law went down to the cafeteria for lunch. Hadn't he just been here? He couldn't decide if the day was creeping by or going too fast.

"I never get tired of it," Dr. Polski said, grabbing a tray.

"Hospital food?" Tommen inquired cheekily.

"Meeting new family members, especially of the newborn kind."

"Yeah. She's...she's something. Small, adorable. Mine. Sh...oot."

The doctor raised a brow but said nothing. They went and sat at a table. The breakfast crowd had gone, but the lunch crowd was no smaller. In fact, it was easily bigger than the breakfast crowd.

Their time was spent mostly with Dr. Polski reminiscing about when Becky was born and the challenges they faced with a special needs child. However headstrong Becky may be or however determined and stubborn she was, she did still have needs and medical issues that had to be addressed.

They returned to the room, no sooner sitting down than the doctor walked in.

"Good afternoon," the man greeted.

Now that things weren't so crazy, Tommen took a better look at the doctor. Dr. Coleman, Travis L. his nametag read. A fraction of an inch taller than Tommen with hair so luscious he could star in shampoo commercials. He wasn't especially strong-looking, a bit soft, but he'd been nothing but helpful and knowledgeable so far.

"And how is our tiny patient today?" he asked, sitting down at Becky's bedside where she still held Maisy who was now dozing. Tommen noted that the doctor looked like he hadn't gotten much sleep.

"She slept good," Becky said. "And she's feeding. She's breathing better and everything seems a lot better."

"Good. All good signs. If I may?"

He gently took Maisy in enormous hands and examined her, commenting on how adorable the little dress was. He peeked in her mouth and noted that things looked good after the surgery.

"So what's next?" Tommen asked. "I mean, her lungs are still crushing her heart, aren't they?"

"They are," the doctor confirmed, returning Maisy to Becky. "So, what we need to do now is figure out how we want to go about managing the enlarged organs. We're looking at lungs, liver, stomach, and kidneys. We have a couple options. The liver we can do just like the tongue. Humans can survive with only half or even a third of their liver. Obviously, we just want to take enough to bring it down to a normal size. The stomach would be similar to bariatric surgery, removing a part of the stomach wall and stapling it back together. There isn't a lot we can do to make the kidneys smaller, but we can remove one of them and let the second one take up the space of both. The hope would be that, in doing all of that, it would create enough room for her lungs to expand and take the pressure off her heart."

"Anti-inflammatories can't do anything?" Mrs. Polski wondered.

"There is no inflammation here," the doctor explained. "These are just large organs. She has organs like what you might see in a six month old or a one year old. They're normal, functioning organs, just too big for her body."

"So, you say they're the correct size for a six month old," Dr. Polski began, "would she not survive until six months and let things progress from there?"

"Her organs will continue to grow at a normal rate. There would always be pressure. By the time she turned one, she would have organs like a two year old. When she turns five, it would be like a six year old at least. This would not resolve itself until puberty, when she starts to grow into her adult body with adult organs. Problem is, I don't believe her heart would last that long under such intense pressure. Already it's working harder than it should. Her blood pressure was sky high as you just saw, and she's not doing anything. Once she starts moving, running around, it could put her into cardiac arrest before the age of two."

"What do you recommend?" Tommen asked. "And if you do remove parts of her organs, will they grow back later and still be enlarged?"

"As she grows, her organs will continue to grow, as one would expect. As for the tissue, essentially, regenerating, that would not be a concern until later in childhood, assuming there even is a problem, as I said again, before puberty. We're looking at right now, what do we need to do before she is one month old? Because I want to be as unintrusive as possible, I would want to do this in small increments. Start with removing a kidney. They are both enlarged, but we take one, the other can survive in its full functioning capacity. It might create enough room for her stomach or liver that we don't need to touch one or either of them, and it could provide more space for her lungs, thereby decreasing the pressure on her heart. I'm trying to minimize the invasiveness of the procedures."

"And we appreciate it," Mrs. Polski told him.

"There is no other way to treat the kidneys?" Tommen wondered. "I mean, I know you can survive with only one, but if something happens, and she's only got one to begin with..." He rubbed his eyes. "I know, I know. We need to make sure she can get to that point. Only looking one month ahead."

"It's hard. I know. No one wants to make these decisions. No one wants to say, 'Go ahead and take organs out of my newborn.'

Believe me, I get it. But this is what we're looking at."

Tommen wanted to tell the doctor to give them a minute to talk about it, think things over. Problem was, there really wasn't anything to think over. This was happening. Here, now, this was what they were faced with. They couldn't put it off for a month or a year. Maisy might not have that long. She couldn't afford for them to hesitate.

"Okay. One step at a time."

"One step at a time," Coleman confirmed. "If things go as well with the kidney as they did with her tongue, we may not need to do anything more. If you're praying people, I would suggest you start praying, if you haven't been already."

"She's a Catholic Jew," Tommen said, grinning and elbowing Becky gently. "She's got it covered."

The doctor commented that he wasn't sure what to make of the statement, but okay, whatever they wanted to do, however they wanted to do it. He was going to go and see when they could get Maisy in.

"I hate this," Becky said once the doctor was gone. "It feels like a high-pressure door-to-door salesman sort of thing. But I don't know what else to suggest."

"Neither do I, sweetie," her mom sighed. "And believe me, I wish I did."

It was an hour before the doctor returned to report that the surgery would not be until the following morning. When asked what they could or should do until then, he simply replied that they should keep her warm and comforted and keep an eye on her condition.

And that was that.

Becky sighed. "She should be at home in her crib."

"She will be," her dad told her. "It might just be a few more days."

"As much as I don't want them doing surgery on her, or touching her at all, I also don't like all this waiting."

The waiting was not as boring as they thought it might be, as nurses came and went frequently. The visits varied from simple welfare checks to drawing blood for tests. Maisy tolerated the fussing and being shifted from person to person, but she was no fan of the needles. Tommen didn't blame her. He didn't like the nurses sticking her either. At the same time, it was a pretty good indication that she was breathing well.

Becky's parents left shortly before dinnertime. After they were gone, she called down to order a meal, and Tommen again visited the cafeteria. Sitting there at the table, alone this time, he texted his dad to let him know what was going on.

"So they're hoping that this will minimize the amount they have to take from her stomach and liver?" his dad asked.

"That's the idea," Tommen sighed. "I don't know. It feels like there should be something more they can do. Something, anything. Something that isn't invasive and doesn't involve removing bits and pieces from my daughter's body."

"I hear you. Unfortunately, this is kind of the way things are right now."

"Yeah."

"I assume you're staying the night again?"

"Yeah."

"Are you going to come home for a shower tomorrow, or do you want me to run you a bag of clothes up there?"

"I'm planning on being home tomorrow for a shower and everything again. I don't know, it just helps me feel a little normal."

"I understand. I'm not going to stop you. You do what you need to do. I'll be by before I go to work tomorrow, okay? Take care of yourself, kiddo."

"Yeah. Thanks."

He set his phone down, picked at his mashed potatoes and gravy a little, then grabbed his phone again to call Nathan.

"What's the news?" the shrink inquired.

Tommen brought him up to speed on things, finishing with, "Is there anything you can do to...equal it, make it so they don't have to do it? Can you just shrink her kidneys?"

On the other end, Nathan sighed. "I don't know. But, now that they have a plan, an idea how to deal with it, I'm more willing to take a look, a general Feel."

"You're going to have to do it now. Surgery's in the morning."

"Fair enough. I assume you're in the cafeteria?"

"You know me too well."

"All right. Obviously we can't explain this to Becky. I'll meet you in the cafeteria. We'll Band, go up to the room, I'll do my thing, and then we'll return. Sound good?"

"Sounds like a plan."

Tommen hung up. Not two minutes later, he spotted Nathan walking toward him from across the room. The shrink sat down across from him.

"How did I know you were going to do that?" Tommen said, trying to sound amused but unable to conjure up the appropriate amount of humor.

"I thought you would be surprised I wasn't here faster," Nathan told him. "Shall we go up now and you can finish your meal later?"

Tommen nodded.

Nathan Banded, bringing all activity in the cafeteria, indeed the whole hospital, the whole world, to a halt. Together they made it back up to the room—having to take the stairs since the elevator was out of the question—and crossed the floor to the bed.

Becky was in the middle of her dinner as well, tomato soup and a grilled cheese sandwich, a fruit cup, and a chocolate dessert, all of it child-sized. Apparently someone hadn't gotten the memo that it was mom eating the food instead of the child. Tommen still found this mildly amusing, and he smiled to himself.

Maisy was back in her glass box, awake, looking around. Because the box could be climate controlled, she did not need a bundle of blankets and lay there in her little red, white, and furry dress.

"As cute as she is, I think she looks more like you," Nathan said.

"Thank—what's that supposed to mean?"

The shrink laughed. "I'm kidding. She's adorable. Before I do anything, I want you to touch her and Feel her first. I want you to know as much as I do about this, and you are going to help me as much as possible."

"Help you?"

"Feel her."

It was non-invasive and virtually painless, but Tommen still felt awful about doing it. All he did was touch his daughter and Feel her. It started out just by feeling her skin. Pink, warm, dry, unbelievably soft, with the finest, tiniest hairs. Then he pushed that Feeling deeper, following the hairs to the follicles, to the lower layers of the skin. From there to the muscles, the bones. Deeper now, but going microscopic, feeling the individual muscle fibers, the pores of the bones. He could have gone all the way to her very DNA, but he refrained, instead skimming through her mid-level, looking around and Feeling all of her organs.

He was no expert at biology, and he had only a basic high school understanding of anatomy, but even he knew something was wrong. Organs were supposed to be nice and snug so they didn't slosh around haphazardly, but these accommodations were positively squished. There was no room for any kind of movement, even for organs to carry out their normal processes. Her stomach was toiling away just to digest what little milk she'd gotten, and it moved slowly through her body. Her kidneys were filtering toxins as they should, but it was too big of a filter for too small of a supply.

He Felt her lungs. Now open and able to breathe, they demanded more air, but there was nowhere for them to go. They pressed against her ribs and constricted her heart. Feeling her liver, normally an exceptionally bloody organ, he found it lacking. Not dry, but it was nowhere near where it should have been.

Frightened, Tommen ceased Feeling his daughter and pulled his hand away as though he'd touched a live wire. He stumbled back a step and looked at Nathan, certain his eyes were as big as dinner plates.

The shrink said nothing, though his expression darkened. He turned his attention toward Maisy and touched her, Felt her. There was nothing particularly exciting about watching someone else Feel; about all it amounted to was just a creepy stranger touching his daughter. Tommen watched Nathan expectantly, looking for thoughtfulness, something to indicate he had a plan; relaxation, something to show that it wasn't as bad as Tommen feared. But Nathan's expression remained stoic and resolute, a man intent on his work, getting a feel for his next project before doing anything.

It was a long couple of minutes, and Tommen found himself starting to pace when Nathan took a calm step back.

"What do you think?" Tommen demanded.

"I think your best course of action is going to be to remove one of her kidneys," he stated. "The kidneys are so big that they're stealing fluids she can't afford to lose. She's becoming dehydrated. It's causing problems in her liver which is causing problems in her stomach so that even though she's eating, she's not getting any nutrition from it. That's not even taking into account her heart and lungs."

"But what about the DNA and —?"

"Tommen, in the time it would take for me to make all of those changes — doing it slowly over a period of days or, more likely, weeks — she would die. She is starving and dehydrating now, as we speak. She needs to lose that kidney so her body can be restored to a functioning balance. That's not even considering her other enlarged organs. This is a problem unto itself."

"Is there nothing you can do? I can Band you for the hours or days you need. Can't you just shrink the organs, remove some of the Matter —"

Nathan shook his head. "Pretending that this isn't a genetic thing, that's just an oops malformation, it is still removing tissue from the body. Once that tissue is removed, it becomes waste. Kidneys filter out the waste. The amount of tissue that would have to come off would overload her kidneys and kill her. Doing it slowly isn't an option.

"But you're a Builder," Tommen pleaded. "You worked with, manipulated the Core of the Wheel, the very nexus of Creation itself! And you're telling me there's nothing you can do?"

"That is exactly what I'm saying. I'm only a Builder, Tommen. I'm not the Author. Your best bet right now is to go forward with the surgery and have one of her kidneys removed. It will slow down or even cease the dehydration. Next is going to be the liver. The liver produces bile. Produce too much bile, break down the food too much too soon, and she doesn't get any nutrition. Do you understand what I'm saying?"

"Yeah. You're saying you're fucking useless."

"I choose not to be offended by your words."

"I choose a lot of things, but I don't always get what I want."

"Tommen," Nathan said. "Take a breath. Calm down. You want solutions. You have one. You want a magic fix. I can't provide that, not in any sense of the word 'safe.'"

"My daughter is at risk of dying. How safe do you think you need to be?" Tommen could feel hot tears rolling down his cheeks and he hated himself for it.

"Tommen, listen to me. Sometimes the answers to your prayers don't come from where you want them to. Sometimes you have to accept help from people you don't know, don't like, or don't trust. I am not the answer you're looking for. Maybe you think this plain old Earthling medicine is subpar and not worth your time and attention, but it may also be your best chance at saving your daughter's life. I wish that I could help, but I can't. Not today. You hate me for it; I can see it on your face. But it's the truth."

"But why?"

"Quite frankly, I don't know. Because. But right now, you need to calm down and take things one step at a time. Face them how they are. This is real life."

"Real life sucks."

"Yes, it does. Now what are you going to do about it?"

Tommen took a breath and wiped his eyes. He put his hands on his hips and looked anywhere but at the man who had just refused to help him, help his daughter. After a long moment, he nodded, still not looking at Nathan.

"Okay," he said. "Okay, fine. We'll just keep going like we have been."

"I'm sorry, Tommen. I am. If you want to talk or need other support, I'm here. But I'm not the doctor you need."

With that, he left. After another long minute, Tommen also left the room, just barely remembering that he had to get back to the cafeteria before dropping the Band. The walk gave him a chance to compose himself and collect his head. The world wasn't ending. They still had a plan. It was just a matter of his Plan B wasn't panning out. But Plan A was still very much an option.

He sat down at the table, Nathan across from him.

"You okay?" Nathan asked.

"No, I'm not okay," Tommen growled. "But sitting here in a Band isn't going to help things."

Nathan took everything in stride, but Tommen had a little harder time maintaining a bit of pleasant small talk to fool the people around them. It only lasted a minute before Nathan excused himself and wished him well.

When he was gone, Tommen stared at the food still on his tray. It was cold by now. Appetite lost, he tossed the remains and started back through the halls, unsure if he wanted to return to the room yet. Problem was, wandering around was decidedly frowned upon by hospital security, and he was forced to go back to the room earlier than he would have preferred.

Becky had finished her dinner, but Maisy remained in her box.

"Tired of being a mom already?" Tommen asked, trying to smile as he sat in the chair. He looked at Maisy, unable to forget what he'd Felt, and terrified of it.

"My arms were getting tired," Becky said. She studied him.

"Everything okay?"

"Yeah." He rubbed his face. "Just stressed."

"Well, kittens and puppies are good for stress relief. But in lieu of those, newborn daughters work pretty well, too."

"I think she's had enough of being held for a while."

"Are you the baby whisperer now?"

"I could be."

"I doubt it."

"Yeah, me too."

They turned on the TV instead. Most of the channels were cartoons, but they agreed that it might be a good idea to catch up on the new cartoons and see what their daughter would be exposed to in the future. Their laughter was nervous.

Tommen held Maisy for a little while in the later evening before claiming fatigue. His body was tired and his eyes hurt, but his mind was still very active. He slept with his back to Becky so she wouldn't see that he was still awake, staring at the wall.

Was there anything more he could do? Or did he have to rely on all of this...Earth medicine? Was the Akari really useless in this instance? Could he do nothing for his daughter? What was the point of having the power of manipulating Creation if you couldn't even save your own daughter's life? It hurt him in a way he could not even begin to describe.

Fine. If the Author wasn't going to help him, maybe he'd ask God. Becky was a Catholic Jew, so she had pretty good standing before the Almighty, but if God wanted to hear a skeptic's prayer more—as one preacher had once said—well, He'd get one.

Tommen didn't actually remember if or what he prayed because he fell asleep. The only reason he knew he fell asleep was because he was suddenly jolted awake by an alarm. Clawing his way back to consciousness, he couldn't remember what he was getting up for, why he needed an alarm. Then it occurred to him that this wasn't a wake-up-and-go alarm, it was a something-isn't-right alarm. It was one of the alarms on Maisy's glass box.

Three nurses were in the room before Tommen could get to his feet. Becky was just reaching for her glasses.

"What is it?" he demanded. "What's going on?"

"Febrile seizures," one of the nurses said. "She's running a temp of a hundred and five."

"Why?" Becky asked.

"That's what we're trying to figure out."

Tommen couldn't say what all they did, but he noticed that they did adjust the climate settings of the box, and they removed the little dress and matching hat, effectively stripping her down to diaper only. It helped some, enough to stop the seizures, but she was still over a hundred. Tommen glimpsed Becky on the other side, watching with wide eyes, chewing nervously on her fist.

"She's dehydrated," one of the nurses said finally. "We need to get a line in and start some fluids."

"Wh-why is she dehydrated?" Becky asked. "She's been feeding."

"It's her kidneys," Tommen told her. "They're too large, so they're taking out more fluids than she's taking in."

The nurses got a line in Maisy's arm and started a fluid bolus. Her temperature remained high and she appeared lethargic, far cry from the fussing earlier when they tried to draw blood. Tommen moved around so he could sit behind Becky, nervously rubbing her neck and shoulders.

Maisy gradually came back to life, though her temperature hovered around a hundred degrees. She clearly did not like the needle in her arm, but there was nothing anyone could do about it; she needed the fluids.

"God, I'm such a bad mom," Becky whimpered, burying her face in her hands.

"You're not a bad mom," Tommen told her. "We don't know what's going to happen, but it's out of our control anyway."

He meant what he said, even if he couldn't believe it himself. Not that she wasn't a bad mom, because he knew she wasn't, but he had a hard time accepting that all of this was beyond his control. There had to be something that someone could do, beyond this weak medicine. He just could not accept Nathan's words.

"So she really does need to have one kidney removed," Becky stated as the nurses relaxed a little.

"Yeah," Tommen sighed. "But maybe it will create enough room in her body for everything else, so she doesn't need more operations."

Another statement he had a hard time believing. He could see she was just as skeptical.

Two of the three nurses departed. The third remained, typing something on the computer near the door.

"If she was dehydrated, does that mean she could be starving, too?" Becky wondered.

"We'll let the doctor make that determination," the nurse said evasively. "And we'll see how things turn out after the surgery."

Sounded like a lot of bullshit and nonanswers to Tommen, a clever way of saying, "We don't know, and we don't know how this is going to turn out." He didn't appreciate either the lack of confidence or the lack of concrete information.

Then the nurse left, and again it was just Tommen, Becky, and Maisy still in her box, still in only a diaper.

"I want to hold her," Becky said, staring at their daughter. "But I don't want her to get too warm." She wiped her eyes. "I don't get it. What do we do?"

Tommen sighed. Pray? Cry? Panic? Go back to sleep? "We wait." He glanced at the clock. "It's two in the morning. Surgery is scheduled for seven. Go back to sleep for a few more hours and..." He let out a breath. " — see how it all turns out. Hope things get better."

"But what if they don't?"

"Then we see what the doctors have to say. I don't know. I don't know what to do. I wish I could just snap my fingers and make it better, but I can't."

After another long minute, Becky took her glasses off and

settled back into the bed. Tommen reluctantly returned to the cot. He wanted to sleep. He wanted to cure his daughter, take away all her problems before morning so that it looked as though a miracle had happened. He ran through his mind everything he knew about the Akari, primarily Matter and Energy. What did he know and how could he apply it here? Could he come up with something Nathan had overlooked? Experience was great, but it could also be an excellent set of blinders. Maybe fresh eyes and a new perspective could come up with something. Necessity was the mother of invention, after all.

Enlarged organs needed to be made smaller. On the flipside, infant body needed to be made bigger. Was it possible to age specific parts of her, so she could grow into her organs? If everything became proportional, then it wouldn't matter anymore that they'd been a little big at birth.

He didn't know if it was possible, or that it would work, and he had little desire to experiment willy-nilly on his own daughter. She was unstable as it was, and he didn't need to make it worse.

Maybe he could decrease the organs' size just a little bit at a time, shave it off instead of cutting off chunks, that way her kidneys could process it better. Make the change gradual.

He didn't know what he was going to do, but if things didn't start getting better, he was liable to try anything.

Chapter Twenty-Six
Noon

Tommen woke, feeling as though he hadn't slept at all. Becky was the one to wake him up as she was on her way to the bathroom. She moved stiffly, but she was getting around better.

It was Saturday now, two days after the birth. His daughter was two days old and all she had known was hospitals. She was supposed to be home by now, sleeping in the crib in their closet, waking up crying because she was hungry, not because she was too hot and having a seizure.

Nothing more had happened since then. Maisy remained safely in her glass box, still in only a diaper, still feverish. Fluids dripped slowly into the line in her arm. Dehydrated because her kidneys were working too well. Her heart was working harder as it was, being compressed by her lungs, but the thickening of the blood meant it couldn't move as well throughout her body. The heart worked harder and beat faster to compensate which raised her temperature. Or that was how Tommen understood it. There was probably a lot more to it, but he wasn't sure about anything anymore. He just wanted this nightmare to be over.

Six in the morning. Nurses had been coming and going for prep work before taking Maisy to surgery, Becky said. If he wanted to go with them down to the operating room, he should probably be up and around.

"They're still not letting you out of their sight, hm?" he asked, trying to sound slightly less than utterly depressed.

"Not until tonight they told me," she replied. "Or maybe tomorrow morning, depending on how well I behave."

"How long have you been up?"

"I only got another hour or so of sleep after what happened earlier. I've just been awake since then. Watching her. Making sure she's okay. Making sure she knows I'm here."

He nodded and kissed her, then wandered off to the bathroom. He hadn't done much the last couple days, but he felt as though he'd worked on the job site nonstop, dirty and sweaty and disgusting. He wanted a shower. Even if he could have taken one right then and there, he probably wouldn't have been ready in time to go with them to the surgery, and he wanted that more than a measly shower. So he did the best he could to freshen up and prepare himself, somewhat, for what lay ahead.

The surgery was scheduled for seven o'clock. The surgeon came in at six-thirty to talk to them, explain what they were going to do, and answer any questions.

Basically it came down to a simple removal of the right kidney and its ureter. The left kidney would remain where it was, no need to mess with it in any way that they saw at this time.

"Why the right kidney?" Tommen wondered.

"It's for the liver, right?" Becky said.

The surgeon nodded. "We want to create more room on the right side for the liver. The more room we create, the less we have to remove."

Tommen shifted in his seat. "How long will it take? What's the recovery time?"

"It's a simple procedure in itself, but we will have to take a little extra time at the end to try and coax the liver into its new resting spot and see how everything is going to fit. She'll be in recovery before ten o'clock. If all goes well, then you should be able to breathe a sigh of relief. Moving the liver down, away from the diaphragm, and allowing the lungs to come down to a more normal resting position, taking pressure off her heart, it will buy enough time to look at things from a little less than an immediate, life-and-death standpoint."

Sounded pretty good to Tommen, and he could see that Becky

desperately wanted to cling to the hope the surgeon was trying to give them. Maisy was living day-by-day right now, even hour-by-hour. This surgery might give them some breathing room for a couple days, a couple weeks even. They had to hope.

Maisy was taken out of the room in her glass box. Tommen followed the surgeons and nurses as far as he could to the operating room before being diverted around to the observation area. There was very little to see beyond the backs of the surgeons, and he could not hear anything they were saying. There was a button in there and a small speaker in the observation room if needed, but they didn't want to talk to Tommen.

Once again, he found himself wondering if they were discussing restaurants or a new movie or something else trivial, something that had little or no bearing on the surgery they were performing or the anxiety with which that baby's parents were waiting.

All the same, even if they were discussing restaurants, Tommen found he could not blame them. Just like his dad could not react to every little thing on the beat, these surgeons could not become overly emotionally invested in every case that came through. No one liked bad things happening to children or babies. No one wished this one anyone else, even a worst enemy. But sometimes, that was just the luck of the draw. Bad things happened, and they had a job to perform to try and make things better. It was their day job, but right now, it was Tommen's life.

And, he figured, as long as they were just meandering their way about their day job, not panicking or shouting orders or suddenly closing the blinds on him, he could tolerate a little casual conversation. Sometimes, being too focused on a job was just as bad as being too distracted. These guys knew what they were doing.

That was what Tommen told himself, though he had a hard time believing it, truly believing it. That seemed to be the mantra lately. His cynicism and paranoia told him everything was going to go horribly wrong and he was going to lose everything. He didn't have much experience with optimism, but there was another part of him that said to stop being so stupid and be grateful that this technology even existed, that there even was hope and a plan to save his daughter. Fifty years ago, a hundred years ago, not only would Maisy have died, but the doctors would have been powerless to save Becky, too. Then he really would have lost everything. This wasn't the ideal, where a snap of the fingers could reveal the problem and a *Star Trek*-esque device could just be waved around to fix everything, but it was a damn good start.

He let out a breath and tried to relax himself. This was not how he envisioned spending his weekend. This was not how he envisioned spending his first week with his new daughter. He wanted to call up everyone he knew and show off pictures of Maisy in every adorable dress Becky had sewn. He wanted the light-hearted ribbing and the new dad jokes, not sympathy or the usual offers of, "If you guys need anything."

Then the surgery was over. Stitches, staples, glue, the hole was closed, dressings were laid over the incision sites, and everything was returned to normal. Maisy was taken out of the operating room, leaving the nurses to clean things up. Tommen abandoned his post and went to meet his daughter, or the doctor anyway.

"How did it go?" Tommen demanded.

"Smooth as warm butter," the doctor replied calmly.

He did not say more at that moment, and Tommen elected to wait on his questions until they were back with Becky and she could hear everything as well.

When they entered the room, Tommen noted her sigh of relief, perpetuated in part by his generally relaxed demeanor. He wanted to convey a sense of everything being okay. They were going in the right directions, just in small steps. But now that this was done, maybe they could rest for a few days and see what became of this.

"So, everything went well," the doctor told them. "Her right kidney was removed to make room for the liver. It went just as smoothly as we could have hoped. It was a little tricky to move the liver where we wanted it to go, but it is in place." He shifted uncomfortably. "Her lungs did move where we wanted them to, so some of the pressure on her heart has been relieved. But..." He paused as if considering his words. "Children, especially newborns, are very squishy and pliable, especially their organs, which is why we're having such smooth success. However, their bones are also very pliable, too. Maisy's lungs, being all cramped up in her chest, are bruised from constant pressure against her ribcage. We're worried that her heart is bruised as well. It's nothing catastrophic at this point, and everything we just did today should help, but it is something that we'll need to keep an eye on over the next few days."

"And she'll be okay?" Becky asked. "For the next few days?"

"All signs say yes. I still want her to stay today and overnight. If things start improving and look on an upward trend by morning, I would even feel comfortable letting her go home for a few days. Hospitals are great places, but honestly, home is where the heart is, and half of healing is purely psychological. Touch, home, comfort, familiarity, I believe it does as much good as anything we do here."

"What's our next step, then?" Tommen wondered. "Assuming things go just swimmingly overnight and she's doing great tomorrow, what are we looking at?"

"It depends on how well she does. The absolute best case scenario is that this is all we need to do. Once the swelling goes down, her liver settles into its new home, her lungs stop compressing her heart, and she grows up healthy, with careful monitoring to ensure all is well. No matter what, I want to see her again soon, like, say, in a week, to see how things are healing up, where her organs stand, and so on. Then we can make the decision whether we need to staple her stomach, remove a portion of her liver, and so on. I don't want to say anything for certain until we see how this right here plays out. It's just too soon at this point."

"Fair enough," Tommen said, nodding and mentally noting everything the doctor said. If Nathan wouldn't help, maybe he could do some of these minor fixes on his own.

"Any questions?"

Tommen and Becky glanced at each other. Sure, they had a million questions, but there was too much uncertainty to even waste breath on them. Most of them were just what if scenarios. Most of the answers would fall into one of two categories: One, they were in a hospital, so things could get taken care of quickly; two, if they weren't in a hospital, get to one quickly so things could get taken care of. After a minute or two, they declined. Then, as the doctor excused himself, Becky spoke up.

"When can I be formally discharged?"

He gave her a cheeky look. "When you stop causing trouble for the nurses." He grinned and shook his head. "No, they tell me you've been good. I'll check in on you before I leave, around seven or so. If you're feeling fine, I'll be happy to discharge you."

He left the room and Becky leaned back in her bed. She folded her arms. "I'm feeling fine now. I want to go home. All of us. I just want to take her and go home. Put her in her crib, show her toys and things, and just...hold her. Why do we have to go through this?"

"I don't know," Tommen sighed. "Maybe you can ask the One Who controls things like that."

He'd never been big into religion since becoming a teenager, and was just beginning to accept the possibility and-or reality of an Author. He wasn't sure about the nuances and where God Himself fit into all of this. But for all of that, he hated to see Becky's faith being shaken like this. She'd managed to stand strong when it was her own woes, her dwarfism and diabetes and the hassle that came with those conditions. But when it came to her daughter? That was a little harder to stomach. How was she going to handle being taken away from all of this to a place halfway across the galaxy?

Tommen would be lying if he said he didn't feel similarly. He could handle color-blindness, hearing loss, and a barbecued arm. To see his daughter fighting for her life in a hospital at only two days old simply killed him. Might as well stick him with a knife because at least that would hurt less.

He texted his dad with an update. It was over an hour before he replied.

"I know it may not sound like it right now, but that's great news. She'll be coming home tomorrow, then?"

"If everything goes well."

"I can hear your doubt through your text. But consider this: what do you think would have happened if Becky hadn't caught it and you brought her home without all of this?"

Tommen sighed. "Bad stuff. Possibly worse because of the extra time it would take to call an ambulance and get her to the hospital. I know. It's just...it's hard."

"I know, kiddo. I'm not saying it's not. Hang in there."

He stared at his phone for a second before putting it away.

"Heading home for a shower and stuff?" Becky wondered.

"I don't know," he admitted. "I don't want to. Mostly I'm hungry."

"You didn't eat breakfast."

"I know. I should, but I don't want to leave, either."

"Go home," she told him. "Take a shower and get something to eat. One of us has to stay sane, and we're both going to go insane if we both stay here, wallowing in uncertainty. Maybe you can double-check and make sure everything is ready and perfect for her arrival."

That sounded like something of a good idea, Tommen decided. He kissed both of them before turning and forcing himself to leave. He didn't want to. He felt like he was abandoning them. At the same time, they were in a hospital, which was arguably the best place for them if anything happened. And if anything happened, medically, there was going to be jack shit he could do about it.

The thought was cold comfort as he walked through the hospital, fishing for his car keys in his many pockets. Even when he found them and got in his car, he sat there for a long moment.

There had to be something he could do. Had to be. He had a wicked arsenal of abilities that could change the physics of the universe. Gravity, Light, Sound, Thermodynamics, Magnetism,

Matter, Time. And all of it was completely useless? He didn't buy that. There had to be some combination of skill and ability that would heal his daughter. Maybe Nathan was just afraid of making things worse, didn't want to use Maisy as an experiment. Tommen could respect and understand that, and he appreciated the caution. But if things didn't improve, drastic measures would have to be taken.

On the other hand, what if things got better? What if this really was all she needed? Remove a kidney, get everything settled, and just keep an eye on her until she hit puberty when things were likely to sort themselves out. Just a little speed bump, starting out in life, but everything else would be comparatively fine.

Tommen arrived home, unsure how he felt about that line of thought. As if he hadn't had enough heart attacks over the last two years, now the Author felt the need to throw this at him. Denied a happily ever after for a cheap scare at the end of a series, a last hurrah to shake things up at the finale, like the never-ending will-they-won't-they in bad romance media. Will they ride off into the sunset? Or will the horse break a leg before they reach the horizon? It was all so frustrating. Couldn't the Author just wrap things up with a pretty little bow and send them on their way?

He figured his grouchy attitude must have showed on his face because when he walked in the door, his dad raised a brow.

"Everything okay, kiddo?" he asked cautiously.

"Fantastic," Tommen growled.

"It sounded like things are going pretty well, maintaining if not improving. Did I miss something?" His dad warily followed him down the hall and paused in his bedroom door.

"When do we get a happy ending?" Tommen asked of no one in particular really, pulling out clean clothes. "At what point do we get to ride off into the sunset without the car breaking down?"

His dad frowned and folded his arms, shifting his stance to lean on the doorframe. "The car is always going to break down, Tommen. The car will break down, the pipes will leak, someone will get sick or laid off from work —"

"But those are easy things. Watching your daughter cling to life when she's barely two days old is not easy. You can't call a mechanic or a plumber for that."

"No, but you can call a doctor. And you have. And she is getting the very best care she can get. Compared to a couple days ago, or even just last night, I think things are getting better. The problem is not the problem. The tedium is the problem, having to wait. What's more, having to hope and trust and maybe even pray a little."

Tommen faced his dad. "If I pray and God doesn't answer, should I have even wasted my time? If I don't pray and she gets better, would it have made a difference? Whether it's God or the Author, someone out there seems to hate me and everyone I love. I have all this great Akari power, and it's fucking useless. Even Nathan won't help me."

"Tommen, listen to yourself. You talk like the world is ending." He continued before Tommen could protest. "I know. Your daughter is your world. But she is getting better. I still remember each and every time you landed in the emergency room because of Tyler. I hated to see it, and I wished I could pummel him myself. It hurt me as much as it hurt you. I just had to remind myself that you were alive, getting the best care available, and to always tell you I loved you and wanted to see you succeed, whatever the bullies said or did."

They stood there, staring at each other.

"I understand that you are conflicted," Walter said softly. "I understand that you wish this all away, make it so it never happened or find a miracle cure. Don't think I don't feel the same way. She hurts, you hurt. You hurt, I hurt. She hurts, I hurt. This isn't isolated. You're not going to want to hear it, but you need to be patient and have just a little faith. It's not easy, and I understand that. But if it's all you are able to do, then do it well. And know that once the emotion has worn off a little, I'm not taking any of this personally, because I know exactly how you feel."

Tommen studied his dad for a moment, then pushed past him to go take a shower. He knew his dad was right in a lot of ways, including the part where he did want all of it to go away and he didn't want to hear logical advice. He just...he wanted to go back in time and fix it before it started.

No, that wasn't right. If he wanted to be really, truly honest, he wanted to go back in time and stop himself from getting into this mess. Maybe it was insisting on more condom use, maybe exercising more self-control and not sleeping with Becky at all. Maybe it would have to go so far as never dating her. Wherever that tipping point was, that place of no return, he wanted to go back and make the other choice.

Maybe it would have saved him unnecessary grief when he was trapped in the in-between dimension. Maybe he wouldn't have felt so wretched about running into battle, the thought of never seeing her again. Maybe he would have been more resistant to Rifun's recruiting if he hadn't worried about Becky being used as a pawn against him. It would certainly have made things easier on his dad.

It wasn't that he didn't love Becky or Maisy, because he did. But if he wanted to go back and do it over again and change things, did that still make him a bad person? Would he have even been aware of all of this, a sort of alternate future? Or could *this* be that alternate future? Now that was a step into *The Twilight Zone*.

And here was an even deeper question: had he chosen this path, or did the Author choose it for him? Was the Author scripting his life, or merely recording his actions? There was a dose of philosophy.

Tommen got out of the shower still feeling rather bitter about the whole thing, but at least he was clean. Some of that pent-up anxiety melted when he got out to the living room and saw his dad. He let out a breath, but before he could say anything, his dad held up a hand.

"It's okay, Tommen. I understand. I really do. Just remember something: the people around you? We are not your enemies. I am not your enemy. Becky is not your enemy. Your daughter is not an enemy. We're all hurting. But we need to stick together. Does that make sense?"

Tommen sighed and nodded. "Yeah."

"Good."

"I'm sorry for unloading on you."

"As I said, I understand, and I'm not taking it personally. As long as you remember that I am not the enemy."

Chastened, Tommen made for the kitchen to grab a bite to eat. He needed to get his head back on straight before returning to the hospital. He needed to be the rock for his wife and daughter, and it did them no good if he was a mess. As he sat at the table to eat a ham sandwich, his dad approached.

"Is there anything you would like me to do?" he asked levelly. "Errands you need run, minor things? I don't know what you've got going, but you can't completely forsake everything outside the hospital."

Tommen rubbed his face. Everything outside the hospital felt so far away. Even being home was more like a dream.

"Do you have all your college textbooks, got everything straightened around there?" his dad wondered, tone somewhat desperate.

"College?" Tommen wondered, giving him a look. "Dad, just as soon as possible, we're running off to the other side of the universe. I'm about to upend Becky's life even more, to say nothing of how things are going to go for Maisy."

His dad sighed. "I know."

He finished his food joylessly, then ambled off back to the bedroom, certain he was forgetting something but not sure what. He grabbed another little outfit for Maisy, something she could wear home. Because she would be coming home. She had to. She couldn't not come home. That would be...more than Tommen could handle.

He returned to the living room and approached his dad, feeling very much like a small child who has gotten in trouble and is now trying to suck up to be forgiven and let out of time out.

"Is there anyone you know of in the Time industry who might

know a few tricks about how to save Maisy? Do you think your hi-tech guy who makes these glasses and hearing aids and watches and whatever else, do you think he might know of something?"

His dad shifted in his seat, expression thoughtful. "I don't know right off hand, but that doesn't mean there isn't someone out there. Do you know what you would need, some kind of contraption or the results? What are you looking for?"

Irritation bubbled in Tommen's gut. Hadn't his dad been paying any attention? Did he not read his texts or understand what his son was saying? Biting back a few choice words, Tommen answered, "Something to shrink her organs back to normal size. I don't want to have to rely on hope that removing one kidney will solve the problem. I don't want to have to take her back to have part of her liver removed or her stomach stapled or whatever else."

If Walter had any misgivings about the request, he was very good at not showing it. He just nodded thoughtfully and appeared as though he really might have an idea as to how to go about fulfilling Tommen's request.

Tommen shifted his stance and sighed, rubbing his face. It was the middle of the day and he felt exhausted. He shook his head. "No, don't bother."

"I didn't say anything," his dad told him.

"No, but...it's still not smart for humans to go to the Wheel. You could be arrested, captured by Borelians...just, forget it."

Now his dad stood from his recliner and met Tommen face-to-face. Tommen had never seen his dad look more sincere or serious than he did in that moment as he said, "Tommen, you started a war to save my life. You went to the edge of the universe and risked everything to look for a cure you weren't even sure existed. The least I can do is try to pay back the favor by trying to save your daughter, my granddaughter."

"But I can't stand the thought of losing her and you. Besides, the doctors have a plan, and she might be coming home tomorrow. If everything turns out well, I don't want to send you off on an unnecessary suicide mission. Maybe wait and see."

His dad looked immensely skeptical, but finally nodded. "All right. I won't go running off just yet. But that doesn't mean I won't be looking into it a little more and seeing what I might be needing to do. If this turns into a long-term thing, well, I didn't want to have to go dark so soon anyway."

Tommen managed a small smile. "Thanks, Dad."

His dad clapped him on the shoulder and guided him toward the kitchen. "Come on. Let's get you back to the hospital before you wear yourself out pacing here."

They took their respective vehicles but both ended up at the hospital. Tommen was becoming somewhat known amongst the nurses and other staff, so he was no longer detained like a mass murderer in the making, but his dad was not quite as well known and was forced to jump through some hoops. It was unclear whether Tommen vouching for him helped or hurt things, but they got through soon enough and were on their way upstairs.

There did not appear to be any chaos around the room, nor did they enter to find Becky weeping or in other distress. In fact, she looked rather calm, nearly content. Maisy was still in her box, right up next to the bed.

"How's she doing?" Tommen asked, crossing the room in only a few long strides.

"Holding steady," Becky said, though she frowned. "She's slower to recover than the nurses hoped she would be. But the important thing is, she hasn't gotten worse." Her voice sounded hollow, as if repeating a happy mantra to try and convince herself that all was well.

"Rest and sleep is the most important thing right now. For both of you," Walter said, approaching. "She looks like she's following orders." He raised brow at Becky.

"I'm resting. I haven't caused any trouble at least since he's been gone."

"That must be a new record," Tommen chuckled anxiously.

Becky swatted at him. Unlike times past, their banter was rigid, forced, hardly anything resembling carefree and light-hearted. Eventually, all eyes turned back to the baby in the glass box.

"Personally, I think she looks more like Tommen," Walter said, evidently trying to bring the mood up a little.

"Well, she acts like him, anyway," Becky said, finally smiling a little. "She woke up earlier, looked at me, farted, then went back to sleep." She managed a small giggle. "If there is anything good about being here rather than at home, it's that I'm not the one who has to change her diapers."

She swallowed nervously, but they were all smiling anyway.

"But, I mean, that's good, isn't it?" Tommen wondered. "That means her kidneys and intestines are working. Or, you know, kidney."

"I guess so. I mean, it wasn't much. But the nurse said that they didn't expect much from her right now. I don't know. I mean, I generally understand babies, but this is just...I don't know."

"Well, you know more than I do. I can't say I know anything about babies, and certainly nothing like this."

"You two make it sound like she's on her last legs," Walter interrupted. "Tommen already told me that this surgery bought her some time and she's likely to come home tomorrow. What are you going to do then? Show her the house, show her the neighborhood. Come on, guys, what were you originally planning to do had everything going just superb from the get-go?"

Tommen and Becky glanced at each other. Honestly, Tommen couldn't remember those plans. It felt like so long ago, certainly more than just a couple days. Then, once it became apparent that they weren't going to get the ideal start they'd wanted, he sort of discarded all of those plans, electing to just play it by ear.

But to that end, he had to play it by ear, by considering what was going on right now and not pandering to every awful scenario his mind could conjure up. His daughter had a successful surgery and had a better shot at getting out of the hospital now than she had twenty-four hours ago. That was a good thing. In another twenty-four hours, she was likely going home. What did he expect to do with her?

"I do want to show her around the house and the neighborhood and everything," he said finally, "and I think she should pay Will a visit so she can apologize for cutting the bachelor party short and stranding him with a bunch of chicken wings."

"Talking about the food or your friends?" Becky laughed.

"Probably both," Walter said.

"Yeah, Chris texted me or something about wanting a bachelor party do-over," Tommen mentioned. "I figure it might have to be a little more low-key so I can show off to them the reason I had to run out on them the other day. And I'll have to brag about her in class, too." He looked at Becky. "Maybe you and your mom can bring her to the campus one day and we'll go out for lunch or something."

His dad shifted his stance. "Tommen."

Tommen knew exactly what his dad wanted, but he ignored and instead opted for a safe, "I figured you would be sleeping."

Walter gave him a look. How long was he going to put off telling Becky about the escape? Was he even going to tell her? Finally, Walter replied with an equally safe, "What time are you getting out of class?"

"I get out by one every day, and then I'll be heading to work after that most days. Friday through Sunday, I don't have class, and Chris said he'd give me Mondays and Tuesdays off so I'm not too overwhelmed."

"All right, so maybe Monday or Tuesday night we can go out to dinner."

"But then you have to work."

"Not every night," Walter protested stiffly. "And I am retiring. Eventually. You make it sound like you don't want to go out to eat with me. What, did I sprout another ear or a third eye or something?"

Tommen shook his head. "No, nothing like that. It's just...your schedule is different from everyone else's. I don't want you to get caught up in something."

"And retirement?"

"Fine. We'll all go out for your retirement party."

"Hm...I don't know about that. A baby at a retirement party might cramp my style."

"You don't have any style. Besides, she's already coming to my bachelor party. Just think about that for a second before complaining about style."

Becky rolled her eyes and grinned, muttering, "Men. I swear." She looked at Maisy. "We're evenly matched now, men and women in the house, but you're too young to partake just yet. So I'm still high and dry."

"Actually, I'd say you're just under four feet," Tommen said, giggling like an idiot.

She swatted him.

"See, there you go causing trouble again," he told her. "I don't think they're going to let you out at the rate things are going." She swatted him again and he playfully cried, "Nurse! Nurse, she's attacking me! Ow! Belligerent patient!"

He wasn't yelling loud enough to actually attract attention, but it was enough to get them laughing. When Tommen finally looked back, after shielding himself from more swats from Becky, he found Maisy was awake and looking at him, smiling in her cute baby way.

Things were going to be okay, he decided. Whether or not there was a reason to mope didn't matter, because it wouldn't solve anything. He had to stay firm, stay positive, and be the rock for the women in his life, even if one of those women was only a couple days old. He had a duty to them to stay strong.

Walter was still hanging around when Dr. Polski showed up, just on his way to the synagogue for evening service. He was overjoyed to see Becky and Maisy were both doing well, and he promised to pray especially for Maisy that Yahweh would heal her.

"Mom would have come today, but she had too many kids to take care of," he told her. "She didn't think their antics would have been appropriate here. She's at work now, but she's thinking about you."

"That's okay," Becky said, though Tommen could see the disappointment on her face. "Tell her that there's a good chance we're going home tomorrow. I'll call her when we're leaving."

Dr. Polski promised to do so, then wished them all well before heading out.

"Are you working tomorrow night?" Tommen asked as Walter made to leave as well.

His dad shook his head. "Nope, not until Monday. I'll be around when you guys get home tomorrow, don't worry."

"Well, at least you'll be able to get a few decent pictures to show the guys. I seem to recall something about them wanting to see if a newborn could fit in one of your hands?"

"We can find that out tomorrow once she's off all the wires," Walter said, though he did blush rather noticeably. He stood from his comfortable position on the couch, looking to ensure he had everything. Then he looked at Tommen. "Come on, kid, what do you say I buy you dinner before I take off? We'll go to the swanky cafeteria downstairs."

"No one says 'swanky' anymore, Dad," Tommen told him.

"Well, I do. You want to or not?"

"Do I get leftovers at least?" Becky cut in.

Tommen gave her a look. "You get to eat off the kid's menu."

"I know, that's why I'm asking." She sighed dramatically and rolled her eyes. "Guess I'll just have to wait until I'm discharged before getting the good stuff."

"Be thankful they're waiting to discharge you until after dinner," Walter told her seriously. "Last time I was admitted, they kicked me out right before lunch."

She got a kick out of that and told them to get lost so she could call down for dinner before the nurses came to discharge her. Tommen left the room in a much better mood than when he'd entered, and he and his dad made their way to the cafeteria.

"She's not going to let herself be discharged until Maisy is, too," Tommen said as they got in line. "She'll fake sugar problems if she has to, but she's not leaving without her."

"I would believe that," his dad said, his tone uncertain as to how he should react.

The cafeteria was crowded and they were forced to take a table that hadn't been cleaned yet. Well, a few crumbs wouldn't kill them, Tommen figured, wiping them onto the floor. He sat and started in on his food. He'd decided to go with standard fare, chicken strips and fries. Across from him, his dad had elected for a slightly healthier chicken salad with a side of vegetables, though he stole several fries off Tommen's tray.

"What happened to not being concerned about your girlish figure?" Tommen wondered.

His dad shrugged. "What can I say? Every so often, I have an attack of conscience."

"Oh, is that what this is?"

"And I'm being nice to the hospital. How would it look if I had a heart attack and the last thing I ate came from their cafeteria? There would be mass hysteria in here. Lawsuits everywhere. I think I'm doing them a favor."

Tommen raised a brow. "I don't think heart attacks come about based on the last thing you ate."

His dad raised a fork. "Maybe not. All the same, if someone suddenly has a medical episode in here, falls out of their chair, it still doesn't look good for the hospital or the cafeteria."

"Maybe, but at the same time, we're in a hospital. This is where sick people are. They've probably had people in here with medical episodes, and you'll notice the cafeteria is still open. I think there would have to be more than one person keeling over out of their chairs for people to really panic like that."

His dad just shrugged and continued with his salad. Tommen noticed that he was constantly looking at the chicken strips, and he guessed his dad was somewhat regretting his choice of lunch.

"When are you going to tell her?" Walter asked pointedly, his tone and expression leaving no room for banter or evasion. He wanted an answer. "We are all extremely vulnerable right now if Julianna wanted to try something. If not for Maisy's condition, I would suggest going now."

"I know," Tommen sighed. "I know. I just don't know that I can heap all that extra stress on Becky right now. And how is a newborn going to handle a portal, never mind a sick newborn? I want to make sure she's healthy and strong enough for that." He rubbed his eyes. "Can you give me just one day? We take Maisy home and sleep one night in our bed as a family like we planned."

"Kid, I'm not the one you have to convince; I'm not the one gunning for you."

"Believe me, I know."

"Then act like it. You have to tell her."

Tommen stabbed at his food. "All right, I will. I'll think of something tonight."

They finished their respective meals in silence. After dinner, Walter wished Tommen a good evening and good luck and said to keep him updated. Tommen reluctantly promised he would. Then they departed, Walter to his car, Tommen back up to the room.

Becky was still in bed, dinner tray pushed to one side, watching something on TV. Maisy still slept in her box.

"How are things up here?" Tommen asked lightly. Becky scooted to one side of the bed so he could sit next to her. "Causing too much trouble for them to want to let you go?"

"Not causing enough trouble, I think," she answered. While there was a glimmer of humor in her voice, there was also a certain sense of worry.

"And Maisy?"

"Maintaining is the best she can do." Becky's voice was tight. "I mean, I get that newborns aren't especially active, running around and whatnot, but she's been quiet and sleepy to the point of lethargy."

"Have you told the nurses?" Tommen got up and went

around to the other side of the bed to look at his daughter. She was sleeping still, and barely roused when he gently touched her.

"Of course I have. They drew blood—she barely put up a fuss, and you saw how mad she was about it the last time—and they're doing tests and stuff, but it takes time."

"Well, with the recent kidney surgery, I don't know, maybe she's just not as fast to recover as me or you. Maybe she's not the tough-as-nails, gung-ho, push through sleet and snow kind of strong that you and I are. Maybe she is going to be a kinder, gentler soul."

"That's great and all, but this is not the time to show it. Right now she needs to be that tough-as-nails and everything else you just said."

Fear crept into Tommen's mind but he beat it back as much as he could. The surgery went well and things were fine. How could they expect a newborn to just bounce back from a major surgery? Sure, children were more squishy and bouncy than adults, but she was literally only two days old, brand new to the world. She was still fragile. Give it time, he told himself. By morning, all would be well, and they would be heading home. He couldn't let himself get wrapped up in his own cynical paranoia. He had to deal with everything as it came and not before.

Nevertheless, he pulled up a chair on the other side of the box and sat to watch TV with Becky, keeping one eye on Maisy. He saw her little belly rise and fall rhythmically as she breathed. Her tiny fingers and toes made small, nearly imperceptible movements. He tried not to dwell on it. She was in a deep sleep. She'd had a tough day and needed to sleep it off. Tommen remembered the surgery he'd had on his arm; he'd been pretty sleepy after that. His daughter had an organ taken out of her body. Why shouldn't she be tired from that? Now that the initial anesthesia had worn off, she was probably feeling true exhaustion as her tiny body tried to figure out what happened and make it better.

They watched TV for a while. To be more precise, the TV was on and they stared at the screen, but for as often as they kept looking at Maisy, watching her, touching her, attending to her every tiny move, well, at least Tommen wasn't sure what was going on in the TV program. He wasn't even sure what they were watching.

It was after eight when some of Becky's brothers and sisters showed up with their families, the kids all wanting to see their newest cousin. The older kids gave their congratulations and were generally more mature and understanding of the circumstances surrounding the hospital stay. The younger kids all wanted to know why Maisy was in a box and if she would be going home in a box. Tommen got cheeky and said that yes, Maisy would be going home in a box, but the nurses hadn't brought the wrapping paper or bow yet. Becky gave him a look and said no, she wasn't going home in a box. She was just feeling sleepy and a little sick, so that's where she had to stay until the doctor said she could go home.

"Going home tomorrow, then?" Nomi asked. "That's what Dad was saying."

"That's what we're hoping," Becky told her. "If she does well overnight."

Tommen could see she had a hard time believing that was going to be the case. In the poor lighting in the room, he watched his girlfriend age twenty years, and he saw what she would look like in her forties, the age lines as she crossed over from youth into maturity. From maturity she would move on to wisdom. In an odd sort of way, seeing her like that only made him love her more.

He looked at Maisy. She'd been sleeping all afternoon and most of the evening. Becky tried to get her to feed, but she wanted none of it. Of course, this only alarmed Becky further and she called for the nurse. There was some deliberation and it was decided that if Maisy wouldn't take by nine o'clock, then they would administer some nutritional supplements via IV. If she still wasn't better by morning, not only would she not be going home, but they would have to consider more drastic measures.

Tommen tried not to get too worried, telling himself that he didn't usually feel like eating after major or minor surgery, but once he had a chance to sleep it off, he was ravenous. Probably Maisy would be up at four o'clock, just squalling and demanding to be fed, among other things. She was a baby and had her own needs. Those needs couldn't simply be scaled down as if she were just a tiny adult. All the same, it was hard to hold onto that hope when she was still in a glass box, attached to tubes and wires.

"You're sleeping here again tonight, then?" Becky asked Tommen after her last relative had gone.

"Is there a reason I shouldn't?" he wondered. "Everything is ready at the house. Just need her. And you."

He almost told her about the escape, but the words jumbled in his brain and caught in his throat. How could he even bring up something like that right now?

She nodded but still seemed uncertain as she watched Maisy. The tiny baby was still sleeping, rousing only to a dreary lethargy at best. She was still this way when a nurse came in to finally administer some kind of nutrition supplement. It wasn't necessarily food, but it would meet her needs until morning when they could figure out what to do next. Either she woke up crying for food or there was a possibility of needing to force feed.

"Why would this be happening, though?" Becky demanded of the nurse. "I mean, if she has an enlarged stomach, I would think she would be screaming for food."

"Maybe, but things are still trying to sort themselves out after surgery," the nurse replied calmly. Her blond hair was brushed back in two French braids. Given how they were still impeccable and not super frazzled, Tommen guessed she hadn't been on shift for very long. She went on, "Even if her stomach is enlarged, if it's being compressed at all different sides, it might be uncomfortable or even painful to feed. Having an enlarged liver may also be giving her heartburn more easily."

"How does a newborn get heartburn?"

"It's not something we typically associate with babies, true, but this is anything but typical. And as Tommen has pointed out, she is still recovering from surgery and may not feel like feeding. A nutritional supplement will help for the night, and we'll see what happens in the morning." The nurse smiled. "Assuming she doesn't wake you up before then looking for breakfast."

It was meant to be encouraging, but Tommen could see Becky wasn't feeling it herself.

They settled in for an uneasy sleep, though they still watched TV from their respective beds. There weren't too many channels that weren't cartoons or other kid's shows, but that was all right. Tommen figured he could use some easy TV, the shows where the bad guy was always pretty obvious (minus a fake mustache here and there), the schemes were ridiculous, and problems could be solved in a day that got condensed down into half an hour, or even fifteen minutes. There was no waiting, no real uncertainty, and the good guys always came out on top.

Tommen hadn't watched cartoons since he was a kid, but Becky seemed to know what was up, from her time as a babysitter and needing to keep kids entertained. Shows he thought might be interesting got skipped over, and ones he thought were dumb were selected instead. But he wasn't going to complain. Whatever it was on the screen, it helped to pass the time.

At some point, he figured he must have slept because the next thing he knew, he was in a field. It was a field he knew well; it was the one that bordered the dark forest. He judged his distance to be about a hundred yards or so from the border, and standing between him and the forest was the white rabbit.

"Long time no see," Tommen commented. Indeed, it had been over a year since he'd seen the rabbit. "Where have you been hiding?"

"Here and there," the rabbit replied, sounding both elusive and like his normal crabby self. "Mostly I've been trying to keep some of the smaller Shadows from trying to sneak over the border and get close to you."

"Yeah, well, I'm fine. Any clue on how to help my daughter now?" His words came out perhaps a little more sharply than intended.

"Let the Author take care of that. I'm here for you."

"Are you a shrink now?"

"I'm not here to be a shoulder to cry on. I'm here to stop you from going in there—" The rabbit gestured toward the forest. "—and making some very bad decisions."

"I wouldn't even need to think about it if someone on this side of the border would help me."

The words came out of his mouth, but it was as if someone else spoke through him. He looked at the forest. He knew what lurked in the depths. The shadows there were not merely solid objects obstructing the light, but they were living, breathing Shadows. The Dragon still hunted him, he knew, but as long as he was on this side of the border, it was a risky endeavor for any Shadow to cross in pursuit.

The next thing he knew, a furious ball of white fur was coming for him through the air. He put his hands up defensively as the rabbit landed on his shoulder, lashing out with its front paws in something very reminisce of a kung fu movie. Then it leaped off of him and disappeared into the tall grass. Tommen could see the grass moving wherever the rabbit went, and he heard what sounded like a scuffle of some form.

A minute later, a Shadow took off out of the grass, like a smoky pheasant taking flight to escape a hound. It made for the forest in a jilted, stunted flight path. The rabbit made a grand leap, easily four or five feet in the air, still clawing after the Shadow. The evil thing got away, and the rabbit got up on its hind legs, yelling at it.

"That's right! I'm still here! He's with me! Get lost you...you...slimy shadowy...thing." He made a sound and turned back to Tommen. "I've never been good with the insults."

"I can tell," Tommen commented lightly. Then, more seriously, "I didn't mean it, what I said. I know it's bad to go in there."

"Then why are you here thinking about it?" the rabbit asked evenly. "Trust, human. It's a concept you humans don't seem to fully grasp, even with each other. You didn't like Chandler telling you that you're splitting off and heading for darkness. You think that what you see in front of you is everything, that this must be the darkness he's talking about. Not always true."

"That's great and all, but if it's so bad, then why not warn me about it? Why not give me the details instead of some vague, pseudo-mystical, spiritual, prophetic bullshit? Knowledge is power."

"Knowledge caused the fracturing of the universe. It's not your place to know or understand, only trust."

"I have a hard time accepting that. Even if I'm on the right track, it doesn't matter if I go nowhere."

"Pithy bumper sticker philosophy," the rabbit said sharply. "It means nothing except by way of an excuse to justify whatever stupidity you plan to do."

"So what do you expect me to do? Just sit idly by and watch my daughter waste away, clinging to life in a tenuous balance between life and death? Sorry, I can't do that."

"First, I expect you to show some measure of respect. Second, yes, I do expect you to sit and wait and trust that the Author is doing everything exactly as it needs to."

Tommen folded his arms and shifted his stance. "Why, so she can weave in some manufactured drama in order to make a good story and keep her audience hooked? That's a tough thing to do in a series that goes on and on. We're at, what, book eight or nine or something? Which one is this? Nine? Ten? Twelve? Fifteen? Oh, well, ratings are going down, let's up the ante a little with some drama at home. Leave the war and politics aside for this one, let's throw in a sick newborn. That's not cliched at all, definitely won't alienate loyal fans who want to read about intergalactic intrigue. Nah, let's take this subplot and blow it up so that it takes over everything. Then suddenly, let's yank the rug out from under poor Tommen. Yeah, that's some great storytelling right there. I bet—"

For the second time in ten minutes, Tommen saw a flash of white fur coming at him, except this time he was somehow aware enough to know that the rabbit was going to do some kind of ninja kick on him with its hind paws. Considering the strength in a rabbit's hind legs, that kick was going to hurt. And it probably would have, if he hadn't woken up at the exact moment that fur met flesh.

Initially, he wasn't sure what had woken him except it may as well have been a tornado siren warning everyone to scramble for basements and bathrooms as death and destruction barreled down upon them. He clawed his way out of the blankets and looked around the room, momentarily stunned by the bright light.

The tornado siren died down into something more mechanical, and much closer. Nurses were in the room, crowded around Maisy in her glass box. One nurse accidentally stepped on Tommen's burned hand. He gritted his teeth and scrambled out of their way. As he stood against the wall, he saw Becky in her bed, tears streaming down her cheeks. And he was forced to wonder whether his daughter really would be going Home in a box.

Chapter Twenty-Seven
Night

Maisy had difficulty breathing that turned into not breathing at all. By the time the nurses got to the room, her heart had nearly stopped. Even when they did get her breathing again, she started coughing up blood and her heartbeat was all sorts of erratic.

Tests showed that her lungs were bruised because of being squished into such a small chest cavity. Similarly, her heart was bruised from the pressure of her oversized lungs. There was also more internal bleeding that they couldn't pin down just by ultrasound, which earned her another trip into the operating room.

Tommen texted his dad who came over just as soon as he could get around.

"What's the word?" Walter demanded.

Tommen shrugged. He had not been permitted to watch the surgery this time, and instead waited in the room with Becky.

"Internal bleeding, they don't know where it's coming from," he said listlessly. "She had blood in her lungs this morning and stopped breathing. Her heart and lungs are bruised. Everything is just going wrong."

"Do they know — ?"

"No. They don't know. We don't know. Nobody fucking knows."

His dad frowned and said nothing as he sat down. Tommen sighed and rubbed his face. "I'm sorry. I don't know why I called you here. It's probably just messing up your sleep schedule and we're not much company, I'm afraid. You should go home and go back to bed, get some sleep before work."

Walter shook his head. "Don't worry about me or what I was doing. Right now, I'm here for you."

It was about four-thirty when Tommen was jolted awake by the alarms and the nurses and everything else. It was five-thirty when his dad arrived. By seven-thirty, as the sky started to lighten, Maisy was still in surgery. No one had any news, and they didn't know who to ask to find out any information. Thinking about it, Tommen wasn't sure he wanted constant information. Just give him the bottom line and let him work out the rest.

But then, hadn't he just been harassing the rabbit about knowledge being power? He pondered his dream for a while. Thinking about it now, it was like watching a stranger go through the motions and say the words, even as he knew it had been him. The rabbit had chased away one Shadow, but had there been more there, whispering in his ear? Driving him back toward the forest? Was that even possible?

If you do not listen, the loudest make no sound, Chandler had told him once. *No one forces you to do anything. It is the beauty and pitfall of free will. You are free to act on your own, but you do not have the luxury of blaming anyone but yourself.*

"I need to step out for a minute," he said suddenly, standing and vanishing from the room.

He left the hospital and wandered through a small garden. It was mostly desolate, but in the summer it was a haven of color and beauty for children, the flowers attracting all manner of butterflies, hummingbirds, and other small creatures. Tommen dug out his phone and dialed.

"Hello?" Nathan answered sleepily just before it went to voicemail.

"Nathan, I need you. Right now," Tommen said curtly. "My daughter is literally dying and no one knows why. She's in surgery right now. We've had no news, and they don't even know if she'll make it. I'll fill you in on the details when you get here, but if this isn't life-and-death, I do not know what is. And she's out of time."

He hung up, hoping it would make the point. He couldn't just sit around and play games, think about all the what ifs and what abouts and everything else. Maisy needed help now. If Nathan didn't do something, then he would. He couldn't do nothing. He couldn't just trust. Trust did not do surgery or save lives.

His real hope was that Nathan would understand the urgency of things and would Band so as to meet Tommen at the door when he returned. Such was not the case, and he returned to the room just as lonely and frustrated as when he left. One look at Becky and his dad told him they hadn't heard anything while he'd been gone.

Nine o'clock rolled around, and a nurse came by. She had no news of Maisy other than she was still in surgery, but in the meantime, Becky could be discharged.

She was taken off the monitors, and the ports were removed from her wrists and arms. She signed her discharge papers and changed into a new set of clothes. While she proclaimed it made her feel a little better, it only paled in comparison to how she would feel once Maisy was returned to her. Tommen could not disagree.

But with Becky discharged, there was no reason for them to remain in the intensive maternity ward. A new room would be assigned to Maisy once they got word of her condition following her surgery. Most likely it would be right in the heart of NICU. But until then, Tommen, Becky, and Walter were made to wait just down the hall from the operating room. Tommen inquired about watching, but was denied.

Tommen knew a few of the reasons why a parent would not be allowed to watch their child in surgery, and none of them were good. While uncommon anyway, for civilians to be allowed to watch an operation, parents just wanted to see, to know what was happening. Taking a newborn away from her mother was akin to separating a mother bear and her cub. You didn't do it without a damn good reason.

So they sat and waited, looked at a TV without watching the program, looked at pages of magazines without seeing the words.

Becky sat on the couch. Any time Tommen tried to get close to her for comfort, she pulled away. Most often she cited pain from her own incisions, but he had a hard time believing it. He looked at his dad whose expression only conjured up sympathy.

Tommen waited for a call or text from Nathan, something to let him know that the Builder was on his way. But it never came. He sent out a few texts of his own but got no reply. He told himself it was because Nathan was Banding to get to the hospital, and Bands and technology didn't always play nice.

It was ten o'clock when a nurse came down to the waiting room, but she was there for another couple awaiting news of their child. Tommen and the other dad exchanged glances, both acknowledging the other's pain without ever saying a word.

Ten-thirty rolled around.

At exactly ten-thirty-eight, another nurse appeared. Seeing how they were the only ones left in the waiting area, Tommen figured he could safely assume this was the news they had been waiting for. She took them out of the waiting room to another room where the doctor was waiting.

"How is she?" Becky demanded. "How's our baby?"

"The doctors were able to find the bleed and stop it," the doctor reported, though his tone was less than enthusiastic. "That was finished up by eight o'clock. Unfortunately, as they were wrapping up, more started to go wrong. To make a long story short, right now we're looking at total multisystem failure. She's going to be taken to the highest level of NICU for twenty-four hour surveillance."

"What do you mean, multisystem failure?" Tommen asked. "What about just taking a small piece of her liver or stapling her stomach or...whatever else you guys were going to do?"

"That was when they were functioning. At this point, even if we did all of that, it's not going to bring back function. We don't know why everything has started to shut down. We're running tests, but...I'm not going to lie to you, I don't know that we're going to get the results back in time."

"You're giving up?" Becky's voice was tight, as if she were about to burst into tears while simultaneously assaulting the doctor, ripping his face off and mauling him like a mother bear. "There has to be something you can do. Something right now that will—"

"We are doing everything we can. Right now, a cocktail of drugs is keeping her systems functioning, but if that fails, then we're looking at life support. But life support can only go so far."

"So you're saying that our daughter is going to die. And there is nothing you can do."

Becky was standing in front of Tommen. She leaned back against him. He put his hands under her arms to keep her from sliding to the floor, even if he felt like doing the same. Instead, he managed to guide her to a chair where she slumped down like a sack of potatoes. Her eyes were red, cheeks streaked with tears.

"I'm saying that we are doing everything we can and we're hoping for speedy test results," the doctor said gently. "But it is a possibility, I'm sorry to say."

Becky wiped her eyes. "How could this happen? Beckwith-Wiedemann isn't normally fatal, especially since she has relatively minor symptoms. What's going on?"

"That's what we're trying to find out. We're also going over the genetic test again to see if something was missed or misinterpreted."

The doctor took them to Maisy who was now in the most intense part of the Intensive Care Unit. This was the life-and-death, now-or-never part of the department. Tommen felt sick to his stomach.

She was breathing again, but it was heart-wrenching to think that it might only be because of the drugs hanging in the bag over her little glass box. It was unnerving to consider that if those drugs didn't do what they were supposed to, then she might have to go on life support.

She was only three days old, for God's sake. Tommen felt his stomach twist like he was going to be sick. He would have nothing to give because he still hadn't eaten. Even the thought of food was disgusting to him right now. Right now, he just wanted to sit at his daughter's side, watch her, stare at her, and will her to be better. He couldn't trade places with her. In this part of the hospital, he couldn't even touch her as everything had to be sterile and controlled.

Maisy slept now, still recovering from surgery. She wore only a diaper, but she was covered in post-op bandages, almost like a mummy.

"I can't believe this is happening," Becky said beside him, her voice garbled from tears. "Are we being punished?"

"I hope not, because I might have a few choice words for that," Tommen growled. He sighed, his anger dissipating. "I hope not."

She took a step back and sat in a chair. She put her head in her hands and sniffed. After a minute, she looked up. "I'm not hungry, but I need to eat. Show me the cafeteria?"

Tommen hesitated for only a second before his dad stepped in, saying, "I'll keep watch."

With that, Walter assumed a protective position, as though he were guarding the president himself. Tommen mumbled a thank you, and he and Becky made for the cafeteria. It was slow going, since Becky was still recovering from the C-section. She refused a wheelchair, but stated that this would probably be the only trip she made today. That was fine with her, she reasoned aloud, because she wanted to stay by her daughter's side and was only coming down anyway because of her stupid diabetes saying she had to eat or bad things would happen. Tommen decided it best to just let her alone.

He carried both trays around the cafeteria, similar to how he'd done it in high school whenever she had to go through the common lunch line. She looked, told him what she wanted, and he just followed orders. He paid for both meals and they scouted out a place to sit.

"This isn't happening," Becky declared, tearing into her food with her fork but eating very little. "This isn't happening. I didn't go through forty weeks of hell just to say goodbye to her after less than a week. I didn't go through all that, or all of this, to not see her come home."

Tommen just nodded, not oblivious to her choice of words. He let it go for now, but somewhere in the recesses of his mind, he hoped she understood that he was just as invested in this. This was still a team effort. This wouldn't be happening at all, in any sense, good or bad, if not for him.

Him as his dick. *There you go, thinking with the wrong head. This is your fault, your own stupidity. Just following your cock to bed. Well, you made your bed, now lie in it.*

Now that's not fair. This could have happened even if you had been perfect little angels, gotten married, and then decided to have children. Bad things happened to good families, too.

But would it have? Is there any way to really know? What if Becky is right and we are being punished? We're trying to make it right. We've stuck together, done everything we can, made wedding plans, trying to be good parents. We've done more than some teen couples out there.

And if it is punishment, is it from God or the Author? Regardless of who it is, what can you do about it? Not like you can just beat down Heaven's door to have words with God. Can't just jump off the page to give the Author a piece of your mind. Even if you did decide to pray to and yell at either one of them, is it really going to change things? Is Maisy going to magically come out of that glass box with all her wounds healed, organs restored?

No. And if God or the Author won't do anything about it, that means I have to, Tommen decided.

His whole mental conversation took place in about the span of three to five seconds. Becky hadn't said anything, or if she had, he hadn't paid attention. But it was then that Tommen knew he would probably be acting alone using abilities he was loathe to try on himself, never mind his three day old daughter currently fighting for her life in NICU.

"Um, I'm going to step outside for a minute," Becky said, standing and abandoning her tray of half-eaten food. "I want to call my parents, let them know what's going on."

Tommen nodded. "Do you want help getting there, or...?"

"No, I'm okay. I'm just going to go sit on a bench or something."

In the movies, even if the woman said she needed to leave or wanted to go it alone, the man still went after her. As the hero, he had to. He would catch her outside the hospital or at the train station or the airport. He would hug her and kiss her and know just what to say to get her to come back, fall in love with him, and live happily ever after.

Tommen remained anchored to his chair. He had no will to move. He had no words.

He had no happily ever after.

This was not the end, not for him. Or if it was, it was a shitty end. Just another plot twist in a series to keep readers reading. What next? Was his dad going to fall ill with cancer? Was Rifun going to bust out of prison with an army of vengeful Akari-bearers? Was Julianna going to send a whole army of her minions to attack Earth? Something else?

Come on, Author, show me what you got. There is no way you're going to top this.

His heart was aching, but his expression remained impassive as he ate his food, tasting nothing.

Becky still hadn't returned after ten minutes. Tommen concluded that she had returned to NICU without him. That was all right, he figured. He threw away the leftover food, returned the trays, and went outside himself to try and call Nathan one last time. He would give the professional Builder one more chance to come and save Maisy. Even if it was largely uncharted territory, even if he was nervous about doing the procedure on the newborn daughter of one of his clients and pupils, he still had the best knowledge of how to go about fixing whatever was wrong.

Nathan did not answer. His phone even rang, suggesting that he wasn't in a Band, but it just went to voicemail. Tommen left a message, trying to be as polite as possible but knowing that he was failing. He was angry, he was upset, he was confused, and he was going to have to go it alone. How to begin?

He didn't even make it back inside the hospital before he spotted Mrs. Polski's van. Probably Dr. Polski was working—even though it was Sunday, being Jewish, the audiologist worked Sunday to Thursday. It was a toss-up whether he would cancel his appointments to come over. He might, seeing how it was a life-and-death situation.

There was no way Tommen would be able to do anything with so many people around. The last thing he wanted to do was Band, try something, and make things worse. To spectators, it would appear as though things suddenly took a catastrophic turn, and it would be hard to try and explain exactly what happened.

Another reason he put it off was as simple as not wanting to making things worse, because the only worse they could get at this point was, well, death. Life support, maybe, if he wanted to get technical, but, fundamentally, death was the next step down. He could never forgive himself if he caused his daughter's death, regardless of how bad she was to begin with. Maybe he would feel differently if she didn't respond to the drugs and actually went on life support.

Habit initially took him toward the maternity ward, but he peeled off at the last second and made for an elevator to go to NICU. Becky had indeed returned without him, and his dad remained faithfully on watch, though he now watched from a chair.

Tommen sat down and stared at the glass box. This was a true NICU box, enclosed on all sides, the top locked, with only a couple small holes in one side to reach in and touch the tiny infant within. For the moment, though, even those holes were covered with clear panels. Oxygen was pumped into the box through a tube. The doctors didn't want her to contract an infection from any germs on their hands. Maisy simply could not survive an infection at this point.

Silence engulfed them, the room quiet except for the blips and beeps of the monitors. There were no windows here, and even the decor was more reminisce of the general hospital than the rest of the children's hospital. This was not a place of cheer and hope, but desperate, last-ditch prayers. And death.

Tommen Banded himself and his dad. Not taking his eyes off Maisy, he asked, "What do you think this would be like if Lily were still the director?"

His dad let out a breath. "If you're asking if I have any ideas, sorry to say...I don't. I don't know that Lily would have been able to do anything. Time extends your natural lifespan, but I don't know that even a One Hundred Base Year Time Capsule would make a difference here. It might buy her a little time, but..." He trailed off and just shook his head. Tommen saw tears glistening in his father's eyes.

All the same, the implication enraged Tommen and he stood angrily. "Are you giving up, too?!"

"What do you want me to do, Tommen?" his dad asked calmly. "Do you think I enjoy sitting here like this? If I knew of a way to help, I would have done it at the first sign of trouble, before it got to this point. But I don't know. What about Nathan?"

Tommen shook his head and turned away, pulling his arms tight to himself and clenching his fists until his knuckles were white and his burned hand screamed in agony at the movement. "I called and told him what was up. I told him to get here as fast as he could. I haven't heard anything. Not a call or a text, not even anything saying he wouldn't be coming. I don't know."

"Have you tried anything?"

"I planned on it, but now I can't even touch her." He gestured helplessly to the glass box. "I just...I don't know. I don't...fucking know. I don't know."

His dad gave him a look that put him in mind of Chandler telling him something very frankly. "Tommen, your daughter is dying in front of your eyes. You have the power to at least try and save her, or buy her more time for the doctors to do their work. And you're going to let a little box keep you and her apart?"

It was like being slapped, but it also provided a sort of mental clarity for Tommen to hang onto. He looked back at the glass box and his daughter within. She was dying, and he had to save her. Obviously no one else would.

He sat down again and released the Band. He couldn't get to her from the outside, to touch her and Feel her, try to heal her that way. Maybe it was time for a little experiment, taking individual concepts he'd learned and trying to string them together. Maybe he could heal her from the inside.

He closed his eyes and bowed his head, as if he were praying. It was possible to do a little mental dreamwalking while awake, he knew. He'd never tried it, but Nathan said it was extremely difficult and very taxing. It required such intense focus that he could pass out just from the attempt. The brain was more active at night, giving it the power and ability to dreamwalk. While awake, well, that was a different story.

But the room was quiet and he had only one goal. He wasn't fighting other thoughts about his day, his job, his schooling or any of the things that might normally float around his mind. He wasn't worried about petty arguments or pithy issues. Even while awake, his thoughts were solely on the wellbeing of his daughter who was lying in a glass box fighting for her life. He didn't want to hurt her, but he couldn't just let her slip from his grasp without trying to help in some way.

The sensation that flooded him was startling enough that he almost jolted back to himself. In his many dreamwalks to Rifun, it was one developed brain touching another. Everything was organized and focused. There were thoughts, dreams, plans, higher brain functions that made human beings human, the ability to think and perceive and wonder and invent. That was what he had been expecting, and perhaps foolishly so.

A newborn had no such development, not by a long shot. Maisy's thoughts were nebulous and divided into only the most rudimentary categories: things she liked, and things she didn't like.

She wanted the things she liked, and she didn't want the things she didn't like. She didn't like being open and exposed like this. She didn't like the Cold Ones. She wanted the Comforting One, the one who held her and drove away some of the things she didn't like. Or she wanted the Strong One, the one who held her close and protected her and also drove away some of the things she didn't like.

Tommen felt his own higher thoughts erode a little as he touched his daughter's infant mind, but it didn't take much for him to realize that Becky was the Comforting One, and he was the Strong One. He put his own words into some of the gaps because Maisy existed entirely in concepts and feelings. She did not yet grasp language.

It was strange and a little eerie, but it also made it easier to navigate. She knew where her pain was, she knew the things she didn't like. He just had to find and fix them.

Tommen quickly discovered that a mental link was only that: mental. He found his daughter's pain and he learned a lot about what was going on, but he couldn't do anything without actually touching her. He needed a physical link to make a physical change.

He also learned that a baby was very easily influenced. As he realized he could do nothing and began to despair, being in Maisy's mind still, she picked up on this dismay, like filling a cup with a tidal wave. He sensed her agitation and worked to wall off his own emotions from her mind. Instead, he focused on the love he held for her, the ferocity with which he would protect and defend her. He let it flood into her, showing her just how much she was loved, how much they fought for her and wanted her to live, to get past these things she didn't like. He showed her a few happy memories of her first few days of life, hoping she might understand.

He could feel her relax, as if drifting off to sleep. Slowly, he withdrew from her mind and scrambled back to his own. It was a minute before his extended dreamwalk reconnected with his more developed higher brain functions, and he opened his eyes.

Maisy was asleep, but, if her posture and vitals were any

indication, she seemed content, even happy. She knew her mom and dad, Comforting One and Strong One, loved her. She knew they were fighting for her and wanted her to live. They wanted to take away the things she didn't like because they didn't like them either.

It helped him to relax, at least a little.

Every half hour, a nurse would come to record vitals and do a general assessment of Maisy. The first time after Tommen's dreamwalk, the nurse commented on how good she looked and how that was a good sign, certainly a step in the right direction. Becky allowed herself to breathe, and Walter nodded and said that was a good thing.

Half an hour later, the nurse returned and did her thing. Nothing had changed, which was neither good nor bad. Maisy was maintaining. At the moment, that was all they could ask for.

Half an hour later, the same thing.

Half an hour later, things returned to where they had been before the dreamwalk. It wasn't a catastrophic thing per se, but it was sum zero on her progress since the surgery.

After that, Tommen did another dreamwalk, showing Maisy love and comfort and strength, letting her know they were all still there and still loved her. Keep fighting, everything was going to be all right.

She did not relax, and when the nurse returned, nothing had changed.

Half an hour later, things were starting to tick downward. Not a plunge, but a gradual move to the negative side.

Half an hour later, the same thing.

During that checkup, as the nurse opened the lid to the box to examine Maisy, Tommen Banded and stood. He went to the box and lifted the lid all the way open. Nathan still hadn't called or texted or shown up, which meant that it all fell to Tommen to do something, anything to save his daughter.

He looked down at her, still wrapped up like a mummy. He couldn't stand to experiment on his daughter, but he couldn't sit by and let her die, either.

He touched her. He Felt her.

The first thing he did was show her love and let her know that he was doing his best to help her.

With that out of the way and hoping that he was keeping his own fear from bleeding into her, he moved his Feeling to the rest of her body. He had a good idea where the problem might be, from his earlier searching, but now he had to get absolutely specific, down to the cells and the DNA if he had to.

Everything was shutting down. The cells were no longer active and were beginning to die. She was on the cusp of total multisystem failure. But what was causing it?

He'd seen a presentation once about the benefits of chiropractic work, relieving the stress on the spinal cord and letting the nerves do their whole job, from the brain to the body and back again. Seemed a logical place to start, Tommen figured. Can't turn on a light switch if the wires are cut.

Moving around a newborn body was much different than an adult body. It was soft and squishy and not fully developed. Her bones were remarkably pliable, her skull plates not yet fused together, among other things. Instead of walking confidently along a concrete sidewalk, this was more like trying to navigate a bounce house or sandy beach, and his progress was slow.

As he got to the spinal cord and followed it back up to her brain, he noted that even here, things were not quite right. The problem was, he didn't know if it was because something was wrong, or if it was just her being so darn young. She didn't have fine motor control or complex brain activity. Her needs, thoughts, emotions, were all very simple.

Then it hit him. Of course they were simple. They were very, very simple. He didn't expect to find a twelve-lane highway of information, sure, but her simple two-lane street was brand new, freshly paved. It shouldn't have potholes in it already. And if he just followed things around her body, traced everything back to its source...he bet it wouldn't really come from her brain. Her brain was just delivering everything to the rest of her body. He had to go back to the one thing that started this whole escapade. The one thing that first tipped off Becky that something wasn't right. Her breathing.

And if he was right, she would have been just fine, or more fine, until her kidney had been removed and everything settled, allowing her oversized lungs to expand and relieve the pressure on her heart. All her lungs did was supply the oxygen to the blood. And from there, it went to the nervous system to be delivered to the rest of the body.

Borelian poison. It was an odd thing to find it and Feel it, and he briefly wondered whether he could contract it through his daughter, just by touching her. This wasn't a medical oddity; it was an assassination.

Fury welled up in Tommen, righteous fury that someone would try something like this. But now that he knew, he knew of a way to fight back.

He quelled the fury long enough to channel more love and determination to his daughter, then retreated from her body. He carefully replaced everything he had touched and returned to his seat before releasing the Band. He watched the nurse do her thing, then leave the room. After a few minutes, he Banded again, just him and his dad.

"I found the cause of her illness," Tommen stated.

"Beckwith-Wiedemann, wasn't it?" his dad questioned.

"No. That was curable and just fine, non-fatal as Becky said." He explained what he had found.

"Borelian poison?" His dad shifted in his seat. "Are you sure?"

"As sure as I've ever been."

"But who could have given it to her?"

"How many nurses do we see a day? How many have new medicines to give her? It could be any of them. Julianna and the Order, maybe the Tacagans, or the Borelians themselves somehow. I don't know. Point is, she's been poisoned. The good news, though, is that I found it in time and we have the cure. Is there still hasax in the freezer?"

His dad stood. "I believe there is."

"Sit down. At least let me release the Band first."

Walter flushed red but sat down. "Sorry. Getting a little ahead of myself."

They resumed their positions, both settling down for a second before Tommen released his Band. He could see his dad squirming a little as he shifted position in his seat, then stood, stretched, and sighed, using just the right amount of melancholy.

"Sorry to say, kids, but I have to get going home to get ready for work."

"Can't you call in?" Becky asked, her voice near pleading. "A cop who's too emotionally imbalanced is only a liability, right? I'm sure they would understand."

Walter ignored the statement, instead giving them both hugs, wishing them well, then giving a long look at Maisy before leaving. Tommen was feeling pretty rotten, but now the weight had shifted to his dad. His dad knew very well now that if he didn't get back in time, his granddaughter could die.

He also conspicuously left his coat, Tommen saw. It would give him the perfect opportunity to Band, run home to grab the hasax, come back to deliver it, then release the Band and claim he'd "just forgotten his jacket." Tommen smiled inwardly. His dad was by no means a fool. He may not have been a spry young man anymore, but he still had his cunning.

Tommen counted off the minutes, trying to gauge at what point his dad would realize he'd "forgotten his jacket." Out the door, navigating his way through NICU, being careful as he was scrutinized by every doctor, nurse, security guard, and janitor, to the elevator, down to the main floor, across the lobby. Oh, wow, it's a little chilly outside. Better put on my—huh? Oh, I seem to have forgotten my coat. I should go back and get it.

Back through the lobby, more scrutinizing, maybe stopped by a nurse or someone trying to be covert about their investigation into his person and presence, to the elevator, up the NICU floor, extensive scrutinizing, stopped again, questioned again, gets past security, twisting and turning through NICU, finds the room and...

Nothing happened. Well, these things were only happening at the speed of Tommen's thoughts, not necessarily real time, he figured. He tried to be good, but his anxiety had won out and his thoughts may have been a little harried. Give it a few more minutes for snafus, interrogations, and getting lost. For as much as they were there in the hospital, they weren't exactly roaming the halls, and the place was a maze.

Fifteen minutes passed. Then twenty. The nurse came in for her half-hour checkup. It was the one with the French braids again. She quietly reported a continuing descent in Maisy's condition, saying that she would give her one more dose of medicine, but if that didn't work, then they were going to have to start planning for life support.

The nurse left. Tommen glanced at Becky who was sitting in a chair, staring at the floor.

"As much as I want her to live, do we really want to force her to stay alive on life support?" Becky asked. "What kind of life is that?"

"Just for a little while," Tommen coaxed. "Just to see if she'll come back around."

Becky said nothing to that, just continued to stare at the floor. Tommen reached over to try and comfort her, but she pulled away. She said nothing. He also remained silent as he retreated back to his space. He let out a breath. Maisy had to live.

Come on, Dad, where are you?

Was he doing everything in real time? Why? Maybe there was something to be said for being cautious and avoiding suspicion, thinking that he was going to poison one of the NICU babies, but that was the whole point of Banding, wasn't it? Maybe something bad had happened. Maybe he'd been in an accident. Maybe security had refused to let him back into the hospital or into NICU, so he had to get creative about his exit and reentry.

Another hour passed and Maisy continued to decline to the point where the life support machines were all set up, just waiting for the moment when she could no longer function without them. As it was, she was barely breathing and her heart rhythm was anything but normal. Tommen went to her several times with love and protection, but even her simple mental state was slipping away. She was confused and sleepy, the defined categories of things she did and did not like starting to blur until it no longer mattered. He still got a positive reaction when he showed her the Comforting One and the Strong One, but it was nowhere near the reaction he'd gotten only a few hours before.

Hang on, Maisy, he pleaded silently. *Help is coming.*

He dug out his phone and texted his dad. "Where are you?"

No reply.

Tommen leaned back in his seat. He'd called Nathan and begged for his help, then heard no word whatsoever. Not a call, not a text, not even a courtesy of a yea or nay. And he obviously hadn't shown up. Now his dad was on a mission to find life-saving medicine, and he, too, had disappeared off the map. That meant that someone was watching them and trying to foil their plans to save Maisy. But how would they know whether Walter was going home to grab the hasax or just getting ready for work? Maybe it didn't matter. They just had to keep them occupied long enough to ensure Maisy died.

On the other hand, maybe it wasn't just occupation. His dad, maybe, because he was only a Time Agent, hardly a match for a seasoned Akari-bearer. But Nathan was a Builder, capable of manipulation the core of Creation itself. Few were dumb enough to try and fight him, fewer still even skilled enough to be a threat. Except...

Tommen stood, trying to make it look slow and natural. It wasn't hard. He'd been sitting down for a while now and his whole body had stiffened up, especially his arm. He had to keep that limber, or as limber as possible.

"I need to walk around," he declared solemnly.

He did not wait for Becky's reply, assuming she even heard him or even cared. She just sat in her own chair, staring at the tiny baby in the glass box whose life was slipping away. Tommen had done the impossible to bring his dad back from the brink of death, and he wasn't about to stop for his daughter.

As soon as he stepped out of the room, he knew something was off. Aside from the way everything was dead silent—and even on a quiet hospital floor, there was still the constant hum of activity—he felt the pressure on his body of being sucked into a Band. He looked around and spotted the only other moving figure in the Band. It was the nurse with the French braids. She leaned against the reception desk, casually playing with her nametag.

"It's a shame, really," she said, not looking at Tommen. "I'm sure she would have grown up to be just like you. But then, that seems like a huge problem, too, because you have caused nothing but trouble."

"Why are you doing this? She's an innocent baby. And whatever politics this is about...I'm not interested," Tommen insisted. "I'm not. I'm out." He gestured toward the room. "This is my life now. Not Time, not the Miaramila, not the Order, not the Akarin, not anyone else. Just me and my family. Who are you, anyway?"

Now she looked up and started walking toward him. As she closed the distance, she began shedding Disguises. The braided nurse turned into a dozen more nurses whom they'd interacted with over the last few days. Then she turned into Dr. Whitmore, the woman who had been overseeing Becky's pregnancy from the beginning. From there she turned into exactly the person Tommen was expecting: Julianna. Five-foot-five at the tallest with dark hair pulled back in a proper bun, face marred by precise scar lines.

She stopped hardly two feet from him. She held something out to him and he gingerly took it. It was Nathan's driver's license.

"Just like reattaching a leg to a stump," she purred. "But I want you to Feel her, too, so you know everything I know. I want you help me as much as possible."

"Where's my dad?" Tommen demanded hoarsely.

She waved a hand dismissively. "Oh, he's just trapped in a Band. Doesn't even realize it, and probably won't until he looks up and sees it's dark. And before you ask, a little voice manipulation is hardly a difficult feat. A dying little grandchild is an excellent reason to ask for the night off." She shifted her stance. "Your father is hardly a threat to me, or anyone at all anymore. You, however, are quite a nuisance, a little brat who needs to be taught a lesson."

"You poisoned my daughter with Borelian toxins."

Julianna grinned and shook her head. She fished a vial of fluid out of her dress. "No. Not Borelian poison, not quite. Derived from it, yes. It is, in essence, bottling the side effects of the toxins. One dose isn't exactly lethal, but with all the medicine little Maisy is getting, well..." She shrugged.

"If you were masquerading as Whitmore, did you somehow alter Maisy's DNA to give her Beckwith-Wiedemann?"

"Well, it is easier to do in a developing body with far fewer cells. I just needed a way to get her to stay in the hospital for a little while longer, buy me enough time to get to the hospital to give her the dose."

"Why are you doing this?" Tommen asked again, chest tight. "She's innocent in all of this. Why not come after me directly? I'm not liked or wanted by any of the factions, so it's not like I have a ton of backup."

Julianna got a look on her face of pure smug satisfaction. It was made even uglier by her scars. "You want to know why I don't go after you? Because it's too easy. Too predictable." She took another step back, her posture that of someone being it total command of the situation. "I've already driven you to murder, Tommen Forbes, and that was just to save yourself, maybe your dad, too. What else are you willing to do to save your daughter? So young, so precious, so innocent, as you say. Has she even known life outside of this hospital?"

She paused and stared at him with malicious intent. Tommen tried to keep his breathing even. *She's trying to provoke you, Tommen. Don't let her.*

"Trying to be the mature adult instead of the impulsive hothead," she went on. "You were willing to start a war to save your dying father. You killed not one but two people to save yourself. How much more is your daughter worth to you?"

"I don't need this," Tommen stated. "And I don't need you or your bullshit. I can go get the hasax myself. And you—" He pointed at her. "You can go to Hell. Only because of my daughter am I even letting you live."

"Oh, now we get into the threats," Julianna said, not even looking concerned. "You learned a lot from Rifun about posture and projecting, if little else as your war record proves. He was a lot better than you at a lot of things. At least when he made a threat, he sounded like he meant it. And he knew how to deliver."

Tommen was fully unprepared for the uppercut as her fist cracked into his jaw. He heard fabric tear and then a foot met his cheek. He stumbled to the side and tried to figure out what just happened. He was on all fours, feeling his mouth and jaw. Other than the sting and the ache, he didn't taste blood and it didn't feel like any teeth were loose.

"I don't have to kill you," Julianna said, walking up and kicking him in the face a second time. Now he tasted blood. "Not physically, anyway. Sometimes, death is too nice, too merciful. It makes you a martyr, a hero of sorts. Maybe you aren't liked by any of the factions, but that doesn't mean you don't have friends who would rally behind your death.

"But a spiritual, emotional, mental death. That's the best kind. Kill your daughter and watch you flail about in turmoil. Watch you descend into darkness and your friends drift away as they don't understand and don't know how to help you. Every suggestion they make is met with apathy or venom. Even your girlfriend will abandon you in the end, leaving you with nothing."

With a snarl, Tommen launched himself straight into Julianna in a full body slam, driving her to the ground. But she was small and slippery and weaseled her way out from under him, getting in a swift kick to his groin as she slithered away. All fury and motivation left him as pain exploded through his body, and he instinctively grabbed himself and curled up to protect the wounded area. He tried to bring his elbows together to protect his midsection, but Julianna stood and swung her foot around to give him a swift two kicks there as well before aiming for his head. He turned his head just in time to avoid a teeth-shattering blow, instead absorbing the force into his cheek. He may have felt his cheek crack, but he couldn't be sure as he took another blow to his damaged shoulder.

Julianna took several steps back. She was breathing hard and some of the primp had gone out of her bun. Tommen could see her dress was torn where she'd forced her way to a kick.

"You're a lover, not a fighter," she cooed. She squatted down to look at him where he lay on the ground. The pain was subsiding and he was no longer rigid in his position. He was relaxed, but still quite sore, and unable to do anything as she suddenly stood and stomped down right on his burned hand. She may as well have kicked him in the balls again and achieved the same effect, except this time he cried out in serious pain. But Julianna did not let up, and instead ground her heel into the burned flesh. Tears sprang to Tommen's eyes and he could feel his nose start to run.

"The Krydik, primitive and backwards. The twins, weak idiots. The bitch, primitive and stupid. Rifun and Cassius, primitive and superstitious. Your dad, an escaped criminal hiding behind the law. And now you, a foolish teenager who has failed at everything he's tried. I will give the Author a chosen one worth respecting, write a book worth reading."

Then she let off. Tommen was sniffing and breathing hard and in some excruciating pain. His whole body felt limp and exhausted. His arm was throbbing something awful and just the thought of moving his legs or hips was nauseating.

"Actions have consequences," Julianna stated. "You seem to think that time, distance, and intent somehow make you immune to this fact. As if the idea that you're a 'family man' now somehow excuses you of your wrongdoing."

"What wrongdoing?" Tommen asked, his voice hardly more than a whisper.

"Poor choice of allegiance, meddling in general, cowardice, treason, and just making things difficult for me. I can't let these go unpunished. It sets a bad example for the masses. You understand."

He coughed and managed to roll onto all fours, every part of his body protesting. "I understand you're a sadistic bitch with a real attitude problem."

He grunted as she kicked him in the ribs, using Force to augment the strike, and put him back on the ground.

"Let me give you a bit of advice. Stay down."

"And let you hurt my daughter?" He again struggled onto all fours. "Not a chance in Hell."

"You know this, do you? Well, only one way to find out."

She went to kick him again, but he was done playing games. He Banded and caught her foot. Instead of throwing her off-balance one way or the other, he yanked. In order to save herself from doing the splits, Julianna was forced down. He pulled again, sliding her across the smooth tile floor under him until her jaw hit his fist as he got up on his knees.

It stopped her dead and Tommen got down on her, pinning her shoulders to the ground. But she did not struggle. Instead, she just got that smug look on her face again.

"You want to get rough? All right. Let's get rough."

Then Tommen felt himself being thrown into the air, a Gravity track easily getting him off of Julianna and straight into the ceiling. Even once he managed to break or counteract the track, she was already back on her feet. Just as his feet touched the ground, she turned a Light trick, the same one he had used. She took all the Light in the room, all the ceiling lights, the desk lights, the computer screens and monitor lights, and amplified all of them so that Tommen had to shield his eyes. Then, just as suddenly, they were gone. The ceiling lights and computer screens went black. Still the bright image was burned into his retinas, and he was momentarily blind.

Something hit him square between the shoulder blades and he pitched forward. Frantically, he reached for his glasses to switch them to night vision. He only just found the right setting and turned to see Julianna bearing down on him like a ghoul in a horror movie when she swung something at him and it connected with his head.

It didn't knock him out, but he was dazed and feeling the darkness close in on him. Then he was being lifted and laid down. He knew the lights came back on, but he could hardly react. Someone was speaking, but he couldn't make out who. He couldn't even really be sure what they were saying, except something about "the final dose." Part of his brain screamed at him to get up. But the rest of him...just wanted to sleep for a while.

He did not dream, though his head still ached the whole time he was asleep. Surely someone would find him, he thought. He must have visible wounds of some form, something to alert someone to mischief.

But nothing happened. And the next thing he knew, he was being lightly shaken awake. His head felt like a lead balloon with an ax in it, like the worst hangover in the history of hangovers. Blinking concussed sleep from his eyes, he found Dr. Polski looking at him.

"*Beth ddigwyddodd?*" Tommen mumbled. (What happened?) He felt his face, fully expecting to find swelling, bruising, anything of the sort. Nothing. Probably Julianna had Banded his more obvious wounds, leaving the head blow just to ensure that he would sleep.

"They're about to take Maisy off life support," Dr. Polski said softly, almost whispering.

Tommen scrambled to sit up. "*Beth? Beth o'r gloch yw hi?*" He gritted his teeth at the pain in his head. (What? What time is it?)

"Are you feeling okay? Do you understand me?"

He paused for a second, trying to bring everything back into focus. But damn it all, his head hurt. He looked at the elderly doctor. The man frowned and gently patted Tommen's shoulder, standing and looking far older than he was.

"What happened?" Tommen asked, finally finding his English. "What time is it?"

"It's just after eleven. Maisy went on life support about four-thirty, but there's nothing more it can do. She's just...deteriorated."

Dr. Polski sounded at once hollow and brimming with emotion.

"Why didn't anyone wake me?"

"Becky thought you would do well to have the sleep. There's just nothing more..." Dr. Polski sniffed hard and took a shuddering breath. "Nothing more anyone can do."

They entered the room. Becky and her mom were there, as well as a doctor and a couple nurses. Tommen saw Becky had been weeping; her eyes were red, cheeks wet and sticky, hair disheveled. Beside her, her mom didn't look much better. Tommen felt his heart twist and his stomach flip. Tears sprang to his eyes unbidden as he turned his attention to Maisy in her little glass box.

She no longer looked like a mummy. Tubes and wires obscured her mummy bandages. Even though the machines were still working, she looked like death, ashen and still.

"We'll take her off life support," the doctor said softly, "so you can hold her in her final moments. I don't expect it will be more than five or ten minutes."

It was a kind gesture, really, but Tommen was hardly of a mind to appreciate it. Instead, he watched, rooted to the floor as life support was removed. Nothing to breathe for her, nothing to shock her heart back into rhythm. Even the tiny IV ports were removed. One of the nurses handed Maisy to Becky. All that was left were a few tiny nodes to monitor her heart.

Tommen took one of Maisy's tiny hands in just his fingertips. Already she was cooler than she should have been, and she barely moved as if to grip his fingers. He closed his eyes and Felt.

It was like slogging through tar. He could feel her systems shutting down. It didn't hurt, in the same way it doesn't hurt to pull off a dead and blackened fingernail. It's just something that happens. But there was nothing coming for her now. Nothing new to regrow. Just one by one, cells dying, giving up, her organs failing.

Even her mind was not as active as it had been. If she had been a roaring bonfire in the morning, now she was little more than the flame at the end of a matchstick. She had only two things on her mind now, the Comforting One and the Strong One. Tommen did his best to reassure her that they were both there.

He paused. What else did he tell her? Would she understand? Was it even worth trying to tell her anything? Would it matter at this point? He decided no. No, the only thing that mattered now was letting her know that she was loved, even as they let her go. It was ripping his heart in half to admit it, but there was nothing left. Even if his dad walked in right now with the hasax, her organs had failed and she was on her way out.

Tommen felt his world collapse around him as all the dreams that never were suddenly vanished. He would not see his daughter have children of her own. He would not see her get married or date, nor would he be consulted as to whether he approved of said dates. He would not see her graduate high school and go off to college. He would not listen to her gripe about her friends and enemies and frenemies and all the drama of middle and high school. He would not cling desperately to his seat as she learned to drive. He would not take her to a daddy-daughter dance. He would not see her get braces or acne or the makeup to try and make it all better. He would not take her to dance or violin recitals or karate tournaments. He would not help her with her homework and try to make her feel better when she got less than perfection. He would not be there to put a bandaid on a skinned knee. He would not walk her to her first day of school. He would not oversee a playdate with all her cousins. He would not see her first steps. He would not see her first tooth. He would not show her the universe.

He hadn't even changed a diaper or wiped up baby puke. About the only thing he had done that was even remotely close to the fatherhood he had imagined was constantly being up and watching over her, being unceremoniously woken up in the middle of the night because something was wrong. And something had indeed gone very wrong.

They'd been played from the very beginning. Julianna had been five steps ahead of them the entire time, taking this joyous occasion and using it to destroy them so completely. And he, idealistic fool that he was, had missed it.

He felt her fading away, like lights turning off in a building at night, one by one until only the desk lamp was left. Even thoughts of the Comforting One and the Strong One were slipping into merely a sensation of fatigue.

It's okay, he told her. *Comforting One and Strong One are here. We'll always be here. You just go to sleep now.* He sniffed and wiped his eyes. *Everything will look better in the morning.*

There was a last moment, a sensation of love and security and contentment, that all was well as long as Comforting One and Strong One were there.

Then she was gone.

Tommen felt it the same way she did, just a little drop off into unconsciousness, as if sleeping. Then she went further than that, just a little drop. Then the darkness closed in, cool and gentle, pushing him out of her mind, out of her body. There was nothing left to touch, and Feeling her would only produce a chunk of flesh.

Becky's wail broke his trance, but he was still slow to come back to himself. Even then, everything was a sluggish blur, mentally speaking. Even though he'd been there, he'd Felt his daughter slip away, he still couldn't process it. In some foolish part of his mind, he was waiting for the monitor to start blipping again, as if her heart had magically restarted. It would be a true miracle.

But nothing of the sort happened. Becky was crying, her parents were holding her, and Tommen just felt like an island. No, not even an island, because islands were still anchored to the land. No, more like a boat, adrift at sea and tossed by the waves.

The nurse came close and nearly got her head snapped off by

Becky, but she just gently reached in to remove the wires. The time of death was noted, March 13th at eleven-twenty-two, and they were left alone.

Tommen didn't know how much time had passed, but finally Becky seemed to come back to herself, enough to make a coherent sentence anyway.

"I want her little dress," she blubbered. "I don't want to see these bandages she should be in her little dress."

So Maisy was put back in her tiny fur-trimmed dress, the one she was supposed to have gone home in. Well, Tommen thought, she'd gone Home.

With Maisy in her dress, Mrs. Polski suggested taking some pictures, just as if they were normal baby photos. Tommen and Becky were both hesitant, but ultimately agreed. These would be the last pictures they would ever have of their daughter. Tommen got out his phone and found a message from his dad.

"I just looked up and saw it was dark and there was a message on my phone from Dean giving his condolences. I know I've been in a Band. Did...what I think happened happen?"

Tommen wiped his eyes and replied, "Yes. She's gone. We're taking last pictures."

"I'm on my way."

His dad showed up in uniform, just as if he'd come from work. Even so, he would not be going back, Tommen knew, not tonight. Just looking at him, the man was a wreck, no matter how hard he tried to hide it. He'd been tasked with saving his granddaughter's life and he'd failed. Tommen knew well how he felt.

But Walter did get the photo the guys at the precinct had wanted to see, whether he could in fact hold Maisy in one of his huge hands. As it turned out, he couldn't. She was just a little too big for that, or maybe it was her dress. Whatever the case, he ended up using two hands to cradle the child.

Maybe it was morbid to be taking pictures with a deceased infant, but Tommen found that it did help a little. They got the pictures they wanted, the pictures they craved so they would always remember little Maisy. When the doctor finally returned to take her away, it was just a little easier to let her go.

Chapter Twenty-Eight
Ashes and Ink

The flowers were baby's breath. Becky thought it would be appropriate. They graced the table where a large photo of Maisy sat next to the little box that held her ashes. It was an adult box for adult ashes, but there was hardly the same quantity of ash inside. Even being a baby, both Tommen and Becky had taken some of the ash and wore them in respective necklaces. Becky's was a heart-shaped kind of locket where Tommen chose a vial.

It was March 27th, two weeks after Maisy passed. He still couldn't think of it as death, no matter how many times he lay awake at night, terrified of going to sleep, reliving that one moment as he felt his daughter slip from this world. It hadn't hurt, just a gentle descent into sleep and then beyond. But he still couldn't think of it as death.

They had not made their escape as planned. Nathan was gone; Godwin, the twins, Kayla, they were all silent, probably gone as well; and there was no need anyway. Julianna wasn't going to kill him. She already had. She'd won.

Sometimes he woke up in the middle of the night, wondering why he was home and not at the hospital.

Sometimes when he was in class and barely able to focus, he thought about how he needed to get to the hospital after he got out, so he could check on his daughter and see how she was doing.

Sometimes at work, he would think about how excited he was to get home and see his family and be able to show off as the protector and provider to his wife and daughter.

He slept terribly, and it was obvious to basically everyone, even complete strangers.

His grades weren't failing, but they were suffering.

He was given easy tasks at work because no one wanted him to fall and hurt himself or get careless with power tools.

Maybe things would be better after the memorial, he thought.

It was held at the Catholic church Becky and her mom frequented, but the Jewish side of the family was a large presence as well, everyone putting aside whatever theological differences they had to come together for the one universal truth: death. It didn't matter who you were or what you believed, from atheists to Christians to Jews to Muslims, Hindus, and everyone else in the world, death came for everyone eventually.

Some sooner than others, it seemed.

Truth be told, Tommen felt a little ashamed of how out of it he'd been lately, and still was. He'd only known Maisy for three days. Even if he wanted to get sentimental, he still couldn't say he knew her for more than nine months. What he was really weeping over were his own lost dreams and everything he'd imagined and conjured up in his head. He mourned for something that hadn't happened yet.

Because it wouldn't happen. And he felt ashamed for feeling ashamed. Why should he be? This was his daughter for crying out loud! This was his product of creation, a tiny being that had been all his. Well, his and Becky's. But it truly had been a miracle of life. Why shouldn't he weep for its end?

Maybe it wasn't just about the dreams that never happened, but his own failure. If it had been just a genetic defect, that would have been one thing. It wouldn't absolve him of all his guilt and shame, but it would be an answer he could more readily accept. The idea that they had been played from the very beginning, that Maisy's DNA had been manipulated so as to put her in the hospital so she could be poisoned—all under the guise of being helped by doctors and nurses—was troubling at best. Then, to uncover the plot, have a plan in place to foil it, to neutralize the poison and bring her back from the brink of death, only to be foiled themselves...it was too much for Tommen to bear some days.

He'd been knocked unconscious, his dad trapped in a Band. Nathan was dead. Miach and Micaiah and Kayla, even Godwin, hadn't made any kind of contact, even to express condolences; Tommen could only conclude that Julianna had killed them, too.

It put a slouch in Tommen's back and a slump in his shoulders. He sat in the front of the church, elbows on his knees, hands folded in front of his face, staring at the picture and the box. He'd long ago stopped crying openly, but his heart still felt as though it had been torn in two. He just had nothing more to give.

He had been the Strong One, the one his daughter depended on for safety and protection. And he'd been unable to protect her, even when he knew what was wrong. He'd failed. Miserably.

He looked around. Becky was nowhere to be seen. His dad was a few rows back on the other side, talking to Dean and Kate of all people who had come to show their support.

His dad was suffering just as much, Tommen knew. First his daughter now his granddaughter he'd failed to protect, and the second time, he'd been part of the rescue team, caught in a trap he'd been unaware was sprung. To look at him, you knew he was hurting, but he still seemed to be weathering it better than Tommen.

Tommen went back to staring at the photo. It showed Maisy in her little dress, the first time around, when they'd still had hope that everything would be all right. Pink and dry and curled up in Becky's arms. She'd been awake at the time, one of the few pictures they had of her with her eyes open, bright and blue and curious, trying to figure out this new thing called life. But as long as she had the Comforting One and the Strong One, she would be okay.

Tommen rubbed his face and looked at the ground. The Strong One. He'd been the one she looked to, one of the few things in her entire world, and he'd failed her.

His heart jumped but his body remained rigid as his dad sat down beside him.

"How are you doing, kiddo?" Walter asked gently. "Between work and school and holing up in your room, I don't see you much."

"Nothing to see," Tommen murmured.

"How are things between you and Becky?"

He shrugged. They still lived together, still slept in the same bed, but they barely spoke to each other. Any attempt he made to try and fix things, show her he still cared, show her that he wasn't trying to close everyone out, she shrugged him off. He was just waiting for the day when he came home and found her gone, moved back in with her parents. Already the wedding had been canceled, or at least "postponed" her mother said, until they got through this difficult time. Problem was, Tommen didn't know that they would, at least, not together.

"How's work?" Tommen asked, trying to turn the conversation off of himself.

"Good days and bad days," his dad answered evasively.

June 10th was his official retirement date, an executive decision once word got to the sheriff that Maisy had gone. His retirement party would be the following day, a Saturday. Despite being short-staffed, Walter's hours were also being tapered off, going from five or six nights a week down to four or five. April would see him down to four, maybe three if he needed it.

Their already stunted conversation was cut short as the priest got up to speak. People meandered their way to their seats. Walter scooted down to make room for Becky who sat beside Tommen with no more warmth than a familiar stranger. Actually, if he had to put words to it, it was like sitting next to your ex in class and having to work on a project together, especially when you and your ex still kind of liked each other but didn't want to admit it.

But this wasn't high school drama where the only thing at stake was reputation and rumors. This was real life. And real death. Tommen looked at his daughter's eyes once more, a glutton for punishment as his heart was ripped in half again.

They stood and sang a hymn. The Jewish side of the family followed this with a Hebrew song of their own, deep and melodic and haunting, echoing in Tommen's mind even after they sat back down.

Tommen had wrestled with a number of questions afterwards. Indeed, he still was. What was the point of giving him a daughter if she was only going to be taken away? He didn't care who answered, whether it was God or the Author or Pango-Pango. Whoever was in charge of these things, why did this happen? Why was evil allowed to run free, Disguising itself as helpful doctors and nurses when really it was just another Kevorkian? And even if she had been allowed to run free, why had he been so blind to it until the very end? Why couldn't he have seen through it, seen the charade?

He ran over in his mind every day at the hospital, every OB/GYN appointment, looking for clues, something to tell him where he'd gone wrong. He could come up with nothing except that he had been far too trusting. He had expected a more blatant, physical attack, something he could stand up against and be the hero. He'd been completely blind to the idea that Evil could Disguise itself as Good. It had always just seemed like something that Good would not allow, it would not allow itself to be impersonated. And even if Evil tried such a thing, there would always be a tell. A fake mustache, an evil goatee, a flash of lightning at just the right time.

But life was not a cartoon. Life was not a movie. Movies and TV were scripted and predictable. Even if it took a sequel of some form, Good always won. But only because the script writer said so.

Sometimes at night, Tommen would hear Becky murmuring prayers in the darkness, whispering and sniffing. She went through Catholic prayers and Jewish prayers in every language she knew, looking for comfort or answers, he did not know.

Tommen wasn't even sure that he wanted to entertain the thought of a Higher Being anymore. Even if God was out there, or the Author, clearly they hated him. Maybe this was punishment for sins he wasn't aware of committing, or maybe they were just vindictive assholes who needed a voodoo doll to poke for divine stress relief. Seven billion people on Earth, plus how many trillions throughout the universe, and he was the one they deemed the crash test dummy in order for the remaining people to have happy, productive lives.

Becky's parents had told him not to lose hope, not to lose faith. God was in control and He loved all His children. Everything would work out for good in the end. If nothing else, just remember that Maisy was in Heaven now with God. She was happy and joyful, with her body exactly as it should be. She wasn't in pain, wasn't suffering. She was watching over them now, proud of her Mom and Dad and wishing them well. Tommen wondered whether she should even go through the trouble of looking down. He also wondered if it had really been worth the trouble to destroy his and Becky's dreams of having a child, just so God could have another soul of a child with Him. Didn't abortion give Him enough baby souls to love without snatching away the souls of children who were wanted?

He didn't know. He didn't understand. To an extent, he didn't care. Nor did he get up to speak at the memorial. He didn't know what he would say. It wasn't like a funeral where you could reminisce about a good long life, school and work and all the crazy antics people did through the years. He couldn't say he really knew her during the pregnancy, and the three days she'd spent in the world had all been in a hospital. Part of it was in surgery, most of it was sleeping in a glass box. And he certainly couldn't hope to explain how he'd Felt her, known her simple mind. He could not hope to explain how her whole world revolved around the Comforting One and the Strong One, how he'd willed love and peace and security to her through a link that sounded as ludicrous as it was magical.

He became very conscious of the vial around his neck. Little more than half a teaspoon of ash, he had held his daughter more in the last two weeks than he had in the three days in the hospital. He took it off only when he showered because he was too afraid that water might somehow get the waterproof vial and destroy the ash. Even so, he was utterly petrified of losing it because it was literally irreplaceable. Jewelry might be an heirloom; it might be treasured. But the ash of a loved one could not be replaced by any stretch of the imagination. Whether it was parent or child, if it went missing or got destroyed, it was gone forever.

The service was short and sweet. Again, it was only the memorial for a newborn baby, not a funeral for a ninety year old woman with hoards of children and grandchildren. There was nothing to say and no words to describe the pain.

His dad and Becky's parents left first to open up the reception room and get everything going there. That had been part of the plan. Tommen, meanwhile, was one of the last to leave. He stared at the ground, then stared at the box. Back at the ground, then up at the box.

It was a simple wooden box, sealed on the inside, stained a rich dark color on the outside, making the woodgrain stand out. The remains of his child sealed inside. The last he would see of her, save for the ash in the vial around his neck. He dug out the vial and stared at it. It was cheap, hardly any pure metals though it was supposed to look like a brushed bronze. At the very least, it seemed sturdy and he wasn't too worried about any of the links spontaneously busting apart or the link on top of the vial breaking. All the same, as surely as he felt the agony of losing his daughter, it was only amplified as he considered what might happen if he lost this vial.

In his peripheral vision, Tommen saw the priest walking slowly across the room, heading his direction. He was not forceful or intrusive. Probably he would ask if he was all right, ask to pray for him. Nothing sounded worse at that moment. Tommen put the vial back under his shirt, stood, and walked out of the sanctuary to the reception.

As per usual, Mrs. Polski had been the caterer for this event, with a huge line of food set up and waiting. The line of people stretched halfway around the room, and it wasn't moving all that fast. To appease the hungry, grumbling masses, the memory boards had been erected at intervals along the projected line.

Being only three days old and not having a ton of pictures, Mrs. Polski and Becky's sisters had gotten creative with their work, to make it look bigger than it was. One display was made up entirely of the ultrasound photos, taken religiously every few weeks. They were Becky's photo strips, as Tommen had been unwilling to give his up, and they were tucked neatly away in one of his Books for safekeeping. There was another display of pictures of Becky when she was pregnant, labels letting everyone know either the month or even the exact week. Suddenly it all felt like so long ago.

Four more displays showcased pictures of Maisy for every day she was in the hospital, each labeled with the day: March 10, 11, 12, or 13.

March 10th, when she was a brand new infant, just lifted from her mother's womb and meeting her family for the first time.

March 11th, when Beckwith-Wiedemann was confirmed and she had to have surgery on her tongue so it wouldn't block her mouth and throat and suffocate her. She'd still been relatively healthy then, and there had been a chance for her to come home.

March 12th, when she began to starve and Tommen and Becky made the hard decision to have one of her kidneys removed to try and make room for the rest of her organs.

March 13th, when the surgery failed and her systems began to shut down, when she went on life support and ultimately died.

March 13th, when Tommen had tried and failed to protect his daughter from a vengeful bitch.

As soon as his presence was noted, he was ushered to the front of the line to grab a plate of food. He didn't know why. He wasn't especially hungry. Actually, he felt sick to his stomach. Still, he got his food and went to sit down.

He chose a middle table, to make it hard for people to get in and out and get to him, but it did not deter them from, once they were through the food line, coming to him and expressing condolences. He thanked each of them in turn, but his words were more mechanical than emotional. Mostly he just wanted all of this to be over so he might be able to move on. He had to get his grades up and he had to get his head back in the game at work.

Pithy sentiment that dissipated as soon as it blossomed.

At least the graveside service was limited to immediate family only, so it was only him, Becky, his dad, and her parents. Where the

Catholic priest had done the memorial service, now the Jewish rabbi oversaw the graveside service. It, too, was short and to the point.

Then they left.

And that was it.

Maisy was gone. She'd been cremated and now she was buried, or she would be later in the day when the family wasn't there to watch. It was the last Tommen would see and know of her, save for the vial around his neck.

With as scattered as Tommen was in his present mental state, he and Becky had ridden with his dad. The ride in had been silent, and the ride home was no different. It was as though they were all deaf, and only outside noise like the rumble of the engine or the whine of the garage door said they were not.

Dress shoes were removed and returned to closets, along with suit coats. Pants, shirts, and dresses were tossed in the washer but abandoned shortly thereafter. No one was hungry.

There was no baby to take care of.

Toys still lay scattered about the living room, and the clothes were still in the dresser. Now, with the memorial over, Becky slowly went to work packing up some or most of the stuff. The toys went away quickly and easily, and it made the living room look huge once it was clean. The clothes she was less enthusiastic about cleaning out for the simple fact that she had made them. She had spent months painstakingly measuring, cutting, sewing, every shirt and skirt and dress and onesie, all for her little girl. Finally she pushed the drawer closed, unwilling to give them up just yet.

Tommen knew better than to suggest that they could have another or otherwise adopt. For one, Becky was still recovering from her C-section and there was a good chance she couldn't have any more kids. For two, and the real reason that kept his mouth wisely shut, was that he knew it would be the same story all over again. Somewhere, deep down, he knew that this hadn't been a one and done deal. He knew that Julianna was keeping tabs on him, and any way that she could hurt him, she would. She would take away all his children, break his heart any way he could, and take every opportunity to take away his happily ever after.

The following morning as he woke up for class, he found himself in a panic. His necklace had gone. His frantic scramble lasted only a few minutes until he found it under the bed. The vial and chain were in tact, but the clasp had broken.

Cheap Chinese garbage anyway, he thought. He pocketed the vial instead and headed off to class. He did not kiss Becky goodbye. Indeed, she rolled over and refused. She had given up her spring semester so she could take care of Maisy. Now she had no reason, no motivation. The most she did now was take care of the house and sometimes go down to her parents' house to continue her sewing.

Tommen checked his pocket frequently throughout the day to reassure himself the vial was still there, wondering what he was going to do to ensure that any fix he made was permanent.

His inspiration came to him the next day in class. He stayed on campus for a little while afterwards, poking around on his phone for a bit before finally getting up the nerve to make a call.

"White Horse Tattoo," the voice on the other end answered.

"Yeah, do you guys do ash tattoos?" Tommen asked, feeling very much like a small child asking for a piece of candy.

"We don't, and we also don't recommend it because of health concerns. It can cause a lot of problems, no matter how healthy you are or how carefully you and we handle the ash."

He thanked them and hung up. He sat there for a few more minutes before dialing a new number.

It took four tries before he found someone at least willing to talk. He set an appointment and hung up. Then he did some texting around to trade days on the job site.

It was still about ten more minutes before he got up the motivation to get in his car and go home. He bypassed his dad in the kitchen and went down to the room he shared with Becky. She was sitting on the bed reading a book. Judging by her posture and her glassy stare, she was staring at the page but not really seeing what was there. Mr. Snuffles was curled up in her lap. Carefully, Tommen set his bag on the end of the bed and dug out his books to start on his homework.

His dad went to work, popping his head in the door to let them know he was leaving and wishing them a good night. It was his way of showing support and maybe try to get them talking again. Tommen knew he meant well, and he didn't stop his dad from doing it, but he feared it was a vain effort.

After another hour or so, Tommen put down his pencil. Becky was still staring at her book. It even looked like the same page.

"I'm getting a tattoo," he stated.

She did not react.

He frowned and was just about to turn back to his work when she spoke.

"Why?"

"Because I don't want to lose the ash."

She looked up, her gaze confused and not quite there. "What does that have to do with a tattoo?"

"You mix the ash with the ink before it's used."

"You can do that?"

He nodded.

She blinked and stared at him for a minute. Tommen knew the look in her eye. She was on painkillers for her surgery.

Finally she asked, "When are you doing that?"

"I'm going to talk to the guy tomorrow after class. Then I guess we'll see."

Becky nodded, a little life coming back to her. She shifted position on the bed. Then, "I want to go with you."

"Thought tattoos were forbidden for Jews and Catholics?"

"God has already taken my child away. What more can He do to me? If this isn't Hell, I don't know what is."

So it was that after class the following day, Tommen raced home to get Becky and get back into the city to meet the artist. Salem Tattoo was in a nondescript part of town, but it was by no means a threatening place. It seemed to be a place for societal outcasts, people with tattoos, piercings, graffiti artists, unconventional musicians, the modern hippie. Becky looked a little disconcerted about the whole thing, but Tommen was quite accustomed to the outcast scene.

The suite was part tattoo studio, part art gallery, and part museum, all of it quite tasteful, as if it might be found in some travel magazine highlighting little-known backroads gems and attractions. It helped to calm Becky down some as she diverted her attention to the art and museum aspect of it. Most of it was centered around mining and all the legends therein, salt and specters, coal and ghouls, copper and the supernatural. At the last second, Tommen spotted a tiny piece about him. Tommen Forbes, the youngest child to ever disappear into the cave. He disappeared in the spring, and if you go into the old salt cave around that time, sometimes you can still hear him laughing, playing games for all eternity. Or so saith the ghost hunting article.

"Can I help you?" a man asked.

"Depends, are you Russ?" Tommen wondered. "One-thirty consult with Tommen."

"Sure, sure. Step into my office."

His "office" was basically just the front desk. Becky came over as well, mentioning her curiosity about the whole thing.

In a way, Tommen kind of hoped that maybe this little endeavor would bring some life back to her, to them, to their relationship. Maybe there was still a little hope for them, that this didn't have to all end in catastrophe. Might be they just had to come to an agreement to not have kids, period, natural or adopted. Maybe it would just have to be the two of them.

"Ash tattoos aren't the most fun anyway, but the way the two of you are sitting there like zombies tells me that this is something really bad," Russ said.

"Our daughter died," Tommen stated flatly. "Three weeks ago."

Russ' eyes got huge and he nodded slowly. "Understood." He shifted in his seat. "Well, I don't need to tell you that tattoos are permanent. It's illegal for me to do you if you're under the influence of alcohol or drugs, but I also have a personal policy of not tattooing if you're under the influence of grief. I feel for you. I do. And, honestly, it's kind of difficult to have an ash tattoo without someone dying. But I don't want you to do something spur of the moment while you're not thinking straight. Not trying to insult, but I just hate to see rash decisions in the aftermath, you understand."

"I understand," Tommen said calmly. He fished the vial from his pocket. "These are my daughter's ashes. And I've already almost lost them multiple times. Just in the last week or so. I can't stand the thought of losing them permanently."

"Same," Becky murmured.

"All right," Russ conceded. "Just wanted to get that out of the way. So then, what are you guys thinking? You want the same thing, different, what are your thoughts? I can tell you right now, looking at your left hand—how far does that go up?"

Tommen rolled up his sleeve. "All the way to the shoulder."

"That's not going to happen. The scar tissue won't be able to hold the ink and it will just bleed everywhere and be a mess."

"Makes sense. But that's not what I had in mind."

"Great. Let's talk."

It was nothing especially complicated, certainly no portraits. Becky had suggested it on the way over, but Tommen put a stop to that idea. They might be nice to start, but if anything went wrong, it was over. Similarly, it had to stand up to the test of time without bleeding, folding, or get scrunched and squished by changing skin. With designs and whatnot, it was more manageable and less traumatic to the image compared to a portrait which kind of needed to be pristine in order for it to not be ugly.

It didn't take long to hash out the details, and an appointment was set for the following Monday.

"Drink lots of water to make sure you're hydrated and your skin is hydrated, and eat a good meal before you come," Russ told them. "Even a small tattoo, you're going to lose blood."

They had to turn over the ash to the artist, which was a waking nightmare in itself. But it was necessary. The ash was going to be fired again in a small kiln, ground up into a fine powder so that it was like silk, then fired a second time before being mixed with the ink. Every precaution was taken to minimize the risk of infection or other complications.

They thanked him and headed out. Tommen knew several people who just got ecstatic over every tattoo they got, as if they won the lottery every time despite losing a small fortune every time. He did not feel this way. He wouldn't even say he felt excited or happy. If he had to pick a word, he might have said relieved. The only way the ash could be taken from him, after this tattoo, was by literally taking his arm off. And if someone was taking his arm off, well then, he had bigger issues in the immediate moment.

Becky was by far more distressed about it. For her, tattoos were evil, demonic. To puncture your skin with a needle like that was to invite the Devil into your blood, into your very being. Tommen wondered if it was really any different than the pills she was taking. He wasn't even sure she was aware of her growing addiction. He made a passing comment about it once, but she made an equally passive comment about her six month recovery time.

"If that's the case, should you be getting a tattoo?" Tommen asked. He was equal parts concerned and trying to give her an out. He didn't want to see tattoo regret, either, especially for religious reasons. "I mean, it is still skin trauma you're experiencing, and your body is already trying to heal from—"

"It's fine," Becky told him. "It's a small tattoo, no worse than if Mr. Snuffles gave me a good clawing."

He was still unsure, but in no mood to argue. Really he was just trying to give her an out. He'd been Banding her here and there to help speed up the healing process. He estimated that she was about halfway through her recovery, even if she didn't realize it.

Neither of them said anything about the tattoos to their parents, nor did Tommen bring it up at work. He simply stated that the reason he'd needed the day off was just...because he did. Sometimes that happened. Chris had been very understanding and supportive about it, and a couple of the guys said they were available if he needed to talk or have a beer after work. Tommen thanked them and tried to make it look as though he was coming back to life, back around to the real world and moving on. He doubted anyone was really fooled.

He himself wasn't even fooled. He still felt a wreck. He was still plagued by either insomnia or nightmares at night.

He hadn't seen Chandler at all, which was just as well, he thought. Chandler had been right. Tommen didn't want him around. The man had known about this. He'd known about Julianna's treachery and her plot to kill Maisy. But he put his blind devotion to the Author over the life of his friend's child. At least, Tommen had always considered Chandler a friend. A guide. A mentor. Did Chandler see him that way? And if he had, why had he kept silent? Why would he have let this happen? Why would he let Tommen sink into this darkness when he'd had the knowledge to prevent it? No. Tommen didn't want Chandler around. The consequences of betrayal cut both ways. Chandler could stay in his cave.

That didn't mean that the loss of friendship didn't hurt, on top of everything else that was hurting. Lying there in the dark, Tommen wondered if he would even feel the tattoo gun, or if the physical pain would come as a relief. The body could only feel so much pain at one time. That was why there was the joke about if your foot was hurting, well, drop something on the other foot. The body could not well process both instances of pain. Perhaps this would be the same way. His mind could not possibly hold on to all the emotional pain while being actively torn open by a fast-moving needle. Could it?

Well, he was going to find out, he thought as his alarm went off. He slapped it off and grudgingly pulled himself out of bed to get ready for class. Monday again. April already. Just a few days shy of what would have been his daughter's one month birthday. Or anniversary? Didn't matter, he decided, because she was gone.

He picked up Becky after class and drove to the tattoo studio. Neither of them said anything about a tattoo to Walter, just that they were going out. Tommen could see his dad was relieved at the prospect, that they were working things out, maybe going to stick together. Maybe that wedding was going to happen after all, so there would be some sort of happy ending. Tommen wondered what his dad would think when they returned with fresh tattoos.

His dad was leery of tattoos, to say the least. All throughout his life, tattoos were reserved for sailors and criminals. Seeing how he had once been the latter, he didn't enjoy "prison being used as a fashion statement." Only in the last decade had tattoos become truly mainstream. Now his son was getting one? More to the point, his deeply religious girlfriend was getting one, too? Well, he'd already convinced her to have sex and they'd had a baby together. A tattoo seemed like pretty small potatoes.

Tommen managed to rein in his sour mood as they walked in the door. Russ greeted them and sent them to a small table to sign waivers and all the other fun paperwork while he took their IDs and made copies.

"Okay, who wants to go first?" the man asked once everything had been copied, signed, initialed, and sealed in blood.

Tommen went first, hopping in the chair and watching Russ with a sharp eye as the man pulled on gloves, and opened up a few new packages of needles. He set out a couple different guns, and rummaged in a cupboard for a small vial of black ink, a special label on it. Tommen wouldn't say he wasn't incredibly nervous. He'd never had a reason not to get a tattoo, other than his dad's wariness, but there was just something so...permanent about it. It wouldn't just fade away in ten years and it couldn't just be undone. Once it was in, it was in. Needles would rip skin and inject ink and then it was all over.

The image was printed on a small piece of carbon paper. From there, Russ brushed some clear gel over the site and carefully laid the image down flat. When he peeled it off, the outline was there in bright purple.

"You going to be all right, my man?" Russ asked, hand hovering over the guns. "Last chance to walk away clean."

Tommen let out a breath. Maisy's ashes were already mixed with the ink. He could walk away clean, but he couldn't get her ashes back. After a minute, he nodded. "Yeah. I'm ready. Go ahead."

The design was the same for both him and Becky, a stylized letter M, about an inch and a half square, maybe closer to two inches for him. He'd elected to get it on the inside of his wrist, right near his pulse. While sweet and sentimental, the road to getting there was far more painful than he'd anticipated. He was not fat by any stretch of the imagination and had no padding to cushion the blow as the needle ripped through thin, delicate skin and over tendons.

How did people do this time and again, coming back on a weekly, monthly or yearly basis? Up and down both arms, legs, their stomachs and backs, neck and head? How did people suffer this to their hands and face? And this was just the outline. There was still the fill, and the whole center of the design was right over those tender tendons. It wasn't just the actual scoring of the needle, but the way Russ had to constantly wipe off the excess ink, irritating the already wounded skin.

"A little more than you expected?" Russ asked, staring intently at his work but apparently knowing how Tommen was feeling. "Listen, man, it really won't take that long. I promise. This is a pretty small piece. But it is a tender area, I won't lie. If you want, conversation can be a good distraction. Doesn't bother me."

Becky was off looking at art and the museum, not wanting to sit there and think about what she was going to have to go through.

"Mind if I ask how your arm got burned?" Russ went on.

"Um, a fire," Tommen answered, pulling his thoughts away from pain and on the conversation. "It was a wildfire. I was trying to save one of my campers."

"Wait a minute, so you're that kid from a couple years ago...?" The man still did not look up, but he grinned as he worked. "Yeah. Cool, man. I saw that on the news. You're a hero, dude."

"Don't feel like much of one."

Capable of saving everyone but my own daughter, he mused. *I can kill, I can start wars, but I can't save an infant in a hospital. Good going, hero.*

The conversation went cold. But, as promised, the tattoo didn't take long. Fill was a pain in the ass and always took longer than you thought it should, Russ explained, but it got done nonetheless.

Finally free of the pain, Tommen forced himself to relax, closing his eyes while Russ got everything cleaned up, just as pristine as when he had walked in, ready to do it all over again for Becky. Tommen opened his eyes and watched as the man wrapped the site in a bandage. Then he handed Tommen a printed paper, titled, "Tattoo Aftercare."

"Keep this bandage on for twenty-four hours," Russ instructed. "I know you want to show it off and stuff, but trust me, keep the bandage on and keep it dry. After that, you can shower with it fine, but don't soak, you know, in a tub or doing dishes or whatever. Wash it twice a day while it heals. You can use lotion. And whatever you do, don't pick the scabs. Otherwise it will pull the ink out and you'll be back here for touchup. The paper lays it all out for you, or you can call for minor questions. If it gets hot, starts weeping, shows sign of infection, don't call me. Call a doctor first. Then call me. Got it? Doctor, then me. In that order."

Tommen nodded. "I understand."

He got out of the chair. Already the pain was fading to a dull throb. He guessed there was some sort of medicine in the bandage.

"All right, my lady," Russ said. "Your turn, if you're sure."

Becky was hesitant, inasmuch as she was taking off her shirt. She definitely wanted Tommen present, just to watch and be a bodyguard, though Russ was nothing less than professional. She was getting the same design, but just above her breast, over her heart. As Russ explained, going over bone hurt quite a bit, as well as tender skin that did not often see sun or otherwise get abused. She could expect it to hurt, though probably not as much as Tommen. Tendons were about the only thing that hurt more.

Tommen half-expected her to make some comment about having a C-section, or for him to say something about the scar. Neither did. Well, condensing three months of healing into three weeks, the scar didn't exactly look fresh. And they'd only said that their daughter died three weeks ago, not that she'd also been born just three weeks ago. Four weeks now. Not that he was counting.

Tommen wasn't sure how he'd looked when getting his tattoo, but if Becky even registered it as pain, it did not show on her face whatsoever. Not a twitch, not a grimace, not even a blink. Studying her, he couldn't even be sure that she'd taken any pills immediately beforehand. He didn't think so. Maybe she just really wasn't feeling it. Maybe the pain from her abdominal surgery had been so great that this was, as she said, little more than a cat scratch to her.

It was fascinating to watch, now that he wasn't the one under the gun, to see the purple lines turn black and watch dark lines appear on light skin. It was a little messy, as Russ wiped away the excess ink and did his best to do things modestly and not just grab her breast to move it here and there. He kept his eyes focused on his work and made no comments.

Then it was done. Russ wiped away the last of the ink with a paper towel, then washed the area again with special soapy water. He did not give Becky the same kind of bandage he gave Tommen. Instead, she was to take hers off in two to four hours, wash the area, then twice daily after that, et cetera. Once she got her shirt back on, he gave her an aftercare instruction sheet and helped her out of the chair like a true gentleman. Tommen felt both annoyed that he was doing it, and ashamed that he himself had not.

"All right, guys, thanks for coming by," Russ said, going through what was probably a scripted speech. "Questions, call me. Problems, call a doctor, then call me. You can find me on social media, and I like the likes. Good for business, makes the world go round."

There were some parting pleasantries, and Tommen and Becky were on their way soon enough. All told, it had taken about two hours for both of them to be done. The pain in his wrist had returned somewhat to a constant throbbing and stinging, as if he'd been stung by a bee. Suddenly he was faced with the daunting task of driving, forcing his hand and fingers to move, using tendons which had just undergone a procedure just this side of major surgery. His left hand was already half-useless, but it didn't matter because his shifter and everything else was on the right side.

It was a painful ride home, say it that way, and he gritted his teeth the whole way. At least his dad was gone to work so he didn't have to see the obvious discomfort. Even Becky looked like someone had put a sharp rock in her shoe.

"You feeling all right?" Tommen asked politely as she meandered her way to the bedroom and flopped on the bed. "Your sugar hold up okay?"

"Fine," she sighed.

"Was it as bad as you thought?"

"It didn't hurt as much as the surgery, if that's what you're asking."

He shrugged, sighed, and sat down at the desk, intending to start on his homework.

"You ever feel like you've just done something to alter the course of your life and there's no way you can go back through that door?" Becky asked, still staring at the ceiling.

"More than you can imagine," Tommen answered honestly. "Why?"

"I got that feeling the first time we had sex. I told myself that, of course you feel that way, you just gave up your virginity, something you can only do once. I told myself that the feeling would go away eventually. We were playing it pretty safe. Nothing was going to happen. But then...or now, I suppose...looking back...I don't know that things could have happened any other way. This was always going to happen."

"So in every alternate universe and every alternate dimension, me and you were always going to meet, always going to have sex, always going to have a daughter who was always going to die?"

The words came out more sharply than he intended, but he wouldn't deny that he was a little snippy about the subject. Still, the look on her face after he said it cut him deeply.

"I'm saying that there is still more to this that we don't understand," she said softly.

Tommen sighed and only just stopped himself from taking his books out to the living room.

"I understand just fine," he said, his voice tight, temper straining against his will. "Believe me when I say I understand very, very well what happened."

It was one of the longest conversations they'd had since Maisy's death, but it was also the last they spoke to each other that night. Tommen knew they were both hurting, both emotional. He knew that he should apologize and try to make amends, try to save what little relationship they had left. He found that he couldn't do it. Not yet.

He knew too much. When it came right down to it, he knew too damn much and couldn't do a damn thing about it. Maybe he'd just gotten lucky, being able to save his dad from Borelian poison. But when it came to saving his daughter, secrecy and lies and trickery and treachery had cost his daughter her life. Because he knew what others did not, what others could not. He'd been an island, a boat adrift at sea and at the mercy of the wind and waves. Hell, he still felt like it. Others saw misfortune. He knew treachery. And at least part of it was his own fucking fault.

The next morning as he got ready for class, after his shower, he removed the bandage from his wrist. The M looked back at him, full and black. Every injury hurt worse the day after, and tattoos were no exception. But he had a way to get around that. He Pinpoint Banded the tattoo site, watched as scabs formed and fell off. In condensing three weeks of healing into just a few seconds, well, he wouldn't be picking any scabs or going out in the sun or soaking in water. The finished image looked crisp and beautiful. He tossed the bandage in the trash.

When he got home from class, his dad was awake and in his recliner, watching something on TV. Suddenly self-conscious, Tommen pulled down his shirt sleeve before walking through the living room. Then, feeling guilty, he returned after dumping his bag.

"Dad?" he asked cautiously, similar to how he'd approached his dad whenever he had to wake him up from his nightmares.

"What's up, kiddo?" Walter was slow to look at him, but appeared otherwise attentive. At least he hadn't gone back to the pills. Just common grief, then.

"Can I show you something? Just so you don't see it and get surprised and ask about it later?"

Now his dad raised a brow, almost his old self. He shifted in his seat. "And what's that?"

Tommen pulled his sleeve up to his elbow and held his arm up to show off the M.

"When did this happen?" his dad asked.

"Yesterday."

"I'm just kind of assuming you Banded it so it would heal faster."

"Yeah."

"Ah. Becky, too, or just you?"

"She did. Not in the same place, but yeah. She doesn't want her parents to know yet."

"Fair enough."

Tommen pulled the sleeve back down. "You're not mad?"

His dad gave him a gentle look. "Tommen, I stopped trying to boss you around a long time ago. You're your own man now. You don't need my permission. It doesn't matter what I think."

Tommen frowned and looked away, saying, "It's an ash tattoo. Maisy's ashes got mixed with the ink."

"I saw your chain broke."

"Yeah. I was so afraid of losing her ashes. It'll be pretty hard to lose them now."

His dad nodded. "Indeed it will."

And that was that. Tommen returned to his room and started on his homework. Becky was down at her parents' house, doing some of her sewing work. There were days when she couldn't be bothered, and days when she could think of nothing else. It was a way to escape. Sometimes she didn't get back until nine or ten o'clock at night.

That night she didn't return. Tommen called her phone about eleven-thirty, fearing the worst, that Julianna had killed her, too. But Becky picked up. She sounded sleepy and said that she would be staying over there for the night. When asked if she was all right, she said she was fine, just lost track of time. He offered to come pick her up. She declined.

It might have been a decent excuse, except her parents' house was literally within sight of the kitchen window.

It was just another knife to his heart, Tommen figured. Had he been too optimistic, thinking that matching tattoos would somehow bring them together and make it all better? Grief could divide people just as readily as it could bring them together. Except, normally, in these situations, weren't the parents usually blaming each other for their woes?

This time around, it seemed as though the divide came from each parent blaming himself or herself, despite the knowledge that there was nothing either of them could have done.

Well, that wasn't entirely true. He knew that there was something he could have done. There was something he tried to do. And he couldn't do it. He'd failed. His daughter was gone.

But Becky was still around. And she was hurting.

He batted it around for a minute longer, then dragged himself out of bed. In the bathroom, he looked at the mark on his wrist. His daughter was gone, but she would always be with him. He couldn't let Becky go the same way.

He got himself cleaned up, then got in his car and drove down to the Polski house. It was dark, but if he'd just talked to Becky a few minutes ago, and if she was hurting as much as he was, she couldn't be asleep already.

Gathering his nerve, Tommen walked up to the door and knocked. No answer. He rang the doorbell and knocked again. A light turned on. It was not Becky, as he had hoped, but Dr. Polski. He demeanor said he was not pleased to be woken up, but it turned confused when he saw Tommen.

"Tommen?" he questioned. "What are you—? You know you don't have to knock; just come right in." He paused and gave Tommen a once-over. "Why are you wearing a suit?"

"Dr. Polski, I realize it's after your normal ten-thirty curfew, but I was wondering if Becky could go out with me."

The doctor seemed to understand what was going on. He smiled and nodded. "I'll see what she thinks. Come in."

Tommen stepped inside and waited politely while the elderly doctor made his way slowly up the stairs to Becky's room. He heard the gentle knock on the door, but none of the ensuing conversation. He hadn't really expected her to leap out of bed and rush down to see her knight in shining armor. For one, he was hardly a knight in shining armor. But he had hoped for some indication of movement, that she would come down to meet her boyfriend who was well past curfew and still had to nerve to ask to go out.

He waited. He heard voices upstairs, but could not make out the words. So far as he knew, she didn't have any clothes here to have to change into, if she were somehow immodest. His heart sank and his hopes plummeted. His suspicions were only confirmed when Dr. Polski returned alone, turning off the lights over the stairs. His expression did not help. The two of them went out on the porch.

"I'm sorry, Tommen," he sighed, and his apology sounded as genuine as anything Tommen had ever heard. "She's...not in a mood to go out right now. Maybe in the morning." Dr. Polski looked away for a moment. "I know what you're trying to do here. Know that I appreciate it. Her mother will, too, when I tell her. I know you were hoping that she would come home to you tonight. I tried to convince her. It's just not happening tonight. But the best thing you can do is keep trying. All right?"

Tommen nodded somberly. "Okay."

Dr. Polski patted his shoulder. "You look very handsome this evening. Go home and get some sleep."

With that, the doctor quietly closed the door and turned off the lights.

Tommen stood there on the porch for a long moment, after the lights had gone out and Dr. Polski returned to bed, hoping that Becky might sneak her way down to meet with him privately. But one minute turned into two, then five. It was only the beginning of April, which meant it was still a bit chilly, and a few snowflakes floated down from the sky, landing in his hair.

Ten minutes passed. His feet were cold there in his thin socks and dress shoes, and a chill wind penetrated his coat. Finally, he sighed, turned and made his way back to his car. As he stepped off the curb, his foot found the only patch of ice on the entire sidewalk, and he slipped and landed square on his back. Once the initial shock had subsided, he might have expected or hoped for some giggling or a sarcastic comment or even some stern order to be more careful. But his whimsical antic went entirely unnoticed except for the howling of the wind.

Chapter Twenty-Nine
Blurry Vision

Becky did return the following day. She apologized for not taking him up on his offer and said it had been very sweet. But her words were tired, as if she were merely indulging him.

She did not move back in with her parents as he expected her to do, though she did end up staying over there once or twice a week. On those nights, Tommen would go over in a suit, sometimes with cheesy flowers or chocolates, asking her father if he could take her out that evening, even if it was just back home. She almost always refused. Even some nights when she did stay home, he would get dressed up and ask if she wanted to go out. Those she did always refuse.

He tried. He really did. But as April turned into May and he was rejected more often than not, it wore on him. He failed. He continued to fail. He couldn't save his daughter, and he couldn't bring back his girlfriend. His girlfriend who, at one time, was set to be his wife, the mother of his child.

He understood that it hurt. He himself was still hurting. The tattoo on his wrist reminded him of that pain every day. But he was still trying. He tried to explain this to Becky on more than one occasion until she finally told him to just stop. She would come around in her own time, she said. She didn't need him pushing it on her.

That hurt, too, but he did as she requested. He stopped pushing. He stopped chasing her to her parents' house like an idiot high school freshman going to pick up his date for the dance. He stopped trying to explain himself.

This wasn't to say that he ignored Becky or excluded her, but if she put up walls, he wasn't going to try and breach them. The walls wouldn't give, and he was getting tired of the fight. It felt like a terrible thing to do, but life wasn't like the movies. They didn't sit down for a heart-to-heart chat, talk for hours, cry their hearts out and bare their souls, ending in make-up sex and a relationship rising from the ashes (he winced at his own pun). Sometimes, things fell apart in the real world.

Instead, they simply existed, living in the same house with a shared grief neither wanted to acknowledge together. Tommen was willing to pick up the pieces and start over, but he couldn't do it alone. He expressed this to Becky in several ways at different times, but she never really responded.

When it didn't hurt, he sometimes found coals of resentment burning against her. Did she think she was the only one suffering? Forget him, their parents were hurting, too, and she was isolating them just as much. And her friends. Yeah, Tommen didn't exactly go brag on social media about his daughter dying, but he didn't disappear completely, making everyone assume the worst. Why couldn't she see past her own selfish grief? If it was shared grief, why couldn't they share it?

Sometimes he found himself looking back over their entire relationship and wondering how he ever thought it was going to work. She was boisterous, manipulative, naive, ignorant, and selfish.

Then he would consider that he wasn't exactly a shining example of humanity either, and the coals of resentment would die down for a time. He couldn't blame her for her faults when he still had issues of his own. To bring any of them up now would not only be wrong, but extremely rude, a cheap shot, adding insult to injury. They were both hurting, both vulnerable. If he was trying to save the relationship, well, you didn't drill a hole in the bottom of a boat and hope it helped to drain the water.

Other times he wondered whether the boat was worth saving. He just couldn't do it alone, and no matter how many times he tried to be there for Becky, let her know he wasn't giving up, she remained distant, cold.

Trying to bring her around other ways did little to help, either. Thanking her for doing laundry, complimenting her cooking, even offering to do it for her since she was still recovering though Tommen had technically Band-healed her the entire six months by now. Sometimes she refused, saying she wanted to do it, that she needed something to do. Other times she would hand it over and walk away quietly.

If it happened to be laundry, Tommen would sometimes intentionally fold things wrong or mess up her system of organization she had going. In the past, she would get all hyped up about it and lecture him about how to properly do laundry, then dissolve into small growls about this was why she did the laundry because they just couldn't do it right. Now, though, if she said anything at all, it would be a passing mention, a lifeless reminder. Otherwise she would silently rearrange things, if she did it at all. She'd sort of adopted Tommen's way of doing things, just fold them up and stuff them in a drawer.

One day, Tommen came home to find all of the baby clothes gone, the dresser completely cleaned of them. While it had hurt to look at them and see them there, reminding him of what could not be, seeing the empty spot where they had been almost hurt more. It was like giving up, finally acknowledging that it had all happened and it was time to clean up, make it as though it never was. He let out a breath and looked at his wrist, the black ink glittering back at him.

He still hadn't gotten around the dismantling the crib in the closet. He couldn't bring himself to do it just yet. Clothes, toys, those things were more finite in his opinion, easily forgotten. It was the crib that really got him, that one thing that spoke to him more than anything else, that one thing that was supposed to be Maisy's. The thought of having his daughter close while they all slept, the idea of putting her to bed, taking her out and holding her, even if it was just to change diapers in the middle of the night. That crib meant more to him than all of the other stuff combined.

Maybe it was because he hadn't had much when he was a baby. His ma used the same little makeshift crib for him as she had for Teo. They didn't have a whole dresser and closet full of clothes, and their toys were just as makeshift as anything else, but the crib was always special.

He couldn't take it apart yet.

The day the baby clothes disappeared, Becky stayed over at her parents' house. Walter also had the night off, and Tommen found himself on the couch watching a movie with his dad.

"So, how's life on the tundra?" Walter inquired.

Tommen shrugged. "Fine."

"The fact that you even understood the reference tells me it's not."

"Becky got rid of the baby clothes today. I don't know what she did with them, maybe took them over to her parents' house or something."

His dad did not reply.

"Do you think it's worth it?" Tommen asked. "Trying to save our relationship?"

"Why wouldn't it be?" his dad countered. "You don't hate each other. You're just trying to process your grief, and in two different ways, I might add. Are you asking for the simple fact that you're not married?"

Tommen felt his face turn red even as his stomach knotted with guilt.

His dad shifted in his seat. "Tommen, men and women deal with stress and grief very differently. As men, we're fixers. We fix things. Something's wrong, we try to fix it. We want to solve the problem so life can move smoothly. Once life is running smoothly again, then we deal with our inner emotions. Women are the opposite. To them, dealing with the emotion is the key, or at least a big first step, to fixing the problem and making life run smoothly."

"How do we make that work, then?"

"I don't know. It's something you have to figure out for

yourselves. The first thing, though, is to make sure you both understand where the other is coming from. You see her as being unresponsive to your efforts to fix things. She sees you as being unresponsive to her emotional needs."

"But every time I try to...cuddle or hug her or sit her down to try to get her to talk, she shuts me down."

"Are you doing it because you want to, because you are responding to her cues of what she needs, or because you see it as something on your checklist of things to do to fix the problem?"

Tommen opened his mouth, then found he had no words.

"Women are mysterious creatures. Like gravity, it's one of the few constants throughout the universe, I think. But to give you the benefit of the doubt, simply because I'm not here all day and I don't watch you guys like little kids, if you want the relationship to work, you have to want it to work. Both of you. You can give it two hundred percent, but if she doesn't meet you, even a little bit, it will never happen." Walter leaned back in his recliner. "I think it's time you two had a little chat about it."

Be that as it may, it didn't happen that night. Or the next day. Or the next. Wednesday morning, Tommen went to class as usual. English again. He hated English, though he'd used it as one of his many methods of trying to bring Becky back around, asking her for help on essays and other things. Since she did not have classes, she could not plead her own homework, but she was hardly the know-it-all Grammar Nazi she had been, ready and willing to point out every mistake as she found it. Instead, assuming she didn't claim fatigue or other non-excuses, she would edit his essays in silence. Her critiques were purely rule-based now. Misuse of a semi-colon, a missed comma or period, spelling mistakes. She said nothing about style or voice or anything that she once said really made a paper stand out. When he asked her about it, she'd just shrugged and said that she wasn't going to tell him how to write his papers.

He'd stopped asking her for help and instead went to the Writing Center to find an editor and tutor of sorts. It was the only way his English grade stayed afloat, soul-wrenching grief or not. His English class met on Mondays and Wednesdays. The day after Maisy's death was a Monday and the first day of class. Tommen had privately told the professor about the ordeal. The professor sympathized and said that if he needed to step out for a minute or do a make-up class a time or two, then it could be arranged. If it was going to become a habit, better to drop the class and come back when his head was back on straight. Now that a month or so had gone by, all sympathy was now revoked and the professor proved to be a real piece of work.

After an essay got returned, in which he just about failed but managed to skate through with a D+, Tommen had also mentioned that his first language was not English.

"How long have you been here?" the prof asked.

"Um, my whole life, but I didn't start speaking English until, like, ten years ago," Tommen replied.

"I once lived in Greece for six years. I was an embarrassment in the language my first day. By the time I left, I was writing prose worthy of the gods. You have to apply yourself. You have to want it."

Needless to say, Tommen did not get along well with his English professor, but the irritation was two-fold. On the one hand, the guy was a prick. On the other hand, he wasn't entirely wrong, just not in the same way.

Tommen knew he had to want it. The problem was, he didn't know what he wanted. Most of the last year had been spent with the sole idea that he was going to have a family. At this point, he didn't even know if he was going to have a girlfriend. He no longer had to fret over being better than a trailer trash parent because he wasn't a parent at all. He didn't have to worry about having to whisk a wife and child to safety across the universe; one was gone and the other was dubious at best.

He never told Becky about any escape plan. He didn't tell her about the real cause of Maisy's death or her genetic defect. He didn't tell her about Nathan or Godwin or any of the factions. He didn't tell her anything at all. Even if he had, he wasn't sure which reaction he expected or would have accepted: laughter, that maybe he'd had some kind of psychotic break; dismissive disbelief, that he was crazy; some kind of odd acceptance; or total silence as she failed to comprehend anything he was saying?

He wasn't even sure there was anywhere to escape to anymore. Godwin, the twins, they were all silent, every text unanswered, every call unreturned. Walter had once briefly inquired about Rifun's status in the jail and was told the man had been transferred to Mt. Olive back in February and Walter was not entitled to any further news. It was very likely, then, that the Miaramila had been completely wiped out by the Order. Without Kayla, there was no good way to find out the status of Hlohi and the Krydik. Had Julianna truly succeeded in taking out all of those with Authored Books as well, reserving Tommen as a mere toy to play with on occasion?

He didn't know what he wanted, truthfully. He wanted things to go back to the way they were, when he had hope and a future, something to look forward to that was good.

You knew, Chandler, he thought bitterly. *You knew and you didn't say a fucking word.*

Suddenly class was over. That was kind of how things went these days. He went to a place, like class, got all distracted by his own thoughts and woes, and then whatever he had been doing was over and it was time to move on. He had a general idea of what had transpired, and he was at least of a mind to write down the homework.

Being Wednesday, he did not go to the library or the Writing Center, but straight to work.

At some point, the house in the new development had sprung up, seemingly overnight. Walls were up, roof was on, drywall was just being finished, and all the pretty things were being put in place, things that helped to cover the construction nakedness. Paint, flooring, cabinetry, things that made a house beautiful and ready to sell, or move in as the case may be.

It didn't become a home until the family moved in. Tommen didn't know a whole lot about the buyers, or maybe he just hadn't been paying attention. Maybe it was a young couple, just starting out, but only if they were already well-to-do. Maybe it was a family, where he had a good job and she was a successful working mother, maybe even a stay-at-home mom. Maybe it was a retired couple, secure in their financial situation and ready to spend a little bit of the money they'd spent their whole lives saving up. Skimping on groceries and the niceties in life, forgoing expensive vacations for more modest day trips, passing on the luxury house for a humble abode, all so that when they retired, they could buy the house of their dreams and fill it with cute and useless trinkets, vacation for months at a time anywhere in the world, and indulge in all their favorite foods they had been denying themselves for years.

Now that they were on to the more beautiful part of the construction, progress seemed to grind to a halt. The original idea had been to build the house as the homeowners had designed and requested, all good and kosher with architects and engineers and sealed with Chris' approval that they could and would get it done. While the bare bones went up, the homeowners would make their final decisions on flooring, countertops, thing of that nature. Chris was usually reluctant to start a project without everything pretty well wrapped up and tied with a bow, but the homeowners assured him that they knew what they wanted, it was just a matter of shopping around and finding the best price. Chris could respect that, so he let it slide. Besides, it wasn't much different than a homeowner having a plan only to change it at the last possible minute, or even in the middle of the project.

The thing about having everything picked out beforehand, even if it got changed later, was that at least there was a plan. Sometimes it was a matter of putting down the original request and letting the couple fight it out later once they, the construction crew, were long gone. The problem now was that the homeowners were dragging their feet and arguing about some of the details now, and there was no plan to fall back on. On top of that, the busy work was running out as Chris tried to keep putting pressure on the homeowners to make up their damn minds. The countertops should have been picked out a month ago because that's how long it would have taken to get them in. The flooring they could run and get at just about any time as long as it wasn't an uber special order where they had to send word by carrier pigeon to underpaid workers in Central America to illegally cut down endangered trees in the rainforest.

In other words, just pick something out! They would probably be remodeling in five years anyway, so what did it really matter? It was the cause of much grumbling from the guys, but especially from Chris.

Probably the only one not complaining to some degree was Tommen, but he figured his woes were a little more serious than picking out new floors and countertops. And when the guys weren't griping about the homeowners being slow to make up their damn minds, often they were trying to cheer him up and bring him back around to the present. Some cracked jokes and pulled pranks, others offered sagely advice. A few tried the tough love stance, getting short with him and telling him to hurry it up on the job site. A few others simply told him that if he needed to talk, the door was open, otherwise, live in the present. It was healthier for his mental state, and safer when around power tools.

Had he already considered all of this? Tommen thought about it but couldn't say for sure. There were a lot of things he didn't remember about the last month or so. Actually, it had to be more than a month. At least two months now, right? Just about. It was just turning into May, so it was about two months, yeah.

Maisy would be two months old by now, he thought bitterly. She would be two months old, doted on by her parents. Becky would fuss over her clothes and try to entertain her with all manner of brightly-colored toys and baubles. She would hold her close when she was upset for one reason or another. Then Tommen would come home, the breadwinner, and hold his daughter to let her know that all was right with the world again. Everything was just fine.

The Strong One. That was how his daughter had seen him. The Strong One, who would protect her from every evil thing in the world, fight off all manner of monsters and yucky vegetables.

Some days, Tommen wondered if that was really what he had seen and felt, or if he was just exaggerating it now to tell himself that his daughter loved him as well as torture himself that he couldn't do more. But what if it was all just overblown in his mind? What if his daughter had merely seen him as a familiar human being who had done nothing but pace and worry and contribute ultimately nothing to her overall wellbeing?

But then, at the end of the day, as he lay in bed, afraid to go to sleep but having little biological choice, he would remember with razor sharp clarity what it had been like to Feel her and touch her simple mind. She had no language yet, no complex thoughts, only simple needs, simple wants. There was what she liked and what she didn't like. And above all, she liked the Comforting One and the Strong One.

He remembered what it had felt like to let her go.

He thought about asking Matt, the self-styled chaplain, about it, then decided against it. Without the greater context, understanding that he really had touched his daughter's mind, there would only be pithy religious answers and nonanswers. God worked in mysterious ways, we don't always understand His reasons, we don't really understand death and won't until we cross for ourselves, God is the Great Comforter, go ahead and yell at God because He can take it.

Tommen knew all of it, but it did little to make him feel better. Sometimes he would glance at Matt, and he would find the man already watching him, his expression saying he knew what Tommen wanted to say, but he wanted him to say it aloud for himself. I need help. I have questions. I'm so confused. I don't understand.

But Tommen did not say anything, and neither did Matt. Or anyone else. Offers were made, but no one really engaged. And they just plodded along in their jobs.

At the end of the day, Chris gathered everyone in the empty living room. It was almost as big as Tommen's entire house.

"All right, guys, here's the deal," Chris began. "The busy work is basically done. It is. You know it, I know it. Fact is, we're going nowhere faster. I've told the homeowners that they have until next week to make up their minds on at least flooring or else we're pulling out of the project entirely. I'm not dancing around this anymore, and I don't want to jerk you guys around on what we're doing, when we're doing it, and so on. It's frustrating, and it's not fair to you guys.

"That being said, tomorrow we're going to be at the warehouse to finish up some of the small projects, the restoration gigs we've got going on. If I get the call from the homeowners, we'll sally forth with whatever they give us, otherwise, plan on small jobs for a few days. Tommen, Ricky, plan on the warehouse unless I call or text you." He looked around. "We good?"

Heads bobbed and they were dismissed for the day. Tommen briefly returned goodbyes as they were given to him, but headed to his car without another word.

He did not go straight home. Rather, he made a detour and headed for Will's house.

If there was anyone Tommen considered a real friend and true confidant during his crisis, it was Will. He couldn't explain it except he found it easier to talk to a man who could only go by words alone, who could not scrutinize his body language or facial expressions or any of the other little visual cues that shrinks used to dissect their patients. Will could only use audio information to form an opinion.

It seemed disrespectful to think of it that way, Tommen mused. Nathan had been just as good a friend, even when he was dishing out tough love. And Tommen had no doubt that he would have come to Maisy's rescue if not for Julianna. Part of him wondered, on several occasions, when Julianna had actually killed Nathan. Had it been months ago, when Nathan suggested they stop meeting for their sessions? Had it been just after Maisy's birth, when Tommen first called to report a problem? And he, fool that he was, had been so trusting that he hadn't even tried to use Test.

Mrs. Shaw opened the door, but it was Graham Cracker who initially greeted Tommen, barking and tugging on his pants wanting to play. Tommen kicked a ball and the little wiener dog scampered after it. While the tiny dog was distracted, he headed down the hall to Will's room. On the way, he passed Eli.

Eli hadn't gotten in trouble lately, and Tommen was still on his shit list, but after Maisy's death, he had expressed what Tommen believed to be very genuine condolences. Ever since then, Tommen was still on the shit list, but Eli no longer ran away from him as though he were about to whip out the handcuffs and arrest him.

Tommen pushed open the door to Will's room. Sydney raised her head. When she saw who it was, she simply yawned and stretched out even more on her dog bed, making a contented noise and sighing as she closed her eyes again. Will was at his desk, swiftly thumbing through a braille book.

"Speed reading for the blind?" Tommen asked, trying to make it sound like a joke.

"Something like that. Sort of trying to finish this up quick. Heard you come in, so it's like, 'Oh, shit, I have to hurry.' "

"No rush, man." Tommen sat down in a heap on the bed, laying down so he could reach and scratch Sydney's ears. "So is Eli going for dreads or what? His hair looks super long."

"Not that I can see," Will said smartly. "Yeah, he says that's what he's going for. Me, I just figure to keep it smooth." He rubbed his shaved head. "Low maintenance, and even if I had my sight, shaving your head you still do blind. Figure it's the only hair style I can do right and do myself. What about you? You got long hair or what?"

Tommen shrugged. "Not long, not short. Could probably use a trim, but I don't feel like making an appointment or even just going to a place and walking in."

"Becky doesn't cut your hair anymore?"

"I haven't asked and she hasn't said anything. I don't know, I think maybe it would get her too close to me or something."

"You still sleep in the same bed, though, right?"

"I don't know, dude. I just don't know anymore. I don't know what's going on in her mind. Honestly, we barely even text each other. I don't know that I've texted her at all this week."

Will closed his book and leaned back in his chair. "Well, I'm no shrink, but I do know that for a lot of people, it just comes down to communication. I remember when you said you would text each other hundreds or thousands of times a day, even during school. Drove your dad absolutely nuts. To go from sixty to zero in one-point-three seconds...that's not good, dude. Someone has to reach or else something's gonna give."

"I know. We've been over this. But no matter what I do, she's a brick wall."

"I don't know what to tell you, man. I'm no doctor, and no counselor either. If you're doing what you can, well, you're covered on your end is the way I see it. Then you just got to decide when a broken relationship becomes dead baggage."

Tommen sighed and rubbed his face. He didn't want to think about that. He didn't want to consider that. He wanted to believe that if he just gave it more time, then Becky might come around. It had only been two months, after all. Not even that, barely seven weeks. Maybe? He wasn't sure. And that alone had to prove that things were still a little warped. He couldn't give up just yet, and he said as much.

"That's all on you, man," Will told him. "Whatever you want to do."

They talked for the better part of an hour, moving away from Tommen and his woes to the good things happening in Will's life. He was making progress in his braille menu endeavor. He'd refined his idea as best as he could and had pitched it to quite possibly every restaurant in the county, chain store and homegrown. Some thought it too complicated. Others liked the idea and "would get back to him." But there were a few that were totally willing and onboard with the idea and were ready to place an order. One was even a national franchise who liked it so much, the owner said he would buy some for the stores he owned, then take the idea to corporate and see if it couldn't be implemented nationwide.

"Well, it's great that you got some hits," Tommen said, "but I'll believe it when I see it on the national chain."

"Oh, I'm right there with you, man, but let me have my moment. Let me indulge a little," Will said, clearly pleased with himself. "Just think of it. A blind man as the CEO of a nationally-known company. Now that's an achievement."

"Power to you if it happens. Just don't forget us little guys when you become rich and famous."

Will waved a hand dismissively. "Please. How can I forget the little guys? You'll be the ones cranking out on the machines while I sit in my corner office overlooking the city."

"Overlooking the city, maybe, but does it do you any good if you can't see your empire?"

"Hey, man, don't push it. You're ruining my vision. Keep it up and you're getting knocked down from VP to grunt."

"What else is new?"

It was one of the few times when Tommen felt almost normal. Not as things had been, tricking his mind into thinking he was going home to a pregnant girlfriend or a new baby, but as if life itself was moving on, that there was a light at the end of the tunnel and things might be okay.

Then he got back in his car and arrived home to a house that was colder than the refrigerator. He tried to be a little upbeat, cordial at least, something less than mopey. He tried to engage Becky, ask her about her day, her plans, her life. She simply responded that she had no life right now and to please leave her alone. Then she returned to her book.

It was the first time she had explicitly asked him to leave her alone. Tommen's mouth snapped closed and he left the bedroom to do his homework out in the living room. About half an hour later, Becky emerged and left the house. She stayed at her parents' house that night.

He half-expected her to stay there, or at least come back just to pack her things. But she returned to their bed the following night. She pulled away at his every touch, every attempt to hug or cuddle, or even just an accidental touch as he was rolling over. She did this for several nights before he finally confronted her Sunday evening. They were in the living room, and his dad was already gone to work.

"What do you want, Becky?" he asked, exhausted in every way a man can be exhausted. "What can I do? What can I say?"

"There is nothing you can do," she told him. "There's nothing you can do, nothing you can say. Tommen..." Tears were rolling down her cheeks. "I want our baby."

"So do I, but it's not going to happen."

He hated to see her burst into full-blown sobs, but it was reality. Also real was the scratch she gave him on his arm as he went to pull her close and she violently wrenched away. She could have stuck a knife in his heart and it would have hurt less.

"We can't stand around wishing for something that isn't going to happen," he told her severely, voice strained.

"What do you want to do, then? Have more kids? It won't bring back Maisy." Becky's words were choked and almost incomprehensible.

"There won't be any kids if there is no us. Period. I can't do anything about Maisy, and believe me, I tried. I think about it every day, wondering if there was anything I could have done, could have suggested. There wasn't." He could have killed himself just for that statement alone. He went on, "Right now, I'm trying to save you, save the us. Tell me right now, Becky. Is it salvageable? Or is it just as dead? Should I keep trying or let you go, too?"

The look she gave him was a physical mirror of the way his very soul was twisting with grief. She tried to stand tall and walk away strong, but she couldn't do it. She ran down to the bedroom, closed the door, and locked it. Creeping down the hall, he could hear her sobs through the door. He sighed and sat down, back against the wall, knees drawn up.

"I'm sorry," he said after a long minute. "I'm sorry that Maisy's dead. I'm sorry that all this happened. I'll even be sorry for getting you pregnant in the first place if it will make you feel better. Neither of us wanted this to happen, but it did. If I could change it, we wouldn't be here right now. I know you're hurting. I am, too. But we can't live like complete strangers forever. I want to help. I know it's a process. I'm not asking for everything to magically get better overnight. Little steps is all I'm saying." He sighed. "Tell me how to help you. Tell me how to save this relationship, whatever we have left of it. I want to, but I can't do it alone."

She did not reply, nor did he hear any movement to indicate she was getting up or unlocking the door. He waited a while, told himself he would wait all night if he had to. That's how it was in the movies. But in real life, nature called at the most inopportune times. He put it off as long as possible, but his bladder won out.

When he returned, he found the door still locked.

"I love you, Becky," he said, just loud enough that he was sure she could hear him. "I just want to know if you love me back."

There was no reply. He waited. No movement. Maybe she fell asleep. After a good ten minutes, he went out to the living room to finish up his homework and watch some TV.

He couldn't say his grades were phenomenal, not like he'd envisioned life after high school, but he'd come back from the brink of failure and was doing pretty good. His exams could still make or break him, but he figured he could get through it if he could concentrate long enough. These days, half an hour was about all his attention span was good for, and he found himself watching mostly cartoons on the TV.

Maisy was supposed to be here with him, sitting on his lap, watching the brightly colored moving pictures, the two of them just loafing around. Becky would come out, say something about TV inhibiting Maisy's tiny developing brain, scold Tommen, maybe swat him playfully with a spoon, then continue on with whatever she was doing, knowing that as long as Tommen had the baby occupied, she might be able to get a little something accomplished, be it cooking, cleaning, or just taking five minutes to herself to finally relax.

Tommen jumped at a hand on his shoulder. He must have fallen asleep. The TV was still on and he was still in his dad's recliner.

"Everything all right, kiddo?" his dad wondered.

He sat up, rubbed his eyes, yawned, stretched, then slouched back into the cushions. "Becky locked me out of the room."

"Things not going well?"

Tommen sighed. "I don't know what to do, Dad. I've tried giving her space, forcing myself on her, being nice, being argumentative. We sort of had it out last night, and I don't even know that there is anything left to fight for."

"There must be," his dad said, sitting down on the couch. "Or else she wouldn't still be here. She would be packed up and moved back in with her parents."

"What if her parents aren't letting her back? What if they're just pushing her to stay here to try and make things better?"

"I think she's defied her parents enough that it wouldn't be a problem for her to move back. And with them hurting just as much, I don't know that they would put up much of a fight if she did say she was going back."

Tommen mulled this over in his mind for a minute.

His dad shifted in his seat. "Tommen, I know that you're still hurting. We all are. And there is no timeline for grief, to reach that moment when everything is normal and 'okay' again. But it has been almost two months and life is moving on. You're almost done with your first semester of college. You need to decide what is worth fighting for and go after it, especially when it comes to your relationship with Becky. As much as you want an answer from her whether she cares, you can't be wishy-washy either. If you are going to try and save the relationship, then you have to go after it until she explicitly tells you to stop. It's going to be hard, and it's going to hurt. You are going to want to give up. Or maybe you'll decide to abandon the whole thing and release her from this, let her go back to her parents or whatever. But you have to decide what you are going to do."

"How do you do it? How do you keep going after all of this?"

"I wonder the same thing sometimes because there are a lot of nights where I find myself on the side of the road with only my thoughts for company. Let me tell you, that is a lonely and scary thing. What did I miss? What could I have done to protect myself? I should have suspected some kind of interference just as soon as you figured things out, so why did I get careless? Could I have done anything more on my own? Could I have found someone in the Time industry to fix things in some way? Why couldn't I help you like you helped me? You started a war for me. And I got caught in a stupid Band, a rookie mistake if there ever was one."

"Yeah, but that was an Akari Band. Force Akari, but still a Band you couldn't see."

"Exactly. And my ignorance was my undoing."

Tommen shook his head. "Your ignorance was your saving grace. Julianna even said so. You were no threat, so she was just going to mess you up a little and let you live with the failure."

"And that's easily the hardest part. Living with the failure and wondering what I could have done differently."

"So we're in the same boat."

His dad just nodded.

Tommen shifted position. "I confronted Julianna. At the hospital." He glossed over the fight they had, how she'd knocked him out. "But at one point, she was talking about everyone with an Authored Book. The Krydik, the twins, me, Kayla. But she also mentioned you."

His dad took an even breath, stood, and went to his bedroom. A minute later he returned with a book. Upon seeing the cover, Tommen could tell it was an Authored Book. Walter handed it to him, saying, "I don't know how it normally works for you special people, but I found it on my bed when I changed into my uniform. There was a bookmark at the passage where I found out Victoria had been murdered."

Tommen took the Book but did not open it. "Why didn't you say anything?"

His dad frowned and said nothing. Tommen sighed, rubbed his eyes, and stood. "I'm sorry. I'll get out of your chair."

"Don't worry about it. If Becky's still got you locked out, might as well sleep where it's comfortable. I'm just going to my own bed anyway."

Tommen nodded, handed the Book back to him, but headed down to the bedroom anyway, gently testing the handle. Still locked. He could pick it; the lock was fairly simple. But she'd locked it for a reason, and she didn't want to be disturbed. He would have to in the morning, but the last thing he needed was to scare her half to death by picking a lock and getting into bed next to her. Even he could appreciate that.

Was his consideration, then, a sign that he did want to fight for the relationship? He didn't know. He just wished he didn't feel as though he were the only one fighting. It would be nice to know where she stood on the issue, other than an immovable point in the past. He couldn't do anything about it. No one could. There was only the here, the now, where he was fighting to save what little he had left, but she wasn't responding. What was he supposed to do? Some said fight, others said walk away. His dad said to make a decision and go through with it whole-heartedly. Did anyone really understand?

He didn't want to go to a support group, especially not alone. He'd never been big on therapy to begin with, and Nathan's disappearance and presumed death effectively barred that door from ever being reopened. Furthermore, he didn't seem to need group therapy as much as Becky did. He was willing to move forward. She didn't appear to feel the same way. And since it was their child, it would only make sense that they go together.

But then, how did he explain the poisoning? How did he explain the Time and Akari elements? To everyone else, it was just a freak medical tragedy. To him, it was murder.

Tommen returned to the living room, this time lying on the couch. His dad moved about quietly, getting ready for bed. On a normal night, Tommen wouldn't have noticed a thing. This morning, seeing how he was already awake, it was the loudest thing in the universe and could wake up a sleeping xur halfway across the galaxy.

Before fully retiring to bed, his dad popped his head out in the living room.

"You going to be all right?"

For a second, Tommen thought about just not answering, maybe feigning sleep. But his dad knew him too well. Finally he answered, "Yeah. I'll have to pick the lock eventually, get ready for school and stuff."

"Try to get some sleep. I'll be here when you get home."

It sounded like something his dad might have said when Tommen was in elementary school still worrying about bullies. He would lie awake in terror of what the next day would bring. On a good day, it was mean words and dirty looks. On bad days, well, he hadn't exactly been a stranger to the nurse's office, the principal's office, or emergency room. His dad would always do his best to comfort him and let him know that he was around, and he would always be home when Tommen got home from school. A lie, given the unpredictable nature of police work, but in the moment, it had assuaged his young fears.

It all seemed so petty now. Would things have been different if Tommen had indeed turned on Tyler and used his Banding abilities to really hurt the kid and try to make it so Tyler never bothered him again? Maybe. Maybe not. Even before he'd left high school, when he was out running around the universe on life-and-death missions, it had all started to feel so small and worthless.

And in just a couple weeks, he would be walking down the aisle for graduation. The original plan was to follow this up by walking down the aisle for his wedding. But that wasn't happening now. Would it happen ever?

He didn't know if he slept, though he did achieve at least a heavy doze between the time his dad went to bed and when he had to get up for class. He made his way to the bathroom first to try and get freshened up, wake up a little and pretend to be excited for the day.

When he went to the bedroom door, he found it still locked. Sighing, he picked it. He no longer needed a lock picking kit; just a little strategic use of Magnetism would do the trick. He pushed open the door.

"Becky?" he asked softly.

She was still in bed, the gentle rise and fall of her chest letting him know she was still alive. She did not respond to his inquiry, which was just fine, he figured. He rummaged around for some fresh clothes. As he was leaving the room, he glanced in the closet. The doors were open, revealing the crib. The last he knew, the doors had been shut.

Curious, he went over and peered inside. A stuffed rabbit lay inside, dressed in one of the little outfits Becky had made for Maisy.

Taking a steady breath, Tommen quietly sneaked out of the room.

Chapter Thirty
Spectator

He'd had one mission. Be discreet, go home, and retrieve the hasax. As far as anyone knew, he was just going home to get ready for work. Deliberately leaving his coat in the room gave him an excuse to return.

He had Banded just as soon as he could, once he figured he was alone in the parking lot. It had been a sunny March afternoon, well above freezing, and the bears were crawling out of hibernation to clog up the streets and make traffic difficult to navigate, especially in a Band when everything stopped and became an obstacle. The sunlight gave people hope and joy after a dreary winter. For Walter, though, he was still hard-pressed to feel anything even resembling hope and joy. He had to get home, had to find the hasax, had to return and save his granddaughter.

In a way, it had felt almost like redemption, a chance to right his wrongs from his despicable first time at fatherhood. Memories of Victoria flooded his mind as he utilized his police training to navigate the streets and the traffic, barely conscious of the fact that his car wasn't exactly built for some of the maneuvers he was pulling off, jumping curbs and whatnot. But he would total his car before he let his granddaughter perish, not while there was a chance at saving her. His son had done it for him; now was his chance to repay his life.

Borelian poison, the beginning and continuing cause of their woes. It never seemed to end. Walter's injuries, Rifun's seizures, Maisy's illness, all of it stemming from those rainbow bastards. But at least now they had a way to fight back. Walter gritted his teeth and pressed on, zooming across the bridge and heading for home.

According to Chen Po, whose work with the Borelian toxins was just starting to make significant headway before he was murdered, the general cure for the poisons was glucose, sugar. It was kind of a catch-all when the specific toxin was unknown, but it took some time to work. He theorized that there might be more specific, more effective cures for each poison in turn — like opiate inhibitors for the blue toxin — but that was about as far as he got before the siege on Tacaga.

There was no way to know exactly which poison was in Maisy's system, and it wasn't impossible that there could be more than one, just to throw off the doctors in the event they did find something unusual. It was a good thing, then, that they still had a small supply of hasax in the freezer at home.

Walter arrived home and headed inside, still holding his Band. Even with Time being stopped, he still moved with a distinct sense of urgency. He could not rest or relax until he got this back to the hospital and saved his granddaughter's life.

Rummaging through the freezer, it was still surreal to think of himself as a grandfather. The next generation of Forbeses had entered the world. Granted, if she married one day, her name would change, but for the moment, she was a Forbes. And who knew? If Tommen and Becky decided to have more kids, there was the possibility of sons in there, too. Although, if they stuck with strictly natural children, Tommen was just as likely as any of his forefathers to have exactly two boys and a plethora of girls. It seemed to be a curse unique to the family. On the other hand, if they decided to adopt, they could easily choose to go the opposite route, have exactly two girls and a crowd of boys.

Walter shook his head and blinked to clear his mind. No. He couldn't start conjuring up future fantasies. He had to stay in the moment and focus on saving the one grandchild he did have. Otherwise, there might not be that future he was so dreamily envisioning.

Panic was creeping into his mind as he dug deeper in the

freezer, uncovering food that hadn't seen the light of day since it was bought months ago. But still no hasax. Had Becky tossed it out, thinking it old, freezer burned waste? Had she possibly used it in one of her culinary creations?

Well, even if he couldn't find the hasax itself, it wasn't about the flower, but the high concentration of glucose. If he had to, Walter would rob a grocery store for a bag of sugar. It might take a little longer than the hasax to work, but if it worked and Maisy got to come home, well, Walter wasn't going to argue the means if the ends meant his granddaughter lived.

Then, in the deepest, darkest corner of the freezer, buried underneath a myriad of frozen vegetables, was the container of hasax. Grinning stupidly, Walter pulled it out of its snowbank and inspected it. Truthfully, he didn't know whether the hasax could be revived to its natural, effective state after being frozen for a year or more, but it was the best plan they had, short of raiding the hospital cafeteria for sugar.

Breathing a sigh of relief, Walter closed the freezer and turned as if to leave.

It was dark outside. As in, pitch black. It had been the middle of the afternoon when he'd left the hospital, a bright, sunny day full of hope. Now it was the middle of the night. The clock on the microwave read eleven-twenty. He hadn't dropped his Band, hadn't changed it at all. That could only mean that someone else had Double-Banded him, let him think all was well when it really wasn't. Eight hours wasn't a lot of time to jump, but maybe it was just enough.

Cautiously, he reached for his phone. The first thing he saw was a text from Dean, but rather than asking where he was, it was a condolence message, expressing sympathy for his loss. He saw there were similar messages from all of his coworkers on night shift: Kate, Arthur, Arnold, all of them.

So either Tommen had called the sheriff before his own father, or else someone had used a Disguise and masqueraded as him, calling into work to ask for the night off on account of the death of his grandchild.

With shaking hands, Walter managed to text his son.

"I just looked up and saw it was dark and there was a message on my phone from Dean giving his condolences. I know I've been in a Band. Did...what I think happened happen?"

A few minutes later, Tommen replied. "Yes. She's gone. We're taking last pictures."

"I'm on my way."

Walter didn't remember sending that text. But he remembered the sound of the frozen container of hasax hitting the floor. He remembered the stinging pain in his knees as they also hit the floor. His stomach lurched and his mind went fuzzy.

They were too late. He was too late. He'd been duped somehow and had failed to save his granddaughter. She'd been depending on him. His son and daughter-in-law had been counting on him. And he'd failed. He'd fallen for a stupid rookie trick, something even an Apprentice ought to have picked up on. Being Double-Banded like that. What a stupid mistake.

But it had happened. Probably it hadn't even been a Time Band, but an Akari Band, something he couldn't detect, therefore, something he couldn't defend against. And it had cost his granddaughter her life.

He Banded so he could weep freely for a minute or two before standing and going out to the garage. Only at the last second did he consider that, as far as Tommen and Becky were concerned, he'd gone to work. He couldn't show up in his civilian clothes.

Walter stumbled drunkenly down to his bedroom, intending to change into a uniform first thing, but taking another minute to weep anew. He'd failed. He'd almost crossed the finish line, but in last place. He held the cure for a dead man, which made it not a cure at all. It was just...useless.

When he finally wiped his eyes clear, he saw something on his bed. It appeared to be a book, and not one from his shelf. *Of Saints and Sinners* it was called. There was a bookmark shoved in the pages. With a trembling hand, he dared to open the book to the bookmarked page, his eyes drawn to the large lettering in the passage.

"Owain choked a sob and stared at nothing for a long moment. Another sob. He wiped his eyes and took a shuddering breath. He put one hand weakly out in front of him.

" 'He snatched Victoria out of her arms, put one hand around...her throat...and he just...squeezed.' Another sob. 'And he just held her there. For over a minute.' He sniffed. 'Then he squeezed again, just to be sure.' A shuddering breath. 'And he let her fall to the floor. The maid ran. All the staff did. They ran and reported the incident to the police.'

"He broke down. His chains echoed in the chapel as his whole body shook. He couldn't stop, and he wasn't sure he wanted to."

Walter wept anew for what felt like an eternity. He knew he had to keep moving, but it was several minutes before he could force his body to move.

Somehow, he managed to get into his uniform. Next thing he knew he was driving. Sorrow and guilt washed over him. He'd tried this time. He'd really, really tried. It just wasn't enough. He couldn't do it. He couldn't save his only grandchild.

More than once he pulled over to compose himself. He was still in a Band, but that didn't mean he was in a position to even be walking, never mind operating machinery. He could still crash into a wall or another vehicle if he wasn't paying attention. And it was hard to pay attention right now.

Nevertheless, he'd made it to the hospital in one piece. His uniform earned him a little less scrutiny from hospital security, especially when they learned that he was the grandfather of a tiny patient who had just passed away. He got all but a royal escort up to NICU. It was meant to show respect, but Walter really just wanted them to all go away. His grandchild dying was bad enough. It was worse when he considered that he'd been tasked with saving her and failed miserably. All because of a stupid mistake.

The guilt and shame and sorrow hit him like a bullet to the

chest when he walked in the room. The news was bad by itself, but to walk in and have it visually confirmed was more than he could bear.

They took pictures, the last pictures they would have with Maisy. All the cute shots of mother and child, father and child, old time grandparents and a brand new grandparent. Walter got the picture his cohorts at the precinct had been begging for, to see if he could hold a newborn in one hand. As it turned out, he couldn't. He blamed the floofy dress, but the point was, he needed both hands.

She had seemed so peaceful, almost as if she were just sleeping during the whole photo shoot. Such a good little baby. It actually helped to ease some of Walter's fears, which was probably the whole point of the exercise. Rather than just yanking the infant away with no closure, give the family time to process and mourn the loss by celebrating her short life just as much as they could. Dress her up, take pictures, and let her go.

After that, there was no reason to stick around the hospital. Becky had been formally discharged, and there was nothing left for Maisy; she was gone. Walter asked his son if they wanted a ride home so he wasn't trying to drive like he was. Tommen thanked him but refused.

So Walter left the hospital, still muddled and confused in his mind, but a little more at peace after the pictures. He drove home, got out of his uniform, and lay on his bed. He was exhausted. He was wide awake. He wanted to weep waterfalls. He was completely numb. Conflicting thoughts and emotions raced through his mind so they were more perception than real, coherent elements he could consider. One thing was for sure, though. He wasn't going to work tonight. Or probably tomorrow night either.

He heard the door open again, and Tommen and Becky walked in the house. Except for a few sounds of shoes being kicked off and a chair being moved in the kitchen, neither said a word. Walter heard them walk down the hall and go in their bedroom. The door squeaked closed. There was no further sound for about half an hour when he heard Becky weeping inconsolably. Walter knew how she felt. He wanted to do the same thing.

After a time, he got up and went out to his recliner. He had to keep his sleep schedule somewhat consistent, or else he would never be able to return to work. But as the minutes dragged on and the morning seemed but a distant dream, he wondered whether it was really worth the effort. He wondered whether he should even return to work at all, or just call it quits now before anyone else got hurt.

Tommen and Becky had elected to have Maisy cremated. They said it had to do with cost, but Walter knew that everyone in the family, himself included as Tommen's sole family member, would have bent over backwards to provide a nice funeral and burial, whatever they wanted. It was impossible to say what their deeper motivations might have been, at least at the time. Some of the ash went into small necklaces that each wore: for Becky, a heart-shaped locket, and for Tommen, a small vial.

The memorial had been held at the Catholic church that Becky and her mother frequented, though Walter had noticed a rather powerful Jewish presence as well, as Dr. Polski invited probably half his synagogue to the event.

The nice thing about tight-knit religious groups, Walter remembered thinking, was that it really helped to cut down on cost as everyone came together for mutual benefit, not just in it for the money. The church only asked for a small fee to help with any cleanup afterwards. Mrs. Polski and an army of women provided the catering and the decorations, including the many display boards with every picture ever taken of Maisy, including the numerous ultrasound images. The men provided the heavy lifting for the women in setting up the reception hall with the tables and chairs and so forth.

Walter had felt guilty about being the only one on Tommen's side of the family. They really, truly did have only each other. There were no distant cousins to call up, and Miach and Micaiah had gone silent. From Tommen's best guess, from his conversation with Julianna, this had been another massive attack, and the twins, Nathan, maybe even all of the Miaramila, were also gone. The first time around may have failed because it had been huge and obvious. Sometimes subtlety could inflict worse damage than force ever could.

And regardless of how he denied it, Tommen had isolated himself. Going from an annoying and excited father-to-be who would show off the ultrasound pictures to anyone who cared to look, to almost completely silent and never seen, it was a little scary, if Walter wanted to be honest. He wouldn't say he didn't understand, but the change was sharp enough to give a spectator whiplash.

So, with Tommen's lackluster permission, Walter had invited a few of the guys from the precinct to come and show their support at the memorial. Dean and Kate showed up, as did a couple others. Will was also present with his mom, and, surprisingly, Eli as well. On top of all that, Walter had seen a number of messages on Tommen's social media page, including one from Eric.

Still, his son looked like the only person in the world as he sat alone in the front. Occasionally, someone would approach him. Polite words were exchanged, but Tommen ultimately shrugged them off. After a while, Walter moved to sit beside his son.

"How are you doing, kiddo?" Walter asked gently. "Between work and school and holing up in your room, I don't see you much."

"Nothing to see," Tommen murmured.

"How are things between you and Becky?"

He shrugged. Walter frowned, but he didn't know what to do, what to suggest. He couldn't just tell them to suck it up and move on. He couldn't tell them that everything would be all right. A medical mystery was one thing, and that was devastating enough. To know that it had been murder? It had to be eating him up inside.

"How's work?" Tommen asked, evidently trying to find any other topic.

"Good days and bad days," Walter answered evasively.

Before either could say more, the service began. Walter stood and moved, allowing Becky to sit next to Tommen. The atmosphere around them was a bit like molasses in January, thick, sludgy, and cold. There was no affection, little comfort, and it almost seemed as though they were unaware of what was even going on, though Walter was sure they were more aware than they let on.

They livened up a bit for the reception, enough to greet people, thank them for coming, and so on. It was still a challenge to carry on a conversation, or at least a light-hearted one. Laughter from other tables seemed sorely out of place and not a little unwanted.

Cleanup was left to Becky's brothers and sisters, and, after the graveside service, the rest of them went home.

Memorials typically provided a sense of closure for a family, a chance to really close the door and move on. It didn't make everything hunky-dory and snap everything back to the normal daily grind, but it helped. And it did, at least for Walter as he returned to work the following evening.

"Thanks for coming to the memorial yesterday," he told Kate after he'd punched in.

She gave him a look. "Oh, Walt, you know the whole force would have showed up if you would have asked, except for this thing called 'coverage.' But we're here for you; you know that. Everything all right at home?"

"A little frosty."

"Well, I probably have no business in it, but don't let them give up on each other, at least not yet. They need to get through this before making any rash decisions, the same as any trauma or major life event. They need to think it through logically before giving in to emotion."

"Don't need to tell me that," Walter sighed.

Kate folded her arms. "And how are you doing?"

He frowned. "It's not fair, but it's also not changing."

She nodded. "Well, you sound a lot better than you did a couple weeks ago."

"I suppose. Guess we'll just have to wait and see. But until then, there's plenty of stuff to do around here."

With that, he grabbed a page off the printer and a set of keys.

About a week after Maisy's death, Dean had called Walter into his office. It was to be expected. The sheriff asked Walter how things were at home, if there were any problems, any reason to suspect there might be more than just grief going through his mind. He asked how his relationship was with his son and his daughter-in-law. He asked a whole myriad of questions that took a good half hour or more to get through.

Walter didn't fight it. There was no reason to. He didn't want to. He wasn't exactly begging to be let go, and if the sheriff had told him that he was retired as of immediately, Walter figured the most he would be was slightly disgruntled.

Instead, the sheriff had given him an official retirement date. June 10th was to be his last night of work, so that when he punched out at whatever-o'clock on the morning of June 11th, he was done and out. It was an intentional date because Tommen's graduation was June 11th. Walter would punch out, go home, maybe have time to take a nap before getting ready to go to graduation, go through all that hoopla, and be ready for a good long night's rest. A way to kickstart getting his sleep schedule back to normal, Dean said. Walter thanked him and headed out.

But for the time being, he sat on the side of the road near a convenience store, waiting for speeders, for burglars, for drunk morons, for any excitement at all. He glanced at his phone about every ten minutes. Once he had gotten his official retirement date, he'd set up a countdown on his phone. It started out at years, a big beautiful zero, and moved all the way down to seconds. A little more than two months, and the seconds kept ticking down.

He'd learned, in the last week or so, that countdowns could be addicting. Counting down the time to the end of his shift, or thereabouts, counting down to his retirement, counting down to the end of the month. Watching the seconds tick down, the minutes go by, the hours wind down, it was all very mesmerizing. At one point, he'd had seven different countdowns going on his phone. It drained his battery life, and he quickly realized it was distracting him, so he finally eliminated all but his retirement clock.

And he sat there. Waiting. Looking at his phone. Waiting. Drinking his coffee. Waiting for something to do but hoping it didn't happen. Excitement came in many forms, not all of them good.

The night wasn't totally boring, but the little blips on the radar weren't really worth noting. Just another night on the beat. Did anyone still say that? Walter mulled it over as he finished up his paperwork. Well, a few people still used terms like "fuzz" and "po-po" so it wasn't unrealistic to think that "on the beat" was still somewhat in style, even if it was just on the fringe.

Then he punched out and went home. All was quiet.

If there was ever a time when Walter wished for things to remain quiet and not happen, those first few weeks after Maisy's death was it. Miraculously, he got his wish. Actually, he thought there may have even been something of an improvement as Tommen mentioned that he and Becky were going to go out for a bit one day.

It gave Walter hope, and he was able to breathe a small sigh of relief, a weight lifted that he hadn't even realized he'd been carrying. Maybe there was a chance that this could all be salvaged. Maybe there was a chance that Tommen and Becky could work through this together. They had each processed their own grief in their own way, and now they were ready to come together and figure things out. Might be they couldn't have any more natural kids, but adoption was always a viable alternative.

Still, the mood around the house remained fairly dull. Usually either Walter or Tommen was gone to work or school, and Becky sometimes went down to her parents' house to work on her sewing, but on those rare occasions when all three were under the same roof, there was a tension as though a bomb sat in the middle of the room, and he who looked at it first would set it off.

Walter wondered whether he had imagined the whole thing, about Tommen and Becky reconciling. Maybe he'd misinterpreted his son's words or tone. Maybe they were trying to come to an agreement on how to split up and have it be as least traumatic as possible. Maybe they didn't even know what was going on, and whatever this outing was, it was just a way to try and figure things out. Death had hit them over the head and put them in a daze, and now they were just waking up, wondering where they were and why they were there.

Whatever the case, Walter wasn't going to stop them or give them any advice. Maybe that was his own fault, but while he was quite an expert in loss, especially loss of family, he wasn't so knowledgeable about how to put family back together. This was something the two of them would have to work out for themselves.

So it came as a bit of a shock when Tommen came home one day and showed him a fresh tattoo. Well, not absolutely fresh, not in the sense that it was still red and swollen, nor was it scabbed and flaking. All the same, it hadn't been there a few days ago.

"When did this happen?" he asked.

"Yesterday," Tommen mumbled.

"I'm just kind of assuming you Banded it so it would heal faster."

"Yeah."

"Ah. Becky, too, or just you?"

"She did. Not in the same place, but yeah. She doesn't want her parents to know yet."

"Fair enough."

Tommen pulled the sleeve back down. "You're not mad?"

Walter sighed and gave him a look. "Tommen, I stopped trying to boss you around a long time ago. You're your own man now. You don't need my permission. It doesn't matter what I think."

Tommen frowned and looked away, saying, "It's an ash tattoo. Maisy's ashes got mixed with the ink."

"I saw your chain broke."

"Yeah. I was so afraid of losing her ashes. It'll be pretty hard to lose them now."

Walter nodded. "Indeed it will."

Tommen meandered away.

Walter had never been overly fond of tattoos. For too many

years, they had been used as signs of slavery and prison, sailors notwithstanding. Especially in his line of work, it was still a way to mark out gang and prison territories and allegiances. And yet, in the modern world, they were becoming very mainstream, used as expressions of art and self. And, if he wanted to be honest, if he'd seen the design just straight on paper, he would have said it looked very nice. As a tattoo, it didn't look bad, either. Walter wasn't exactly going to run out and get one for himself, make it a trifecta, but maybe he could rethink some of his prejudices against tattoos. The ash part of it was a little creepy in his opinion, but it was his son's choice.

But that was neither here nor there. It didn't change the past, and it didn't change much in the present, either, except that his son now had a little colored skin on his wrist. Otherwise, they just plodded along in day to day life.

April moved along slowly, or maybe it only felt like it. The tenth, they were all feeling it as they silently considered that Maisy would have been a month old. One month into his planned grandparenthood and he wasn't being woken up by a crying baby in the next room. He wasn't being called upon to babysit in an emergency or so the frazzled new parents could have an evening to themselves.

Instead, all the toys got cleared out of the living room, making it look big and empty, an echoing museum of what should have been. The clothes were a little slower to disappear. Neither Tommen nor Becky ever said what happened to them. Walter imagined they first went down to her parents' house, just for safekeeping and to open up a little more room in their bedroom. From there, it was anyone's guess. Maybe they would be given to one of her relatives when they had kids. Maybe they would be donated to the church or the synagogue. Walter didn't know, and he didn't ask.

He figured he should probably get his act together to start packing and preparing to go dark. In a moment of grim humor, he mused that there was no longer any real reason to fight it. He wasn't battling his conscience anymore, wanting to be a present grandfather but needing to go dark. That whole excuse, that whole reason, was gone. Even his own safety seemed like less of an excuse. If Julianna wanted to kill him, she could have easily done it on his failed rescue mission.

His new reason for his sloth, he told himself, was wanting to keep an eye on his son. Walter no longer felt confident leaving Tommen alone, not like that. Sure, he could go to work and the grocery store and wherever else he needed to go, and his fear and paranoia level was minimal. But to go dark and leave his son so completely, he wasn't sure how either of them would handle it. They both had the means to visit the other anytime, anywhere. But Tommen was both prideful and isolated. He wasn't likely to seek out help on his own. It didn't help that Nathan was missing, presumed dead.

So Walter continued to procrastinate on going dark. Even if he did pack up, he still wasn't sure where he wanted to go. All of his original plans had been upended, and he'd been too muddled to give any serious, considerate thought to it. Maybe he could retire to Florida or Arizona. Maybe he should go back to Wales. Maybe he could or should go anywhere in the entire universe. He didn't know.

Sitting on the side of the road again, he checked his phone for probably the twentieth time. One month, two weeks, et cetera, et cetera, until retirement. May was just around the corner.

The weather was rather pleasant, Walter thought. It was no longer frigid cold, but neither was it sweltering hot yet. It was at just that perfect temperature where, if you did get a little warm from working hard or whatever, there was usually a light breeze just around the corner to cool you off. He had his window cracked just a touch to allow for such airflow, even as he checked his phone yet again. One month, two weeks, yadda, yadda, five seconds...four seconds...three seconds...two seconds...

"629, you have a copy?" It was Kate.

Walter turned down the car radio and picked up the mic. "Go ahead."

"I'm in pursuit, heading toward your location. Can you give

me a block?"

"Yes, ma'am."

All he really had to do was nose his car onto the road and position it just so.

That was the bad part about the nice weather. More people doing stupid things. They assumed that just because it was warm and the sun was shining that they were invincible. Maybe they fancied themselves the star, the hero of an action movie where there would always be a way out from under the hand of the law. Maybe they were fighting for or against these law enforcement officials, but either way, the boys in blue just got in the way of either saving or destroying the world.

And maybe Walter had been watching a little too much TV in the last month or so. He needed to get back to the library and read some intelligent, well-thought-out literature, get his brain cells on a mental treadmill. He thought about his Authored Book. He hadn't read it yet, was a little afraid to, honestly.

The man Kate was pursuing was smart enough to stop his car before crashing into Walter's cruiser broadside, but then he made the mistake of trying to flee on foot. With a little creative Banding, Walter caught the guy, tackling him and putting him in handcuffs before he could react. He was a feisty one, though, wrangling him back to the cruisers. Allan had also shown up and was busy checking out the guy's car where several different drugs were found stashed in a hidden compartment in the center console. The man himself was high on something.

The excitement of police life, Walter mused once it was all cleaned up and they were heading back to the station. At least it helped to pass the time. He checked his phone again. It had eaten up a few minutes, anyway.

He really needed to stop looking at that thing. As exciting and addicting as it was, it was also depressing. Only a few minutes? Only a couple hours? Only a day? Sometimes, especially at work, whole years would pass in a single night. Robberies, domestics, homicide, suicide, those took up a few months just by themselves. Walter sometimes wondered if Time had messed with him more than he thought, warped his perception of time.

But that was neither here nor there, he thought. It is what it is. At this point, he just had to take things as they came, but he was learning to look ahead, be hopeful, and make plans again. It wasn't helping his preparations for going dark any; it was more of a mental shift.

As April turned into May, he found himself able to focus and concentrate more. He got back into the conversation around the precinct. As Kate so eloquently put it, the wilted flower had come back to life. There were jokes for weeks about wilted flowers after that, and Kate knew she would never live it down, starting those jokes. But all the same, Walter laughed at the jokes. He got in on the fun, and felt almost normal again. The rest of the guys mentioned that it was good to have him back before he retired a grouchy old depressed miser. Walter wasn't sure how he wanted to take that, but he went along with it, anyway. It was good to be back.

That wasn't to say he didn't hurt, sitting alone in his cruiser, checking his phone, thinking about ways he might have been able to save Maisy. But he was healing.

At home, the hurt was much more obvious. For all of them. For a while, it had seemed as though things might have been getting better between Tommen and Becky, but maybe that was just what Walter had wanted to believe. He couldn't be too sure. But whether it had or hadn't, they certainly weren't anymore. The two rarely spoke to each other that Walter saw, and it wasn't even an angry silence between them. They did not appear to blame each other for what happened. Rather, the silence was thick and murky, depressed. Each one blamed himself, and each was unsure how to reconcile himself to the other.

It might not have been so bad except for the unique burden that Walter knew his son carried. He knew it had been an assassination. From what he explained, Julianna had been orchestrating this from the beginning, even masquerading as Dr. Whitmore a time or two in order to infiltrate Maisy's DNA in the womb, in order to give her Beckwith-Weidemann, in order to force her into a hospital stay, in order to administer the poison. Tommen had missed all of it until the very end, and he blamed himself.

As May dragged on, Walter watched his son try to move on, move forward. The problem seemed to be that Becky wasn't ready for that yet, and Tommen didn't want to move forward without her. Tommen's guilt and cynicism warred with his realism, as he tried to balance his own self-loathing with the knowledge that there was absolutely nothing he could do about it anymore. Maisy was gone. Her ashes were tattooed into his skin. It was time to take the first step forward, into healing, back into the real world. Be part of life again instead of mere spectators. Becky hadn't made that break yet. She knew perfectly well that her daughter was gone, but her heart hadn't let her go yet.

One afternoon, Tommen had confided in Walter his confusion. It was not the first time he had done this. Walter had pointed out that Becky was probably dealing with standard postpartum depression, and heaping a huge helping of death and despair on top of that was definitely not helping things. It might actually take more time for her to recover.

The prospect clearly did not go over well with Tommen, but it was an acceptable and logical conclusion, and he carried on.

The counter on Walter's phone finally ticked down to under a month until his retirement. It made him a little giddy, honestly. He was going to retire. A lot of men complained that they couldn't retire until sixty-five, maybe seventy, and even then, some of them had to work part-time to supplement their paltry income. Walter wanted to look at those men and politely inform them that he was two hundred years old and this was the first time that he was going to be retired. So suck it up, buttercup, and let him enjoy it.

He wasn't even sure what he was going to do. Forget about where he was going to live, how about what he was going to fill his time with. Travel he had at his fingertips, but what about daily life?

He thought about his mentor, Mark. Years could go by without hardly a thought given to the man anymore, but now Walter considered him more deeply. Mark had been killed in Vietnam, but his life before that had been a small-time farmer in one of the Dakotas.

Maybe Walter ought to follow his example, at least for a little while. True, he didn't expect to wake up at the crack of dawn every day to go milk thirty cows and hitch up the horses to plow — or even start up a tractor to plow, for that matter — but a handful of chickens and ducks he could do. Maybe keep a small garden. Just enough to keep him occupied and say that some of his food came from his own hard work.

He shook his head as if to clear it. Good grief, he wasn't on his death bed. He might be able to do that for a season so he could relax and unwind from years of police work and other harrowing feats, but if he had the time, he might as well live a little. Yeah, yeah, there were all sorts of points and jokes to be made about having Time and manipulating Time, but there just seemed to be something freeing about the idea of not having any obligations to meet or shirk. To not have to Band to get in a five-minute break sounded absolutely wonderful.

But for the moment, he still had to work.

He was still addicted to his phone, however, watching the seconds tick down. Watching as four weeks turned into three.

At some point, sitting on the side of the road, he did the back calculation. Three weeks until retirement meant nine weeks since Maisy's death. She would have been two months old last week, Walter mused. She would be three months at his retirement and Tommen's graduation.

He tried to remember Victoria around that age, and was both alarmed and ashamed to say he could recall very little. Maybe it was his behavior from way back then or just the length of time, or maybe it was both. Sorry to say, he knew only what she looked like, but almost nothing of who she had been.

He took a moment to breathe. Victoria's death had been scar tissue for a long time, but Maisy's death had stabbed him in the same place and so much deeper. Even now, the wound was scabbing, but could still be easily ripped open, if he thought about it for more than a few seconds, if he dwelt on his failure.

The radio squawked, bringing him out of his teetering mental state. He was here; he had a job to do.

It started out fairly straightforward. A family was having an evening dinner party, sitting out on the patio when a dog suddenly burst through the bushes and ended up attacking a little girl, about ten years old. One of the uncles grabbed a gun and shot it dead. Walter knew the girl would be tragically disfigured for the rest of her life, and it was now his job to ensure that whoever owned the dog owned up to the crime.

The dog had only a simple chain collar, no tags, but Animal Control found the microchip in the back of its neck. With a fancy scanner, they were able to pull up the information on the chip, including a phone number. Walter called the number.

The man on the other end turned out to be a dog breeder, and the only adult dogs he had were his breeding pair. Both were accounted for. Yes, all his puppies were accounted for as well, and even so, they were only ten weeks old, only a threat in their cuteness.

No, none of his dogs or puppies had escaped in the past. No, he'd never had any problems in the past either.

Yes, his breeding dogs were registered. The puppies were also able to be registered. No, he didn't do it himself because that automatically added a premium on the price, and he didn't want to exclude families who only wanted a purebred pet. If someone intended on showing or whatever, they could register the dogs themselves. Same with the microchips. He did it to be polite and in case one did run off. He notified his buyers that they could change the information, but it was on them to take it over.

Yes, he kept a record of his buyers, but he'd been breeding for some time. That was a lot of puppies to go through, and who was to say that some dogs didn't get sold later on down the line?

Something about the man's demeanor was just a little off, Walter thought, but he tried to play it cool. Just a cop investigating a horrendous accident. If the man was just the breeder, then he was just the breeder.

All the same, he paid the man a visit that night about ten o'clock. He gathered a little preliminary information and said someone would be following up if they needed anything else. The man thanked him, offered his condolences for the girl who had been attacked, and politely saw Walter off his porch. Inside, Walter had noticed the house looked clean with the exception of five puppies running around like a pack of sugared-up banshees, scattering toys and tipping over an end table.

What followed over the course of a week or two was an extensive investigation into the breeder's life and his clients, even if the breeder didn't know it. Many of his clients fell into two categories: people who wanted to show dogs and needed a purebred registered animal, and families who wanted a purebred pet.

But there was another class of buyer in the mix, and on the first day of June, there was a raid on a dogfighting ring. Walter had been there for the raid just by sheer luck of being on third shift. After all, no one ran a dogfight at one in the afternoon. No, it had to be at one in the morning.

Thirty dogs were seized, over seventy people arrested, including the breeder, and the story became headlines all over West Virginia. There was a frenzy in the media and the precinct, and the family of the girl who got mauled wanted the ringleader's blood and, more importantly, his money, in order to pay the medical bills. Walter didn't blame them.

It had been sheer luck, really. At one particular fight in the abandoned barn they used as their arena, one of the bait dogs managed to escape. The fighting dog gave chase and the humans around failed to capture it before it, too, got out. When the medical examiner got through with the fighting dog, he did report finding remains of the bait dog in its stomach. After that little snack, the fighting dog went on a rampage, tearing through garbage, eating a few small mammals, then finding the girl.

It was exhausting, Walter thought, looking at his phone. Less than a week until retirement now. The thought was surreal. He was almost retired. This time next week, he was going to be back on a normal sleep schedule. He wouldn't have to wake up to an alarm every morning, wouldn't have to worry about whether his next night at work would be his last, wouldn't have to wonder what would happen to Tommen if he didn't come home. He wouldn't have to worry about what his next shift would bring, if it would be a calm night on the side of the road, a tiring night of drunk driving and break-ins, or a major sting operation to break up a dogfighting ring.

Instead, he could sleep in, go where he wanted when he wanted, and spend his evenings hosting dinner parties if he wanted. He wasn't much of a host, but the point was that he wouldn't be out on the beat somewhere, waiting and wondering what was going to happen next.

It helped to relax him a little, though that could be a dangerous thing. How many guys had he known were about to retire, bragging it up, and letting their guard down so that they were killed or critically injured in the days before their retirement? He had to be on high alert up until he punched out the morning of the eleventh.

All the same, it would be nice to be able to relax a little, he thought. He was tired of being on constant high alert, and going home was hardly a reprieve.

Becky was more distant than ever, a wisp of a breeze compared to the tornado she had been. Walter could see it was killing Tommen to try and stick by her, cheer her up and everything else, when she did not even seem to realize his existence. She went through everything mechanically, a robot who cooked dinner, did laundry, and cleaned house. Several times, Walter tried to engage her and ask if she was ready for school in the fall, ask how she was going to balance that and her sewing business. She merely replied that yes, she was ready, because she had nothing else to look forward to. And she would balance it because she already had, and because she wasn't adding anything new into the mix.

Walter kept a close eye on both of them, but there was only so much he could do. He talked to her parents about it a time or two, but there really wasn't a whole lot they could offer. Healing was as much a matter of will as anything physical. They really didn't know what to do or suggest. They'd offered to help her move back in with them, but she declined, and they weren't going to force her.

Still, it made him very uncomfortable. But if they could hold out until his retirement, then he could be a little more present. That way, when they had problems during the day, he could be there to help instead of sleeping through it all.

At the same time, he didn't know how much good it would do to be home during the day, especially through the summer. Since finishing up his first semester of college, all Tommen did was work. Twelve hours shifts were pretty much the norm, but fourteen and sixteen weren't uncommon, especially with this next big project they were doing. Another picture-perfect, magazine-worthy mansion nestled in luscious mountain hills. At least this one didn't involve ripping into the side of a mountain, Tommen said, just leveling one a little.

"And you have Saturday off, right?" Walter asked. "I don't want you to suddenly come to me with some 'work emergency' and try to get out of walking for graduation."

"Yes, I have it off," Tommen mumbled.

"I know you're not excited about it, but do it for me at least."

"What's the point, though? I mean, everyone always knew me as 'that kid' for one reason or another. The fighting, the kidnapping, the shooting, the one who got his girlfriend pregnant. Now I'm going to be that kid whose kid died. And I'm going to be on stage in front of everyone."

"For all of five seconds," Walter pointed out. "You're not valedictorian or anyone giving a speech, so you don't have to address the entire congregation. You sit there, listen, and go up on stage when they call you to give you your diploma."

Tommen growled and rubbed his face. "Only because you want me to. And that's the only reason. I don't want to go. I don't want to do it."

Walter chuckled. "Believe me, kid, there are plenty of things I have had to do that I didn't want to. Black-tie fundraisers were the bane of my existence when I worked at city, shmoozing local politicians and rich people, pretending to love them just so we could secure a tiny bit of funding and maybe have enough for ourselves at the end of the day. Graduation is pretty darn mild compared to that, I think. You'll survive."

His son said nothing.

"Is Becky going to come?" Walter ventured.

Tommen shook his head. "No. She doesn't want to be seen by anyone from school."

Walter almost said he understood, then refrained. It might sound discriminatory. They were both hurting and they were both pretty well-known at school. Why should he be more empathetic to Becky's refusal to go while forcing his son? Maybe because he was still a bit of a sucker for a woman in distress, same as Tommen. Thinking about it, though, he elected not to say anything.

"Are you ready for retirement?" Tommen asked, trying to change the subject.

"I've been ready for the last few decades, I think," Walter answered.

"Have you figured out what you're going to do with yourself?"

"Not really."

"I see you at least got a few boxes, even if they are still empty."

"Yeah. At least I made it that far."

"Do you know where you're going?"

"I still haven't decided."

"You've only got so long. It's June now. I thought you put an arbitrary deadline on yourself. Labor Day, wasn't it? Spend the usual tourist season, Memorial Day to Labor Day, getting packed and ready and out the door?"

Walter shrugged helplessly. "I know. And I've been terrible about it, but my bigger concern lately has been you and Becky."

His son's expression turned unreadable, and the conversation ended shortly thereafter. Part of the reason was the awkwardness, and the other part was Walter needing to get to work.

Only a few more days, he mused on the drive in. Just a few more days of, "Do you know why I pulled you over?" and "You have the right to remain silent," and "Please, God, let me punch out on time."

"Evening, Walt," Kate greeted. "Still watching that countdown on your phone?"

"I now have it set to show the days, hours, minutes, seconds, milliseconds, and whatever comes after that."

"Desperation," Arthur quipped.

Walter grinned and shook his head. "No, I got rid of it. I figured I can let myself be surprised."

"Surprised, yeah, right," Kate laughed. "The only surprising thing is that it took so long. You should have been out of here years ago."

"I haven't been here for years."

"Then you get my point."

He waved a hand dismissively. "Yeah, yeah, I know. I should have retired after the warehouse or when Casey was doing his spring cleaning. My stupid pride wouldn't let me."

Kate rolled her eyes. "Men and their egos. I swear."

"Now a pretty little lady like you swearing? My goodness. Didn't your mama teach you nothing?"

She swatted him and he laughed, saying, "What are you going to do? Fire me?"

"No," she told him, smiling smugly, "but I can put you on

toilet duty from now until you leave."

He faltered just a bit at that, but she grinned and sent him out on the road instead.

Only a couple more days, he thought, looking at his phone. It was Thursday night now. Tonight and tomorrow and all would be well. Tommen's graduation, his retirement party, and then he was home free. At least for a little while. He still had to figure out what he was doing, where he was going, and what his plans were.

Used to be that his plans had been just to survive. Whether he was a criminal on the run or a man trying to discover his place in a new era with Time-bending abilities, sometimes his greatest goal for the day had been to go to sleep and wake up the next morning. Then he had his goal to find Tommen, either learn what had happened to him in Forbes Cave or find him and raise him as his own. He had done that. Now what did he do?

It certainly helped to have a plan in mind when starting out on a new journey. It helped to guide him where he wanted to go, and it gave him a reason to set off. Simple need—because if he didn't then everyone would eventually start to see that he wasn't aging—just wasn't quite cutting it, apparently.

He found himself calling Pat the following day after he got off.

"You can come move into my neighborhood," the retired officer said. "Lots of retired folks around here."

"No way. You might start rubbing off on me. I want ideas on things to do. You can't even really garden in Arizona, can you?"

"Container gardens, mostly, but then you're shelling out for a ton of potting soil. That's what my wife does, but I also know it's her way of coping."

"Your cancer back?"

"Ah, they're running some tests, but I know myself. It's back."

"See? That's another reason I can't come down there. You'd all die on me." He forced a nervous laugh.

He could imagine Pat shrugging as he said, "It's what happens when you get old, Walt. Grim Reaper is coming for you, too, someday."

"Yeah, well, I'd like to have a few words with him about taking my granddaughter before me."

Pat grunted his agreement. "Well, listen, Walt. Even if you don't move down here with the rest of us old people, it'd be nice of you to visit one last time."

Walter let out a breath. "Yeah. I'll do that. I'll let you know my plans, or you call me if your plans are a little different. Got me?"

"I git you. Now don't go getting all sentimental on me. Like I said before, I've made my peace. We all die in the end. Just come visit me once and make me happy."

Walter promised he would. More words were exchanged and the conversation ended.

He hung up, feeling more dejected than anticipated when he'd picked up the phone to call his friend. Somehow this was turning into a summer of loss as he lost or gave up everything he'd worked so hard for the last ten years or so. It could easily make men bitter or depressed, but he knew he couldn't succumb to either of those things. Put simply, his son still needed him.

Maybe that was what he could do. Maybe he could talk Tommen into going to college somewhere else, assuming his scholarships would let him. Tommen could go to school, and Walter could hang around in a nearby town or city. Close, but independent of each other in daily life.

But what about Becky? Would she go with Tommen? Would she move back in with her parents? She'd been pretty silent about her thoughts and feelings lately. Walter didn't want to suggest something and make it seem as though they were just kicking her to the curb. Sorry, you didn't recover from tragedy in a convenient timeframe, so we're leaving without you. On the other hand, would Tommen want her to come with them if she did agree, or was he already mentally moving past her?

It was hard to know, and with Tommen gone to work presently, Walter could not ask. That was all right, he figured. It was his last night at the precinct. One last shift, then graduation, then getting everything back on track. Assuming he could catch Tommen on a day when he wasn't working, then they could have that discussion. Conversations would be a lot easier to have when he wasn't sleeping the morning way and didn't have to hurry up and get to work in the middle of the afternoon.

His retirement wasn't officially scheduled until after Tommen's graduation. All the same, someone had brought in celebratory cupcakes, just to whet their appetite.

"Last night, Walter," Kate told him, picking out one with green frosting and sprinkles. "I don't want to hear any reports of you goofing off out there. Or else I'll keep you here around the clock for the next week, as a start."

"Only because you insist," Walter said, sighing dramatically. He bit into a chocolate cupcake with pink frosting. "But know that I don't want to hear any reports about you goofing off after I'm gone. Or else your punishment will be me coming out of retirement."

"Oh no! Not that! Anything but that!"

"There you go. So you better behave."

Kate gave him a look. "You run a hard bargain, Walt."

"What can I say? It's a gift."

With that, he finished off his cupcake and left the break room. Then he went out and grabbed a set of keys for the last time.

Chapter Thirty-One
Chasm

Tommen, I'm leaving."

The announcement had come the Tuesday before graduation, after Tommen had gotten home from work but before he got in the shower. Actually, it was just after he'd taken his shoes off in the kitchen. Maybe she thought that he could digest the news while in the shower, mull it over in his mind instead of blurting out the first thing that came to mind. Maybe she thought that if she didn't say it immediately when he got home, then she would freeze and it would never be said. He preferred to think it was the latter.

"Moving back in with your parents?" he guessed, sighing.

Surprisingly, she shook her head. "No. I'm going to live with an aunt who's out in Wyoming. I can't stay here. I can't stay close. I need to get out, get away."

"Running away won't bring Maisy back."

"Staying here isn't doing much either," Becky countered.

"Why leave, though? Why tell me this now? What...? What haven't I done that you've wanted me to do? What about us?"

"Tommen..." For a second, Tommen thought she would clam up and retreat. Then she took a breath and answered, "I don't know why it happened. I don't understand why Maisy died. Maybe it was punishment, maybe it was chance. I don't know. At this point, I don't think it matters. But looking back, I've gone down some roads I'm not proud of. I don't want to just try and make it right or fix it, constantly bandaid it over and over again. I want to do it right from the beginning. As far as relationships go, I don't think you're part of that."

727

"Why can't we start over? Get married, take over the house, go to school. Maybe we fucked up this time, but let's start over. Together."

Becky shook her head, tears streaming down her cheeks. "I can't, Tommen. It's just not going to happen. I'm leaving."

She could have stabbed him in the heart and it would have hurt less, Tommen thought.

"Is there anything I can do or say to make you change your mind?" he asked helplessly.

"No. And I know I haven't responded to it or said much lately, but don't think I haven't noticed how you've tried. I know about all the times you came to my parents' house with flowers or whatever, trying to be that awkward kid from high school. Those nights I cried myself to sleep."

"Then why—?"

"We're not those people anymore, Tommen, and I think that's what kills me the most. We're not those people. We're adults now. We screwed around like consequences would never catch up to us. But they did. And we've suffered. And I think...I think we both need a fresh start. Away from each other. You have good schooling, good prospects, and everything else."

"And you don't? You've got your own business, a schooling and career path completely laid out, and almost your entire family is here. My dad is still moving, and when he's gone, it's just me here. If anyone should leave the area, it's me."

But Becky just shook her head again. "I can't stand the thought of being around my family here. Thanksgiving? Christmas? They're five or six months away, and it makes me want to puke. My sewing business? I hate it. I haven't even enjoyed sewing since Maisy died, since all my hard work and care went to total waste. I don't even want to look at a sewing machine. As for school? I don't know. I'll keep going like I am just because I have the scholarships and everything lined up, the internship, too. But I just don't know."

He forced a nervous laugh. "Do the people in Wyoming even

know what genetics is?"

Becky managed a small smile. "Believe me, I'm surprised the people in West Virginia do, so Wyoming can't be any worse."

Okay, there was that.

"I already have my plane ticket," she went on. "I just need to pack a few things."

"When are you leaving?"

"Friday night."

"How long have you been planning this? Does your aunt even know you're coming?"

"Yes, she knows. We've been making plans for about a month, and I've already talked to one of the schools out there. I can transfer everything and pick up where I left off."

"Do your parents know?"

She nodded and said quietly, "Yes."

"Why wait to tell me?"

"I wasn't sure how you'd react."

Tommen frowned. "After all we've been through, considering you said the exact same thing about the pregnancy, do you really think so little of me that you were afraid I would get angry?"

"I don't know."

He shook his head. "You're leaving, but really, you haven't been here for months. There's nothing for me to be angry about."

She said nothing to that. After a moment of silence, she said, "Most of my stuff is either being sold or going to my parents, but I still have some packing to do. Maybe I can get my packing finished before your dad gets started on his."

It was wry humor, but Tommen wasn't really sure what to make of it. He watched her walk away and turn to go down to the bedroom. His bedroom. Because it wouldn't be theirs anymore.

He quietly collected a change of clothes and headed into the bathroom. He stared at himself in the mirror for a good fifteen minutes.

His dad said he looked just like his pa at this age. Tommen

stared at his reflection as if he might have a *Lion King* moment and his pa would come and speak words of wisdom. What did he do? What did he say? Should he accept it meekly? Should he fight to the bitter end? What would be the point? It sounded like she'd been planning this for a month now. He, ignorant of this fact, had continued to try and woo her back to him, with no obvious success.

Tommen stared at his reflection, trying to imagine his pa being so young, trying to remember his pa at all. His memories were few and scattered, helped only because of his jaunt into the in-between dimension where he'd been able to do a little time traveling and see his parents and siblings. His intimate knowledge, though, was still sorely limited.

Finally he got in the shower. He couldn't think of anything to do or say. He couldn't conjure up any way to fix things, make them better. Was she running away? Or was this really what was best for both of them? How would things have been different if they'd been married? Was there really any difference? Other than names and rings, their lives were pretty darn intertwined. And her leaving definitely felt like a divorce, just with far less paperwork.

Tommen tried to recall whether Becky had been wearing her ring just now. He couldn't remember. Surely she didn't plan on wearing it after leaving. What did he do with them, then? They were past being returned, and he didn't want to just hang onto them in hopes of maybe, possibly finding someone else someday, because he would always know that they were meant for him and her. And he would always remember what transpired.

Next step would be to pawn them, he supposed. Maybe he could make a few bucks back. If he'd been of an age, he might have stopped to get a drink on the way home. As it was, he could probably still Band and do the same thing. He wouldn't even have to spend the money. Ha! Maybe take the pocket change and buy himself some dinner. Dinner for one.

His mood was grim. His shower took longer than normal, and even when he was out, he took his sweet time getting dried and dressed.

Maisy was gone. Becky was leaving. His dad was leaving by necessity. What did that leave for him? School? Physics hardly interested him, and he really wasn't planning on studying the trades. He'd gone into construction mostly for the money, either to pay for school or support a family. One no longer seemed important and the other clearly wasn't happening. What ambition did he have? What was his drive? Altruism? Sounded great, but when did he get a break?

What was it about him that made the universe hate him so much? Was it God, the Author, sheer random chance? Whatever the source was that caused or allowed these things to happen to him, was there anything he could do about it? He did his damnedest to do good, be good, but it never seemed to be enough. There was always some existential, celestial being out there who could just flick him right back on his ass at any moment. How was he supposed to stand up to that? And at this point, what reason did he have to try?

He returned to the bedroom to find Becky packing, dividing things between boxes and a couple duffel bags. Most of the stuff went in the boxes. Over the next few days, they would either go to her parents' house or one of many charities. Some of the stuff went into the duffel bags, the things she would be taking with her. She took her favorite clothes, a few trinkets. Tommen noticed that she kept the stuffed rabbit, still dressed in one of Maisy's outfits.

She couldn't let go, Tommen mused. She couldn't let go on her own, so she was taking a knife and cutting the cord forcibly, sawing off a limb in order to escape a trap. Tommen had seen several animals in his illegal traps attempt something similar, gnawing on their legs in order to get free. It hurt like hell and there was no clean way to do it, but right now she was incapable of freeing herself any other way. She wanted to be free, but she was so confused and afraid that she wasn't able to process the locking mechanism to simply open the trap, so she resorted to this instead.

Unfortunately, for as much as he understood the analogy, he was unable to make her see things the same way. In fact, she managed to turn the situation around and say that it only proved how the whole thing had been a trap from the very beginning. Yes, she may bear scars when this was all over, but at least she would know enough not to fall into any more traps.

It was then that he noticed that she was not wearing her ring. Indeed, all three were sitting on the bookshelf, untouched, alone amid his trinkets while hers had been packed away.

There was nothing he could say or do to change her mind, it seemed. By Thursday, he was helping her pack, or at least take boxes to the various charities as she dictated.

He considered telling his dad. It wasn't as if Becky had said not to, or that he wouldn't notice when she suddenly wasn't around anymore. But he refrained. No need to get him all worried and ruin the last few nights of work he had left. Let him enjoy his countdown and all the shenanigans at work. What were they going to do, fire him?

Tommen let out a breath. Maybe he should just go with his dad wherever he moved to next. Get away from this place and all the shit he'd experienced here. Looking out the window or going into the city, he hardly recognized his home anymore. He remembered this land being wild and free, unexplored and full of mystery and possibility. Now it was grown up and modern, full of danger and despair. Or maybe it was just him, being an adult and experiencing adult life. Well, adult life sucked. The real world sucked.

It was as good a plan as any, he thought, getting off work Friday afternoon. He hadn't told any of the guys about Becky leaving, either. He didn't need to come off as a weakling basket case. He went to work to do a job to make money. It wasn't Book Club, and it wasn't group therapy. It was work.

That mentality both helped and hurt, he thought. On the one hand, it helped him to focus, to push his problems to another part of his mind so he could work effectively. On the other hand, he did kind of want to tell someone, but there was still something weird about approaching Matt. Tommen wasn't sure how to approach a chaplain, and he could never forgive himself if something happened to Matt, too, after Nathan.

He didn't tell Will about it, either. The guy was on a roll with his braille menu invention, attracting the attention of other manufacturers and restaurants, business-minded folk and the like. If Will was to be believed, there were even a few investors sniffing around his turf, waiting to see how this was going to turn out. He'd sent out his first shipment of menu kits to half a dozen restaurants and had been interviewed for the local paper. Life was going great for him. There was no need to bother him with Tommen's tales of woe.

And, as he thought about it on the way home, was it really a tale of woe? He'd said it himself that she was leaving, but she hadn't been around for months. Virtually nothing would change except he would be cooking his own meals again and doing his own laundry. Conversation, affection, love, that was all long gone. He was basically a bachelor again, and Becky was kind of like his sister now instead of his girlfriend.

He felt ashamed to think of her that way and to reduce everything down to such a level. It felt dishonest and cynical.

Arriving home, he stayed in his car for a minute or two. He'd told Becky he would take her to the airport. She'd agreed, but he still wondered whether she wouldn't have left while he was at work.

This was it. This was the last day they were living together, probably the last day they would see each other. He rubbed his face. He remembered the first day they met in AP Physics. Within a week she had blackmailed him and gotten him to turn over some of his prized furs. She was clever and bright, spunky and not afraid to speak her mind. She was three-foot-nine but walked like she was ten feet tall. Obviously someone forgot to inform her of her shortcomings because she bulled her way through life like nothing could stop her.

Nothing, except the loss of a child and an entire future she had envisioned for herself and their family.

Taking a breath, Tommen got out of his car and went inside.

To his surprise, she hadn't sneaked away while he was at

work. But neither did she chastise him about being late. At the same time, her flight wasn't until eleven, so they weren't exactly cutting it close.

"You thought I'd sneak away," she stated, evidently reading his expression.

"The thought had crossed my mind," he responded diplomatically.

She nodded. "It crossed mine, too, honestly. It would be easy. Obviously it was expected to some degree. But I couldn't bring myself to do it. It wouldn't be fair to you. Wouldn't be right."

"When did you want to leave?"

"Well, if you hurry up and shower and change, my mom said she would make dinner for us first."

Sounded as good as anything, Tommen figured.

The idea of going over to her parents' house was daunting. He hadn't been over there for a while, trying to get Becky to come home. He hadn't been over there for dinner since before March, when everything had been happy and hopeful. Things would be different now, a different atmosphere, different conversation. What did her parents think of him now? Did they blame him for the misfortunes? Did they wish their daughter had never met him? Did they pray for evils to befall him?

He had a hard time believing that, seeing how they'd seemed mildly pleased with his attempts at bringing Becky home. He'd tried. He really had. Probably they had tried for over a month to talk her out of leaving. If they couldn't do it, and he couldn't do it, then no one could. She was leaving and that was that.

The best he managed to muster up was nice pants and a nice shirt. He couldn't see a reason for anything fancier than that. He didn't even feel like getting this dressed up, but there were standards that the Polskis liked to maintain. Becky respected him enough to not sneak away when she had the chance. He would return the favor by respecting her parents. Except for the time Dr. Polski clocked him in the jaw, they had been nothing but good to him.

In a way, he felt as though he'd betrayed them as well. If not for him, Becky would still be healthy and happy, on her way to school and a bright future not marred by death and destruction. They had trusted him to be a gentleman, be the Chivalrous Welshman, and do the right thing. Instead, he brought on an unplanned pregnancy, hardship and heartache and family drama, and death. In the end, it really was all his fault, not even considering the Time aspect of it. He'd been unable to control himself as a stupid, horny teenager, and disaster ensued.

He returned to the kitchen where Becky was pulling on her shoes. They were regular shoes, a little pair of flats she broke out for special occasions. At his confused look, she said, "It'll just be easier to get through security with these than my big, clunky, metal-framed shoes. You never know, they could be bombs. Plus they'll feel better on the plane, sitting down for a long time."

Tommen wordlessly agreed and carried her bags out to his car. This was his last chance to get her to change her mind, but he didn't know what to say. He'd exhausted every argument, and some of them only seemed to drive her more into certainty that she had to go. He'd tried everything he could think of.

In the movies, the hero always knew what to say. Even if the lovers were destined to separate, there was still something he could say to soften the blow, to let her know that he still cared but he was happy for her, whatever she did in life. No matter what, they could still be friends, confidants, the perfect couple that could never be even as loyal fans screamed at the screen for them to get back together. Then those same fans would take to the Internet to publish swaths of fanfiction detailing their ideal endings and other fantasies.

But this was not a movie, and if this was a book or a Book, it was shaping up to have a pretty shitty ending. This was supposed to be his happily ever after, not a happily never after. He was supposed to be riding off into the sunset on a big white stallion, the knight in shining armor and his fair maiden, who wouldn't be a maiden come morning. This was more like a soap opera.

They scooted down the short distance to her parents' house. Dr. Polski met them at the door, giving them both massive hugs. Tommen was caught off-guard and nearly had his ribcage crushed before being released to remove his shoes and enter the grandiose mansion. Mrs. Polski was in the kitchen still cooking, but wiped her hands and paused long enough to also hug them, much more gently than her husband.

The older couple was happy to see them, but Tommen noticed that their attitude was of sorrowful resignation. They didn't want to see Becky leave, but they couldn't convince her to stay, either. They did not appear to harbor any ill will toward him for it, but he still wasn't sure how he wanted to approach them anymore. Even just going to see Dr. Polski for an annual checkup suddenly felt like an awkward endeavor.

The dinner spread proved to be all of Becky's favorites, which Tommen supposed was to be expected. It was her mom's way of trying to get her to stay, reminding her of all the good food and good fun, reminding her that there was no cooking like Mom's cooking. Problem was, Tommen thought, Becky was just as good a cook and had made plenty of good food for him and his dad over the last year.

But that was where the nudging and trying to get her to stay ended. It was all subtle. Overt conversation was focused more on how Aunt Cecilia was doing, where she was living, what the little town where she lived was like, the people, the community college just a few miles away. Apparently Aunt Ceci also had chickens, ducks, and a few goats she kept more as pets than anything else, and they got along splendidly with her two dogs. In a moment of dry humor, Tommen wondered what it would be like to see bull-headed Becky take on a goat. That would be something to see.

Then the talk turned to college. Becky had already contacted the school and set up her classes for the fall semester and double- and triple-checked that her scholarships had all transferred and were good and valid. By the time those ran out, she would at least have her Associate's and should be starting on her internship. The internship was paid, which was a good thing. It meant that any job she got, she would be able to save a majority of the funds for whatever she needed as far as big life purchases, like a house.

Tommen was not oblivious to the fact that they never actually mentioned the name of the town where Aunt Ceci lived, nor the name of the college or anything that could be identifying. It was as though she were vanishing into a ghost land, and he was not permitted to follow. He wondered if Aunt Ceci really lived in Wyoming. He wondered if Aunt Ceci even existed, given that he couldn't recall her ever coming up in previous conversations.

Dessert was no different than dinner, all of Becky's favorites, all of it delicious. Mrs. Polski tried to pack some up for her so she could take it on the plane, but Becky stopped her, saying it would probably get confiscated by a jerk TSA agent who forgot his dinner and so decided to graze off of the unsuspecting patrons passing through the airport. On top of that, she wasn't even sure if it was allowed anyway. After all, lasagna bombs were a huge problem these days. Dangerous and sticky to clean up. Plus it just stained everything around it.

Mrs. Polski relented, but did not seem too thrilled about it. Half of her existence was providing for her family at the intersection of good food and a safe home. Now she could give neither to her youngest daughter. Dr. Polski looked much the same way, except his provisional intersection came at the corner of fueling dreams and protection from danger. He, too, was unable to give either of those to Becky right now. The best either of them could give was a prayer and a hope.

Then the time came to leave. Becky still hadn't changed her mind, not that anyone had really been trying anymore. This was happening. Short of an angel or God Himself descending to tell her to turn back, Becky was leaving West Virginia and heading to another state. She was leaving Tommen and going to live with her aunt.

So they returned to the entryway to grab their shoes. Becky slipped on her shoes and lingered for a moment to speak to her parents while Tommen quietly headed outside to wait. He leaned against his car, not saying a word, not telling her to hurry up. This was all on her.

"Tommen."

He turned, surprised, to find Dr. Polski approaching.

"Just so you know," the doctor said, "we don't blame you."

"It's my fault this all happened," Tommen stated.

The old Jewish man shook his head. "No. It is simply the will of God. And who are we to dictate it? I know it's not a satisfactory answer. We wish we could see and understand everything, and I would be lying if I said I did not doubt myself and my faith during this time. But know that we do not blame you, and we do not hate you. Helen and I still think of you as a son, and you are free to approach us for anything as a son."

Tommen nodded. "Thank you."

There was so much more he wanted to say, but he didn't want to unload on the man. Why would God let this happen? If God hated abortion, why did He find it necessary to kill living babies? If marriage was sacred, why would He let them split up? Too many unanswered questions swirled through his mind, but in the moment, he could only express some measure of gratitude toward the Polskis.

The closest Mrs. Polski got to him was the porch, where she managed a small smile and a wave. Tommen dipped his head toward her, and she returned the gesture. Dr. Polski hugged Becky one last time before opening the car door for her. He closed it behind her, then went to stand beside his wife on the porch, watching them pull away.

"You can still change your mind," Tommen said quietly as they neared the bridge.

"No, I can't," Becky replied simply.

They crossed the bridge and Tommen skirted the outside of the city to get to the airport.

Was it really almost three years since the standoff in the hangar? It felt like so long ago, such a petty thing. That part of his life was over. So, too, was this chapter, as Tommen took Becky to the airport.

Friday night meant that traffic was thick and congested as the work day ended and nightlife began. People loosened ties, loosened belts, opened wallets, and opened themselves. Bars were crowded, stores stayed open a couple extra hours, and the city police were out in force.

Then they were past the city. At night, the only traffic out here were big trucks coming on or off the interstate, only a few scattered cars going here and there. Tommen was one of two vehicles heading for the airport. Parking was easy enough to find, though the price was no less ridiculous, even for short-term parking. Still, his sense of decency told him to suck it up and go in with her. It would be the last time he spent any money on her, might as well make it count. He grabbed the ticket from the dispenser and the wooden arm went up.

He found a spot to park. As soon as he shut off the engine, he jumped out and hurried around to the other side to open Becky's door for her.

"Still trying, aren't you?" she asked.

"Right up until the plane leaves," he told her.

She said nothing to that, just made for the trunk. He got there before she did and hefted the duffel bags on his shoulders.

"Chivalry to the end," she stated.

"I don't know about that. A lot of my actions toward you have been less than noble."

She frowned and managed to climb up into the trunk where she turned around and sat. She patted beside her. Sighing, he set down the duffel bags and sat down next to her.

"Well, my actions and attitude toward you haven't always been stellar, either," Becky said. "I know I'm crass and stubborn and have kind of a big mouth. I blackmailed you within a week of meeting and I've chewed on your backside a number of times for petty, stupid things."

"Maybe, but you're also smart and clever and you certainly knew how to keep me on my toes," Tommen said, finding it in him to laugh.

They sat there for a minute or two.

"Remember the time, a few weeks into class, Mrs. White accidentally gave us a project meant for her AP Chemistry class?" Becky asked suddenly. "And none of us said anything because it was totally awesome?"

"Oh, the one where we mixed the chemicals and almost set off the fire alarms and the sprinklers because we had no idea what we were doing?" He grinned and nodded. "Yeah, I remember that. I also remember we got in a lot of trouble for it."

"Yeah, but it was like, she was the one who gave us the project. How were we supposed to know it was for another class?"

" 'Maybe the use and mixing of chemicals should have given you an idea,' " Tommen said in his best impersonation of Mrs. White. " 'These chemicals are dangerous and expensive, and bad things can happen if you don't know what you're doing.' "

Becky giggled. "Yeah, so let's give them to high school students; they're known for their maturity. Then we ended up getting two weeks of straight book work. No movies, no demos, no projects, nothing but strict book work. Every quiz, every section review, every question answered in complete sentences even if it was multiple choice. Oh, God, she punished us so hard for that."

Tommen leaned forward, elbows on his knees. "All seems like so long ago now. So petty and stupid. But at the time, it was the most important thing in the world. Study hard, get good grades, get loads of scholarships, go to college, get a high-paying job, make money. And if you're not happy with that, go back to school, change your career, make more money." He shook his head. "They don't teach you about the important stuff. Budgets. Family. The daily grind."

"They just set you on the track and tell you to aim for the horizon," Becky agreed. "They don't tell you that you never reach it."

"They don't tell you that the finish line is wherever you make it, that sweet spot where you know you're supposed to be. It may not be perfect, and there may be problems, but it's just right for you. No one but you."

Becky shifted beside him. After a second of hesitation, she scooted close to him and leaned on his shoulder. "I think we may have settled in a swamp filled with quicksand. We can fight the muck and do everything we can to stop it, but I think it was a sinking ship from the beginning."

"And that's why Maisy was taken from us?"

She got off his shoulder and looked away. "I don't know. I don't think we'll ever know what could have been."

"Or what could still be." He looked at her. "You can still walk away. You don't have to get on that plane. You don't have to go to Wyoming."

"Yes, I do. My sweet spot is still out there somewhere, and I don't think it involves you. Your sweet spot is still out there, and it doesn't involve me."

Tommen sighed and frowned. "Why did we do all this, then?"

"Because we were young, dumb, horny teenagers who didn't know any better, who didn't think anything bad could happen to them because we are the heroes of our own stories. And nothing bad — nothing really bad — ever happens to the heroes. And I think real life sort of smacked us in the face."

"Yeah, with a load of bricks."

"And this is what's happening now."

He nodded. "Yeah. This is happening."

Becky studied her hands, folded neatly in her lap. "I don't hate you, Tommen. I don't blame you. I don't even know that I don't still love you. That's what makes this hard, because we're not fighting and screaming and each wishing the other would fall off a random cliff. But it's still the right thing to do."

"Is that why you're still sitting here in my trunk?"

"Honestly, I had hoped to kind of remind you of the bad things that I had done to you, get you to not like me, maybe even start an argument."

"You were looking for a way to make me push you away and

make that severance more severe, more final."

She just nodded.

"I would be lying if I said I wasn't trying to do the same thing mentally, but I can't do it. Because I do still love you, Becky. I wish I knew a way to convey that in such a way that it would make you stay, but I've run out of ideas."

"So maybe stop trying," she suggested quietly. "Maybe if we stopped trying to force the issue, it will simply resolve itself in the future. Maybe our paths will cross again, or maybe they won't. I don't know."

Tommen let out a breath and got out of the trunk. "Well, the least I can do is help you get there. If we're not going to fight and argue, then I'm still obligated to carry your bags."

She smiled at that and climbed out as well. He grabbed the bags and she led the way into the airport.

The last time Tommen had been in here, he and his dad had gone to speak with security so they could be taken to one of the hangars for a hostage negotiation. That was pretty much where his friendship with Eric and Varad had ended, once they understood his secret second life. And now his relationship with Becky was ending here. Tommen decided he did not like this airport.

Once Becky had checked in with the airline, they ended up procrastinating again, a short distance from the security checkpoint. That would be the first part of the split, as it was a place where Tommen could not go. The split would be final only after Becky's plane took off.

They reminisced some more, about high school, about friends, about work, about home. How foolish they had been back in high school, thinking they had this all figured out. That was one thing that public education was good at, Tommen thought, making the students believe that they knew everything there was to know and that the classroom was the end-all of knowledge. Less than a year in real world and he felt as unprepared and as dumb as ever. He'd like to go back in time and punch his younger self a few times, tell him all the stupid shit he was going to be involved in. His younger self would just laugh.

At long last, Becky could delay no longer. She already knew she was probably going to have a hard time getting through security. Dwarfs were notorious for being terrorists, after all. She could be hiding a bomb somewhere in her abundant body. Tommen couldn't help but laugh.

He knelt in front of her and gave her a hug. It was a massive hug, one that said he didn't want to let go because he knew it would be the last one he gave her. He could feel tears running down his cheeks into his beard, but he didn't care. He loved her. He didn't want her to go.

In the movies, the hero always knew what to say. At the very least, even if he started walking away, she would come running back to him, leap into his arms, kiss him, and proclaim her undying love, that they could work it out and be together.

But this wasn't a movie, and he knew that wasn't going to happen.

When he was done hugging her, he kissed her. Her body momentarily went rigid with surprise, but she did not fight it and instead kissed him back. It was not helping his ability to separate and let go, but he needed it. If he wanted to be totally honest, he kind of wanted to have sex with her, too, one last time, but that wasn't going to happen. That would certainly be taking it too far.

Becky pulled away, grabbed her carry-on and walked away without a word and without looking back, leaving Tommen kneeling there on the floor. The TSA agent at the desk gave him a sympathetic look.

Feeling disgusted with himself, Tommen stood with the intent to walk away himself, but he made it only as far as the bench they'd just been sitting on. He watched Becky go through security. She did indeed have a harder time getting through security and was taken aside for a patdown. Because dwarfs were notorious bombers, after all.

Then she was through and disappeared into the terminal.

After a long moment of staring, waiting for her to come running back, Tommen concluded that it just wasn't happening. She was leaving, and leaving him behind. And she was taking part of his heart with her. He looked down at the "M" tattooed on his wrist. She had one just like it on her chest.

They would be two people, a thousand miles apart, sharing a tattoo and all the hurts and joys that went with it, and no one would ever really understand. A thousand years from now, archaeologists would dig them up, find the scars, and wonder how they came to be separated. Maybe poetry and songs would be written about it. Or maybe he was just trying to look for any silver lining in the thundercloud hanging over his head.

But there wasn't any.

He headed out to the parking lot and sat in his car. He glanced in the back seat. Maybe she'd forgotten something, maybe left him a note in the seat for him to find. Nothing.

He sat there for an hour and a half until what he was sure was her plane took off into the night. And that was that. She was gone. Out of his life, heading for a small town in Wyoming, or wherever she was really going.

It was another ten minutes before he could compose himself well enough to drive, and he hated himself for it. He hated the sympathetic looks the toll booth operator gave him as she handed over his parking receipt. He hated how much he had to pay just to use the parking lot for a couple hours, but he also knew that it was primarily his fault for sitting there and waiting for the plane to leave. And he hated himself even more.

Then the wooden arm went up and he was on his way, navigating the twisting lanes and trying to figure out which way to the exit. Must be another layer of security, Tommen thought, stall a terrorist long enough to catch him simply by confusing the hell out of him and getting him all turned around so that he returned to the airport as if turning himself in. But he made it out eventually and started toward home.

The house would be empty and dark. His dad was at work. Becky was gone. Their daughter had been gone for months now. Everything that should have been would never be.

He was sick of it.

If he was the hero of his own Book, then why did it feel like the Author was still jerking him around constantly? Why did it feel like he was constantly running out to the end of his chain and strangling himself, only to find that his leash was getting shorter and shorter? Was the Author dictating his moves or simply recording them?

He concluded that she was probably just recording them, because otherwise that would mess with free will. But she could manipulate everything around him, nudge things here and there, maybe pass him a stray thought or two to influence him or someone else. There was no booming voice from above, just a simple whisper, a passing thought. Almost as bad as the Dragon except pretending to be good. If the Author—hell, if God was so powerful, why didn't He stop this? Why did He allow bad things to happen?

Oh, ye mere mortal, it is not on you to understand.

If there is a plan, then that implies that there is a reasonable amount of control over the situation and the people in it. So then it comes down to being unable or unwilling to give us just a little sliver of understanding. If a man is stumbling around in the dark, and someone has a match, is it not the right thing to do to light that match and help the man? I'm kind of stumbling around here.

His more refined thoughts were a bit scattered, Tommen knew, but he knew what he meant, and he knew what he meant to do. If he was the hero of his own story, well, his story sucked. It was a tragedy filled with nothing but death and despair and war and all the terrible things in life. And if anyone was out there with any shred of power or willingness to direct him, well, it would be a now or never instance. Either he was in control of his life or he wasn't, and there was no other way he could think of to test that theory.

He pulled in the garage and went in the house. He didn't even bother taking off his shoes as he crossed the kitchen in two strides and hit the living room. When he turned to go down the hallway, he stopped dead in his tracks. Chandler stood in the doorway to his bedroom.

"I know what you're thinking, Tommen," Chandler said. "And I can't let you do this."

"You! Knew!" Tommen shrieked. "You knew what was going to happen! You knew! About all of it! You knew and you didn't say anything! My daughter might still be alive except for you!"

"No she would not," the Native man said in a firm voice. "And neither would you. Or Becky."

Tommen swallowed hard, wiped his eyes, and nodded. "Great. So in the end, nothing changes."

"Unless you want it to change. You want to prove yourself, prove your own theory, you can do that. Right now."

Tommen started down the hallway, fully intending to go into his room, fully expecting that Chandler was merely apparitional, maybe a figment of his imagination or just a phantom. He did not expect the man to be entirely solid. Tommen bumped into him, stopped, then steeled himself. Without taking a step back, he whispered, "Get out of my house. You're right. I don't want to see you again. I'm tired of your riddles and your bullshit. Go back to your cave, Chandler. You are not welcome here."

He knew Chandler took a step back, but in the time it took for Tommen's eyes to flit from one focus point to another, the man was gone, as if he had never been there at all.

Tommen entered his room and went to the closet. He pulled down all the stuff that had been accumulating up top since Becky had moved in. A few shirts, a couple pairs of pants, trinkets and small items. Then he found his Books. Nine of them including one he hadn't seen before. He stared at them. He had half a mind to burn them, then refrained. There were other copies out there, and it would serve no purpose. Eventually, everyone would know of his shame. And in the end, they would all see how he had taken back control of his life.

He found his gun case, the one he'd gotten for his birthday last year. He twisted the combination, flipped the locks, and opened it to find...it was empty. There was a picture of a gun and note in his dad's handwriting.

"Sorry, kiddo. I'm too worried about you, and if something bad really is happening, you have other means of self-defense."

Tommen slammed the case shut and snarled his frustration. Then he got up and went out to his dad's bedroom. In the nightstand next to the bed, he pulled open the drawer. The case was there, and it wasn't typically locked. It wasn't locked today, but neither was there anything in it, just another note saying, "Don't do it, Tommen. Call me, call 9-1-1, or call the hotline." He'd written down the hotline below that.

He looked in the closet, went to the big gun case. He knew the combination to the digital pad, but was unprepared for a new secondary spin dial lock on the handle as well. Had his dad really been this concerned? Was it just generic concern? Had Tommen ever given any indications before about this?

He was crying now, but he couldn't say why except sheer fear and panic. Heat of the moment was one thing, but this was getting drawn out far too long.

Wiping his eyes, Tommen sullenly returned to his room. The Books sitting on his bed mocked him, taunted him. Well, there was more than one way to do this. He climbed on his bed, looked at the ceiling, and removed his belt.

Epilogue

Walter had heard or read numerous stories about people hearing a voice from Heaven telling them to get home immediately, only to find that their home was burning down or being robbed or some other catastrophe. Normally, he dismissed the literal voice from Heaven as being a gut instinct. Divinely inspired, maybe, but probably more gut instinct than a literal, Biblical voice from Heaven.

Today was the day that challenged those beliefs. He'd been doing little more than sitting at his desk doing paperwork when he felt as though he'd been arbitrarily picked up out of his seat and pushed to his car, ignoring any probing questions from the others in the office, his only thought as one of needing to get home immediately. Something wasn't right. He couldn't say for sure whether a divine voice had spoken out loud, but it was certainly a force that couldn't be easily argued with as he raced home, Banding just as soon as he got out into the road.

The house was quiet. Tommen's car sat in the garage. Walter paused as he pulled up behind it, the garage door still opening. Walter could see the heat still rising from the hood. He hadn't been home for very long. There were no obvious signs of mischief, but Walter still told himself to be cautious.

Walter all but jumped out of his car and ran inside the house.

"Tommen?" he called.

There was no answer. Dirty tracks indicated that the teenager hadn't removed his shoes before walking through the house, and Walter followed the down the hall to Tommen's room where he pushed open the door.

It was a full five seconds before Walter could pinpoint the source of the unearthly sound that echoed in the room. It was coming from him.

Tommen had punched a hole in the ceiling and tied off to one of the rafters. He hung just off the end of his bed.

Running more by instinct than logic, Walter climbed up on the bed and drew his knife. Tommen had gotten creative with his leather belts; Walter simply grabbed on near one of the buckles and, using every bit of inhuman strength he could muster, starting sawing and pulling.

The belt gave. Tommen crumpled to the floor. Walter, unprepared for the sudden snap, wobbled and fell off the bed, knocking his head on a bookshelf so that spots danced before his eyes. He scrambled to all fours and crawled over to his son, pulling the belt out from around Tommen's neck. Bruises had blossomed where the belt had been, and there was damage to his throat, but his neck wasn't broken, and he was still warm. Walter felt for a pulse, found none, and he wasn't breathing. With shaking hands, Walter got on his radio.

"Central from 629."

"Go ahead, 629."

"I'm at 5555 S. Deering Rd. with an 18 year old male, attempted suicide by hanging, CPR in progress, requesting an ambulance."

"Copy that, dispatching an ambulance to 5555 S. Deering Rd. Do you require additional law units?"

"Negative on that. Scene is clear."

Dispatch might have said more, but Walter wasn't paying attention. He pushed up Tommen's shirt and started compressions, sweat dripping down his forehead.

For too many people every day, this is the end of the story.

That's it.

The end.

Side characters no longer matter.

Plotlines no longer matter.

Whatever was going on, whatever events, dates, plans, or occasions, whatever unanswered questions, they all end here.

They don't matter.

And you will never know what happens next.

Author's Note

The Chivalrous Welshman is at its end. Years of war and drama and heartbreak and laughter, and this is where it stops. Like driving into a rock wall or off a cliff. Sure, there is still stuff going on—with Miach and Micaiah and the Miaramila and the Akarin and the Order and everything else—but when it comes to suicide, none of that matters anymore.

This ending was simultaneously one of the easiest and most difficult to write, and I have no illusions that someone out there doesn't feel the same way about reading it. Someone I know once said it this way, "Suicide is death by Satan."

To be quite honest with you, Reader, as of this writing, I don't know whether Tommen survives, if Walter or medics are able to revive him. I know my original plans, but so many of my original plans have been altered or tossed completely that I don't consider them reliable. If he does survive, he certainly won't be the Chivalrous Welshman anymore. Even if Tommen lives, the Chivalrous Welshman is dead.

As for the rest of the story, whether or not he lives, the continuation of the *Timekeeper Chronicles* will be found in *The Fifth Horseman*. This will provide the answers regarding Julianna and Miach and Micaiah and Kayla and the Akarin and the Miaramila and the Order. It will just do it without the Chivalrous Welshman.

If you are in crisis, get help. Call 9-1-1 or your local help center. Don't be a statistic.

Don't let this be the end of your story.